THE
AERONAUT'S
WINDLASS

BY JIM BUTCHER

The Dresden Files
Storm Front
Fool Moon
Grave Peril
Summer Knight
Death Masks
Blood Rites
Dead Beat
Proven Guilty
White Night
Small Favour
Turn Coat
Changes
Ghost Story
Cold Days
Skin Game
Side Jobs *(anthology)*

The Codex Alera
Furies of Calderon
Academ's Fury
Cursor's Fury
Captain's Fury
Princeps' Fury
First Lord's Fury

The Cinder Spires
The Aeronaut's Windlass

JIM BUTCHER

THE CINDER SPIRES

THE AERONAUT'S WINDLASS

orbit

www.orbitbooks.net

ORBIT

First published in Great Britain in 2015 by Orbit

1 3 5 7 9 10 8 6 4 2

Copyright © 2015 by Jim Butcher

Interior Illustrations by Priscilla Spencer

The moral right of the author has been asserted.

A CIP catalogue record for this book is available from the British Library.

HB ISBN 978-0-356-50365-3
C format 978-0-356-50468-1

Printed and bound in Great Britain by CPI Group (UK) Ltd, Croydon CR0 4YY

Papers used by Orbit are from well-managed forests
and other responsible sources.

MIX
Paper from
responsible sources
FSC® C104740

Orbit
An imprint of
Little, Brown Book Group
Carmelite House
50 Victoria Embankment
London EC4Y 0DZ

An Hachette UK Company
www.hachette.co.uk

www.orbitbooks.net

For Prima and Sirius, Silent Paws

HABBLE MORNING

HIS MAJESTY ADDISON ORSON MAGNUS JEREMIAH ALBION

House Lancaster

Lancaster Vattery

House Bayard

North Spiral

House North

House Astor

Spirearch's Manor

West Spiral

Central Market

East Spiral

House Windham

House Corvus

South Spiral

House Byron

Shipyards

FIRST CITIZEN AND SPIREARCH

SPIRE ALBION

PS

HABBLE LANDING

Wayist Temple

Lumber Yards

House Fairfax

North Spiral

House Elliot

House Price

West Spiral

House Hood

Central Market

East Spiral

House Edge

South Spiral

House Gladstone

Black Horse Inn

Shipyards

LOWER LEVEL

UPPER LEVEL

North Spiral

West Spiral

Verminocitor's Guild

East Spiral

South Spiral

SPIRE ALBION

PS

■ ■ ■ Prologue ■ ■ ■

Spire Albion, Habble Morning,
House Lancaster

Gwendolyn Margaret Elizabeth Lancaster," said Mother in a firm, cross voice, "you will cease this nonsense at once."

"Now, Mother," Gwendolyn replied absently, "we have discussed the matter at length upon multiple occasions." She frowned down at the gauntlet upon her left hand and rotated her wrist slightly. "The number three strap is too tight, Sarah. The crystal is digging into my palm."

"Just a moment, miss." Sarah bent nearer the gauntlet's fastenings, eyeing them over the rims of her spectacles. She made a series of quick, deft adjustments and asked, "Is that better?"

Gwendolyn tried the motion again and smiled. "Excellent. Thank you, Sarah."

"Of course, miss," Sarah said. She began to smile but glanced aside at Mother and schooled her expression into soberly appropriate diffidence.

"There has been no discussion," Mother said, folding her arms. "Discussion implies discourse. You have simply pretended I wasn't in the room when I broached the subject."

Gwendolyn turned to smile sweetly. "Mother, we can have this conversation again if you wish, but I have not altered my intentions in the least. I will *not* attend Lady Hadshaw's Finishing Academy."

"I would be more than pleased to see you enter the Etheric Engineering Academy along with—"

"Oh!" Gwendolyn said, rolling her eyes. "I've been working with those systems in the testing shop since I could *walk*, and I'm quite sure I will go mad if I have to endure two years' worth of introductory courses."

Mother shook her head. "Gwendolyn, you cannot possibly think that—"

"Enough," Gwendolyn said. "I *will* enter the Spirearch's Guard. I *will* take the oath. I *will* spend a year in the Service." She turned to regard her reflection in the long mirror, adjusted her skirts marginally, and straightened the lapels of her short bolero jacket. "Honestly, other daughters of the High Houses take the oath. I cannot imagine why you're making such a fuss."

"Other Houses are *not* the Lancasters," Mother said, her voice suddenly cold. "Other Houses do not rule the highest habble of the Council. Other Houses are not custodians of the sternest responsibility within all of Spire Albion."

"Mother." Gwendolyn sighed. "Honestly, as if the people living in the lower levels of the Spire are less worthy somehow. And besides, those great vats and crystals all but mind themselves."

"You are young," Mother said. "You have little appreciation of how much those crystals are needed, and not only by those of Habble Morning or the Fleet, or of all the planning and foresight that must go into producing a single crystal over the—"

"The course of generations," Gwendolyn interrupted. "No, apparently I have not been enlightened to your satisfaction—I would, however, submit to you that another repetition of this particular bit of pedantry seems unlikely to correct the situation, and that therefore the least frustrating course of action for all involved would be to abort the attempt."

"Gwendolyn," Mother said, her eyes narrowing. "You will return to your chambers in the next ten seconds or I swear to God in Heaven that I shall beat you soundly."

Ah. Now they came to it. Gwendolyn suppressed a flash of purely childish fear, and then one of much more reasonable anger, and forced herself to consider the situation and the room in a calm and rational manner.

Mother's outburst had been so entirely appalling as to freeze Sarah in place. The maid was perfectly aware that such a display of emotion from one of the leading ladies of Habble Morning was not something that should be witnessed by the hired help. Mother, in her anger, had been quite inconsiderate, since Sarah didn't dare simply leave the room, either. How was the poor girl supposed to react?

"Sarah," Gwendolyn said, "I believe I heard Cook mention that her back was still giving her trouble. I would appreciate it if you ease her duties this morning. Would you mind, terribly, delivering Father's breakfast to him, and sparing Cook the stairs?"

"Of course not, Lady Gwendolyn," Sarah said, bobbing in a quick curtsy. She flashed Gwendolyn a swift smile containing both gratitude and apology, and moved from the room with sedate efficiency.

Gwendolyn smiled until Sarah had left the room, then turned and frowned faintly at Mother. "That was not very thoughtful of you."

"Do *not* attempt to change the subject," Mother said. "You will take off that ridiculous gauntlet at once or face the consequences."

Gwendolyn arched one eyebrow sharply. "You realize that I am armed, do you not?"

Mother's dark eyes blazed. "You wouldn't *dare*."

"I should think I would have no need to do such a thing," Gwendolyn replied. "However, I care to be beaten even less than I care to live out my days in this dreary mausoleum or one precisely like it. I daresay that at least in the Service I should find *something* to interest me." She lifted her chin, narrowed her eyes, and said, "Do not test me, Mother."

3

"Impossible child," Mother said. "Take her."

Gwendolyn realized at that moment that Mother's threat and outrage alike had been feigned, a pretense that had distracted Gwendolyn until a pair of the House armsmen could approach her silently from behind. She took a quick step to one side and felt strong hands seize her left arm. Had she not moved, the second man would have had her right arm in the same moment, and her options would have been far more limited.

Instead she seized the wrist of her assailant, pivoted her weight into him, robbing him of his balance, breaking the power of his grip at the same time, and continued her smooth circular motion into a throw, dumping him over one hip and onto the floor at the feet of the second armsman. The fallen man tripped the second, who struggled to push up from the floor. Gwendolyn lifted her skirts slightly and kicked the second man's arm out from beneath him. He dropped down onto the first man with a surprised grunt, and glared up at her.

"I'm terribly sorry," Gwendolyn said. "It isn't personal." Then she gave him a calm, sharp kick to the head. The man let out a short grunt and dropped limply, stunned.

"Esterbrook!" Mother said sharply.

Gwendolyn turned from the two downed men to find Esterbrook, captain of House Lancaster's armsmen, entering the room. Esterbrook was a lean, dangerous-looking man, his skin worn and leathery from years of the pitiless sunlight borne by aeronauts and marines. He wore a black suit and coat tailored in the same style as the uniform of the Fleet Marine he had once been. He bore the short, heavy, copper-clad blade of a Marine on one hip. The gauntlet on his left hand was made of worn and supple leather, though the copper cagework around his forearm and wrist was as polished and bright as Gwendolyn's newer model.

Gwendolyn focused her thoughts at once, stepping away from the stunned men and lifting her left hand to present the crystal held against her palm to Esterbrook. She sighted her target, the captain's grizzled head, in the V shape made by the spread of her first and second fingers. By the time she had, her gauntlet's crystal had awakened to her concentration. Cold white light blazed from it, changing all the shadows in the room and causing her mother to blink and squint against the sudden radiance.

"Good morning, Captain Esterbrook," Gwendolyn said in an even tone. "I am well aware that your suit is lined with silk. I feel obliged to advise you that I am aiming at your head. Please do nothing that would require me to put my training to such tragic and wasteful use."

Esterbrook regarded her from behind his shaded spectacles. Then he reached up very slowly with his right hand, removed them, and blinked a few times against the etherlight of the weapon Gwendolyn held trained upon him. His eyes were an eerie shade of gold-green, and his feline pupils contracted into vertical slits against the light.

"Quick," he commented.

Gwendolyn felt herself smile slightly. "I had an excellent teacher, sir."

Esterbrook gave her a very small portion of an ironic smile, and tipped his head to her in acknowledgment. "Where in the Spire did you find someone to teach you the Way?"

"Cousin Benedict, naturally," she replied.

"Ha," Esterbrook said. "I kept smelling the perfume on him. Thought he'd taken up with a woman."

Mother made a wordless, disgusted sound held tightly within her throat, barely audible past her tight-closed lips. "I have expressly forbidden your close association with him, Gwendolyn."

"Quite, Mother, yes," Gwendolyn agreed. "Captain, if you would be so kind as to disarm yourself, please."

Esterbrook stared at her for a moment more, and then the lines at the corners of his eyes deepened. He inclined his head to her, then moved only his right hand to unbuckle his sword belt. It fell to the floor.

"What are you doing?" Mother demanded of him.

"My lady," Esterbrook said in a polite tone, "Miss Gwen holds a deadly weapon, and one which she is fully capable of using."

"She won't use it," Mother said. "Not upon you. And not upon her family."

Gwendolyn felt a surge of frustration. Mother was quite right, of course. Such a thing would be unthinkable—but she had no intention of continuing to live her life cloistered within Lancaster Manor, venturing out only for the constant, meaningless, regular, deadly dull, *boring* routine of balls, dinners, concerts, and school. She could not allow Mother to call her bluff.

So she shifted her arm very slightly and unleashed radiant etheric energy from the crystal against her palm.

There was a howling scream of suddenly parted air and a blinding flash. It was followed an instant later by a deafening roar, like thunder, and a marble statuette sitting on a side table just behind Esterbrook exploded into dust and flying fragments. The fragments rattled and bounced around the room in the silence after the blast, and grew quiet only a few seconds later.

Mother stood staring with her mouth open, her face pale, half of her body already coated with fine marble dust. Esterbrook was coated with the dust as well, but he hadn't moved or changed his expression.

"Captain," Gwendolyn said. "If you would be so kind as to continue."

"Miss," he said, bobbing his head again. Moving very slowly, and keeping his left arm completely still and at his side, he unbuckled the straps of the gauntlet and let it fall to the floor.

"Thank you, Captain," Gwendolyn said. "Step aside, please."

Esterbrook looked at Mother, spread his hands in a silent, helpless gesture, and took several steps back and away from his weaponry.

"No," Mother snapped. "No." She took three quick strides to the chamber's fantastically expensive door, made from wood harvested from the deadly, mist-bound forests of the surface and bound in brass. She twisted its key until it locked, and then withdrew it. She returned to her original position with her chin lifted in outrage. "You will *obey* me, child."

"Honestly, Mother," Gwendolyn said, "at the rate we're going, we'll bankrupt ourselves redecorating."

Gwendolyn's gauntlet howled again, and part of the door was blown to splinters and twisted brass. The rest was wrenched from its brass hinges and flew out into the hallway beyond, tumbling once before it crashed to the ground.

Gwendolyn raised her arm until the crystal at her palm was parallel with her face and walked calmly forward, toward the door. The armsmen behind her groaned and began to gather themselves together. Gwendolyn felt a flash of relief. She hadn't wanted to inflict any serious harm upon the two men. Benedict had informed her that, with blows to the head, one could never be sure.

"No," Mother breathed, as she walked by. "Gwendolyn, no. You can't. You don't understand the horrors you might face." She was breathing very quickly and . . .

Merciful Builders.

Mother was *crying*.

Gwendolyn hesitated and stopped walking.

"Gwendolyn," Mother whispered. "Please. You are my only child."

"Who else, then, will represent the honor of the Lancasters in the Service?" Gwendolyn looked at her mother's face. Tears had made clean tracks through the thin layer of dust.

"Please don't go," Mother whispered.

Gwendolyn hesitated. She had her ambitions, of course, and her proper Lancaster reserve, but like Mother, she also had a heart. Tears . . . tears were unprecedented. She had never seen her mother weep except once, with laughter.

Perhaps she could have been . . . somewhat more thoughtful about how she had approached her decision to enlist. But there was no more time for discussion. Enrollment for the Guard was this morning.

She met her mother's eyes and spoke as gently as she could. And she would not cry. She simply would not. Regardless of how much she might wish to.

"I love you very much," she said quietly.

Then Gwendolyn Margaret Elizabeth Lancaster walked out over the shattered door and left her home.

Lady Lancaster watched her daughter go, tears in her eyes. She waited until she heard the large front doors of the manor close to turn to Esterbrook.

"Are you well, Captain?"

"A bit surprised, perhaps, but well enough," he said. "Lads?"

"Lady Gwen," said one of the guardsmen, touching his cheek and wincing, "hurts."

"You didn't show the opponent sufficient respect," Esterbrook said, amused. "Go get some breakfast. We'll work on takedowns this morning." The men shambled out, looking rather embarrassed, and Esterbrook watched them, evidently pleased. Then he paused, and blinked at Lady Lancaster. "My lady . . . are you crying?"

"Of course I am," she replied, pride swelling in her voice. "Did you *see* that? She stood up to all three of you."

"All four of us," Esterbrook corrected her gently.

"Gwendolyn has *never* had a problem standing up to *me*," Lady Lancaster said in a wry tone.

Esterbrook grunted. "Still don't see why you feel a need for such dramatics."

"Because I know my daughter," she said. "And I know very well that the only way to absolutely ensure that she pursues any given course of action is for me to forbid her to do so."

"Reminds me of someone else who insisted on joining the Service, my lady," Esterbrook said. "Let's see. . . ."

"I was quite young and willful at the time, as you know very well. But when I left it was nothing like that."

"Indeed not," Esterbrook said. "As I recall it, my lady, you reduced *three* doors to splinters on your way out, not one."

Lady Lancaster eyed the captain and sniffed. "Honestly, Esterbrook. I'm all but certain that you're exaggerating."

"And half a dozen statues."

"They were tasteless replicas."

"And a ten-foot section of stone wall."

"Mother was standing in the door. How else was I to leave?"

"Yes, my lady," Esterbrook said gravely. "Thank you for correcting me. I see now that there is no comparison to be made."

"I thought you'd see it that way," she said. "You have good sense."

"Yes, my lady. But . . ." Esterbrook frowned. "I understand that you wanted to steer her toward the Service. I'm still not sure I understand why."

Lady Lancaster eyed him thoughtfully for a moment. Esterbrook was a faithful soldier, an invaluable retainer, and a lifelong friend and ally— but the warriorborn's feline eyes tended to focus best on their immediate surroundings. She had no doubt that Esterbrook, if she so requested, could close his eyes and tell her the exact location of any object she could name in the room. But he'd have no idea where they were before the room's most recent redecorating, or where they should go now that the centerpiece statue had been destroyed. The warriorborn dealt best with the present, whereas she, like the Lancasters before her, had to concern herself with the far past—and the near future.

"Events are in motion in the Spires," she said quietly. "Signs and portents appear. No fewer than four Fleet aeronauts have reported sightings of an Archangel, and swear that they were neither drunk nor sleeping. Spire Aurora has recalled her embassy from Spire Albion, and our fleets have already begun to skirmish. The lower habbles have become increasingly restive and . . ."

Esterbrook tilted his head. "My lady?"

"The crystals are . . . behaving strangely."

Esterbrook arched a skeptical eyebrow.

Lady Lancaster shook her head. "I don't know how else to explain it. But I've worked with them since I was a small child, and . . . something isn't right." She sighed and turned to regard the shattered door. "There are dark times ahead of us, old friend. Strife such as has not been seen since the breaking of the world. My child needs to see it for herself, to learn about those who will fight against it, to understand what is at stake. She'll do that in his service, as she cannot anywhere else."

"Strife," Esterbrook said. "Strife seems something of a handmaiden to Lady Gwen already."

Lady Lancaster looked at the shattered door and at the drifting dust, still swirling in the wake of her daughter's passage.

"Yes," she said quietly. "God in Heaven, Archangels, merciful Builders, please. Please go with my child."

■ ■ ■ Chapter 1 ■ ■ ■

Albion Merchant Ship *Predator*

Captain Grimm flicked the telescoptic up off of the right eyepiece of his heavy goggles. The Auroran airship was a faint blot against the thick clouds below, while *Predator* was hidden high above in the aerosphere by the glare of the sun. A storm was roiling through the mezzosphere, the layer of heavy cloud and mist that lay beneath them, but there was still time to reach the enemy vessel before the storm began to interfere with the ship's systems.

Grimm nodded once, decisively. "We'll go in on the currents. General quarters. Run out the guns. Spread the web, top, bottom, and flanks. Full power to the shroud. Set course for the Auroran vessel."

"Sound general quarters!" Commander Creedy bawled, and the ship's bell gave three quick rings, repeated in a surging clamor. "Guns, make ready!" The command was echoed down the length of *Predator* as the gun crews raced to their turrets. "Spread the web 'round the clock!" Leather-skinned men in goggles and surplus Fleet aeronautical leathers leapt into the masts and rigging of the airship, shouting back their compliance. Creedy grabbed the end of the speaking tube and called, "Engineering!"

"Engineering, aye," came the tinny-sounding answer.

"Full power to the shroud, if you please, Mister Journeyman."

"Full power to the shroud, aye. And tell the captain to blow the hell out of them before they can touch our shroud. That storm's too close. He times the approach wrong and we'll be naked."

"Maintain discipline, Mister Journeyman," Creedy said severely.

"Maintenance is what I do, idiot," snapped the engineer. "Don't tell me my business, you jumped-up wollypog."

"Let it go, XO," Grimm said very quietly to Creedy. He was smiling, if only barely, at Journeyman's response. The etheric engineer was quite simply too valuable to replace and the man knew it.

The taller, younger man scowled from behind his own goggles and folded his arms. "He should be setting an example for the other men in his compartment, Captain."

Grimm shrugged a shoulder. "He isn't going to, Commander. You can't squeeze blood from a stone." He folded his hands calmly behind his back. "Besides. He might be right."

Creedy gave the captain a sharp look. "Sir?"

"It's going to be very close," Grimm replied.

Creedy stared hard at the Auroran ship and swallowed. It was one of the rival Spire's *Cortez*-class ships—a large merchant cruiser much more massive than the *Predator*, carrying heavier guns and bearing a thicker shroud. Though the *Cortez*-class ships were officially trading vessels and not warships, they were well armed and had been known to carry an entire company of Auroran Marines. This ship, Grimm was sure, was the vessel responsible for the recent losses in Albion merchant shipping.

"Prepare boarders, sir?" Creedy asked.

Grimm arched an eyebrow. "We are bold and daring, Commander, but not maniacs. I'll leave that to Commodore Rook and his friends in the Fleet. *Predator* is a private vessel."

"Aye, sir," Creedy replied. "Probably best if we didn't linger about."

"We'll rake their web hard, force them down, drop a buoy, and let Rook go after them," Grimm confirmed. "If we stay for a slugging match, that storm could come boiling up and disrupt our shroud."

"And theirs," Creedy pointed out. Good XOs did that in the Fleet, playing the devil's advocate to the captain's plans. Grimm found the practice mildly irritating. If he hadn't owed Creedy's sister a favor . . .

"They have more and larger guns than we do," Grimm replied. "And much more ship than we do. If we hang naked in front of a *Cortez*, the worst captain in their fleet would send us all screaming down to the surface."

Creedy shuddered. "Aye, sir."

Grimm clapped the young man's shoulder and gave him a brief smile. "Relax. When Fleet disciplines young officers so decisively, they do it to make an impression—so that when they return to their duties in Fleet, they won't repeat their mistake. They mean to put you to work again, or it would have been a simple discharge. They'll not leave you habbled for long. Then you'll be clear of *Predator* and in a properly armored hull again."

"*Predator* is a fine ship, Captain," Creedy said stoutly. "Just . . . a little more fragile than I'd like."

And, Grimm thought, considerably *less* fragile than he knew. "Buck up, XO. Even if we don't bring a prize ship back with us, the bounty for laming her and leaving her to Rook will earn us a tidy bonus. A hundred crowns a head, at least."

Creedy grimaced. "While Rook rakes in hundreds of thousands of crowns in prize money. And buys his House a few more Councilors."

Grimm closed his eyes and lifted his chin slightly as the men unreeled the nearly transparent ethersilk webbing. He didn't need to watch to know the way the etheric web would change as the power runs carried electricity to it, making it stir and rise, becoming seemingly weightless. It caught the invisible currents of etheric energy coursing through the aerosphere, and the translucent silk strands, spread like great cobwebs for a good two hundred feet around the vessel itself, caught the force of the unseen etheric currents coursing through the skies and began pulling

Predator forward. The slender ship gathered speed rapidly. The wind rose, cold and dry. Distant thunder from the sullen storm rumbled through the thin air.

The thought of Commodore Hamilton Rook gaining even more influence in the Spire didn't particularly trouble Grimm. Most of the affairs of Spire Albion didn't trouble him. Let the trogs in the Spires chew one another's lips off, if that was what suited them. As long as he had *Predator*, he had everything he needed.

Kettle, the sailor at the control grips of the ship a few feet behind and above Grimm and Creedy, let out a short whistle. Grimm turned and lifted an eyebrow. "Mister Kettle?"

The grizzled sailor nodded down toward the approaching storm with his chin. "Skipper, you might consider a steeper descent than normal. Gravity will get us there quicker, and if the exchange doesn't go well, we can just go right on past them into the clouds."

"Mind yourself, aeronaut," Creedy snapped. "If you have a suggestion, you can pass it to the captain through me. Those are the regulations on a Fleet vessel."

"XO. This isn't a Fleet vessel," Grimm said quietly. "This is *my* ship. Let me think."

Mister Kettle's suggestion had merit. The extra speed of the dive would make the gunnery tricky, but their ship was sound, and they shouldn't need miraculous shooting to disable the enemy ship in a surprise attack—and they would commence the engagement a few moments sooner, ahead of the storm. He far preferred their chances if the *Predator*'s shroud was intact around them.

Creedy, who could ride out a storm without blanching, began to look a little green at his captain's views of Fleet regulations. But he glanced over his shoulder at Kettle and valiantly attempted to continue to do his duty as he saw it. "A steep dive seems unnecessary, sir. In all probability they won't even realize we're upon them until the guns open up."

"We're a long way from home, XO. I'd rather not deal in probability." Grimm nodded back to the older sailor. "We'll do it your way, Mister Kettle. Inform the gun crews to adjust their firing angles."

"Aye, sir."

Grimm tilted his head and considered the strong breeze blowing across the deck. "Mister Creedy," he said, "have the men rig sail, if you please."

Creedy paused and blinked in surprise. "Captain?"

Grimm didn't blame the younger man for his reaction. Few airships utilized wind-sails these days. Steam-driven propellers and the new screwlike turbines were the preferred means of locomotion in the event that a ship dropped out of the aerosphere or was becalmed in some portion of the sky without etheric currents strong enough to propel a vessel. But sails had advantages of their own: They didn't require bulky, heavy steam engines to function, and they were—compared to steam engines, at least—nearly silent.

It was funny, Grimm mused, how often in life a bit of judicious silence could come in handy.

"Keep them reefed for now," Grimm said. "But I want them ready."

"Aye, sir," Creedy said, with even less enthusiasm than a few moments before—but he relayed the commands firmly.

After that, there was little to do but wait as the *Predator* took position for her dive. Standard battle gear included a harness with a number of attachment points on it. A lifeline was a six- to nine-foot length of heavy, braided line of leather with a clip on either end, and every man was required to have three of them on him when general quarters was sounded. Grimm and Creedy both hooked a pair of lines to the various rails and rings set about the airship for that exact purpose, cinching them in tight.

Once fastened in, Grimm paused to straighten his uniform. As the captain of an Albion merchant ship, he was not strictly required to wear one, but the crew had commissioned one for him after their first highly successful run as privateers. It was identical to the uniform of Fleet, but instead of his leathers being colored deep blue with gold trim, they were jet-black trimmed in bloodred. The two broad stripes of an airship captain adorned the end of each sleeve of his long coat. The coat's skull-shaped silver buttons had seemed a bit excessive to him, but he had to admit that they did lend the outfit a credibly piratical air.

Last of all, as always, he cinched tight the strap of his peaked cap, securing it tight to his head. Aeronauts considered it very bad luck for the captain to lose his cap when his ship dived into battle, and Grimm had seen too many odd things in his day to be entirely liberated from the superstition himself.

It took several moments to cover the miles of distance between the Auroran vessel and *Predator,* and tension mounted the entire while, thick in the chill air, its rigidity visible in the spines of the gunners and aeronauts. Ship-to-ship combat was the most destructive violence known to man, and everyone on *Predator* knew it.

Grimm played his role as he always did. The men were permitted to be nervous and fearful—it was the only sane response to their situation, after all. But fear was a disease that could swell and spread, incapacitating crews and bringing on the destruction that had been dreaded in the first place. The captain was allowed no such luxury as fear. The men had to be sure—not only suspect, but be absolutely *certain*—that their captain knew precisely what he was doing. They had to *know* that their captain was invincible, infallible, immune to defeat. That sure and certain knowledge was critical to the crew—it allowed them to ignore their fear and to focus their minds upon their duties, as they'd been trained to do.

Men who functioned as trained, even in the hellish fury of an aerial battle, were absolutely vital to victory. Such a crew tended to suffer far less injury and loss of life—and Grimm would sooner hurl himself off

Predator's ventral mastworks than needlessly spend a drop of his crew's blood. So he did what he could to make them fight as efficiently and ferociously as possible.

He did nothing.

Grimm stood calmly on the deck, his lifelines neat and taut, his hands folded behind him. He stared ahead and allowed himself to show no emotion whatsoever. He could feel the eyes that shifted to him from time to time, and he stayed steady, a reassuring and confident presence.

Creedy attempted to emulate his captain, with limited success. He clutched one rail so tightly that his knuckles had gone white, and his breath was coming too hard through his flared nostrils.

"XO," Grimm said quietly, smiling. "Perhaps your gloves?"

Creedy looked down at his hand and hurriedly removed it from the rail. He spent a moment fishing his gloves from his pockets and donning them.

Grimm couldn't blame the young man. This would be his first battle aboard *Predator*, a civilian vessel. Built of little more than wood, she was not clad in the sheets of brass and copper-shrouded steel armor a military vessel boasted. Should enemy fire penetrate her shroud, every blast would inflict hideous damage upon the ship and her crew alike—and a lucky shot could destroy her core crystal, unleashing a blast of energy that would spread both ship and crew across miles and miles of sky.

Creedy's fears were grounded in years of experience upon warships of Spire Albion's Fleet. Everything he knew told him that he was about to engage in a battle that could very well end in mutual annihilation, that Grimm was taking a horrible risk.

It wasn't the XO's fault that he had never fought upon *Predator* before.

It was time. His ship was in position, perhaps a mile and a bit more above the Auroran vessel.

"Sound maneuvers!" Grimm called.

The ship's bell began to ring in a rapid staccato, a last warning to the ship's company to secure safety lines before *Predator* went into battle.

Grimm felt a wolfish grin touch his mouth. He reached up to tighten the band of his peaked cap in preparation for the dive, and nodded slightly to one side. "Mister Kettle," he said, "you may begin your dive."

■ ■ ■ Chapter 2 ■ ■ ■

AMS *Predator*

Grimm stood firm as Journeyman cut the power to the lift crystal's suspension rig, and *Predator* dropped from the sky like a stone.

An attack dive was a small vessel's maneuver. The actual fall would inflict little damage on a vessel of any size, but the sudden reduction of speed on the far end of the dive could be a severe strain upon her timbers. Larger ships, with their far heavier armor, suffered more from such pressures, and in order to decelerate slowly enough to ease those strains, a large ship had to lose so much altitude that it often could not return to the level of the engagement effectively. A truly efficient combat dive required a brief, severe period of reduction in speed, and Grimm had read accounts of battleships and dreadnoughts that had attempted a dive, only to have their lift crystals tear themselves entirely free of the ship when attempting to arrest their descent too rapidly. Sane captains rarely tried a combat dive with anything heavier than a light cruiser — but for a relatively tiny destroyer-size ship like *Predator*, the dangerous feat dwelled at the heart of battle doctrine.

Kettle kept his hands firm on the control grips, riding the ship into the dive, keeping her steady with the maneuvering planes mounted on her hull and in her tail. The etheric web still hauled the ship forward as before — but now she was rushing down as well, coming toward the Auroran ship almost directly out of the midday sun.

The deck began to buck and jolt as their speed built. Timbers moaned and flexed in protest, the pitch rising steadily. Only the safety lines of his harness held Grimm in place, and he was once more glad to be a man of only middling height—poor towering Creedy was trying to imitate Grimm's stoic posture, and his head was being yanked about randomly as the ship bucked its way into battle.

The Auroran grew larger and larger, and the sound of *Predator's* straining timbers continued to rise in tone and volume. All ships made their own individual sounds during a dive, though no one was sure precisely why. Grimm's midshipman's tour had been aboard a destroyer named the *Speck*. It had howled like a damned soul when it stooped upon a victim. Other ships wailed like enormous steam whistles. Still others took up a regular pounding rhythm, like the beating of some vast drum. Once, Grimm had been aboard the light cruiser *Furious*, which literally boomed out enormous snarls as it charged to combat.

But *his* ship outdid them all.

When *Predator* sailed into war, she *sang*.

The rapid winds and rising shrieks suddenly blended into a single harmonious tone. Lines in the rigging and the yards and the masts themselves quivered in time, and began giving off their own notes of music, in harmony with one another. As the speed increased, the chord rose and rose, and built and *built*, until it reached a crescendo of pure, eerie, inhuman fury.

Grimm *felt* the music rise around him, felt the ship straining eagerly to her task, and his own heart raced in fierce exultation in time with her. Every line of the ship, every smudge upon her decks, every stain upon the leathers of his aeronauts leapt into his mind in vibrant detail. He could feel the ship's motion, forward and down, could feel the wind of her passage, could feel the rising terror of his crew. One of the men screamed—one of them always did—and then the entire crew joined in with *Predator*, shrieking their battle cries together with their ship's.

The ship would not fail them—Grimm knew it; he felt it, the way he could feel sunlight on his face or the rake of wind in his hair.

And he also felt it the instant their speed, their course, and their position were absolutely perfect.

"Now!" he thundered, raising his arm in a single, sharp motion.

Kettle pulled the altitude throttle from zero back up to its normal neutral buoyancy, and hauled hard on the steering grips. Though Grimm couldn't see it, he knew what was happening: The engine room would have seen the throttle indicator, and even now Journeyman and his assistants would be unleashing power from the core crystal back into the lift crystal again, and the ship suddenly groaned as she began to slow.

At the same time, *Predator* pirouetted upon her center axis, leaning over to her port, and brought her port-side broadside to bear upon the Auroran ship. Even with the protection of his goggles' dark lenses, the flash of seven etheric cannon forced him to wince and look away as they sent their charges screaming toward the Aurorans.

Each cannon was a framework of copper and brass around a copper-clad barrel of steel. A row of weapon crystals was suspended in the exact center of the barrel's length upon copper wires, and when the weapon was activated, it behaved in much the same manner as a common gauntlet—except on a far larger scale. Then the energy of a cannon crystal was added to the outgoing rush of power, and the result was pure destruction.

A cannon bolt unleashed massive energy upon impact. A single hit from one of *Predator*'s cannon, if placed in precisely the right place, could incinerate most of an unarmored vessel. Seven such weapons turned their fury upon the Auroran ship, targeting the tips of her masts, where her etheric web spread out around her. Grimm watched intently for the results of the first salvo.

In theory, the light cannon aboard *Predator* could fire a bolt that would strike effectively from nearly two miles away. In practice, it took a steady ship, a steady target, skilled gunners, and no small amount of luck to hit something at more than half a mile, perhaps more if they used the heavier chase gun, *Predator*'s only medium cannon. A light ship's defense was in its agility and speed, and they rarely cruised stably when they went into battle. Such cold-blooded trading of fire was for the heavier warships, armored to withstand multiple hits and carrying weapons ten times the size of *Predator*'s arms.

His gunnery crews were all veteran aeronauts of the Fleet, and he would match them against any active warship's crew. Though *Predator* was moving swiftly, the target stood barely two hundred yards off her beam, and the men had known the exact angle at which Kettle would hold the ship.

Ships did not dodge broadsides at this range. One could hardly see a cannon's blast in flight. It simply moved too quickly. There was the flash of the gun and the flash impression of a glowing comet dragging a tail of sparks, and then impact upon the target, with a barely detectable delay in between.

Not a single crew missed its target.

And not a shot landed.

Instead, there was a flash of emerald illumination perhaps twenty yards short of the enemy vehicle, as the cannon blasts struck the enemy ship's shroud.

The shroud was a field of energy generated by a ship's crystal power core. When a cannon blast struck the shroud, it illuminated like a hazy, spherical cloud flickering with lightning, absorbing the incoming fire and dispersing its energy safely before it could strike the ship. Shrouds were a strain upon a ship's core, a tremendous demand upon the core's energy reserve. One did not simply sail along with the ship's shroud raised and in place.

Grimm's eyes widened as time seemed to stop.

Predator's cannon had ripped deeply into the enemy's shroud, the energy of the blasts chewing away at the defensive field, almost all the way to the Auroran's hull. But they had not inflicted any damage.

The Auroran vessel's shroud was up and in place.

Therefore she had seen *Predator* coming.

Therefore she had been watching.

Therefore the Auroran had *intended* to be spotted, sitting fat and lazy on a sluggish current just above the mezzosphere, a perfect target—and she would be ready to return fire.

Even as Grimm flashed through those thoughts, he saw signal rockets flare out from the Auroran—as if the shrieking thunder of discharged cannon wouldn't have alerted the Auroran's allies.

Creedy screamed in fury. He had obviously reached the same conclusions Grimm had, and he'd likely thought that it would be his death scream. After all, no ship the size of *Predator*, unarmored, could survive the weight of fire the Auroran could throw back at her.

And an instant later, the Auroran returned fire.

The deck was nearly bleached away by the flash of light that spilled forth from *Predator*'s shroud when the Auroran guns spoke. The enemy ship carried twelve light cannon in her broadside to *Predator*'s seven, and if they were slightly less powerful individually, the difference was hardly worth noticing. The enemy fire lit up *Predator*'s shroud like a bank of fog, and wiped it away almost before it could be seen.

But her shroud held, stopping the worst of the enemy fire no more than a dozen feet from her hull, and bathing the ship in the sharp smell of ozone.

Creedy's scream broke off in a shocked, choking sound.

Grimm would laugh about that later, if he survived the next few moments. For now, he had a maneuver to complete—and then a trap to escape.

"Kettle!" he boomed, signaling with his hands at the same time, "complete the dive and take us into the mist!"

"Aye, sir!" answered the veteran pilot; then he set his feet and hauled on the steering grips, his teeth clenched, his neck straining with the effort.

Predator had stooped upon the Auroran from above her and to her starboard. Now, as they dived beneath her, Kettle rolled the ship again, far onto her port side, presenting her starboard broadside to the Auroran's lower hull and ventral rigging.

Again *Predator*'s guns howled their fury, but this time there was a difference. Leftenant Hammond, the starboard gunnery officer, had spotted the enemy's shroud, and in the bare seconds between that stunning revelation and his crews' chance to fire he had reassigned targeting. Now *Predator*'s guns fired in a rippling sequence, one after another— each aimed exactly amidships on the Auroran.

Ripple fire was an old tactic for hammering through a ship's shroud, though it took tremendous training and skill to pull off. The first shot blew aside a portion of the shroud, creating a cavity in its defenses. The second lanced in deeper, into the opening created by the first, before it also claimed its portion of the shroud. Then the third and the fourth and so on.

The number six gun's blast left black scorch marks on the enemy's hull.

Number seven's shot exploded almost exactly in the center of the enemy's belly.

There was a roar of released energy, a flash of hellishly bright light. A section of hull a good thirty feet across simply vanished, transformed into a cloud of soot and deadly splinters that flew up through the ship above them, hurled like spears by the force of the blast. Fire consumed the hull around the hole, and roiled and boiled through the vulnerable guts of the Auroran ship above them. Shattered ventral web-masts fell from the ship, only to become tangled in their own rigging and in the finer, nearly invisible shimmers of her ventral web. The sudden drag and the abrupt absence of her ventral web changed both the ship's propulsive balance and her center of gravity, and she began listing heavily to port. The blast had also smashed one of her two ventral planes to splinters, and as she rolled, she began to yaw as well.

Creedy, Kettle, and every crewman on the deck let out fierce, savage cries of triumph. Though they had by no means dealt the Auroran a mortal blow, she was, for the moment, severely lamed. She was still deadly, with her more numerous guns, bloodied but whole behind her mostly solid shroud, but in a duel between the two ships, *Predator* would now have the upper hand.

Grimm didn't watch the secondary explosions in the other ship, as flickering discharges of etheric energy found volatile crystals aboard the Auroran, probably upon the gauntlets in a weapons locker. He had already flipped his telescoptic back down and was raking the surrounding skies with his gaze and the telescopic lenses, searching for whomever the Auroran had been signaling.

The second vessel rose out of the mists of the mezzosphere, murky clouds roiling off of her spars and rigging, boiling down off of her plated flanks and leaving her armored sides gleaming as she rose into the harsh light of the sun. The banner of the armada of Spire Aurora flew bold from both dorsal and ventral masts, two blue stripes on a field of white, with five scarlet stars spangled between the blue stripes. Across her prow was painted in gold: ASA *Itasca*.

Staring at her, Grimm felt his bones turn cold. *Itasca* was a ship of legend, with a battle record stretching back more than five hundred years, and the Aurorans considered her a fine prize to be given to veteran captains on the fast route to their own admiralty. Grimm couldn't remember her commander's name at the moment, but he would be one of the Aurorans' best.

Worse, *Itasca* was a battlecruiser, a vessel designed specifically to run down ships like *Predator* and hammer them into clouds of glowing splinters. She could take the full punishment of *Predator*'s guns without flinching, and her own weapons—some four times Grimm's own broadside, and nearly as heavy as those of a battleship—would slam aside *Predator*'s shroud and destroy the ship and crew behind it in a single salvo. Worse, trusting in her armored plates and shroud, *Itasca* could stand off and fire accurately from a range *Predator* could never hope to match. Even worse, she had an armored warship's multiple power cores, and could store, deploy, and charge a far greater length of web than *Predator*, so that even with her vast additional mass, Grimm might not be able to outrun *Itasca* before her guns brought the race to a premature conclusion.

The only thing they had going for them was blind luck: The Auroran warship had come up from the mist almost two thousand yards away—though Grimm thought it worth noting that if *Predator* had come down at the standard angle of attack instead of at Kettle's more daring dive angle, *Itasca* would have come up barely a hundred yards to port. *Itasca*'s captain, whoever he was, had been lucky in positioning his vessel—after all, the Albion privateer could have dived down on the merchant cruiser from any angle, and *Itasca*'s captain had no way of knowing from which way he'd come. But he'd outthought Grimm and predicted his attack successfully. That was the kind of luck a smart captain made for himself.

"Kettle!" he snapped. "Dive, now!"

The helmsman's hand was moving toward the throttle in instant obedience even as he blinked in surprise—and then looked past the captain to see *Itasca* turning her overwhelming broadside to them.

The ship dropped again, without any maneuvers warning, catching many off guard. There were screams. Grimm saw Leftenant Hammond fly upward from the deck, held down by only a single safety line—the gunnery officer had to have rushed up and down the line of gunners, giving his crews instructions in rapid succession in order to pull off his ripple-fire maneuver. Grimm thanked God in Heaven that the man had remembered to keep one line secure despite his haste.

For an instant, Grimm thought he'd avoided engaging *Itasca* entirely— and then, just as *Predator* reached the top layer of the mists, *Itasca* opened fire.

Grimm's ship was a small target, as ships went: *Predator* was barely more than a destroyer in terms of mass. She was moving fast as well, and at an oblique angle. Considering how far away *Itasca* rode, it would take a fiendishly skilled or lucky gunner indeed to place blasts on target, especially with crews whose eyes were used to the dimness of the mists and now rose into the brilliance of the aerosphere.

Someone on *Itasca* was skilled. Or lucky.

The blast of the warship's heavy cannon ripped a hole in *Predator's* shroud as easily as a stone hurtling through a cobweb. The round burst at the top of the rearmost dorsal mast, and only the steep angle of *Predator's* renewed dive saved her. The explosion tore her topside masts away completely, hungrily devouring her entire dorsal web in a lace-work of fire as it went. Shards and splinters of wood went flying, and Grimm heard crewmen scream as a cloud of deadly missiles ripped into the starboard gun crews. Shrapnel hit the main crystal of the starboard number three gun, and it went up in a green-white flash that killed its crew and left a gaping wound a good twelve feet across in the ship's flank. An aeronaut named Aricson in one of the adjacent crews screamed as the section of deck to which his safety lines were fastened went flying out and away from *Predator*, dragging him with it. He shrieked in terror for an instant, and then man and scream both vanished into the mist, as the swirling sea of fog reached up and swallowed *Predator* whole.

"Evasive action!" Grimm ordered. The distant screaming roars of the *Itasca's* guns continued, and he heard the hungry hissing of blasts streaking through the mists around them, making them glow with hellish light. They had been lucky to survive a single glancing hit. Thirty guns raked the mist, and Grimm knew the enemy ship would be rolling onto her starboard side, giving the gunners a chance to track their approximate line of descent. If the same gunner or one of his fellows got lucky again, *Predator* would not be returning home to Spire Albion.

Kettle turned the steering grips hard as the cold mist enveloped them, and the ship slalomed lower into the mezzosphere while Grimm waited for the round that would kill his ship and his crew, forcing himself not to hold his breath. All the while, *Predator* sang her defiance to the mists, the chord shifting and changing with each alteration of her course, and the sound drifted up behind them like mocking laughter.

Grimm clenched his fists and ground his teeth. It was all very well for his ship to behave in such a fashion, but he sometimes wished that *Predator* could *think* as well as taunt the enemy. There was nothing to be done for it. Grimm simply had to hope that the mists of the mezzosphere would muffle and confuse the source of the sound, giving *Itasca*'s gunners no clear target.

He waited for as long as he dared, nearly a minute, and then screamed, "Pull her up!"

Kettle signaled the engine room, and their wild descent began to slow. A few measured breaths later, *Predator* leveled out, and they simply waited, everyone on deck entirely silent while Kettle struggled to trim the wounded ship as she completed her dash.

After a time, Grimm slowly exhaled and bowed his head. He reached up and wearily removed his goggles. The wet air felt cold and sticky against the skin around his eyes.

"They aren't chasing us," Creedy breathed, bringing his own goggles down.

"Of course not. *Itasca*'s too damned big," Grimm replied. His voice sounded hoarse and thin in his own ears. His neck and shoulders felt as if they'd been replaced with bars of brass. "A monster like that can't dive with *Predator*. Besides, no Auroran captain would try to follow us in this murk for fear of looking ridiculous. Two blind men can't have a very dignified chase."

Creedy snorted through his nose.

"Damage control," Grimm said quietly, unfastening his safety lines. "Make sure Doctor Bagen has everything he needs to see to the wounded. Call the roll. I'll be in my cabin."

Creedy nodded, looking slowly around them. "Sir?"

Grimm paused.

"This ship's shroud . . . it's extremely powerful for a vessel of this size."

The young officer hadn't actually asked the question, but it hung unspoken in the air between them. Grimm didn't like prevarication. It complicated life. But though he thought the young officer was a decent enough sort, he wasn't ready to extend that much trust. Not yet. So he gave the XO a flat gaze and said, "See to the ship, if you please, Mister Creedy."

Creedy snapped to attention and threw him an academy-perfect salute. "Yes, sir, Captain."

Grimm turned and went to the privacy of his cabin. He closed the door behind him and sat down on his bunk. The battle was over.

His hands started to shake, and then his arms, and then his belly. He curled his chest up to his knees and sat quietly for a moment, shuddering in the terror and excitement he hadn't allowed himself to feel during the engagement.

Aricson's scream echoed in Grimm's head. He closed his eyes, and the purple blotch the dying number three gun had burned on his retina hovered in his darkened vision.

Stupid. He'd been stupid. He'd been tearing huge swaths of profit from the Auroran merchant fleet. It had been inevitable that they would eventually respond to him. Some idiot would probably say that the fact that they'd sent *Itasca* to deal with him was a high compliment. Said idiot wouldn't be visiting the families of the dead men to give them his condolences and their death pay. He knew that he'd made sound decisions given what he'd known at the time, but some of his men were dead because of them nonetheless.

They were dead because he'd commanded them, and they'd followed. They'd known the risks, to a man, and every one of them was ex-Fleet. Things could have gone immeasurably worse than they had — but that would be little comfort to the newly minted widows back at the home Spire.

He sat and shuddered and regretted and promised dead men's shades that he wouldn't make the same mistake twice.

He was the captain.

By the time Creedy arrived with the damage report, Grimm had reassembled himself.

"Captain," Creedy said respectfully. "I don't think your accomplishments have been properly appreciated at home."

"Oh?" Grimm asked.

"Yes, sir," Creedy said. Controlled admiration crept into his tone. "I mean, for the Aurorans to dispatch *Itasca* to mousetrap a lone privateer . . . when you think about it, it's really a kind of compliment, sir."

Grimm sighed.

"Captain Castillo is one of their best," Creedy went on. "His attack was nearly perfect, but you slipped right through his fingers. If you were a captain in the Fleet you'd have merited tactical honors for . . ."

Creedy's face reddened and his voice trailed off.

"There are worse things to happen to a man than being drummed out of the Fleet, XO," Grimm said quietly. "Casualties, then damage reports. How bad?"

"Bad enough," Creedy said. "Five dead, six injured—shrapnel, mostly, and a concussion from an aeronaut in engineering who unhooked his second line too soon."

Grimm nodded. "The ship?"

"The dorsal masts are stubs. We'll need to get to a yard to replace them. We had to cut the rigging loose and drop it, so we lost most of the dorsal web. There's a hole in the gun deck where the number three gun was—we'll need a yard to repair that, too. And we blew two cables in our suspension rig."

Grimm took a slow breath. The suspension rig was the central structure of the ship, built around the main lift crystal. The weight of the entire ship hung suspended from the rig, and was distributed through its cables. There were eight of them, any two enough to bear the weight of the entire vessel . . . but the more cables broke, the more likely it was that those remaining would break—especially during any high-speed maneuvers. The loss of the occasional cable was expected, but was never to be taken lightly.

"You're saving the best for last, I think," Grimm said.

Creedy grimaced. "Chief Journeyman says there are fractures in the main lift crystal."

Grimm stopped himself from spitting an acid curse and closed his eyes. "That second dive, so soon after the first."

"That was his theory, sir. He's cut power to the lift crystal, and is running extra to the trim crystals to make up the difference in buoyancy and keep us afloat."

Grimm smiled faintly and opened his eyes. There would be no prize money on this trip, and no bounty, either. The trim crystals that helped adjust the ship's attitude were expensive, and using them to help maintain the ship's lift would be hard on them, but replacing them was a standard operating cost. The large crystals sufficiently powerful to suspend airships were another matter—they were far rarer and much more bitterly expensive. Only a power core cost more, assuming one could be found at all.

Where would he get the money?

"I see," Grimm said. "We'll simply have to replace it, I suppose. Perhaps Fleet will put in a word with the Lancasters."

Creedy gave him a smile that contained more artifice than agreement. "Yes, sir."

"Well," Grimm said. "It seems we need to return home. A bit earlier than we'd planned, but that's all right."

"Set course for Spire Albion, sir?"

"We're in the mist, XO," Grimm replied. "We can't take our bearings until we get back up into open sky. Where *Itasca* is doubtless hunting for us."

A low, groaning tone rumbled through the cabin's portal. After several seconds it rose higher and higher and higher, into a kind of distorted whistle, and then faded away.

Creedy stared out the portal and licked his lips. "Sir, was that . . . ?"

"Mistmaw," Grimm replied quietly. "Yes."

"Um. Isn't that a danger to the ship, sir?"

"Swallow us whole," Grimm agreed. "They aren't usually aggressive this time of year."

"Usually?"

Grimm shrugged. "If it decides to come eat us, we can't stop it, XO. Our popguns will only make it angry."

"The beasts are that big?"

Grimm found himself smiling. "They're that big." He inhaled and exhaled slowly. "And they're attracted to powered webbing."

Creedy glanced out the portal again. "Perhaps we should cut power to the web and reel it in, sir."

"I think that would be very wise, XO," Grimm said. "Though I expect Journeyman cut power to the web within a moment after we pulled out of the dive. Unfurl the sails. We'll spend the night moving with the wind, come up sometime tomorrow, and trust that *Itasca* won't be sitting there waiting for us."

Creedy nodded. Once again the strange, long call of the sounding mistmaw vibrated through the cabin. "Sir? What do we do about that?"

"The only thing we can, XO," Grimm said. "We stay very, very quiet." He nodded a dismissal to Creedy and said, "Raise sail. The sooner we get moving, the sooner we get back to Spire Albion."

■ ■ ■ Chapter 3 ■ ■ ■

Spire Albion, Habble Morning,
Tagwynn Vattery

Bridget sat in the dim vaults of the vattery, back in the shadowy corner where the cracked old vat had been removed. She wedged her back against the corner and held her knees up close to her chest. She was cold, of course. The chamber was always cold. She noticed only when she paused to think about it: She'd lived too much of her life in this room for it to be truly uncomfortable.

"Bridget?" called her father's deep voice from the entrance of the chamber. "Bridget, are you back here? It's time."

Bridget hugged herself harder and pushed a little farther back into the corner. The rows and rows of vats scattered the sound of his voice, sending it bouncing around the chamber. She leaned her head against the cold, reassuring solidity of the cinderstone wall and closed her eyes.

This was her home.

She didn't want to leave her home.

Her father's voice, gentle and deep, came again. "Take a few more moments, child. And then I want you to come out, please."

She didn't answer him. She heard his gentle sigh. She heard the doors to the chambers shut, leaving her with the quietly gurgling vats and the faint glow of a few scattered secondhand lumin crystals.

It wasn't fair. She was perfectly happy doing exactly what she'd done ever since she was a small child. And it was a good and necessary duty. Her father's vats provided the finest meats in all of Habble Morning, after all. Without someone to tend them, people would starve. Or at least eat inferior meat, she supposed. Personally, she took pride in her craft. She'd rather starve—to death, if necessary—than eat that ridiculous rubbery chum that Camden's Vattery produced.

It was ridiculous. Her family wasn't one of the High Houses, except in a fussy technical sense. She and her father were the only remaining members of the Tagwynn line, for goodness' sake, and it wasn't as though they were running out buying new ethersilk outfits every other week. Or at all. They lived no better than anyone else in Habble Morning. She hadn't *asked* to be born to the lineage of some overachieving, bloodthirsty Fleet admiral, no matter how respected a role he played in the history of Spire Albion. It wasn't as though she and her father enjoyed any particular privileges.

Why on earth should she submit to an outdated, rigidly traditional *obligation?*

She felt a small surge of outrage and tried to ride it into something larger and more determined, but it dwindled and flickered out again, leaving her feeling . . . small.

She could pretend all she liked. She knew the real reason she didn't want to spend her year in the service of the Spirearch.

She was afraid.

There was a rustle and a very light thump, and she looked up to see one of her favorite people bound lightly from the top of the next vat, land in silence only a few feet away, and sit down, regarding her with large green eyes.

"Good morning, Rowl," she said. Her voice sounded little and squeaky in her own ears, especially compared to her father's basso rumble.

The dark ginger cat purred a greeting and padded over to her. Without preamble, he climbed into her lap, turned a lazy, imperious circle, and settled down, still purring throatily.

Bridget smiled and began to run her fingers lightly around the bases of Rowl's ears. His purr deepened and his eyes narrowed to green slits.

"I don't want to go," she said. "It isn't fair. And it isn't as though I can actually help anyone with anything. All I know is the vattery."

Rowl's purring continued.

"We don't even own a gauntlet or a sword, unless you count our carving knives. We don't have enough money to get them, either. And even if we did, I don't have the faintest idea of how to use them. What am I supposed to do for the Spirearch's Guard?"

Rowl, having had his fill of getting his ears rubbed, stretched and turned over onto his back. When she didn't begin immediately, he swatted lightly at her hand with a soft paw, until she started scratching his chest and belly. Then he sprawled in unashamed luxury, enjoying the attention.

"But . . . you know Father. He's so . . . so good about honoring his obligations. When he gives his word, he keeps it. When he sets out to accomplish something, it's not enough simply to accomplish it. He needs to be the *best* at it, too. Or at least try to be. He served his time. He says it's important for me to do it, too." She sighed. "But it's a whole *year*. I won't get to see him at all. And . . . and the neighbors and the people in this corridor. And . . . and the vats and the shop and . . ." She bowed her head and felt her face twist up in pure misery. She gathered Rowl in her arms and hugged him to her, rocking back and forth slightly.

After a few moments, the cat murmured, "Littlemouse, you are squishing my fur."

Bridget jerked guiltily and sat up, loosening her embrace. "Oh," she apologized, "please excuse me."

The cat turned to meet her eyes with his and seemed to consider that for a moment. Then he nodded and said, "I do."

"Thank you," Bridget said.

"You are welcome." The cat flicked his tail back and forth a few times and said, "Wordkeeper wishes you to leave his territory?"

"It isn't that he wants me to go," Bridget said. "He thinks it is important that I do so."

Rowl tilted his head. "Then it is a duty."

"That's how he sees it," Bridget said.

"Then there is no matter for consideration," the cat replied. "You have a duty to your sire. He has a duty to his chief. If he has agreed to loan one of his warriors to his chief, then that warrior should go."

"But I'm not a warrior," Bridget said.

The cat looked at her for a moment and then leaned his head forward to rub his little whiskery muzzle against her face. "There are many kinds of war, Littlemouse."

"What is that supposed to mean?" she asked.

"That you are young," the cat said. "And less wise than one who is old. I am wiser than you, and I say you should go. It is obvious. You should trust a wiser head than your own."

"You aren't any older than I am," she countered.

"I am cat," Rowl said smugly, "which means I have made better use of my time."

"Oh, you're impossible," Bridget said.

"Yes. Cat." Rowl rose and flowed down onto the floor. He turned to face her, curling his tail around his paws. "Why do you wish to dishonor and humiliate Wordkeeper? Would you change his name?"

"No, of course not," Bridget said. "But I'm just . . . I'm not like him."

"No," Rowl said. "That is what growing up is for."

"I am *not* a child," she said.

The cat looked around speculatively and then turned back to her. "Rather than do your duty, you are hiding in the darkest corner of the darkest room in your home. This is very wise. Very mature."

Bridget scowled and folded her arms over her stomach but . . . she said nothing. She was acting like a child. Rowl was right. He generally was, but did he have to be so irritating about it?

"You are afraid," Rowl said. "You are afraid to leave the territory you know."

Bridget felt the tears welling up again. She nodded.

"Why?" Rowl asked. "What is there to fear?"

"I don't know," she whispered.

Rowl just sat, green eyes penetrating.

Bridget bit her lip. Then she said in a very small voice, "I don't want to be alone."

"Ah," Rowl said.

The cat turned and vanished into the deep shadows of the chamber, leaving her feeling smaller and colder and even more alone than before.

Bridget wiped at her eyes with her sleeve and swallowed the tight feeling in her throat. Then she stood up. She left her hand against the cool stone for another long moment, and tried to think of that familiar sensation coursing into her, infusing her with strength. Rowl was right, in his smugly annoying way. Her family did have a duty. There might not be much left of House Tagwynn, but it was still a good House. After all her father had done for her, after all the love he had given her when her mother passed, she owed him more than embarrassment—even if no one thought it embarrassing but him.

It was only a year. Only one . . . long . . . strange . . . lonely . . . terrifying year.

She walked slowly to the chamber door.

When her father opened it, she looked up at him. Franklin Tagwynn was an enormous block of a man, his shoulders almost as wide as the doorway. His arms were thicker than many men's legs, and the muscles sloping up to his columnar neck were like slabs of stone. He wore his white apron, and his belt with its vatterist's carving knives. His rumpled hair was the color of bare iron, and his eyes looked tired and concerned.

She tried to smile for him. He deserved it.

His answering smile was tired, and she knew she hadn't fooled him. He didn't say anything. He just enfolded her in a gentle hug. She put her arms around his solid warmth and leaned against him.

"There's my brave girl," he said quietly. "My Bridget. Your mother would have been so proud of you."

"I'm not brave," she said. "I'm so afraid."

"I know," he said.

"I won't know anyone," she said.

"I expect you'll make friends quickly enough. I did."

She huffed out a tired little breath. "Because I've made so many friends in the Houses already."

"Bridget," he said, his voice a gentle reproof. "You know you've never really tried."

"Of course not. They're pompous, spoiled, egotistical brats."

His chuckle was a low rumble against her cheek. "Yes. I know that they seem that way to you. But you had more responsibility thrust on you than most children when you were young—especially the children of the Houses. You had to grow up so fast. . . ." He leaned his cheek against her hair. "I can hardly believe it myself. Seventeen years went by so *quickly*."

"Daddy," she said quietly.

"I know you haven't cared much for the other children of the Houses, but they aren't all bad. And most of them will grow up. Eventually. You'll see." He leaned back from her and held her at arm's length.

"There's something I must speak to you about. One more responsibility I must ask of you."

She nodded. "Of course, Father."

He rested his huge hand fondly on her head for a moment, smiling. Then he said, "I need you to look after someone for me."

She tilted her head and blinked. "Pardon?"

Behind her father, two cats sauntered into the room. The first was a very large grey male, a muscular beast with many scars in his otherwise smooth fur, and notched ears. The second was Rowl. The ginger cat sat down behind and slightly to one side of the grey, and his whiskers quivered with amusement.

Her father spoke very seriously. "Clan Chief Maul has decided that it is time for the Spirearch to recognize his tribe as citizens of Habble Morning, which, to his way of thinking, obviously means that his line is no different from one of the other High Houses. As such, he acknowledges his obligation to detach a member of his family for service to the Spirearch. I offered you to Rowl as a guide, to help him learn the ways of the Spirearch's warriors."

Bridget blinked for a moment and then felt her face turning up into a wide, wide smile. "Wait . . . are you saying . . . are you saying that Rowl is going with me?"

"No," Rowl said smugly. "*You* are going with *me*. It is much more important that way."

Chief Maul glanced at Rowl in what might have been vague disapproval. The younger cat blinked his eyes once, slowly, and seemed to Bridget to be insufferably pleased with himself.

"This is an important duty," her father said. Laughter sparkled in his eyes. "And I know it will be a sacrifice for you. But are you willing to do this, for the sake of House Tagwynn's good relations with the chief and his clan?"

Bridget turned to Rowl and held out her arms. The ginger cat padded over and leapt up into them, nuzzled his cheek against hers again, and settled down comfortably. His softness was a favorite blanket, and his purr was as familiar as one of her mother's barely remembered lullabies.

"Well," Bridget said. She nuzzled her cheek against Rowl's fur. "If it's for the House of Tagwynn, then obviously it is my solemn duty. I'll manage."

▪ ▪ ▪ Chapter 4 ▪ ▪ ▪

Spire Albion, Habble Morning

For Gwen, the following two weeks were absolutely dreadful.

"I really don't quite see the point of all this," she panted. Her legs hurt. Her feet ached. Her chest felt as if it were on fire. All in all, she saw little reason for this running about the Spirearch's manor, and they'd done so for increasing amounts of time every single day during their training.

"It's good for you," Cousin Benedict said. He was a tall, lean young man less than two years older than Gwen herself, with tawny brown hair cut into a soft, thick brush. He wore the same exercise uniform Gwen did, though he loped along beside her lightly, without any apparent effort at all.

There was no detectable strain in his voice. None at all. The rotten, cat-eyed, thoroughly disgusting lout.

"It's all very well for you," Gwen gasped. "You've done it before."

"For the last two years, yes," Benedict agreed.

"You aren't wearing these ridiculous clothes."

"I'm wearing exactly the same clothing," Benedict countered.

"Yes, but you're *used* to them. Augh, pants, how do you stand *running* in these things?"

"Better than I would in skirts, I daresay," he answered. "I thought you'd love the running, Gwen. I personally grew to find it invigorating."

Gwen sputtered. "Invigorating? Benedict Michael Sorellin-Lancaster, you may personally kiss my—"

"As you wish, coz," Benedict said, smiling. "I must say, you're shaping up rather nicely."

Gwen kept pushing herself to keep moving, and felt that she hardly had the energy to regard the compliment with the proper suspicion. "What?"

The tall young man smirked. "You were barely able to complain at all the first few days. Just listen to you now. You've had something to say all the way to the end of the run."

Gwen glared daggers up at her larger cousin and let out an incoherent growling sound. It was all she could manage as the crew of training Guardsmen rounded the corner and pounded their way down the final length of wall to the courtyard. As they ran, people in the market watched them pass—Gwen herself had seen this peculiar practice of the Guard on many occasions. She had been aware that she would perforce engage in the same activity upon joining, but no one had told her that it was so very . . . taxing.

"Company!" bellowed the grey-haired Captain Cavallo as they reached their destination. "Halt! Fall out, people."

The grey-clad Guardsmen staggered to a ragged stop. Though the new recruits had set off in a neat formation, four abreast, that hadn't lasted long, and the crew that flopped down onto the cinderstone floor did so in an unruly, panting mob. The shapeless tunic and trousers that they'd run in were all identical, and all of them were dampened with sweat.

The veterans came to a relaxed stop, their breathing controlled, and stood grinning at the recruits or else speaking quietly to one another. Gwen disliked being gawked at by absolutely anyone, though that blocky blond Reginald Astor annoyed her more than most. He thought himself handsome, and was, in an irritatingly self-assured way, and he always had a habit of staring when she was disheveled and covered with sweat, with her uniform sticking to her in a most unladylike fashion.

She looked up with a scowl and found Reginald staring again, an insolent smile on his face.

She glared at him and said to Benedict, "I don't suppose you mentioned to Reggie how much I dislike his gawking."

Benedict looked down at her, smiling. "It would only make him be more obvious about it."

"Such a needless trial," Gwen muttered. "In addition to the needless trial we're already undergoing."

"Would you like me to go protect my helpless little cousin, then?" Benedict offered.

Gwen frowned for a moment. Benedict's offer was tempting, and it shouldn't have been. Normally she would have been perfectly comfortable with the notion of bracing some leering cad and pinning his ears back properly. For some reason, though, allowing her cousin to manage such a thing for her seemed . . . simpler.

Perhaps it was the exhaustion of all the running and classwork. Cavallo lectured the recruits for several hours every afternoon about the various habbles, their laws, and their relationships with one another—and while her own tutors had long since given her a similar grounding, it seemed that they had left a good many things out of their lessons. Or at least they had never made any particular effort to bring the ramifications of all those dry facts to Gwen's attention, and she had found herself stammering like a perfect nitwit when confronted with them during the captain's lectures.

Gwen was unused to being less than excellent at anything she pursued. She was not an excellent runner. She was not an excellent student of Spire politics; nor did she seem to be able to gain a proper grasp of the morning inquisition classes, a subject to which she'd had no prior exposure whatsoever. Oh, she had done well enough in the practice hall, when it came to the use of gauntlets at least, but her blade work remained every bit as inept as it had ever been, and she felt glumly certain that when live blade training commenced in a few weeks, she would continue working with a wooden training blade.

Being incompetent was surprisingly draining upon one's confidence. And annoying.

Was that why she didn't want to deal with Reginald? Was she afraid that she would find herself insufficient to the task of dissuading him? She'd had a considerable amount of practice in insufficiency of late. What if it had become a habit?

Nonsense, she told herself firmly. It appeared that she was going to have to face a great many challenging circumstances if she was to remain a Guardsman—and she *had* to remain a Guardsman. Any other outcome was unacceptable, since it would mean returning home and admitting to Mother that she had been correct.

Now, *that* was something that could not be borne.

"I will deal with him," Gwen said firmly. "But thank you, coz, for offering."

Benedict nodded as if that had been the answer he expected all along. "May I recommend you wait for a bit of privacy? A young woman bracing a peer in public is one thing—a recruit who confronts a veteran Guardsman that way is another matter entirely."

"I'll consider it," Gwen said.

Benedict did his best not to wince, Gwen could tell, but he didn't try to gainsay her, either. "Very well."

She sat for a time, breathing hard, her legs and feet aching most unpleasantly. It would pass, though. Already she felt she had recovered better from this run than she had after a night's sleep subsequent to her first run, two weeks before. Gwen had to admit that the exercise was quite practical. Each level of the Spire was simply enormous, and if one could maintain a hard pace for hours at a time, it would not be difficult to outrun an enemy or to catch some kind of criminal. Thieves, she felt sure, did not run as a matter of daily training—they wouldn't have someone like Cavallo pushing them. Were they the self-motivated sort, they would hardly be thieves, would they?

When Gwen looked up again, most of the recruits and veterans had moved back into the walled courtyard of the Spirearch's palace. Only Reginald and a handful of his cronies remained outside, along with Gwen and one of the largest young women Gwen had ever met. The girl was a quiet one, and her blond hair was long and thick. She had shoulders as wide as some men, thick wrists, and strong-looking hands and forearms. Her name was . . . Bother. Gwen couldn't remember her introducing herself to anyone. Actually, Gwen couldn't remember her speaking at all, unless questioned by an instructor in the classroom. The other recruits all referred to her as the cat girl.

The cat in question came scampering out of the courtyard and ran over to the large young woman. It was a ginger-colored beast and would have been quite appealing had it not been such a filthy creature. Cats lived in all the crawl spaces and vents and other unsavory, dank, vermin-infested regions of the Spire as a matter of course.

One would see cats now and again when moving about the habble, but they rarely associated directly with humans. Occasionally a household might be adopted by a cat or a small group of them, and some businesses found it wise to offer them food in exchange for their services as exterminators. It was a much simpler arrangement than refusing to pay the cats, and then finding one's stores emptied without a trace in the dead of night. She had heard of cats who had been employed as tenders and guardians for young children—but such arrangements were almost always business-oriented. Gwen had never heard of a cat who showed affection.

The lithe creature flowed into the cat girl's lap, turning in several circles and rubbing against her as he did. He nuzzled her cheek with his nose, and sniffed curiously at her sweaty uniform. The girl absently ran her hands over the cat's fur, and the beast settled down to enjoy the attention.

"What I want to know," said one of Reginald's group, "is what, pre-cisely, that vermin is doing running loose about the manor."

"It's quite unnatural," Reginald agreed. He folded his arms and re-garded the cat girl speculatively. "It makes one wonder what could mo-tivate a reasonable person to shelter such a pest."

At that, the cat girl looked up at Reginald. The large young man gave her his widest smile. "Well, how about it, Bridget, love? What rewards do you reap from having the beast nearby?"

The cat girl—that was right; her name was Bridget . . . something-or-other—looked at Reginald for a few seconds before answering. Her face was a neutral mask. "You wouldn't understand."

That drew a round of chortles from the young nobles. "Really?" Reginald asked. "And why is that?"

Bridget frowned thoughtfully for a moment, choosing her words with deliberate care. Then she nodded slightly to herself and said calmly, "Because you are an ass, sir."

Had the cat girl slapped him across the face, she could not have drawn a more startled reaction from the young noble. Reginald opened his mouth silently a few times, and then said, "Excuse me."

"I'm sorry," Bridget said. She rose, still holding the cat in her arms, and raised her voice slightly, enunciating the words. "You. Are. An. Ass." She smiled faintly. "Sir."

Gwen felt her eyebrows climb toward her hairline.

"You . . . you cannot speak to me in such a way," Reginald said.

Bridget and the cat regarded him with unblinking eyes. "Apparently I can, sir."

Reginald's eyes flashed with anger. "You shouldn't even be here," he snarled. "Your House died decades ago. You and your father are nothing but the last few scraps of meat clinging to a rotting bone."

Something shifted.

Gwen couldn't tell precisely what had happened, but the air was suddenly thick. Bridget's face never moved. Her eyes didn't narrow; nor did she bare her teeth. She said nothing. She did not so much as twitch a muscle. She only stared at Reginald.

It was the cat, Gwen realized. The beast's eyes seemed to have grown larger, and the very tip of his long tail had begun to flick left and right in slow rhythm. The cat stared at Reginald as if he were preparing to spring upon him with murder in mind.

When Bridget spoke, her voice was hardly louder than a whisper. "What did you say about my father?"

Gwen rose hurriedly. Reginald was a practiced duelist, and while most such confrontations ended in only mild injuries, it was quite possible for one or both participants to be killed when tempers were hot—and she was abruptly certain that the heavy silence now gathered around the cat girl was a thundercloud of undiluted rage.

An insult like the one Reginald had delivered was ample grounds to demand satisfaction, though she was certain the ass hadn't deliberately set out to provoke the reaction. If, however, Bridget was as upset as Gwen suspected, that might be exactly what he got—and Reggie, for all his oafishness, was more than competent with both blade and gauntlet. Bridget was very nearly as bad with blades as Gwen was, and her gauntlet work was atrocious. A duel could not end well for her.

"Excuse me," Gwen said, walking over to Bridget as though nothing at all were happening.

Bridget's eyes and those of the cat both flicked toward Gwen at the same time.

Goodness, that young woman was tall. She had at least a foot on Gwen. "We haven't been introduced," Gwen said pleasantly. "I'm Gwendolyn Lancaster."

Bridget frowned faintly. "Bridget Tagwynn."

Gwen cocked an eyebrow. "The House of Admiral Tagwynn?"

The corner of Bridget's mouth twitched, perhaps in irritation. "The same."

"How wonderful," Gwen said, a slight edge to her tone. "He was the finest naval commander in the history of all of Spire Albion. In fact, the Spire might not be here at all if not for his courage and skill. You come from one of the greatest families in our history."

Bridget frowned again. Then she ducked her head in a small, awkward bow. "Thank you."

"She comes of a footnote in Albion history," Reginald said, his voice sullen. "What has her family done for the Spire lately? Nothing. Their house grows meat, for Heaven's sake, like a common trog."

Bridget's eyes went back to Reginald. "You say that as if it is an insult, sir."

"And what is that supposed to mean?" Reginald demanded.

"That I would rather be a common trog than an ass of House Astor, sir."

Reginald's face turned bright red. "You dare cast an insult into the face of my House?"

"Not its face," Bridget said, arching an eyebrow. "Its ass."

"You vile little trog," Reginald said. "You think that because you've been to the Spirearch's Manor, because you are in training for the Guard, that you are worthy of such an honor? You think you can yap and taunt your betters because of it?"

"I'm not sure," Bridget said. "I'll let you know once I meet someone better than me."

Reginald's eyes blazed, and with a snarl he ripped one of his gloves from his belt and flung it hard at Bridget's face.

Bridget never moved—but Gwen did. She snatched the glove out of the air and turned to face Reginald. "Reggie, no."

"Did you hear that bloody slab?" Reginald snarled. "Did you hear what she said about my House?"

"And what you said about hers," Gwen said. "You started this, Reginald Astor."

"Stay out of this, Gwendolyn. I demand satisfaction!" His furious gaze went back to Bridget. "Unless the famed courage of the House of Tagwynn has dwindled away to nothing along with its bloodline."

Bridget's frown deepened and her mouth opened slightly. She glanced aside at Gwen and said, "Miss Lancaster . . . did this man just challenge me to a duel?"

"Hardly a man," Gwen replied. She looked up and met Bridget's eyes. "And yes. He did."

"Lunatics," Bridget breathed. "Must I accept?"

"If you don't," Gwen said, "he can litigate. The Council could assess a punitive fine against House Tagwynn."

"Could?" Reginald said. "Would. I guarantee the High Houses would rule harshly against such a display of disrespect to one of the leading Houses of Albion."

Bridget looked at Gwen again. "Is that true?"

"Courts are never certain," Gwen said. "But . . . it probably is."

"But I never insulted the Astors. Only him."

"He's the heir to the House, I'm afraid," Gwen said. "The Council may not make that distinction."

Bridget closed her eyes for a moment and muttered beneath her breath, "When will I learn to keep my mouth shut?"

"You don't have to do this," Gwen said.

"We're barely holding on as it is," Bridget said. "If . . . if we were fined, my father would have to sell the vattery."

Reginald barked out a harsh-sounding laugh. "Which is why insignificant little nothing Houses should show more respect to their seniors. You should have thought of that before you spoke."

The cat's claws made scratching sounds against the sleeve of Bridget's shirt. She put a hand on the beast, as if restraining it.

"Apologize," Reginald snarled. "Now. And I will forget that this happened."

Bridget paused again before she spoke. Then she squared her shoulders, faced Reginald, and said, "But I wouldn't." She glanced at Gwen. "How does this work? Do we fight right now?"

Gwen blinked up at the large girl. "You . . . actually intend to accept his challenge?"

Bridget nodded her head once. The cat made a low, eager growling sound.

Gwen sighed. "It doesn't happen here. You'll need a second, someone to accompany you, help you prepare, and to schedule the duel. You'll also need a Marshal to adjudicate it."

Bridget blinked. "That . . . seems like a needlessly complicated way to do something so adolescent."

"There are excellent reasons for it," Gwen said.

"I see," Bridget said. "How do I accept his challenge?"

Gwen wordlessly held out the glove.

"Ah," Bridget said, and took it.

Reginald nodded tightly, and gestured at one of the young nobles beside him. "This is Barnabus. He will be my second. Have your second contact him. Good day." He spun on a heel and marched away, into the palace, taking his entourage with him.

Bridget and Gwen watched them go. After a moment Bridget said, "I didn't need your help."

"Pardon?" Gwen asked.

"Your help. I didn't need you to come over here and make things worse."

"*Worse?*" Gwen asked, startled. "In what way did I make things worse?"

"I didn't ask you for your help. When you got involved his idiot pride was at stake. He was forced to start defending the honor of House Astor for fear of showing weakness to a Lancaster." Bridget shook her head. "If you weren't there, all I had to do was stop talking. It would have left him with nowhere to go."

"I was trying to *help* you," Gwen said.

Bridget rolled her eyes. "Why do all you people in the High Houses think that you are the only ones who can possibly manage matters that are none of your bloody business? Did you even consider the fact that I might not *want* your interference?"

Gwen folded her arms and scowled. She . . .

She hadn't, had she? Not for one second. And of course Reggie had been more stung by Bridget's words, because he wanted Gwen, and resented being humiliated in front of her. Gwen hadn't thought things through. She'd simply charged into the situation, attempting to pour oil on troubled waters—only she'd set the oil on fire instead.

As a result, it looked like someone was going to get burned. She couldn't leave things in that state, not when she'd helped put them there. She couldn't bear it if anyone were hurt because of her foolishness—well, perhaps if it was Reggie, and if he wasn't hurt too badly, but she'd feel awful if anything happened to Bridget.

"You might have a point," Gwen said quietly. "But that doesn't matter now."

"Why on earth not?" Bridget asked.

"Have you the faintest idea of what is involved in a formal duel?"

"Two fools."

Gwen found herself smiling faintly. "Other than that."

Bridget seemed to withdraw into herself. She hunched down a little, as if trying to hide her height. She frowned down at the cat, stroking its fur. "Other than that . . . no. I have no idea."

"Reginald does," Gwen said quietly. "You might not want my help, Miss Tagwynn—but as of now, you most assuredly need it."

■ ■ ■ Chapter 5 ■ ■ ■

Spire Albion, Habble Morning

Bridget regarded the nobleman uncertainly. "I'm not at all sure about this, sir."

Benedict Sorellin-Lancaster stood facing her, in the gloom of what could only loosely be considered early morning in Habble Morning's marketplace, outside the training compound of the Spire-arch's Guard. He was a tall man, as tall as her father, but lean with youth and a natural inclination. Benedict gave her a smile that he probably meant to be reassuring, but it showed a little too much of his larger-than-average canine teeth. "That's the problem, isn't it?" he said. "You aren't sure and you need to be. Come on, then. I need to assess what kind of physical strength you have. You'll not hurt me, Miss Tagwynn, I assure you."

"It seems . . . improper," she said, frowning. Of course she wouldn't hurt him. But even had that been her intention, Benedict's golden, vertically slit eyes showed him to be warriorborn, with the blood and the strength of lions in his limbs. "Are you quite sure this is sanctioned by the Guard?"

"Normally, open-hand combat is taught after your initial training course, but there's no regulation that says you've got to wait that long to learn. As long as it's your time you're spending, and not the Guard's."

"I see," Bridget said. "That seems equitable. How should I attack you?"

Benedict's face remained serious, but his eyes suddenly sparkled.

Bridget's stomach did an odd little shuffle-step, and she looked down straightaway.

"Just come at me," he said. "Try to pick me up."

Bridget frowned but nodded at him. "I see," she said. She took several steps closer to the young man and said, "Excuse me, please."

"Don't say 'excuse me,'" Benedict chided. "You won't be saying 'excuse me' to Reggie on the dueling stage—"

Bridget bent, faintly irritated by his tone, got a shoulder beneath Benedict's stomach, and dragged him up off the floor. He wasn't much heavier than a slab of red meat from one of the large vats back home, and she lifted him, held him there for a moment, and then continued the motion, tossing him over her back and onto the cinderstone floor behind her.

She turned to find him sitting on the ground, staring at her with his mouth slightly open.

"I'm sorry," she said. "Was that acceptable?"

"You . . . uh," Benedict said. His golden eyes glinted in the gloom. "You're . . . rather fit, Miss Tagwynn."

"I work for a living," Bridget said. She regretted the words almost instantly. She hadn't meant them as an insult to him, implying that he did not, but a prickly scion of one of the great Houses of Albion could readily interpret them that way.

But no anger touched his eyes. Instead his face spread into a slow, delighted smile. "Oh, Maker of Ways," he breathed, and the sound flooded out into a bubbling laugh.

Bridget liked the way his laugh sounded. She found her mouth tugging up into a small smile. "I beg your pardon, sir?"

"We should issue *tickets* to this duel," he said. "Reggie could spend his life trying and still not live it down."

"I beg your pardon?" Bridget repeated. "Whatever do you mean?"

"The duel," the young man said. "He challenged you, which means that you have the right to choose the location of the duel and the weapons to be used."

"How nice for me," she said. "But I still don't follow."

Benedict pushed himself back up to his feet, smiling. "You don't choose a weapon at all. You make it an unarmed duel."

Bridget tilted her head. "That does seem less likely to result in someone being maimed or killed for no good reason. But I don't know how to fight that way."

"I do," Benedict said. "The basics are reasonably simple to learn. And you're strong enough."

Bridget frowned. "But . . . presumably Reggie has had a great deal more training than I have. And while I am quite strong for a woman, I am surely not much stronger than he is. Would that not mean that he would have little difficulty in overcoming me?"

"That depends on what path you take," Benedict said.

Bridget felt her frown deepen. "My path . . . You aren't going to attempt to convert me to your religion, are you? I hope you are not, sir. That would be awkward."

Again, that easy laugh rolled forth. "Those who follow the Way have no need to proselytize. One does not convert to the Way. One simply realizes that one already follows the Way."

"God in Heaven, not that speech again," came a new voice. Gwendolyn Lancaster appeared from the gloom, dressed in the plain grey exercise clothing of the Guard, just as they were. It was difficult for Bridget to reconcile the absolute confidence in the noblewoman's stance and voice with her utterly diminutive size. Bridget felt quite certain that even without training, she could break Miss Lancaster like a ceramic doll.

"Dearest coz," Benedict said, his voice turning even more pleasant. "You are looking . . . particularly *Gwennish* today."

Gwendolyn arched one dark brow sharply at that statement and then said, "What are you doing on the ground?"

"She threw me here," Benedict said, his tone pleased.

Gwendolyn frowned at him, and then her eyebrows lifted. "*Did* she?" Her eyes turned to Bridget. "She doesn't look warriorborn."

"She isn't," Benedict said. "But she works in a vattery. I don't suppose I weigh too much more than a side of red meat, do I, Miss Bridget?"

"Not much more at all, sir."

Gwen narrowed her eyes. "Oh, you aren't thinking . . ."

"For Reggie? I most *certainly* am," Benedict said. "It's perfect."

"Stop it," Bridget said at last, exasperated. "Both of you. Stop it this instant. It's like you've both read a book that I haven't and you won't stop talking about it. It's most impolite."

"I'm sorry," Gwendolyn said. "I take it you weren't raised to be as underhanded and devious as Benny and me."

Bridget blinked. Goodness, that the noblewoman would just *say* it outright like that seemed very, very bold. But at the same time . . . somewhat reassuring. Gwendolyn Lancaster might have been many things, but at least she didn't seem as smugly capable of self-deception as many of the other children of the High Houses. "I would not care to make such a judgment of your families," Bridget said carefully. "But . . . no. It would seem not."

Rowl came padding out of the darkness, silent, as always, offering no explanation of where he had been, as always. Bridget bent one of her knees slightly, hardly needing to think about it, and he used it as a springboard to hop lightly into her arms and then flow up onto one of her shoulders. The cat nuzzled her cheek and she leaned her head in toward his slightly.

"Listen carefully, Littlemouse," Rowl said, in an almost inaudible tone. "I have sought word upon these two. They are dangerous."

Bridget flicked her eyes toward the cat and gave a tiny fraction of a nod to tell him that she understood. Being called "dangerous" by a cat could mean a great many things, but it was generally delivered as something of a compliment. She thought the two nobles to be rather self-involved and entirely overflowing with arrogance they hardly seemed to know existed, but she had learned long ago not to treat a cat's opinion lightly.

So she said to Gwendolyn, "Please excuse me, Miss Lancaster. You were saying?"

Gwendolyn had tilted her head, her bright eyes studying the cat sharply. "I was saying that if you can come near to matching Reggie in physical strength, then you can fight a duel he cannot win."

"I don't really care if anyone wins," Bridget said. "I just want everyone to walk away alive, and for this nonsense to be over."

Gwendolyn blinked and suddenly flashed Bridget a smile that looked as warm and true as an aeronaut's sunrise. "You have an absolutely wretched attitude about fighting a pointless duel for the sake of pride. Did you know that?"

"Thank goodness," Bridget said.

"The point is," Benedict said, rising easily to his feet, "that if you can offer him anything like a real fight, there's no way he can win the duel. If he defeats you bare-handed, it likely won't be by much, and he looks like a brute and a bully. And if you defeat him, he'll forever be the Astor who was beaten soundly by—" Benedict broke off and gave Bridget a slight smile.

"By the vattery trog," Bridget said. She smiled slightly. "That . . . would be quite the vile thing to do to him."

"Wouldn't it, though," Gwendolyn said, beaming.

"But . . . I'm not going to do that," Bridget said.

"Why under Heaven would you not?" Gwendolyn asked. "He more than has it coming."

"Possibly," Bridget allowed. "But to humiliate him would be to invite some other kind of indirect reprisal—if not upon me, then upon my father. My father is a good man. I won't see that kind of mischief brought to him because of me." She looked at Benedict. "Is there some weapon that we could use that would allow him to win without slaughtering me or looking like a fool?"

"There's no weapon, tool, or clockwork in the world that could make Reggie not look the fool," Gwen said in an acid tone.

"I don't care about victory," Bridget said. "I don't care about making him look bad. I just want to move on with my life as if we'd never traded words."

"You're right, coz," Benedict said, nodding slowly. "She has a wretched attitude about dueling for pride."

The two traded another, longer look, which again made Bridget feel that she'd skipped the necessary background reading needed to understand.

"Food?" Gwendolyn suggested suddenly. "The two of you came out here so early, you've missed breakfast call. Inquisition class is in half an hour, and you don't want to run on an empty stomach after that." She looked up at Rowl and added, "And for you as well, Master Cat. I'm buying."

Rowl said smugly, "This one has her priorities well sorted. Tell her my favorite food."

"Rowl," Bridget said. "That is not how one goes about such things."

She looked up to find both of the Lancasters staring at her.

"You speak Cat," Benedict said. "I mean, I'd heard that some people claimed to do it but . . . For goodness' sake, you sounded exactly like a cat just now."

"He has no idea how terrible your accent is," Rowl observed.

Bridget rolled her eyes at the cat and said to Benedict, "Yes, of course. Do you . . . not have any cats in residence at House Lancaster?"

"Certainly not," Gwendolyn said. "Mother wouldn't hear of it."

"We do, actually," Benedict said, cutting over Gwendolyn smoothly. "The servants have an arrangement with several cats to handle vermin. But as far as I knew, it's an old understanding, and no one there has ever actually communicated directly with a cat before."

Gwendolyn blinked several times. "How is it that you know that when I do not?"

"Because no one tells you anything, coz," Benedict said. "Perhaps because you spend so much time with Lady Lancaster and often do not pause to think before you speak."

Gwendolyn tilted her head to one side as if to acknowledge a fair point. Then she blinked again and said, "Then I am afraid that I have been quite rude. I have neither introduced myself to your companion nor sought introduction to him. Please convey to him my apologies, if you would, Miss Tagwynn."

Bridget looked carefully at Gwendolyn for a moment, waiting for the flash of mockery that would appear in her eyes, as they would have in Reggie's, but it didn't come. She seemed sincere. Imperious and obsessed with protocol—but sincere.

"What is this she asks, Littlemouse?" Rowl said, leaning forward to peer intently at Gwendolyn.

"She seeks an exchange of names," Bridget told him, in Cat. "Human names, not cat names. She feels she has wronged you by not seeking it sooner."

Rowl stiffened in indignation. "Has she?"

"Perhaps not intentionally," Bridget allowed. "She wasn't sure what to think of a cat appearing among humans. I suspect she genuinely seeks to avoid giving offense."

Rowl's tail lashed back and forth. "What would Wordkeeper say of her?"

Bridget smiled slightly. She knew precisely how her father would treat Miss Lancaster. "He would ask her to tea and extend all courtesy."

Rowl nodded his head sharply, once, a very human gesture. "Then

I will also extend courtesy. Tell her my name, and that she has not yet earned a cat name of her own, but that breakfast is a good start."

Bridget turned to Gwendolyn and said, "Miss Lancaster, this is Rowl of the Silent Paws tribe, kit to Maul, chief of the Silent Paws."

"A prince of his house, as you are of yours, coz," Benedict noted.

Gwendolyn evidently had the grace to avoid looking skeptical at this pronouncement. She gave Benedict a decidedly unreadable look, which only made him smile.

He had, Bridget thought, a very nice smile.

Gwendolyn turned back to look at Rowl seriously and said, "Welcome, Sir Rowl, to . . . the human part of Habble Morning. It would please me very much to buy you breakfast, if you would permit it."

Rowl promptly plopped down into Bridget's arms, his throaty purr needing no translation. "A *very* good start," he murmured.

"Yes, Miss Lancaster," Bridget said. "That would be fine."

■ ■ ■ Chapter 6 ■ ■ ■

Spire Albion, Habble Morning

Rowl watched Littlemouse and her fellow humans behaving foolishly, and wondered how soon she would need him to intervene and set things right.

Once more they had slept less than all the humans in the Spirearch's Guard, and once more the human Gwendolyn and her half-souled cousin thought that they were preparing Littlemouse for some kind of combat, which was ridiculous. The best way to prepare for fighting was to fight. Any kitten knew that.

Currently Benedict was having Littlemouse practice falling, which was similarly ridiculous. One didn't *practice* falling. One simply landed on one's feet. Yet over and over, Littlemouse fell from her feet to her back, sometimes alone, sometimes helped along the way by Gwendolyn or Benedict. Rowl had been suspicious of this activity at first, assuming that it would be used as an excuse for Gwendolyn to eliminate a rival female, or for Benedict to claim mating rights with Littlemouse. But over the past few days it had proven to be more foolish than nefarious, and did not seem to harm Littlemouse to any significant degree, so Rowl permitted it to continue.

It seemed a shame to waste so much of one's time—and to miss so much sleep—in such a fundamentally stupid activity. If they'd only asked Rowl about it, he could have explained it to them.

Benedict began to show Littlemouse how to make him fall to the floor. What was the point of learning to do such a thing slowly, and obviously with considerable cooperation from Benedict? Did Little-mouse think that a foe would behave in such a way?

Rowl sensed a pressure change in the air against the fur of his flank and his whiskers, and lazily tilted an ear in that direction. There was a whisper of motion, utterly inaudible to anyone but a cat, with all the commotion the humans were making to cover it, and Mirl emerged from the shadows.

"Rowl," said the black-furred female. Mirl was a small cat, but swift and intelligent. She was one of Maul's Whiskers, his spies and hunters. Only a tiny ring of green was visible around her large, dark pupils, and the only way to see her in the gloom was by the dim shine of her eyes.

"Mirl," Rowl replied lazily.

Mirl prowled to his side and sat, studying the humans. "What are they doing?"

"They mean to teach Littlemouse to fight," Rowl said.

Mirl considered them gravely. "I see. Have they begun yet?"

"They seem to think so," Rowl said. "What news from my father?"

"He sends his greetings and says that you are to do your duty or he will notch your ears."

Rowl flicked his tail and yawned. "I know what I am to do. Is that all?"

Mirl twitched her ears in an amused flick, but her tone became more serious. "He says that Longthinker has confirmed the reports of the Silent Paw scouts."

Rowl moved his eyes to the smaller cat. "The new things in the air shafts?"

Mirl blinked her eyes in affirmation. "So say the Shadow Tails, and the Quick Claws, and half a dozen other tribes besides them. Cats have gone missing in other habbles as well—but none have seen what took them."

Rowl made an irritated sound in his chest. "That seems cowardly."

"To me," Mirl said, "it seems skillful."

"That as well. Are we then at war?"

"Not yet," Mirl said. "Maul says that first we must know whom we would war against."

"What does Longthinker say we face?"

"Longthinker . . . is not sure."

Rowl looked at Mirl sharply. But he said nothing. His tail lashed back and forth restlessly. Longthinker was not cat, but he was clever, wise, and honorable. If he did not know what threat now stalked the Silent Paws and other tribes in their own home tunnels, it must be something strange indeed—or something new.

"Please tell my father," Rowl said, "that I advise a declaration of war immediately—without restriction. We will be better served by immediate aggression than by too much caution. Let us hunt and destroy them before they have a chance to nest."

"I will tell him your words," Mirl said. She twitched a careless whisker. "He will not heed them."

Rowl ignored that last remark with the disdain it richly deserved.

Mirl sat beside him and watched the humans flopping about. "I have seen such a thing before."

"This fight-teaching?" Rowl asked, his tone dubious.

"In the Temple of the Way, in Habble Landing," Mirl said.

"What were you doing all the way down there?" Rowl asked.

"My duty as a Whisker," Mirl replied loftily. "They did something resembling this, only there were more of them and they wore different kinds of clothing."

"Did they look this foolish?"

Mirl tilted her head thoughtfully. "Many did. But others seemed less foolish."

"In what way?"

"They moved less poorly. Not so well as a cat, of course."

"Of course," Rowl said.

"But they were much less clumsy than most humans." She used a paw to comb the fur of one ear. "Perhaps it works." They both watched Littlemouse take a particularly hard fall. "Eventually."

"They *are* rather slow, humans," Rowl mused. "Do you really think it has potential?"

"She hardly need be *much* less clumsy to make another human look so," Mirl said. "Whom is she to fight?"

"A young male. He aimed words of pain at Wordkeeper. In reply, Littlemouse slapped his ears with her words. Now they plan to fight."

"They *plan* to fight?" Mirl said, mystified. "Why does she not go find him in his sleep and fight him then?"

Rowl yawned. "I have no idea. But he will not find her in *her* sleep. If he tries, I will rip out his eyes."

"Sensible," Mirl said. "Though a human is no easy prey. Not even for the mighty Rowl."

"A proper Whisker should not make so much noise," Rowl growled.

Mirl rose and bowed her head in a mirror of the human gesture. "Yes, mighty Rowl."

Rowl fetched her a swift rap on the nose (though not with his claws extended), but Mirl avoided it with lazy grace, her eyes dancing with laughter. She sauntered off, flicking her tail mockingly. "You are almost as handsome as you think you are, you know."

"You are too quick and too clever for your own good," Rowl replied calmly. "Keep your wits about you in the tunnels. I would prefer it if you did not go missing."

"Don't make a foolish mistake that gets you killed while protecting your human," she replied.

"Will I see you again soon?"

"Perhaps," Mirl said. "It depends on my mood."

Then she glided back into the dark the way she had come.

Rowl watched her go, the insufferable female. He stared after her for a moment, his tail lashing thoughtfully. Insubordinate—but quick. And beautiful. And never, ever boring.

Perhaps he would compose a song for her.

Once "fighting" practice was over, things that mattered could be done. Rowl took his customary place in Littlemouse's arms and accompanied her to breakfast in the marketplace.

The marketplace was a sea of stalls and small buildings set in the center of the habble, surrounding the Spire Lord's manor. About a quarter of the stalls were made of spirestone, originally placed there by someone the humans called the Builders. The remainder were made mostly of brick, their doors and vending windows now covered with hide stretched over frames. Some of the more well-to-do shops used wood from the jungle-covered surface, painstakingly transported up miles of Spire.

Littlemouse carried him toward the stall that smelled the best and was one of the few that were occupied this early in the day. Human Benedict seemed to know the owners of the stall personally, for they greeted him by name each morning. It was probably due to his hunger—the half-soul's body burned hotter than other humans', almost exactly as hot as a cat's, and he had to eat more frequently than other humans. Rowl waited while Benedict ordered for everyone and paid with the small pieces of metal the humans valued so dearly.

Once that was done, the food was made, and the humans went to a nearby table to eat. Rowl took his seat beside Littlemouse, who placed a roll of bread and meat in front of him. Rowl tore it open with his claws and waited for the little gouts of steam to clear. It did not matter how delicious the food tasted—burning one's tongue was an undignified experience and he did not intend to repeat it.

"What do you think of the training, Rowl?" Benedict asked politely, after the human had wolfed down one of the rolls whole.

Rowl eyed Littlemouse. In his judgment, she did not seem to have made up her mind whether or not to favor these two humans with her loyalty, but she clearly regarded human Benedict as a potential mate. It would be discourteous of him to jeopardize her chances of propagating her species. "It seems painful," he said to Littlemouse. She translated this into the human tongue, smiling wryly.

"It can be," Benedict said. "But in an actual fight, you might be injured and need to function anyway. Little pains now could save a life later."

"Cutting Reggie's throat in his sleep could do so as well," Rowl said, and eyed Littlemouse. She rolled her eyes, translating that, and human Gwendolyn promptly began choking on some of her food.

Rowl calmly took a few bites from the cooler edges of his dumpling.

"Quite a direct soul, isn't he?" Gwendolyn managed after a few moments.

"You have no idea," Littlemouse said.

"There is a good reason to limit the conflict to something less . . . decisive," Benedict said, addressing Rowl directly. "Reggie is a member of a large and powerful family. The man who will be his second is also an Astor, of a cadet branch of the House. If anything permanent happens to Reggie, the second will report it and they might seek vengeance."

"I would think they would be glad to rid themselves of a fool," Rowl replied.

Human Gwendolyn made a snorting sound when Littlemouse translated and took another bite of her breakfast.

"To a degree," Benedict allowed. "But if they tolerate harm to a member of their House, others might see it as a sign of weakness."

"Ah," Rowl said. "That makes at least a little sense." He considered the situation gravely. "But Littlemouse does not have a large House to take vengeance on her behalf should Reggie do something permanent to *her*."

Benedict seemed uncomfortable when Littlemouse translated that. "There is . . . a certain amount of truth in that. But it is not in the interests of anyone in the habble for duels to be lethal. Pressure could be brought against House Astor if such actions were taken."

"If he kills Littlemouse," Rowl asked, "would the House of Lancaster then war upon the House of Astor?"

Benedict and Gwendolyn exchanged a long look. "I . . . don't think so."

"Then this pressure you speak of is a paw without claws," Rowl said. "It will do nothing to truly prevent his action."

Gwendolyn abruptly leaned across the table, looked hard at Rowl, and said firmly, "If any such thing happens to Miss Tagwynn, Master Rowl, I will personally challenge Reggie with gauntlets and blow a hole in him large enough for a cat to leap through. You have *my* word on that."

"Not only have I already lost the duel," Littlemouse murmured, "but I've been killed as well. Why are we wasting breakfast on a dead woman?"

Rowl looked up at Littlemouse and said, not unkindly, "You were already fool enough to become involved in this. It is time to let wiser heads than yours sort it out. I promise that once I am sure that you are not blindly walking into your own death, I will let you lose the fight on your own."

Littlemouse scowled at Rowl.

"What did he say?" Benedict asked, blinking back and forth between them.

"That he wants a bath," Littlemouse said in a decidedly threatening tone.

"Really, Littlemouse," Rowl said, nibbling another bite. "You must at some point begin to grow out of these childish outbursts."

"Oh," Littlemouse said, her face flushing. "You can be so *infuriating*."

"You are only angry because you know I am right," Rowl said, in the tone one ought to use when one knows one is obviously correct and the other is entirely wrong.

Footsteps approached through the gloom, and Rowl looked over to see the human Reggie's associate approaching the breakfast table. He watched without moving, but settled his feet into a good place to allow him to throw himself at the enemy's eyes should he attempt anything harmful.

A few seconds later, Rowl's humans became aware of the human approaching. He came to a stop at their table and lifted his chin. "Benedict. Gwen. Miss Tagwynn."

Rowl narrowed his eyes.

"Good morning, Barnabus," human Gwendolyn said in a chill tone. "You're going to support him, are you?"

The human Barnabus shrugged, apparently unfazed. "The challenge was formally given and accepted, Gwen. He means to see it through."

"That doesn't mean that *you* have to be the one who seconds him," she replied.

"He's blood," Barnabus said simply. "Besides, if I don't, some hothead will."

Benedict shook his head. "He's got a point, Gwen. I'm sorry you got dragged into this, Barney."

Barnabus shrugged. "Miss Tagwynn, may I ask who is serving as your second?"

"Me," said humans Benedict and Gwendolyn at the same time.

And even as they did, Rowl let out his most violent and raucous war cry, and hurtled at human Barnabus's eyes.

The human was taken utterly off guard. He flung up his arms and fell backward. Rowl landed with his weight on the human's chest and rode him all the way to the spirestone floor. The human fell even more clumsily than Littlemouse did, and hit with a huff of expelled breath, briefly stunned.

Everyone there, in fact, looked briefly stunned.

Rowl sat calmly on his chest, leaned over close to human Barnabus's face, and snarled, "I am Rowl, kit of Maul, lord and master of the Silent Paws—and *I* am her second."

Littlemouse translated this in a startled, jerky voice. Human Barnabus stared at Rowl with wide eyes and then looked back and forth between him and Littlemouse, listening.

"You can't be serious," Barnabus sputtered in response.

Rowl batted him sharply on the nose with enough claw to draw a few drops of educational blood and let out another growl. "Pay attention, human. Littlemouse will meet the Reggie in unarmed battle in the market, in the light of noon, seven days hence."

Barnabus stared some more, eyeing the cat and then Littlemouse's translation. "Benedict," he said a moment later. "Reggie picked an idiotic moment to indulge his taste for duels, but this is beyond the pale. A *cat* as her second? What will people think?"

Benedict pursed his lips thoughtfully. "If it were me? I'd probably think that Reggie was one of the scum of the Great Houses, throwing his weight around against someone like Miss Tagwynn. But I think you're missing the point, here, Barney."

"And what point would that be?" he demanded.

"*Him*," Benedict said, and pointed at Rowl.

Rowl lashed his tail, never looking away from human Barnabus's eyes. He held them for a moment, then rose and calmly prowled back to his breakfast.

Littlemouse asked, in Cat, "This is what Maul wants?"

"Obviously," Rowl said. He might have sounded smug—not that he

69

didn't deserve to feel that way, of course. The human Barnabus had been entirely at his mercy.

"I'm sure I don't understand," Barnabus said, staring at the cat.

"I'm sure you don't, either, sir," Littlemouse said. "But you will. In one week."

■ ■ ■ Chapter 7 ■ ■ ■

Spire Albion, Habble Morning,
Ventilation Tunnels

Grimm strode toward the Spirearch's Manor, his booted steps striking the stone floor with sharp, clear impacts, and reminded himself that murdering the idiot beside him in an abrupt surge of joyous violence would be in extremely bad taste.

"Perhaps her time has come," said Commodore Hamilton Rook. He was a tall, regal-looking man, provided one desired a monarch whose nose was shaped like a sunhawk's beak. His black hair was untouched by silver, which Grimm was certain was an affectation. His face and hands were weathered and cracked from his time aboard his ship, a battlecruiser called *Glorious*, a peer of *Itasca*, if not even remotely her rival. He was refined, well educated, exquisitely polite, and an utter ass. His Fleet uniform was a proper deep blue accented with an unseemly amount of golden braid and filigree, and bore three gold bands at the end of each sleeve. "What say you, my good Francis?"

Grimm glanced aside and up at Rook. "As ever, I ask you not to call me Francis."

"Ah. The middle name then, I suppose? Madison?"

Grimm felt the fingers of his sword hand tighten and relax. "Commodore, you are well aware that I prefer Grimm."

"A tad stuffy," Rook said disapprovingly. "Might as well call you 'Captain' all day, as though you still had a true commission."

Extremely bad taste, Grimm thought. Appallingly bad taste. Historically bad taste. No matter how joyous.

"I had hoped your recent successes might have made you less insecure," Rook continued. "And you haven't answered my question. My offer is more than generous."

Grimm turned down a side corridor out of the main traffic of the day in Habble Morning. "Your offer to pay me a quarter of her worth to break my ship into scrap? I had assumed you were making some kind of stillborn attempt at humor."

"Come now, don't romanticize this," Rook said. "She's been a fine vessel, but *Predator* is outdated as a warship, and undersize as a ship of trade. For what I'm offering you, you could secure a merchant vessel that would make you several fortunes. Think of your posterity."

Grimm smiled faintly. "And the fact that you would secure her core crystal for your House's inventory is beside the point, I suppose."

Crystals of suitable size and density to serve as a ship's power core were grown over the course of decades and centuries. Core crystals were not expensive; they were *priceless*. In Spire Albion, all current crystal production was under commission to the Fleet, leaving a set number of core crystals available to private owners—most of whom would not part with them at any price. Over the past two centuries, the Great Houses had been steadily acquiring the remaining core crystals. Certainly they could be had from other Spires, but so far as Grimm knew, no one in the world could match in power or quality the crystals the Lancasters produced.

"Of course it would do no small amount of good for the standing of our House," Rook replied. "But it's an honest offer nonetheless."

"No," Grimm said.

"Very well," Rook said, his voice tightening. "I'll double it."

"No. Twice."

The larger man took a step in front of Grimm and stopped, glaring.

"See here, Francis. I mean to have that crystal. I've seen the damage report your engineer turned in. You were lucky to make it back to the Spire at all."

"Was I?"

"You need entirely new power runs, a new main lift crystal, and at least *three* new trim crystals! I've seen your accounts. You've nowhere near enough money to afford them."

"She's wounded," Grimm said firmly. "Not a derelict."

"Wounded," Rook said, rolling his eyes. "She can barely limp up and down the side of the Spire on a tether. *Predator* isn't an airship any longer. She's barely a windlass."

Grimm suddenly found himself facing Rook, his hands clenched into fists.

Rook apparently did not notice that detail. "I am making you an open and friendly offer, Francis. Don't force me to resort to other means."

Grimm stood silently for a moment, staring up at Hamilton Rook's sneer. "And what means, sir," he asked quietly, "would those be?"

"I can pursue it in the courts, if need be," he said. "Report on the dangerously slipshod handling of your ship. Report on the number of casualties you've suffered. Report on the complaints and accusations of criminal behavior other Spires have forwarded to the Fleet."

Grimm ground his teeth. "I incurred those accusations while acting on the Fleet's behalf, and you know it."

"And would be ordered to deny it," Rook said, his smile widening. "Honestly, Francis. Do you really think the Fleet would rather stand by you, a disgraced outcast, than suffer a public humiliation like that?" The smile vanished. "I *will* have that core crystal, Grimm."

Grimm nodded thoughtfully. And then, quite quickly and with no restraining gentleness whatsoever, he slapped Commodore Hamilton Rook across the face.

The smack of the impact echoed down the empty corridor. Rook reeled back, stunned by the fact of the blow more than the force of it, and stared at Grimm with wide eyes.

"*Predator* is not property," Grimm said in a calm, level tone. "She is not my possession. She is my home. Her crew are not my employees. They are my family. And if you threaten to take my home and destroy the livelihood of my family again, Commodore, I will be inclined to kill you where you stand."

Rook's eyes blazed and he drew himself up to his full, intimidating height. "You arrogant insect," he snarled. "Do you think you can slap me about without paying for it?"

In answer, Grimm took a quick step forward and did it again. Rook tried to flinch away from the blow, but Grimm's hand was too quick for him. Again the sound of the slap echoed down the hallway.

"I'll do it any damned time I please, sir," Grimm said in the same level voice. "Take me to court. Let me tell the judges and the public record precisely what incensed me enough to strike you. You will be publicly humiliated. If you hoped to keep any shred of your reputation, you would have no choice except to challenge me to a duel. And, as the challenged party, I would insist upon the Protocol Mortis."

Rook leaned his head back slightly from Grimm, as though he had opened his pantry to fetch cheese and found a crawlyscale waiting for him instead. "You wouldn't dare. Even if you won, my family would have your hide."

"I'd change my flag to Spire Olympia," Grimm said. "They'd be glad to have me. Let the Rooks attempt their little game with the captain of an Olympian vessel. Do you think your corpse is worth that, Hamilton?"

Rook clenched his fists at his sides. "That's treason."

"For an officer of the Fleet, yes," Grimm said, baring his teeth. "But not for a disgraced outcast like me."

"You wretched little nothing," Rook said. "I should—"

Grimm took a step forward, never breaking eye contact, forcing Rook to take a step back. "You should what, *Commodore?*" he said. "Say nasty things behind my back? Challenge me to a duel? You haven't got the spine to look in a man's eyes when you kill him. That's something else we both know."

Rook clenched his teeth, seething. "I will not forget this, Grimm."

Grimm nodded. "Yes. One of your many excellent failings, Hamilton, is that you forget favors and remember insults."

"Indeed. My House has a long memory—and wide vision."

Grimm felt a surge of anger threaten to shatter his demeanor, but he suppressed it from everything but the tenor of his voice. "Wide vision? Is that how you style it? Know this: If anything happens to any of my men, or to any of their families—anything, no matter how small—I shall hold you personally responsible. I shall denounce you to the Admiralty and the Council within the hour. And in the duel that follows, I shall kill you and cast your body from the top of the Spire—and not necessarily in that order. Am I perfectly clear, Commodore?"

Rook swallowed and took another half step back.

Grimm pointed a finger at him and said, "Stay away from my home. Stay away from my family. Good day, sir."

Then the captain of *Predator* turned precisely on a heel and continued marching toward the palace.

Grimm hadn't been walking for two minutes when a calm, amused voice spoke from the darkness of an unlit side corridor. "What's happened to you, Mad? You've acquired a few shreds of discretion. I remember a time when you would have braced that pompous twit in the middle of the habble market at noonday."

Grimm snorted and didn't slow his steps. "I've no time to fence with you, Bayard."

A small, slender figure of a man appeared from the gloom and fell into step beside him. Alexander Bayard wore a commodore's uniform almost precisely like Rook's, if not quite as richly fashioned. It was also a great deal more weatherworn. Bayard loved to spend his days aboard ship out on the deck of his flag vessel, the heavy cruiser *Valiant*, whereas Rook hid from the elements whenever he could.

"Yes," Bayard said easily. The smaller man lengthened his strides to match Grimm's. "I've heard. You've a ship that can barely stay afloat and no means to repair her, so I'm certain you're in quite the rush to clear port again."

"Don't make me duel you," Grimm said.

"Why on earth not?" Bayard said, putting a bit of extra swagger in his step. He had dark, glittering eyes and hair that had gone magnificently silver decades before its time. "You'd lose and we both know it."

Grimm snorted.

"You're a true tradesman of violence, my stiff-necked friend," Bayard continued. "But you've no ice in your soul and not a speck of reptile in your blood. It takes calculation to win a duel against a reptile, and you've always been impatient."

Grimm found himself smiling. "You've just called yourself a reptile, Commodore."

"And so I am," Bayard agreed. "I'm a viper who plays every angle to his advantage." His smile faded slightly. "Which is why I'm in uniform and you aren't, I'm afraid."

"There was no point in both of us being drummed out," Grimm replied. "You know that I don't hold it against you, Alex."

"You needn't. I'll do it for you. And as for Rook . . ." Bayard shuddered. "If it comes to a duel, I hope you will call upon me to be your second."

"I find it unlikely that I should be so desperate," Grimm said. "I suppose that if everyone else says no, I may consider you."

"Excellent. A day in advance at least, if you please. My mistress would never understand if I walked out on her abruptly."

Grimm barked out a laugh. "Neither of you is married, and you've been seeing each other exclusively for . . . eleven years now?"

"Thirteen," Bayard said smugly.

"God in Heaven. And yet you persist in the fiction that she is your mistress even now. Why?"

A boyish grin spread over Bayard's face. "Because scandal, old friend, is ever so much more enjoyable than propriety. Such things are the spice of life."

"You're a degenerate," Grimm said, but he was smiling widely now, and the rage and frustration he'd felt at his encounter with Rook had faded away. "How is Abigail?"

"Rosy cheeked, starry-eyed, and content, my friend. She sends her love."

"Please convey my warmest respects," Grimm said. He cocked his head to one side and regarded Bayard. "Thank you, Alex."

"Rook would try the patience of an Archangel," Bayard said, inclining his head. "You are not without friends, Grimm. Don't waste another moment in concern for the fool."

"I would not consider the time spent thrashing him wasted."

Bayard let out a rich, warm laugh. "Few would, I daresay."

They came to a dim section of largely unused tunnel, where the lumin crystals were spaced widely apart. Grimm put his hand lightly upon the tunnel wall to guide his nearly blind steps. "You didn't just happen upon me when I needed a boost in morale. You were following me."

"Obviously."

"Why?"

"I think you need to speak to the Spirearch."

"That's where I'm going now," Grimm said.

"Ah, yes," Bayard replied. "But you see, he is not in his manor. He sent me to bring you to him—"

Bayard stopped abruptly in his tracks. Grimm followed suit almost instantly. The tunnel was full of whispering sound: the echoes of their steps, of their voices, the distant empty exhale of air moving through the Spire's vents, and their own breath.

Grimm was never sure, after, what tiny hiccup of sound or what flicker of motion in the gloom gave the ambush away—his instincts simply screamed that danger was at hand, and he drew his sword in a liquid whisper of copper-clad steel. Beside him, he felt as much as heard Bayard do the same, and then something, some *thing*, shrieked in the dark and a cannonball of howling hot agony hurtled into his chest.

■ ■ ■ Chapter 8 ■ ■ ■

Spire Albion, Habble Morning,
Ventilation Tunnels

There was no time to react and no room to wield even the short, straight blade of his sword. Grimm fell before the horrible, painful weight and thrust at it with an arm, shoving something that snarled and spit and drew blood with teeth and claws. The creature was perhaps the size of a large child. It flew up and away from him.

"Grimm!"

"I'm fine!" Grimm snapped, rolling swiftly to his feet. He tore his jacket from his shoulders and wrapped it swiftly around his left arm. "Cats?"

"I think not. No cat ever made a sound like that."

The howling sound repeated itself from either direction of the tunnel. "More than one of them," Grimm said.

"Back-to-back," Bayard replied, and Grimm felt the sudden, wiry pressure of the other man's shoulders pressed against the middle of his back.

"I should be friends with taller people," Grimm panted.

"Bite your tongue, old boy, or I'll hack apart your ankles."

There was another motion in the dark and the creature flew at Grimm again. This time he interposed his leather-wrapped arm, and felt claws and teeth sink into it. Grimm let out a shout and spun to his left, slamming the creature against the stone of the Spire's wall. He continued the motion of the spin with his right arm, thrusting his short blade home into the thing, and felt the weapon bite sharp and deep. A warbling shriek like nothing he had heard before filled the hallway, even as he heard Bayard cry out, "Hah!" A snarling cry came from somewhere behind Grimm.

Grimm had no time to turn to Bayard. The creature was thrashing madly, its claws biting into Grimm's arm even through the layers of thick leather hide. He struck with the sword as swiftly and viciously as he knew how, praying that he didn't misjudge its length in the dark and impale his own arm. He could see nothing but a vague shape struggling against him, but he could feel hot blood splashing from the wounds his blade inflicted.

The thing let out another scream and then it was abruptly gone. Cries echoed up and down the halls from both directions, fading as they retreated. Grimm instinctively found Bayard again, and made sure his back was against the other man's for the next several moments. They both gasped for breath. Grimm's wounded arm throbbed and burned in a most unpleasant fashion.

"Cowards," Bayard panted a moment later, when it was clear that the attack was over. "Bloody cowardly things."

"Indeed," Grimm said. "Shouldn't we be running now?"

"Absolutely," Bayard said. "But half a moment. I've a light here somewhere."

Grimm waited impatiently while Bayard's clothing made rustling sounds. "Ah!" he said. "In my weskit. I'd almost forgotten." A moment later there was a dim source of pale blue light as Bayard removed a lumin crystal the size of a fingernail from one of his pockets and held it up.

The tunnel was unsightly. Blood that looked black in the pale light was splattered everywhere—more near Grimm than Bayard. Bayard himself was scarcely mussed from the action. His sword, though, was stained dark to half the length of its blade.

"God in Heaven, you're a sight," Bayard said, lifting an eyebrow. "There's more blood than man." He looked past Grimm to the heavy splatters on the wall. "My word, old boy. You missed your calling as a butcher."

"Tried," Grimm said. "But I couldn't manage. I had to settle for the Fleet."

"Bitterness does not become you, my friend," Bayard said. His dark eyes flicked around the hallway. "How's your arm?"

"Painful," Grimm said. "I'd as soon not unwrap the coat from around it until we're somewhere where we might find bandages."

"Best we move deliberately, then," Bayard said. "It would be rather funny to watch you run until your heart pumped all your blood out, but I'm afraid Abigail would be cross with me. She might refuse my attentions for hours. Even days."

"We can't have that," Grimm said. He shook as much blood as he could from the blade of his sword, and then grimaced and wiped it off on the leg of his trousers not already soaked with the stuff. He returned the weapon to its sheath just as Bayard finished wiping his sword clean with a kerchief and offered the cloth to Grimm.

"You might have said something," Grimm growled.

"That outfit's ruined anyway."

Grimm glowered at him and opened his mouth to say something more, when Bayard abruptly pitched sideways and began to fall.

No, that wasn't it at all, Grimm thought. Bayard was standing perfectly still. His friend hadn't fallen—*Grimm* had. He could distantly feel the cold spirestone floor beneath his cheek. Bayard's mouth was moving, but the words seemed to be coming at him from several hundred yards down the tunnel, and he couldn't quite make them out. Grimm tried to put a hand beneath him and push himself up, but his limbs wouldn't move.

"Bother," Grimm mumbled. "This is rather inconvenient."

Bayard leaned down and peered closely at Grimm's face. The last thing Grimm remembered of the moment was the feeling of being hoisted up onto Bayard's slim, wiry shoulders.

Grimm opened his eyes and found himself in a warm, dim room. The ceiling was made of hardened clay—one of the most common construction materials for the more modest residences within Spire Albion. It hadn't been painted white, but instead was covered with a colorful and rather fanciful mural that looked like it had been done by a particularly enthusiastic child. It made little sense, containing seemingly random images of airships, the sun, some sort of odd-looking plants that only partially resembled trees, and an image of the moon that was much too large in relation to the sun opposite it. Strange creatures occupied the same space, none of them familiar to Grimm, though he might have seen some of them in his more fanciful childhood storybooks.

The room was lit by dozens and dozens and dozens of tiny, nearly dead lumin crystals, collected in jars of clear glass. Their light was a nebulous thing, showing everything clearly and seemingly originating from nowhere. It was a small, spare chamber, sporting a student's desk and a small and overstuffed bookshelf. He lay on a bed of woven ropes with a thin pad over them, and blankets had been piled over him until they more threatened to smother him than keep him warm.

He began to push them away, only to find that his left arm had been bound to his chest. Both arms were wrapped in what seemed to him irrational amounts of cloth bandages. They weren't white. Instead they had been made from a broad spectrum of every color and texture of cloth imaginable. One of the strips had little pink heart shapes alternating with bright yellow suns.

Grimm sat up, wincing at the pain from his arm. He had a number of other cuts on his upper body, apparently, which were also covered in bandages and some kind of pungent sterilizing ointment. He didn't remember receiving the minor wounds, but that was hardly unusual in combat. There was a foul taste in his mouth, and his throat burned with thirst. A pitcher and mug on a tray on the bed's nightstand stood ready, and he poured the mug full of water and drank it down three times running before his body began to relent.

Someone tapped on the door and then opened it. Grimm looked up to see a young woman enter the room. She was dressed . . . not so much untidily, he decided, as *randomly*. Her grey shirt was made of ethersilk, patched in several places, and looked as though it had been tailored for a man almost two hundred pounds heavier than she was. Though the shirt was long enough to serve as a gown itself, she wore a green undergown, with rustling skirts that fell to the floor. As she walked toward him, he saw that she wore stockings instead of shoes—green and white polka dots on one foot, and orange and purple stripes on the other. She wore an apron— but it looked to be made of leather, and was burned in several places, a smith's garment rather than kitchen wear. Her hair had been dyed in crimson and white stripes, and then braided so that it resembled a peppermint candy. One lens of her spectacles was pink, the other green, and the band of her too-large top hat was fairly bursting with folded pieces of paper. She wore a necklace from which depended a glass vial of nearly spent illumination crystals, and she carried a covered tray in her arms.

"Oh," she said, pausing. "He's awake. Goodness. That was unexpected." She tilted her head, peering at him first through one lens of her spectacles and then through the other. "There, you see? He's fine. He's not mad. Except that he is. And I should know." She carried the tray to a small table against one wall and whispered, "Should we tell him how improper it is for a gentleman not to wear a shirt when there is a young lady present? It isn't that we don't appreciate the view, because he's quite masculine, but it does seem like something one should say."

Grimm blinked down at himself and fumbled for the bedcovers with one hand, pulling them up. "Ah, please excuse me, young lady. I seem to have lost my shirt."

"He thinks I'm a lady," she said, and beamed at him. "That's quite unusual, in my experience."

Grimm racked his mind for the proper thing to say in such a circumstance, and found little. "To be called a lady?"

"Thinking," the young woman said. "Now, here is some fresh soup, which doesn't taste very good, but he should eat it all because the poison thinks it's even worse."

Grimm blinked. "Poison?"

The young woman turned toward him and came close enough to lay a hand on his forehead. "Oh, dear. Is he feverish again? No, no. Oh, good. Perhaps he's just simple. Poor dear."

Before she could turn away, Grimm caught her wrist in his hand.

The young woman . . . no, he decided, the *girl's* breath seemed to catch in her throat. Her entire body went stiff and she breathed, "Oh, dear. I hope he doesn't decide to harm me. He's quite good at doing harm. It took forever to clean off all the blood."

"Child," Grimm said in a low voice. "Look at me."

She froze abruptly. After a silent second, she said, "Oh, I mustn't."

"Look at me, girl," Grimm said, keeping his voice gentle and calm. "No one is going to hurt you."

The girl flicked a very quick look at him. He saw only a flash of her eyes over the spectacles when she did. One was an even, steady grey. The other was a shade of pale apple green. She shivered and seemed to sag, her wrist going limp in his hand.

"Oh," she breathed. "That's so sad."

"Who are you speaking to, child?"

"He doesn't know I'm talking to you," the girl said. The fingertips of her free hand rose to the crystals in the little bottle around her neck. "How can he hear me without realizing something so simple?"

"Ah," Grimm said, and released the girl's wrist very slowly and carefully, as he might a fragile bird's body. "You're an etherealist. Forgive me, child. I didn't realize."

"He thinks I'm the master," the girl said, ducking her head and blushing. "How can he be so clever and so stupid all at once? That must hurt awfully. But perhaps it would be more polite if we didn't say anything. He seems to mean well, the poor thing. And he's conscious, mobile, and lucid. We should tell the master that it looks like he'll survive."

With that, the girl scurried out of the room, nodding to herself, her soft litany hanging for a moment in her wake.

Grimm shook his head. Whoever the girl was, she'd been serving her apprenticeship for a goodly while, despite her apparent youth. All etherealists were odd and became more so as they aged. Some were a good bit odder than others. The child was at least as strange as any other etherealist he'd met.

He went to the tray and uncovered it. There was a bowl of soup and several flatbakes, along with a spoon that would have been modest had it not been made from dark, glossy wood. He tasted the soup, bracing himself for the bitter taste of most medicines, and found it surprisingly bland but pleasant.

He fetched out a stool, sat down at the desk, and devoured the soup, along with the flatbakes and two more glasses of water. By the time he finished, he felt almost like a human being. He took note of a plain robe that had apparently been left for him, and managed to tug it on one-handed and belt it at the waist.

No sooner had he finished than there was a heavy thump upon the door to his chamber.

"Ow," said a man's voice. "Damnation to you." The latch rattled several times and the man sighed in a tone of impatience. "Folly."

"He doesn't mean to hurt your feelings," said the girl in an apologetic tone. "He's just too brilliant for you." The door opened, and the girl stepped back hurriedly without meeting Grimm's eyes.

A man entered the room holding a rumpled handkerchief against his apparently bleeding nose. He was a scrawny specimen except for a small potbelly, and it made his limbs look out of proportion, almost spidery. His hair was a dirty grey mop, his face covered by sparse white stubble. He was dressed in a suit about two decades out of date, in sober shades of brown and grey, and large, soft slippers made of some kind of creature with green-and-black-striped fur. Too old to be middle-aged, too young to be elderly, the man had eyes that were a vibrant shade of blue Grimm had seen only in the autumn skies high above the mists. The man walked with the aid of a wooden cane tipped with what might have been a weapons crystal from a ship's light cannon. It was the size of a man's clenched fist.

"Ah!" he said. "Aha! Captain Grimm, welcome, welcome, so good to be able to speak to you when you aren't delirious." He glanced aside at the girl and mumbled out of the corner of his mouth, "He's not delirious, is he?"

The girl shook her head with wide eyes that didn't leave the ground. "No, master."

Grimm was quite unsure how to respond with courtesy to such a greeting, but he settled for bowing slightly at the waist. "We haven't met, sir. I'm afraid you have the advantage of me."

"Yes, we did, tomorrow," the old man said. "And no, you aren't, and the last is a matter for debate, perhaps. What do you think, Folly?"

Folly bit her lip and touched her vial of crystals. "He doesn't realize that Captain Grimm is quite uncomfortable because he doesn't know anyone's name."

"Untrue!" the etherealist stated with conviction. "He knows his own name, I daresay, and at least one of yours. He's had seconds and seconds to transfer that knowledge into his memory. Unless, of course, he remains delirious." The old man squinted at Grimm. "You're quite sure that you are lucid, sir?"

"At times I wonder," Grimm replied.

Something very young and very full of mischief flickered far back in the etherealist's eyes, and his face stretched into a wide smile. "Ah. Ah! A man of modesty, either so false that it may be true or so true that it seems entirely false. I can see why Bayard speaks so well of you, sir." The old man touched the tip of his cane to the floor far to one side and sank into an elaborate bow of dancelike grace. "I am Efferus Effrenus Ferus, at your service, sir. And that's Folly."

"Folly," the girl said, and bobbed a curtsy toward the far corner of the room.

"Sweaters," Ferus said soberly. "Sweaters, dear. And two pairs of socks, one of them wool. Oh, and fetch me a gentleman's hat of a size no larger than six and then soak it in vinegar."

The girl curtsied again and hurried from the room.

Ferus beamed. "Such a sweet child. And she always remembers perfectly. Now, then, Captain." He turned back to Grimm. "You have questions, I answers. Shall we see if they match?"

"Please," Grimm said. "I appear to be your guest. Have I you to thank for caring for me?"

Ferus's shoulders sagged in evident disappointment. "Apparently they do *not* match. I was going to say strawberries." His lips compressed and he shook his head. "You aren't very good at this game, Captain."

"I take that to mean that you did help me, sir."

Ferus waved a hand. "Bayard did more for you than I did, I daresay. But that said . . . yes, I was compelled to employ my skills on your behalf."

"Skills, sir?"

The etherealist nodded. "Today I am a physician with the cure to a condition hardly anyone ever contracts. If you'd asked me twenty years ago, I'd have told you it seemed a very poor long-term investment with very little commercial viability. But here we are."

Grimm found himself smiling. "Indeed. Here we are. Thank you for your help."

The old man beamed and drummed the end of his cane on the floor. "Just so, just so. Whatever beastie it was tried to eat you, it left a good many dangerous structures behind in your blood—quite rude, sir, quite rude, and most unfair."

"Poison?" Grimm asked.

Ferus waggled his hand back and forth. "Yes. No, actually, not even remotely, but for purposes of this conversation, yes."

Grimm frowned. "Ah. Um. Am I in any danger?"

"You're dead as a stone, man!"

"I am?"

"Yes. No, actually, not even remotely, but for purposes of this conversation, yes." Ferus nodded at his arm. "You've clouded the issue. I should check your wound to ensure my work was thorough. Do you mind?"

"No," Grimm said. "I suppose not."

"Excellent," Ferus said. Then he turned and left the room, banging the door shut behind him.

Grimm stood for a moment, frowning. Then he shook his head and began to seat himself again.

"Ack!" cried Ferus from the hall. "No, stop *moving*, man! How am I supposed to see anything with you dancing jigs about the room?"

Grimm froze in place. "Ah. Is . . . is this better?"

"You look rather awkward, halfway down like that. You aren't by chance having a bowel movement of some kind?"

Grimm sighed. "No."

"Well, try not to until I'm finished."

"Ah, Master Ferus. If you don't mind my asking, how exactly are you examining me? Surely you can't see the wound from out there?"

"Untrue!" Ferus said. "From out here I can see little else! There, done. I do good work, if I do say so myself." Footsteps shuffled up to the door and then stopped warily perhaps a foot away.

The doorknob rattled again fitfully and then went still.

"Bother," Ferus said. "Confounded thing. Why do you mock me?"

Grimm walked across the room and opened the door.

Ferus let out a sigh. "Thank you, young man, thank you. Were I your age I'm sure I would learn the trick of it straight off, but the mind, you see. It goes rather stale."

"It's the least I could do," Grimm said.

"Incorrect!" Ferus proclaimed. "The least you could have done would be nothing! Goodness, I hope you're brighter than you seem. We've really no more time to waste upon your education, Captain."

"No?" Grimm asked. "And why not?"

And in an instant the old man changed.

His previously animated voice went low and steady. Something shifted in his spine and shoulders, conveying a sense of perfect confidence and strength wildly at odds with his innocuous stature. And most of all his eyes changed: The sparkle in them transformed, distilled itself into a muted fire that met Grimm's gaze without expectation or weakness.

Grimm became abruptly certain that he was standing before a very dangerous man.

"Because, Francis Madison Grimm, we've come to the end," Master Ferus said.

"The end? Of what?"

"Of the beginning, of course," the etherealist said. "The end of the beginning."

Chapter 9

Spire Albion, Habble Morning

I can't believe you're going along with this," Gwendolyn told Benedict. She tried to keep her voice pleasant and neutral.

Her cousin eyed her and slipped a half step farther away from her as they walked together toward the duel.

"Oh, please," Gwendolyn said, allowing her tone to become openly cross. "Now you're just teasing me."

Benedict smiled very slightly. "Rowl seemed insistent."

"Rowl," Gwendolyn said, "is a *cat*, Benedict."

"Have you ever tried to stop a cat from doing what it wants to do?" Benedict asked her.

"No, of course not. There are no cats in House Lancaster."

Benedict barked a sharp laugh. "That again."

Gwendolyn felt her face heat slightly. "I've never seen one there," she continued, as if he hadn't interrupted her at all. "The point is, Benny, that if I spent a lifetime thinking they were little more than clever beasts, you can be sure that many others have as well."

"And?"

"And word has spread. *Everyone* in the habble will be watching this duel today. This will be the first time House Tagwynn has impinged upon the awareness of the Great Houses in a generation. Can you imagine what they're going to be saying about Bridget and her father if she shows up with a bloody *cat* as her second?"

"I can," Benedict said, his voice maddeningly calm. "Yes, indeed."

"Now, what is *that* supposed to mean?" Gwen demanded.

"Honestly, coz, I know you're still a recruit, but I can't very well go explaining everything to you. You've seen everything I have. You've had the same education I have. You have an excellent mind—when you bother to bring it in on a consult with your temper, I mean. Use it."

Gwen scowled at him. "I have. It tells me that the name of Tagwynn is in danger today," she said. "And it's there because of my own stupidity, and that we can't allow them to come to harm because of my mistake."

"Yes," Benedict said. "All true. But take it a step further. What are the consequences of today?"

Gwen pressed her lips together for a moment before speaking. "If she loses the duel, the Tagwynns will be both a laughingstock and a highly visible target of economic opportunity. At the very least, their income might suffer. It's probable that one of the hungrier Houses with interests in that market will find a way to buy out their vattery or legislate them out of business."

"True," Benedict said. "And if she wins?"

"That's a far worse circumstance," Gwen said. "If she beats Reggie, she incurs the ire of a major House. 'Might' and 'probably' transfigure to 'will' and 'certainly.'"

Benedict nodded. "House Tagwynn, House Astor, yes, you've done the math." He considered. "Well. Two-thirds of it, anyway."

"What do you mean, two-thirds?"

He held up a forefinger. "You've accounted for the Tagwynns." He held up the next finger. "You've considered the Astors." He stuck his thumb out to one side. "What about the cats?"

Gwen let out an impatient breath . . . but then she paused.

"There are really cats inside House Lancaster?" Gwen asked. "And I've just never seen them?"

Benedict spread his hands as if displaying that fact's self-evidence.

"But . . . I suppose it does not necessarily follow that *they* have not seen *me*."

"Ah," Benedict said, his tone pleased. "The light dawns."

Gwen considered that for several steps. "Are they truly that intelligent? I know the little beasts are clever, but . . ."

"It is often very useful for others to think you less intelligent than you are," Benedict said, his tone amused. "It works particularly well against those who aren't as intelligent as you in the first place."

Gwen blinked. "Goodness."

"I must admit that I hadn't thoroughly considered the situation before meeting Rowl," Benedict said. "It's just a theory, coz—but it seems sound."

"It . . . does, doesn't it?" Gwen said. She looked up at Benedict shrewdly. "You've never been known for your acute political intellect, Benny. Most of the House considers you a distant and disinterested observer— not a political asset."

Her cousin looked pained. "And I shall remain so in their eyes, if you please," he said. "Politics is the purview of scoundrels, tyrants, and fools. I only observe because I prefer not to become their victim."

Gwen snorted. "You're safe from everyone but me," she promised.

"Oh, dear."

His stomach made a rumbling noise and Gwen smiled up at him. "Hungry?"

"I've eaten," he replied.

"You're warriorborn, Benny," Gwen said firmly. "Your body needs more fuel. There's nothing wrong with that."

He pressed his lips together, and his feline eyes became remote.

Gwen let out a mental sigh. She knew how much Benny disliked being born different, and the pains to which he went to conceal those differences. She knew he never moved as quickly or as powerfully as he could have during runs or in combat training. He carried lumin crystals with him and employed them in the darker sections of the habble, despite the fact that his feline eyes had no need of them. He ate on a rigid schedule in the Guard's dining hall, downing exactly the portions dealt out to each recruit—despite the fact that he could quite literally starve to death on a diet that would be more than adequate for anyone else.

Benny was a wonderful, sweet, dear idiot, Gwen thought.

"We're eating before the duel," she said firmly. "Come with me."

"Gwen," he protested.

"I'm hungry," she lied smoothly. "And you wouldn't be so rude as to make a lady eat alone, would you? Come along."

Benedict scowled. "I haven't any money with me."

"I have lots," Gwen said cheerfully. "Come along."

"Honestly, Gwendolyn," he muttered. "You simply cannot take a hint."

"Oh, I am more than capable of it, coz," she said airily. "At the moment I choose not to. Shall we have those dumplings you like?"

Benedict's stomach rumbled. Louder.

He eyed her. "That's cheating."

"I have no idea what you're talking about," Gwen said, and gave him what she liked to think of as her very firm smile, the one where she locked her jaw. She spoke through her teeth. "Now. Come. Along."

Benedict glowered for a moment more and then sighed. "You're going to insist, aren't you?"

"I'm a lady of House Lancaster, Benny. You are a gentleman of House Sorellin-Lancaster. I shouldn't need to." She smiled. Firmly.

Benedict rolled his eyes, plucked a white handkerchief from his pocket, and gave it a solemn wave. "I yield."

Gwendolyn beamed. "Commendable."

The little stall where a stout, silver-haired old couple named Beech served hot food to order was off to the side of the main market area, out of the immediate swirl of trade and foot traffic. The backs of other stalls formed a little C-shaped alcove where a few simple tables and chairs had been set out, creating the impression of seclusion.

Gwen marched up to the stall but found no one in sight. "Hello?" she called. "We've come for some lunch!"

"We're not quite ready yet," called a voice from inside the stall.

"Become ready," Gwen called back, a merry edge in her command. "I'm glad to pay very well for your trouble."

There was a sigh from inside the stall and then an older man with eyebrows approximately as thick as his wrists appeared from the pantry in the rear. Mister Beech blinked once at Gwen and then said, "Miss Lancaster? This isn't your usual hour. What are you doing here?"

"Securing your profit margin for the day," Gwen said, smiling and dropping a coin purse on the counter. It jingled invitingly. Neither the sound of the coin nor her smile seemed to displease the vendor. "I'm in need of one of your dumplings before noon."

"Simple enough, miss, coming up. And for the young sir?"

"Two more of the same," Gwen said firmly.

"Coz," Benedict protested. It was, Gwen thought, a decidedly feeble protest, undermined by another rumble from his stomach.

"Right away, miss," said Mister Beech, and he turned to his stove, where a pan of oil awaited, and produced a number of sausages from an insulated cold cabinet. Mrs. Beech appeared from the back, her grey hair held back under a kerchief, stirring vigorously at a batch of dough. She spread some flour on a board and plopped the dough onto it to begin kneading it with swift, confident hands.

"I'll hear no back talk from you, Benedict," Gwen said, offering him a tart smile. "Or rather, I shall hear none from your belly, for an hour or two at least. Honestly, it's most unbecoming a Lancaster, grumbling and growling like that."

Benedict rolled his eyes again, but his mouth quirked at the corners.

"Fortunately for me, I am not so limited as you poor, pure Lancasters, having the Sorellin bloodline to broaden my mental, emotional, and artistic horizons."

"What's that?" Gwen asked, and propped a hand to her ear, raising her voice slightly. "I'm certain I didn't hear you correctly over the sound of your belly howling. It almost sounded as if you were questioning the utter and unquestionable superiority of the House of Lancaster."

Benedict's smile widened. "Go play with your crystals and let the rest of us get on with the real work, eh?"

"For shame, sir," said Mister Beech, peering up at Benedict from beneath his bushy eyebrows, his eyes glinting with amusement, "to speak so of the young miss's family."

Gwen gave Benedict a triumphant smile. "There, you see? The Lancasters have the support of the people."

Benedict laughed. "You're only taking her side because she's paying."

"The young sir is wise," commented Mrs. Beech.

"Aye, he is, he is," agreed the old man—as Gwen counted out a generous number of coins into his palm. She stuck out her tongue at Benedict cheerfully and said, "Thank you both very much."

A rather bookish-looking man of middle years entered the alcove, muttering, ". . . just don't see how that's going to work." His clothes, though fine, were rumpled and askew, and his violet weskit was an affront to the sensibilities of a generation against the plain brown tweed of his coat and trousers. His hair was brown and overgrown, muddled with strands of grey, and his hands were long fingered and fine. He was writing in a journal with a pen fitted with a glowing crystal, muttering to himself as he did. "Good day, Mister and Mrs. Beech," he said without looking up. He stifled a yawn with one hand, and then continued writing. "A double of your finest and with some coffee, if you will. Nice and dark." The pen flew over the page, scrawling out a line of some sort of figures Gwen didn't recognize.

"Good day, Addy," said Mrs. Beech, her voice warm. "Up all night again?"

"The curse of an academically inclined mind, I'm afraid," the man replied. "Miles and miles of different ways to think the same old useless things." He never stopped writing as he spoke, and he bumped into Gwen with the edge of his journal. "Ah, pardon me, sir."

"Sir?" Gwen asked in an arch tone.

"Yes?" Addy asked, finishing a line with a flourish and beginning the next.

Gwen cleared her throat, quite obviously indicating that she expected him to look up.

"Out with it, man," Addy said. "If you've something on your mind, just say it! I'm a bit too pressed for time to dance about!"

Gwen's eyes narrowed and turned steely. How dared this person be so discourteous to a lady? And most particularly to a lady of House Lancaster?

"Coz," Benedict said quickly, putting a hand on her arm.

She shook it off. "A moment, cousin," Gwen said. "I am faced with a distasteful quandary."

"But—"

"Benedict," Gwen said in her sweetest, gentlest voice.

Benedict grimaced and took a small step back.

Addy, if such was his name, was still writing, all but ignoring her. Intolerable!

"Mmmm?" he asked absently. "Quandary?"

Gwen's voice came out cold and precise. "Whether to settle for a tongue-lashing for someone so impolite, or to take offense at this slight and demand satisfaction, as is my right!"

Addy blinked several times and only then did he look up at Gwen. "I say. Really? Demand satisfaction?" Mirth bubbled underneath the words, as if he could hardly contain laughter. "You're considering challenging me to a duel?"

"I will have your name first, sir," Gwen snapped.

"Does it matter?" Addy asked.

"Of course it does," Gwen said. "I would know which House has been so slovenly as to allow one of its scions to wander about Habble Morning without the manners God gave a goat."

"Goats are actually rather gentle, sensible creatures," Addy replied in a mild tone, "and they rarely burst into duels. Certainly not after an all-nighter." He sighed. "Miss, *should* my name matter?"

"What?" Gwen asked.

"My name," Addy said. "Are my actions not my own? Should it matter if I belong to a low House or high? Am I any more offensive as a common citizen than as one of the aristocracy?"

Gwen blinked several times. His questions were so odd that they might have been phrased in a foreign tongue. Then she said, "Of course it should matter. I judge you no commoner by your clothes, sir, but if you are, I can hardly castigate you for your lack of graces when no education in such matters has been yours."

Addy tilted his head sharply to one side, and his dark eyes glittered. "You would hold me *more* accountable if I belonged to the aristocracy?"

"Of course," Gwen said. Her tone suggested that the man was an idiot. "Protocol between members of the Houses is the standard by which appropriate respect is given to one's peers—respect that keeps those Houses from feuds and civil war. It is your duty to behave properly, sir. To those whom much is given, much is required. Of course I expect more of you."

A slow smile spread over Addy's face. "How interesting." He looked past Gwen to the two vendors. "How long?"

Mister Beech was already moving to draw a brass-wire basket from the heated oil, and he began setting the dumplings out onto square bits of cloth. "Coming up now."

Addy nodded at him and turned to Benedict. "All right," he said. "Would you be so good as to introduce me to your cousin, sir? I think I like her."

Gwen blinked several times. "I beg your pardon?"

Benedict drew in a deep breath and eyed Gwen with fond exasperation. "Coz," he said. "You really must learn to shut your mouth from time to time. You'll taste less shoe leather." Straightening his coat, he bowed and said, "Gwendolyn Margaret Elizabeth Lancaster, daughter of Lord Minister and Lady Lancaster, it is my . . . singular pleasure . . . to introduce you to His Majesty Addison Orson Magnus Jeremiah Albion, First Citizen and Spirearch of Albion."

Gwen stared at Benedict in shock for a second.

Her stomach absolutely disconnected itself from the rest of her vitals and plunged into some unimaginable abyss.

She slowly turned her gaze to the pleasantly smiling Spirearch. Then her face began to turn very, very hot.

"Miss Lancaster," the Spirearch said with a small, pleased bow. "What a unique pleasure it has been to make your acquaintance."

Gwen stared at him, appalled. "You don't . . . you don't look like . . . your portrait."

"I was younger and a good deal angrier when it was painted," he replied. "I don't blame you one bit, Miss Lancaster. I haven't been to a public function since you were a small child, I should think. There's no reason at all you should have recognized me."

"I . . . I just . . . s-sir . . ." Gwen stammered. She felt her hands twitch, and could only assume it was because the endless hours of instruction in protocol had instilled the proper forms into her very nerves. He smoothly captured her hand and bowed over it.

"Young lady, you are every bit as beautiful as your mother was when she was your age. Ah, breakfast! Or lunch. Lunchfast, perhaps," the Spirearch said, as the Beeches produced the fresh, hot dumplings and glasses of chilled juice on a serving tray. "Would the two of you care to join me?"

"I . . . we . . ." Gwen gave Benedict a rather desperate look.

Benedict took a moment to smile at her and, she realized, to bask in the expression on her face. He was clearly enjoying the situation with an absolutely sadistic amount of amusement.

"We should be delighted, sire," he replied.

"Excellent!" the Spirearch said. "There are fine tables just there, I think." He picked up the tray, smoothly leaving coins for his own dumpling on the counter as he did. He favored Gwen with a polite smile and a nod in the proper direction. "Ladies first?"

Gwen took a slow breath. Then she said to Benedict, "I am a perfect idiot," and began walking to the tables.

The Spirearch lifted an eyebrow and glanced up at Benedict.

"That's Gwennish for, 'I apologize,'" Gwen heard him say soberly behind her. "After you, sire."

They set to the food in an awkward silence that soon changed to an appreciative one.

"My word, that's good," Benedict breathed. He obviously tried to restrain himself, but just as obviously was having trouble doing anything but cramming the entire mass of dumpling into his mouth all at once. His food disappeared in large bites.

Gwen had just offered the most appalling insolence to the monarch of Spire Albion. She felt as if whatever she'd had at breakfast that morning might come up, and barely touched her own dumpling.

"The food here is better than anything I could get in the manor, without waiting for hours," the Spirearch acknowledged. "The Beeches moved up to Habble Morning from Habble Landing ten years ago. I offered them a position on my staff, but they preferred to make their own way. I like that."

Benedict nodded, but he didn't stop chewing.

"So, Master Sorellin," the Spirearch said. "I'm surprised to see you back this year, after what happened last spring."

Benedict shrugged a shoulder. "It hardly left a scar."

"Too bad," the Spirearch said, his eyes sparkling. "I'm told young ladies swoon over them."

Gwen lifted her eyebrows. "Benny? Whatever is he talking about?"

Benedict suddenly looked uncomfortable and kept his eyes focused on his food.

"Benedict was serving a year with the Guard," the Spirearch said. "I sent him as part of a small team down to Habble Risen to track down a missing shipment of weapons crystals. The thieves who had them declined to yield up their prize."

Gwen's eyes widened. "You were in battle?"

"It wasn't a battle," Benedict replied quickly. "Just a scuffle over getting through the door of their hideout. Hardly worth mentioning."

"A scuffle in which a Guardsman was badly wounded," the Spirearch said. "And in which your cousin killed two armed men who were beating one of his fellow Guardsmen with clubs. After that, he pushed six more back through their own front door despite all they could do to hold it against him. One of them stabbed him in the arm for his trouble."

"It wasn't much of a wound," Benedict said. His face looked flushed.

"He saved a number of lives," the Spirearch said, "including those of his companions and most of the thieves—never mind the havoc that could have been loosed if those crystals had flooded the black market." He blinked and looked at Gwen. "He received the Order of the Spire. I assumed you knew."

"To my knowledge, he never said anything about it," Gwen said, staring hard at Benedict. "This is the first I've heard of the matter. You told me you hurt your arm in a sparring match, Benny."

Benedict ducked his head and picked up the second dumpling. The first had vanished with unseemly haste, despite his efforts to slow down.

The Spirearch smiled. "Miss Lancaster—may I call you Gwen?"

"Of course, sire."

"Excellent. But you must not call me 'sire.' Addison will do nicely."

Gwen hesitated. "Sire . . ."

The Spirearch waved his hand. "I know the protocol. But it was created two centuries ago, when Gregor the Strong united the habbles and formed the Council—when he still had active executive power and an army to back it up."

"Sire . . . Addison, sir," Gwen stammered. "You are still the Spirearch."

He laughed. "The monarchy was a necessary evil at one time, Miss Lancaster. Now I'm largely obsolete, and quite content to have it that way. Your father and the Council manage the affairs of the Spire by consensus, and all the habbles are represented in a fashion that at times borders upon being fair. The only armed forces we need within the Spire are the Guard—and they generally coordinate humanitarian efforts. I don't rule, Miss Lancaster; nor did my father or grandfather. I just try to help my people when they need it."

"You *are* the Spirearch, sire," Gwen insisted. "All the nobility honor you. All are honored to serve you."

"Merciful Builders, but you're young," he said with a whimsical smile. "Wait until I issue some sort of proclamation that cuts into their bank accounts, and I suspect they'd honor me with a mob and clubs." He shook his head. "It's tradition, true, for young nobles to volunteer to serve in the Guard, a mark of status. But it's an arbitrary one in many ways. If I attempt to push past my boundaries, I expect some other activity might suddenly replace the Guard for high-profile service to the community."

"Not everyone feels that way, sire," Benedict said quietly. "Not all of us see you as a relic."

"Not the Lancasters," Gwen added.

"Perhaps not," the Spirearch said thoughtfully. "But be that as it may, I'm interested, Gwen, in why you wish to join the Guard."

"I am the only child of my father's line," she replied.

"And as such may be excused from such duty with no loss of honor to you or your family. No one would think ill of you for avoiding your term of service."

Gwen lifted her chin slightly. "I would, sire."

The Spirearch sat back in his seat and eyed her for a moment. Then he said, "I will show you no favoritism whatsoever, Miss Lancaster, despite your importance to your father's house. You will be given assignments like any other recruit. Some of those assignments might carry you into danger. More young men and women than I care to remember have been hurt or killed in the line of duty while following my commands. Do you understand?"

"Yes. I do, sire."

He finished the last few bites of his dumpling with a pensive frown. Then he turned to Benedict. "The same goes for you, Master Sorellin. I choose those best suited to the tasks at hand based upon their ability. You've been put into harm's way in my service and might be again."

"Yes, sire," Benedict said, as if the Spirearch had stated that water was wet.

Addison nodded and said, "We're to have about forty new recruits this year, and as many returning veterans. I'll see you both at the palace at the end of the training cycle to take your vows and sign your contracts."

"Of course, sire," Gwen said. "Sire . . ."

"Miss Lancaster," the Spirearch said reprovingly.

"Addison," she said, and then added, "sir."

He smiled, mostly with his eyes. "Yes?"

"Had I known who you were earlier . . ."

"You would have been well within your rights to react in precisely the same way, Miss Lancaster," he said firmly. "Please excuse me for my rudeness. It's very seldom I get to be impolite for fun—and I'm afraid I have a rather depressingly low sense of humor. I trust you will forgive me."

She felt her cheeks heating up again. "Of course, sire."

There was a sudden deep, hollow chime. Someone was ringing the bells at the center of the habble's common area, near the marketplace.

Benedict tensed. Then he popped the second half of his second dumpling into his mouth in a single bite. Gwen pushed her dumpling toward him automatically, and he scooped it up in what was clearly an unthinking, instinctive reaction.

"Ah," the Spirearch said. "I believe I saw something in the notices about a duel to be fought today. I may have heard that the situation has the potential to be quite messy and ugly for those involved. You wouldn't know anything about it, would you, Miss Lancaster?"

His voice was calm, even whimsical, but there was something in his words that carried the hint of steel.

"I suspect you know very well that I do, sire."

His teeth showed briefly. "Then I suspect that you plan to see it to the end."

"We do," Benedict said in a quiet voice.

The Spirearch nodded. "A great many eyes are on what you do today, Miss Lancaster—among them my own."

Gwen swallowed. The great chime tolled several more times and then fell silent.

The Spirearch glanced toward the source of the sound and nodded in what was undeniably a dismissal. "The Tagwynns are good people.

House Lancaster has always had my respect, miss. I expect today's events to vindicate that respect."

Gwen could recognize a command when she heard it, and her heart suddenly beat a little faster. This situation was no longer a simple mess caused by her lack of judgment. The attention of the Spirearch meant that it had ramifications for her House as well.

"Yes, sire," she said, her throat dry. "They will."

■ ■ ■ Chapter 10 ■ ■ ■

Spire Albion, Habble Morning

Bridget felt sure that she was going to be sick and throw up in front of half the habble.

"Littlemouse," Rowl said in a low, stern tone from her arms. "Straighten your back. Lift your chin. Show no fear. Give your enemy nothing."

"That's very good advice, miss," said the master of arms in a similar tone, though speaking the human tongue. He was a tall, spare man, the threads of silver in his hair standing out sharply against his all-black outfit. They were waiting in the common area of the market of Habble Morning, near the dueling platform, and the grizzled warriorborn man had just finished ringing the chimes.

"You speak Cat, Mister . . . ?" Bridget flushed. "I'm sorry. I don't know your name."

"Esterbrook, miss," he said with a slight polite bow. "I don't speak it well but I understand enough. All wise folk do."

"I like him," Rowl said from Bridget's arms.

She smiled faintly and tried to follow Rowl's advice. "I apologize if I do something improperly, Mister Esterbrook," she said, "but I'm afraid I have little experience in these matters."

"Wise folk don't," Esterbrook said calmly, giving her another smile. "It's simple enough, Miss Tagwynn."

"I'm unclear as to what role a master of arms plays in a duel when it's being fought . . . unarmed."

"Oh, my part doesn't change," Esterbrook said. "My office is filled by several of us old soldiers, with one of us covering each day of the week. My job is to do everything possible to make sure everyone lives. I seek to resolve the cause of the duel before any blood is shed, and then I ensure that the protocol of the duel is followed and that no one interferes in what happens."

She frowned. "Who would interfere?"

"His second, perhaps," Esterbrook said. He glanced at Rowl. "Or yours."

Rowl gave a contemptuous flick of his ears and looked away.

"And . . . if someone does not follow the rules?"

"I'll stop him," Esterbrook said. "It is within the rights of my office to take any steps necessary to do so, up to and including the taking of life."

Bridget blinked. "Goodness."

"Duels are serious business, miss," Esterbrook said quietly. "Though these arrogant sprats growing up these days don't seem to think so. They shouldn't be entered into lightly."

"They shouldn't exist at all," Bridget said.

Esterbrook seemed to think about that for a moment. Then he shook his head. "They . . . serve a purpose, if they're kept within a strict structure, and if death doesn't result too often. There's something to be said for having the means to directly confront someone who has wronged you—for there to be a reason for these glib-tongued louts to show an ounce of courtesy and to guard their words."

"Ah," Bridget said, flushing slightly. As the glib-tongued lout in question, she was currently on the receiving end of this facet of the habble's law. "I'm not sure everyone would agree with you. We're a civilized society, are we not?"

Esterbrook blinked. "Since when, miss? We're a democracy."

"Just what I mean. We have dispensed with violence as a means of governing ourselves, have we not?"

"The heart of democracy is violence, Miss Tagwynn," Esterbrook said. "In order to decide what to do, we take a count of everyone for and against it, and then do whatever the larger side wishes to do. We're having a symbolic battle, its outcome decided by simple numbers. It saves us time and no end of trouble counting actual bodies—but don't mistake it for anything but ritualized violence. And every few years, if the person we elected doesn't do the job we wanted, we vote him out of office—we symbolically behead him and replace him with someone else. Again, without the actual pain and bloodshed, but acting out the ritual of violence nonetheless. It's actually a very practical way of getting things done."

Bridget blinked several times. "I've never thought of it that way," she confessed.

"It is one of the only things we respect about your people," Rowl put in. "Though, of course, cats do it better."

"Quite possibly," Esterbrook agreed. "Ah. Here comes the physician. And your esteemed opponent, it would seem."

Bridget looked around them. People were appearing from all over the market in response to the chimes—dozens of people, in fact. And only a moment later, she was quite sure that dozens had become hundreds. She felt her throat turning very dry, to go along with her fluttering stomach and her racing heart.

Fear was really quite tedious. She wanted to be rid of it as soon as possible.

A small man with silvery hair carrying a physician's valise and wearing a very sensible, no-nonsense suit approached Esterbrook, and the two exchanged handshakes. Esterbrook introduced the man to Bridget, though a few seconds later she had completely forgotten his name. The crowd *continued* to grow. At lunch, on a weekday? Hadn't these people anything better to do with their time? Bridget frowned at the crowd and restrained herself from rubbing Rowl's ears, which the cat would have found undignified in public.

Reginald Astor appeared out of the throng, along with not only his second, but half a dozen other men of the same general age and rank. He was dressed just as she was, in a plain grey training uniform. They approached as a group, Reggie swaggering in the lead.

Beside her, Bridget felt Mister Esterbrook grow tight with coiled tension, something she sensed on a level below conscious thought—it was, she thought, almost the same sense she felt from a suddenly angered cat.

"Master of Arms," Reggie said, throwing the warriorborn man an exaggerated bow. "It's about time we did this, isn't it?"

Esterbrook narrowed his feline eyes but inclined his head in respect. "I am indeed the master of arms. My name is Elias Esterbr—"

"Details," Reggie said. His eyes were focused intently on Bridget. "There she is, the little trog with her little scavenger."

The idiot couldn't have known that it was a word the cats considered a deadly insult. Rowl catapulted up from his resting place in Bridget's arms toward Reggie, and it was all she could do to keep hold of the suddenly furious cat.

Reggie reconfirmed his idiocy by bursting out in laughter, though at least his second had the wit to take an alarmed step back. "Goodness!" he said in a merry voice. "Is the kitty upset with me? It's not as though I'm launching a suit to have the vicious little thing drowned."

"Rowl," Bridget hissed in Cat. "Settle down."

"I *heard* him," Rowl snarled.

"And he will be dealt with," Bridget said, "in the proper order of things. First he is mine."

Rowl let out a spitting snarl of frustration and then settled down again, though his body remained quivering-tight with tension.

"Mister Esterbrook," Bridget said, looking from Rowl to the man. "I am ready to begin, sir."

The warriorborn nodded. "In accordance with Spire law, I beseech you both to resolve your differences in some less dangerous and destructive manner. No matter how well managed, loss of life and limb remains a possibility of any duel. I now ask you, Mister Astor, if you will retract your grievance and avoid the dangers inherent in a confrontation."

"She insulted the honor of my House," Reggie said loftily. "She will apologize for it or I will have satisfaction here and now."

Esterbrook turned to Bridget. "Miss Tagwynn, will you offer such an apology?"

"Let me be clear that I never offered House Astor an insult, Mister Esterbrook," Bridget said. "Nor did I insult Reginald. I simply described him in accurate terms. If he finds himself insulted by the truth, it's hardly my concern."

A low, quiet round of chuckles went through the crowd.

"But in any case," Bridget said, "I stand by what I said. Truth does not become untruth simply because its existence upsets the scion of a High House."

Esterbrook's eyes glinted and he nodded once. "Let the record show that neither combatant finds a way to resolve their differences peaceably. We will therefore proceed to contest. Mister Astor, is your second present?"

"Yes, here, of course," Reggie said, beckoning his cousin Barnabus forward.

"Miss Tagwynn, is your second present?"

"I am," Rowl said, in Cat.

Esterbrook nodded seriously, and another murmur ran through the crowd, a mixed sound of amusement, disgust, confusion, excitement, and other things Bridget couldn't quite make out.

"Point of order!" Reggie said, in a voice meant to carry to the entire crowd. "This is a violation of duel protocol. Miss Tagwynn has arrived without a second."

Esterbrook looked at Reggie with a blank expression. "Oh?"

"The law states," Reggie continued, "that a duelist's second must be a citizen of a habble in good standing with the law." Reggie sneered at Rowl. "And as I see no such person here, I can only conclude that Miss Tagwynn did not bring a second. I insist that she be prosecuted for acting in contempt of Spire law, and her House fined appropriately."

Bridget's stomach plunged. It happened only on rare occasions, when someone felt the need to punish a House that had not left itself vulnerable in any other way, but when fines were levied for violations of Spire law, they tended to be outrageous. Even the smallest of the fees that could be forced upon her father would quite literally beggar him.

"Master Astor," Esterbrook said, and to Bridget's surprise, his own voice was pitched to carry as well. "When it comes to supporting the letter and spirit of the law, your dedication and zeal are selectively remarkable." He reached into his coat and produced a folded writing sheet. "I have here in my possession an affidavit, reviewed and notarized by Judge Helena Solomon. It states that one Rowl, heir apparent of House Silent Paws, has with the rest of his House pledged his support to His Majesty, Addison Orson Magnus Jeremiah Albion, First Citizen and Spirearch of Albion. Further, the affidavit states that he resides within Habble Morning and that no outstanding fines or warrants have been levied against him. As such, he is, in fact, a citizen of the habble, in good standing."

"What?" Reggie said. "House *what*?"

Esterbrook diffidently offered him the writing sheet.

Reggie snatched it and stared, reading. His cheeks turned bright red, and the crowd began to murmur again.

Bridget's gaze fell on a plain, rather dumpy man standing not too far away, in the first row of gawkers. Unlike the others, he was not speaking to anyone else. There was something familiar about him, something that reminded her of her primary schooling days, but she couldn't pin

down the proper memory. His greying hair was shaggy, his suit years out
of style, and if he hadn't been the only person in sight who appeared
absolutely calm and undistracted by Esterbrook's pronouncement, she
might never have taken notice of him. She felt his eyes meet hers. A
glitter of mirth passed through them, and he gave her a wink.

Bridget blinked. That was rather bold of him, whoever he was. Was
he one of her father's business associates, someone she'd met when she
was much younger? She was sure she would have remembered. And
why was she gawking at the man when, she realized, one of the most
important legal precedents in the Spire's recent history had just been
made? *Cats* had been declared *citizens* of the habble. Apparently with
all the rights and—much more critically—the responsibilities that status
implied. Cats and humans had enjoyed a long-standing arrangement—
but one that was entirely unofficial, and which either side could violate
without necessarily creating enormous repercussions. But Esterbrook
and his proclamation had just changed that balance immensely—and
perhaps not, Bridget realized with dismay, for the good of all involved.

"This is not . . ." Reggie sputtered. "*Cats* are not eligible to . . ."

"According to the law, sir," Esterbrook said calmly, "they are. Have
you any other complaints to make before we proceed, sir? Or perhaps
you have changed your mind, and would be willing to simply abandon
this fruitless course."

Reggie narrowed his eyes, his gaze locking onto Bridget and Rowl.
"You're making a mockery of a noble tradition, beast-man."

Esterbrook's feline eyes narrowed to slits, and there was a hint of a
growl deep in his chest when he spoke. "I simply execute the responsibilities of my office, Master Astor. If that displeases you in some fashion
it is not my concern."

Reggie's friends took note of the growl and gathered in close around
him.

Just then there were footsteps behind Bridget, and Gwendolyn Lancaster and Benedict Sorellin appeared from the crowd. They were both dressed in civilian clothing, Gwen in a pearl-grey dress, vest, and jacket, and Benedict in a simple, rather dismal black suit. Both of them, Bridget noted, were wearing gauntlets, the thick copper wire of the weapons' cages wrapping around their left forearms.

"Are we too late?" Gwendolyn asked. Bridget had no notion whatsoever how the prim little noblewoman managed to load so much arrogance and confidence into her seemingly fatuous tone. "I *do* hope we haven't missed the display of courage and grace that this little event promises to be. Goodness, Reggie, here you are. With six friends." She gave Astor a blindingly white smile and counted them, moving her hand in a seemingly unconscious gesture. "One, two, three, four, five, six."

Gwendolyn, Bridget noted, used her gauntlet-clad left hand to count. The copper cage glinted in the noonday light.

"I thought two were all that were needed for a duel," Benedict said, his tone weighted with exaggerated confusion.

"Indeed," Gwendolyn replied. "Reggie seems to have become befuddled."

"I can help," Benedict said. And then his manner changed, the false drama vanishing. He simply stared at them, no expression at all on his face. "Come, boys. Let's the five of you and I leave Reggie and his second to this business. I'll buy you each a round and you can decide which fight you want to watch."

"Which fight?" Gwen asked. "Whatever do you mean?"

"They have a choice," Benedict said. "Watch Reggie fighting Bridget. Or me. Fighting them. One will take a great deal less time than the other."

"Sorellin," Esterbrook growled, his tone full of gentle reproof. "I'll have no brawling here."

"Sir," Benedict said with a nod. "It won't be a brawl, sir."

Esterbrook seemed to consider that for a moment, and then nodded. "Very well, then."

Bridget thought, with some satisfaction, that Reggie's crowd of hangers-on looked rather nervous. They were trying for arrogant, but the way they had all unconsciously moved a few inches back from Benedict was rather telling.

"You can't threaten *me*, Sorellin," Reggie snarled.

Benedict blinked several times. "Reggie, my old friend, I wouldn't disturb your business today for the world. You know exactly where you reside within my personal regard. I would never harm a hair on your head."

"I might," Gwen put in cheerfully. "I've got this lovely new gauntlet and I've never actually used it on anyone."

Esterbrook cleared his throat.

"Oh, piffle, I didn't use it *on* you, only *near* you," she said to him. "But, Reggie, let me be perfectly clear. You sought this duel, and you're going to have it. You and your second, and your friends can watch like everyone else. There will be no distractions, no moments of confusion, no mysterious objects flung from the crowd. Just you on the platform." She smiled even more widely. "Do you understand?"

"Miss Lancaster," Esterbrook said in a heavy tone. "I am quite sure that the young man has no intention of dishonoring the House of Astor this day with any such action."

"Unless," Bridget added, "he's . . . perhaps afraid of me."

Gwen glanced up at Bridget, her eyes shining. "Unless that."

"Enough," Reggie growled. "Master of Arms, commence." He turned to his friends and said, "Go watch with the Lancasters. Make sure they don't interfere."

Gwen turned to Bridget, nodded firmly up at her, and said, "If you find it quite convenient, make him cry. There's such a nice turnout for it."

Bridget found herself letting out a brief breath of a laugh, and she suddenly found the sickness in her stomach diminishing.

"Just breathe," Benedict advised her. "Relax. Let him make the first mistake. Believe me: You can count on Reggie for that." He gave her shoulder a quick squeeze with his fingers and smiled at her.

Then her friends turned to Reggie's pack of bullies, and they all departed in a group with Gwendolyn and Benedict, all of them smiling politely at one another and walking as if they expected the others to leap upon them in the instant they lowered their guard.

Esterbrook looked around at the crowd for a moment and shook his head. He muttered something under his breath about the Great Houses and their theater, and then turned to Bridget. "Miss Tagwynn," he said. "As the challenged party, you may decide which of you will take position on the platform first."

"Very well," she said. "Where will Rowl stand?"

"On the ground beside the platform. Only the two seconds and myself are permitted within ten feet of it. That's the rule."

"I will not be able to see from there," Rowl said. "You should change the rule immediately."

Esterbrook grunted and thought. Then he turned and picked up one of the large chimes in its heavy metal frame. It must have weighed three hundred pounds if an ounce, but the rather lean-looking man moved it as if it had been a living-room chair, putting it beside the nearest corner of the platform. "There, sir cat," he said. "So that you can see. Does that suit you?"

Rowl considered the chime gravely and then calmly leapt onto it. He took a few steps about before sitting down and saying, "It will suffice. Barely."

"Excellent," Esterbrook said. "Miss Tagwynn?"

"I'll go first," she said. "Let's get this over with."

"As you wish, miss," Esterbrook said.

And a moment later Bridget found herself standing upon a platform looking out over the crowd that had gathered to watch the duel. There were . . . more people than she had ever seen in her life in any single place, and she absolutely could not let herself think about the number of eyes that were upon her. She might simply scream. So instead she took Benedict's words to heart and started breathing in a slow, steady tempo, focusing upon her surroundings and her opponent.

Reggie climbed onto the platform at the opposite corner, his second standing on the ground just behind him. As he stood up, the crowd let out a cheer and began clapping and shouting and whistling. The sound was enormous, terrifying, like the rumbles of thunder that sometimes reached down into Habble Morning during the fiercest thunderstorms of spring.

"Littlemouse," came Rowl's voice from behind her. "Remember who you are. This creature wants to take it from you. Do not let him."

She turned to give the cat a glance and a quick nod. Then she turned to face Reggie again.

Esterbrook hopped lightly up onto the platform and went to stand in the center of it, holding a simple red kerchief in his right hand. The symbolism of the color of the cloth was not lost on Bridget. The color of blood. This was a place of blood and pain and death, and any of them were a possibility in the next few moments.

Focus. She had to focus. She kept breathing and systematically blocked out everything but herself, the platform, Reggie and the cloth.

Esterbrook restated the circumstances of the duel for the public, and that Bridget had chosen to face her challenger in unarmed combat. Reggie was smirking at her. It was meant to be a smug, confident expression, but . . . she fancied she could see something darker and uglier hiding within his eyes. He might not even know it was there, she realized—but he hated her. Or at least he hated something that, at this moment, happened to be Bridget-shaped.

Reggie had been trained. He knew how to fight this way. She'd been training, too, but she knew so very little.

Victory isn't about the quantity of what you know, Benedict had assured her during the past days, *but the quality.*

She hoped he was right.

Esterbrook raised the kerchief. In a moment he would drop it. When it touched the surface of the platform, the duel would begin.

Just breathe. Focus. Concentrate. Breathe.

He released the kerchief.

And a sudden low, urgent shriek went through the air, piercingly loud.

The crowd froze. Bridget looked around in confusion, only to see Reggie standing, looking upward, with his mouth wide-open. Esterbrook's expression was, for an instant, one of disbelief. Then, as the sound droned on and on, rising and falling in a slow ululation, his expression turned grim.

Thunder, louder than even the storms of spring, began to rumble through the very stone of Spire Albion.

For some reason her eyes settled on the man in the crowd who had winked at her earlier. His face contained neither confusion nor fear as he stared up at the translucent vaulted ceiling of Habble Morning. His expression was full of a cold, steely rage. He turned at once, sharply, while everyone else was still looking around, and began stalking through the milling crowd, moving swiftly and in a straight line, as if by some effort of sheer will he made the folk of Habble Morning find other places to be than in his path.

Bridget found herself standing beside Esterbrook, though she had no recollection of stepping forward. "What is this sound?" Bridget asked him, shouting over the racket. "What's happening?"

"Air-raid siren!" Esterbrook shouted back. "The first in twenty years! You need to take shelter, Miss Tagwynn! Spire Albion is under attack!"

Chapter 11

Spire Albion, Fleet Shipyards

Creedy!" Grimm called as he made his way over the mist-shrouded gangplank from the airship dock in the Fleet ship-yard atop Spire Albion, and onto *Predator*. "With me!"

"Captain on deck!" called Kettle, down in the hold. "Mister Creedy to the deck!"

"My cabin," Grimm said with a grimace, and headed that way.

"Aye, sir," Kettle said. Then in an astonished voice he said, "Captain. Your clothes . . . Sir, you're wounded."

Grimm sighed and looked down at the borrowed outfit Ferus had lent him. It was not, strictly speaking, an actual suit, having been made from two or perhaps three vaguely similar suits, none of them particularly fine. He'd rigged his wounded arm into a sling. "Aye, aye, summat came out of the vents and tried to make a meal of me in a side tunnel. My own fault for taking a shortcut."

"Bloody hell," Kettle said, clearly angry. "Doesn't Habble Morning employ verminocitors anymore?"

"No permanent harm done," Grimm said, giving Kettle a quick wink. "How many men are on shore leave, do you know?"

"We've a quarter crew aboard," Kettle said. "The boys are off seeing some duel happening in the market today. Couple of highborn sprats going bare-knuckle, 'twould seem. There's a group bet against a bunch of those rascals from *Glorious*."

"I hope they make out," Grimm said. "They'll need to, after what *Itasca* did to our accounts."

"Never fear, sir," Kettle said. "The boys will be fine." He finished folding the long web of ethersilk he'd been untangling, secured it with leather ties, and then stowed it in one of the lockers beside the base of the rigging—despite the fact that the masts and spars were currently missing from the ship's upper deck, not yet having been replaced. "Let me get the door for you, sir."

"Thank you," Grimm said. Kettle opened the door to his cabin and Grimm stepped in, turning to pass his sheathed sword to Kettle. "See this cleaned for me, would you? Bit hard to manage with one hand."

"Aye, sir," Kettle said, accepting the weapon and shutting the door behind him.

Grimm settled down in his chair. His wounded arm ached quite uncomfortably, though Ferus assured him it was healing. Folly had presented him with a small jar of rather sharp-scented unguent, and he was supposed to apply it to the wound every time he changed the dressing. Something else he would have to ask for help with. Mister Bagen, the ship's doctor, would doubtless find it tedious and complain interminably about the haplessness of wayward captains.

Creedy knocked and entered when Grimm bade him do so. The tall young officer had to duck his head a bit to keep from bumping it on the ceiling.

"Sit, sit," Grimm said. "You look like you're apologizing for something, just standing there."

Creedy smiled faintly and settled on the bench along the cabin's wall, opposite the bunk. "Kettle says you were injured, sir."

"Some damned creature came out of the vents, I suppose," Grimm replied. "Worse attacks have happened."

"Bad luck," Creedy said. "We've had a bit of a run of it, haven't we?"

"I suppose that depends on how one regards it," Grimm replied. "We had a rather good bit of luck in surviving an engagement with a *Cortez*-class and *Itasca*, after all. We're here to tell the tale."

"That's true, sir," Creedy said. He bit his lip. "You were gone overnight. I hope you don't mind that I granted the men liberty."

"They'd have hung you from a spar and taken it if you hadn't," Grimm said. "Keeping a quarter crew aboard was the right decision."

Creedy looked slightly relieved and nodded. "Good." He glanced up at Grimm and said, "Captain . . . I don't want to overstep my place, but . . ."

"Go ahead. Ask. Pour us a drink while you're at it."

Creedy looked relieved to be given some orders to follow while he spoke his mind, and he drew glasses and bottle from their usual places. "Sir, I've been taking a survey of the damage."

"How accurate was Journeyman's estimate?"

"Spot-on, sir," he replied, somewhat reluctantly. "The blighter is insubordinate, but he knows his job."

"Yes, he does," Grimm said, accepting the glass Creedy offered him.

"Sir," Creedy said, "the estimate for repairs is . . . considerable."

"I'm aware," Grimm said.

"I'm afraid that . . . times being what they are, there might be those in the High Houses who might begin to put pressure on you to sell."

"Really?" Grimm said. "Well, I suppose they have the right to make offers."

"I'm afraid they might be more aggressive than that, sir," Creedy said earnestly.

"If they get out of line, I'll just slap them around and threaten them until they stop," Grimm said.

At that Creedy all but spat out some of the drink he'd just taken. He managed to choke it down and after a moment managed a chuckle. "My sister told me you had an odd sense of humor, sir."

"I suppose I do," Grimm said.

"But . . . joking aside. What are you going to do with her, sir? I mean, I don't know if you'll be able to get a loan, not in these times. If you won't sell her and you can't repair her . . . what?"

Grimm studied the young man for a moment. Creedy seemed almost painfully earnest, and Grimm had always thought well of the young man's family, but . . . Rook had obtained a description of *Predator*'s wounds sooner and more thoroughly than he should have. Someone had talked, and while Grimm had no reason to suspect that it was an act of malice in general, or Creedy's act in particular, it was perhaps best to employ a modicum of caution.

"Let me worry about that, XO," he said. "There are several possibilities to explore, and I'm going to examine them all. Meanwhile, we stick to Journeyman's proposal for refitting her. I saw to having the death benefits paid before my, ah, little adventure in the ventilation tunnels. We'll replace her spars and her web out of what's left of our current funds, as well as the bulkheads and the number three gun emplacement. There's enough money to do that much, and it will be your concern. I'll secure the new crystals we'll need."

"Sir, uh. I thought we might take on a cargo."

"Cargo?" Grimm asked. "In her shape?"

"No need to strain her, sir," Creedy said quickly. "But . . . a short run could yield some quick, modest profit."

"A short run . . ." Grimm frowned. "You mean down to Landing, don't you?"

"There's always cargo coming and going from the lower habbles, sir," Creedy said.

"In barges. In scows," Grimm said quietly, "and on windlasses. *Predator* is an airship, Commander."

"With all due respect, sir," Creedy said, looking down, "she isn't. Not right now. Not until you've secured the funds to mend her."

"I'll consider it," Grimm said, and managed to avoid growling as he did. "Thank you for bringing it to my attention."

"Sir," Creedy said, "it might take you several years of work to earn it that way, but it would be honest work at least. There's no shame in it."

"And no joy, either," Grimm said. "Not for me, not for the crew, and not for *Predator*. You can't expect a cat to change his fur for you because you think it would be better."

Creedy blinked at that. "I . . . I don't understand."

"A ship is more than wood and crystals and ethersilk, Byron," Grimm said. "Some thick-skulled vat counters have always said it was nonsense, but the men on the ships know better. Airships aren't just vehicles—and the men who treat them like more than that get more out of them."

"In the academy, we were taught that it has never been conclusively—"

"I went to the academy, too, thank you," Grimm said. "The academy is where knowledge begins—not where it ends. You're a solid man. You'll understand in time."

"If you say so, sir," Creedy said dubiously.

"I do," Grimm said. "But for now, why do we not consider ways we might—" He stopped abruptly. There was a faint, faint sound, something he had heard before, hauntingly familiar.

Then he placed it—a high-pitched humming, like an etherwasp gliding effortlessly on an etheric wind, but louder, wider, deeper.

It was the distant war cry of an Auroran destroyer—if he remembered correctly, the *Ciervo*.

But that would mean . . .

Grimm bolted to his feet and flung open his cabin door. He stomped onto deck, bellowing, "General quarters! General quarters!"

Creedy came out after him, gave him the briefest of stunned looks, then whirled and started ringing the ship's bell.

Grimm hurried to the speaking tube and shouted, "Journeyman!

Get your drunken ass out of that chair you think I don't know about and run up the main crystal! Get us off this dock and bring up the shroud!"

Journeyman didn't reply, but only seconds later the planks of the deck began to quiver and vibrate as *Predator's* main power crystal stirred to life—and less than a minute later she let out groans and squeaks of protest from her battered timbers and began to rise.

"Kettle, the lines!" Grimm bellowed—but he didn't need to do it. Kettle was already taking an ax to the heavy lines that secured *Predator* to the dock, cutting the wounded ship free.

Meanwhile, *Ciervo's* war cry grew louder and louder and louder. Around the shipyard, vessels of the Fleet began to call general quarters as well, the alarm bells ringing in strident cadence. Somewhere in Habble Morning, immediately below the shipyard, an air-raid siren began to wail.

And then the enemy was on them.

Ciervo—Grimm was sure of it now—appeared out of the mists above in a screaming dive that took her streaking down past the shipyard at a steep attack angle. Her guns spat thunder and howling light into the docked airships and into the shipyard itself, detonations flinging men and equipment about like tea leaves whirling in a stirred cup.

And behind her, following her same dive, were half a dozen more vessels like her.

Fire began falling from the far side of the shipyard, marching toward *Predator* in a swath of hellish destruction. Even as Grimm watched, *Chivalrous*, a heavy cruiser three times his own ship's size, vanished into a cloud of fire and light and screams of anguished ship and crew. Other ships were struck, though the heavier vessels, even without their shrouds up and active, were only minimally harmed by the light guns of the enemy destroyers. The oncoming fire destroyed a merchant ship named *Tinker* only a hundred yards from *Predator*. Then another merchant vessel called *Surplus* blew into flaming splinters only fifty yards away, in the neighboring slip. Splinters and bits of metal—and worse—flew past

Grimm in a deadly cloud, some of the pieces so close that he heard them go by.

Grimm planted his feet as he felt his ship wallowing up off of her dock, lifted his chin, and wondered whether he'd realized the danger in time to stop the Auroran squadron from finishing what *Itasca* had begun.

The fire of the final ship in the column fell upon *Predator.* . . .

And shattered into light and whistling shrieks against his ship's now-active shroud, the light blinding without his protective goggles. Grimm held himself perfectly still, as if his entire field of vision had not at all been converted into a tapestry of dancing colors, and then the screams of the diving vessels faded abruptly as they plunged past the edge of the Spire and on down into the mists below.

Grimm blinked his eyes until he could see again, and scanned the misty sky around the shipyard. He saw what he'd been afraid he would see, and turned to Creedy calmly. "Form a shore party to bring the crew back to duty," he said. "Tell Kettle that he's acting armorer. Crew to be armed with gauntlets, sidearms, and tunics immediately."

Creedy only stared at Grimm, stunned. His eyes flicked around the shipyard, where dozens of fires had begun to blaze, consuming the costly wooden structures that had been erected to expand upon the original spirestone design. People were screaming and dying.

"Creedy!" Grimm snapped.

"Sir."

He repeated his orders.

"Aye, sir," Creedy said, blinking, and set about them. Given a task, Grimm thought, Creedy was excellent at seeing it through. Within a moment he had dispatched Kettle with an armed shore party, and put Journeyman in charge of distributing weapons to the crew and preparing more for quick issue when Kettle returned. "I don't understand, Captain," he said when he was finished. "Why arm the men?"

Grimm pointed at a bit of debris floating lightly on the wind. A stray current of air or ether sent it gliding down to the deck of *Predator*. It was a small rectangle of ethersilk. He picked it up and held it out to Creedy. The square of silk stirred and rippled in the shipyard's etheric eddies, moved just as it might by wind, though in a slower, more graceful manner.

"Is that . . . ?" Creedy began.

"The etheric sail from a boarding rig," Grimm confirmed. The flag-size squares of ethersilk were used to help propel and guide the flight of a parasail. With decent etheric currents, a well-managed parasail, and a bit of luck, a man could climb, descend, and alter course. In the Fleet, such rigs were used in boarding actions, with Marines leaping from their airship and using them to glide down to the enemy vessel.

Grimm held up a few broken cords fastened to the ethersilk and said, "It would appear that they frayed and snapped when the rig opened. Whichever poor bastard was using it as part of his gear is on his way to the surface now. The Aurorans always were cheap about the equipment for their Marines."

Creedy finally understood and stared up into the pale mists overhead. The sun was a dull circle. Some days the top of Spire Albion could see open blue sky. Today the typical blanketing mist had reduced visibility to a few hundred yards at best.

"You think there are enemy Marines on the way?"

"This isn't a full Fleet assault," Grimm said. "The Spire's batteries were surprised by that dive, but you can be sure they're ready now. If the Aurorans intended to seriously assault Albion, their battleships would have blanketed the shipyard batteries with fire the instant their own ships had completed their pass."

"Then this was a raiding force?" Creedy asked.

Grimm frowned, looking at the yards. The Fleet vessels had not re-acted as swiftly as *Predator* and her crew, but they were now in the process of leaving the shipyard, gathering together two hundred feet above the Spire, concentrating their armor and firepower. Albion's home fleet consisted of a corps of twenty *Roc*-class battleships, absolute leviathans a hundred times the mass of *Predator*—and correspondingly sluggish and slow to respond. They were accompanied by a screen of lighter vessels, around fifty cruisers and destroyers of various tonnages. All of them had sounded general quarters and were under way.

Grimm watched the Fleet lurching into motion, which he suspected to be futility in action, and jerked his chin up toward the mists above them. "You've got to admire how well the Aurorans managed that pass of the Spire, and in mist like this. But those destroyers can't lock horns with the home Fleet, or with the Spire's batteries. They damaged or destroyed a few lighter ships, but they couldn't possibly have hoped to inflict serious harm to home Fleet."

"You think the attack was a distraction," Creedy said.

"Why do it otherwise?" Grimm nodded overhead again. "I suspect there's a troop transport up there, dropping its complement."

"Merciful Builders," Creedy said, his eyes widening in understanding. "They knew the Fleet would mobilize. They wouldn't have any choice."

"Precisely," Grimm said. "If they can get a body of troops into the Spire, God in Heaven only knows what mischief the Aurorans could manage. And as we speak, every Marine in home Fleet is aboard his ship. Up there. Where he can't defend the Spire."

"We've got to tell Fleet," Creedy said.

"I'm an exile, and you've been habbled, Byron," Grimm said quietly. "All I have is a theory and an old piece of ethersilk. Even if we could get word to him, do you think Admiral Watson would stand down?"

Creedy's face looked pained, frustrated. He nodded slowly, his eyes thoughtful. Then he said, "The men are a fine crew, but they aren't professional soldiers—and a regiment of Auroran Marines will outnumber us three to one. They'll tear us— That is, we'll never defeat them."

"We needn't defeat them," Grimm said, "but only slow them down. Bayard has a crooked mind but it works perfectly well. He'll realize what's happening before long."

"Yes, sir," Creedy said quietly. "What are we to do?"

"Gather the crew, arm them, and defend the Spire, Mister Creedy," Grimm said. "Make ready to repel boarders."

Chapter 12

Spire Albion, Habble Morning

To shelter, then," Benedict said, turning to Gwen as the sirens wailed. "Back to Lancaster, I think."

Gwen stared around at the rising panic spreading through the market. "I . . . Yes, the house is supposed to be under a structural strongpoint of some kind, but . . ."

Bridget hopped down from the dueling platform and caught Rowl as he jumped up into her arms. The cat's eyes were very wide, his head jerking back and forth as he tried to track all the frantic movement.

"My father," Bridget said. "I need to get to my father."

"Wait," Gwen said, catching Benedict's wrist as he was turning to go. There was something in her that was screaming for attention, and she had to take a moment for the thought to crystallize.

The young man arched an eyebrow and looked down at her—but he waited.

Then there was a hideous sound, as if a thunderbolt could scream in anguish and rage. Part of the translucent ceiling of Habble Morning suddenly burned with a light brighter than any mist-shrouded noonday sun. The very floor beneath their feet shook with it, and a pall of dust fell from the ceiling high overhead. A second later there was another shrieking impact, and another, making the spirestone of Albion toll like a titanic bell.

Dust fell in a choking haze, and the screaming redoubled. Pieces of masonry that in the past had been used to repair the not-quite-invulnerable spirestone fell, some of them larger than a man.

Gwen took note of them and simply lifted her chin. The stones would fall where they fell. Panicked flight might as easily carry her beneath a falling mound of masonry as save her from it. Her father had always said that when one most wanted to panic was when one most needed to think clearly, so despite the falling stone, Gwendolyn Lancaster stood quietly.

Then she spoke in a slow, firm tone, realizing the truth of the words even as she said them. "We are members of the Spirearch's Guard. We don't run from trouble. We run toward it. We should report for duty."

Bridget blinked at that, and her expressive face showed a flicker of fear, then resignation, and then annoyance. "Oh, bother. I should have remembered that myself."

Benedict smiled with tight lips. "Ah. I had rather hoped to get the two of you stowed in some nice safe strong room, but . . . you're right, of course. We should."

"Benny, don't be tiresome," Gwen said. "Where do we go?"

Again the Spire shook with thunder, and more rock fell. Screams began nearby, high-pitched and terrible. Gwen could not be sure whether it was a man or a woman or a child.

"There," Benedict said, nodding toward the source of the sound. "Our first duty is to protect and aid endangered citizens. Follow me." The three of them and Rowl started forward through the panicked residents and dust-filled air, Benedict's tall, lean form leading the way.

A waterfall of shattered stone roared down abruptly, only a few yards away, and Gwen absolutely could not believe how violently *loud* the impact sounded. Small chips of stone flew out, one of them stinging as it struck her hip. She saw Bridget flinch, and a tiny spot of blood appeared on her right cheek.

They ran perhaps fifty strides, the screaming growing louder, and suddenly from out of the haze of shattered stone the shape of a mound of rubble appeared. Someone was pinned beneath a large piece of masonry. Some of the dust had been matted into scarlet mud. He was clearly in agony.

"Benedict, lift the stone," Gwen said. "Bridget, help me slide him out."

"Wait," Benedict snapped. "If he's bleeding under there, the rock could be holding the injury shut. We have to be ready to stanch it immediately when we get him out. We need cloth for bandages."

Gwen nodded sharply and promptly reached for the hem of her skirt and started tearing it into strips. "Bridget," she said.

Bridget knelt down and started to do the same thing, while Benedict crouched beside the trapped man. Then Gwen's cousin let out a swift curse.

"It's Barnabus Astor under all this dust," Benedict said.

"Bad luck," Gwen noted, still tearing. "If there were any kind of justice, it would be Reggie there."

Between the two of them, Gwen and Bridget managed to reduce the outermost layer of Gwen's skirts into strips and folded pads. Once it was done, Benedict nodded and said, "Bridget, haul him out when I lift. Don't dawdle."

"I won't," Bridget said seriously.

Then Benedict turned to the fallen stone, a mass the size of a small coffin, dug his fingers beneath one edge, and heaved with the entire power of his lean frame. For a second nothing happened. The muscles in Benedict's back and shoulders swelled out and shook. But then there was a groan and the rock shifted ever so slightly. Poor Barnabus let out a shriek of new agony, and then Bridget was dragging him out from beneath the rock.

There was blood, Gwen noted, what seemed an entirely unnecessary amount of it. A few weeks ago she'd have had no real idea what to do about it, but their first long day of weapons training had been composed entirely of lessons in how to deal with injuries like this one. Gwen slammed a thick pad of cloth over a spurting wound in Barnabus's leg, then wrapped strips of cloth around it, tightened them, and tied them off. The young man let out another breathless gasp of agony as she jerked the knots tight.

"That will do to get him to safety," Benedict said, panting. "Bridget, I'm going to pick him up. I want you to get his wounded leg up onto your shoulder. Keep it elevated, eh?"

"Of course."

Thunder roared again, and stones began to fall nearby. There was a low, deep groaning sound from overhead, and Benedict's face went white. "Hurry!"

He scooped Barnabus in his arms and Bridget immediately braced the wounded man's leg on one of her shoulders.

To Gwen's great alarm, rocks began to fall more rapidly all around them. "We've got to get out of the atrium! There, a side tunnel."

"Go, go, go!" Benedict shouted, and began to half run, half shuffle toward the relative safety of the smaller tunnel.

Just as they slipped into its cool dimness the tower groaned again, and suddenly a section of masonry the size of an average home crashed down onto the space they'd just vacated. The noise was deafening. The dust became a throat-closing, choking pall.

"Farther in!" Gwen gasped, and they continued their retreat down the dim side tunnel, into what rapidly became blackness.

Finally they reached a turn, and once they'd rounded the corner the air suddenly grew sweet again, the gentle current flowing down the tunnel evidently dispersing the dust, and they came to a halt. "Light?" Benedict asked, coughing.

Gwen reached up to the small crystals on her earrings with the fingers of her right hand and willed them to life one at a time, just as she would have done to discharge a gauntlet. The tiny crystals winked alight. It wasn't particularly bright light, but contrasted with the blackness it was dazzling.

Benedict lay the wounded man on the ground and examined his injuries. "Bother," he said quietly. "Barney, old man, I'm afraid you've sprung a few leaks."

Barnabus answered through the pained clench of his teeth. "Normally that only happens when I've been engaged in epic drinking."

"We'll put some corks in you, then, until we can get you to a physician."

Bridget turned to Gwen and started ripping at the second layer to her skirts, while Benedict examined the bandage Gwen had put in place. Evidently he thought it sound, because as Bridget handed him more cloth, he moved on to other injuries and began stanching them in turn. Gwen ran out of skirt before Barnabus ran out of injuries, leaving only one thin layer of skirts between her legs and the cold air of the habble.

"Come on, then," Benedict said. "Keep the bandages coming."

"I hardly think so," Gwen said. "Benny, take off your shirt and we'll rip it to bits."

Benedict shot her a glance, then eyed her last layer of skirts and grunted understanding. He slipped out of his jacket and weskit, and stripped off the shirt beneath in a single ripple of motion, passing it back to Bridget.

Gwen sometimes forgot that her cousin was, like all warriorborn, a particularly athletic-looking, masculine specimen of a man lined with hard, lean muscle. The effect was impressive. Bridget blinked at his unclothed torso in such shock that his tossed shirt fell through her hands as if they'd suddenly gone numb. "Oh," she said. "My."

Gwen arched an eyebrow and felt herself smiling. So it was like that with Bridget, was it? Well. God in Heaven only knew that Benedict deserved someone's affection. Amongst the families of the High Houses in general, the warriorborn were considered . . . unseemly—and best put to use as armed retainers or bodyguards—and certainly *not* as members of a House.

Gwen nudged Bridget with an elbow. The girl blinked again, shook herself, and went back to tearing cloth as the air-raid sirens continued out in the habble's main atrium.

"Hang in there, Barney," Benedict said as he worked. "I know it hurts, but I think we'll keep your body and soul knitted together."

Barnabus answered with a faint, pained grunt, his eyes closed.

"I still don't understand why this is happening," Bridget said. "Airships attacked the Spire? Whose?"

"The Aurorans, most probably," Gwen answered.

"But why would they do such a thing?"

"Economics, mostly."

"What?"

"The government of Spire Aurora is greedy, corrupt, and inefficient," Gwen said. "Taxes are quite high. Each habble struggles against its neighbors to claim funding and favors from their government, and the actual business of government is generally neglected. As a result, their enterprises suffer and do not grow—while their population does. So once every generation or so, the Aurorans become aggressive. Their Fleet gobbles up outposts, and in the past entire Spires, plundering their wealth to keep their own Spire going, and getting a lot of their own people killed to reduce the pressure on their population."

Bridget sounded baffled. "They want to go to war . . . for *money*?"

Gwen snorted. "You'll never hear them say that. They always manage to find or contrive a rationale. But in the end they are nothing more than glorified pirates. Tension has been building between their Armada and our Fleet for a year or so—mostly raids on Albion merchantmen, and small-scale engagements with Fleet ships."

"Didn't think they'd move this soon, though," Benedict put in. "I don't think anyone did."

From the darkness just outside the little circle of light Gwen's earrings cast, there was a quiet, rather unnerving feline sound.

Bridget tensed and looked down the tunnel. "Rowl says someone is coming."

"Thank God in Heaven," Gwen said, peering. "Perhaps it is some of the Guard." She called, "Hello? Who is that, please?"

A few moments later, eight men in uniforms of the Spirearch's Guard stepped into the outskirts of Gwen's light. Two of them were carrying a stretcher, its occupant covered by blankets. Another, wearing the weapon-crystal insignia of a junior officer, touched a finger to his brow and said, "Miss."

"Lieutenant," Gwen said. She didn't recognize the man, but that was hardly unusual. The Guard had several dozen outposts throughout the Spire, with most of two thousand individuals serving. "I'm quite glad to see you. We've a wounded civilian here. Can you help us?"

"Sorry, miss," the man replied. "I'm afraid we've duties of our own to attend to."

"Gwendolyn," Benedict said.

Gwen shot Benedict a glance. He never called her by her full name. He was waiting for her to look, his face calm, but his eyes were intent. "I'm sure the lieutenant regrets the need to fulfill his duty. It's nearly miraculous that he is in motion at all this soon after a surprise attack."

Gwen frowned at her cousin. Then Benedict flexed his left wrist, his gauntlet hand, in a slow circle, and with a cold shock Gwen realized what he meant.

The attack had happened only moments ago. The four of them had been involved in it, had seen it happening, and yet they'd barely had time to duck into the tunnel for safety and apply rapid field dressings to poor Barney Astor. Yet here stood a full squad of the Guard, already armed and organized and carrying a casualty on a stretcher. And, Gwen noted, wearing large field packs as well.

No one could have thrown that together in mere moments, not in the terror and confusion currently raging through the habble. Not unless they'd known the attack was coming.

And who would know better than the enemy? An enemy wearing Guard uniforms, operating in secret—an enemy who would have no compunction in killing anyone they came across in order to maintain their disguise.

Someone like herself, for example.

Gwen's heart started pounding so loudly she fancied she could hear it.

Benedict gave her a microscopic nod, then deliberately closed his eyes and turned back to the wounded man.

Closing his eyes. He'd done that on purpose, so that she could see it. Why?

Ah. Obviously, yes.

Gwen pivoted back to the false Guardsmen, raised her left hand, and discharged her gauntlet into the officer's face from less than five feet away.

■ ■ ■ Chapter 13 ■ ■ ■

Spire Albion, Habble Morning,
Ventilation Tunnels

There was a truly blinding flash of light. When one discharged a gauntlet, the light was bright enough to clearly show the bones of one's hand through the seemingly translucent flesh. The force of the gauntlet's blast screamed into the echoing expanse of the tunnel, smashing into the officer like a blazing sledgehammer. It flung his abruptly limp body to the ground as if he'd been bludgeoned with an enormous club.

Then Gwen willed away the light of the little crystals on her earrings and plunged the tunnel into blackness.

She couldn't see a thing but a blinding swirl of colors—and her own eyes had been at least partly shielded from the light of the gauntlet's discharge. The false Guardsmen who had been able to see the crystal directly would be in even worse shape. Absolutely no one would be able to see in the sudden contrast of brilliance and pitch-blackness.

No one but one of the warriorborn.

Gwen dropped to the floor as a sudden sound she had never heard before, a snarl indistinguishable from the coughing roar of a large hunting cat, burst forth from the blackness. There was a quick, scuffling sound of boots pressed sharply against the stone floor, an exhalation, and then a cry of pain in the darkness. There were more scuffling sounds, a voice shouting something in Auroran, more screams, and then the flash of a gauntlet gave her a burned-picture image—two men were already on the ground, and Benedict was locked in grips with a third man, whose gauntlet had gone off while Benedict, fighting bare-handed, held it aimed at a fourth enemy.

That flash image gave Gwen only an instant to understand where her cousin stood, and an even briefer time in which to act. She aimed her own gauntlet wide of Benedict's position and triggered another shot, sending a blast in the general direction of the disguised invaders. She had no idea whatsoever whether she'd hit friend or foe, but thought it a very good idea not to remain in the same place, in case any of the Aurorans had the same idea she'd had. She rolled to her left until her shoulder fetched up rather painfully against a cold stone wall.

There were the sounds of more movement in the darkness, scuffling noises, blows struck—and then a short, sharp gasp.

Bridget.

God in Heaven, in the frantic moment of danger, Gwen had forgotten about their companion.

"Stop, Albion!" snarled a voice in a heavy accent. "Or the girl dies."

Light rose again, this time from one of the intruders, holding up an illumination crystal. Four forms lay on the ground, utterly still, and as Gwen blinked her eyes, struggling to peer into the new illumination, she saw Benedict holding a fifth man by the throat all but entirely suspended from the ground, with his boots barely resting on the floor. There was blood on her cousin's hands and splattered across his naked chest.

The invaders holding the stretcher had dropped it. There was not a casualty beneath its blankets—instead it had been stacked with leather satchels set with fuses. They'd had only a brief introduction to the devices in their munitions lectures, but Gwen knew enough to recognize a military-grade explosive charge when she saw it.

Only a few feet to her right, one of the invaders stood behind Bridget. He held her throat in one hand, and with the other had trapped one of her arms behind her. Fresh burn marks on his uniform at one shoulder suggested that the second blast of Gwen's gauntlet had found a target.

Bridget's eyes were wide and furious, her neck bent at an angle that suggested she was in pain. Her captor stared at Benedict over Bridget's head, the light of the crystal gleaming off of his feline eyes.

"Put him down," growled the enemy warriorborn.

Benedict bared his teeth, but her cousin released the fifth man, who slid to the floor like so much limp vattery meat, and let out a low groan. Gwen took time to note that the remaining invaders were now spread out, the nearest two kneeling so that those standing behind them had a clear field of fire. All of them held gauntlets aimed and ready—several of them pointing directly at Gwen. She, unfortunately, did not have her own gauntlet aimed at them—and she rather thought that if she moved her left arm at all, she'd never know it when they fired.

"Three men in three seconds," the Auroran said to Benedict in a low, flat tone. "Not terrible. But I'd have taken you if the little girl hadn't gotten lucky with the second shot."

Benedict lifted his left hand, his gauntlet's crystal smoldering with light.

The Auroran smiled very slightly and drew Bridget a little more fully between himself and Benedict. "How sure are you of your aim, Albion? Fire and my men will kill you and your little girl. And once you're dead, I'll kill this one and move on."

"Shoot him, Benedict," Bridget grated. "He smells. I would rather—"

The Auroran flexed his fingers slightly, and Bridget's words abruptly ceased. He put his lips close to her ear and said, "The men are talking."

"If I stand down," Benedict said, "you'll kill her anyway. What reason do I have not to at least take you with us?"

"My word," the Auroran said. "You go down. That's how it is. But you can save them. Stand down and I'll tie these others up and leave them unharmed."

Benedict stared at the other warriorborn for a silent moment. Then he said, "Give me your name."

The Auroran inclined his head. "Diego Ciriaco, master sergeant, First Auroran Marines."

"Benedict Sorellin, Spirearch's Guard," Gwen's cousin said.

"Benedict Sorellin," Ciriaco said, "you have my word."

"Remember my name," Benedict said.

And then he lowered his gauntlet, an oddly calm expression on his face.

"Will," the Auroran told him. Then he turned to his fellow Aurorans and said, "You will fire on my command."

Gwen abruptly realized that while her gauntlet was not pointed at any of the armed men facing them, it *was* pointed at something else.

"You will *not*," she snapped in a sudden cold tone, doing everything she could to copy her mother's furious, imperious voice of command, the one she used only on special occasions. "If anyone fires or harms any of us, I swear to God in Heaven that I will discharge my gauntlet into your explosives. It would not be the end I had hoped for, but it will be quick, and if I die defending Albion from Auroran invaders, I should not count my life wasted. Can you say as much, Mister Ciriaco? Can your companions?"

There was a moment of utter, crystalline silence.

Then Ciriaco let out a low hiss and snarled, "Hold fire."

Benedict's teeth shone in a hard smile. "In that case, sir, perhaps I could offer to accept *your* surrender. My terms will be a great deal more generous than those you offered me. Release the young lady, lay down your arms, and you will be taken as prisoners of war."

Ciriaco snorted. "Only to be tortured for information by your masters? I prefer the explosion, sir."

"Then we are at an impasse."

Ciriaco grunted an acknowledgment. "True enough. But that balance will inevitably change. Someone will be along."

"I assure you, sir," Gwen said, "I will have no compunctions what-ever about blowing up any number of your fellows who might have the appallingly bad taste to interrupt us."

The warriorborn stared at her, his face unreadable. "Conversely, miss, if more of your own people appear, your threat seems rather di-minished. How many of your own folk are you willing to kill along with all of us?"

"Even in a draw, the advantage is mine," Gwen said. "While I keep you pinned here, you cannot complete whatever objective it is that you have been given. You do not hold a winning hand."

He showed his teeth. "Yet. How long, do you think, before your people sort out enough of this mess to send armed patrols through the side tunnels? Hours? A day?" He nodded toward the unconscious form of Barnabus Astor. "How long does your wounded man have before he succumbs? I know when to expect my people. And I know that they'll be armed. It shouldn't surprise me at all if in the next moment, a long gunner shot you dead from far down the tunnel and out of your sight before you even realized the danger. Time is on my side, miss, not yours."

Gwen felt a cold sensation in the pit of her stomach.

"Surrender," Ciriaco said in a hard voice. "Save who you can." He eyed Benedict. "Surely you see. Tell her."

"To the best of my knowledge, sir," Benedict said in an apologetic tone, "no one has ever been able to tell my dear cousin anything. At all."

The Auroran's expression darkened as he turned back to Gwen. "There is no path to victory for you here."

She showed him her teeth. "Yet," she said with a certain vicious satisfaction. "We shall all, I think, wait and see."

◼ ◼ ◼ Chapter 14 ◼ ◼ ◼

Spire Albion, Habble Morning

Grimm hated personal combat.

Aboard an airship, combat was a tide, a storm, a force of nature. Men died, yes, and it was horrible and it haunted him—but they died at the mercy of forces so powerful that it hardly seemed a merely human agency could be involved. Most often one never saw the face of the enemy, only his ship, hanging like a model in the sky, often looking quite serene and beautiful.

That was an illusion, of course. Pain and death were the reality.

But battle was a distant thing in airships. Detached. Clinical. One pitted one's mind and skill and the heart of one's crew against another captain doing precisely the same thing. One saw what the enemy did to one's own ship, but only rarely did one have a clear, horrible view of what one had perpetrated upon the enemy. Most important, a good commander could make decisions that protected his crew and brought them victory, the ship moving at his will like a single, enormous living being.

Personal combat was a very different world.

Kettle returned with the majority of the crew within moments, and Mister Journeyman was waiting to issue weapons and tunics lined with ethersilk. The tunics were old, the silk harvested a generation ago at the very latest, and they would be of use only against an indirect blast from moderate range—but they were the best Grimm had been able to find for his men, and they were a great deal better than no armor at all.

"We're ready, Captain," Creedy said. The large young man had donned his sword and gauntlet. "Where should we go?"

"Where there is need," Grimm said. "It stands to reason that . . ." He paused as Kettle approached with his sword, its sheath lashed to a baldric. It took a bit of consideration to settle the belt across Grimm's chest so that his sling wouldn't tangle in it, and so his unwounded right arm would be able to draw the weapon.

"Captain," Creedy said. "What are you doing?"

"I'm not about to send the crew somewhere I'm not willing to go, XO," Grimm replied. "Thank you, Mister Kettle."

"Captain," Kettle said. "Your gauntlet?"

Grimm wiggled his left arm in its sling and sighed. "I could scarcely aim the thing, I'm afraid."

"Captain," Creedy said. "You're wounded. You shouldn't go."

"Nonsense," Grimm replied.

Creedy ground his teeth. Then he turned to Kettle. "Mister Kettle?"

"Sir?" Kettle asked. There was, Grimm thought, a certain amount of skepticism in the honorific.

"As our dear captain is determined to put himself in unnecessary danger, I am tasking you with the personal responsibility of watching over him. I don't want you more than a step away from him until this is settled. Clear?"

Kettle's expression relaxed, and for a second something almost like a smile graced it. "Crystal, sir."

"Bah," Grimm said. "I could order you not to do so, you know."

"What's that, sir?" Kettle asked in an overloud voice. "I couldn't quite hear you. My ears, the explosions, you see, sir."

Grimm eyed him, but Kettle remained amiably, apologetically deaf. Creedy's expression was set into a stubborn frown. Grimm looked around and noted other crewmen observing the exchange, and sighed. "Fine, fine." He gave them both an irritated glare, but his heart wasn't really in it. "As I was saying, it stands to reason that the boarders won't attempt to land on the Spire's roof in the shipyard. There are Marines here on duty, batteries, ships, crews. Had they intended an open assault, they'd have landed already."

"Where, then?" Creedy asked. "Do you think they're headed for Landing?"

A fair question. The enterprising inhabitants of Habble Landing had spent a generation investing in wearing a hole in the spirestone outer wall of their habble, and then constructed an airship port of their own, out of wood, on the exterior wall of their level of the Spire. Where before there had been only two entrances to Spire Albion, the roof and the base, there were now three. Transport times of goods throughout the many habbles of Spire Albion could be cut in half, and the craftsmen and merchants of the Spire had been swift to take advantage of such an opportunity—and now Landing possessed nearly as much wealth as Morning.

"Perhaps," Grimm said. "But even there, they'd have a real fight on their hands to get in. I believe they'll go in another way."

"The ventilation tunnels?"

"Precisely. They'll get as many of their Marines into the tunnels as they can and set them about the business of weakening Albion from within."

Kettle whistled through his teeth. "The mouths to those tunnels aren't but maybe four feet by four, and right on the side of the Spire. No ledges or nothing, Captain. Hell of a difficult target for a Marine flying a parasail."

Grimm started walking toward the gangplank. "Industry and determination, Mister Kettle, can transform the difficult into the routine," Grimm said. "We can assume they'll move from the ventilation tunnels into the side tunnels, and from there proceed to their objectives. There are a number of possible targets for them to assault within Habble Morning, and they may try for the shipyards as well. Our mission is to keep them bottled up in the side tunnels. We needn't hunt them down—I daresay our own Marines will be happy to do it once they return."

Grimm looked over his shoulder and saw his crew following him, some of them still buckling their swords and gauntlets into place.

Kettle had found most of them in a remarkably short time—eighty-seven men, only nine short of her full complement. It seemed they had all been together, and rather nearby, to place their bets on that duel.

How many, Grimm wondered, would still be alive when the sun set?

"Mister Creedy, pass the word to the officers, if you please. Make sure every single one of them understands our goal and that I expect it to be met regardless of what happens to the officers or myself. They are to inform the men in their squad the same way."

"Aye, Captain," Creedy said, and immediately turned to begin walking backward, speaking in terse tones to the first of the crewmen behind them.

"Mister Journeyman," Grimm called, without turning his head.

"Aye, Captain?"

"You stay."

An incredulous, absolutely acidic epithet split the air.

"I believe the phrase you used was 'jumped-up wollypog'? If you are too valuable to show proper deference and courtesy to my XO, you are certainly too valuable to risk in a firefight with Auroran Marines, Journeyman. That's how it is."

The engineer's ongoing curses faded into the background as Grimm began to trot forward, and his men came with him.

They descended a spiral ramp that led from the shipyard to Habble Morning, fighting against confused traffic heading in the opposite direction. The habble was in chaos.

The bombardment from the Auroran destroyers had not struck the habble directly, but enough of the energy had transferred through the spirestone to dislodge a significant amount of masonry used to buttress and repair the Spire's roof. There were screams and the scent of smoke on the air. That was terrifying. If an enemy was lurking, he could be fought—but if smoke began to fill the habble or its tunnels, it could kill every one of his men without a blade being drawn or a gauntlet discharged.

Members of the Spirearch's Guard rushed here and there, rescuing those who had been trapped in the rubble or tending to the injuries of the wounded. It was a dutiful reaction to the crisis, but not a well-ordered one. They moved in small groups of three or four, with no obvious coordination. No one was attempting to direct or calm the traffic on the atrium's streets, as far as Grimm could tell.

"Sir!" Creedy said, pointing.

Grimm swiveled his gaze to the far side of the habble—where flickers of brilliant white light played intermittently against the far wall, changing the buildings between into black outlines.

"Firefight," Grimm said. "Good eyes, XO. Shall we greet our guests?" Without waiting for an answer, he set out at a rather slow if steady lope. His arm hurt abominably, but there was nothing for it. Habble Morning occupied the entirety of the Spire, most of it beneath a vast atrium nearly two hundred feet high, and it was the next-best thing to two miles from one side of the great cylinder that was Spire Albion to the other. They had to hurry, but arrive with enough breath to aim steadily and ply their blades.

The run was like some kind of appalling dream. Most of the buildings seemed little damaged, but occasionally one would appear that had been crushed by falling masonry. The wounded lay on the spirestone floor or wandered dazed through the streets. Grimm ground his teeth against the need to stop and help a small child who had obviously

suffered a broken arm. The poor waif was in agony, but not in danger—
which might not be true if the invaders managed to set enough of Habble Morning on fire, or blow up vatteries or water gardens, or murder
the Spire Council—though Grimm had mixed feelings on the sort of
loss *that* might constitute—or any of a number of other acts of war that
could have been under way.

Perhaps a quarter of an hour passed while they ran—an eternity during
any battle. By the time they reached the spot Creedy had seen, Grimm
had assumed that it would most likely be over. He was mistaken. As they
approached, they could hear the howling discharges of gauntlet fire.

Grimm came to a panting halt just around the corner of a large
house, one of the original dwellings from the Building, made of spirestone seamlessly fixed to the habble's floor. The firing came from the
other side.

"Stern," he said, fighting to keep his voice steady and calm. "Get a
look; come back quick, no dawdling."

"Captain," said a slender, dark-haired man a good many years
younger than the average crew member of the *Predator*. Stern had been
a grubby midshipman in the deployment that had ended Grimm's career, and had (against Grimm's express instructions) followed him from
the Fleet onto *Predator*. He had remained small and thin as he grew
into an adult, and could move as quickly and quietly as any warriorborn
when he needed to do so.

Creedy was blowing hard after the run, his face red. "Captain," he
gasped. "Are we where I think we are?"

"Lancaster Vattery," Grimm said. "They've come for the crystals."

"God in Heaven. If the Aurorans destroy them . . ."

"Then Fleet will have to fight a war without replacement crystals or
additional vessels," Grimm said.

Which was, he reflected, saying something very nearly the same as
"losing a war."

Stern came hurrying back to the group. "The vattery is made of spirestone," he reported, "so there's no blasting a way in. Lancaster retainers are holding the door so far, but there aren't enough of them to keep it much longer."

"And the enemy?" Grimm asked.

"Captain," Stern said, his voice worried. "They're the Spirearch's Guards."

"Nonsense," Grimm said promptly. "Likely they're Aurorans wearing false uniforms. How many?"

"I made it two dozen—but they've taken up positions, sir. They're shooting from cover."

Creedy blinked. "What? If they want to destroy the vattery, they should be storming the door. Shouldn't they? Every minute they're here makes it more likely that they'll come under attack themselves. Why wait?"

"Mmmm," Grimm said, and narrowed his eyes, thinking. "Why wait?" Then he felt his lips bare his teeth in a smile. "Why indeed. Because they *are* waiting. Perhaps they're expecting reinforcements. Stern, where are they positioned?"

"There is a masonry wall around a little garden between the vattery and the house, Captain. It's been chewed up by gauntlet fire, but they're using it for cover."

Grimm nodded once. "Creedy, take two squads and flank them from the far-side rear, if you please. I'll take the rest and make sure that the enemy is too busy looking at the near-side front to notice you. Don't dawdle now."

The XO nodded, pointed to two other officers, and beckoned. He started away at a run, and the others followed.

Grimm turned to the rest of the crew and said, "These boys are better at this kind of fighting than us, but there are a hell of a lot more of us than there are of them. So we treat this exactly like a boarding action.

Aggression, aggression, aggression, and stay together. God in Heaven be with you."

He led his crew to circle the house and enter the field opposite from where Creedy's team would appear. When Creedy got there, he and his men would be behind the Aurorans' cover, blasting away at invaders trapped against a stone wall. They would wreak havoc on the foe.

Of course, it also meant that the Aurorans would have a very strong defensive position against Grimm and his men, but there was no helping that. The howl of gauntlet fire filled the air, the light flashing swift and bright in a thick, deadly curtain of energy.

Grimm drew his sword, lifted it, and cried, "Albion!"

The crew's weapons leapt into their hands, and they roared, "Albion!" in furious unison.

Grimm rounded the last corner, followed by seventy howling aeronauts, and sprinted toward the Auroran position.

Chapter 15

Spire Albion, Habble Morning,
Lancaster Vattery

Two seconds.

Grimm and his crew had two whole seconds of surprise and confusion in which to advance on the enemy. Two seconds was a great deal of time when measured in units of life and death. They had covered perhaps half of the open ground before the Aurorans managed to gather their wits and an officer began barking orders, redirecting their aim.

The glow of a couple of dozen weapon crystals lit the dimness, shining like spotlights, and they began to pour fire into Grimm's crew—mostly from gauntlets, but also from several long guns. Grimm's men returned fire as they ran—wildly inaccurate, for the most part, but anything that helped make the Aurorans flinch or seek cover was desirable. Then it was horrible sound and blinding light and the feel of spirestone beneath his boots as he ran, sword aloft.

Two seconds more.

By the end of it, twenty of his men were down, most of them screaming, some horribly still. Others had been hit in their ethersilk tunics, and though they staggered as they ran, they kept going.

Grimm saw the blast that hit him, slamming home into his ribs.

For an instant he faltered, looking down—but the suit the old etherealist had lent him was evidently lined with ethersilk of the highest quality. The blast had felt like little more than a stiff punch, unpleasant but hardly deadly, and though it had burnt and torn the outer layer of the suit's coat, the silk beneath was unmarred.

And then Grimm had reached the blast-pocked walled garden. The wall was more decorative than functional, being only about as high as his stomach, except where gauntlet blasts had lowered it in gaps to only a couple of feet high. Grimm stomped his boot down onto one such gap and leapt into the garden and past the rank of men defending the wall, making room for the men coming behind him.

He saw a pale face before him and whipped his sword in a quick strike, felt it hit. Then there was a flicker of steel, and he ducked beneath one of the inward-curving talonlike blades of the Auroran Marines, and parried a second blade of the same kind.

Then Kettle bounded through the gap in the wall, sweeping one large boot into the teeth of the man defending the opening as he did. The helmsman landed, his gauntlet hand stretched out behind him, and put a blast into the head of another defender.

And after that it was frantic motion, reflex, and terror. Steel flashed, gauntlets screamed, and his crew fought to press into the garden, to put enough men through the wall to make the weight of numbers decide the matter.

The Auroran Marines disagreed.

These were hard-bitten men, professionals who were trained to excel in the mayhem of battle. They recognized the danger of losing the wall, of being surrounded by a numerically superior force, and they fought savagely, viciously. Grimm found himself driven back, Kettle by his side, while the crew kept trying to follow the pair of them in—only to be cut down, mercilessly and precisely, by the Auroran long gunners or the blades of the enemy Marines.

Grimm felt the momentum shift, felt the gathering determination of the Aurorans as they realized that they outclassed their opposition. In a few seconds more, he judged, the attack would be repulsed—leaving himself and Mister Kettle subject to the attentions of enemy gauntlets.

And then Creedy's squad arrived.

They didn't shout. They ran in relative silence, their footsteps masked by gauntlet fire, by howls and screams, and took up position along the opposite wall of the garden. Creedy made it happen with excellent discipline. He made sure every man was at the wall, gauntlet lifted, arm braced, aimed and ready to fire before he gave the order.

The Aurorans, fully focused on repelling Grimm's assault, suspected nothing until the moment Creedy's first salvo felled nearly half of them. Grimm lunged forward, driving his sword into the breast of an officer whose silk had absorbed the blast that struck him. Kettle, at his side, intercepted a wild swing from another foe with his own blade, bellowing, "Albion!"

As he did, his fellow aeronauts surged forward with a roar, copper-clad blades in hand, vaulting the low wall or leaping through the gaps, swamping the stunned invaders in their numbers.

The surviving Aurorans lasted rather less than two seconds.

"Creedy," Grimm said a few moments later. "Report."

"Eleven dead," Creedy said in a subdued, solemn voice. "Two more who won't last long. Seventeen incapacitated by their injuries and as many walking wounded, sir. I've sent those wounded who can move back to *Predator*, with word to send Doctor Bagen at once."

Grimm grunted. "The Aurorans?"

"Three live. They might not survive their injuries."

"Have Bagen see to them the moment he's finished with our own. I should think that the powers that be will want to speak to them, eh?"

"No doubt, sir," Creedy said. "I've put some of the older, calmer hands to guard them."

"Good man," Grimm said. "Send someone to the vattery and let them know that we're not trying to murder them."

"I thought there might be nervous men with gauntlets inside, so I went myself, sir," Creedy said.

Grimm felt his lips quirk. "I see that they didn't blast you," he noted.

"No, sir," Creedy said, his tone serious. "Armed retainers of Lancaster, sir, former Marines, very good discipline. They're staying at their post, and their commander has gone to secure the household."

From outside the garden, where the wounded had been laid out together, there was a low, groaning scream of pain. Grimm looked up wearily from where he sat on a bench in the garden itself. There was a small burbling brook and a pool there, along with several dwarf trees and abundant green ferns, quite beautiful but for all the blood and corpses. The dead men stank of offal and excrement, the way they always did. It seemed undignified for a man's last remnants to be so foul, but that was the way of it. Grimm tried to ignore the smell and the motionless forms alike.

There were always unpleasant consequences to a battle.

He rose wearily, straightened his back, cleared his throat, and looked into the middle distance. "That was work well-done, Mister Creedy. In the battle and after. I've known men who didn't have half as much composure or sense in their first close-quarters action."

Creedy hesitated awkwardly before replying. Captains did not say such things to their junior officers in Fleet. Creedy frowned at nothing in particular, which also happened to be in the middle distance. "Sir," he said.

"Yes, I don't like it either," Grimm replied. "But as I cannot put you in for a combat ribbon or a commendation for unusual competence under fire, we must make do."

"I . . . Yes, sir."

Grimm nodded. "When time serves, I shall buy you a drink and we'll not speak of it again."

"I . . ." Creedy nodded. "I should think that perfectly acceptable, Captain Grimm."

"Good," Grimm said. "That's done. As soon as Bagen gets here, gather the men and get ready to move. There are a great many more Aurorans out there somewhere, and we'll need to be ready to respond."

"We captured four of their long guns intact, sir. Shall I issue them to the men?"

Grimm nodded once. "Excellent notion. Give one to Mister Stern. He's a fine shot. Have him pick a squad to use the rest."

"Aye, sir," Creedy said, and left to see to it.

"Captain," Kettle said from where he'd been standing, silent and discreet, a long step away. His tone was a warning.

Grimm turned to find a tall man approaching in a black suit tailored almost exactly to the lines of a Marine's uniform. He wore a blade and a gauntlet, and his short brush cut of hair was grizzled. Even before Grimm saw his eyes, he'd pegged the man as warriorborn from his lean build and grace.

"Captain Grimm, I presume," the man said.

"Aye," Grimm replied. "You've the advantage of me, sir."

The tall man offered his hand and Grimm shook it. "Esterbrook," he said. "First armsman of House Lancaster. I'm glad for your intervention, Captain. Four to one are stiff odds."

"The Aurorans seemed to think so," Grimm replied. "Six of you held off two full squads of professional Marines. Impressive."

"Brief," Esterbrook said. "Otherwise you'd need to use words like 'tragic' or maybe 'noble sacrifice.' Thank you."

Grimm found himself smiling up at the man. "What can I do for you, sir?"

"Lord and Lady Lancaster were in the residence and saw much of what just happened. They wish me to convey their thanks and their condolences for your losses, and to inform you that they have already sent for their personal physicians and that they're preparing space in the house for your wounded. You needn't fear that your men will lack the best care available."

Grimm felt something ease in his gut that he hadn't known had been paining him. "I . . . Please, sir, convey my heartfelt thanks to the Lancasters."

Esterbrook nodded. "Will." He looked around and then at Grimm again. "You're Francis Madison Grimm? Captain of the *Perilous*?"

Grimm felt his shoulders tighten. "Former acting captain, sir. I am he."

"I heard the Admiralty broke your sword. For cowardice."

Kettle made a growling sound.

Esterbrook glanced up, arching an eyebrow at Kettle. But then he turned back to Grimm, clearly waiting for an answer.

"They did, sir," Grimm said.

Esterbrook showed his teeth. "But you'll charge a dug-in position of Marines. With one arm in a sling."

"It was necessary to do it," Grimm said. "We all serve, sir. Some with more glory than others."

Esterbrook seemed to consider the multiple meanings in Grimm's answer and said, "Right. The Admiralty has its head up its nethers again."

Grimm arched an eyebrow and said nothing. Behind him Creedy shouted out an order, and the remaining aeronauts began to gather together. Bagen had arrived, as had two other men with the distinct confidence and focus of physicians in a crisis. His men were being cared for. He felt his chest ease as if it had been suddenly cut free from tight leather bonds.

Esterbrook looked at the gathering men and said, "You're moving out?"

"I can't imagine that the crystal vattery was the enemy's only target," Grimm replied. "And I do not think the men we took down were operating alone. They seemed to be waiting for some other support to arrive."

Esterbrook nodded. "What I thought, too. I'd offer to send a few men with you, but . . ."

"Others may yet attack the vattery, and your duty is to the Lancasters," Grimm said. "Albion must not lose the vattery. I'll leave a squad with you to help secure it until the Marines or the true Guard arrives."

Esterbrook ducked his head once. "I'm grateful to you, Captain. I have wounded of my own. Where are you headed next?"

"I intend to patrol the perimeter of the atrium and—"

With no warning whatsoever, a ginger tomcat sailed over the garden wall and sprinted toward them. Kettle let out a brief sound of surprise, his hand darting toward his sword on reflex. The cat hurtled up to Esterbrook and slid to a halt with a long, chewy-sounding burble of throaty sound.

Esterbrook blinked down at the cat and held up a hand. "Wait, wait, slow down."

The cat seemed to bound back and forth in place, stiff legged, as if he could barely keep himself from breaking into another sprint. The stream of agitated feline sound continued.

"The beastie's gone mad, sir?" Kettle asked.

"Not mad, I think," Grimm said. "Mister Esterbrook, can you understand him?"

"I only speak a bit," Esterbrook said. "'He's . . . there,' 'danger.' 'Help.' Those I understood." He shook his head. "What danger? Who needs help?"

"Wait," Kettle said. "I know they're clever beasts, but . . . you mean the things actually *talk*?"

The cat turned two frantic circles and then darted over to the corpse of a fallen Auroran Marine in his stolen uniform. He stopped to make sure they were all looking at it and then deliberately swiped at the dead man's chest, hissing.

"More of them?" Esterbrook asked. "Like that one?"

The cat made another sound that Grimm could have sworn was an exasperated affirmative.

"Merciful Builders," Kettle breathed. "Is the man serious?"

"My bosun on *Perilous* kept a cat aboard," Grimm said. "The little monster was not to be underestimated." He looked up at Esterbrook. "Is this creature known to you?"

"Yes," Esterbrook said at once. "He is. His name is Rowl."

"Then it would appear I know where I'm going next," Grimm said calmly.

Rowl whirled to look directly at Grimm, wide eyes intense. Then he let out another mrowling sound and darted back toward the wall of the garden. He leapt to the top and paused to look back over his shoulder.

"Mister Creedy!" Grimm called. "We're moving out!"

"Aye, sir!" Creedy said. "Where are we headed, Captain?"

Rowl leapt down and darted into the dimness, pausing thirty yards later to look back.

Grimm started moving, Kettle at his side. "At the quick march, Mister Creedy. Follow that cat."

■ ■ ■ Chapter 16 ■ ■ ■

Spire Albion, Habble Morning,
Ventilation Tunnels

Bridget had never really given much thought to what it might be like to be held prisoner with her captor's hand quite literally threatening to choke the life out of her, but she felt quite sure that she would never have imagined that the experience would primarily be tedious.

At first she had been racked with confusion and fear, but in the standoff that came after she had been taken, she felt increasingly humiliated, insulted. What kind of fool was she to let herself be taken prisoner and used against her own Spire by its enemies? And right in front of Benedict?

The Auroran warriorborn Marine Ciriaco held her back firmly against his chest, with one arm wrapped around her stomach and the other hand lightly holding her throat. Initially she had thought that she might be able to take him off guard and throw him, but at the slightest shift in her weight, Ciriaco's hand would close and shut off her air entirely.

After several minutes of tense silence, Bridget turned her head enough to see part of Ciriaco's face. "Just so you know," she said, "you're holding me uncomfortably. My back is going to start cramping. When it does, I'm not going to be able to hold still."

"I'm sure you'll be missed," the Auroran replied calmly, giving a little twitch of the fingers around her throat by way of demonstration.

Benedict, his eyes locked on the Auroran, let out a low and utterly inhuman-sounding growl.

"Careful, boy," Ciriaco drawled. "If you let it out right now, it's not going to end well for any of us."

"I'm quite serious," Bridget said. "Sir, if my back starts to cramp and I begin to spasm and you kill me for it, my friend will most certainly come for you and matters will devolve."

From where she still lay on the floor, aiming her gauntlet at the explosives, Gwen said, "One might even say 'explosively devolve.'"

The Auroran grinned at that. "Damnation, but I admire women with spirit. But it's been my experience that prisoners who do anything at all are prisoners who are trying either to escape or to kill me. So you don't get an inch."

"There's another option you haven't considered," Bridget said.

"And what is that?"

"Take me. Leave your explosives here and depart."

"Nonsense," Gwen said.

"Miss Lancaster," Bridget said in a very cross and rather loud tone, "would you *please* stop helping me. Your only solution necessitates, as its linchpin, the deaths of everyone standing in this tunnel. Why not let me take a pass at finding something a bit less sweeping?"

Ciriaco let out an almost musical chuckle Bridget could feel along her spine. "I'm listening. Why would I do such a thing?"

"Because it salvages as much as possible from the situation," Bridget said.

"I need those explosives."

"You don't get them," Bridget said in a frank tone. "In very nearly every scenario that might play out here, you do not retain the explosives. If our reinforcements arrive, you do not get them. If your people arrive and someone doesn't make a perfect shot before my associate knows it is happening, you do not get them. If no one shows up, you do not get them. If my back cramps up and the chain of events progresses as we expect, you do not get them."

The Auroran made a rumbling sound.

"But consider: If you retreat and take me with you, you have the means to prevent my friends from opening fire—the threat to my life. Nor will you be pursued—if you leave the explosives, they will have little choice but to remain with them to prevent you from using them for their intended purpose."

"If not the explosives, then what profit do I have from this proposal?"

"You get to survive the hour," Bridget said. "Your men survive. You get to escape into the tunnels and fight another day."

Ciriaco grunted his acceptance of the statement. "And what do you get?"

"You don't get to blow up whatever you'd planned to blow up," she replied. "And both of my friends survive the hour."

He growled. "And what do *you* get, miss?"

"Raped and murdered, likely," she said. "But as that decision will hardly be up to me, there seems no point in dwelling on it. I'm a bit new to this sort of thing, Sergeant, but it seems to me that standing around hoping for some soldier who might or might not come along to be perfectly stealthy and to make a perfect shot at the correct target on his first attempt seems to be a course of action with a very low probability of success—especially when any failure or incorrect decision on his part means that everyone dies in an explosion. By contrast, my proposal guarantees your immediate survival and gives you hope to survive the future, to possibly negotiate better terms for a surrender, or even to escape Albion altogether."

One of the other soldiers evidently spoke Albion, because he looked from Bridget to Ciriaco and said something in a tense voice. The warriorborn Marine snapped out a brief, savage-sounding answer.

"By all means, discuss it," Bridget said. "The more we talk, the more likely we'll find some sane way to end this." And, Bridget thought, it would give Rowl more time to find another solution. She only hoped he had better sense than to stage some sort of one-cat surprise assault. "Sergeant, surely you must see that—"

Ciriaco's fingers tightened again, shutting off her air, and he said in a mildly irritated voice, "You people can't get enough of the sound of your own voices, can you? I'm thinking."

"She doesn't say it well," Benedict said in a low, hard voice. "But she's right. Whatever your mission was, you've little chance of accomplishing it as planned now. And the longer you stay here, the more likely it is that something bad happens to all of us."

"Something tells me," the Auroran said, "that you aren't going to just stand there while I walk away with the girl."

"That will depend," Benedict said.

"On what?"

"What happens to her," he said. "Treat her with respect and release her unharmed, and we're all just soldiers."

"And if I don't?"

Benedict was quiet for a moment before he said, "It's personal."

Bridget, who had not been able to breathe during this exchange, slapped the fingers of one arm against Ciriaco's steely forearms, as if tapping out of one of Benedict's holds in training.

"Hmm?" Ciriaco said. Then, "Ah, yes." His fingers loosened, and Bridget sucked in a lungful of air. The motion shifted her weight by some minuscule degree.

And, so quietly that she almost thought she'd imagined it for a moment, Ciriaco made a sound of pain.

Bridget froze, considering that. That was right; the Auroran had taken a gauntlet blast to the shoulder. She could still smell the stench of charred cloth and what might have been burnt flesh. The wound had been significant enough that he had feared to challenge Benedict to battle. In fact, now that she considered it, the hold Ciriaco had on her was hardly an efficient one. A few weeks of training did not make her an expert, but she knew that he could have been holding her locked quite easily with his right arm, freeing his gauntlet hand. Instead, his left arm was wrapped around her midsection—and not particularly tightly.

Why not? Obviously because he *could* not. He might not be able to lift his arm at all. That would explain why he wouldn't allow her to shift her position. His left arm might be a good deal less strong than he would like her to believe—and she was tall enough that if she altered her posture, the fingers on her throat would not have as sure a grip. Granted, the fingers of his right hand held her windpipe like a vise, and were perfectly sufficient to the task of killing her—or to dissuade her from testing the strength of his left arm.

There might be a way for her to escape, she realized. But it all depended upon the Auroran's resolve. How willing was he to kill her?

"Albion," Ciriaco said. "Do not for one second think that I'm afraid of your taking things personally."

"If you're not afraid, let go of the girl," Benedict said.

"I'm fearless," Ciriaco replied in a dry tone, "not stupid. And as smart as it would be to accept her offer, it isn't going to happen."

Bridget turned her head toward him again. "Why ever not?"

"Because I am a loyal son of Aurora," Ciriaco said. "And I have a duty. I'll fulfill it or die trying." After a moment he said in a softer tone, "And, miss, however this turns out—if we'd taken you, I'd have gutted any man who tried to lay a hand on you. If it had to be death, I'd have given it to you clean and quick."

"To be clear, you are not a rapist," Bridget said, "but you are a murderer."

"You seem to have it surrounded, miss," he said.

He sounded entirely sincere—which made any attempt to exploit his weakened arm something best left to a moment of desperation.

Though her back began to twinge again, and she feared that moment was rapidly drawing nigh.

The two groups fell into a tight, withering silence for a moment more. And then the rather eerie voice of a cat echoed through the dim hallway.

"Littlemouse," Rowl said. "Help comes."

Ciriaco tensed at once at the sound, looking up and down the hallway as though seeking its source, but even the remarkable eyes of the warriorborn were not able to see into blackness from a small and relatively well-lit area.

"This may be your last opportunity, Sergeant," Bridget said. "Walk away."

Ciriaco made a growling sound in his chest. "Cats are a vicious little plague, but they don't frighten me either, miss."

Several of the other Aurorans spoke in their home Spire's tongue, a quick, terse exchange, which was ended when Ciriaco growled the same phrase he'd used a moment before. Then his eyes widened and he snapped out another order. The Aurorans looked at one another, but lowered their gauntlets and started backing out the way they'd come.

"Stay with me, miss," Ciriaco said in a low tone. "Albion—you, step over by your little friend on the ground. We're going."

Benedict narrowed his eyes, but then his nostrils flared, and he nodded as if in understanding. He took several steps until he stood over Gwen.

"Remember," he said to Bridget, "our first lesson."

Bridget blinked at him.

The first thing to learn, as he had often repeated while instructing her, was how to fall.

Of course . . . that hadn't been the first *lesson*, had it?

It seemed rather suicidal, but . . . perhaps Benedict's judgment in these matters was better than her own. So though it made her heart race with sudden, quivering terror, Bridget moved. She braced her feet and clamped her hands down onto Ciriaco's right forearm, bending forward with all of her strength, much as she would when tossing a side of beef forward and over her shoulder.

And several things happened very quickly.

First, something like a collar of fire closed around her neck. Ciriaco was no novice of battle—instead of being thrown over her shoulder, he took a smooth pair of steps, circling around her, and as a result he was only lifted a few inches clear of the floor.

As soon as she felt his weight pivoting away from him and onto her own legs, Bridget pushed her body back as hard as she could—and slammed his wounded shoulder between her body and the spirestone wall. He let out a startled snarl of pain, and the deathly grip on her throat loosened.

A crackling lance of etheric energy burned across Bridget's field of vision and struck one of the Auroran Marines square in the head. He went down in a heap of motionless limbs. The first bolt was followed by three more half a heartbeat later, and though two failed to score, the other struck an Auroran in the thigh, sweeping his leg from beneath him and slamming him to the floor.

Bridget had no chance at all in pitting her muscles against the warriorborn's stony strength. Both of her arms did not serve to overpower his single limb.

So she kept slamming her body against his wounded shoulder, seized upon a single one of his fingers with both of her capable hands, and bent it back savagely.

Ciriaco screamed a furious word, and then Bridget found herself flying forward though the air, until she struck the far wall of the tunnel. It was a rather startling experience, particularly the sudden stop. Her arms and legs stopped working properly, and as she bounced off the wall she felt herself falling, and she couldn't breathe.

She wound up on the floor, and then the two crystals the Aurorans had been using for light winked out, leaving nothing but blackness broken only by dazzling flashes of etheric light.

The floor seemed quite cool and comfortable for some reason, and she was content to remain there. The flashes of light ceased their bickering, and a moment later she felt Rowl's nose gently nuzzling her cheek. She made the effort to move her hand and assure him that she was all right.

Then she heard voices and light sprang up in the tunnel. A great many men with weatherworn clothing, weatherworn faces, and odd, heavy-looking tunics had appeared. They were all armed with gauntlet and blade but for four who carried long guns, their copper coils gleaming, their overheated barrels giving off trickles of steam as they boiled away the water from their little storage tanks.

One man appeared from their midst, and Bridget picked him out immediately as their leader. He was of only average height, his suit was rather mismatched and patchy, and one of his arms was held in a sling, but there were the marks of gauntlet fire on the suit, and he was sprinkled with blood that did not appear to be his own. The man moved with an absolute surety of purpose, with unbroken focus, and the men around him deferred to him with an obvious, silent respect that could not have been expressed in words. He took a quick look around and said, "Excellent shot, Mister Stern."

A slender little man holding a long gun touched a finger to an imaginary cap. "Baker made the good shot, sir. Legged him. We've got a prisoner to talk to."

"Good work. See to him."

"Aye, Captain."

The man turned and approached Bridget.

Rowl immediately stepped up onto Bridget's chest, sat, and regarded the man with narrow eyes and a low growl.

"Excuse me," he said to the cat. "But you did wish me to help her, did you not?"

The cat's eyes narrowed further.

The man extended his hand to Bridget and asked, "Can you rise, miss?"

Bridget made a hushing sound of reassurance to Rowl, took the man's hand, and slowly rose, gathering Rowl into her other arm as she did. "Yes. Thank you, sir." It hurt to speak.

The man inclined his head politely. "My name is Grimm." He looked over to where a tall and very handsome younger man was helping Gwen to her feet. "Mister Creedy, detail a squad to secure those explosives, if you please."

"Aye, Captain," said the tall young man.

Bridget suddenly felt a bit dizzy, and then Benedict was at her side, one of his hands beneath her elbow, offering her gentle support.

"The Aurorans," she asked him. "What happened?"

"They took your advice—minus the part where they abducted you, for which I cannot help but feel grateful," Benedict replied.

"I was going to lift him and throw him like you told me," Bridget said, "but it didn't work. I'm sorry."

Benedict blinked. "Is *that* what you thought . . . No, no. I caught the scent of Captain Grimm and his men coming once Rowl returned, and thought a cross fire was imminent. I meant for you to *fall*."

Bridget blinked. "Oh. It's . . . In retrospect, it's rather obvious when you phrase it in that manner."

Benedict lifted her chin gently with a couple of fingers and peered at her neck. "I must admit, though—he certainly didn't see it coming." He poked at her throat gently with his fingertips.

"Ow," Bridget said calmly.

"A physician should look at this," Benedict said, his voice worried.

Gwen had gone to Barnabus's side and looked up from the wounded man. "Him, too. He seems to be unconscious." She rose and went to Grimm. "Captain, can you spare any men to help us with our wounded?"

"Of course, miss," Grimm said, inclining his head in a little bow. "I'll have them taken to where my own men are being treated at House Lancaster, if that suits you."

Gwen arched her eyebrows rather sharply and said, "I suppose that will do."

"Mister Creedy," Grimm said. "You will take a squad to get the civilians to safety and the prisoner and confiscated material to a secure location. I will continue the sweep and meet with you back at House Lancaster. Mister Stern, take point again, if you please. . . ."

And as quickly as they had come, most of the aeronauts and their captain departed.

The tall young man saw to the loading of the explosives back onto their stretcher, and men to carry them, and made sure the captured Auroran wasn't going to bleed to death or bolt. Then he turned to them and said, "Ladies, sir, if you could come with me, please. We shouldn't linger here until we're sure it's clear of more of the enemy."

Bridget still felt somewhat confused. "Benedict," she said, "I'm sorry but . . . I don't understand. Is the fighting over?"

His expression darkened. "No," he said quietly. "I think it's just getting started."

▪ ▪ ▪ Chapter 17 ▪ ▪ ▪

Spire Albion, Habble Morning,
House of Master Ferus

Folly sat up in her bed in the little loft over the master etherealist's library, covered in a cold sweat, her heart racing, her breath heavy. She sat there dully for a mute moment. Terror left a sour miasma in the air around a person—not something one could smell, even if she had the sharpest of noses, but she always felt that she could detect its stench, for some reason.

"Teacher," Folly called. "It would seem I've had the dream again."

"Did you catch it?" the master called back. "If you didn't, I should say that the dream has had you."

Folly sat up and looked around her little loft. Her stacks and stacks of jars full of little-used illumination crystals—she would never understand the phrase "burnt out" in reference to the crystals that no longer responded to an average human will—gave the entire place a soft aqua glow. She turned to check her dream catcher.

Between two stacks of glass jars was a funnel web woven of individual strands of ethersilk. Folly checked the web and the small etheric cage at the narrow end of the funnel, built of a neutral crystal in a frame of copper wire.

Really, Folly thought, it was quite a good thing that she was an etherealist's apprentice, because she would have made a remedial spider. The funnel web had dozens of sagging strands, and several of them had even parted completely, their loose ends floating away from her fingers as she brushed them near. It was lopsided, the curl of the spiral didn't close in a steady curve, and there were several obvious lumps in the design, where her knots and glue-work had been clumsy.

But, she thought, that didn't mean that it was necessarily a *bad* web, especially for someone who had never had the same opportunity to learn afforded every spider.

And the little crystal in the etheric cage was glowing with sullen, flame-colored light.

"I am a successful self-taught spider, I think," she called down to Ferus.

"I always hoped you would grow into one," Ferus said. His chair scraped on the floor, and footsteps approached the ladder to the loft. The ladder groaned as he came up it and eyed the trap. "By the Builders, Folly. What a marvelous little gnatcatcher you are!"

Folly smiled and bounced a little as he spoke, reaching for the cage.

The small assembly promptly retreated from her outreached hand, and the crystal seemed to strain against its copper cage, buzzing and vibrating against the metal like an angry wasp. She blinked several times and took her fingers away from it, reminded of the unpleasant relationships enjoyed between some spiders and some wasps.

"Ah!" Ferus cackled. "Ah, you *did* it. I thought as much!"

"I just told you that I did it, teacher," Folly pointed out.

"Not you," Ferus said in a testy voice. "I was speaking of the Enemy."

Folly tilted her head and regarded the little copper framework. "There's an Enemy?"

"God in Heaven, yes," Ferus said. "I'm sure I told you. I distinctly remember doing so."

"Perhaps that was tomorrow, teacher."

"It may be," Ferus said. "But yes, quite. Enemy, capital E."

"If one is to have an Enemy, one might as well have a respectable one. And this dream? It is an Enemy sending?"

"I rather suspect it was more of a Folly *taking*," Ferus replied. "Give it to us; let's have a look."

Folly considered the problem for a moment, then carefully reached her hand down on the far side of the copper cage. She moved her hand toward it, and it began to buzz again, moving away. She herded it over to the edge of the loft, and Ferus caught it handily as it leapt away from her.

"Excellent," he said, his tone pleased. The old etherealist leaned down to peer at the crystal. "Let's see what's been on your mind, eh?"

His eyes glittered brightly and then the old man fell silent, staring.

Folly rose from her bed, took off her nightclothes, and put on clothes that felt right for today: a red stocking, a grey stocking with blue speckles, a plain dress of yellow cotton, and a dozen brightly colored scarves that she tied in a row down each arm, using her teeth to finish the knots. Then she strapped on a pistoleer's gun belt, minus the unreliable weaponry, and filled the holsters with small mesh sacks of dim little etheric crystals instead. They were not used to being carried that way, but it would be a good learning experience for them, she thought. She completed the outfit with several more scarves that went around her neck and wound a long knitted scarf about her head. It was hot, but she thought it suited today, and she felt ever so much better once she had finished dressing.

She had time to dress and to sit down and begin telling all of her little crystals good morning when the master let out a long, slow breath and lowered the etheric cage with its sullen crystal heart. He looked awful. His face was grey, his eyes sunken.

"Teacher?" Folly said. She moved to the edge of the loft and crouched beside him, reaching out to touch his head, which was fever-hot. "What did you see?"

"A sending indeed," he said. "This was no dream, no etheric echo, my girl. I believe it was a message."

Folly blinked. "A message? Sent by ether? Is such a thing possible?"

"A moment ago I would have said that it was not," he replied, his eyes still far away. "But it would seem that someone has worked out how it might be done—though just as clearly they had no idea that they might be overheard."

"You think I've been eavesdropping in my dreams? I trust that is not an assessment of my character, teacher."

"No," he said slowly. He often spoke so when his mind was fully focused on some task. "No, child. Your nightmares of late—you've been hearing their whispers for what? Two weeks now?"

"About that, yes," Folly said. "But, teacher—how is it that I heard them and you did not?"

"That is an excellent question. I will give it consideration." He took a slow breath and then said, "By the way, we're at war as of an hour ago. I didn't think it was worth waking you for."

"I may have missed this . . . dream message, otherwise," Folly said seriously. "I suppose it would be disorienting to have an Enemy but no war."

"Let us not make assumptions," the master said.

"Then I will make a question or two, if you do not mind."

"Rarely."

"You say this was a message. To whom was it sent?"

"Points for grammar, Folly. Mmmmm." Ferus rubbed at his chin. "Another etherealist, almost certainly."

"Are there any others in Habble Morning?"

Ferus shook his head. "Not for . . . a great many years now. The nearest is Bernard Fezzig down in Habble Solace, I think. But he's utterly mad, you know."

Folly carefully straightened one of the hundreds of jars of exhausted crystals that had inexplicably become slightly misaligned. "The poor man."

"It happens to the best of us," Ferus said, and slid back down the ladder, bouncing the trapped etheric message in one palm. He had,

Folly noted, forgotten to put on his clothing that morning, except for a pair of thick black socks and his sleeping cap. "I have an intuition."

"Is it a fine one?"

"I think we shall need that grim captain."

"Captain Grimm?"

"Don't correct my grammar; it's an aesthetic choice of word order. But yes, that fellow whose arm had been infected."

"What shall we need him for?"

"He seemed capable. And polite. And it's so rare to meet someone who is actually polite for the proper reasons." He paused. "Is it cold in here?"

"You need to put on your warm robe, teacher," Folly suggested diffidently.

"Ah, yes, I knew I'd forgotten something, child. Thank you." The master picked up a robe—there were several he'd absently discarded over the past few weeks strewn about the library floor—and put it on inside out. But he was very busy thinking; Folly could tell from the set of his jaw. He was doing very well just to get his arms into the proper holes when he was in that state of mind.

Folly finished touching each jar of little crystals and then carefully climbed down the ladder. It wasn't until she was halfway across the room that she heard a sharp, heavy crashing sound from the front hall.

Ferus's head whipped around toward the sound, his eyes glittering fever-bright, flicking left and right at random distances. He lifted one hand to point, and his voice was a silken snarl. "Folly, by that wall, down low."

Folly hurried to obey. When the master scanned that many futures that rapidly, and spoke in that voice, one really had to be quite stupid to do otherwise. She dropped into a low crouch, kept her feet beneath her in case she needed to run, and reached into her holsters to give her little crystals reassuring pats, in case they had become frightened.

Ferus nodded and absently held out his right arm. The crystal on the head of his cane let out a soft chime as he sent out a current of etheric energy from his fingertips, and then the implement sailed gracefully across the room and into his hand.

Just as it did, the doors to the library crashed open, and three men wearing uniforms that closely approximated those of the Spirearch's Guard entered the room. They carried all manner of soldierly equipment, including gauntlets and blades. One held an ax that he had just used on Ferus's fine wooden door, and his companions both advanced with their gauntlets raised and glowing. They discharged the gauntlets within a second of one another, and brilliant energy flooded the room, a torrent of destruction meant to rip the old man facing them to shreds.

Folly winced, and experienced something she felt quite sure was pity for the poor fools.

Ferus simply lifted his cane, and the crystal at its tip drew in the deadly bursts of etheric energy as a sponge soaked up water. He held the cane forth, and the crystal continued to drink down etheric force from the weapons crystals of the enemy gauntlets, yanking the power from them in one long, continuous burst.

Gauntlets were not designed for that kind of steady discharge of energy, and they began to shed heat almost instantly. The copper wires that served as a cage for the weapons crystal, encasing the user's forearm, smoldered, heated, and began to glow. The two men let out pitiable screams and fell, scrambling with leather straps and buckles that scored the fingertips of their right hands even as they tried to unfasten them.

The third man looked at the other two and showed a spark of intelligence. He stripped his gauntlet rapidly, dumping it on the floor. But then he ruined his brain's hard work by drawing his copper-clad sword and advancing on the master, holding his ax in one hand, the sword in the other.

Ferus gave his head an impatient shake, lifted his cane, and sent a

single, flickering dart of searing light across the room. It flew in a sinuous, erratic pattern, winding around a column and beneath a table and
slithering through several stacks of books before hammering into the
broad side of the ax's heavy, copper-covered steel head.

The bolt melted a hole three inches across through the steel, sending out an enormous burst of sparks and flares of flickering fire, and the
man yelped and dropped the weapon, turning to stare with wide eyes at
the master.

Ferus said calmly, "You are trespassing, sir. Begone. While you still
can."

With each word, a brilliant, tiny wisp of light like the first flickered
out of the crystal and began orbiting around the master's white-fringed
head in a beautiful, deadly crown of etheric fire.

The man licked his lips and then looked behind him. His wounded
companions had managed to rip the gauntlets from their arms, and had
drawn their short, straight swords. He turned back to the master and
bared his teeth.

"Don't," Ferus said, his voice softening. "Please don't. There's too
much pain on that path."

The two men on the floor gained their feet. The third man took a
deep breath.

"Folly," the master said. "Close your eyes."

Folly did, at once.

There was a guttural shout from the intruder. There was a volley of
hissing sounds and a chorus of shrieks.

Then screams.

And silence.

And the smell of burning meat.

Folly swallowed and rose slowly. She cracked open one eye, and
then the other. The master hadn't said she had to keep her eyes closed
indefinitely.

He was unharmed. He stood in the same spot, his head bowed, the crystal of his cane now dark again, resting against the floor as though the implement had grown too heavy for him to hold.

Folly did not look at what was left of the intruders in their disguises. It was disturbing, and she was at the limits of her skills as a spider already. She needed no further bad dreams. She carefully did not let herself cry, though she wanted to very much. It pained the master to see her cry, and she would rather be burned to death herself than to give him pain. He'd had so much of it already.

She reached his side and touched his arm gently. "Are you all right, teacher?"

She watched his hollow, weary eyes stare for long heartbeats at the scorched not-men who now littered their library floor before he answered. "What have we learned today, Folly?"

"That one ought not to use etheric weapons against an etherealist?"

"While what you say is very true, I was hoping for a different context."

"Ah," Folly said. She considered for a moment and said, "Someone sent these men here to kill you, specifically."

"Good. Continue."

"They had to know where you lived. Therefore someone who knows you, or knows of you, is responsible for them."

"Correct," the master said. He lowered his voice to a preoccupied mumble. "I confess, I did not catch the faintest glimpse of this future."

Folly frowned suddenly, wrinkling her nose. She knew she could not actually smell it, but her mind told her that she could feel the stench filling her nose.

Fear hovered around Efferus Effrenus Ferus, master etherealist.

"You know," Folly said. "You know who sent them."

"I think so."

"Who is it, teacher?"

"An old friend. A friend who has been dead for a decade."

Folly considered the words for a moment before saying carefully, "That does not seem probable."

"Oh, aye," the master said. "It's utterly mad. But there it is."

"Teacher, I don't understand."

"There's no rush," he said in a very soft voice. "You will soon enough."

Folly bowed her head a little. "Teacher?"

"Yes?"

"What shall we do now?"

"Fetch my dueling suit, if you would," he said. "Also three feathers and a tack hammer. Ready my collection. Oh, and pack a bag."

"A bag?"

"A bag. With . . . food, clothing, books, that sort of thing. We'll be leaving the habble."

Folly blinked several times. "What? We will? To go where?"

"First we'll go see the Spirearch and get him to give us the grim captain," he said.

"And then?"

Something dark and hard rose for a moment in the master's eyes, and the look made Folly shiver.

"And then," he said quietly, "we shall visit an old friend."

▪ ▪ ▪ Chapter 18 ▪ ▪ ▪

Spire Albion, Habble Morning,
Spirearch's Manor

Twelve hours after the fighting ended, Grimm wanted nothing so much as a bath and his bunk on *Predator*. He ached for them, in fact. When he was this weary, his sleep would be too deep to be disturbed by dreams of the men he had lost in the fighting. He could put off, for at least one night, being haunted by the faces and limbs that had been crushed, scorched, and mangled by the first battle of what could be a long and costly war.

Instead of resting, though, he and Creedy followed a slim, aging, gentlemanly sort of fellow named Vincent from the entry hall of the Spirearch's Manor down a hallway with polished wooden walls and floors, decorated with some of the finest art in Spire Albion. According to the engraved brass plaques beside each piece, there were paintings from the giddy days of the New Dawn, two centuries before, sculptures from the Olympian master McDagget, and other pieces, some of them attributed to relatively unknown artists currently working in Spire Albion. They were exquisite, Grimm thought. He approved of the taste of whoever had decorated the hall.

They were shown into what appeared to be a study, also furnished entirely in wood and lit with candles rather than lumin crystals. There was a large desk with five chairs set neatly in front of it.

Vincent nodded to the chairs and said, "If you will wait here, sirs, he will be with you shortly."

"Of course," Grimm said. He and Creedy sat while Vincent departed.

It was perhaps a matter of two or three minutes before a door in the rear wall of the study opened and the Spirearch came into the room. He was a man of no impressive height and what might charitably be called a scholarly build—but Lord Albion's eyes were sharp and hard, and he moved with a brisk, no-nonsense sort of energy as he approached them. Grimm and Creedy rose at once to meet him.

Albion came around the desk to offer his hand to Grimm. "Captain Grimm," he said. "I hear extraordinary things about your service to the Spire in the face of the surprise attack."

"Sire," Grimm said, bowing his head slightly. "This is my XO, Byron Creedy."

Creedy mumbled something Grimm couldn't understand, and shook the Spirearch's hand with a kind of numb shock on his features.

"Well," Albion said, "I know how tired you both must be, so sit, sit, and I'll be as succinct as possible." They sat, while Lord Albion rested a hip against the edge of his desk, looking down at them with calm assessment clear in his eyes. "I'm afraid you made a serious mistake today."

"Sire?" Grimm said.

"You proved yourself extraordinarily capable, Captain," Albion said. "I can hardly let something like that go unremarked."

"I don't understand, sir," Grimm said, frowning.

"Captain, your clarity of thought in the face of unexpected disaster is a rare quality. It's a poor reward for such heroism, but I'm afraid that I must insist upon continuing to use you for the good of my Spire."

Grimm was quiet for a moment. He wanted to sink into a tub of hot water and soak away the violence and fear of hours of skirmishes with Auroran Marines. He wanted to sleep. Hadn't his men given enough?

"Sire," he said in a measured, quiet voice. "I have already offered such skills as I have in the service of Albion. The Spire made it quite clear to me that I was not needed."

"The *Perilous* incident, yes," Albion said. "I'm familiar with what happened. Or perhaps I should say, I am familiar with both the history of what happened and with what actually transpired. You didn't have to accept your discharge quietly, Captain. But you did."

"It was what was best for the Fleet, sire," Grimm said.

"An arguable point, I think," Lord Albion said. "But your sacrifice was without doubt a good thing for the Fleet, if not for you personally."

"I didn't join Fleet to serve myself, sire," Grimm said.

"The best never do." Albion gave Grimm a faint smile. "But your previous difficulties are irrelevant, Captain. The Spire Council is, as we speak, voting to declare a state of war with Spire Aurora. The Spire needs every capable commander it can get."

"I hardly think the Fleet will welcome me back in any capacity, sire," Grimm said in a voice that came out diamond-hard, though he hadn't meant it to. "No one wants to work with a proven coward."

"I do," Albion said. "I'm not talking about returning you to the Fleet, Captain. I want you for myself."

Grimm blinked. "Sire . . . what I did today was what any competent, professional commander would have done in my place. It does not qualify me for a position in your personal service."

"Perhaps, Captain, judgments about what qualifies a given individual for the Spirearch's service might best be made by the Spirearch," Lord Albion suggested, his eyes sparkling with quiet humor.

Grimm shifted in his chair uncomfortably. "Sire . . . I'm no diplomat, so with your leave I'll just say it, and beg your pardon ahead of time if this comes out sounding unpleasant or disrespectful."

Creedy's eyes widened slightly, but he stayed as silent as a stone.

Albion arched a brow. "Oh, by all means, Captain, speak."

"I don't like it here. Spending more than a few weeks in this dreary old mausoleum makes me feel as if I can't breathe. I don't understand how any of you can stand it day in and day out. I'm an aeronaut, sire, living on a deck since I ever could remember. I belong in the sky. I belong on my ship. It's the only place that feels . . . right. Thank you for your offer, but I don't want another job."

"I understand," Lord Albion said. "But you proceed from a false assumption. I don't want your service as an adviser on my staff, Captain." He folded his arms and narrowed his eyes slightly. "I want an airship helmed by a captain I can trust."

Grimm and Creedy traded a surprised look. "Sire?"

"I have need of a ship to serve as transport and support for a mission for my Guard," Albion said. "I've decided that I want *Predator*, along with her captain and crew, to fill that position."

"What if they don't want to do it?" Grimm asked.

Creedy made a choking sound.

"I can be a very persuasive person," the Spirearch said.

"You have no legal authority to do that," Grimm said.

"You're right. But I mean to see it done all the same."

Perhaps it was the fatigue, but Grimm found himself growing genuinely angry. "Sire," he said stiffly, "*Predator* is not for sale. *I* am not for sale."

That brought a wolfish flash of a smile from Lord Albion. He pointed a forefinger at Grimm and leaned forward slightly. "*Exactly*, Captain. Exactly. You've served Albion as a privateer for eighteen months now. This would be no different."

"That's . . . very generous, sire," Grimm said cautiously. "Perhaps, though, you have not been made aware of *Predator*'s state of repair. She's in need of refitting. It may be some time before she's skyworthy." *Decades, perhaps*, Grimm thought. "She's running on nothing but her trim crystals."

"I'm not an aeronaut, Captain," the Spirearch said apologetically, "or an aeronautical engineer. What does that mean, precisely?"

"She can only go up and down," Creedy said in a helpful tone. "And she has to do it very slowly."

"Ah," Albion said, brightening. "As it happens, that is precisely what I need your ship to do."

Grimm narrowed his eyes. "Meaning what, exactly?"

"I'm sending a team to Landing," the Spirearch replied. "It needs to be done quickly—before dawn, if possible. I'm sure that your ship is adequate to—"

Grimm rose, his heart pounding harder and louder as his anger grew. "Sire," he all but snapped. "With all due respect, there is ample transport to Landing. Send them down in a barge or a windlass."

Lord Albion's head drew back slightly, his eyebrows lifted in surprise. "Captain, I am not sure why the idea upsets you so."

"My ship isn't a barge. And she's bloody well no windlass," Grimm snarled. "And while I'm alive she never will be. Not for the Fleet, not for the bloody Spire Council, and not for you, sire. Thank you for the offer, but I cannot help you. If you will excuse me, please. I must see to the needs of my wounded and dead. Creedy."

Grimm turned to leave and Creedy lurched up out of his chair to follow, his face pale.

Albion sighed audibly. Just as Grimm reached for the door, he said, "That's a shame, Captain. I wish we could have worked something out. Do you perhaps know someone in the market for new lift and trim crystals for a ship *Predator's* size? It seems I'll have some spares on my hands."

Grimm froze with his hand on the doorknob. He tilted his head and then turned slowly, inexorably back toward the Spirearch.

Albion gave him a feline smile. "Do this work for me, and you'll be making the trip down to Landing with top-of-the-line replacements from the Lancaster Vattery. I'm told your engineer can have them installed and calibrated within a week."

"You . . . would do that?" Grimm breathed. "In exchange for *what*?"

"This job," Albion said. "One job. Take my team to Landing. Provide whatever support you can for them while they are there. Bring them back here when they're done."

"One job," Grimm said.

"Frankly, Captain, my hope is that you will see the advantages of my offer and will be inclined to work with me on an ongoing basis. But if you want nothing to do with me after this, so be it. Keep the crystals and go your way."

"If I did, you'd be throwing away a fortune."

Lord Albion shrugged. "I prefer to think of it as an investment in the future, Captain Grimm. What say you?"

Grimm exhaled through his nose. The anger was still burning, but smoldering alongside it was . . .

Hope.

Unattainably valuable replacements for *Predator's* damaged crystals, waiting to be installed. His ship rising above the mists again, to sail in the blinding light of the sun. His crew's livelihood secured. And yet *Predator* would be bound to no one but her captain.

Freedom.

Grimm realized with a sudden shock of purely mental impact that nothing on earth could convince him to turn down such a deal.

"I say . . ." Grimm began, slowly. Then he sighed. "I say that you are a manipulative son of a bitch, sire."

"Each and every day of the week," Lord Albion replied, nodding. He met Grimm's eyes. "And I don't turn my back on *my* people, Captain."

He hadn't said, *The way that Fleet does*, but it hung unspoken in the silence after his words.

Albion lifted his hands, palms out, as if signaling the end of a bout, and regarded Grimm with a frank gaze. "It's as simple as this: I need you, Captain. The Spire needs you."

Grimm clenched his right hand into a fist for a moment, and then relaxed. "Mister Creedy."

"Captain?"

"Return to *Predator*. Inform Engineer Journeyman that he has work to do. Make ready to sail to Landing."

■ ■ ■ Chapter 19 ■ ■ ■

Spire Albion, Habble Landing

Major Renaldo Espira, Auroran Marine, walked calmly through the cramped, crowded streets of Habble Landing dressed in local clothing, carrying a crate marked with the logo of one of Landing's water farms. Though there was much excitement and the buzz of talk and rumor in the habble, evidently the authorities of Habble Landing had not yet realized the extent of his battalion's incursion into Spire Albion, and no checkpoints or patrols had yet been established. He could still move about in relative freedom.

The initial assault had come off with as much success as any combat mission could reasonably expect. He had yet to hear from the assault teams striking Habble Morning, but his Marines' months of training in the precision maneuver of parasails had paid off handsomely. Already better than four hundred of the five hundred men under his command had made contact and begun to concentrate, and there had been reports of fewer than twenty men who had failed to target one of the Spire's many ventilation ports properly.

It looked as though, barring bad luck, he would have more than enough men to attain his objectives, and if he was able to see the most daring raid in the history of any Spire to completion, his fortunes in Spire Aurora would be secured for life.

Espira wove his way through the hectic streets of Landing. Most habbles in every Spire had modified the original spaces as designed by the Builders, adding in fortifications, additional housing, more vatteries, whatever was needed—but the inhabitants of Landing had done so to an extent that was little better than madness. They had actually divided their habble's vertical space in half, in effect creating two duplicate levels of the same habble, one stacked atop the other. It meant that the normally spacious ceilings of a basic habble had been turned into close, looming things, and they made Espira feel as if the ceiling were slowly coming down on top of him.

If that madness was not enough, they had then filled both of those spaces to overflowing with more masonry and wooden construction than Espira had ever seen. The streets had turned from broad walkways into cramped, narrow affairs, where no more than three men could have walked beside one another. Houses and businesses were pressed together wall-to-wall, and the doorways were by necessity narrow ones. One literally could not walk twenty steps on the streets of Landing without brushing body-to-body with a fellow pedestrian.

This wasn't a habble. It was a warren for rats.

And yet . . . there were expensive wooden doors on nearly every home. In places, entire homes had been constructed of wood—and they did not look particularly lavish, either, being built with a sturdy, bland functionality that suggested the residences of craftsmen and tradesmen. Yet the amount of wood that went into building a single such residence would have sold for enough money to keep a man in food and drink for a lifetime.

Rats, indeed. Greedy, gnawing, thieving *rats*.

Let them flaunt their wealth. Things would change.

He stalked through the narrow streets and wound his way down an alley between two buildings to an old, rotting wooden door. He paused to knock at it, three measured strokes followed by two quick ones, and it opened at once.

Her batman, Sark, stood on the other side of it. The fellow reminded Espira of a hunting spider—he was warriorborn, tall, gaunt, with long, slender limbs and hands that seemed a little too large for the rest of him. His hair was black and short, and covered his face, head, neck, and what showed of his hands in a sparse, spidery fuzz. Sark had the feline eyes of his kind, one of them set at a slight angle to the other, so that Espira could never be sure precisely where the man was looking.

"What?" Sark asked. His tone suggested that he would rather have killed Espira than spoken to him.

Espira had not become the youngest major in the history of the Auroran Marine Corps by allowing himself to be intimidated by hard men. "Is she here?" Espira asked Sark.

"Why?"

"There's a problem."

Sark looked at, or slightly past, Espira and made a growling sound.

Espira lifted his chin and narrowed his eyes. "This is above your pay grade, Sark. Unless you'd prefer to explain to her why you turned away the man who came with a warning of a threat to her plan."

Sark didn't move for a moment, as still as any spider who senses that prey is coming near. Then he made a throaty sound and stepped back from the door, leaving it open.

Espira walked in boldly and pressed his crate of vegetables into Sark's hands as though the man were a common servant. Sark accepted the burden, but his crooked eyes narrowed. Espira could feel them crawling over his back as he walked past the batman and down the gloomy hallway to the copper-clad steel door to her chamber.

He knocked and waited rather than entering. He was bold, not suicidal.

After a moment, a woman's voice said, "Come in, Major."

Espira opened the door, which moved easily and soundlessly on its hinges, and entered the room beyond. It was a luxurious chamber, a sitting room by design. Lumin crystals glowed in wall sconces. A large sculpture of Spire Albion resided in one corner of the room, with walking space all around it. Opposite the Spire was the graceful shape of a large harp nearly five feet high. A trickling fountain that had been carved into one wall made quiet whispering sounds, and the water fell into a small pool filled with floating flowers and small, slithering forms that could only barely be glimpsed beneath its surface.

She sat in one of two chairs near the pool with a serving table placed between them. She was preparing two cups of tea, her motions calm and precise, somehow ritualistic. She wore a dark blue, conservative gown, well fitting, elegant, and expensive. She was neither young nor old, her lean, predatory features were intriguing, and something in the reserve of her movements whispered that a searing sensuality might lurk beneath her perfectly composed surface.

It was her eyes that made Espira uneasy. They were the cold, flat grey of the mists that covered the world, and she rarely blinked.

Espira made her a proper and polite bow. She remained still for a moment, and then nodded to the second chair. Espira approached and sat. "I pray you will forgive this intrusion, Madame Cavendish, but it was necessary to speak to you."

Instead of answering, she passed him a cup of tea on a fine ceramic saucer. He accepted it, of course, with a smile, and bowed his head in thanks.

Madame Sycorax Cavendish was a very proper woman. Anyone who behaved toward her in any other fashion, so far as Espira could tell, did not survive the experience. So he smiled, waited until she had taken up her own cup, and sipped tea together with her.

The tea, he noted, was his favorite—Olympian mint, and braced with the perfect amount of honey. Obviously his visit had not taken her by surprise. She'd had no way to know he was coming; yet, dammit, she'd known anyway.

Her flat eyes watched him steadily over the rim of her teacup.

He suppressed a shudder.

"Renaldo," she said. Her voice was extraordinary, mellow, warm, and soft, the kind of voice that could give rest to weary convalescents—or gently lure an aeronaut to his doom on the surface. "You know I enjoy your visits. Is there something I can do for you?"

She would not be pleased by his news, but there was no helping that. "Our command post has been discovered."

Her cold eyes narrowed ever so slightly. "Oh?"

"A verminocitor stumbled across it in the pursuit of his duties, I'm afraid," Espira said, keeping his tone neutral, simply reporting objective facts. "He was captured before he could escape and warn anyone of our presence."

Madame Cavendish arched an eyebrow. "Captured?"

Espira pressed his lips together for a second, then nodded. "The Verminocitors' Guild of Landing requires them to work in pairs. He claims that he was working alone, that he didn't want to split the contract with one of his fellows."

"And he volunteered this information?"

"His story didn't change, even after vigorous inquisition," Espira said. "But we are too close to our goals to allow some small mischance to undermine us now. We need to be sure."

"I see," she said. She took another small sip of tea, her expression thoughtful. "You would like me to determine his veracity."

"In essence," Espira said. "Better safe than sorry."

"One might say," she murmured, her voice silken, "that more foresight would have prevented this unfortunate event from coming to pass."

He'd seen men die just after the woman used that particular tone of voice. Espira took a moment to consider his reply carefully. "One might also say that the view behind us is always clearer than that before. There are always unforeseen problems. The most vital skill a commander can possess is to recognize them when they appear and adapt to overcome them."

Madame Cavendish tilted her head, as if considering that statement. "I suppose that is a practical mind-set, for a military man," she allowed. "Thus you have sought out the support of an ally to adapt to this adversity."

"Indeed, madame," he said. "You know how highly I regard your judgment and your skills."

The barest hint of a smile haunted one corner of her mouth. "Major. I know precisely what you think of me." She resettled her fingers on her teacup and nodded slightly. "Very well. I will assist you."

"You are most gracious, madame," Espira said, rising. "Time is of the essence, so—"

Madame Cavendish's voice came out in two pulses of dulcet music, and the lumin crystals in the walls flickered a sullen scarlet in time with them. "Sit. Down."

Espira's heart abruptly leapt into his throat, a thrill of something like distilled panic flashing through his belly. He arrested his momentum and clumsily—quickly—took his seat again.

Madame Cavendish's mouth widened into a smile, and she said, as if explaining to a child, "We're still having tea."

Espira's mouth felt very dry. "Of course, madame. I pray you, please excuse my . . . enthusiasm."

"I should think most successful soldiers bear the same burden," she replied, still smiling. They sipped together for a few more minutes, the silence deafening. Then Madame Cavendish put down her cup and saucer and said, "I trust you have arrangements in place to dispose of the remains, once I am finished."

"I do."

"Wonderful," she said. She picked up a matching serving plate artfully arranged with a number of foods appropriate to the setting and offered it to him with a smile. "Do have a scone, Major. I made them myself."

■ ■ ■ Chapter 20 ■ ■ ■

Spire Albion, Habble Morning,
Spirearch's Manor

Gwendolyn Lancaster took the lead as they followed the Spirearch's batman deeper into the manor. Barely half a day had passed since the Auroran attack, but a good many things had changed—not the least of which was that she and Bridget, along with the rest of the recruits, had exchanged their training uniforms for the functional livery of the Spirearch's Guard—a simple white shirt with dark blue trousers and jacket, the arms and legs seamed with gold piping.

"I cannot but think that this seems ill-advised," Bridget said from behind her. "A war has begun. Have we therefore somehow mystically acquired the knowledge we need to serve in the Guard?"

"I should say it is a practical act, Bridget," Gwen replied. "We have, after all, already faced the enemy and triumphed."

Bridget sounded doubtful. "'Triumph' seems . . . an awfully evocative word when compared to what actually happened."

"We met the enemy with deadly force, foiled their designs, and survived," Gwen said.

"And were *rescued* by those aeronauts."

"We were most certainly *not* rescued," Gwen said. "Not by aeronauts and most specifically not by a man who was cast out of the Fleet for cowardice."

"This should be interesting," Benedict said. "What did happen, then, dear coz?"

Gwen sniffed. "My plan embraced the necessity of cooperation to overcome greater numbers. We kept the enemy pinned in place until the proper amount of force could be brought to bear against them. We were the anvil to the hammer of our reinforcements."

"Is she serious?" Bridget asked Benedict.

"Sweet Gwen lives in a very special world," Benedict replied soberly, even kindly. "Apparently it looks only somewhat like the place in which we mere mortals reside."

Gwen turned and gave her cousin a narrow-eyed glare. "In function, which part of my description is inaccurate?"

At that, the tall young man frowned. After a moment he shrugged and said, "The part where you make it sound like that was your plan all along, instead of something you desperately improvised on the spur of the moment."

"Of course I improvised it on the spur of the moment," Gwen snapped. "They ambushed us."

"But . . ." Bridget said. "Gwen . . . the fight started when you discharged your gauntlet into that officer's face."

"It is hardly my fault if they did not ambush us more effectively than they did," Gwen replied. "And if they had, or if I had not done what I did, none of us would be here right now." She walked a few more steps before saying, "And in any case, we did keep our heads in the midst of a great panic, and we saved poor Barney's life. Which is what trained members of the Guard are supposed to do, I believe."

"That is certainly true," Benedict said with a note of approval in his voice. "I should say as well, coz, that I have never seen you flinch in the face of adversity, but one can never tell how a given person will react to real combat. You more than lived up to my expectations. Nerves of steel."

"Thank you, coz," Gwen said in a more subdued voice.

She didn't turn to look back again. The flash of her gauntlet's discharge kept playing back through her thoughts. The Auroran officer had been taken completely unaware by her sudden blast. There had been a slightly confused expression on his face, as if he hadn't quite heard the last phrase she'd said, and wished her to repeat it. She hadn't realized until much later how young the man had been. In the panic and concern for Barney, in the dust and the blood, she had seen a man in a uniform. But in her mind's eye, she had gradually discerned that he had been little older than she was, and certainly no older than Benedict.

A young officer, perhaps one of the elite new crop of the Auroran Marine Corps, chosen to lead a small team on a straightforward but important support mission, bringing explosives to an assault team at a critical target. In the eyes of the men who planned the attack, it must have seemed an ideal assignment for a bright young prospect—simple, unlikely to lead to direct combat, in which an officer with an agile mind would be far more valuable than one experienced in battle, especially if he had the watchful eye of an experienced noncommissioned officer like Ciriaco to guide him. Surely to some commander it seemed a fine mission to set a new rising star upon his ascendancy.

And Gwendolyn had wiped the life from him as swiftly and as surely as the darkness swallowed shooting stars in the night.

She wanted to feel remorse over it, to regret what she had done. It seemed to her that it was the sort of thing a decent person should feel. But when she sought for such emotions within herself, she mainly discovered a profound relief that she and her companions were still alive.

But she couldn't stop thinking about his face.

The blast had left a ruined mass where his face had been. She'd had to shoot him there, of course—there'd been no way of knowing whether he wore ethersilk beneath his false uniform. She kept seeing his face in that brief, fatal flash, kept putting words into his mouth that had matched his expression. *Beg pardon, miss? Could you repeat that, please? What on earth are you doing?*

Whatever would she have said in reply? *Why, making a corpse from someone's beloved child, sir.*

She hadn't eaten since.

Lord Albion's batman reached the end of the richly appointed hallway and knocked on the door. At a word from beyond the door, he opened it for Gwen and her friends and bowed slightly, waving them in.

Gwen swept into a room that was decorated and arranged like a small private study, but which was, in fact, something much more. Oh, certainly the desk and the lights, both lumin crystal and candles, were studious enough, as were the bookshelves, packed thick with many more volumes than they had been designed to hold. It was the subject matter of some of the titles that made it seem otherwise—the histories of Albion written by Dagget and Deen were common enough, but the set by Montclaire that had been outlawed two centuries before, due to the scandalous rumors they had spread about the first Spirearch of Albion, were another matter. One rather thick volume was titled *Means of Execution Through the Ages*, and was placed with an elegant balance of nonchalance and availability at the eye level of anyone entering the room. As threats went, it was nearly subliminal—and perhaps it was placed there for that very reason.

Behind the desk, in a case, were miniature replicas of each and every airship in the Aetherium Fleet of Albion, from the mighty battleship *Dreadnought*, the size of Rowl, down to the tiniest destroyer, *Energetic*, no larger than Gwen's smallest finger. There were several spaces in the case that had recently been emptied. Those spots showed a lack of fine dust where the bases of the models had rested. The ships destroyed in the Auroran attack, perhaps?

Opposite the replicas' case, behind the desk, was a large section of wall that had been papered with a variety of maps, from large-scale renderings of the known world down to ancient copies of the schematics of Spire Albion. Gwen had seen similar maps in her father's study. They were continuously updated, hyperaccurate charts of both geography and etheric currents, the ones used by the Fleet and kept in secret storage by ship captains, with orders to destroy them should the ship be in danger of being taken.

All in all, Gwen thought, for a monarch who had claimed to be rendered obsolete by the tides of history, Lord Albion seemed to be following the game rather closely.

This was no study.

In every way that mattered, it was a throne room.

Two men occupied the room. One of them was the Spirearch, obviously, seated behind his desk, looking as affable and unthreatening as he had the first time she'd met him. The other was the outcast officer, Captain Grimm. He stood in the corner nearest the miniatures with one arm in a sling and his back against the wall. He was dressed in the very clothing he'd worn when his men had come charging down the tunnel, though perhaps his coat was stained with even more blood.

Lord Albion rose, smiling, as they entered. "Ah, the heroes of the truly desperate hour. Had that group managed to carry their explosives to their companions, Albion might have suffered a crippling and permanent loss in the form of our largest crystal vattery. Please be seated."

Gwen and Bridget stepped into curtsies, which Bridget had not quite gotten the hang of. Benedict swept into a polished bow, and then each of them sat down in one of the five chairs in front of the Spirearch's desk, with Rowl settling on Bridget's lap.

"Sire," Benedict said. "How may your Guard serve you?"

"You could start by leaving out the honorifics," Albion replied. "At least while we're in here. I know I'm the Spirearch, and you obviously do as well. That seems to me sufficient, and it will save time."

Benedict said, "Ah." But he frowned as he settled back in his chair. "In that case, how may your Guard serve you?"

"By waiting a moment," Albion said. "I'm expecting two more."

Not half a minute later, the doorknob to the study rattled. It made a few fitful clicking sounds, and then a man's voice sighed audibly. "Blast and curse the confounded things. Folly?"

The door opened and a rather odd old man entered. He was dressed in a bottle-green suit that looked as if it had fit him properly at some point in the last few decades. It had an odd sheen on it, as if . . .

Gwen arched an eyebrow. God in Heaven, the man wasn't wearing a silk-lined suit. He was wearing a suit made *entirely* of ethersilk, with what had to be multiple layers of the expensive material.

A girl with the bearing of a servant or apprentice followed him into the room, her eyes on the floor. She was dressed in a collection of cast-off clothing worn in very odd ways, and her eyes were rather unsettling, one a grey-blue, the other a fiery green-gold. She carried a jar of what looked like common, expended lumin crystals, which she held as one might an infant. The other hand was stretched out behind her, dragging a pair of small children's wagons in a little train. Both had been filled to overflowing with all manner of apparently random articles.

"Addison!" the old man cried, hurrying in. He peered owlishly at Grimm, standing in the corner. "Ah!" he said. "Exactly who I was looking for! I need this man."

Lord Albion lifted an eyebrow. "Yes," he said, drawing the word out a bit. "That's why he's here."

"That was deucedly clever of you, Addison," the old man said. "However did you manage it?"

"You told me about him yesterday, Master Ferus," said the Spirearch in a patient voice, "and advised me to secure his services."

The old man's head rocked back. "Really? Are you quite sure?"

"Entirely," Albion said. "There were only so many experienced, independent captains with damaged ships willing to take you to Landing to choose from."

"Extraordinary," Ferus muttered. "And you're sure he's the proper one?"

"I am. Master Ferus, this is Captain Grimm. Captain, I believe you have met Master Ferus?"

"I have indeed," the outcast replied.

"Hah," Ferus said. "Aha, Captain. I told you, did I not, that you and I would meet today?"

"As I recall it, you did."

"I thought as much," Ferus said, nodding. "Very well, then. Shall we get going?"

Albion cleared his throat. "Master Ferus. If you please, could you possibly share the reason you need the good captain's vessel?"

"To find the Enemy, of course," Ferus said. "There's mischief afoot."

"Ah," Albion said. He did not say it with much enthusiasm. "Is there anything more specific you can tell me?"

Ferus considered that. "Doorknobs are extremely complex technology."

Albion nearly failed to suppress a sigh. "Do you think Landing is in danger?"

"Of course it is. We all are."

"It's not impossible," Grimm said quietly. "Except for Morning, Habble Landing is the largest center of commerce in the Spire. If the Aurorans have more explosives and use them on the docks, it would cause chaos. I'm not an economist, but a very significant portion of Spire Albion's interhabble trade passes through Landing at some point."

"Seventy-five percent," the Spirearch provided.

"God in Heaven," Grimm said. "Is it that much?"

"Every habble charges for passage through its portion of the transport spirals," Albion said, nodding. "Transport by barge or windlass is cheaper, faster, and safer. By bypassing some or all of the tariffs, a merchant can as much as double his profit margin."

"And if the shipyard at Landing were destroyed? How much harm would it do the Spire?"

"Incalculable," Albion said. "Eventually the shipyard at Landing would be rebuilt—but the economy would be crippled or paralyzed in the short term, and our capacity to support a war effort would certainly be greatly reduced until it was functioning again."

"Excuse me, si— Ah. That is, excuse me," Gwen said, trying to sound properly respectful while utterly ignoring the propriety of the Spirearch's title. It felt clumsy and wrong, like trying to sing with a mouthful of breakfast. "I don't understand. If the Aurorans wanted to destroy the Landing shipyards, why not just do it with their ships?"

"Presumably," Grimm said, "because the only ships fast and quiet enough to slither in past our patrols are their destroyers. Their weapons are destructive, but relatively light. It would take them time to pound the Landing yard to splinters, and the Landing defense guns and our Fleet would object. It takes armored capital ships to accomplish something like that. Their larger guns will destroy the target far more rapidly, and their armor and heavy shrouds will enable them to stay until the job is done."

Bridget frowned. "I thought the Aurorans who entered the Spire had been defeated and captured."

"Would that they had," Albion said quietly. "The ships that strafed the Morning shipyards managed to evade the Fleet, but Captain Bayard got *Valiant* in close enough to the enemy formation to confirm the presence of an Auroran troop transport."

"I don't know what that means," Bridget said.

"Auroran troop transports carry a full battalion of their Marines," Benedict said quietly. "Around five hundred men."

"How many have been accounted for?" Gwen asked.

"Forty-nine," Albion replied. "Those taken in the attack on Lancaster Vattery and several men who evidently attempted to parasail into the vents and missed their target. Their bodies were found on the surface."

Gwen imagined men, their parasails tangled and collapsed, screaming as they fell nearly two miles through the mist, faster and faster and faster. She tried not to shudder. "I . . . see."

"I'm not sure I do," Benedict said. "What is our part in this to be?"

Albion spread his hands. "You three are, I am afraid, a remainder, as it were."

"Sire?" Gwen said. "Oh, bother, I'm sorry. Excuse me?"

Lord Albion rose and took a couple of the large maps down from the wall behind him, revealing a to-scale rendering of the entire Spire. "Spire Albion," he said. "Ten thousand feet high, two miles across. There are two hundred and fifty habbles, of which two hundred and thirty-six are occupied. As many as four hundred and fifty heavily armed enemy Marines are in here with us—somewhere. Do you remember how many Guardsmen are in active service, Miss Lancaster?"

"A little more than three thousand," she said.

Albion nodded. "Mister Sorellin, do you know how many Marines serve in Home Fleet?"

"A full regiment," Benedict replied. He glanced at Bridget and added, "Fifteen hundred, more or less."

"Precisely," Albion said. "Forty-five hundred bodies to protect two hundred and thirty-six potential targets." He spread his hands. "I've been forced to dispatch them all up and down the Spire."

"But why?" Bridget asked. "Wouldn't it be wiser to fight the Aurorans with all of them? I mean, it seems to me that forty-five hundred men could see to five hundred foes."

"We do not yet know where the Aurorans are, and our numerical advantage means nothing until we do," Albion replied. "More important, some enemies are far more dangerous than mere soldiers, however formidable. Right now rumors are spreading, and fear spreads with them. Fear kills. Before all else, order must be maintained—and that means reassuring the citizens of Albion that they are protected."

"And you're sending us to protect Habble Landing?" Gwen guessed.

"In a way," Lord Albion said. "The Auroran Fleet knew precisely from which angle to attack Morning's shipyards to minimize the effectiveness of defensive fire. They sent their troops into the Spire, and they evidently know its tunnels and vents well enough to remain hidden, at least so far. They knew exactly where to find the Lancaster Vattery, and their uniforms were all but identical to ours."

Gwen frowned, thinking. "No one of those things seems particularly important but . . . when you put them all together . . ."

Lord Albion smiled at her, clearly waiting for her answer.

"There's a hidden hand in this," Gwen said. "Someone who knows the Spire." She blinked. "Someone who lives here."

"Top marks," Lord Albion said. "There is a traitor among us. Perhaps even within my Guard."

Rowl looked up at Bridget and made a sound.

Bridget translated, "That is why you are sending kits to do a hunter's job."

Albion looked at Rowl and nodded. "Precisely. I need to send someone I can trust. When this operation was being planned, none of the trainees had reported for duty. The enemy's operation pattern suggests intimate knowledge of the workings of the Guard and Fleet alike."

"What about me?" Benedict asked.

Albion waved a vague hand. "Oh, come now. It isn't you, Sorellin."

Gwen thought that her cousin didn't know whether to look relieved or somewhat insulted, but he managed to nod at Lord Albion.

"So you're sending us?" Bridget asked. "Um. To do what? I only ask because it seems that it will be easier to follow your orders if we have actually heard them."

Lord Albion's eyes crinkled at the corners. "I've dispatched a number of small teams of recruits on various errands, to various habbles. I'm sending you to Habble Landing with Master Ferus so that you may assist him in his inquisition."

"Ah," Gwen said, nodding. "If I may be so bold, what are you to be looking for, Master Ferus?"

"You apparently are," Master Ferus said. "And I'm all but certain I'll know it when I see it."

Albion did smile that time. "Landing has more residents and more people constantly coming and going than any other habble in the Spire. It's a hotbed for information and black-market trade. If there is anything to be learned about our guests or of the viper in our midst, it will be learned there."

"Ah," Ferus said in a more subdued voice. "Yes, precisely. I will also be gathering information."

Albion pointed a finger at Benedict. "Your sole concern during this operation is the physical well-being of Master Ferus. He is of critical importance to the security of Spire Albion. You are to stay with him at all times. You are to protect him. Whatever happens, he must return safe. Do you understand?"

Benedict nodded soberly. "I do."

Albion's gaze moved on to Bridget. "I'm sending you and Mister Rowl because if there's trouble afoot in Landing, the local cats will know it. They rarely have cooperative dealings with any human, but I believe they may make an exception in your case. You are to serve as Master Ferus's liaisons with the local cats."

"I can do that," Bridget said.

"What about me?" Gwen asked. She was sure that she had kept her impatience out of her voice, but Lord Albion's eyes smiled again.

"Miss Lancaster, having taken note of your talents and your obvious, ah, determination to stay your course, regardless of how ill-conceived it may be, I am sending you along to be a smoother."

"A what?"

"Your duty is to smooth the way for Master Ferus's inquisition. The inquisition must keep moving forward. You are to avoid, overcome, or knock down any obstructions that may block his path."

Gwen found herself frowning. "I'm not sure I understand how to do that."

"I'm not sure you understand how to do anything *else*," Benedict quipped.

Gwen fetched him a quick kick in the ankle with the side of her foot.

"Captain Grimm," Albion continued, as if he hadn't noticed, "will be transporting you down to Landing, and will be ready to lend you his support and that of his crew should you have need of them." He looked back and forth between them. "Do you understand your objectives? Do you have any questions?"

"Um," Bridget said tentatively. "What it is we're doing, exactly?" She hurried to add, "Oh, I understand that each of us has a responsibility to help Master Ferus, but we still don't know what we're to be helping him *with*."

The Spirearch regarded her gravely. "Do you know what the phrase 'operational security' means, Miss Tagwynn?"

"No."

"It means that not everyone has all the information," he said. "That way, if you are spied upon, or captured and interrogated by the enemy, it will not benefit them. You cannot accidentally let slip secrets you have not been told. You cannot be tortured and forced to reveal information that you do not possess."

Bridget's eyes opened very wide. "My goodness."

"I leave it to Master Ferus to decide how much each of you must know to perform your duty adequately," the Spirearch said. "He will inform you at his own discretion. Until such time as he does so, you have your duties. Is that clear?"

"It seems simple enough," Bridget said.

"The most difficult things often are," said Lord Albion. "Pack for the trip, and do it swiftly. You leave within the hour."

■ ■ ■ Chapter 21 ■ ■ ■

Spire Albion, Fleet Shipyards

B ridget held Rowl in her cradled arms as they walked up the spiral ramp leading from Habble Morning to the shipyards on the Spire's rooftop, and tried to keep her breathing steady.

"Honestly," Rowl said. "What are you so concerned with, Little-mouse?"

"I've never . . ." Bridget said. "I've never really been . . . outside."

"There are many things you have never done," Rowl responded. "To be frightened of them is of no use to you."

Bridget glanced over her shoulder, where Benedict was walking with Master Ferus, never more than a couple of strides away from the old man. He'd shouldered his own pack and an enormous duffel apparently meant for Master Ferus and his apprentice, and carried them absently, his eyes sweeping everywhere, even here in Habble Morning.

"I'm not frightened," Bridget replied. "I'm . . . simply considering the possibilities."

"Such as falling off the Spire?" Rowl asked.

Bridget swallowed. "Yes."

"Or some enormous monster flying in from the mist and devouring you?"

"I'm certain the tower's defenses are perfectly adequate to repel mist-maws."

"Or being driven mad by the light of the sun?"

Bridget's fingers immediately went to her neck, where her goggles with their protective lenses hung. "Rowl, my friend, you are at times a perfect little monster."

Rowl gave his tail a disdainful flick. "I am a perfect everything."

"You speak with the cats, Miss Tagwynn?" asked the man walking beside her. Captain Grimm, his arm still in its grimy sling, looked like a man who should be collapsing from exhaustion, but his voice was steady, polite, his eyes alert.

"Imperfectly," Bridget said. "Though, honestly, I think most of them understand every word we say. Except when they don't, of course."

He glanced at Rowl, smiling. "An unkind thing to say of a hero."

Rowl flicked his tail again, his expression unrepentantly smug.

Bridget smiled at that, and rubbed her nose against Rowl's furry head. "He *is* a hero. And a tyrant."

The cat looked up at her and yawned.

Grimm let out a short bark of laughter. "Aye, aye. The cat who lived on *Perilous* was much the same. He didn't take orders well, and we were lucky to have him."

"This one," Rowl said, looking at Grimm. "This one seems smarter than most humans, Littlemouse. I have decided that he may stay."

"Given that it is his ship that will carry us," Bridget said, her tone dry, "that seems very practical."

Grimm seemed to infer Rowl's portion of the exchange, and inclined his head slightly to the cat. "At your service, sir. Ah, the guard station, good."

Their small group had reached the top of the ramp leading up to the shipyards. A large metal grate had been lowered over the doorway out, and at least twenty Marines stood on guard at it. Gwendolyn Lancaster had evidently taken her duty seriously—she was already there, speaking quietly with a senior sergeant, showing him the letter of authorization from the Spirearch. The Marine did not look pleased with her. Gwen frowned, put one fist on her hip, and said something to the man with a rather tart expression on her face.

The Marine's weather-beaten face grew redder, but he growled and jerked a hand in a quick motion. One of his men went to the grate and began pulling on a rope that lifted it, opening the way to the shipyards.

Light, nearly as bright as the flash of a discharged gauntlet, poured down the ramp from the outside world. With it came a breath of wind and air that was much colder than that of the habble in which Bridget had grown up. There was a strange scent to it—wood, and burnt wood, and metal, and something else, something sharp and fresh. Bridget's heart started pounding.

Captain Grimm said something to her, but she wasn't sure what. They walked up the ramp and into the sharp-scented air and the dazzling light.

It was *bright*, painfully bright, like suddenly understanding a truth she would prefer to be anything else. She had to blink her eyes closed as the cold air hit her in the face, an utter shock of sensation. She had never felt anything like it.

Then she remembered, in a panic, how dangerous it was to let the light touch her unprotected eyes, and she fumbled blindly at the goggles around her neck. It was difficult, with only one hand to use, but she finally managed to lift them to her face and hold them there with her quivering fingers.

The dark lenses reduced the glare of the light and she could suddenly see.

For a moment she wished she couldn't.

There were structures and airships and people everywhere in the shipyard, but that was of distant, secondary importance. She looked up and felt as though she might simply fall over onto the ground out of sheer disorientation.

There was no ceiling.

There was no *ceiling*.

She looked up, and up, and up, and up, and there was simply *nothing* overhead, nothing but a light, fine veil of mist that rose into infinite distance above her. She felt an irrational conviction that she was balanced on a precipice, and that a single misstep might betray her and send her body flying up into the void. She jerked her eyes back down to the floor. She fought away a sudden, overwhelming impulse to throw herself prone and hang on to the solid spirestone floor for dear life.

"Easy," she heard Captain Grimm saying. "For some, the first time is a shock, Miss Tagwynn."

"I'm sorry," she managed to say. "I don't mean to make a scene. Normally I am quite composed."

"You're doing better than I did," Grimm said. "I lost my breakfast, and couldn't make myself look up again for days."

"What did you do?"

"I kept trying until I looked up," he said. "It got better. Don't be hard on yourself, miss. It will pass."

"*I* think it is very interesting," Rowl said in a calm, pleased tone.

Bridget choked off something that might have come out a laugh or a sob. She wasn't sure which. She still felt dizzy, sickened, but clearly this problem wasn't going to solve itself. The sky wasn't going anywhere. So she took a deep breath and forced herself to lift her eyes again.

She could see a burning orb, outlined in the mist. The sun. She had never seen it like this, without it being filtered and diffused through the translucent sections of spirestone around the habble. It burned like no candle or crystal she had ever seen.

"That's . . ." she breathed. "That's lovely."

Grimm glanced up and then smiled. "A bit of a dingy view," he said. "When time serves, you should see what the sky *really* looks like."

"You mean," Bridget asked, pointing, "up there?"

She turned to find Captain Grimm staring up and smiling serenely.

"Up there. Up in the deep blue sky. If you think the sun is beautiful, wait until you see it without all the mist. And the moon. And the *stars*. There is no beauty like that of the stars on a clear night, Miss Tagwynn."

"But," she said, "isn't it dangerous? To see such things? I thought men who did went mad."

"Oh, you'll need goggles during the day; it's true," Grimm replied. "Airships sail in etheric currents, and they interact oddly with sunlight. If one doesn't protect one's eyes from them, it can do strange things to one's mind."

Bridget glanced ahead of them at Master Ferus. "Is that . . . is that why Lord Albion's man is so . . . so odd?"

"He's an etherealist, Miss Tagwynn," Grimm replied. "For most of us, etheric currents flow around us, like a stream of water flowing around stones. But for some folk, etheric energy doesn't go around—it courses right through them. They draw it to them." He shook his head. "Goggles are sufficient for the likes of you and me, miss, but there's no protection for a man like Master Ferus."

"He's mad?" Bridget asked in a quiet voice.

"So is his apprentice, though less so," Grimm said. "Master Ferus is the fourth etherealist I've met in my lifetime. They've all been mad. The only question is whether or not it shows."

"Oh," Bridget said. "I do not mean to pester you with more questions, Captain, if you have duties to see to."

He shook his head. "By all means, miss, ask. I am to provide you with my support, after all. Presumably sharing what modest knowledge I have falls into the purview of that duty. Ask your questions."

"Thank you. The etherealists—can they really do what the stories say?" asked Bridget.

"It depends on which stories you've heard, I suppose," Grimm said.

"The usual, I think," Bridget said. "*Burnham's Tales. The Stories of Finch and Broom.*"

Grimm smiled a bit and spread his hands. "Well. They are perhaps a touch overblown."

"But etherealists really can do such things?" Bridget asked. "Call lightning with a word of power? Make a mystic gesture and fly?"

"Try not to think of it that way," Grimm said. "Etherealists are, in many ways, simply etheric engineers."

"Etheric engineers cannot call lightning, sir. Or fly."

"No?" Grimm asked. "But they can design etheric weaponry, such as gauntlets, long guns, and cannon, can they not? Can they not design an airship and send it aloft into the sky?"

"True," Bridget said. "But those are . . . they're weapons and ships. Of course they do that. They design and build devices to a function. It's what they do."

"My point is that an etherealist does the same sorts of things, miss. It's just that he skips the troublesome part in the middle."

Bridget found herself smiling. "Oh," she said. "Is that all he does?"

Grimm winked at her.

"Are they dangerous?" she asked.

He was silent for a moment before he said thoughtfully, "Anyone can be dangerous, Miss Tagwynn. Etherealist or not." He smiled at her, but then his face sobered. "But between the two of us, I think they are capable of more than we know. For myself, I think it wise to keep a very open mind."

They had walked down the length of the shipyard as they spoke, and had come to a large boarding ramp that led up to an airship.

"Captain Grimm," Bridget asked, "is this your vessel?"

"Aye," Grimm replied, unmistakable pride in his voice. "This is *Predator*, Miss Tagwynn. I take it you have not been aboard an airship before?"

Bridget shook her head, staring up. "I've never even seen one."

Predator was, Bridget thought, rather impressive. The main body of the ship seemed to be a large and oddly contoured half tube suspended between three rounded towers that rose up at either end of the ship and in her very middle. Folded along her flanks were a number of bundled rods of some kind that looked like they could be folded out, and old-style canvas cloth hung from them—sails, she realized, made to be extended horizontally, along the ship's flanks. Other masts had been folded against her belly, which was held clear of the stone of the shipyard by heavy struts that supported the vessel's weight. And, she saw, two more masts on the ship's main deck rose up above the ship, their yardarms spread, with more sails reefed against them. Running up the length of both masts were large metal rings that encircled twisted lengths of ethersilk sail—the ship's etherweb.

Most airships she had read about had steam engines in place as their secondary propulsion system. The only ships that favored sails were those operated by the fleets of very poor Spires—or by scoundrels, such as pirates, smugglers, and the like, who were willing to dare the dangers of the mists rather than sail in open skies.

Positioned all around the vessel, at the bases of the masts, she could see large reels lined with the netlike woven ethersilk webs that harnessed the etheric currents that would drive airships faster than any other transport in the world. She understood the principle simply enough. The more webbing one let out of the reel, the more etheric energy it could catch, and the faster it would drive the ship forward. Of course, the web had to be charged with electricity in order for it to function, so airships were limited in the amount of web they could charge by the strength of their power cores.

And there were the weapons.

The gun emplacements protruded bulbously from the ship's deck, the copper-barreled cannon snouts nosing out from a costly rotating ball assembly that would allow the gun crews to swing the cannon forward and aft as well as up and down. She had no way to judge how large the weapons were in comparison to others of the breed, but they certainly looked formidable.

One of the gun emplacements, Bridget noted, was simply missing. There were a number of freshly cut boards around it, suggesting that it had been damaged in some fashion, necessitating the removal of more wood in order to provide a stable platform to replace the missing assembly.

And the entire ship, she realized, was made of wood, so much wood that it beggared her imagination. She remembered how proud her father had been when they had been able to afford the polished wooden service counter at the vattery, and how careful he was to clean and maintain it. It had cost a week's profit for enough wood to build a counter ten feet long and three feet wide.

And *Predator*, Bridget realized, was a dozen times that length, and as high as a two-story house. *All* of it wood.

There were men on the ship, moving all over it. Men carrying crates and bags up the boarding ramp, men on lines hanging down the side of the ship, applying oil to her hull, men atop the towers, men climbing the masts and working with the reefed sails, men scrubbing down the deck, men inspecting the weapon emplacements, men coiling costly ethersilk webbing more neatly onto its reel.

There was a small army aboard this vessel, Bridget realized, each of them performing some kind of specific task. And it was a good thing there *were* so many of them. They might not have survived the confrontation in the tunnel without the aeronauts, whatever Gwendolyn seemed to think.

"If you will excuse me, Miss Tagwynn," Captain Grimm said. "There are many things to which I must attend before we can leave."

Bridget inclined her head. "Of course, sir."

He nodded and bowed slightly at the waist. "Someone will be down momentarily to show your party where to go." He ascended the ramp, weaving between several men carrying various burdens without missing a step.

Rowl was staring up at the ship, his eyes intent, tracking motion, his ears pulled to quivering attention, straight forward. "Littlemouse," he said. "That looks interesting."

"Not too interesting, I trust," Bridget said. "Airships are quite dangerous, you know."

"Dangerous," Rowl said, contempt dripping from the word. "For humans, perhaps."

"Don't be foolish," she said. "There could be any number of hazards in there. Machinery, electrical wiring, weaponry—if you go exploring, you might find something that could hurt you."

"If one doesn't, one is not truly exploring," Rowl replied. "But since you worry so badly, and since I know you will not stop speaking of it, regardless of how foolish you sound, I will remain near you—to make sure that *you* do not run afoul of hazards aboard the ship, of course."

"Thank you," Bridget said.

"But those tall . . . ship-trees, standing up on top."

"We call them masts," Bridget said. She had to use the human word for them. The tongue of the cats had the occasional shortcoming.

"Ship-trees," Rowl said in an insistent tone. "Those interest me. I will climb them."

"All the way up there?" Bridget asked. She felt slightly dizzy just thinking of the view from the mast tops. "It seems unnecessary."

Rowl turned his head and gave her a level look. Then he said, "I sometimes forget that you are just a human." He flicked his ears dismissively and looked back up at the masts. "A cat would understand."

"Just so long as the cat doesn't fall," she said.

Rowl made a growling sound, an expression of displeasure that needed no special skill to understand. Bridget smiled. She couldn't help it. The little monster was so full of himself that she couldn't help but tease him from time to time.

She hugged Rowl gently and rubbed her nose against the fur on his head.

Rowl growled again—but with much less sincerity.

Suddenly there was a presence beside her, and Bridget looked up to see that the etherealist's apprentice was standing next to her. The girl with the oddly colored eyes stared up at the ship—but not, Bridget noted, at the features to which her own eyes had been drawn. Instead, the girl seemed to stare intently at the featureless planks of *Predator's* flanks, and left Bridget with the slightly unsettling impression that the girl's mismatched eyes were peering straight through the wood.

"Oh, my," the girl said, ducking her head enough to make it clear that she was speaking to the jar of expended lumin crystals she still held cradled in one arm. "Have you ever seen one like that?"

"Beg pardon, miss?" Bridget said politely.

"Oh, they're talking to me again," the girl told the jar. "Why must people always talk to me when I leave the house?"

Bridget blinked several times at her response. What did one do in such a situation? It seemed unthinkable that they should stand together looking at such an impressive creation and not carry on some sort of polite conversation.

"I . . . I'm afraid I don't know your name, miss. We are to be working together, it seems. My name is Bridget Tagwynn, and this is Rowl."

The girl smiled and said to the jar, "This is Bridget Tagwynn and Rowl, and we're to be working together."

Bridget frowned. The girl's response had not been rude, precisely. It had simply been so disconnected from the situation that etiquette utterly failed to apply. "May I know your name, please?"

The girl sighed. "She wants to know my name, but I'm simply awful at introducing myself. Perhaps I should tattoo 'Folly' on my head and then people can just read it."

"Folly," Bridget said. "It is a pleasure to meet you, Folly."

"She seems very sweet," Folly told the jar. "I'm sure she means well."

Rowl said, "This girl has too many things in her head, I think."

Folly replied, "Oh, the cat is right. All the things I've forgotten plus all the things I haven't. I keep forgetting over which ones I need to throw a dust tarp."

Bridget blinked again. Before she left the vattery, she could have counted on one hand the number of people she'd met who actually understood Cat. She glanced down to find Rowl staring into infinite distance, exhibiting no reaction. Bridget knew the cat well enough to know that he had not been surprised.

Gwendolyn and Benedict caught up to them, finally, with Benedict staying close to a bemused Master Ferus's side.

". . . simply saying," Benedict said, "that perhaps you could have gained the guard's cooperation without resorting to threatening to arrest him for impeding an inquisition."

Gwendolyn frowned. "Ought I have threatened to charge him with treason, do you think? That one bears the death penalty."

Benedict gave his cousin a rather hunted look. "Gwen, you . . . I don't even . . . I can't possibly . . ." He shook his head, mouth open for a second.

A very small smile touched Gwen's mouth, and her eyes sparkled.

Benedict sighed and shut his mouth again. "Touché. I'll stop telling you how to do your job now, coz."

"*Thank you,*" Gwen said.

Bridget smiled slightly at the exchange, and even Rowl seemed amused.

Not a minute later, a very tall young man, dark haired and square jawed, descended briskly from the ship and approached them dressed in an aeronaut's leathers, his goggles hanging around his neck. He came to a stop before them, gave them a bow, and said, "Ladies and gentlemen, I am Byron Creedy, *Predator's* executive officer. Master Ferus, Captain Grimm has asked me to bring you and your party aboard at your earliest convenience."

The old etherealist blinked and looked up from whatever private thoughts had preoccupied him. He looked the young man up and down, nodded, and said, "Convenient would have been yesterday. Now will suffice."

Creedy arched a brow at this answer, but he bowed his head and said, "Then if you would all please follow me? Welcome aboard *Predator.*"

■ ■ ■ Chapter 22 ■ ■ ■

AMS *Predator*

wendolyn Lancaster looked around *Predator* with what she felt was well-earned skepticism. It seemed that in following the orders of the Spirearch, she had fallen in with scoundrels.

Oh, granted they had been fierce enough in battle—and granted that they had, in fact, quite possibly saved her life. Probably, even. But after asking a few questions of passing crewmen, she had determined that the help of Captain Grimm and his men had gone first to the Lancaster Vattery. Possibly that had been coincidence at work, but Gwen's father put precious little store by such notions.

The crystals her family's vattery produced were quite literally the most valuable resource in the world, the most expensive piece of equipment one could purchase. It seemed to strain coincidence that the captain of a ship in dire need of replacement crystals should happen to wander by the vattery. It seemed an equal stretch that he should then proceed to rescue the heir apparent of House Lancaster, purely by happenstance.

She supposed that a military-minded man might have deduced that the Lancaster Vattery would be a prime target of attack—but if Grimm had managed to piece all of that together in the chaos of the attack, he was the tactical equal of old Admiral Tagwynn himself, and Gwen hardly thought that the Fleet would have cast out a captain of such ability. Of course, coincidences happened, and this could be one. But if it was *not* coincidence, then it meant that Captain Grimm had known enemy movements and intentions.

It was possible that she was doing a courageous and capable man a grave disservice, but a determination to protect the vattery was something that had been fed to her with her mother's milk and drilled into her during every hour of every day that had passed since. As theirs was the only crystal vattery in the Spire capable of producing core crystals, there simply was no alternative but to take every precaution possible. So while she felt a regret that perhaps Grimm deserved better of her, she faced her duty squarely, and kept a quiet, calm eye upon the man.

She mounted the steps to the airship's bridge—the conning tower at the forward end of the ship. The roof of the tower had a small raised platform at the rear, where the ship's steering grips were. The pilot would stand upon it, with the clearest view of anyone aboard of what was in front of the airship. The captain and his executive officer stood on the deck in front of the pilot, enjoying a similar view. Gwen supposed clear sight of the ship's surroundings would be quite vital in wartime.

At the moment, the view was rather pedestrian. The mists had thickened as *Predator* cast off from her pier, and the ship currently hung in cloudy limbo, the sun only a dim suggestion somewhere far above. The dull black walls of Spire Albion stretched out ahead and astern of the airship on its left (or "port") side. A pair of heavy lines were fastened to a long tether cable that ran down the side of the Spire, in order to prevent winds from causing the ship to drift away from the tower. A pair of long poles set out to the side of the ship kept winds from pushing it *into* the tower, too. They had already been under way for a quarter of an hour, and the black stone of the Spire rolled slowly upward as the vessel sank down into the mist, heading for the shipyards of Habble Landing.

The pilot, a rather hard-looking man whose name was Kettle, took note of her presence first, and cleared his throat loudly.

Captain Grimm and Commander Creedy looked back at Kettle, and then at her. They glanced at one another, and then Creedy came over to her wearing a polite smile. "Miss Lancaster," he said. "How may I be of service to you?"

Gwen straightened her dark blue uniform jacket and said, "I wished to ask you a few questions, sir, if that is quite all right?"

"Certainly, miss."

Gwen nodded. "Are you the same Byron Creedy who lately served on the battlecruiser *Glorious*?"

Creedy's friendly expression suddenly became very closed. "Indeed, miss. I had that honor."

"Were you not habbled by the Fleet review board for conduct unbecoming an officer and a gentleman?"

A muscle along the young man's jaw twitched, and Creedy gave her a brief, stiff nod.

"I see," Gwen said. "I may be required to place the success of our inquisition and our very lives in your hands, Commander. I need to know what kind of man you are, and whether or not you will be there to help if I should call upon you."

"Thus far, miss," he replied in a very precise, polite voice indeed, "the captain and crew of *Predator* have been there to help you even when you have *not* called. Or so I judged the situation we found in the tunnel."

"Forgive me, sir," she said. "But we have little time and I fear I must be direct and plain. You were cast in disgrace from the active service rolls of the Fleet. Your captain was exiled from the service entirely. Many of your crew members have similar service records with the Fleet. It is quite the collection of men in disgrace."

"Perhaps, miss," Creedy said with a coolly lifted chin, "you would prefer to travel the remainder of the distance to Landing without enduring the disgrace of our company."

"Byron," said Grimm in a gentle, firm tone.

Creedy glanced over his shoulder, let a breath out through his nose, and then turned back to Gwen to speak in a low, hard voice. "Miss, if I were you, I would have a care what you had to say about the captain in front of any of his officers or crew—myself included. None of us particularly care to hear ill spoken of the man, and none of us will care who your parents are if you insult the captain. Do I make myself understood?"

Gwen arched an eyebrow at him. "Have I said anything that is untrue, Commander?"

"You have said nothing untrue," he replied. "You have also said nothing that is complete. There is more to the world than what a review board publishes about an officer or aeronaut, Miss Lancaster. Guard. Your. Tongue."

And with that, he gave her a rigid bow and strode off the bridge. His boots thumped solidly on the deck and the stairs as he left.

When Gwen turned back to the front of the ship, she found Grimm standing two feet from her. The man had not made a sound to give away his approach, and Gwen had to force herself not to flinch as she found him facing her.

He was, she thought, a rather striking man. He wasn't beautiful. His features weren't balanced. He had a rather heavy brow, which gave him a slightly brutish look—one that was belied by the glitter of intelligence in his dark eyes. His cheekbones were sharp and wide, and contrasted with his thick jawline. His mouth was narrow, though whether that was its natural form or simply his current expression, Gwen couldn't say. He was of unimpressive height, but well muscled, and he had the look of a man who could do heavy work for hours without tiring. His hands were blocky, square and strong, and he carried himself with the rigidly proper posture of the Fleet, despite his disgrace.

It was the blood on him, she thought, that made her uneasy. He had not yet changed out of the clothes he had worn in battle, not even the sling that cradled one of his arms.

"Captain Grimm," she said calmly.

"Miss Lancaster," he replied. "Why were you provoking my executive officer?"

"Because I've always found that people's reactions are more honest when they're tired, and I wanted to test his before he went to his bunk."

He seemed to consider this for a moment and then nodded. "And you're speaking to me now for the same reason, I take it."

Gwen gave him a tight smile. "Something like that."

The captain grunted. "You're too young to be that ruthless."

"My nanny and several instructors told me the same thing," she said. "Your men still think well of you after the battle, Captain. That's remarkable."

"Do you think so?"

Gwen shrugged. "There are many Fleet captains whose men would sour on them if they suffered the casualties your crew did in battle."

"There are many Fleet captains who are idiots," he replied.

"Your men do not seem to have been fazed."

"It was a fight that needed to happen," Grimm said. "They understand that. I didn't kill those men. The Aurorans did. They understand that, too."

"All the same," Gwen said. "I asked around about you, Captain Grimm. I have some questions for you as well."

"I'm certain that you do, miss. Please proceed."

Gwen nodded. "What can you tell me about the *Perilous* incident, Captain?"

Grimm's weary expression never flickered. "I have nothing to say about it."

"That's what everyone seems to think," Gwen said, nodding. "The records of the inquisition afterward have been sealed. Not even my father's influence could acquire them."

"It's done," Grimm said. "It's in the past, and best left there."

"So the Admiralty seems to think," Gwen said. "A Fleet captain dead in midcruise, his executive officer beaten into a coma. Three young lieutenants left to bring a warship and her crew safely home through pirate skies. Lieutenants Grimm, Bayard, and Rook, to be precise."

Grimm regarded her impassively.

"To this day, no one is sure what happened on *Perilous*," she told him. "But she came home with heavy losses—and when the dust cleared, Lieutenants Rook and Bayard had been promoted to lieutenant-commander, while Lieutenant Grimm was summarily drummed out of the service for cowardice in the face of the enemy."

His voice turned dry. "I am somewhat familiar with the tale, miss."

"It gives me serious concerns," Gwen said. "Are you a coward, Captain?"

The man stared at her with those shadowed eyes for several moments before he said, his voice very soft, "When needed, miss. When needed."

Gwen tilted her head. "I'm not sure what to make of that answer, Captain."

"Good," he said shortly. "Mister Kettle, if you would send for me a quarter of an hour before arrival."

"Aye, Captain," said the pilot in a laconic tone.

Grimm gave her a short, brief bow. "Miss Lancaster," he said. Then he turned and walked wearily down the steps to the deck.

Gwen watched him cross to the center tower and enter his cabin. The man did not seem much like a scoundrel to her. Nor did he seem to be a coward. She frowned thoughtfully, until she felt the weight of the pilot's gaze on her. She looked up at Kettle and said, "Do you believe what they said about him at the court-martial?"

Kettle grunted and peered ahead for a moment, and Gwen thought he had simply declined to answer. She had turned and begun to leave when he said, "Miss Lancaster?"

She paused. "Yes?"

"I didn't know him when he was in the Fleet, miss, but . . ." Kettle took a slow breath, his lips moving slightly, as if composing his answer before he spoke. Then he nodded and turned his eyes to her, his expression intent. "Miss Lancaster, spirestone is heavy. Fire is hot. And the captain does his duty. No matter what it costs him. Understand?"

Gwen regarded Kettle's unshaven face for a slow breath and then nodded slowly. "I believe I'm beginning to. Thank you, Mister Kettle."

"It's nothing, miss."

"How long will it take us to reach Landing?"

"Another hour of travel. Then we wait in line for a berth. Few hours, probably. We'll ring the ship's bell when we arrive."

"Thank you," Gwen said, and she turned to leave the pilot to his duties.

Interesting.

Her father had always said that a man could be fairly judged by the quality of his allies and that of his enemies. Captain Grimm seemed to have a number of rather staunch allies, despite his disgraced status, apparently including Lord Albion himself. And despite what had happened to him, his pride was unbowed. If what Kettle said was true, then Grimm was a rather remarkable man—perhaps even the kind of man who could match tacticians of historic brilliance, the kind that made coincidences happen, rather than letting them happen to him.

Perhaps he had saved her family's vattery and her life because he had believed it his duty to do so.

Or perhaps not.

Time would tell.

■ ■ ■ Chapter 23 ■ ■ ■

AMS *Predator*

Grimm's dreams were unpleasant, and concluded in a hectic racket that eventually resolved itself into the sound of someone knocking firmly at the door to his cabin. Before he'd had time to realize that he was actually awake once more, his legs had already swung out of his bunk, and he was sitting up by the time he muttered, "In."

The door opened and Stern leaned his head into the cabin. "Begging your pardon, Captain."

Grimm waved a dismissive hand. "We're there already, Mister Stern?"

"Still waiting for a berth," the wiry young man replied. "But you've got a visitor from the Fleet, sir."

Grimm gave the young man a sharp glance, and then a brisk nod. "I'll be out momentarily."

"Aye, Captain," Stern said, and shut the door again.

Visitors from Fleet? Now? At least Grimm had been able to wash himself down at a basin of water before he slept. Now he rose, dressed himself as best he could in clean clothing, and awkwardly tied off a fresh sling for his wounded arm. He raked a comb through his mussed hair several times, scowled at himself in a small mirror, and eyed the stubble of a beard that marred any chance he might have of presenting himself in an officer's proper condition.

Of course, he wasn't an officer of Fleet anymore, was he?

Grimm shook his head, tried to shake off the bone-deep exhaustion he still felt, failed to do so, and went out of his cabin anyway.

"Captain on deck!" Stern barked as Grimm opened his door. Grimm stepped onto the deck to see every crewman in sight stop whatever they were doing, turn toward him, and snap him a perfect Fleet salute. He kept himself from smiling.

"Mister Stern," Grimm said beneath his breath. "Why is it that the crew bothers with formal protocol only when a serving member of Fleet comes aboard?"

"Because we like to remind the uptight bastards that on this ship, you're in command, Skipper. Regardless of what Fleet thinks of you."

"Ah," Grimm said. He lifted his voice slightly. "As you were."

The crew snapped out of the salute with near parade-ground precision and returned to their duties. A dapper little figure in the uniform of a Fleet commodore swaggered across a boarding plank laid out between *Predator*'s deck and that of a Fleet launch, hovering alongside Grimm's ship. The man hopped down onto the deck and shook his head in bright-eyed amusement. "Permission to come aboard, Captain?"

"Bayard," Grimm said, stepping forward and offering the other man his hand.

"Mad," Bayard said, trading grips with him. "Good God in Heaven, man, I knew *Predator* had been injured, but . . . Were you talking to strangers again?"

"To Captain Castillo of *Itasca*, briefly," Grimm replied. "I took my leave before the conversation could go any farther than it did. What are you doing here, Alex?"

"We heard that you'd been injured again while playing hero during the attack, and Abigail insisted that I look in on you."

Grimm gestured to his arm. "The rumor mill is performing to specifications, I'm afraid. I already had this when it started."

"I remember," Bayard said. "So. You repelled an assault by Auroran Marines . . . with one hand."

"My crew did the majority of that."

Bayard made a little *ah* sound. "Naturally. While you stood about offering critique, I suppose."

"It's as if you know me."

Bayard's teeth shone in a sudden smile. "And you had no further injuries—from a critically pilloried crewman, perhaps?"

"A few scrapes and bruises. I'm well."

"That will ease Abigail's mind greatly," Bayard said. "Now, about that brandy."

"What brandy?"

"The excellent brandy you're about to pour me in your cabin, naturally," Bayard said in a cheerful tone—but his eyes were quite serious.

"I see," Grimm said, nodding. "I suppose if it gets rid of you more rapidly, it's a worthy investment. This way, Commodore."

Bayard grinned. "And to think that they call merchant captains uncivilized."

Once inside the cabin, Grimm shut the door behind them and turned to his old friend. "All right. What's this really about?"

Bayard made a half circle out of the fingers of his right hand and frowned down at them in puzzlement. "That's odd. There's no drink there."

Grimm snorted. Then he went to the cabinet and came back with a couple of small glasses of brandy. He offered one to Bayard. Bayard took it, lifted it, and said, as he ever did when they drank together, "Absent friends."

"Absent friends," Grimm echoed, and the two of them drank.

"It's official," Bayard said after. "The Spire Council has declared a state of war with Spire Aurora."

Grimm frowned. "Inevitable, I suppose."

"Inevitable and ugly," Bayard said. "We're already sending out word to call in our ships in First and Second Fleets alike. The Admiralty, in its wisdom, has decided to remain in a defensive posture until we have concentrated our entire Fleet presence."

Grimm felt his eyebrows rising. Aerial warfare was the very soul of sudden and overwhelming violence. A commander who surrendered the initiative to the enemy was a commander who might well be obliterated by a surprise offensive at the time and place of the enemy's choosing before he could ever give the order to engage. "What?"

Bayard flopped down onto Grimm's narrow sofa. "Exactly. This raid has rattled old Watson rather badly, I'm afraid."

"Why?"

"Because the enemy set this attack up to manipulate him and they succeeded. They jerked him around like a puppet on strings. If some poor fool hadn't been randomly wandering by the Lancaster Vattery . . ."

Bayard lifted his glass to Grimm.

Grimm rolled his eyes.

". . . Watson's response might have cost Albion its most precious resource." Bayard sloshed down a bit more brandy. "So he is proceeding with utmost caution in order to avoid falling into another such trap."

"Unless, of course," Grimm said, "they're trying to manipulate him into sticking one of his feet to the floor and piling up all our ships in one place."

"Exactly." Bayard sighed. "Every element of First Fleet is currently sailing in a giant circle around the Spire to watch for trouble, like some kind of bloody carousel. Several of us tried to talk sense into him, but you know old Watson."

"He's a rather brilliant defensive tactician," Grimm said.

"I agree," Bayard said. "The problem is that he's an inept defensive *strategist*. We should be dispatching ships to hammer the Aurorans hard in *their* home skies, force *them* to think defensively. The damned fool's *encouraging* them to take the initiative."

Grimm frowned down at his drink and said, "What does this have to do with me?"

Bayard scowled. "Don't give me that. You're Fleet, Mad. Same as me."

"The Fleet rolls say otherwise."

"There's a *war* upon us," his friend replied. "This is no time for petty grievances. We need every skilled captain we can get. I want you to come back."

"I have been dishonorably discharged. I *can't* come back."

"You're an experienced combat commander," Bayard countered. "And you've won more than a little respect for your actions at the Lancaster Vattery. The prime minister of Albion himself watched you defend his home, his people, and his livelihood through his study window. If you come back to Fleet and offer your services, I think the winds are right to make it happen—and there happens to be a captain's slot I need to fill in my squadron."

Grimm looked up sharply.

"*Valiant*," Bayard said simply. "I need a flag captain."

Something lurched inside Grimm's chest, something that he'd forgotten over the past decade—the voice of a much younger, much less experienced Francis Madison Grimm, determined to win command of a Fleet ship of his own. He wasn't sure whether it felt like fireworks exploding in his chest or the vertigo of a drunken tumble down a flight of stairs. "You're insane. I never commanded a Fleet ship."

"Yes," Bayard said, his voice hardening. "You did."

"Not officially," Grimm spat. "Not on paper. And no officer, no matter how popular or favored, is given a bloody heavy cruiser as his first command."

"Rules are made to be broken," Bayard replied. "What they did to you wasn't right. I don't see how reversing that injustice could be wrong."

"I'm working for the Spirearch now," Grimm said.

"I know. But this is your chance, Mad. To make it all right. Come back to Fleet command with me. Offer to rejoin."

Grimm narrowed his eyes. "You want me to go to them. You want me to go to them with my hat in my hands and ask them to let me back in, pretty please, your lordships."

"*War*, Mad," Bayard said, leaning forward. "This is bigger than me. It's bigger than Hamilton Rook and his family. It's even bigger than your wounded pride. We *need* you."

"Then I look forward to being notified, in writing, of the clearing of my name and the restoration of my rank and standing in Fleet," Grimm said.

Bayard's face became furious. "Dammit, Mad. You have a responsibility. A duty."

"You're right about that much, at least. But my duty to Fleet ended years ago. I have other responsibilities now."

Bayard simply stared, anger radiating from his every pore. Grimm met his gaze without hostility and without yielding.

After a moment, Bayard seemed to deflate. He made a disgusted sound and finished off the brandy in a gulp. "Damn your pride."

Grimm finished his own glass and let the liquor burn down his throat, half-afraid that the turmoil in his chest might set it alight. "Alex . . . what you're asking me to do—I won't do it. I can't do it. I can't."

Silence fell.

"Abigail said as much," Bayard said finally. "But I had to try."

"Thank you," Grimm said. "Truly."

Bayard moved one shoulder in a shrug, set his glass aside, and rose. "I also wanted to give you some advance warning—your XO is about to be put back on active duty. They're calling in everyone they've habbled and every reservist they can from the merchant fleet."

"I suppose that's hardly surprising," Grimm said, rising with him.

"How is he?" Bayard asked.

"He'll do," Grimm said in a firm tone. "When?"

"A week at the longest," Bayard said.

"I'll make adjustments," Grimm said, and the pair of them walked back out on deck together. "Please give Abigail my regards."

"You'll need to have a meal with us soon," Bayard said. Then he grimaced. "Wartime permitting."

"I should enjoy that."

"This . . . arrangement you have with the Spirearch," Bayard said. "Will it last?"

"Perhaps. Perhaps not."

"Then I reserve the right to speak to you on the subject again."

"My answer shall not change."

"No. I don't suppose it shall." Bayard glanced up, and then tilted his head a bit to one side. "Captain," he said. "What is that at the very top of your forward mast?"

Grimm looked up, following Bayard's gaze to where a small, solid form was outlined against the sunlit mist. "Apparently," he said, "it is a cat."

■ ■ ■ Chapter 24 ■ ■ ■

Spire Albion, Habble Landing

Rowl found the view from atop the foremost of the two ship-trees to be less exciting than he had assumed it would be. Oh, he could see over the ship itself well enough, though based upon his understanding of the vessel's name, as if it needed one, he felt that its master should have been thanking cats for the obvious inspiration, at the very least. Perhaps there was an arrangement to be reached here. Certainly, if they named something after cats, even the dimmest of humans must understand that there was recompense to be discussed.

The vessel itself had proved to be interesting. He had seen Little-mouse safely ensconced in a small room with a cup of hot drink, which tasted terrible but which she insisted upon having frequently in any case. After that, he had gone exploring. There were many hallways and rooms upon *Predator*, as well as a number of things that needed chasing and catching. Probably not eating, though, unless he was truly hungry. Rowl felt sure that Bridget's fragile feelings would be crushed if he denied her the pleasure of sharing her meat with him.

There was certainly a place for a cat on a construct such as this, provided he didn't mind the company.

Once he had inspected the vessel, he had promptly climbed the ship-tree, but the only things of interest to be seen from there were the humans moving about the ship, and honestly, it would be a long and dull day indeed before they proved more than momentarily interest-

ing. A smaller ship, possibly also bearing a name inspired by his people, came alongside *Predator*. A human of significantly less clumsiness
than most came aboard, a small male, and despite its diminutive stature, it moved with a warrior's confidence and wore a very large and
fine hat.

Such hats often signified humans who considered themselves important, which was adorable for the first few moments and trying ever
after.

The visitor had, however, entered the ship as if waiting to be permitted on another's territory, which was the proper way to do things. Rowl
had begun to approve of the human Grimm, who had thus far acted
with less than utter incompetence in every aspect of his life. If Grimm
was able to command such respect even from humans with very large
hats, he might make suitable help, and even humans were wise enough
to realize that good help was the most elusive of quarries.

Rowl followed the conversation Grimm had with the visitor. It seemed
largely to be concerned with inexplicable human madness, though he
understood the anger and raised voices that signified what might have
been a bloodletting. As so often happened with the fickle beasts, it did
not develop into a proper battle, and the visitor left in apparent defeat.

Shortly after that, there was some activity between the tall second in
command, and a human operating several long levers with colored
cloth on the ends. They were apparently signals of some kind, because
the humans peered down at something below them for a time, after
their flags waggled. What they saw seemed to satisfy them. The ship,
which had been motionless, finally descended toward a wooden platform that, apart from minor details, looked almost precisely like the one
they had just left.

Rowl found that disappointing. It seemed a great deal of trouble for
him to spend half a lifetime bored up a ship-tree to gain very little in
the way of an interesting change of environment. But such things were

to be expected when dealing with humans. He would remain patient until they fumbled past such foolishness. Was he not, after all, a cat?

He descended the ship-tree. It was rather less enjoyable than the climb had been. It was an activity better suited to humans and their spidery fingers. He would have to see to it that there was a human prepared to climb up and carry him down with proper dignity next time. Perhaps it would be an opportunity to test the capability of human Benedict. Clearly he was unworthy to be the mate of Littlemouse, but perhaps with the right guidance some kind of adequacy could be nurtured.

Rowl returned to the little room where Littlemouse and her companions were drinking their stinking water, and leapt up to grip the handle upon its door, hanging from it long enough to make it come open. Then he prowled in and shut the door again with a press of his shoulders.

The human Gwendolyn blinked at him several times and then said, "When on earth did he leave? *How* did he leave?"

Littlemouse nodded at him and said to human Gwendolyn, "He is a cat, Miss Lancaster. Asking such questions is an exercise in futility."

Rowl leapt up onto Littlemouse's lap and nuzzled her cheek affectionately. He liked Littlemouse. She was far less stupid than most humans.

"The ship is landing," he told her. "We should go see what this new habble looks like at once."

He waited for Littlemouse to repeat what he had said to the other humans. Honestly. He sometimes felt that humans simply had to be *deliberately* obtuse. What was so difficult about understanding civilized and excellently enunciated speech? His father had often opined that, in fact, humans really were exactly as foolish and helpless as they seemed—or that life was simpler if one assumed it to be true, at any rate. But Rowl was not yet sure.

A moment later, an acutely unpleasant sound of metal striking metal sliced across the deck. It was one of those human noises that had been, he felt sure, created for no purpose whatsoever but to annoy cats.

The sound did seem to galvanize the humans, though. Littlemouse and her companions rose and began fussing about the way humans often did. The humans who operated the ship did the same, and after a pointless delay for the humans to collect all their toys and keepsakes, he was finally able to take his rightful place in Littlemouse's arms and herd them all in the proper direction.

They descended from the ship onto a wooden platform that seemed to simply hang in open air from the side of the Spire. He had to give humans credit where it was due—they did seem to have a knack for building interesting places for cats to explore. They walked over the creaking wooden planks, their steps echoing.

"Littlemouse," he said, "if the human platform fails, will we not fall to the surface?"

He could hear her heart speed up, and her hands became somewhat clammy against his fur. "Nonsense. I'm certain it will do no such thing."

But she began to walk slightly faster.

Littlemouse and her companions joined a rather large herd of humans who were standing around doing nothing interesting or profitable. They stayed there interminably, only occasionally taking a step forward. Honestly. Was it any wonder their clan chief had finally begged Rowl's father for the guidance and support of the Silent Paws?

At last they funneled through a relatively tiny opening in the wall of the Spire along with a column of similarly placid humanity, and took their turn wasting even more time by talking to armed humans who were not even so important as to have large hats. And only after all of that indecipherable human ritual was complete to their satisfaction did they enter Habble Landing.

Rowl reminded himself that cats were eternally patient, and that he would not simply explode if he did not fling himself from Littlemouse's arms and go exploring. Which was not to say that he *could* not do so if he wished, because cats were also their own masters. He decided that his patience was practically legendary—which was fortunate for Littlemouse, or Rowl would already have taken care of this problem or mystery or whatever it was while she was still milling about in the line to talk to the armed humans at the entrance to Habble Landing, thus robbing her of the glory of success.

Though, now that he thought about it, he was the most important member of the party. Any glory gained was rightfully his in any case.

He decided to tolerate the situation for the present. But if the humans became unmanageable, he might have to take steps. And who could blame him? Not even his father would assert that it was practical to manage *five* humans. It was a well-known fact that humans became more addled than usual when running in herds.

Habble Landing was fascinating. For one thing, the ceiling was only half the height of other habbles he'd seen. It was still far above even Littlemouse's head, but the more enclosed space reminded him of the ducts and ventilation tunnels that were traditionally the territory of his people. And it was *thick* with humanity. Habble Morning was considered to be a well-populated habble, but Habble Landing absolutely teemed with people by comparison. Hundreds and hundreds of them were coming and going through the hole in the Spire wall. Dozens of humans who were selling trinkets and keepsakes (all of which Littlemouse would say were absolute necessities for a human) were lined up along the walls in neatly arranged stalls—and this wasn't even the market area.

Voices filled the air, so many of them that it was impossible to pick out a specific conversation—taken as a whole, the voices created a low murmur that sounded a bit like the sighing of air through a junction point in the vents. Scents were thick, too—foul smells that always came with humanity, savory smells of various foods, and absolutely fascinating scents he could not identify.

"Goodness," human Gwendolyn was saying. "Have you ever seen so many people coming and going?"

"It would be a lovely setting for slipping an enemy agent into the Spire," human Benedict agreed.

Human Folly was apparently frightened of something, though she was in no danger that Rowl could see. Her heart beat very quickly, and she stank of nerves strung tight. She kept her eyes on the floor and stayed within inches of the senior male of the group, Master Ferus. The older man's eyes were almost closed, as if he wanted an observer to think he was nearly sleeping, but Rowl could see them flicking around in an almost feline fashion, taking in the sights just as he was.

"Master Ferus?" human Gwendolyn asked. "Where should we go, sir?"

"Hmm?" Ferus said. "What's that?"

"Lodging, perhaps?" Littlemouse suggested.

"Ah, excellent, yes." He glanced back at human Benedict. "Young man, do you know of a decent inn?"

"I believe there are a great many of them in the habble, but I stayed at the Guard house while I was here," human Benedict said in an apologetic tone. "I do know that we should be able to hire a runner who can assist us."

Human Gwendolyn frowned. "Should we not stay there as well? This is an official inquisition for the Spirearch, after all."

"We can't make it official, and we can't stay at the Guard house," Littlemouse said. "If there is a traitor amongst the Guard, and we march in and announce our intentions, we might as well blow trumpets everywhere we go."

"Quite right," Master Ferus said. "Quite right. A runner, then."

Human Gwendolyn seemed to take that as a command. She nodded and strode off through the crowd. Rowl waited with infinite patience. There were many things to see and smell. One human vendor had a great many little creatures in little cages. Some of them had wings, and some scales, and some fur. Rowl managed to sort out scents to their owners and studied them thoughtfully. Then a gentle stir and shift in the direction of the ventilated air announced the arrival of afternoon, as the sun began to warm the other side of the Spire, and brought with it a deliriously savory scent of cooking meat.

Rowl whipped his head to one side to stare in the direction from which the scent came—and noted, as he did, that human Benedict had wit enough to smell it, too, and was showing exactly the same interest. The human's stomach made growling, grumbling sounds.

Human Gwendolyn returned shortly, in the company of a rather scrawny little human kit. The little human's hair was a mess, its face was dirty, its clothing ragged, and Rowl, who found humans drearily like one another most of the time, could not tell whether the apparent runner was male or female.

"This is Grady," human Gwendolyn announced. "He has graciously consented to guide us to an inn."

"Aye, aye," said the little human. "Just come with me, ladies and gents, and we'll get you squared away with a clean bed and a hot meal."

"Good, good," said the oldest human. "Proceed."

"Yes, sir!" said the little human. "Right this way!"

They followed the little human from the gallery that led to the ship-yard, and into a side tunnel, where he produced a medium-size lumin crystal and made everyone utterly blind to anything happening more than a few paces away. Humans were inconsiderate that way. Rowl could see perfectly well, after all. It was hardly his fault if humans couldn't tell the difference between mere dimness and true darkness.

Which was ironic, because they were, as a whole, among the dimmest creatures he knew.

They walked a short way through the side tunnel and then exited into a long, narrow street where the human buildings crowded in close on every side and thrust up from the floor all the way to the ceiling in many cases—but the building heights were uneven and jagged overall, like so many broken teeth. The street was only dimly lit, and there were considerably fewer humans walking along it than they had seen near the shipyard.

Rowl found that . . . inconsistent. The presence of danger brushed along his fur as the little human led Littlemouse and her companions down the street, and Rowl found himself gathering and releasing his muscles. He could not pinpoint any particular threat and yet . . .

Littlemouse, wise enough to look to a cat for guidance, noticed Rowl's reaction almost immediately. Her own posture became tenser, her eyes flicking around, searching for any threat just as Rowl did.

Suddenly Rowl heard soft footfalls behind them, and he turned his ears quickly to listen in that direction.

"Littlemouse," he said quietly. "We are being hunted. Behind us."

She looked down at him, but did not swivel her head to look over her shoulder toward their pursuers. Excellent. Such a gesture would have alerted the hunters to the fact that their prey had sensed them. Littlemouse was so clever—for a human, of course.

"Benedict," Littlemouse said quietly. "Rowl thinks someone is following us."

Human Benedict frowned at her, but did not ask questions. Instead, Rowl saw his nostrils flare, and he began to use his eyes, looking around him, though he did not turn his head.

"Damn," human Benedict said a moment later. He took a step forward, drawing even with Master Ferus, and tapped human Gwendolyn on the shoulder. She turned to look up at him, but didn't stop walking. Human Benedict leaned down to speak quietly to her. "Coz, I'm afraid we've been marked."

Human Gwendolyn frowned. "Marked?" She looked down at herself. "Did someone put something on my dress?"

Human Benedict let out a breath through his teeth. "Marked, coz, as prey. We're being paced and followed."

"By whom?"

"Footpads, most likely," human Benedict replied. "There are several gangs that operate in Habble Landing."

Human Gwendolyn narrowed her eyes. "I see. And which person has marked us, specifically?"

"To your left," human Benedict said. "About ten feet behind us, dark brown coat, black hair, about twenty. He's keeping track of us by watching our reflections in windows as we pass them. And there's another one ahead of us, on the right, in that slouchy hat."

"I see," she replied. "What is the usual course of action for dealing with such things?"

"Avoid them."

"We've already failed at *that*," human Gwendolyn said, her tone irritated. "What else?"

Human Benedict sounded a bit flustered. "Coz, how should I know? I've never been marked by footpads before."

She considered that, and nodded. "I see."

Then, without hesitating for more than the time it took to take a step, human Gwendolyn turned, raised her gauntlet, and discharged it.

An almost invisible bolt of force and heat howled through the air and slammed into the stone wall of a building's front side, not two feet from the head of the footpad pacing them from behind. The light made Rowl duck his head to shield his eyes, and the force of the blast threw chips of stone from the wall, sending them skittering around the street.

The footpad (and perhaps a dozen other humans who happened to be nearby) let out a shriek and flinched back, staring at the smoking, scorched gouge in the stone. He lost his balance and fell to the ground and onto his rear. The entire street, in fact, froze in its tracks, everyone staring at little human Gwendolyn.

She stepped toward the footpad, her gauntlet's crystal still glowing in her palm, and raised her voice to a pitch and volume that would carry it to the entire street. She pointed the forefinger of her right hand at the stunned footpad and said, her voice hard, "You."

The man just stared at her.

"Run home," human Gwendolyn said. "Do it now. And inform your masters that *we are not prey.*"

Her words echoed around the stone building fronts for a few seconds.

Then the footpad's mouth twitched a couple of times. He gave a jerking, frantic nod, scrambled to his feet, and dashed away down the street and out of sight.

Rowl turned his eyes back to human Gwendolyn, impressed. That was precisely how one should deal with a would-be predator. Human Gwendolyn's instincts and response had been practically non-incompetent.

"Maker of the Path," human Benedict swore beneath his breath. "Coz, you just discharged a *gauntlet* on a *crowded street.*"

"And stopped us from being attacked by thugs," human Gwendolyn replied. "No one was hurt. Honestly, coz, we have no time for this sort of nonsense." She took a step forward and knelt down to stare in the eye the little human who had led them there. "Grady," she said in a sweet tone, "why did you bring us here to be attacked?"

"I didn't!" the little human said, his face bloodless. "I wouldn't! I won't, miss!"

"You just happened to bring us down a crowded chute full of men seeking targets to mug? Is that what you want me to believe?"

The little human swallowed. Then he said, "I know another inn, miss. Right by the gallery, out in the open. I could take you there if it pleases you."

"Fool me once, shame on you," Gwendolyn said. "Fool me twice, and I may feel inclined to blast you purely on principle."

The little human stared at her, agog.

"Boo!" Gwendolyn shouted, and stamped her foot.

Grady turned and sprinted off.

"Are you certain you don't want to blast the ground at his feet as he runs away?" Benedict asked, his voice dry.

"Don't be tiresome, Benny," Gwendolyn replied. "If we can't trust one runner, we can't trust any of them. There's no guarantee that the next time it might not be Auroran agents instead of simple thieves waiting for us. Present me with options."

Benedict frowned for a moment and then shrugged. "There's one place we can go where I feel certain we can at least get honest guidance, if nothing else."

"Excellent," Gwendolyn said. "Let us proceed."

"This way," Benedict said, and they started walking again. After a moment or two, human Benedict turned to look directly at Rowl. "Thank you," he said.

Rowl yawned, feeling rather pleased with himself for having saved his humans from footpads, and said, "It is what I do."

■ ■ ■ Chapter 25 ■ ■ ■

Monastery of the Way, Habble Landing

Bridget walked carefully through the cramped passages of Habble Landing, trying to pay attention to any other sources of potential danger—but she felt as if she'd been sent to the store without anyone telling her what she was supposed to buy. What would danger look like? She supposed that if it was overt and obvious, just anyone could see it coming, but she had no idea of what an ambush might resemble before it actually began to happen. She saw no one in a great black cape, or twirling a waxed mustache, which all the villains in the theater seemed to have, though she supposed true villains would rarely do one the courtesy of identifying themselves and declaring their intentions in a forthright manner. It was one of the things that made them villains, after all.

She kept one eye on Rowl constantly. She would never admit it to the little bully aloud, but he probably had a much better idea than she of what might prove a threat. He was already even more insufferably pleased with himself than usual today, having warned them of the footpads. If she admitted it to him, he would never let her forget it.

Rowl, for his part, looked and sniffed and flicked his ears this way and that, taking in all the sights and sounds of the busy, even maniacally industrious habble.

The crowded labyrinth of vendors' stalls and counters near the airship docks had been only a foretaste of the habble proper. There were more shops in operation in one quadrant of Landing than in the entirety of Habble Morning! And they had divided their vertical space in half, so that there was a whole second level above them presumably filled with even more enterprise.

Entire lengths of cramped street were dedicated to specific crafts and businesses. There was a street of tinkers and smiths, the air hot and filled with the sound of metal on metal. There was an entire street of papermakers, the smell of their labors so appalling that Rowl buried his nose beneath Bridget's arm until they were past. There was a street of vatteries, next to the street of tanners, next to the dye makers, and absolutely everyone seemed to be in a great hurry, passing their slower-stepping group with grumbles and dire glares.

The people were just as dazzling in variety. She'd always assumed that Habble Morning was the most cosmopolitan habble of the Spire, the absolute hub of Albion culture, but though visitors weren't precisely unheard-of there, there was simply no comparison to be made.

In the space of ten minutes, she spotted half a dozen different groups of foreigners moving through the streets of Landing. She saw a group of ruddy-cheeked Olympians in their traditional green-and-gold garb, most of them wearing the device of their home Spire's laurel wreath upon their breasts or pendants or rings. Not five steps later, a pair of women with the golden-brown skin marking them as Nephesians strolled by wearing long, sweeping skirts in half a dozen fine, pattern-slashed layers of different colors. They were followed by a tall warrior-born man with the nearly black skin and ice-blue eyes of an Atlantean, wearing an airship captain's coat of indigo, and not long after that she spotted a crew of rather small, lean, worn-looking men and women whose faces were marked with the fine, swirling ritual scars of Pikers.

"Is this your first time out of Habble Morning, Miss Tagwynn?" Benedict asked her.

Bridget jerked her eyes away from the Pikers rather guiltily. "Is it so obvious?"

"Totally understandable," he said. "After all, something like seventy percent of the residents of Spire Albion never leave their home habbles at all."

"I should think it would reduce one's chances of being preyed upon by footpads," she observed.

Benedict grinned. "Oh, of course. Crews like that never pick on anyone from their home habble. Too easily identified to the authorities. And their leaders would never allow it."

"Leaders?" Bridget asked. "They aren't just . . . like, packs of marauding ventrats?"

"Naturally not," Benedict said. "Far too messy and chaotic, and therefore easily stopped. Everything they do has to be coordinated and carefully organized."

"Organized robbery?"

"Among other things, yes," Benedict said. "Smuggling, the sale of dangerous intoxicants, trafficking in weapons, in medicines, in flesh." His eyes darkened slightly. "All controlled and precisely applied by the guilds."

Bridget blinked. "The guilds? Like the Vatterists' Guild?"

"I doubt it's much like the Vatterists' Guild in Habble Morning," Benedict replied. "All of the guilds are in competition here, and most of them engage in one kind of shady activity or another. Some are worse than others, but as a rule, if someone gets his head broken in Habble Landing, it was because one of the guilds decided it needed to be done."

"It would seem to be a great deal of trouble to manage a group of men who would do such things," Bridget noted.

"Indeed it is."

"Wouldn't it be simpler for them to . . . just do honest work?"

Benedict showed his teeth. "Probably. But there will always be those who seem to think that simply taking what they need through strength is easier and more enjoyable than working to create it. Certainly it leaves them more leisure time."

"I don't understand," Bridget said. "Why would guilds that behave this way be permitted to exist?"

"Any number of reasons," Benedict said. "If there is a law, someone will work to break it. That's human nature. The guilds have a certain code of conduct to which they adhere that makes them a somewhat less appalling proposition than independent criminal activity. They are the devil we know." He pursed his lips. "And they are extremely powerful."

"Not more powerful than the Guard, surely."

"More focused than the Guard," Benedict said. "Much harder to find than the Guard. And of course, they aren't burdened by the restrictions of Spire law. Atop that, they also control a number of legitimate businesses, and through their influence can significantly alter habble politics. They command a combination of fear, respect, money, and professional craft that makes conflict with them a difficult and dangerous proposition."

Bridget frowned, thinking about that. "Then . . . pardon me if my understanding falls short, but did not Gwendolyn just issue a rather blatant public *command* to these powerful and dangerous men?"

"Yes," Benedict said placidly. "Yes, she did."

"Oh, dear," Bridget said. "That seems . . . less than ideal."

Benedict shrugged, his feline eyes constantly sweeping the streets as they walked. "Perhaps. Perhaps they'll respect it as a show of strength. Men like that tend to refrain from unprofitable enterprises such as preying upon victims who can fight back—and the Lancasters can certainly do that."

They turned down a final cramped street, and as they did, Bridget could actually see the tension go out of Benedict's lean frame, and his face relaxed into a smile.

"What just happened?" Bridget asked.

"This is safe territory. We're close now," Benedict said. "The guilds won't operate in this portion of the habble."

"Why not?"

"They've been taught that it is more trouble than it's worth," Benedict said.

They passed through a last bit of street crammed with buildings and suddenly emerged from the warren into the open space of a standard-height habble ceiling, stretching out fifty feet overhead. The rest of the habble's buildings simply ended, the twin levels connected by a heavy deck and several large wooden stairways, as if their designers had simply forgotten to carry the conversion of the original space beyond the point they had just passed.

Before them stood a solid wall of masonry ten feet high, set with a single heavy gate of bronze-bound wooden beams. In front of the gate sat a man in a rather odd-looking saffron robe, the material loose-fitting around the upper arms, but bound in by wraps on his forearms. His pale head was shaved entirely bald, and he sat with his eyes closed, his legs crossed, and his palms resting lightly on his knees. A simple rod of copper-clad metal about three feet long rested on the floor beside his right hand.

"Oh," Bridget said. "Is that a monk of the Way?"

Rowl stirred in her arms and looked up at the man, the cat's ears focused forward and his tail twitching with interest.

"Oh, I can't do this," Master Ferus said. "Sir Benedict, would you mind?"

"Of course, sir," Benedict said. He raised his voice a little and said, "This is Brother Vincent. He has gate duty because his handwriting is terrible."

Brother Vincent smiled without opening his eyes. "Sir Benedict. Have you come to teach or to learn?"

"Shall we find out together, brother?" Benedict asked.

Brother Vincent smiled and did not open his eyes.

Benedict promptly unbuckled his sword belt and stripped off his gauntlet. He held them out to Bridget and asked, "Do you mind?"

She blinked and then assured him, "Not at all." It took a bit of juggling to hold Benedict's weapons and Rowl at the same time, but she managed.

"Thank you, miss," Benedict said. Then he turned and began stalking toward Brother Vincent on cat-quiet feet.

"What is happening here, precisely?" Gwendolyn asked Master Ferus.

"Tradition," Ferus replied, watching Benedict with bright eyes.

She frowned. "Meaning what, precisely?"

"Isn't it traditional for a Lancaster to know something about tradition?" Master Ferus asked acerbically.

Folly gave a little curtsy to no one in particular, and then told her jar of crystals, "The monks take their guardianship of the temple very seriously. They won't allow anyone to enter casually. One must prove to the monks that his desire to enter is sincere."

Gwendolyn lifted one delicate eyebrow. "And how does one—"

Silent as darkness itself, Benedict sprang upon Brother Vincent.

"Oh," Gwendolyn said. "I see."

Bridget had never seen the warriorborn move so quickly, but somehow the monk was already on his feet, and the two men met in a flurry of blows and counterblows that made Bridget's heart skip several beats. She could barely see what they were doing, they moved so quickly, and it was laughable to think that she might be able to anticipate what might happen next. By comparison, her own knowledge of unarmed fighting was, she could see now, a pebble beside a Spire.

And then something terribly complex and lightning-quick happened, and Benedict wound up with his face pressed against the spire-stone floor while Brother Vincent held one of the warriorborn's arms straight out and up behind him at what seemed an extremely uncomfortable angle. The monk stood over him with one foot braced against his back, until Benedict grimaced and slapped the floor twice.

Brother Vincent obligingly released his arm, and the younger man lay quietly for a moment before gathering himself and rising to his feet. He rolled his shoulder several times, wincing. "What was that?"

"It would seem," Brother Vincent said, "that you have come to learn, young knight."

"I was fairly sure of that five minutes ago. You never showed me that combination."

"Didn't I?" Brother Vincent asked, smiling. "Goodness. Such an oversight. But I'm sure I haven't forgotten to show you anything else."

"I'm sure you didn't forget, brother," Benedict replied, his tone wry. "I think you just want me to come visit more often."

Brother Vincent smiled and clasped Benedict's shoulder with one hand for a moment. "It took time to soften your skull enough for ideas to slip in, but you proved a good student eventually. It is good to see you, son."

Benedict smiled and the two exchanged a bow. "Brother, we've come to the temple for help."

Vincent's dark eyes became troubled. "You know that we do not involve ourselves in politics, Sir Benedict."

"Nor would I ask you to do so," Benedict said. "Perhaps you could spare a cup of tea and a few moments of conversation?"

Brother Vincent studied Benedict's face for a moment before his gaze turned to take in the young man's companions. Bridget felt slightly uncomfortable beneath that gaze. It seemed as though the man could see a great deal more of her than he had any right to. Brother Vincent's stare lingered on Master Ferus the longest, and he sighed. "Then the rumors are true. War again."

"And the walls have ears," Benedict said.

"Of course, of course," Vincent said. "I'll get someone to cover my post. Do bring your companions inside."

Benedict nodded, and beckoned the rest of them. Bridget walked over to him and passed his weaponry back. "That was amazing," she said.

"That was typical," Benedict said, smiling. "Amazing would have been if I'd beaten him."

"How do you know him?"

"He was my mentor when I first came, several years ago," Benedict said. "I was considering joining the monks at the time."

Gwendolyn made a slight sniffing sound. "Ridiculous, Benny. You'd look wretched in saffron."

"It's not my best color," Benedict said gravely, nodding.

"He mostly wore purple back then," Brother Vincent said cheerfully.

"Purple?" Bridget asked.

"Bruises," Benedict clarified, smiling. "I was the kind of student who sometimes had difficulty listening."

"A teacher can always find other paths," Vincent said. "Ladies and gentlemen, won't you please come inside. Welcome to the Temple of the Way."

■ ■ ■ Chapter 26 ■ ■ ■

Spire Albion, Habble Landing,
Temple of the Way

Gwendolyn watched Bridget hand her cousin's weaponry back to him and carefully did not smirk. For goodness' sake, Gwen had been standing just as close to him, and with empty arms as well, and yet Benny had turned to the girl with the cat almost instinctively when he began to disarm himself.

Benedict had expressed to Gwen his determination to avoid entanglements with a wife in no uncertain terms on any number of occasions. He had even been something very nearly rude to Mother when she had pressed one too many partners upon him at a dance two years ago.

It was not as though there were no young ladies interested in him. Oh, granted, none of the highest tier of eligible ladies would have considered a union with a young warriorborn, even if he'd been a full member of House Lancaster—well, perhaps if he'd been the heir, she supposed. But the ladies of the lesser Houses could very well better their position through a union with Benedict.

There was also, she thought, always That Sort of Person, who would gladly seek a tryst with one of the warriorborn simply for the thrill of something so outré. Benedict was of course a fine-looking young man. He had been pursued by any number of young (or youngish) widows when he came of age, but he had ignored them all with steady, polite reserve.

Now he spoke quietly with Bridget and the Wayist monk, and Gwendolyn felt immensely pleased for him. She had known Bridget long enough to feel certain that she had no designs on Benedict for the sake of his endowments, monetary or otherwise. And while Bridget seemed to have very little in the way of social graces, such things could be learned. Anyway, courage and integrity were more important, and the girl had those in excess. The name of Tagwynn still carried weight in some corners of the habble, too. Mother could be convinced to bless such a union.

Of course, Benedict would be sure to make a hash of things if left to his own devices. Thank goodness he had someone to smooth the way for him—when the time was right, naturally.

Gwendolyn smiled in satisfaction and followed the monk into the temple with the rest of her group.

She was entirely unprepared for what she found in the interior of the temple. She had expected a rather simple arrangement—and indeed it was, in the extreme. But the monks had transformed the courtyard behind the temple's heavy gate into a garden so lush and thick that even those in her family's estates simply could not compare.

Every square foot that could be spared, she saw, had been devoted to planters of masonry filled with rich black earth transported painstakingly from the surface. Each planter supported a fine net of silken threads above it, spangled with small lumin crystals that glowed like a thousand stars, bathing the whole of the courtyard in rich silver radiance. Beneath the woven nets of light grew fruit trees, grapevines, rows of vegetables and grains—as well as flowers, small trees, ferns, and leafy bushes she could not identify. Foodstuffs growing from the filthy soil of the surface, rather than in a proper water garden treated with nutrient-bearing vatsand. The very thought was somewhat nauseating. Why do such a thing?

The *smell* of the place was simply shocking. It filled the air with a riot of scents, sharp and pungent, rotten and sweet, and above all, very, very *alive*. The air itself seemed different, thick and swollen with moisture. The impression of the whole was that of rampant life, growing as wild as the deadly green hell covering the surface of the world, and she felt her heart speed up in an immediate, irrational reaction of instinctive fear.

Her rational mind told her that clearly there was no danger here. Any number of monks were moving quietly through the plants in their saffron garb, trimming and tending and weeding. Insects buzzed through the air, many of them striped with yellow and black. Bees? Goodness, she hadn't known anyone had been able to successfully transplant a colony to Spire Albion. As far as she knew, only the Pikers had managed to successfully manage beehives, and their near-monopoly of the honey and mead market provided the cornerstone for their economy.

Well. If this garden could support something as fragile as bees, surely the place couldn't be all that threatening, regardless of how nightmarish it might look. She took a breath and steadied herself, and pressed forward through the vegetation, following her cousin and Brother Vincent.

There must have been two hundred feet of the bizarre gardens between the gate and the temple proper, which rose up to a height of four stories and was built of excellent masonry. The building looked nearly as square and as solid and as fixed as if it had been made of spirestone by the Builders themselves. Despite its height, it managed to appear squat and thick, as if determined to resist the sheer *idea* of any assault, much less the actual attack that might spring from such a notion. Two more of the monks, armed as Brother Vincent had been, stood at the main doors of the temple, and watched in stoic silence as Gwendolyn's group followed their guide within.

Gwen expected the inside of the temple to match its stony exterior, but to her surprise she found that it was warmly lit and decorated with paintings and banners bearing proverbs in Wayist script. Some of the paintings, though they depicted iconic figures of the Wayist faith, had been masterfully produced. In their own way, they were a match for the collection they'd seen in the Spirearch's Manor.

The floor was made of stone blocks, but was painted a deep green color, except for a brown path that wavered back and forth down the hallway. So many feet had walked upon the painted path that in its center, the paint had worn away and the stone itself had been worn down along with it. With the others, Gwen found herself naturally following the depression along the hallway, the soles of her feet an inch below the proper level of the floor.

"The meal room?" Benedict asked.

"It seems simplest," Brother Vincent said. The monk looked over his shoulder and smiled at Gwen. "You seem surprised, miss."

"It's . . . very lovely in here, really," Gwen found herself replying. "It's not at all like it appears to be on the outside."

"Is anything?" asked Brother Vincent with a small smile.

"Here we go," Benedict said beneath his breath.

Gwen arched an eyebrow at her cousin and turned back to Brother Vincent. "Wouldn't it be faster to walk in straight lines rather than wandering back and forth like this? This way does not seem sensible."

The monk's smile widened. "Did anyone forbid you to do so?"

"Well, no," Gwen said.

"Why aren't you walking the way you believe to be sensible, then?"

Gwen blinked. "Well . . . it was obviously the way everyone walks here, I suppose."

"Did you wish to avoid offending our sensibilities?"

"No. Not exactly," Gwen said. "It just . . . it seemed the proper thing to do."

Brother Vincent nodded. "Why?"

"Because . . . well, look at it. The stones are all worn down where everyone has walked."

"Do you feel you should walk the same path because so many have walked it before you came, miss?"

Gwen glanced at Benedict, but her cousin only looked back at her in silence, apparently interested in her answer. "No, of course not. Except yes, in a way. I hadn't really given it any thought."

"Few do." Brother Vincent bowed his head and turned to continue leading them down the hallway, and Gwen had the sudden impression, from his body language, that he was a teacher who had just concluded a lesson.

She felt her back stiffen slightly. "Brother Vincent," she said, in what she felt must be a tempered, yet iron tone. "Are you trying to trick me into becoming a Wayist?"

She couldn't see his face, but from where she stood she could see his cheeks round out as he smiled. "In the void, there is no distinction of east and west."

Gwen blinked slightly at that. "I know all of those words, and yet when strung together like that I have no idea what they mean."

The monk nodded. "Perhaps you are choosing not to hear them."

Gwen sighed in exasperation. "Benedict?"

Her cousin turned to walk backward for a few paces and smiled. "He's like that, coz. I don't know what he means, either. It's his way."

The monk carefully did not turn, and Gwen suddenly felt that the man might be laughing at her. So she sniffed once, lifted her chin firmly, and started walking in a straight line down the hall, Wayist custom be damned.

She tripped on the irregular surface a few seconds later, and all but fell. After that she lowered her chin enough to make sure she could watch where she put her feet.

"Pardon me, Brother," Master Ferus said a moment later. "But might I trouble you to show us the collection, if it isn't too much trouble? My apprentice has never seen it."

Brother Vincent's face lit up as if the etherealist had just offered to cook him a fine meal. "Of course, sir. It's on the way, after all."

Master Ferus beamed. "Excellent. Attend, Folly."

"Yes, master," the apprentice said.

"Collection?" Gwen asked. "What collection?"

Vincent's eyes gleamed. He stopped at a very large, very heavy door, and opened it with a gentle push of his hand. The enormous thing swung open wide silently and smoothly to reveal an immense chamber beyond.

"Ladies and gentlemen," he said in a quiet, vibrant tone. "The Great Library of Spire Albion."

Gwen felt her eyes widen.

The Great Library was huge—it must have taken up three-quarters of the space of the entire temple all by itself. The ground floor was filled with shelving and worktables, and every inch of shelf space was crammed with books—books of every size and shape and color. Why, the collection here beggared the one at her academy—that had been a library of nearly three thousand volumes, and it wouldn't have taken up a tenth of the space of the ground floor of the library—and there were three tiers of shelves circling the outer wall of the library above the ground floor, each accessed by balconies and multiple series of staircases. More monks moved around the upper floors, dusting and tidying the shelves. All in all there were more books in the library, Gwen felt sure, than she had seen in the entirety of her life outside it.

A dozen saffron-robed monks were seated at the tables, copying volumes by hand, while younger initiates carried paper, sprinkled sand over pages to dry the still-wet ink, and performed any number of other tasks to support the effort. Gentle music drifted through the air, from a pair of monks playing wooden flutes in elegantly interwoven melodies.

Gwen stared for several silent seconds and then realized that she was attempting to calculate the approximate value of the books, based solely upon their materials. The paper for each book was representative of more wood than its volume would suggest. House Lancaster had a library of several hundred volumes, but it was one of the wealthiest Houses in all of Spire Albion. Habble Morning's academy had nearly a thousand volumes collected over two centuries, some of them quite old and valuable. But this place . . .

The Great Library could scarcely have been more costly, in a purely monetary sense, if its walls and floors had been coated with gold.

But that was, she supposed, in keeping with the rest of Habble Landing. Entire *buildings* had been made of wood here, in their mad division of their working space. She had known the local economy was vigorous, but she'd had no idea that the level of commerce taking place here dwarfed that of Habble Morning itself. All that construction would have required milling of the wood, resulting in mountains of sawdust. Perhaps that had been the source of raw materials for the paper in the volumes before her. That might have lowered the price—but all the same, the books represented a genuine fortune, amongst a group of men and women who were known for their pathological avoidance of excess or material gain.

It also went a great way toward explaining why the monks so strongly discouraged casual visits to the temple, she supposed. Her own family's vatteries weren't precisely open to the public, either.

"Oh," Folly breathed out loud. The oddly dressed girl was staring at the library with round eyes. "Oh, is that . . . ?"

"Oh, yes," Master Ferus replied.

"I've never . . . never felt this in our library, master."

"Felt what?" Ferus asked. His voice was gentle but his eyes, thought Gwen, were rather sharp.

Folly was silent for a moment before she said, "I am not sure."

"Think on it," Ferus suggested. He turned to Brother Vincent and asked, "Might she remain here, quietly, while we take tea, Brother? I give you my word that she will give you no offense."

Brother Vincent bowed at the waist. Then he stepped aside and murmured something to one of the apprentices before moving back toward the group. "Miss, please do not touch any of the volumes without consulting with one of my order."

Folly tensed when the monk spoke to her, and cradled her jar of little crystals close to her chin. "Oh, he spoke to me. Ought I tell him that I understand? No, of course not—he knows now, because I asked you about it."

"There," Master Ferus said, with a pleased smile. "Now, about that tea?"

Brother Vincent studied the etherealist's apprentice for a speculative moment, then smiled at Master Ferus and said, "This way."

The monk led them to a modest dining hall featuring low, round tables made of copper-clad iron surrounded by sturdy cushions instead of chairs. Gwen was unsure of the dignity of such . . . novel seating, but she managed to sit down upon one of the cushions with what she felt sure was acceptable grace, and within moments they were sipping at cups of hot, excellent tea, sweetened with scandalous portions of honey. Rowl had a small bowl of his own. The cat wasn't satisfied until Bridget had spooned twice as much honey as anyone else had into it.

Once they had all sipped (or lapped), Brother Vincent nodded and turned to Benedict, who sat at his right. "Very well, then. Tell me."

Benedict made a round of introductions, and gave a concise account of the events of the past days, including the purpose of their own visit to Landing.

"In short," he said, "we need a place to stay that is free of any undue influence of the guilds. It was my hope that the Walker could be convinced to allow us to operate from here, Brother. It's the most secure place we could ask for."

"Walker?" Gwen asked.

"The foremost brother or sister at the temple," Brother Vincent said, smiling. He turned back to Benedict and shook his bald head. "I'm sorry, son. The laws of our order are precisely that. The Wayist temples do not take sides in political disputes of any kind."

"But this is your home," Gwen blurted. "If the Aurorans conquer Albion, they conquer you along with it."

"The Temple of the Way in Spire Aurora operates quite peacefully," Brother Vincent said in a mild tone. "We would deeply regret the loss of life that such a conquest would necessitate. We would help the wounded and the bereft in any way that we could. We would peaceably protest any inhumanity perpetrated by either side, and accept the consequences of that protest. But we are neither soldiers nor warriors here, Miss Lancaster. That is not our path."

"I don't remember asking you to fight anyone for me, Brother Vincent," Gwendolyn replied. "I have recently discovered that I have something of a knack for it."

"Should we permit you to use the temple as the base of your inquisition, it would create the impression of partisanship with the Spirearch. We deeply respect his authority and his restraint, but the purpose of our temple is to serve all humanity—not merely the inhabitants of one Spire."

Benedict smiled without much humor. "Which is the answer I expected you to give, Brother. Perhaps you have a suggestion as to where we might stay in relative safety. It's been a while since I was last here, and even then I didn't know the habble as well as the order does."

Brother Vincent took a long, slow sip of his tea, his eyes narrowed in thought. "If you're searching for an entirely honorable proprietor in this habble, I hope you brought considerable supplies to sustain you." He returned Benedict's faint smile with one of his own. "It's all the money, I think. It does strange things to some people."

"Surely some must be better than others," Benedict said.

"Some certainly appear to be," Vincent replied. "Whether the truth matches the appearance is another matter. I have often heard it said that anything in Landing has a price—especially loyalty."

Gwendolyn lowered her cup and stated, "We don't need an honorable innkeeper, Benny."

Her cousin blinked at her. "We don't?"

"Not at all. We simply need one who sells his loyalty with adequate integrity." She turned to Brother Vincent. "Is there an innkeeper who, when bought, remains bought?"

The monk raised his eyebrows. "A mercenary innkeep?"

"It is the quickest way, and we are in something of a hurry," Gwen said.

Vincent seemed to muse over that for a moment before saying, "Giving you even so little a thing as our advice strains the neutrality the order has worked hard to cultivate."

"What if we were not asking Brother Vincent?" Gwen said. "Suppose we ask my cousin's old teacher Vincent for a recommendation?"

"Sophistry," the monk said. "And threadbare, at that."

"We're simply having conversation over tea," Gwendolyn pointed out firmly. "It isn't as though the Spirearch has written requesting your aid."

Brother Vincent pursed his lips. "I must carefully consider the impact my actions might have on the order and other followers of the Way."

"While you're at it," Gwen said, "perhaps you should consider the impact your *lack* of action might have on the Wayists of Spire Albion— along with all of their neighbors. Surely they are included in the rolls of the humanity you say you wish to serve."

Brother Vincent blinked several times. Then he said in a mild tone, "You don't take hints terribly well, do you, Miss Lancaster?"

"Perhaps I'm choosing not to hear them," Gwen replied in a honeyed tone.

Something that looked suspiciously like a newborn smile suddenly danced in the monk's eyes.

Gwendolyn smiled brightly back at him.

■ ■ ■ Chapter 27 ■ ■ ■

Spire Albion, Habble Landing,
the Black Horse Inn

Bridget walked along a bit behind Benedict, whose eyes constantly scanned the streets around them as they walked from the temple to the inn Brother Vincent had named. She really shouldn't have been chattering at him on the way there. After all, it was his duty to watch for danger and protect Master Ferus from any attack. How could he do that effectively while she was hanging all over him?

"What did you discover, Folly?" Master Ferus was saying to his apprentice.

The oddly dressed girl frowned for half of a minute before she spoke. "Frozen souls."

"Ah!" Ferus said, raising a finger. "Yes, near enough. Well-done, child."

Folly beamed and hugged her jar of crystals to her chest. "But why haven't I ever felt anything like that in our study?"

"It is primarily a matter of density," Ferus replied. "One needs more than a handful of trees to see a forest."

Folly frowned at that. "It seemed as if . . . they spoke to one another?"

"Nothing quite so complex as that, I think," the etherealist said. "Some sort of communion, though, definitely."

Bridget cleared her throat and said tentatively, "Excuse me, Master Ferus?"

The etherealist and his apprentice turned their eyes to her. "Yes?" he asked.

"I do not mean to intrude, but . . . what are you talking about?"

"Books, my dear," Ferus replied. "Books."

Bridget blinked once. "Books do not have souls, sir."

"Those who write them do," Ferus said. "They leave bits and pieces behind them when they lay down the words, some scraps and smears of their essential nature." He sniffed. "Most untidy, really—but assemble enough scraps and one might have something approaching a whole."

"You believe that the library has a soul," Bridget said carefully.

"I do not *believe* it, young lady," Ferus said rather stiffly. "I know it."

"I . . . see," Bridget said. "Thank you for answering my question."

"You are welcome."

They kept going, following Benedict, and eventually came to the inn on a well-traveled portion of the streets leading to the gallery outside the shipyard. A sign hanging outside featured, as many of them did, the drawing of a fantastic animal that supposedly existed long ago—most of the inns in Habble Morning were so decorated, Bridget knew. The lettering beneath proclaimed the building to be the Black Horse Inn.

They went in and found the usual for such a place—a common room where food and drink were served, in essence a small pub or restaurant. The ceiling was really quite low. Benedict had to duck his head a little to avoid bumping it against the heavy beams supporting the second floor. The air was thick and smoky, too. Several men and women sitting huddled at the tables were holding pipes that smoldered with whatever weed they burned within them. Which was, strictly speaking, against the guidelines laid out by the Merciful Builders in the High Manual. Apparently they had viewed smoking as a serious sin.

But then, Habble Landing did have something of a reputation as a place of disinclination to piety. It was, after all, the home habble of the Wayist Temple, and had only a few small chapels to God in Heaven.

Here the guiding principle was the interest of business. And apparently at the Black Horse Inn, business was excellent.

There were three score people at least crowded into the common room, occupying every table. Two women were weaving as rapidly as they could through the room, carrying food and drink to the tables and taking away empty plates and cups. Back in the kitchen, dishes rattled and voices spoke loudly but without heat, evidence of a business operating at its full, focused speed.

"A moment, a moment, ladies and gentlemen," called a round-cheeked man in a rather plainly made jacket of silvery-grey raw ethersilk. Only after he'd said that did he take a look at them. Bridget saw his bright, rather closely set eyes take in Gwendolyn and Ferus's excellent (and expensive) clothing at a glance, and he came forward, rubbing his hands together to smile broadly at them. "We're quite busy, as you can see, but we'll clear you a table in a moment."

Benedict's stomach made a noise audible even over the chatter of the room. "Wonderful," he said.

"We also have need of lodging, sir," Gwendolyn said. "We've been told your establishment can serve our needs."

The innkeeper rubbed at his neck. "Ah, miss. I see. We'll be happy to get a hot meal into your bellies, travelers, but I'm afraid my rooms are all spoken for."

"I beg your pardon," Gwen said, smiling. "I'm not sure I heard you correctly."

"Well, miss," the innkeeper said, "times being what they are, what with an attack and maybe a war and so on . . . we've no rooms to rent, I'm afraid."

"They're full right now?" Gwendolyn asked. "Every one of them?"

"I'm sorry, but they are," the innkeeper lied. It was patently obvious from the expression on his face. Perhaps, Bridget reflected, turning down money was not something an entrepreneur of Habble Landing was emotionally equipped to take in his stride. But why wouldn't he simply rent her the rooms, if that was the case? Ah, it doubtless had to do with . . .

"Who is renting them?" Gwen asked brightly. "Perhaps I could make some sort of bargain with that person?"

"That's not any business of yours, miss. Meaning no offense, but I don't go blabbing about my customers or their business."

"I'm sure we can reach some kind of understanding," Gwendolyn stated.

"No rooms," the innkeeper said, his jaw setting stubbornly.

Gwendolyn Lancaster narrowed her eyes.

They decided to take their dinner in their suite, rather than shouldering their way into the Black Horse's common room. One of the women from downstairs delivered it on several stacked trays. The food came in hot and fresh, on the best plates the Black Horse had to offer, along with genuine silverware and several rather expensive bottles of mistwine.

Once the food had been set out on the room's small table, the serving woman left, and Folly shut and latched the door carefully behind her. The etherealist's apprentice looked wan, as if she hadn't eaten in days. Once the door was closed, the girl immediately hurried to the corner of the room farthest from it and settled down on the floor, holding her little jar of crystals carefully.

"Coz," Benedict said, opening the first bottle of mistwine, "I'm afraid you may have a thing or two to learn about bargaining for the best possible price."

"It isn't my task to save money," Gwen replied rather tartly. "I'm here to save time."

"Impossible, impossible," Master Ferus said. "Time is time. We can barely even see it, much less alter it."

Benedict poured the wine into their glasses calmly, despite his stomach's rumblings, before he seated himself and began to fill his plate. His motions, Bridget noted, were not hurried—but she could see the cords in his neck standing out with the effort of his restraint.

"Not time, then," Gwen said, "but trouble. Yes, we paid five times the price—"

"Ten times," Benedict interjected gently.

Gwen waved her hand. "The point is, we aren't wasting hours running back and forth to the temple until we find another inn."

"Point, child, a fair point," Master Ferus said.

"Littlemouse," said Rowl rather pointedly from the floor, "where should I sit?"

Bridget calmly cleared a little space on the table, put some roasted fowl on a small plate, and lifted Rowl up to the table to sit before it. The cat made a pleased, throaty sound and began nibbling away. "If I may ask," Bridget said hesitantly, "what is our next move?"

"Exploit the environment," Master Ferus said around a mouthful of beef. "The room below is an excellent place to sample the local climate for signs of unusual activity. Sir Sorellin, perhaps you would be willing to employ your talents to go down and listen? Pretend to be drinking, but don't become impaired."

Benedict swallowed hurriedly and cleared his throat. "Master Ferus, I fear that the Spirearch's orders prevent me from doing any such thing. I'm to stay within arm's reach of you."

The old etherealist blinked. "Oh, I suppose your orders could be interpreted that way, couldn't they?"

"Interpreted literally," Benedict said. "I'm afraid so."

"That being the case," Ferus said, "I will accompany you. It will add verisimilitude to have someone who is genuinely drunk at the table." He shook his head sadly. "Death is light as a feather, duty as heavy as a Spire, what?"

"Ah," Benedict said.

"Master Ferus, is that wise?" Gwen asked.

"It's an ancient proverb, handed down from the time of the Builders," Ferus replied. "Chronologically speaking, it is wisdom of the highest order."

"Not the proverb," Gwen said. "You, inebriated. It seems to me that you might have more difficulty pursuing your mission if you are drunk."

"I should far rather be drunk than *eaten*, Miss Lancaster," Ferus said in a serious tone. "As should we all. Very well, that's settled."

Gwen blinked.

The etherealist took a slow sip from his glass and nodded owlishly. "Master Sorellin and I will confront and destroy several more bottles of this rather excellent mistwine, and see what news can be passively gleaned. Meanwhile, the rest of you will go with Rowl and Bridget to make contact with the local cats. If anything out of the ordinary is happening in Habble Landing, they'll have noticed it."

Rowl looked up from his food to say, "He said my name first, Little-mouse. He has an excellent sense of priorities."

Bridget eyed Rowl and then looked back at the old man. "Master Ferus, forgive me, but I'm not sure exactly how long it might take to make contact. Cats are not known for their forthright hospitality when it comes to meeting strangers."

"I'll help," Gwen said calmly.

Bridget sighed. "I . . . think your help, in this particular endeavor, might be counterproductive."

Gwen frowned. "In what way?"

God in Heaven, she really doesn't realize what she's like when she's bearing down on some poor soul, Bridget thought. Aloud, she said, "Cats don't react well to, um, to . . ." She faltered and looked over at Benedict, silently pleading for help.

"Gwenness," Benedict said.

Gwen lifted an eyebrow. "In what way, precisely, did you mean that remark, coz?"

"In precisely every way," Benedict replied. "Your diplomatic efforts so far have consisted of instigating a duel, threatening detachment of Fleet Marines with charges of treason, throwing away a tidy little fortune in bribes, and abruptly discharging a gauntlet into an otherwise nonviolent situation."

"But—" Gwen began.

"Twice," Benedict said mildly.

Gwen regarded him steadily and gave her next bite of fowl a particularly stiff jab of her fork.

"I don't mean to insult you, Gwen, but . . . cats don't react well to the kind of pressure you bring to bear," Bridget said, "especially not when they're dealing with . . ."

"Invaders," Rowl muttered.

". . . newcomers," Bridget finished mildly.

Gwen rolled her eyes and said, "Very well. I shall keep myself out from underfoot, then."

"It's just for the first meeting," Bridget said quickly.

Benedict frowned at Bridget. "You shouldn't go alone."

"She isn't," the etherealist said. "Folly will be with her."

Bridget glanced at Folly. The girl was bouncing her little jar of crystals gently, and singing them a very quiet lullaby.

Benedict arched an eyebrow and said, "Ah."

"It's all right," Bridget said. "Fewer people mean less noise. Rowl will be able to hear potential threats well before they can come near enough to harm us."

Rowl groomed one of his front paws modestly.

"Right, then," Master Ferus said. "That's settled as well. Go forth; good hunting. Sir Benedict, let's get drunk."

■ ■ ■ Chapter 28 ■ ■ ■

Spire Albion, Habble Landing Shipyards,
AMS *Predator*

Grimm descended from the deck to the engineering section just as the engineers were carefully opening the crates marked with the crest of the Lancaster Vattery.

"Ah!" Journeyman cackled, rubbing his broad, callused hands together. The stocky, balding engineer was sweating despite the pleasantly cool afternoon. They had grounded the ship and throttled down her core crystal only about half an hour before, and the excess heat shed by the ship's power conduits had not yet dissipated. Currently electricity was running only to the lumin crystals and the kitchen. "Finally! Carefully now, man. If you crack one of my new crystals I'll hoist you up on a spike!"

Grimm cleared his throat calmly.

Journeyman squinted over his shoulder. "Ah," he said. "That is, I will report you to . . . to . . . the proper person in the chain of command, who will make decisions about discipline that are not mine to make."

"Always good to maintain discipline in your section, Chief," Grimm said pleasantly. "Even in a civilian vessel."

Journeyman flicked Grimm a quick salute and snorted. "*Preddy*'s a warship, Skipper. We all know that."

Grimm shrugged a shoulder. "When need be, Chief. Are the new parts up to spec?"

Journeyman waved a hand vaguely at the far workbench, where eight green-white crystals the size of a man's head sat in an orderly row in a long crate, like eggs in a nest. "Those are the new trim crystals, and they're first-rate. You can still smell the solution from the vat on them."

Grimm glanced at Journeyman sharply. Trim crystals of varying quality were often to be found, but never *new* ones. New trim crystals tended to be more efficient and more sensitive to varying degrees of current, and then gradually degraded with use. A ship with new trim crystals was slightly but significantly more maneuverable than one without—which was why they were universally snapped up by the Aetherium Fleet as rapidly as they were produced. "They're *new*?"

Journeyman gave Grimm a gap-toothed grin. "Bet you a fancy silk suit on it, Skip."

Grimm shook his head slowly, partly in answer to Journeyman and partly in slowly dawning realization of the amount of debt into which he had been placed. *Predator* would have been nimble even if the Spirearch had provided used lift crystals—with new ones she could dance with the finest in the world.

The last crate finally came open with a groan, and the engineering crew carefully broke it down around the last crystal, an enormous, oblong shape the size of a bathtub, its emerald surface faceted so finely that except for a few glitters of light upon it, it looked round and smooth. The lift crystal would socket into the suspension rig, the ship's structural foundation, and when they were in flight, all the weight of *Predator* would be spread across the crystal's surface.

"*Gorgeous*," Journeyman crooned, approaching the crystal with his hands outstretched. "Oh, you beautiful thing. Come here. Come here."

Grimm arched an eyebrow. "Ought I leave the two of you alone?"

Journeyman sniffed haughtily and then knelt down beside the crystal, running his hands over its surface. He muttered to himself, then started pulling probes and gauges from his tool belt. He popped a pair of engineer's optics over his nose, flicked several different lenses into place, and squinted at the crystal's surface, prodding and muttering.

Grimm gave him several minutes to study the lift crystal before he cleared his throat again. "Mister Journeyman?"

"Been some kind of mistake, Skip," Journeyman muttered.

Grimm leaned forward. "Mistake? How so?"

Journeyman hooked up a set of probes to a power outlet and touched them to the big crystal. Radiant spirals of light began to flow through the crystal just beneath where the probes touched. Journeyman eyed the spirals through his optics, then flicked them out of the way with an annoyed hand and did it again, this time watching a gauge to which the probes were attached. "Yep. Definitely a mistake."

"What's wrong with it, Chief?"

"Oh, not a damned thing, Skip," Journeyman said. "Brand-new, and one of their Mark IVs to boot. Efficient as hell."

Journeyman, Grimm reminded himself, was a genius with etheric technology. That was why they had managed to return home to Albion with an almost completely nonfunctional lift crystal in the first place— Journeyman had rigged the trim crystals to carry a load for which they had never been designed, and more or less burned them out in the process. He was a damned fine engineer, but at times Grimm wished he could be a bit less of a genius child entirely absorbed by his toys.

"Then what's the mistake, chief?"

Journeyman turned to squint at Grimm. "This is a battlecruiser's lift crystal, skip, or I'm a shiny new wollypog ensign."

Grimm grunted, frowning. Capital ships used multiple heavy crystals to maintain their altitude, and the crystals tended to be denser and more complex, which made them more energy efficient. The sheer mass of the large ships' structure and armor demanded nothing less. If what Journeyman said was true, that lift crystal could easily keep a ship thirty-five times *Predator*'s mass aloft. They'd have to be careful of how much power they fed to the crystal, or its raw power might tear it free of the suspension rig entirely. It was altogether possible that *Predator* might be able to *climb* faster than she could *dive* with a crystal like that to lift her.

"What kind of altitude could she take us to, chief?"

Journeyman scratched his ear with one broken-nailed finger. "Seven, maybe eight miles? Way higher'n we could breathe without tanks, anyway. For all practical purposes, she won't have an operational ceiling. And she's real efficient at lower altitude. Won't have to dump a quarter of the power we used to from the core into this sweetheart to keep us in the air."

One of the engineering crew let out a low whistle, and Grimm felt himself in heartfelt agreement with the sentiment. The largest part of a ship's power budget was allotted to its lift crystal. Less energy spent on keeping the ship afloat meant more power that could be used for other systems. They could get more speed out of the etheric web by charging it more highly, increase the density of *Predator's* shroud, and fire her cannon until their copper barrels melted. The Spirearch had given them parts of such quality that, when combined with her exceptional core crystal, *Predator* was about to become the fastest airship in Albion's Fleet, as fierce as any military vessel in her own class, with the ability to pour fire from her cannon that a cruiser might envy.

It didn't mean that *Predator* could take on a true armored warship like *Itasca*. But she would be far more elusive and difficult to bring down with a lucky shot—and any ship lighter than *Itasca* would get a very nasty surprise if it engaged Grimm's little ship.

"I love you," Journeyman said to the lift crystal. He kissed it and spread his arms across its surface in an embrace. "I love you. You big, beautiful beast, I want you to marry me. I want you to bear my children."

"Chief," Grimm said reproachfully, but his heart wasn't in it. Addison Albion had come through on his promise to a degree that Grimm could scarcely encompass. Grimm tried to calculate the cost of the Spirearch's largesse, and realized that he couldn't. Crystals like that weren't for sale. They were priceless—and they would make his ship into something far more swift and fearsome and efficient than she had ever been before.

The Spirearch had known that Grimm had no intention of taking service to him, but he had sent these crystals anyway. How did one, in good conscience, pay back a debt that by its very nature could not be calculated? How could Grimm turn his back on such a gesture of faith and walk away after a single errand? If there was a way to do so, he certainly did not see it.

Lord Albion, Grimm decided, was something of a judge of character.

"How long until you've got them all installed, chief?" he asked.

Journeyman looked up from the crystal and squinted around the section, evidently gathering his thoughts. "Trim crystals won't take but a day," he said. "They're standardized, and we can swap them out pretty quick. This lovely beast, though . . ." He rubbed his hands over the lift crystal's surface again. "This might take some time. Our suspension rig can handle her, but not until I make some modifications."

"How long?"

"And then there are the power runs," Journeyman said. "We'll have to install some resistors to reduce the current or those trim crystals will have us spinning upside down in midair the first time Kettle tries to bank. And we'll have to lay new runs to the web nodes, so that we can feed more current to the web."

"How long?"

"And there's the Haslett cages to consider, too. I'll have to calibrate them to account for the increased efficiency, and the core's cage, too, to let us run up a thicker shroud."

"Chief," Grimm said, keeping his patience with effort, "how *long*?"

Journeyman shrugged. "A month, maybe?"

If Grimm knew his engineer, he'd still be fussing over and massaging his new crystals into increased performance six months from now.

"There's a war on, chief. How long for the quick and dirty necessities, just to get us moving?"

Journeyman's face wrinkled as if he'd just caught a whiff of something foul. "Skipper," he protested.

Grimm let a hint of calm, cool steel creep into his voice. "I'm a captain. Humor me. How long."

The engineer scratched at the back of his neck, muttering. Then he said, "Maybe a week?"

"Run 'round-the-clock work shifts," Grimm said. "And if you can find any bonded local engineers, we'll hire them on."

Journeyman stared at Grimm as though Grimm had just suggested that the engineer should prostitute his mother to pirates. "In *my* engine room? Skip!"

"Do it, chief," Grimm said. "That's an order."

Journeyman muttered a bit more savagely under his breath. "A few days, then. For that, you get the most pathetic, slipshod, half-assed, rickety, unreliable, accident-prone potential disaster in the history of the airship."

"I have every faith in you, chief," Grimm said, turning to go. "Draw funds as you need them and get to it."

■ ■ ■ Chapter 29 ■ ■ ■

Spire Albion, Habble Landing

Four weeks ago, Bridget had lived a quiet and sensible existence, she thought. She worked with her father, took care of their customers, and often visited her poorer neighbors, bringing gifts of meat that hadn't sold and needed to be eaten. She attended school every other day, and occasionally ventured to the market to purchase what their home and business needed. She had been to the amphitheater half a dozen times to attend musical concerts, and gone biweekly to services at the Church of God in Heaven.

And now, she thought, she was wandering through a strange and possibly dangerous habble, her only companions a cat who regarded himself as the world's preeminent being, and a rather reedy girl who kept up a steady, muttered conversation with her jar of used crystals. What if she got lost? What if she came upon more footpads? What if she found the enemy before she made contact with the local cats?

At least in Habble Morning she'd had the implied authority of her uniform to hide behind. Now she wore only her regular clothes. Granted, the wide sleeves of her blouse concealed the gauntlet on her left hand almost completely—but she'd scarcely had time to learn to discharge one without killing someone by accident, much less doing so by conscious intention. She doubted her ability to hit a target more than three or four feet away if it came to a genuine combat situation.

She wasn't sure whether that made her better off than if she was completely unarmed, or worse.

Rowl rode on her shoulder, his head held at a high, cocky angle, as though he had recently conquered the place, laying a benign gaze upon his realm and subjects as their little party walked through one of the wider and more crowded tunnels of the habble's first level. The cat's nose never stopped twitching, and his ears flicked around alertly.

"Honestly, Rowl," Bridget murmured. "Are you certain you're watching for the local cats?"

"Even the sharpest eyes cannot see what is not there, Littlemouse," Rowl replied serenely. "Keep walking. Over toward those cooking places."

"I bought you a dumpling not half an hour ago," Bridget protested.

"Those smell good to me, and I want to smell them some more," Rowl said. "Any other cat worth the name would feel exactly the same way. Perhaps we will see them there."

"And perhaps as long as we're there, you'll have another bite?"

"Perhaps I shall."

"I should make you carry your pay around yourself."

"Metal circles," Rowl scoffed. "They are a human madness. A human should deal with them."

"He's right," Folly put in, from where she walked so close to Bridget's flank that Bridget feared to turn toward her too quickly lest she strike her with an elbow in the process. "Money is a madness, a delusion-illusion. It's not made of metal, really. It's made of time. How much is one's time worth? If one can convince enough people that one's time is an invaluable resource, then one has lots and lots of money. That's why one can spend time—only one can never get a refund."

"I see," Bridget said, though she didn't. "Well, in any case, shall we go over there?"

Folly leaned down and whispered to her jar, "She spoils the cat."

"A privilege I do not give to just anyone," Rowl said smugly.

Folly suddenly stopped in her tracks and let out a harsh hiss.

Bridget turned to the other girl as pedestrians nearly walked into her back and began to pour impatiently around her. The etherealist's apprentice was standing with her back ramrod-straight, her mismatched eyes very wide.

"Folly?" Bridget asked.

"It's here," Folly said in a whisper. "It's watching. We would tell Bridget about it if we could."

They were getting a few glares and mutters now as they slowed the foot traffic around them. Bridget didn't mind glowers and low curses—but she found herself very much concerned that their disruption of foot traffic called a great deal of attention to the two young women. It was quite the opposite of operating covertly.

She took Folly's arm firmly and guided the girl onto a side path. "Folly?" she asked. "What's here? What's watching?"

"Bridget doesn't know about the grim captain's visitors," Folly said, her eyes darting around. "But they're looking at us right now."

Bridget blinked. "Captain Grimm's visitor? Do you mean that commodore?"

"The one with the very large hat," Rowl added helpfully.

"She doesn't understand," Folly said to the jar. "These came before that, when the master treated the grim captain, on the day before they met."

"I'm a bit confused," Bridget said politely. "Master Ferus treated Captain Grimm before meeting him?"

Folly whispered to her jar, "If she keeps repeating everything I say, this is going to take much more time." She glanced around them and slowly exhaled. "There. I think . . . I think yes, there. We're alone now."

"Folly, I need you to help me understand," Bridget said. "Are you talking about Aurorans?"

Folly blinked several times and then said, her tone thoughtful, "She brings up an excellent point. Possibly. I feel awful, and I think I'll sit down."

The etherealist's apprentice sat down on the ground as if entirely exhausted, her knees curled up to her chest, her eyes sunken. She leaned her head back against the spirestone wall.

"Miss Folly," Bridget said, "are you quite all right?"

Folly patted her jar as a mother might a restless child and said, "It's all right. Bridget doesn't know how hard it is to hear things. Tell her that we're just tired and we need a moment."

"I see," Bridget said. She tilted her head, studying the other girl thoughtfully. She'd regarded Folly as someone who must have fallen into some kind of premature dotage, but . . . her answers were canny enough, if phrased quite oddly. Folly had said that she would have told Bridget something if she could, though by the simple act of saying as much, she had accomplished it.

"I noticed," Bridget said, "that Master Ferus seems to have difficulties with doorknobs."

"She doesn't know that the master is far too brilliant for such things," Folly said, nodding.

"And you," Bridget continued thoughtfully, "seem to have difficulty speaking directly to others."

"Oh, she uses her eyes and what's behind them as well," Folly said to her jar with a weary little smile. "That's two in one week. Perhaps I should write down the date."

"Remarkable," Bridget said. "Miss, I am very sorry if I said anything to offend you or if I haven't paid attention when you meant me to hear something. I didn't understand."

Rowl leaned down to peer at Folly. "She seemed no more ridiculous to me than most humans."

At that, Folly looked up and beamed a smile at Rowl. "Oh. He doesn't know that that's the kindest thing anyone's said about me since the master called me a gnatcatcher."

"And now we're back to being very odd," Bridget said. "But I shall try to make allowances for it, since we're to be working together."

Bridget felt Rowl's paw tap her cheek, and she turned her head in that direction.

The side lane where they'd stopped was dimly lit, even by the standards of Habble Landing. It reminded her of the tunnel where the footpads had lurked. For a second she didn't see whatever Rowl had warned her about—but then there was a flicker of light, and she saw a pair of green-gold eyes staring at them from the shadows, and around them was a grey-furred shape. A cat.

Bridget made a basket of her arms and Rowl leapt down to them, and then to the ground. The ginger cat ambled calmly down the alley toward the other feline. Then he sat down a few feet away from the other cat, ignored him entirely, and began to fastidiously groom his paws.

The stranger cat emerged from the gloom and sat down a bit closer to Rowl. Then he, too, promptly ignored the other cat and began grooming.

"Oh," Folly asked her jar. "Do you think Bridget knows if that is . . . cat diplomacy?"

"They've never explained it to me, but it's more of a power struggle, I think," Bridget replied. "I'm fairly sure it's about establishing which of them is the least impressed by the other."

"I wonder what is being established."

"A more capable cat is never impressed by a less capable cat."

"Oh," Folly said. "I see what she's saying now. They're seeing which of them is the proudest."

Bridget sighed and nodded. "Or at least which has the biggest ego."

"By ignoring each other," Folly said.

"Yes."

Folly frowned down at her jar. "I don't know all about cats, like Bridget, but it seems to me that this could be a prolonged contest."

"It often is."

"I wonder what we should do to hurry things along," Folly said to her jar.

"Hurry two cats?" Bridget asked, smiling at Rowl. "No. The cats didn't come to our habble looking for our help, Miss Folly. This is their custom, their way. We shall wait."

"We shall wait for three hours, apparently." Folly yawned to her jar of crystals.

"One learns patience, working in a vattery," Bridget said. "It doesn't matter how much one wants a batch to be done. It won't happen any faster. It's the same with cats."

Folly leaned down to her jar and whispered, "I don't think cats grow in vats, but we shouldn't say so aloud, for that might hurt her feelings and be unkind."

"You know what I meant," Bridget said, "though that was very amusing."

The other girl smiled downward, clearly pleased. "So few people understand my jokes. Usually they just give me very strange looks."

"I'm the girl who associates with cats," Bridget said. "Please believe that I know precisely the look you mean." Bridget checked on Rowl again, but the two cats remained locked in their war of mutual indifference. "I've been thinking about what the Spirearch said earlier. About the nature of Master Ferus's mission."

"She means 'secret mission,'" Folly said to her jar.

"Did he tell you what he was up to?"

Folly traced a fingertip along the outside of her jar. It might have been Bridget's imagination, but the tiny crystals inside seemed to give off the faintest glow of light where Folly's fingertip touched the glass. "Bridget doesn't understand the master very well," she said. "He guards knowledge like a banker guards coins."

"So you don't know exactly what he's looking for, either."

Folly smiled faintly without looking up. "He gave me a few pennies. They're quite frightful."

Bridget frowned. "But surely it isn't difficult to deduce that he means to locate the Auroran infiltrators and foil their plans."

"Bridget's logic seems sound," Folly said. "I was thinking almost the same thing."

Bridget nodded. "We're seeking the help of Albion cats to thwart the Aurorans. But they've been so successful at keeping their movements concealed that we still have no idea exactly where they are. That seems a remarkable accomplishment, to descend through the vents of half the habbles of a Spire without being observed by a cat somewhere. They must be doing something to make sure they go unseen. Do you think it possible that the Aurorans are also using cats as scouts, Folly?"

The etherealist's apprentice ducked her head a little at the mention of her name. The pitch of her voice dropped to a bare, low whisper. "Not cats. Not cats."

"Not cats," Bridget said. "It's something else, then. Something that frightens you."

"It's a terrifying penny," Folly said to her little jar. "I'm slightly mad, but not a fool. If Bridget knew, she'd be as afraid as I am."

Bridget felt a chill run neatly up her spine and leaned toward Folly, speaking more quietly. "You mean . . . something from . . ." Her mouth felt quite dry and she swallowed. "From the surface?"

It wasn't unheard-of for the creatures of the surface to gain access to a Spire. In fact, the smaller beasts did so regularly. A Spire contained literally hundreds of miles of ventilation tunnels and ducts, water channels, cisterns, sewage channels, and compost chambers. Metal grates were regularly installed where they could be, but constant contact with the outer atmosphere degraded their cladding and eventually left them vulnerable to iron rot.

Cats did far more to protect the residents of any Spire than humans realized, by hunting and killing such intruders. Granted, the lovely little bullies would have done so in any case, and not simply for food, but because they loved the hunt. Most folk tended to assume that cats preyed solely upon rodents and the like, which was certainly true, but in fact by working cooperatively, a tribe of cats could stalk and bring down prey considerably larger than themselves.

Sometimes, however, something too large and too dangerous for cats to handle managed to enter a Spire's tunnels. That was why every habble employed verminocitors, men and women who hunted such predators professionally, who maintained and repaired the defensive grates, and who tracked and killed nightmarish interlopers before the beasts could begin hunting the people of a Spire.

But those were wild creatures. If, somehow, the Aurorans had managed to train something from the *surface* to fight with their military . . . There were many stories and books and dramas written around the concept of some misguided soul attempting to tame the creatures of the surface, to train them to do their will. Such fictional figures universally met an identical fate: agony and death at the hands of their would-be pets—generally after a great loss of life.

Wild beasts could not *be* tamed. They could not *be* controlled. That was, after all, what made them *wild*.

"They don't belong here and they want to destroy us," Folly said to her jar, her eyes sick, but her tone matter-of-fact. "All of us. They don't care what Spire we call home."

"Well," Bridget said. "If the Aurorans truly are playing with that fire, it's only a matter of time before it burns them."

"I once had a dream of the world," Folly said. She gave Bridget's face a quick, flicking glance before looking down again. "And it all burned."

Bridget felt a shiver gather at the nape of her neck, and she said nothing. She looked away, back toward Rowl, waiting.

Chapter 30

Spire Albion, Habble Landing,
the Black Horse Inn

Benedict fetched their drinks when the bartender waved at them, and Master Ferus seized his rather large mug of beer with obvious enthusiasm and began tilting it back at once.

"Goodness," Gwen said, shaking her head. "I'm quite certain that a gentleman does not simply *attack* a drink so."

Ferus lowered the mug and wiped foam from his upper lip, beaming. "No, indeed, he does not. Fortunately I am absent any of the qualities that make a gentleman, and thus need not bother with the gentlemanly approach." He waved his empty mug at the bartender and said, "Another, Sir Benedict!"

Benedict, who had just sat, gave the old man a rather lopsided smile and then rose again, without complaint, to make another trek across the room and back. He came back with one enormous mug in each hand, and set them both down before Ferus.

The old etherealist beamed and said, "A man who plans ahead. Foresight, always foresight, it's the first trait of any formidable person at all."

"I just hoped to be able to sample mine before I had to get up again," Benedict said, and sipped demonstratively at his own drink. "How is your tea, coz?"

"Perfectly tepid," Gwendolyn answered, but she added a dollop of honey to it in any case, stirred it, and sipped. Even scarcely warm tea was tea, thank goodness, and something that felt very normal amidst all the strange events of the past few days. "Master Ferus . . . my word."

Ferus lowered the second emptied mug, coughed out a quiet, rather unobtrusive little belch, and smiled at her. "Yes, child?"

"I take it that you are not obliterating your good sense for no reason whatsoever."

He narrowed his eyes at her and gave Benedict a shrewdly conspiratorial glance. "Doesn't miss much, does she?"

"Despite what everyone tends to think, no," Benedict agreed in a polite tone. "I think she rather enjoys letting everyone believe she's too self-absorbed to notice anything that's happening around her."

"It's either that or let them think I'm some vapid twit. Like Mother," Gwen said. "I simply can't bring myself to stoop that low."

Ferus nodded sagely. "No, not a bit like your mother. Can't have that." He took the third mug in a comfortable grasp and smiled. "In fact, you are quite right, Miss Lancaster. There is a method to my madness. Well. To *this* particular madness, at any rate." He took a deep draft from the third mug, though at least he hadn't finished it in a single gulp.

"And what would that be?" Gwen prompted him.

"You must understand something of what we do," Ferus said, "or this will seem like foolishness."

"We? Etherealists, you mean?"

"Precisely," Ferus said, with another politely suppressed belch. "A great deal of what we strive to achieve happens as . . . as an instinct, I suppose one might say. We touch upon forces that others cannot sense."

"You mean the ether."

Ferus waved a hand in a rather exaggerated gesture. "That's simplifying a monstrously complex concept to its barest core, but yes, that will do. We sense etheric forces. Most people do, to some degree, though they rarely realize it."

"I'm sure I don't know what you mean," Gwen said.

"In fact, you do," Ferus replied. "That gauntlet you're wearing, for example."

"Yes?"

"What do you feel in it?"

"Nothing in particular," Gwen replied. "The crystal is a bit cool against my palm, but it always is."

"In strictest point of fact, miss, it isn't," Ferus said. "If you found yourself a thermal meter and compared the crystal's temperature to that of your skin, you would find them to be almost precisely the same."

Gwen frowned. "I assure you, sir, it is quite cool."

"It isn't," Ferus replied. "What you feel is the etheric energy that courses through the crystal. But your sensation of it is . . . something your mind was not sure what to do with, when you first encountered it. A wonderful place, the mind, but if it has any kind of disappointing failure, it's that it always attempts to put new things into the context of things which are already familiar to it. So your mind apparently decided, upon encountering this new sensation, that it might just as well label it 'cold' and get on with your day. And you are far from alone—it's one of the more common reactions to the first direct exposure to an intense field of etheric energy."

"The crystal on my gauntlet tingles," Benedict said, nodding. "A bit like when you've fallen asleep on your hand and the blood comes rushing back in. Though I'd never heard it explained in quite those terms before, Master Ferus."

"That sounds like nonsense," Gwen said. "Something is cold or it isn't, sir."

"Ah!" Ferus said, pointing a finger at her. "I had no idea you had an interest in philosophy! Splendid!"

"I beg your pardon," Gwen said. "I never mentioned philosophy."

"Didn't you?" Ferus replied. "You just heard Sir Benedict confirm that his experience with a weapons crystal was significantly different from your own. There is but one reality; that is true—but the two of you experience it in slightly different ways. The older you get, I should think, the more you will come to understand that the universe is very much a looking glass, Miss Lancaster."

"Meaning what, precisely?"

"That it reflects a great deal more of yourself to your senses than you probably know."

"Rubbish. If I look at a blue coat, I see a blue coat. The fact that I'm looking doesn't change that."

"Ah," Ferus said, raising a finger. "But suppose that what you see as the color *blue* is the same shade that Sir Benedict sees when he looks at something you would call *green*."

"But that doesn't happen," Gwen said.

"How do you know?" Ferus replied. "Can you see with Sir Benedict's eyes? And if you can, I should love to know the trick of it."

Gwen blinked several times. "So you're saying that it's possible that when I see blue, he sees green?"

"Not at all. He sees the color blue," the etherealist said. "But *his* color blue. Not yours."

Gwen frowned. She opened her mouth to object again, thought about it, and put her teeth together. "And if Benedict does, then perhaps everyone else does, too?"

Benedict smiled down at his cup. "It would do a great deal to explain the aesthetic tastes of House Astor, you must admit."

"Ugh," Gwen said with a shudder. "Yes, those people simply cannot coordinate their wardrobes properly."

"Now then," Ferus said, after another pull from his mug. "That's something perfectly simple and relatively minor—colors. What if other fundamental aspects of life seem quite different to others? What if their experience of heat and cold is different? What if they sense pleasure or pain differently? What if, to their eyes, gravity draws objects sideways instead of down? How would we know the difference, eh? We've all learned to call the same phenomena by certain names from the time we are quite small, after all. We could see things in utterly unique and amazing ways, and be quite ignorant of the fact."

"That sounds remarkably slipshod," Gwen said. "I'm sure that God in Heaven would not have created the world and its residents in such a ramshackle fashion."

"Ah!" Ferus said, beaming. "There, you are a philosopher already! A great many reasonable folk who have gone before you have put forth a similar argument."

"The real question, of course," Benedict said, "is why on earth it matters. After all, we seem to have a common frame of reference for blue, and when she says 'blue' I know what she is talking about, even if my blue is her green."

"It matters because it is philosophy," Ferus replied with an expression of sly wisdom. "If all philosophers took questions like yours seriously, Sir Benedict, they'd find themselves straight out of a career, now, wouldn't they?"

Gwen sipped at her tea, frowning some more. "But . . . I'm not saying that I agree with your proposition, of course, Master Ferus, but let us suppose that you are correct, for the sake of argument."

"Let us suppose," Ferus said.

"Then it would mean that . . . for all practical purposes, each of us lives in our own . . . universe-Spire, would it not? Perceiving all of it in our own fashion."

"Go on," Ferus said.

"Well," Gwen said, "if that is the case, then it seems quite remarkable to me that we've managed to establish any kind of communication at all."

Ferus arched an eyebrow. "Quick study, Miss Lancaster, very quick. Indeed. When we connect with our fellow mortal souls, something quite remarkable has happened. And perhaps one day, if we all work at it diligently and manage not to exterminate one another, we may even be able to see through one another's eyes." He beamed. "But for now, we'll have to make do with making good guesses, I suppose. Food for thought." He finished the third mug in another pull and waved for more.

Benedict cleared his throat. "Master Ferus, I'm afraid we've wandered from the original point."

"Have we?"

"Why are you getting drunk?" her cousin prompted gently.

"Ah!" Ferus said. He held out his empty mug to Benedict. "Would you mind terribly?"

"Your turn, I think, coz," Benedict said easily.

Gwen sighed, and fetched another pair of mugs for the etherealist.

"Lovely," Ferus said, and gulped some more. "Perceptions of etheric energy change from mind to mind, just as you and Sir Benedict demonstrate with your weapons crystals. And if one changes one's mind, that also changes the nature of those perceptions. This will allow me to perceive those energies in ways in which I would not normally be able to do so."

"You're getting drunk," Gwen said slowly, "so that you can experience etheric energy differently?"

Ferus held up his mug and said solemnly, "Think of it as goggles for one's mind, instead of one's eyes."

Benedict sipped at his drink, frowning. "You think you'll be able to sense the Aurorans' weapons crystals?"

Ferus waved a hand. "No, no, there are so many of those things about, it would be like searching for a needle in a barge-load of needles."

Gwen turned her teacup idly in her hands and said abruptly, "You think there's another etherealist here, don't you? And you think that . . . by changing your mind, it will be easier for you to find him."

Ferus nodded, though the gesture made his head wobble a bit. "Top marks." He put away another mug, and this time his finishing belch was rather louder. "Extrapolate."

Benedict suddenly smiled. "If you could sense him, he could sense you. So you are also changing your mind to make that more difficult."

Ferus slurred his sibilants severely. "Astute, sir, sincerely astute." He peered down toward the bottom of his mug. "Though I confess, I have not changed my mind quite this thoroughly in some time."

"Why?" Gwen asked. "I mean, why do you believe there's another person like you here?"

"It's complicated," Ferus said. "Or I seem to remember that it is, at any rate."

"The Auroran Fleet," Benedict said thoughtfully. "Their attack was precise. As if they'd had some kind of beacon to show them exactly where to dive through the mists. Could an etherealist manage such a thing, sir?"

"I daresay," Ferus said.

Gwen set her teacup aside. "And have you . . . changed your mind sufficiently to locate this person?"

Ferus eyed her and then his mug, unsteadily. "It would seem not. But it's likely a question of distance, methinks. If we get closer, I'll have a better sense of it."

"And that's why you're contacting the local cats," Gwen said. "To give you an idea of where to start looking."

"Time," Ferus said. "There's no time for a search pattern." He closed his eyes for a moment, and Gwen thought that he suddenly looked several years older, and several years wearier. "There's never enough time, you know."

Gwen traded a frown with her cousin. "Sir?"

Ferus shook his head. He took a swallow from the mug and put it down again. "Time to slow down now, I think."

Gwen nodded, and felt somewhat relieved. "Too much of such an indulgence can be dangerous, sir. What now?"

"Now?" Ferus sighed, without opening his eyes. "Now we wait."

"Is that wise, sir?" Benedict asked politely. "You do say that we're short on time."

"We always are," Ferus said. "At the moment it is all we can do, I'm afraid. Best get comfortable."

Gwen and Benedict traded another look, and Gwen nodded firmly. "In that case," she said, "I shall ask for properly hot tea."

▪ ▪ ▪ Chapter 31 ▪ ▪ ▪

Spire Albion, Habble Landing Shipyards,
AMS *Predator*

The door to Grimm's cabin opened a few inches and Kettle said, "Skipper, something you'll want to see."

Grimm blinked his eyes open, long-accustomed reflexes swinging his legs out of his bunk and his feet to the floor before he was able to focus his gaze. Night had fallen and the cabin was lit only by the light of a few large lumin crystals that were hung around Landing's shipyards, shining wanly through the small windows. He felt as though some kind of gum were squeezing his eyelids shut, but he knew it was nothing more than simple weariness. He must have been asleep for less than three or four hours for his body to feel so reluctant to get out of his bed.

"Skipper?"

Grimm felt an irrational surge of annoyance at the pilot and promptly clubbed it into submission. Kettle hadn't slept much more than Grimm had, and the man wouldn't have woken him if it wasn't important. "I hear you, Mister Kettle. I'll be out directly."

"Aye, sir," Kettle said quietly, and closed the door.

Grimm fumbled a lumin crystal to life, quickly washed himself from a basin of tepid water, and dressed. Captains did not arrive to address a crisis looking like an unmade bed. They were always calm, confident, and neatly turned out. If an enemy battleship was about to unleash a full broadside on a ship, the captain would face it with his hat straight and his cravat crisp and square. Anything else undermined the faith of a crew, increasing the chances of casualties, and was therefore unacceptable.

That said, a captain knew very well how time-critical any number of issues could be. On a Fleet ship, Grimm would have had a personal valet to manage a good many things and save him considerable personal time on a given day—but *Predator*, as a private vessel, could not afford the luxury. The upshot being that it took him nearly four minutes, instead of three, to cleanse himself, dress, buckle on his sword, tug his hat on firmly, and appear on the deck. His arm ached restlessly without its sling, and he could have done with a shave, but all things considered, it could wait until morning.

"The time, Mister Kettle?" Grimm asked as he emerged.

"Sixth bell," Kettle replied. "Three o'clock, sir."

Grimm strode to the ship's starboard rail and scowled up into the misty night sky at the vessel that was making its descent to the landing slip beside *Predator*'s.

She was a large armed merchantman, a third again *Predator*'s size, flying a Dalosian flag this night. She'd been painted smuggler-black all across her hull, though there were sharp white marks painted on her decks to show the way to her crew in darkness. Like *Predator*, she had masts for raising sail when the use of her web was not possible, though Grimm knew her sails to be stained storm-cloud grey and smudged with black smoke. A blazon of garish red paint at her prow named her the *Mistshark*.

"There, you see, sir?" Kettle growled. "What's *she* doing here?"

"Whatever it is," Grimm mused, "I think we can safely assume it is unlikely to make our sleep more restful."

"Could be we have a problem with that new number three gun, skipper," Kettle suggested darkly. "Maybe it goes off completely by mistake. Blows that bitch clean out of the sky. Terrible accident, sincere regrets, we all go to the funerals."

"Now, now, Mister Kettle. You know I would never condone such an action." He glanced aside and added in a whimsical undertone, "At least, not when it could be traced back to *Predator*." He narrowed his eyes, scanning the decks of the *Mistshark* for familiar faces. "Still, you know she took that slip intentionally. Make ready a side party if you would. She'll be here to gloat in a moment."

"There could be a horrible accident with a gauntlet," Kettle growled.

"If you please, Mister Kettle," Grimm said, keeping a firm note of reprimand in his tone.

"Side party, aye, aye, Captain," Kettle said, and stomped off, muttering under his breath.

Grimm nodded and went back to his cabin. He picked up his nicer bottles of liquor, his cutlery, his gauntlet, and a number of small, valuable objects, placed them all in his heavy cabinet, and locked it. Then he made the bunk neat and turned up his crystal lamps to their brightest levels. By the time he had finished, he could hear men on the deck of *Mistshark* shouting. Her captain would be on the way.

Grimm went back out on deck and eyed the other ship. A lean woman of an age with him but half a foot taller was coming down the gangplank onto the pier.

"No," she said firmly to the burly one-eyed ape of a man walking beside her—*Mistshark*'s first mate, Santos. "I absolutely forbid it. Unless you can find a way to make it look like it was someone else's ship that had the accident."

Santos spat out a curse, scowling, and put his hands on his hips. He glowered at his captain and then up at the deck of *Predator*.

The woman took notice of Santos's reaction, and turned on a low, heavy bootheel to gaze up at Grimm. Her expression turned into a perfectly amused smile. She wore an aeronaut's dark leather pants, a white blouse with roomy sleeves, and a tailored vest bearing intricately embroidered designs. She swept a hand up to her head and doffed her cap, giving him a formal bow, her arms spread at her sides.

Grimm scowled.

When she straightened again, the woman replaced her cap and said, "My dear, dearest, lovely Francis. You look absolutely delightful."

Grimm folded his arms and continued to scowl.

The woman laughed. "Francis, I do hope that in your usual charmingly predictable and courteous way, you have prepared to receive me. I'm coming aboard. With your permission, of course."

"Kettle keeps asking me to let him shoot you, Captain Ransom."

"But you never would," Ransom replied, smiling. "Not Francis Madison Grimm of the Albion Aetherium Fleet. Even though he isn't."

Grimm gave her a sour smile. "Let's get this over with, shall we?"

Ransom put a hand to her chest and made a sad face. "Oh, sweet Francis. You wound me with your lack of enthusiasm."

"I shall certainly wound you if you try to take anything that isn't yours while you're here."

"Everything's mine, Francis," she replied in a merry tone. "The only question is whether or not it *knows* it is yet."

Grimm jerked his head toward *Predator*'s gangplank in a peremptory gesture, and walked toward it without ever quite turning his back entirely on Captain Ransom.

The woman strode down the pier and around to *Predator*'s gangplank with steady, quick strides, and came up the ramp like a visiting monarch.

"Side party," Kettle snarled. "'ttention!"

Tension indeed, Grimm thought. Half a dozen armed men, three on either side of the gangplank, snapped to attention, and every single one of them kept his hand on his sword, his gauntlet primed and gently glowing. Kettle faced the gangplank and gave his best glare to Captain Ransom as she came up to the deck.

"Sweet Kettle," Ransom said. Something quite predatory came into her smile. "Does your knee still ache when it rains?"

"Aye," Kettle snarled. "And I make it feel better by breaking the noses of mouthy, sucker-punching, welching, treacherous Olympian bi—"

"Mister Kettle," Grimm said, his tone hard. "Captain Ransom is my guest. You will maintain courtesy and discipline aboard my vessel or I shall terminate your contract. Do I make myself perfectly clear?"

Kettle looked over his shoulder at Grimm sullenly. He grunted. Then he turned and snapped off a textbook salute to Captain Ransom.

Ransom returned it genially. "Permission to come aboard?"

"Granted," Kettle said through clenched teeth.

Grimm stepped forward and cleared his throat. "Conditionally, Captain Ransom. I believe you are familiar with my terms."

Ransom beamed and unfastened her gauntlet. Kettle stepped forward, warily, to accept it. Then she unbuckled her sword belt and passed that over as well. "Satisfied?"

"And the knives in your boots, if you please," Grimm said.

She reached down and withdrew two slender copper-clad blades from the tops of her boots, smiling without a hint of shame or repentance as she surrendered them. "I only put them there to give you an excuse to gaze at my lower half, Francis."

"How thoughtful," Grimm replied, his tone disinterested. "What's that at the small of your back?"

Ransom reached behind her, and every man in the side party rattled their swords to make sure they'd come clear of their scabbards if need be.

Her smile widened and she produced a small silver flask. "A lovely drop I picked up in Ethosia. You'd like it."

"Fool me twice, shame on me," Grimm said. "You won't be needing it."

She rolled her eyes and passed the flask over as well. "Don't you touch a drop of that flask, Kettle."

"No worries there," Kettle growled. "I know where it's been."

Ransom ignored the comment loftily. "Anything else, Francis?" She bobbed an eyebrow at him. "Should I strip out of my clothes as well?"

"That shall not be necessary," Grimm replied stiffly.

Ransom winked at him. "I do so appreciate the courtesy that is always shown me when I visit the second-fastest ship in the sky."

Grimm felt a flicker of utterly irrational annoyance at the mention of the race, and had to fight to keep from clenching his jaw. "It is how decent, civilized people behave, Captain Ransom. Though I suppose that to someone of your level of moral fortitude, it must seem remarkable."

She barked out a quick laugh. "I would say you'd scored a touch, Francis, if I had the least shred of desire for your good opinion." She strode across the deck breezily. "Don't bother to show me the way to your cabin, Captain. I'm sure I'll find it in the same place."

Grimm watched Ransom walk away, and permitted himself a slow exhalation and a narrow-eyed glare. Kettle stepped up next to him, his eyes wary.

"That woman," Grimm said quietly, "drives me quite insane."

Kettle grunted. "Why'd you marry her, then?"

Grimm followed her to his cabin and shut the door behind them. He leaned his shoulders back against the door and folded his arms over his chest, mostly to use his right arm to support his wounded left. "All right, Calliope," he said. "What are you going to make me regret this time?"

She tossed her hat casually onto his writing desk, settled onto his bunk, and stretched out along it with a smug assumption of the space. "Perhaps I missed you. Can't I pay an old friend a social call?"

"Friend," he said, his tone carefully devoid of emotion. "Empirical evidence suggests that you cannot."

She smiled, the expression impish, her green eyes sparkling in her strong, square face. Had an artist painted Calliope, no one would accuse her of extraordinary beauty, but somehow it was present in any case—in the way she held her head, the glitter in her eyes, in her sheer physical confidence. A still-life image of her was something of an oxymoron. Calliope was never still. Even when she was seemingly motionless, he could see her mind at work, sorting ideas, seeking solutions, cataloging the space around her. To see her beauty, one had to see her in motion.

"You've grown so cynical since the Admiralty cashiered you for obeying orders, Francis," she said. "It's most unbecoming."

Grimm simply stared at her.

Calliope rolled her eyes. "I'm almost certain that I remember you having a sense of humor sometime in the murky past, at the dawn of history."

"We used to have a lot of things," Grimm said in a neutral tone. "What do you want?"

"I want to make you an offer. An easy job with an excellent profit margin."

"How believable," Grimm said. "But I'm afraid I'd rather not lose another year's earnings to your amusements."

"It isn't about money," she replied.

"Since when?" Grimm said mildly.

"I'm doing quite well for myself now," Calliope replied. "Why, not a month ago we stumbled upon a damaged *Cortez*-class merchantman. She'd had a battlecruiser escort, but apparently it went haring off in pursuit of some dim-witted band of amateur pirates who had made a mess of attempting to take her. Her entire belly was as naked as a newborn. Took the ship and her cargo, sold them, and ransomed back her crew. I've enough money to bathe in at the moment."

Grimm snorted and opened his door. "I believe I've heard enough. Good day, Captain Ransom."

"No," she replied, her eyes hardening. "You haven't heard enough. Not yet. Hear me out. Give me one minute. If you don't like the offer, I'll go."

Grimm twisted his mouth into a frown. "We're done here."

Calliope sat up, her brows knitted, her gaze intense. "Mad," she said very quietly. "Please."

Grimm stared at her for several seconds. Then he shut the door again. "One minute," he said.

"Due to a clerical error, I find myself double-booked," she said. "I've half a load of vatsand bound for Olympia and the other full of medicine bound for Kissam. I can't make both deliveries in time. Help me out by taking the Olympia run, and I'll split the net profits with you."

"In theory, I should think a ninety-ten split would be more reasonable," Grimm said.

"You want ninety percent of *my* cargo?" Calliope asked.

"Ten percent and a solid reputation is a great deal more than nothing and a broken contract," Grimm said. "Theoretically."

She narrowed her eyes. "There's no point in trying to argue with you over this."

"None whatsoever. I'm not the one who needs help."

She pressed her lips together and then nodded once. "You leave me little choice, it would seem."

"In fact, I leave you none at all. I'm not available. That battlecruiser you mentioned gutted *Predator*. It'll be days before we can put sky under her again."

Calliope frowned. "What? She's not skyworthy?"

"Yet," Grimm said.

Those green eyes slipped into calculation and seemed to reach some sort of conclusion. She rose abruptly and reached for her hat. "Then I suppose I should seek help elsewhere. I'm sure someone would like the work."

Grimm nodded and opened the door for her. Captain Ransom strode out of the cabin and over to the gangplank, where Kettle warily returned her effects. She glanced back over one shoulder at Grimm, just for a second, and then departed the way she had come.

Kettle came over to his side. "What did she lie about?"

Grimm shrugged. "I'm not certain. All of it, likely. Said she had an easy-money job for us."

Kettle snorted.

"Precisely."

"And you told her no," Kettle said, rather carefully.

"Of course I did."

The pilot sagged a little with evident relief. "Ah. Fine. It's never good news when she shows up."

Grimm found himself frowning thoughtfully. "No. No, it isn't."

"Sir?"

"*Mistshark* arrives just as the Spire comes under attack?" Grimm asked. "Are we to think it a coincidence?"

Kettle grunted. "What do you mean?"

"The Spirearch sent us down to Landing to smoke out an enemy force," Grimm said. "And it just so happens that by chance, the fastest ship in the sky is docked in the Landing Shipyard?"

Kettle scowled. "*Predator* only lost that race because Santos sabotaged our main Haslett cage."

"Regardless of how it happened, she won," Grimm said. "She claimed the fame and glory. Such renown is a marketable commodity."

Kettle's frown deepened. "You think she's enemy transport?"

"I am disturbed by the presence of inordinate levels of coincidence,"

Grimm said. "I want eyes on *Mistshark* at all times, reporting anything, no matter how trivial. See it done."

Kettle nodded. "Aye, sir."

Grimm narrowed his eyes thoughtfully. "And after that . . . send Misters Journeyman and Stern to my cabin, please."

Kettle's concerned frown twisted up into a little smile and his eyes glittered with a sudden malicious light. "Ah. Yes, sir. I'll be delighted to."

Chapter 32

Spire Albion, Habble Landing,
Ventilation Tunnels

Major Espira seized the sword from the hand of the Auroran Marine braced at attention in front of him. He held up the weapon and inspected it minutely before snarling, "You've allowed the copper to wear through, right there, Marine." He held up the weapon a few inches from the Marine's eyes, so that the tiny spot of brown-red rust was clearly visible. "The iron rot's already begun. Can you see that?"

"Yes, sir," the Marine said.

"Why do we clad iron and steel with copper, Marine?"

The man's cheeks colored slightly. "To prevent iron rot from destroying the weapon, sir."

"Excellent. You do know. And once the iron rot sets into the steel, how long will it be before it spreads from this point and turns the entire thing to rust?"

"A few days, sir. Give or take."

Espira nodded. "This weapon will not kill whom you need it to kill if it shatters on the first stroke, or snaps when you attempt to draw it from the scabbard. I don't mind if your carelessness kills you—but it might also kill your brothers in arms, myself among them, when you fail to fulfill your duty."

The Marine swallowed, staring ahead, and said nothing.

"Well? What have you to say for yourself, Marine?"

"No excuse, sir," he replied.

Espira passed the weapon back with a sharp motion and said, "Report to the armorer, scour the rust off, and seal the bare spot with lead. Once that is done, you will perform maintenance on every spare weapon in the armory—and you will do so with flawless attention to detail. Understood?"

"Yes, sir," the Marine replied, saluting.

Espira glared all the way down the line of Marines from Second Company's first platoon. "In fact, why don't all of you prepare your weapons and gear for inspection? *Again*. When I return in one hour, each and every man of you will turn yourselves out like Auroran Marines, or God in Heaven bear witness, I will send every one of you up the ropes."

The faces of more than twenty hard-bitten professional soldiers went pale in a single wave of acute unease, and Espira let the silence weigh heavy before he said, "Dismissed."

The Marines all executed a drill-ground right face, despite not being ordered to, and marched quietly and efficiently away from the intersection chamber and back down the length of ventilation tunnel to their designated bivouac area.

"Barely looked like a real spot to me, Major," rumbled a deep-chested voice from behind him.

Espira turned to find Sergeant Ciriaco standing a few feet away, having approached in total silence. The warriorborn Marine threw him a crisp salute, which Espira returned with equal precision. "Sergeant. Once upon a time, the first sergeant I worked with taught me to keep nervous men focused on their mission with familiar routine and fear of my wrath if they deviated from it."

The other man relaxed, smiling a bit. "Did he? He teach you anything else?"

"Only to never expect him to arrive in a timely fashion," Espira said, not quite allowing himself a smile. "Where is Lieutenant Lazaro?"

Ciriaco's feline eyes glinted with buried rage. "Dead, sir."

Espira tilted his head. "How?"

"He ignored my advice and made a bad call," Ciriaco said. "Ran into what he thought were civilians tending wounded after the air strike. He tried to bluff his way past them instead of shooting them and moving on with our payload."

"Why?"

"One of them was a pretty girl. Looked like a porcelain doll. He was young, sir."

Espira frowned and nodded. Chivalry was a virtue held in high esteem in the upper echelons of Spire Aurora. It took young officers time to learn how seldom it could be indulged in combat. Unfortunately, actual combat could often be abruptly, lethally parsimonious in the matter of how much time it gave young soldiers to learn. "What happened?"

"They caught on to him, and the little doll lit up his face with a gauntlet from about two feet away."

Espira grunted. "Damn. The boy had promise. At least it was quick. The vattery?"

The sergeant shook his head. "Waited for the strike team to rendezvous but they never came, and we never got the explosives to them. Some kind of reserve Fleet officer with far too much initiative assembled a militia, brought it into the tunnels, and intercepted us. I presume the vattery team is dead, sir."

"Bah," Espira said. "It was only a side errand, and a sensible gamble, but it would have been a nice feather in our caps to have destroyed that damned crystal shop of theirs." He tilted his head, frowning at Ciriaco. "Are you shot, Sergeant?"

"A bit," Ciriaco said. "It'll pass. Damn fool Lazaro. Lost half the squad." He squinted down the hallway after the departed platoon. "Would you really send them up the ropes, sir?"

"Half a tithe of my strength? Don't be absurd. But at the moment, they need something to fear more than a Spire full of angry Albions."

Ciriaco's nostrils flared and his eyes shifted to one of the other tunnels leading off from the intersection chamber. "That why she's here?"

"Mind your tone, Sergeant," Espira said to the larger man. "You're one of the finest soldiers in Spire Aurora—but we all have our orders."

"Yes, sir."

Espira nodded, and then followed the sergeant's glance to the darkened tunnel. Madame Cavendish's batman, Sark, stood at the entrance to the tunnel, a sober, frightening figure in black, his walleyed face locked into an expression of perpetual boredom. No one with half an ounce of brains in his head would mistake him for anything but a lethal sentry.

Espira had been blocking it from his attention deliberately, with constant attention to the men—but now that all voices had fallen silent, he could hear it again: a high, pitiable, hopeless keening sound that came drifting brokenly out of the darkness.

"Ren?" Ciriaco asked in a whisper.

"A verminocitor stumbled onto the base," Espira replied, equally quietly. "We caught him, but not his partner. He says he was alone. She is here to verify his story."

"Knives?" the warriorborn guessed.

Espira shook his head and suppressed a shudder. "She took nothing with her."

"She's a mad beast," Ciriaco said.

"She is *our* mad beast," Espira corrected him. "Be glad she is on our side."

The warriorborn narrowed his eyes, staring intently at Sark, and rolled one of his shoulders stiffly, as if it pained him. "No, sir, Major," he said. "I don't think I will."

Just then footsteps sounded in the black hallway, firm and decisive. A moment later Madame Cavendish emerged from the darkness. She paused at Sark's side, and her batman handed her a small towel. It was only then that Espira noted that her nails and fingertips were wet and scarlet. The sobs in the tunnel continued unabated.

The etherealist calmly discarded the cloth and walked over to Espira. Sark loomed in her wake.

"Major," she said, "we have had a stroke of luck. He was indeed working alone, though he believes there will be a search for him in the next twenty-four hours or so."

"Disappear the body, ma'am?"

"God in Heaven, no," she replied. "That would only make the Verminocitors' Guild turn out in increasing numbers, searching more and more tunnels to find one of their own. Take the body and leave it where it will be found in the next few hours. Then there will be no search."

Espira nodded slowly, struggling to keep his face neutral. He looked down at the darkness from which weak sounds of despair still drifted. "He's alive, ma'am."

"What is left in that tunnel is a technicality," Cavendish said. "But it wouldn't do to have him found with sword strokes and blast wounds in him." She mused for a moment and then smiled. "Send him up the ropes."

Espira felt his throat tighten again, and his stomach twisted at the idea of doing that to any man, much less a hopeless, broken one. "Ma'am?"

"No more than a minute, or there won't be enough left to be identified," Cavendish said. She paused and then said, her voice harder, "Do you understand, Major? Do you know how long a minute is?"

Espira ground his teeth but said, "Yes, ma'am."

"Very well. Do your best not to interrupt my preparations again, won't you, dear? I'm expecting guests, and I must be ready to receive them."

With that, she turned and began walking calmly away. Sark watched them in silence until she was several paces away, and then he turned to follow her.

Ciriaco waited until Sark was gone to let out a low, leonine growl.

"We work with the materials we are given, Sergeant," Espira said.

The sobbing continued in the darkness.

"Ren," Ciriaco said quietly, "don't order me to send a living soul up the ropes."

"Of course I won't, old friend," Espira said quietly. "Break his neck. Send up the corpse. Dispose of it as Madame Cavendish specified."

Espira could feel Ciriaco's gaze on him, and then the warriorborn Marine sighed and nodded. "Yes, sir."

■ ■ ■ Chapter 33 ■ ■ ■

Spire Albion, Habble Landing

Bridget had nearly fallen asleep when, a number of hours later, both bored-looking cats abruptly whipped their heads in the same direction, ears pricked forward as if they'd heard something—although Bridget hadn't, beyond the normal muted noises of later hours in the habble.

After a moment frozen, both cats simultaneously rose, stretched, and yawned.

"Folly, wake up," Bridget said. "It's time."

Folly blinked her eyes open from where she'd been dozing with her head against the wall and looked around, apparently disoriented. "Whose time is it?"

"Shhh," Bridget said, listening intently.

"Adequate?" Rowl asked the other cat.

"So it would seem," the strange cat replied.

"Introductions?"

"Appropriate."

Both cats turned at the same time and sauntered toward Bridget and Folly, walking exactly shoulder-to-shoulder.

Folly peered sleepily at them as they approached, and whispered to her jar, "I wonder which of them won."

Bridget felt her eyebrows lifting. "I . . . I believe it was a draw," she whispered back. "This is a formidable member of his tribe." She sighed.

"Just our luck, when we're in such a rush, to meet someone who could ignore Rowl for so long."

"Ought we stand up?" Folly asked her jar worriedly. "Won't it be seen as disrespect if we do not?"

"A human who is sitting down is a human who cannot possibly pounce on a cat faster than the cat can spring away," Bridget replied. "Stay sitting. It's more polite."

"Oh, Bridget makes it perfectly sensible," Folly said, smiling. "I'm so glad I wondered aloud."

Rowl prowled over to Bridget and settled comfortably in her lap.

"Oh," said the strange cat. "They belong to you. I had wondered why they waited about."

"This one belongs to me," Rowl said, leaning his head up to nudge the underside of Bridget's chin. "That other one works for me."

"With you," Bridget said, beneath her breath.

Rowl flicked a careless ear. "It's the same thing." He turned to the strange cat and said, "I am Rowl, kit of Maul of the Silent Paws. This is Littlemouse. That one has not yet earned a real name."

"Her name is Folly," Bridget put in, saying all but Folly's name in Cat.

"No real name," agreed the other cat. "I am Neen, kit of Naun of the Nine-Claws."

"I have heard of the Nine-Claws," Rowl said. "They seem perfectly adequate."

"I have heard of the Silent Paws," Neen replied. "I find nothing overly objectionable about them."

"The humans of my habble sent Littlemouse here to ask for help from cats."

Neen lashed his tail thoughtfully. "That seems overly intelligent for humans."

"I thought the same," Rowl said. "Littlemouse, ask."

Bridget stared calmly at Neen, matching the cat's enigmatic, confident expression as best she could. "If it is not too much trouble, I would like to speak to your clan chief."

Neen tilted his head and returned her stare. "It almost sounds like a cat."

"It sounds precisely like a cat," Rowl replied, some of the hair along his spine rising. "Littlemouse is mine and I will thank you to remember it."

Bridget ran a hand down Rowl's spine in just the way he most preferred and hastened to add, "I know that this request is unusual, Neen, kit of Naun, but it is very important to the Spirearch, Lord Albion, and it may be that only the Nine-Claws can help us. I beg your indulgence in this matter, and will accept whatever decision you make in it."

Neen lashed his tail left and right for a moment before rising and saying, "It is Naun's place to decide, I think. Remain here. Naun will see you. Or he won't. Farewell, Rowl's Littlemouse." Then he turned and vanished into the shadows.

"Goodness, so abrupt," Folly muttered.

"Cats are not to be rushed," Bridget said. "On the other hand, it's rather difficult to slow them down, once they've decided to start." She traced Rowl's ears with her fingertips and said to him, "I take it we should wait."

"You should," Rowl said approvingly, turning in a circle and then lying down in her lap. "I, however, am weary from all that diplomacy. I shall sleep."

The Nine-Claws kept them waiting for all of half an hour.

Then a pair of large male cats appeared from the shadowed hallway. They sat down at the very limits of Bridget's vision, where the yellow-gold gleam of their eyes was the thing she could best see.

"Folly," Bridget said. She touched Rowl's back lightly, and the cat lifted his head at once. "Of course," he said, and yawned. "Now they are quick."

"It's as though they have no consideration for others at all," Bridget said in a dry tone.

"I suspect that they do not," Rowl growled. "But this is their territory. We must show them . . ." He shuddered. "Respect."

Bridget nodded firmly and said to Folly, "Let Rowl walk first. Stay even with me, shoulder-to-shoulder, and try not to look at any specific cat for more than a second or two—it makes them uneasy. Very well?"

"Don't worry," Folly said to her jar. "I'm here to protect you."

"Yes, thank goodness for that," Bridget said, rising as Rowl climbed out of her lap. She offered a hand to Folly and hauled the slender apprentice etherealist to her feet.

Rowl looked back and up at them, his expression enigmatic, then turned and prowled forward.

They followed the pair of male cats into darkness that rapidly swelled and swallowed them. Bridget would have been blind if not for Folly and her jar of expended lumin crystals. There must have been several hundred of the little crystals in the girl's container, each producing a faded remnant of its original glow. Any one of them could have barely produced light enough to be seen from the corner of one's eye—but taken together, they cast a very soft, nebulous radiance that at least allowed Bridget to follow the cats without walking into a wall or tripping over debris on the tunnel floor.

The pair of warriors—they could be nothing else, given their size, their silence, and their arrogant demeanor—led them into the ventilation tunnels of the east side of the Spire. While the Builders had created Spire Albion in the shape of a perfect circle, each habble was laid out as a square fitting within that circle. The extra spaces, at the cardinal points of the compass, were filled with a variety of supporting structures—cisterns, ventilation tunnels, waste tunnels, and the like. Cats generally preferred the smaller ventilation tunnels for habitation. Bridget could barely squeeze into one of the little tunnels and still wriggle forward, and she devoutly hoped that Naun would meet them in one of the larger tunnels or intersection chambers.

It took them only a few minutes to reach a large intersection chamber where, apparently, the Nine-Claws had decided to receive them. It was a roomy space, with ceilings that stretched up out of the meager light of Folly's jar, forty feet wide and perhaps twice as long. Eight ventilation tunnels intersected at this point, and the moving air of the Spire's living breath swirled around the chamber, a constant, droning sigh.

The far side of the chamber featured several pieces of wooden furniture, including a footstool, a wooden chair, a high barstool, and an impressive, darkly stained table. They were lined up in that order as well, obviously as stairs leading up to what amounted to a dais.

A score of warrior cats were arrayed on the various pieces of furniture or on the ground at their feet—up to the large table, where a single, heavily muscled tomcat of purest black sat with his eyes mostly closed. On the barstool, just below the level of the table, sat Neen, with a bored expression, though his tail lashed left and right in agitation.

"He has his *own* furniture?" Rowl demanded, under his breath. "Oh. That is simply outrageous. What is he doing with those? Cats have no need for such things."

"Why do I suspect you're going to want me to buy some for you?" Bridget asked.

"That is not the point." Rowl sniffed. "We will discuss such matters later."

Bridget kept herself from showing any teeth when she smiled and looked carefully around the large chamber. There were a great many cats looking on. In the wan light Folly held, she could see little of them but for indistinct shapes and the flicker of reflections of green-gold eyes.

Hundreds of them.

"Oh, my," Folly whispered. "There are certainly more cats here than I have seen in the duration of my life. And oh, look. Kittens."

Bridget arched a brow sharply, and turned her head to follow the direction Folly was pointing out to her jar. She did indeed spy several tiny sets of eyes, many of them coming closer as the curious kittens crept forward, noses extended, their ears pricked toward the visitors. *That* was odd. Cats did *not* expose their kittens to humans. Even Bridget and her father, with their strong relationship with the Silent Paws, had seen kittens no more than half a dozen times in her life.

And now the Nine-Claws had received them in the very same communal chamber where their kittens were being cared for. In fact . . .

"This is all of them," Bridget breathed to Rowl. "This is the entire clan. Kittens and all."

Rowl narrowed his eyes and made a quiet sound in his throat. "Impossible. Too many tunnels must be watched and guarded and held against encroachers." But even as he said it, Bridget saw his eyes scanning the room, taking an approximate count of their hosts.

"They're nervous," Folly whispered. "Banding together for safety."

"Cats don't do that," Bridget said, or began to say—but she stopped herself. Cats absolutely operated in groups to hunt and defend territory more safely. But they certainly did not ever allow themselves to appear to be doing such a thing. Such a lack of independence would be seen as unacceptable.

Even a "team" of cats working together tended to be a loose coalition more than anything, and lasted no longer than was necessary. Clan chiefs like Maul or Naun maintained their position through a dense, complicated network of one-on-one relationships, through building a general consensus, and when necessary through the exertion of personal pressure where possible, and force when necessary. Getting half a dozen cats to agree upon almost anything was the next-best thing to impossible.

Getting several *hundred* to move together, to abandon their individual territories, to share a single living space was . . .

. . . unheard-of. Literally. From all she knew of cats, Bridget would never have believed such a tale if someone had told it to her.

What in the name of God in Heaven was happening in this habble?

Rowl strolled forward through the chamber as if there weren't enough potentially hostile cats surrounding them to smother them all to death beneath their sheer weight. As deaths went, Bridget thought, being asphyxiated by warm, soft, furry little beasts seemed a bit less ghastly than some she had considered lately, but nonetheless she preferred to avoid it. Rowl, generally speaking, knew very well what he was about—but when his natural ability and confidence failed, the results tended to be the sorts of events one felt obligated to write down in one's diary. She hoped, rather fervently, that this would not be one of those occasions.

Rowl went straight to the lowest stool and mounted it as calmly as if it had belonged to him, and the cats who sat there were forced to give way awkwardly at the last moment or else find themselves bowled over. Rowl proceeded up the pieces of furniture until he reached the high stool upon which sat Neen. Once he had reached that, Rowl calmly took a seat beside his counterpart and faced Naun attentively.

Naun watched this display with narrowed eyes, and the tip of his tail twitched once or twice. Then he eyed Neen.

Neen idly lifted a paw, cleaning it fastidiously. He was not precisely ignoring his clan chief—but he was, Bridget felt, walking near some sort of boundary.

Naun's voice was a deep growling tone. "You are Rowl of the Silent Paws."

"I know that," said Rowl. After a moment he added, "Sire of the Nine-Claws."

Naun growled in his chest. "Arrogant. Just like the other Silent Paws who have visited my domain."

"I know that, too," Rowl said. "You know why I have brought these humans to you."

"Yes," Naun said. His green-gold eyes flicked to Folly and Bridget. "They believe we owe them some sort of service."

"Sire of the Nine-Claws," Bridget said, taking a small step forward.

That drew the eye of every cat there. Bridget felt rather abruptly severely unnerved by the attention of so many consummate predators, however small each of them might be individually. She swallowed and kept her voice steady. "Lord Albion, the Spirearch, sent us to request your aid in a matter in which we believe only the Nine-Claws can help us."

Naun peered at Bridget and tilted his head this way and that for a moment. "Is that some kind of trick, kit of Maul? Like when the humans make those hideous dolls appear to speak?"

"It is no trick, sire," Rowl said easily. "This is my human, Little-mouse."

"And it *speaks*," Naun mused.

"As I told you," Neen noted.

The elder Nine-Claw eyed his kit and considered his own front paws for a moment, as if deciding whether or not he needed to choose one with which to reply.

Rowl feinted at Neen's nose with one paw and the other young cat flinched. Instantly every warrior cat in the place was on its feet, and Bridget felt almost certain that she could actually *hear* the mass of fur upon spines suddenly springing straight up. The air whispered with hundreds of low sounds of feline warning.

Bridget found herself holding her breath.

Rowl ignored the chorus of angry growls with a certain magnificent indifference to reality, looking at Neen in strict disapproval.

"Respect your sire," Rowl said severely. "Or you will oblige him to teach you, here and now, when he obviously has greater concerns before him."

Neen blinked at Rowl several times. He took note of the room, and all the cats staring at him, and abruptly became disinterested, looking out at nothing in particular, his eyes half closing.

There was a long silence. And then Naun let out a low sound of amusement, and his ears assumed a more relaxed, attentive angle. Bridget felt her pent-up breath slowly easing out of her again, as several dozen of the watching cats joined their clan chief in sharing their amusement.

"You have courage, Rowl Silent Paw," Naun noted. "Or you are mad."

"I know that, too," Rowl replied. "Will you hear Littlemouse's request?"

"Littlemouse," Naun said, his gaze traveling up and down Bridget's large frame. "A fine name for her."

"She grew more than was expected," Rowl explained. "It was most inconsiderate, but what can one expect?"

"Humans rarely concern themselves with the needs of cats," Naun agreed. "And those who do are rarely to be trusted."

Rowl lifted his chin. "Littlemouse, kit of Wordkeeper, is exceptional."

Naun studied Bridget with unblinking eyes for a time. Then he said, "Rowl, kit of Maul, you are a welcome guest in my domain."

Rowl tilted his head sharply to one side. "Whatever do you mean, sire?"

Naun's unreadable eyes, for an instant, were hot with rage. "The Nine-Claws are no friends to humans. No matter to whom they belong." The older cat turned to stare hard at Bridget. "Littlemouse, kit of Wordkeeper, you and your companion are unwelcome here. You will depart immediately. You will not return to these tunnels; nor will you attempt to make contact with my clan. Should you refuse to abide by either of these commands, your lives are forfeit."

Bridget opened her mouth, startled. "But . . . sire, surely if you would only hear me out."

"I *know* why you are *here*," Naun snarled, rising to all fours. "I know you seek to enlist our aid as eyes and ears in the coming conflict, but you will not have it. The war is a human war. It is not a cat war. The Nine-Claws will not care if your enemies slaughter every last man, woman, and child—it is all the same to us. We will go on as we have with whatever batch of humans rules this habble."

Bridget bit her lip. Well. That was unacceptable. She couldn't simply return and explain to Master Ferus that the cats had said no, and what might be his next idea? Miss Lancaster would *surely* not simply abide by that conclusion. But what could be done? Within this setting, Naun's word was law. And though most people thought cats to be little more than vicious little vermin, good mostly for killing even worse little vermin, Bridget was perfectly aware that cats were willing and able to bring down human beings if they chose to do so. Naun could absolutely make good on his threat. If Naun so ordered it, none of them would leave this chamber.

Even so, Bridget had a duty to perform. She had no intention of failing in it. She squared her shoulders and took a deep breath, ready to try again.

Folly abruptly seized Bridget's wrist, and the slender girl's fingers felt like cold, hard bronze.

"No," Folly hissed. "Can she not see it?"

"See what?" Bridget whispered back.

Folly turned her head slowly, her eyes raking over the chamber, the shadows, the silent, tense forms of the Nine-Claws clan.

"They are *afraid*," Folly breathed, barely audible, her lips hardly moving at all. "They are being *watched*."

Bridget's mouth suddenly felt dry, her throat tight. "Here? Now?"

Folly nodded her head in so slow and slight a motion that Bridget almost thought she had imagined it.

Naun turned, the motion deliberate, his dark fur rippling in the dim light of Folly's jar, speaking in a slow, heavy voice. "You will be shown from this place and put on a path back to the human quarter of the habble." He paused to glance over his shoulder at Neen and said, his voice heavy with weariness, "Show them to the ropes."

■ ■ ■ Chapter 34 ■ ■ ■

Spire Albion, Habble Landing,
Ventilation Tunnels

Rowl, Littlemouse, and the slightly odder-than-usual human girl walked in a circle of Naun's hardiest warriors, half a dozen big, battle-scarred toms, most of whom were nearly Rowl's size. Each warrior wore a pair of fighting spurs — curved metal blades fashioned by humans and attached to leather cuffs that wrapped around a cat's rear legs. The spurs were sharp enough, when used properly, to be more than a little dangerous.

Rowl felt that the escort was largely symbolic. None of them were his match, spurs or not, and Littlemouse, of course, was both armed and an exceptional human, with strength that had even impressed the half-soul, Benedict. It would take a dozen experienced warriors, at least, to bring down a human like Littlemouse.

Rowl growled in his throat. The first to try it would not live long enough to touch her.

And that was what this was about. Naun had extended his hospitality and with it his offer of protection — to Rowl. He had made no such offer for Littlemouse and Folly. Clearly Naun had no love of humans, for which Rowl could hardly blame him. As a matter of history, cats had usually come to regret entanglements with humans. Humans were fickle, prone to changing their minds without warning or reason. There were very few reliable human beings, even with the half-souls among them—which was why those such as Littlemouse and Wordkeeper were so very exceptional. It was why no sane cat allowed kits to come anywhere near human beings. Humans seemed to feel that it was perfectly acceptable to teach kits to accept food from their hands as a matter of course, rather than teaching them the importance of hunting skill and self-reliance.

Once one had to depend upon someone else for food, one had to depend upon someone else for life itself. To give humans such power over cats was an abomination, but it was far from the only indignity or injustice that humans had meted out over the centuries—including active hunts of cats, at times, blaming them for things no cat would have done for any reason, attempting to poison their food supply or their water. Cats and humans regularly clashed in places where their understanding of the local human population was incomplete, and mutual pain was the inevitable result of such a breakdown of basic comprehension. If Naun had suffered through something like it, or if those he cared for had suffered, it could easily drive him to irrational hatred of even exceptional humans like Littlemouse.

There were only a few reasons Naun would send them from his territory on a course so different from the one they had taken when they arrived, none of them pleasant. Certainly, Rowl thought, Naun meant for something to happen—something of which he did not (and perhaps *could* not, if Folly was correct) speak aloud. Rowl's instincts kept repeating calmly that Naun intended to expose them to some kind of danger.

Which was perfectly fine. Rowl could handle any reasonable amount of danger, and between himself and Littlemouse he felt that there were few challenges that need occupy his thoughts with undue concern. The real question to him was why Naun would do such a thing. It seemed somewhat rude, especially to a visiting clan chief's heir, but then, Rowl did not yet know everything that was happening—practically everything, he felt certain, but there might be some nuance to the situation, or to Naun's motivations, that the local clan chief intended to show him. Or it could be simple treachery.

Rowl had no preference. In either case, he would deal with the problem and then respond to Naun in whatever manner was most appropriate and tasteful. When had he done anything else?

The little group reached the mouth of a side tunnel, and the leader of the escort of Nine-Claws toms came to a halt. "There," the cat said. "Down that tunnel. Keep going and it will lead you out into the human section of the habble."

"Will it?" Rowl asked calmly.

"Yes."

"But you aren't going there," Rowl said.

"No."

"You are stopping here," Rowl said.

"Yes."

"Because you are afraid."

The other cat stared at Rowl with flat eyes.

Rowl yawned his unconcern. "If you wish to keep those eyes," he said pleasantly, "move them elsewhere."

"Rowl," Littlemouse breathed in protest. Littlemouse was such a tender, sensitive thing. Threatening to rip out someone's eyes was probably something she regarded as shocking, no matter how sincere Rowl might be, or how well earned the threat had been. Rowl looked up at her fondly, then turned his attention back to their escort.

The threat drew a response from the rest of the Nine-Claws present, and they all turned to stare at Rowl.

Rowl returned their gazes one by one. And one by one they turned disinterestedly away from him, as if they'd found their conflict to have suddenly become unspeakably dull.

Rowl lashed his tail in satisfaction and said to Littlemouse, "Shall we?"

"Of course," Littlemouse replied. "Would you like me to carry you?"

Rowl considered the question gravely. "No," he decided. "You should be ready to use your gauntlet instead."

Bridget's eyebrows went up, but instead of protesting, she calmly rolled her sleeve all the way up and away from the gauntlet. As Rowl understood it, there was no real need for such an action, as long as Littlemouse didn't use the gauntlet too much—but the copper cages around the devices grew very hot after a time, and could set cloth aflame.

Folly, meanwhile, stared at the new tunnel's blackness with wide, frightened eyes. Rowl approved. Fear was wisdom in a situation like this, and he was pleased that Folly was obviously intelligent enough to know it. He hoped that she would use the fear to make her cleverer, rather than more foolish, but that was asking much of a human, relatively odd or not.

"I wonder," Folly said to the jar, "could we go another way? A way that is not down this tunnel?"

"Unlikely," Rowl said. "Naun means us to walk down that tunnel. To refuse him would be to challenge his rule."

"Oh, dear," Folly said.

"I think you should walk on my right," Littlemouse said to Folly. Littlemouse was afraid—Rowl could hear her elevated heartbeat—but her voice was as calm and regular as a cat's. He felt that he deserved most of the credit for teaching her that. "That way I can lift my gauntlet hand without bumping into you."

"Oh, yes, she's quite right," Folly said, nodding, and stepped up to stand a little behind Littlemouse and to her right. "But one of us should tell her that I would prefer another tunnel—any other tunnel at all in the world—to this one."

"Hold the lights up, please?" Littlemouse asked. "The sooner I can see a potential threat, the sooner I can attempt to blast it."

Folly solemnly lifted her little jar of crystals to her chin.

"Thank you," Littlemouse said.

"I will go first," Rowl told her. "Please do not tread upon my tail. I find it demeaning."

"I haven't done that since I was eleven," Littlemouse said, smiling.

"Yet," Rowl said. Then he flicked his tail left and right and started down the tunnel. After he had taken a few steps, the clothing of the humans rustled and they began walking steadily along behind him.

There was a strange scent in the tunnel, and Rowl noted it immediately. It was creature flesh—he knew that much—something that had come into the Spire from the surface, its scent pungent and unsettling in his nose. There was the foul taint to it that Rowl had learned to associate with poisonous, inedible kills while he was still a fuzzy little kit. So something particularly strange and perhaps particularly dangerous had recently been in this tunnel.

Rowl objected. Granted, the Nine-Claws territory was not his to defend, but it seemed grotesquely inappropriate that something should go to all the trouble of coming this far up the Spire from the surface, only to prove utterly useless as food after it should be hunted. It seemed very rude to make a cat go to all the work of hunting and killing it and then not provide the victory feast after the successful conclusion to the hunt.

"Ahead," Folly breathed. "Something. The ceiling."

They had to walk another forty steps (fewer for the humans, he supposed) before even his eyes could make out something in the near-perfect shadows of the tunnel's ceiling. The ceiling was perhaps two or three pounces above them, and made of conventional stone, rather than spirestone. The humans of Habble Landing had halved the height of the tunnels as well, though Rowl was sure he did not know why they would do such a foolish thing. To provide more tunnels for the top half of their habble, Rowl supposed.

There was, Rowl noted, a hole in the ceiling, as wide as the length of his body and tail. From the hole trailed dozens of long lines of some kind, something like all the long ropes on Grimm's airship, but made of different material than those had been. They stirred gently in the breeze of the tunnel. As they did, they reflected hundreds of tiny, random colors of light from the jar Folly carried.

It was a moment more before Littlemouse and Folly were able to see the lines, and at that point their steps slowed and stopped.

"What . . . what is that?" Littlemouse breathed. "What are those ropes made of?"

"Ethersilk," Folly whispered.

"Ethersilk *rope*?" Littlemouse asked, her mouth open. "Who could afford to make such a thing?"

"It isn't rope," Folly told her jar. "But she doesn't know that. She's probably never seen what it looks like before it's been harvested."

"Harvested?" Littlemouse asked. Then she drew in a short, sharp breath. "Silkweavers. That's what you mean, isn't it?"

Folly stared at the hole as though she could not look away and nodded in silence.

Bridget shook her head. "But they live on the surface, and in the mists. They don't . . . To weave a strand that big, they would have to be enormous. And God in Heaven, what lunatic would attempt to *tame* them? Fools have been trying to domesticate them for their silk for two thousand years with no success. With no *survivors*."

"In my opinion, humans are sufficiently foolish to attempt it again," Rowl noted.

"Oh!" Folly said suddenly, and staggered back several steps, flinching away from some unseen threat. "Watch out!"

Rowl stared at the odd human, and for a baffled second nothing happened.

And then there was a chorus of high-pitched, eerie sounds, and dozens of silkweavers plunged through the hole and plummeted toward them.

Rowl had never seen one of the creatures before, but he had learned his people's lore about the silkweavers, along with a nightmarish menagerie of creatures like them. He knew them, knew how they hunted—and he knew how to kill them.

The first movements proved to be half a dozen creatures about half of Rowl's own size, he estimated. They had a dozen legs, spread out along either side of a lean, hard-scaled body that made them look something like overly enthused silverfish. Their heads, however, were bulbous, sporting short muzzles that opened in three parts that were all serrated along the inside. Streamers of silk issued from their rear parts, providing a kind of drop line that they would use to control their fall.

The fresh-exuded silk, Rowl remembered, was quite adhesive and presented additional danger. It would not do to be hasty. So he contemplated his actions carefully, until the silkweavers had fallen almost halfway to the tunnel floor.

And then he moved.

He bounded up not at the lowermost of the falling silkweavers, but at the highest. He slammed both front paws into the thing, stiff-legged, and shoved it back. Rowl used the momentum to twist in the air and land on his feet, his head already tracking to see the results of his attack.

His victim swung in a wide arc, its silk line tangling with those of its companions. The silkweavers let out whistles of distress, as the sticky silk at their rear ends clung to other lines and weavers alike. One of them became hopelessly tangled, and two more had legs wound up in twists of silken line. The other three managed to escape the tangle and drop to the floor.

Rowl pounced on the first and batted it as hard as he could with his paws, knocking it away, onto its side. The second got the same treatment—and then the third leapt upon Rowl.

The warrior cat had been waiting for the stupid things to get around to that. He flung himself in the direction of the silkweaver's leap, flipping himself onto his back in a sinuous motion as he did. The silkweaver came down, poisonous jaws questing for his flesh, and he held it away with his front paws—while raking savagely with the claws on his rear legs at its vulnerable underside.

The silkweaver's legs convulsed as Rowl hit something vital, and the cat flung it off of him contemptuously. Neither of the other two had risen to their many legs yet, and were still thrashing on the stone floor. He pounced on the nearest, got a good grip on its underbelly with his jaws, and before it could curl and bite him, he shook it savagely, ripping the frail underbody open. It let out a shriek like the first, legs thrashing, and tumbled free, leaving a mouthful of its vitals behind.

Rowl spat the foul-tasting things out of his mouth and turned toward the third silkweaver—only to see Littlemouse's large, sturdy shoe come crushing down on the thing like a column of living stone. The silkweaver was quite simply no match for that kind of mass and strength, and it didn't so much die as explode in every direction. Rowl whirled toward the tangled silkweavers, leapt upon one of them, and killed it with his jaws, taking care to avoid the silk himself—and while he did, Littlemouse stomped the remaining two silkweavers into splatter marks on the floor.

Handy, humans, Rowl thought. Clumsy, slow, and not always terribly bright, but they were very, *very* strong, through sheer, inarguable mass. He now saw his father's wisdom in desiring to keep a few of them around the home tunnels. They could manage annoying problems that might prove awkward and time-consuming for cats.

Rowl looked around calmly for more foes to defeat, but he'd run out of enemies with which to amuse himself. Just as well, he supposed. They tasted horrible, and it would take him a week to get all of their goo and stench out of his fur.

"Well, I have saved you both," Rowl said to the humans. "Though I will concede, Littlemouse, that you were not entirely useless to me in this matter."

"Thank you," Littlemouse said gravely. She examined the bottom of her stomping shoe and shuddered. "Ugh. How revolting."

"How useless," Rowl said, disgusted. "It was barely a fight at all, and we can't even eat them."

"Just as well," Littlemouse said. "They have a poisonous bite, do they not?"

"Were any of us bitten?" Rowl asked.

"No."

"Then no," Rowl said simply. "They obviously did not." He gave her gauntlet a pointed glance. "An unused weapon is not a weapon at all."

"I didn't have time to aim it before they were bouncing all over the floor," Littlemouse said. "And after that, they were all around you. You did ask me not to step on your tail with my boots. I assumed you would not want me to step on it with my gauntlet, either."

Rowl considered that and nodded. "That does not seem unreasonable, I suppose. Presumptuous, but not stupid."

"Thank you," Littlemouse said, in that tone of voice that sometimes made Rowl wonder whether she was in some way mocking him. He couldn't be sure. Littlemouse was woefully lacking in ears, and had no tail whatsoever. How on earth was one supposed to know what was going on behind those enormous, myopic eyeballs without some kind of cue?

"So that's what that is like," the odd human was saying. She shivered. "Weavers, weavers, run."

"Folly," Littlemouse said. "It's all right. They're dead. We've killed them."

Folly shook her head in a jerky motion and jabbed a finger upward. "Bridget doesn't know," she whimpered. "Bridget doesn't. There, there, there!"

And with that a *flood* of silkweavers poured from the hole in the ceiling. They were all more or less the same size as the first group of the creatures—but there were more of them. Not dozens. Not scores. Hundreds. Hundreds and hundreds of them, pouring out like water in a chorus of shrieks, a rattling thunder of clashing serrated jaws, swarming down the already hanging silk lines like inverted aeronauts. Like fleets of them.

It was just possible that there were too many for Rowl to exterminate alone.

"Run!" Littlemouse bellowed. She grabbed Folly, and Rowl flung himself into a run beside them. The etherealist's apprentice and the two Guardsmen, neither of whom were guarding anything or, in point of fact, *men*, took off down the hallway at a frantic sprint.

A chittering tide of silkweavers boiled along behind them.

■ ■ ■ Chapter 35 ■ ■ ■

Spire Albion, Habble Landing,
Ventilation Tunnels

Just before the original six silkweavers hurled themselves at them, Folly had watched it happen.

It had been quite unnerving, really. She had stared at the hole in the ceiling and suddenly felt the utter, irrational certainty that six silkweavers were hurtling out of it. She could see nothing, and yet she felt that she could have counted the spiky hairs on their many legs if she'd cared to do so. While her eyes told her the space was empty, every primitive nerve in her body had fired off howls of panicked warning, and she had been able to do nothing but flinch and scream.

It was a second later before the silkweavers actually appeared, and Folly, confused, had simply stared as Rowl and Bridget dispatched them. She hadn't been stunned for very long, really—that cat had moved with an utter disregard for the superior numbers of the foe and, for that matter, of gravity. Within a handful of seconds, the six silkweavers had died.

Folly saw the conclusion of the fight in her thoughts a few seconds before it actually ended.

Which could only mean . . .

She had successfully tracked a possible future.

"Oh," she heard herself say. "So that's what that is like."

And then a stirring in the ether, like the first that had warned her of a malicious presence beyond the hole in the ceiling, slithered through the air—only this one was far, far larger. Folly immediately tilted her head to one side, struggling to track the sensation. Her eyes slipped out of focus because they were of no use, no use at all, and she shuddered as she realized what she was feeling—another possible future coalescing before her mind's eye.

And this future included more silkweavers. Hundreds more.

"Weavers," she breathed. "Weavers. Run."

"Folly," Bridget said. "It's all right. They're dead. We've killed them."

Folly shook her head as the malicious presence in the ether suddenly looked *back* at her, a shock of immaterial sensation as unsettling as a sudden scream in one's ear. That presence seemed to focus on her, and then it began to rush closer.

That was when Folly understood, for the first time, the nature of the Enemy her master had warned her about.

Those hadn't been silkweavers that Rowl and Bridget had dispatched. They'd been *puppets*.

"Bridget doesn't know," Folly said to the empty air, struggling desperately to latch onto the same sense of distilled instinct that had let her track the future of the initial attack. The invisible sense of a thousand images blurred through her mind, like a hundred people singing different songs all at once. It was painful, and she felt that she had glimpsed only the barest trace of possibility. She could possibly escape, and Rowl might have a chance but . . . "Bridget doesn't," she said aloud.

She looked around wildly, trying to find more futures, a path to survival for all of them, but it was like trying to catch a specific gnat out of a cloud of them. Bright chances flitted by nimbly, and Folly struggled to understand them before they vanished. There was one. And there. And there. She was barely aware that her mouth was moving. "There, there, there."

Even as she spoke, the future coalesced into certainty, and she had less than a second's premonition before the silkweavers physically poured down from the lair above them. She needed a future with life in it, and sought desperately—while a hideous horde of painful, increasingly probable futures assaulted her thoughts like pieces of stinging hail striking her skull. It was new and odd and utterly terrifying, for some part of her actually lived through each future she saw.

She fought to hang on to it, but she could not retain the vision, and it vanished.

"Run!" Bridget bellowed, and Folly felt herself being propelled. She stumbled into a run beside the taller girl, and the horde of little silkweavers came after them.

She struggled for a few seconds more to attain enough clarity and calm to see the future, to find some path to survival, and then abandoned the effort. That was the mark of a true master etherealist—the ability to look into the future in any circumstance, no matter how dire—and it required a level of self-mastery and concentration that she had clearly not yet attained.

Bridget twisted to unleash the fury of her gauntlet into the swarm behind her, but she might as well have been tossing stones at a grease fire for all the good it did. Of course, looking on the bright side, there were so many silkweavers that Bridget could hardly *miss*, could she? So at least they had that going for them.

But the silkweavers were gaining.

Folly forced herself to order her thoughts, as the master had so often practiced with her. It would have helped if she could have sat down in a nice lotus position and breathed quietly for a while, but the silkweavers seemed unlikely to extend that courtesy to her, so she made do with synchronizing the beat of her thoughts to that of her pounding heart and running feet, and the etheric world opened itself to her.

Everything changed.

The world faded into an utterly black void, ablaze with traceries of etheric light. The tiny crystals in her jar twinkled brightly, and the weapon crystal of Bridget's gauntlet glowed like a miniature sun. Rowl and Bridget appeared to her as phantoms, partially illuminated by the glow of etheric energy passing through them, but mostly to be seen as shadows where that energy was absent.

Pulsing streamers of energy flooded through the walls and floor of the Spire, the spirestone drawing it from the sky and conducting it down through its matter to the earth—a lightning rod being continuously struck. She cast a glance over her shoulder and saw the horde of silk-weavers shining like an out-of-control fire, every single creature ablaze with clouds of light. Using this portion of her mind to see, Folly could peer through the seemingly solid stone as if it had not been there at all, though it was a rather dizzying, disorienting activity within a Spire. There were myriad flows of energy, going generally downward, but also lancing back and forth through channels in the spirestone, placed there by the Builders so that the Spire's systems could support the lives of its residents. If a truly complex clock had been manufactured out of trans-lucent glass, Folly imagined, her current quandary might be an experi-ence similar to trying to find a single part located somewhere within it.

They needed a smaller tunnel, something that would let them pass through easily but bottleneck their pursuers, slowing them, and Folly found one at hand. Now, if she could only find an etheric nexus, there might be more possibilities open to her.

"That way!" she shouted to her jar, and abruptly turned down a much narrower passage with a much lower ceiling.

"Folly!" Bridget shouted in protest—but it wasn't as though the larger girl had any choice in the matter of which way to go: Folly had the only light. Bridget slipped on her silkweaver-slimed shoes, righted herself, ducked, and plunged into the smaller tunnel after Folly. Rowl entered behind Bridget, letting out a snarling, hissing cat scream of warning at the foremost silkweavers as he did, and the three of them fled down the much more constricted hallway.

Their footsteps were loud in here, their breathing deafening. Bridget had to run in a crouch—but the tide of silkweavers pursuing them had to slow at the entrance, like water pouring from a small hole in a large vessel; their pursuers were no fewer in number, but fewer could approach them at once, and that was very nearly the same thing, for Folly's purposes.

Though, now that she considered it, Folly had never regarded herself as the sort of young woman who had *purposes*, precisely. That was potentially a troubling development—not nearly so troubling as being torn to pieces by thousands of silkweavers, of course, but it was a matter upon which to be deliberated—assuming, of course, that she survived the next few moments.

Folly led them down the choked hallway, slowing her steps slightly so that she could sweep her ether-focused gaze around them for further options. And then, suddenly, she was able to see one of the things that might change the situation—a nexus.

Flows of etheric energy coursed down from half a dozen directions, pouring into a single downward-flowing conduit—and at the point where they merged together, excess energy overflowed the conduit, spreading out into the air of the tunnel in a gossamer backwash. That cloud of etheric force all but sang to Folly, and she rushed forward in a desperate sprint, panting, fumbling for her pistoleer's holsters as she went.

"Folly!" shouted Bridget from behind her. "Wait!"

There wasn't time—not if the tide of silkweavers was to be stemmed quickly enough to save Bridget's life. Folly ripped out the two mesh sacks of quiescent lumin crystals from the holsters and gave them a quick snap, one at a time, dumping their contents onto the floor of the tunnel. Then, without hesitating, she smashed her jar of crystals down to the stones as well.

And for an instant the tunnel went completely dark. Folly could see, of course, by the fey illumination of her ethersight, but she supposed it must have been a terrifying moment for Bridget, who unleashed a despairing shriek.

But that, Folly supposed, was only because Bridget had never seen what an etherealist, even an imperfectly trained one like Folly, could do with a supply of ready energy and vessels to contain it.

"All of us together now," Folly admonished the crystals, and felt their sleepy, rather muzzily confused sense of aggregate agreement—and then she seized upon the freely flowing etheric energy with her thoughts and sent it coursing down into the crystals.

Infused with energy far beyond that which had originally been stored within them, the little lumin crystals' radiance swelled from faint, ghostly glows to a thousand merry pinpoints of radiance, a sudden well of white light.

Shrieks of surprise and distress arose from the silkweavers, a surge of raw sound compressed by the narrow confines of the tunnel into a sledgehammer. Folly did her best to ignore its impact, and staggered only a little. Then she threw her hand out toward the tunnel down which they had just fled, giving the flows of energy a quick mental nudge, and sent a spray of little crystals flying down the silkweaver-filled hallway in a glittering cloud that scattered among the silkweavers in an entirely random distribution.

The next part was tricky, and Folly hoped that the crystals remembered her endless practice sessions. Lumin crystals were designed to accept a charge of etheric energy and output a steady trickle of light. But light was really just one of any number of possible expressions of energy. Weapons crystals did the same thing, only with heat and force. Lift crystals expressed that energy in a form of inverted gravity. And the most complex crystals of all, power-core crystals, expressed their energy in another form—electricity.

There was no difference between a lumin crystal and a power-core, really, except that the power-core crystal was grown with the complex pathways needed to route etheric energy into a rising surplus, converting it into bottled lightning. There was no reason a little lumin crystal could not do the same thing, assuming that someone was willing to provide them with a blueprint of the necessary structured paths.

So Folly, as quickly and ably as she could, imagined the precise sort of pathways her little crystals would need to employ. That was a fairly elemental exercise, but doing it a *thousand times*, all at once, was something of an ambitious effort, more so than any she had successfully used in her practice sessions. Of course, the practice sessions had been embarked upon with the precise goal of providing her with the skill she'd need for a moment just such as this.

Goodness, think of what trouble they'd be in if Folly hadn't practiced.

So because it was right and necessary to do so, she simply imagined a thousand different complex, unique little paths for her baby lumin crystals, all at once. Well, she shouldn't exaggerate, really, since that was boastful. There were nine hundred and eighty-seven crystals on the floor. So she modestly imagined nine hundred and eighty-seven patterns, one for each little crystal, to show them how to use the energy she was feeding them.

And the hallway behind them—and every silkweaver in it—was suddenly wreathed in a latticework of blinding, blue-white lightning.

The noise of it was really quite startling, a cloud of individual *snap-cracks* that sounded rather similar to the discharge of a weapons crystal—only since there were nine hundred and eighty-seven of them, all within the same second or two, the noise was equivalent to a small army firing a fusillade within the confines of the little access corridor. The heat was fearsome as well, and with the heat came a blast of wind that was, Folly felt, really quite unnecessary to the process, neither adding significant fearsomeness to the unleashed energy, nor accomplishing anything other than to knock Folly and Bridget down soundly, and to scatter her matrix of lumin crystals hither and yon.

Folly lay on the floor after, because it seemed the proper thing to do. She blinked several times up at the ceiling and realized that, without her ethersight, she could not be sure she was in fact looking at the ceiling at all. When one assumed, one quite frequently was correct, but it was hardly a constant.

There was etheric energy spilling from the nexus still, and Folly waved her hands at it vaguely, sending it out toward her little crystals. Without Folly's thoughts to guide them, they were once more innocent of the knowledge of how to turn etheric force into violent death. The little crystals began to glow cheerfully, lighting the entire length of the access tunnel.

Folly turned her head to find Bridget staring, most definitely, at the ceiling. The larger girl had a scorch mark on her chin, and a long scratch along her hairline that had bled toward her eye without obscuring it. She blinked several times and then looked around them dazedly.

Folly turned her head the other way to find Rowl standing over her. The cat's fur stood straight out in every direction, though there were uneven gaps here and there where it had been singed away. The cat's expression, Folly noted, was very catlike.

Rowl swatted her nose firmly with one paw, claws sheathed. Then, with massive dignity, he rose and firmly turned his back on Folly to walk over to Bridget, nuzzling her and letting out an encouraging purr.

Folly continued to lie meekly on the floor. Rowl, she thought, probably had some sort of point. She really hadn't expected quite *that* much excitement. What would the master think? He did so disapprove of showing off. And besides, she felt quite thoroughly exhausted, at least as sleepy as her brood of tiny crystals.

Bridget sat up slowly. She turned her gaze up and down the hallway. The air was full of the stench of scorched silkweavers, though there really wasn't a great deal left of them—a leg here, a bit of shell there, a fang there. The hallway was black with fine ash.

The former vatterist shook her head slowly and said in an awed tone, "Folly. Your little crystals did this?"

"Don't brag," Folly admonished her crystals firmly. "You couldn't have if I hadn't shown you how."

Bridget blinked several times. "*You* did this."

Folly sighed and closed her eyes. She really did feel quite tired. "As an exercise," she mused aloud, "it was really quite simple. Not at all easy, but quite simple."

"I don't . . ." Bridget began. "I had no idea . . . That was . . ."

Folly had been trained for this as well. Most folk had no idea how formidable an etherealist's skills could be when applied properly. When they learned, their general reaction was, she had been assured, one of understandable if irrational fear. Which was a shame, because it had seemed that Bridget might have been a rather lovely friend, and she really didn't want to start crying. It would be perfectly awkward.

". . . amazing!" Bridget finished. "God in Heaven, Folly, I thought we were finished. Well-done!"

Folly blinked open her eyes and stared at Bridget for a moment. Then she felt herself smile, and she looked down very quickly, as Bridget's shape went all blurry. How odd that suddenly her tears did not feel awkward at all.

Then Rowl let out a sharp hiss.

Folly felt it at the very last instant, too late—the awful attention of the awareness she'd sensed before, while they were searching for the

Nine-Claws. It was the Enemy; she felt almost certain. She couldn't think of a better sobriquet for the malevolent presence that had been driving the silkweavers like an enormous threshing machine intent on murdering them. It was as if the spirit of hatred itself had been given a mind and a dark will, and was eager to convey its malice through the medium of the hideous creatures of the surface.

What kind of creature could have such a horrible will? How could such an intangible thing be fought? In a lifetime of strangeness, Folly had never heard of such a thing before, and she found that it frightened her a very great deal.

That same Enemy presence now sent a trio of the little creatures—burned and mangled but alive and obviously dangerous—toward Folly's weary, recumbent form.

Everything happened very, very quickly. Rowl let out a shrieking snarl and flung himself on the silkweaver farthest to one side. Then there was the howl of a discharging gauntlet, and the second silkweaver vanished, burned and blown to bits by the blast of Bridget's gauntlet.

The third silkweaver flung itself onto Folly's face—

—and was intercepted just short of it by Bridget's fist. The larger girl simply drove her arm down like a steam engine's piston, crushing the silkweaver to the spirestone floor and ending its attempts on Folly's life with a perfectly brutal finality.

"Oh," Folly breathed. Her heart was racing painfully. "Oh, my."

"There," Bridget said, nodding in satisfaction. "Rowl?"

The cat had finished dispatching his opponent and approached, shaking one of his front paws in pure distaste. "They are the last," the cat reported. "Can I use my metal circles to hire a *human* to clean my paws? Is there a human who could do so competently?"

"I shall do it," Bridget said, rising. She winced and touched her cut lightly.

"But I desire competence," Rowl protested. "You are too rough with your wet cloths. If you would only use your tongue, as is proper—"

"I think not," Bridget replied firmly. "I know where your paws have been." She offered Folly her hand. "Can you rise?"

Folly took her friend's hand and rose. She wobbled for a moment, but Bridget steadied her until the hall stopped spinning hatefully about.

"Rowl," Bridget said. "Are these silkweavers grown?"

"They are grown as much as they ever shall be," Rowl said with satisfaction.

"You know what I mean."

"I do not think they are mature," Rowl replied. "My people's lore suggests that adults are two or three cat-weights, or larger."

"Hatchlings," Bridget said, frowning. "Could little silkweavers like this have spun the lines we saw back at the hole in the ceiling?"

"Oh," Folly said. "Oh, Bridget is clever. In a very horrifying sort of way. No, these little things could not have done so."

"Adults had to lay eggs, and spin those lines," Bridget said. "But . . . if only the hatchlings remained to attack us . . . ?"

Rowl growled. "Indeed. Where are the adults?"

Folly's heart began to race in real panic this time. "Oh," she breathed, her instincts screaming to her precisely where the Enemy would direct its deadliest weapons. "Master."

■ ■ ■ ■ Chapter 36 ■ ■ ■

Spire Albion, Habble Landing,
the Black Horse Inn

It was well after midnight, Gwen felt simpleminded with exhaustion, and the Spirearch's master etherealist was leading the bar in an enthusiastic round of "Farmer Long's Cucumber," a song that featured a number of shocking concepts Gwen had scarcely encountered before that night, along with what seemed to be an infinite number of verses.

"Really, Benedict," she complained. "I'm sure I've no idea where you could have learned such a crass piece of exploitative trash."

". . . and she hid it there again!" Benedict sang, grinning, before turning to his cousin. "From Esterbrook, naturally."

"The cad. Are you almost out of verses, at least?"

Benedict took a sip of his drink, his expression scholarly. "Marines on an airship apparently make a custom of writing more verses to their favorite songs during their tours of duty. Only the best—"

"You mean most obscene," Gwen interjected.

Benedict bobbed his head in acknowledgment. "Only the best are retained, but even so after several centuries of sailing tradition . . ."

Gwen arched an eyebrow. "You're telling me that they're going to go on all night, aren't you?"

"Well past that, if they don't get tired of it," Benedict said. He squinted up at the cheery, ruddy-cheeked etherealist. "One wonders, though, where Master Ferus learned them."

"I was once a Marine, of course!" Ferus bellowed. Then he and several customers of the pub shouted in unison, "*Semper fortitudo!*"

Gwen sighed.

"*Fortitudo*, Miss Lancaster," Master Ferus said, and plopped from the table down into his chair with the grace (or at least the drunken recklessness) of a much younger man. "An old, old word, even by my standards. Do you know what it means?"

"Strength," Gwen said promptly. " 'Always strong.' "

"Ah, but what *kind* of strength?" Ferus asked, over the roar of a new singer taking over more verses of the song.

This one featured Farmer Long's cucumber falling in a mud hole, and Gwen wanted nothing to do with it. "Sir?"

"There are many, many kinds of strength. *Fortitudo* refers to something quite specific." He poked a finger at Benedict's biceps in demonstration. "Not this kind of brute power, not at all. It means something more—inner strength, strength of purpose, moral courage. The strength required to fight on in the face of what seems to be certain defeat. The strength to carry on faithfully when it seems no one knows or cares." He swirled his cup and eyed Gwen. "And the strength to sacrifice oneself when that sacrifice is what is required for the good of others, even when one could offer someone else up instead. Especially then."

Gwen smiled briefly. "How, um . . ."

"Pointlessly trivial?" Ferus suggested quickly.

"I was going to say 'interesting,' " Gwen said in a mild tone.

"And that's as close to diplomatic as she gets," Benedict noted.

Gwen kicked her cousin's ankle beneath the table. "Master Ferus, it grows late."

"Indeed," the etherealist said, and stifled a yawn with one hand. "Perhaps we should consider discontinuing our investigation until we have heard from our field agents."

"You mean the cat?" Gwen asked.

"Quite." Master Ferus suddenly peered at Benedict. "I say, boy. What's caught your interest?"

Benedict's feline eyes were focused on the bar at the far side of the room, where the master of the house was speaking in a low voice with a newcomer, his expression intent. The fellow was a broad, burly man in green aviation leathers and a greatcoat trimmed in the thick grey-brown fur of some creature of the surface, making his already massive shoulders look inhumanly broad. The coat's sleeves bore the two broad rings of an airship's captain. His square face was ruddy and getting ruddier, and he slammed a blocky fist down onto the bar hard enough to be heard even over the singing crowd. "What!?"

One thick fist shot across the bar and seized the innkeeper by the front of his suit.

The frantic innkeeper darted a nervous glance over toward their table, and spoke in a low, hurried voice to the burly aeronaut.

"Ah," said Benedict. "I think now I see why our host was so reluctant to rent you the room, coz. He'd already promised it elsewhere."

"That isn't a Fleet uniform," Gwen noted.

"It is not," Benedict said. "Not a uniform at all, really. He must be a private captain."

"Olympian, I should think, from the colors and the fur trim of his coat," Master Ferus put in. "Olympian and, it would seem, possessed of a fury. Which is funny, if you know enough history."

The Olympian released the innkeeper after a few more low, choice words, and then stalked toward their table, scowling. Gwen studied him the way she'd been taught to consider possible opponents, and found herself growing alarmed. The man moved far too lightly on his feet for someone with a build so powerful, and his balance (as one might expect from an aeronaut) was excellent. Worse, his eyes were quick and alert, sweeping the room as he moved, the mark of a man who was on guard for trouble.

Gwen had attained some modest skills in the hand-to-hand combat arts of the Wayists, but she had, or so she thought, no illusions about her ability to deal with a much larger or better-trained opponent without the element of surprise to support her skill. "Benny?" Gwen said. "Unless you think we should shoot him . . ."

"*I'm* not the one who bought his bed out from under him, coz," Benedict said. "This situation looks like it needs smoothing to me."

"I'd rather not be transmogrified into paste while trying it," Gwen said.

Benedict sat back in his chair, his eyes amused, and said diffidently, "Did you, however briefly, consider *talking* to him? Just for the sake of novelty?"

"He doesn't look like a man who would react well to threats."

"An extremely fine coat," Master Ferus mused. "They don't give those to just anyone, do they?"

Benedict arched an eyebrow at the etherealist and said to Gwen, "I said *talk*, as opposed to *threaten*. Though one hardly need struggle to see the possibility that you might not understand the distinction."

"You make me sound like a perfect ogre," Gwen said.

"But an articulate, wealthy, and very stylish one, coz," Benedict said. "Beautiful, too. Try it. Just for fun. And if it doesn't work out, we can always grind his bones to make our bread later."

"Or," Master Ferus mused, "be ground, as the case may be."

The Olympian captain reached their table, slammed his fist down on it hard enough to make all of the crockery and utensils jump up off the surface, and demanded, "Get out of my room."

Gwen didn't mind the threat display so very much. God in Heaven knew she'd made a few herself in the past several days. But neither did she care for it, nor feel terribly frightened by it. She was, after all, wearing a gauntlet—but then, she noted, so was the Olympian.

"I'm very sorry to have inconvenienced you, sir," Gwen said. "But my associates and I required the room. It might be better if you looked elsewhere."

The man, who had been staring hard at Benedict, turned his eyes to Gwen for a flickering glance before tracking back to the warriorborn. "She speak for you?"

"For purposes of this discussion, I'm afraid so," Benedict replied.

"Fine," the man said, and turned to face Gwen, looming over her. "Then you. Go gather up everyone's things and get them out of my room, girl. Now."

She recognized the tone of absolute authority in the man's voice, and she did not care for it at all. "Introductions," she said crisply.

That gave the Olympian an instant's pause. "What?"

"You have not introduced yourself, sir," Gwen said, her voice hard. "I should like to know your name before I exchange another word with you."

The man straightened, his eyes narrowed, and then he shook his head. "Bloody Albion fussbothers . . ." He took a deep breath, visibly controlling more vile language, and then said, "Pine. Commodore Horatio Pine, of the Half Moon Merchant Company out of Olympia. And I don't give a tenth-crown who you are. That suite is reserved for my captains and myself, and we've just walked a mile on the surface to get to this bloody Spire and nearly got shot up by your own bloody Fleet when we finally made it through. I am in no mood for games."

Gwen nodded. "My name is Gwendolyn Lancaster of the House of Lancaster—yes, before you ask, *those* Lancasters, the ones who made the crystals that are most probably keeping your ships in the air, sir—and while I sympathize with your plight, I am afraid that I still require those rooms."

"So yourself and your friends can do some comfortable drinking?" Pine spat. "I've got wounded men who need good rooms and the attention of physicians, and this bloody habble is packed to the roof. Get out of those rooms, or by God in Heaven and the Long Road both, I will leave you all unconscious in an alley and move my men in anyway."

"Perhaps such brutish thuggery is how things are done in Olympia," Gwen said, her voice lashing out like a whip's crack. "But in Albion, sir, there is rule of law, and I shall be pleased to defend myself against any such violence."

Pine narrowed his eyes. Then he said to Benedict, "You sure she speaks for you?"

Benedict sighed and leaned forward to lightly thump his forehead down onto the table. Several times.

"I didn't threaten him!" Gwen protested to her cousin.

There was a sharp sound of crockery breaking, and Gwen turned to find that Master Ferus's mug had dropped from suddenly limp fingers. He made a soft sound and twitched several times. Then he shivered and his eyes closed.

Gwen traded a look with Benedict, and held up a forestalling hand to Commodore Pine. "Master Ferus?" she asked after a moment. "Master Ferus, are you quite all right?"

Ferus opened his eyes, rose calmly, and said in a level tone, "Sir Benedict, I wonder if you would be so good as to draw your sword. Miss Lancaster, prime your gauntlet, if you please." He took his chair and slid it over to Commodore Pine. "This, sir, is for you. You'll find it quite wieldy, I expect."

Pine blinked several times. "What?"

"Gwen," Benedict snapped, rising and drawing his sword, his eyes everywhere.

Gwen swallowed and instinctively put her back to Benedict's and, as Master Ferus had instructed, primed her gauntlet, the weapon crystal on her palm swelling to glowing life.

And then the doors of the Black Horse exploded open, and high-pitched, alien shrieks filled the air.

Chapter 37

Spire Albion, Habble Landing,
the Black Horse Inn

The doors to the Black Horse slammed into the walls framing them, and what could only be a creature of the surface world squeezed inside.

The thing was leathery and enormous, double or triple the mass of the largest man Gwen had ever seen, but it somehow managed to compress itself and come through the door without slowing down. Its segmented body was something like a spider's, but with four sections instead of two, elongated grotesquely, and some kind of dark grey carapace covered its back in flexible, articulated plates. It had too many legs to be a spider, too, all of them thick and massive at the base, covered in thickets of some kind of spine or rigid, sharp-looking hairs.

Its head was hideous, Gwen thought. It was half-shrouded in protrusions of its armor, wide and flat, with a nest of beady, gleaming eyes on either side—and a set of massive jaws hinged to great, bulging muscles along its skull.

It slammed the door to the Black Horse closed—and then its rearmost legs spun a coil of some viscous grey substance onto the door behind it.

"Silkweaver!" someone cried.

The room erupted into panic. Patrons lunged up out of their seats, screaming. Some of them ran toward the stairway to the private rooms. Most fled toward the opposite door or the kitchen. A handful drew swords and raised gauntlets.

The silkweaver gave them no time to attack. It flung itself to the far side of the room, hurling its massive body into a luckless patron in aeronaut's leathers, smashing the man into the spirestone wall of the inn with an audible cracking of bones. The silkweaver then slammed the other door closed and once more webbed it shut, while its eyes scanned the room—looking, she realized, for a target. As it did, it distractedly seized a reeling patron with its long front set of limbs and slammed the man to the floor with casual, lethal power.

"Dear God in Heaven," Gwen breathed, a chill settling in her belly. "It's intelligent."

"Impossible," Commodore Pine snarled, gripping the chair in both meaty hands and stepping back to stand even with Benedict and Gwen. "Silkweavers are beasts."

"That's not a silkweaver," Master Ferus said in a matter-of-fact tone. The etherealist leaned forward and plucked a pitcher of beer from the table. "It's a marionette. Some sort of puppet, at any rate."

Pine scowled at Master Ferus as the man began to take a long and determined pull from the pitcher and then turned his glare to Gwen. "How drunk *is* that man?"

"He's an etherealist," Gwen said, "and quite."

"Ah?" Pine blinked, eyed Master Ferus with decided apprehension, and said, "Ah."

"We have to get Ferus out of here," Benedict said in a low, tense voice. "It's here for him."

"Quite!" burbled Master Ferus from the midst of another drink. He coughed and wiped at his mouth. "Quite, yes. It's been sent to stop me from interfering."

"With *what*?" Pine demanded.

"I really have no idea," Ferus said happily. "I've been changing my mind all night. Which is why it can't find me, I presume."

Gwen watched in horror as the silkweaver waited until several folk had pressed toward the doors to the kitchen together, and then it simply flung itself at them in another fantastically powerful bound. It struck them like a runaway freight cart, making wreckage of bodies in a chorus of screams. Its many legs struck like deadly clubs at whoever survived the impact. A drunken armed patron discharged a gauntlet into the thing from no more than a foot away, but the silkweaver's carapace shed much of the force of the blast, and the attack did little more than melt a small crater into its hide.

The weapon *did* get the creature's attention, though, and it turned, lightning-quick for something so large, and its jaws opened into three parts that closed on the armed man's gauntlet wrist and severed it from his body as neatly as the Lancasters' gardener clipping a rose stem.

After that, the silkweaver began spinning again, and barricading the door to the kitchen with grisly corpses and silk webbing. The folk remaining in the room were fleeing toward the stairs, the only exit remaining to them.

"Stairs," Benedict said in a harsh voice.

"No. We can't run. We have to kill it," Gwen heard herself say in a hard, vicious voice. "Gauntlets are useless against that armor. If we trap ourselves in narrow hallways and tiny rooms, we play to its strengths, and it will murder us all one at a time. We're still Guardsmen, Benedict."

"With orders to protect Master Ferus."

"We protect him by *killing* that horrible thing before it hurts any more Albions," Gwen spat. "Right here, where we have room to use our numbers against it, while we still have them to use."

"Little girl's right," Commodore Pine grunted. "Rats take me, that's a huge one. But not invincible. If we can get to its belly, we can kill it. Nothing but blubber and arteries down there. A shot to its head might do the trick, if anyone can make it around the armor."

Gwen nodded sharply. The silkweaver had its head shrugged down behind its knobby armored shoulders as it worked—a difficult target, and one that would not sit still once someone pointed a weapon at it. She turned to the etherealist. "Can't you do anything?"

"I'm afraid my cane is upstairs in the suite," Ferus said apologetically. "It would have given me away. Without it, I can't do anything significant."

"Go *get* it," Gwen said through clenched teeth.

Ferus opened his mouth and stared at Gwen helplessly, then waved his hands and said, "But . . . there are *doorknobs*. And I've sent Folly off to talk to cats."

Gwen gave him a level look, but there probably wasn't time for the etherealist to get his cane before the silkweaver came again in any case. She turned to the other survivors still in the room. "You lot!" she shouted at them, a group of older men pressed into a small defensive clump, just as she and her companions were. "When it goes for the stairs, we shall attack it together from all sides!"

"*Semper fortitudo!*" bellowed Master Ferus.

"*Semper fortitudo!*" a grey-haired, blocky man in a dockworker's jacket answered. "We're with you! Everyone together!"

"Are you insane?" screamed another patron, a younger man in another separate knot of younger men. "That thing will kill us!"

"Oh, God in Heaven, man, *do* gather up your scrotum and fight!" Gwen snarled.

Benedict blinked.

"Even if we can engage it," Commodore Pine said, "if we can't get to its belly we can't kill it. It'll just hunker down under its shell."

Gwen looked sharply around the room and found a possible solution. "Should that happen, I shall make sure it does not have the luxury to remain still. Benny, can you keep its attention for a few moments?"

"As you wish, coz," Benedict said, baring his pointed canines in a savage smile. "Planning to threaten it with treason?"

"You simply won't let that go, will you?"

"It's about to come again," Master Ferus said calmly.

The silkweaver compacted a last pair of grisly corpses into the doorway—one of them, Gwen thought, might still have been moving—sealed them in tight with its silk, and swarmed up onto the bar, its weirdly segmented eyes scanning the room as its legs danced restlessly, as if eager to pounce upon another target.

Benedict obliged the creature, gliding out into the open floor directly between the enormous silkweaver and the staircase, sword in hand, and turned to face it alone, isolated from any of the defensive pockets of survivors. The silkweaver was a predator, a creature that sensed vulnerability and attacked it. It leapt at him at once, as swift and deadly as when it had slaughtered the dead strewn about the floor of the tavern.

But the silkweaver's previous victims had not been Sir Benedict Sorellin, warriorborn of Albion.

Gwen darted toward the bar and tried to keep an eye on her cousin, but it was virtually impossible. Not because she couldn't see him—simply because he, and the silkweaver, were moving too fast for her to properly comprehend what was happening.

The silkweaver's massive form moved like lightning, like some engine of destruction, its clublike limbs hammering the ground with cracks of impact like heavy steam pistons slamming the spirestone floor—but no matter how fast the creature moved, or how quickly it struck, its blows never found flesh. Benedict somehow stayed fractions of an inch ahead, or to the side, or beneath the sweeping limbs, dancing back before the onrushing silkweaver, his feet hardly seeming to touch the floor. When the silkweaver's jaws snapped at his face, they met with nothing but a short, vicious strike of his sword.

The beast shrieked in pain and charged Benedict furiously, following her cousin out into the center of the room—and Gwen realized that Benedict had led the creature there intentionally, to expose it to attack from all sides.

"Now!" Gwen shouted as she reached the bar. "Attack!"

Commodore Pine let out a bellow, hefted his chair, and charged the silkweaver, and the other surviving patrons of the Black Horse joined him. Some of the men had swords, and Gwen saw at least one gauntlet in evidence, but most were armed with chairs and knives. Their faces were pale, their voices cracking in screams that were more of terror than ferocity, but they knew as well as Gwen did that once a large predator of the surface began to spill human blood, it would not stop until it had killed every living person it could reach. Something about the taste of it maddened them, drove them to a savagery that was far beyond that of a mere hungry animal, though no one had ever provided an explanation as to why.

Two of the younger men fell before they could even reach the silkweaver with their improvised weapons, clubbed down by lightning strikes of its many limbs. The rest closed on the silkweaver's flank, knives and swords stabbing, and the creature scuttled sideways, lashing out as it went, sending up more screams—until Commodore Pine closed from the opposite side of the silkweaver and brought his heavy chair down through a ponderous, swooping arc with all the strength of his stocky frame.

The chair had a wooden seat, but the rest of it was made of coppered iron. It had to have weighed forty pounds if it weighed an ounce, and Pine swung it with such force that the impact bent and twisted it. The silkweaver's armor might have protected its vitals from the shattering power of the blow, but nonetheless the force of the Olympian aero-naut's strike slammed the beast to the floor, sending its legs out in a wide sprawl and stunning it for a portion of a second.

In the brief half instant of weakness, Benedict attacked.

With the same coughing roar Gwen had heard in the tunnels, Benedict closed on the silkweaver, his sword striking once, twice, three times, spinning in swift, heavy, vicious circles. Benedict wielded an exceptionally dense, weighty sword that had been intentionally created for use with his enhanced physique, and Gwen knew it would strike with terrible power. Three of the silkweaver's limbs went spinning away from its body amidst gouts of violet fluid, and it staggered back, rough limbs slipping on the bloodied spirestone floor.

Pine shouted, banging the twisted chair down onto the silkweaver with less effect the second time, and then was struck in the chest and sent flying back. The silkweaver's rear sections swept left and right like a curling tail, battering three more men and sending them reeling, but the old Marine and several of his companions began driving their blades toward the creature's belly and its vulnerable flank.

The silkweaver shrieked as more violet blood flowed, and whirled on the men with unmistakable fury. They raised their weapons, but were simply no match for the thing, their knives and short swords unable to penetrate the creature's shell once it had faced them. It rushed them, tearing and smashing, breaking bones and rending flesh. Benedict roared again, but even his blade could not penetrate the silkweaver's armored shell and thudded futilely against it, slicing scrapes and fissures in the hide, but drawing no blood. Even when he discharged his gauntlet nearly flush against the thing's hide, it did nothing to distract the silkweaver, and men screamed and fell before it—leaving Benedict standing alone.

The silkweaver whirled on her cousin, flailing with its severed stumps of limbs, sending a spray of fluids at his face before it rushed forward.

Benedict reeled back as the thing's blood filled one of his eyes, and began to dodge and weave again—but now the floor was slick with scarlet blood and violet, and the silkweaver was not charging with blind violence. Instead it circled, forcing Benedict to retreat from it in a spiral, and it wasn't until a few seconds later that Gwen realized that as it had advanced, the silkweaver had laid a strand of sticky ethersilk on the floor behind it.

"Benny, look out!" Gwen screamed.

Benedict's boot touched the silk strand on the floor, and adhered to it almost instantly.

Her cousin fell.

The silkweaver rushed forward for the kill.

Benedict's gauntlet went off with a howl, his blood-shrouded face twisted into a snarl.

The silkweaver wrenched its body, and the massive humps of armor around its relatively tiny head shielded it from harm.

And then a lumin crystal tore itself from its sconce, flew across the room like a blazing star, and struck the silkweaver precisely between the eyes.

"*Semper fortitudo!*" Master Ferus slurred in a bellow. "Over here, you great gawking thing! Leave that boy alone! I'm the one you're looking for!"

Had Gwen doubted the silkweaver's intelligence before, its reaction would have convinced her of its awareness and purpose. At the sound of Ferus's voice, the thing whirled with blinding speed and spent an endless second simply focused upon the old etherealist in what could only have been a shock of recognition. And then it let out the most bloodcurdling shriek it had uttered yet.

A second lumin crystal darted from a sconce and bounced off the silkweaver's head. The creature's weirdly segmented eyes seemed to flinch away from the cool blue light. "Come on, then!" Ferus snarled. "What are you waiting for, an engraved invitation?"

The silkweaver screamed again and rushed at the old man.

Gwen found herself in motion.

She seized a glass bottle of the most potent liquor in the tavern in her right hand and flung it toward the empty space between the silkweaver and Master Ferus. Then, as the bottle tumbled, she raised her gauntlet. There was no time for careful sighting. Instead she relied upon the hours and hours of practice she had put in to sense the precise moment to blast the tumbling bottle.

She triggered her gauntlet, and white light leapt from the crystal on her palm across the room to the bottle. It exploded at once into a rapidly expanding shower of blue flame—a shower that fell directly onto the silkweaver's back and head. Fire suddenly wreathed the creature, burning skin and blackening armored hide, sending it staggering, thrashing and bucking in pain.

"Master Ferus!" Gwen shouted, and sprinted toward the old man. It seemed to take an endless amount of time, but could only have been a few seconds. She reached the etherealist's side just as the silkweaver shuddered and its wild contortions ceased. Still aflame, it spun toward the etherealist again and once more rushed forward, making a horrible, hissing sound as it came.

Gwen pushed Master Ferus behind her and raised her gauntlet. The burning silkweaver was coming fast, its agonized body still contorting strangely, its small head thrashing. Gwen would have only a single chance to kill the creature, and she dared not waste it.

She planted her feet firmly, straightened her back, squared her shoulders, and took a steadying breath. Then she sighted carefully between her fingers and waited.

The silkweaver came on, hissing and charging, burning and smoking, its mouth and clublike limbs smeared with blood.

When it was no more than five feet away, Gwen loosed the bolt from her gauntlet.

Then there was an impact so vast that she could scarcely credit it as anything but a delusion, a sense of rapid, brutal motion, and a blossom of agony in her skull.

And then nothing.

■ ■ ■ Chapter 38 ■ ■ ■

Spire Albion, Habble Landing,
Ventilation Tunnels

Bridget stared for a moment at the remains of the silkweavers, then turned on her heel and walked decisively down the passageway—back toward their nest.

"My goodness," Folly breathed. Bridget had helped her collect her scattered crystals, most of them smeared with fine ash, some with more gruesome remains, and the girl had refilled the mesh bags in her holsters and was fixing the lid back onto her jar. "What is Bridget doing?"

"Hundreds of little silkweavers didn't just pop out of the air," Bridget said back firmly. "They hatch from eggs, do they not? Something must have laid the eggs."

"She is of course correct," Folly whispered to her jar. "But it seems to me that is an excellent reason for us not to go back in that direction. Doesn't it seem that way to you?"

"If there was a mother present, would she not have attacked us as well?" Bridget asked. "Rowl?"

The cat, prowling along at Bridget's side, paused to flick ashes off of one paw, his expression irritated. "It stands to reason, Littlemouse."

"Then the mother is not present," Bridget said. "We should look at the lair. It could be that we will learn something."

"Or be webbed up. Or poisoned. Or eaten," Folly said in a small voice. "Eaten all up."

Bridget paused and looked back at the ethcrealist's apprentice. "Folly," she said, "I understand that you're frightened. I am too. But we were sent out to get information—and what do we have to show for it?"

Folly didn't look up at Bridget, but frowned down at her gently glowing jar of crystals.

"If you don't want to go," Bridget said, "then we can walk back to an illuminated hallway and I'll go myself, if you'll lend me your jar."

Folly clutched the jar of little crystals to her bosom and bit her lower lip. "Oh, no. No, no, I couldn't do that. That would be a violation of trust."

"We have a mission," Bridget said. "We'll need the light."

"We?" Rowl asked smugly.

"Oh," Bridget said, scowling down at the cat for a moment. Then she looked up at Folly. "Please, Folly. We'll do just a little more, and then we'll go back."

Folly took a deep breath. Then she nodded, very quickly, as if eager to get the motion over with.

Climbing the ropes was difficult, and it was made no easier by the fact that Rowl insisted upon riding up on her shoulders.

"Why do you breathe that hard?" the cat asked her curiously. "Does it help in some way?"

Bridget made an incoherent snarling sound, secured her feet on the too-narrow length of ethersilk wedged between them, and strained to push her arms up another foot or so.

"Your shoulders are shaking," Rowl noted. "It isn't very comfortable for me. Are you sure you're doing this correctly?"

Bridget ground her teeth and kept climbing.

"It's perfectly simple," Rowl said impatiently. "Watch."

And with that the cat seized the length of ethersilk with his forepaws, taking it firmly in his stubby grip. Then he hunched up his rear quarters, lifted his back paws, and sank his claws into the ethersilk line. He slid his front paws up, and with effortless grace shinnied up the last three feet of line and disappeared into the opening in the masonry ceiling.

"You see?" his voice came down. "You should be more like that. It's faster, and one need not puff like a steam engine."

This time Bridget managed to growl, ". . . kill that cat . . ." putting as much threat as she could into the words. Then she hauled herself laboriously up the last few feet, heaved her upper body over the edge of the hole, and tried not to panic at how exquisitely vulnerable she felt, lying on her belly in what was presumably a silkweaver nest.

There was a strange, acrid odor thick in the air, a scent that made her skin crawl, and she could see almost nothing in the darkness. Had a foe been present, Rowl would have warned her—that was, after all, why he had proceeded into the nest first, bless his fuzzy, arrogant heart—but even Rowl couldn't sense everything, every time.

Bridget wasn't sure she wanted to come any farther up. If a silkweaver should leap at her, she wanted to be able to drop back down at once. Of course, if she did so, and lost her grip on the lines, she would fall twenty feet to the spirestone floor. Statistically, she had heard, surviving such a fall was a toss of the coin. Granted, the chances of surviving the poison of a silkweaver were worse.

Bother, she didn't need mathematics. She needed to look and get it over with, and get *out* of this horrible place.

She primed her gauntlet, and the crystal on her palm glowed and crackled with power, sending a wash of tingles up her arm to the elbow—but it hadn't really been designed for illumination, and the light from it seemed to spread out and accomplish nothing practical. All it really did was to leave her blind to anything more than a few feet away.

But at least, she supposed, its glow managed to make her into a much better target than she'd been a moment before.

"Folly," Bridget called, trying to keep her voice steady. "Send up the light."

Bridget expected the etherealist's apprentice to tie the jar to the line of ethersilk so that Bridget could haul it up. Instead she heard Folly open the jar. Bridget grunted and pulled herself the rest of the way up, so that she could turn and peer back down through the hole at the other girl.

Folly took the end of the ethersilk line in her hand, closed her eyes for a moment, and then slipped it into the jar of gently glowing crystals. She said something quietly, speaking in the same tone of voice one might use when addressing small children—and then there was a flickering of light amongst the crystals, and their quiet luminance abruptly spread into the ethersilk line and up it, like water flowing through a pipe.

Bridget watched in amazement as the light spread up the line, branching out into the other strands of ethersilk it crossed, until it passed into the silk at the edge of the hole and beneath her, and then on into the silk-covered chamber beyond, until the entire thing pulsed with a muted, aqua glow.

Rowl let out a quiet sound, an expression of pure emotion Bridget had heard only a few times in her life, when a cat was impressed but did not wish to acknowledge the fact.

The nest was covered in ethersilk. The walls, the floor, the roof, like some vast cocoon, spreading from the hole in the floor up to the height of the spirestone roof above, with walls composed of more silk—it was, Bridget thought, stunned, the fortune of a commoner's lifetime, the silk representing enough value to buy her father's vattery whole, a dozen times over.

She gave her head a small shake and forced herself to look past the treasure the silk represented. She scanned the nest again, straining to see details. There were tiny nodules of silk all over the floor and lower walls of the nest, each the size of an adolescent's fist. Some sort of . . . cradles for the little silkweavers? Each bore a similar funnel pattern, where the silkweaver would obviously have eased into the cradle.

High above the floor of the nest was a much, much larger cradle, one seemingly large enough to host three or four of Bridget. The silk-weaver matriarch's bower?

And between the enormous bower and the tiny cradles were more funnel shapes, much larger than those below, yet smaller than the one above.

None of them, as far as Bridget could see, were occupied.

"This is why the Nine-Claws were all huddled together," Bridget breathed.

"This is what Naun wanted us to see," Rowl said, his tone that of a teacher correcting a student.

"Also that," Bridget said quietly. Then she nodded. "Let's go back. Master Ferus must know of this at once."

■ ■ ■ Chapter 39 ■ ■ ■

Spire Albion, Habble Landing Shipyards,
AMS *Predator*

Grimm spent the evening filling in for the ship's cook, who had been given leave along with a quarter of the ship's crew. Unfortunately, Journeyman hadn't bothered to inform the cook or his assistant that he'd brought an extra twenty men aboard to labor in the engine room. Journeyman was a simple soul, and the length and breadth of his universe could be described in precisely the same terms as the area of the ship's engineering spaces. The evening meal had therefore been woefully inadequate, and someone had to step in.

Creedy had been nearly apoplectic when Grimm had calmly removed his captain's coat from his shoulders and donned an apron. In Fleet, such a thing would never have been conceived. A ship's captain was her master and the right hand of God in Heaven Himself, and concerned with matters of such grave importance that minor issues like food for the mortals in his command were entirely beneath him.

"I'll get someone else to take this duty, sir," Creedy said stoutly.

"The nonessential personnel are already on leave, XO," Grimm replied. "All the remaining hands are fully engaged in installing the new systems and making repairs. You know that."

"But, sir," Creedy said. "What will the crew say?"

"What they *won't* say, Byron, is anything like 'my captain allowed me

357

to go hungry while demanding that I work without cease,'" Grimm said.

Creedy moved his arms in an abortive gesture of frustration. "Sir . . . it just isn't natural for a ship's master."

"Nonsense. The Olympian Navy holds that a captain should know the details of every position in his ship's company by working them with his own hands, stem to stern. It's the only way to be sure you know what each man needs from his captain in order to be able to perform his duty."

Creedy's handsome face screwed up in protest. "We are not Olympians, sir."

"Surely as Albions we need not believe that we already possess all the sum of the world's wisdom. Are we not better bred than that, Mister Creedy?"

"But . . . sir, you can't possibly expect me to . . . to take my meal from you as if you were any other cookie in the galley."

"Indeed not," Grimm said gravely, and held out a second apron. "As I still have only one reliable arm, I require your assistance. Coat off and look sharp, Mister Creedy. There are tubers need peeling."

Kettle walked through the crowded mess hall and brought his bowl and spoon back up to the galley counter after the meal, grinning broadly at Creedy.

The XO scowled at him. There were bits of something, perhaps shavings of tuber skins, in his hair, and he'd cut his hand twice. Grimm had cleaned and covered each wound carefully before sending the young officer back to work, and Creedy's temper was worn thin. "Do you have a problem, Mister Kettle?"

"No, sir," Kettle drawled. "Just wanted to give my compliments to the skipper on his captaining."

"His captaining?" Creedy asked.

Grimm kept a grin from spreading over his mouth.

"Yes, sir, indeed. The hands and I all agree he's a damned fine captain."

Creedy regarded Kettle without humor. "I see."

"Best captain in the sky, maybe."

"I understand," Creedy said.

"There's rarely been a finer captain, we reckon," Kettle said expansively.

"You have made your position clear, Mister Kettle," Creedy all but snapped. "I'm sure the captain appreciates it."

Kettle nodded and put the bowl down.

Creedy snatched it up, scowling.

"So, Skip," he asked, with perfect innocence. "When will Waller get back into the galley, so you can get back to captaining?"

"Why, Mister Kettle," Grimm said. "One is tempted to think that you do not approve of your captain's cooking."

"No, sir!" Kettle said. "You'll never hear me complain, sir. I'm just a much bigger admirer of his captaining, sir."

"Mind your heading, Kettle," Creedy snapped. "Why, I should—"

Grimm put a gently restraining hand on Creedy's shoulder. "Cook should be back on board by midnight, I daresay."

"I'll spread that around," Kettle said, nodding to them pleasantly, and went back to his place at a table.

Creedy frowned after him for a moment and then turned to Grimm, lowering his voice. "Sir . . . the men shouldn't be able to criticize the captain openly like that."

"I didn't hear a word of criticism, XO," Grimm replied. He grunted with effort and dumped the last of the simple stew he'd made of the insufficient meal Waller had left behind into a large bowl, which held a double-size portion of the . . . food. "Kettle was merely expressing himself. That man knows how to complain flawlessly." He looked at Creedy. "You had a few mouthfuls when you could, Byron. I saw you. What did you think of my stew?"

Creedy looked suddenly discomfited. "It was . . . perfectly nourishing, sir. With salt, practically palatable."

Grimm smiled and began cleaning up.

Creedy blinked several times. "Sir . . . do you mean to say you made . . . *that* . . . on purpose?"

"Command is about more than knowing the protocol, Byron," Grimm said. "Whose fault was it that not enough dinner had been prepared?"

"Mine, sir," Creedy said stoutly. "I should have kept an eye on Journeyman, sir. His section was extraordinarily busy. There are small grounds to reprimand him."

"By the book, perhaps. But you and I were both supervising different sections of the ship, and he's the chief of the engine room. He should damned well be thinking about his men and the hired hands, as well as his systems."

"That's . . . a very fine distinction, sir."

Grimm shook his head. "The men know exactly what happened. And there are reprimands that have nothing to do with the book." He carried the double-portion bowl over to the counter. "Mister Kettle," he called.

The pilot looked up. "Aye, Skip?"

"The chief hasn't come up out of his precious engine room to eat. Perhaps you and some of the men can see to it that he sits down long enough to feed himself."

Kettle eyed the double-portion bowl askance and then slowly beamed. "Aye, Captain. He's working so hard, he deserves nothing less."

Creedy watched Kettle pick up the bowl and head out. Virtually every man in the mess hall went with him.

"What are they going to do?" Creedy asked with a certain amount of fascination.

"Watch Chief Journeyman eat every bite without salt, I should think, upon peril of their extreme displeasure," Grimm said. "And go very hard on him the entire time for forgoing such a basic responsibility and costing them a decent meal."

The young officer frowned. "Sir . . . it seems a bit hard on the men to proceed this way."

"Nonsense, XO," Grimm said. "The food was technically nourishing and they all ate their fill. We've done our penance in their eyes for not making sure the problem was avoided in the first place." He winked at Byron, and started shrugging back into his coat. "And after all, we can hardly have them *wanting* their captain to cook dinner when someone screws up by the numbers, now, can we? After all, I have a ship to run."

Creedy considered that for a long moment before he said, "You have a devious mind, sir."

Grimm looked up at the tall young officer and dropped his voice into a more serious register. "Strategy and tactics, discipline and protocol are necessary, but they're just the beginning. You have to know people, Byron. How they think, what motivates them. Watch. Learn."

Creedy stared at Grimm for a long moment. Then he nodded and said, "I will."

"Good man."

"You've hardly slept, sir," Creedy said. "I'll take the next watch. Go get some rest."

"Good of you," Grimm said, and took up his coat again. "I'll be in my cabin if I'm needed."

Grimm nodded to Byron, tried to ignore the pervasive ache that had spread from his injured arm out into every other fiber of his being, shambled to his cabin, hung up his coat, and flung himself down on his bunk without bothering to undress. He was asleep before the faint scent of Calliope's perfume that still lingered on the covers could bring back memories, unhappy or otherwise.

A sharp rap at his door brought Grimm abruptly out of his first sound sleep in days, almost before it had begun. He managed to sit up and swipe the rather less-than-captainly drool from his chin before the door opened and Creedy poked his head in with an apologetic expression. "Sir?"

Grimm suppressed a groan. Captains were not subject to such mortal infirmities as sleep deprivation. "Yes, XO?"

"Several of the men came back early from their leave, sir. They say there's been some kind of situation involving your passengers, sir. Trouble. People were killed and injured."

Grimm swung out of his bed at once and rose, ignoring the protests of his weary body. At least he was still dressed. "Kettle and an armed party of four to be ready to leave with me, including the men bearing the report. Doctor Bagen and his bag will accompany us. We leave immediately, to be briefed en route to Master Ferus's party."

"Aye, sir," Creedy said with a brisk nod, and withdrew from Grimm's cabin, bellowing orders.

Grimm took his wounded arm out of its sling long enough to properly don his coat, then added the sword belt and the sling again. The damned thing was a nuisance. The moment his arm was serviceable, he'd toss the blasted sling over the side of the Spire.

It seemed likely that would happen faster if he could only get several hours of sleep, all in a row.

He checked to be sure that his sword would draw smoothly, slid it firmly back into its scabbard, settled his hat onto his head, and strode out to meet the moment.

✻　　✻　　✻

A deckhand named Harrison guided them to the Black Horse, an inn and pub. Even at the late hour, well after midnight, a small crowd had gathered around the place.

"Don't know what happened exactly, sir," Harrison was saying. "But there was screaming like souls in Hell from inside, and what looked like smoke from a fire."

Another crewman named Bennett saw them coming and hurried over, flicking Grimm a quick salute. "Sir. Been watching it since Harry and the others left, sir."

"And?"

"No one has gone in or come out. The doors won't open, sir. But your passengers are inside. I was having a drink in there earlier, and that elderly fellow was leading a round of 'Farmer Long's Pickle.'" He nodded toward a couple of uniformed Guardsmen over by the doors. They were young men, their uniforms not quite tidy, perhaps the least valued of their garrison, to be drawing the late shift. They seemed somewhat at a loss for what to do. "These lads seem to be out of their depth, sir."

Grimm sighed and said, "Boarding ax, Mister Kettle."

Kettle turned to one of the other men of the party, and caught a heavy-headed boarding ax as it was tossed to him. The thing was part ax and part sledgehammer, meant for battering down the doors or bulkheads of an enemy ship, not for true combat. It would make short work of the doors of the inn, Grimm judged.

"With me," Grimm said, and strode toward the young Guardsmen, Kettle at his back.

They turned to him with a mix of uncertainty and anger on their faces. "Here now," said one of them. "What's this, then?"

Grimm eyed the young man steadily. In moments of confusion,

young soldiers were often comforted by authority figures who seemed to know what to do.

The Guardsman's back stiffened a little, and he nodded. "Captain," he said, with at least a pretense of respect.

Grimm nodded back. "Guardsman," he said. "I have friends inside that building. I see that the doors have not been opened."

"They're stuck fast," said the second Guardsman. "There are people inside shouting, but it's a demon's torment to hear them."

"I've an ax here," Grimm said. "Perhaps you would care to use it."

The Guardsmen looked at each other. While the Spirearch's Guard might have been popular with the scions of the great Houses of Albion, for a symbolic year or two at least, the majority of its long-term members were common men and women with widely varying backgrounds—and most of them had less extreme levels of endemic confidence.

"Bloody wooden doors are expensive," muttered the second Guardsman. "It'll be a month's pay to replace one."

"Bill it to Captain Grimm of the airship *Predator*," Grimm said. "Kettle."

"Aye, sir," Kettle said. He fired off a crisp salute and strode confidently toward the door.

"Can he do that?" the first Guardsman asked the second.

"Um," the second said.

"Guardsmen," Grimm said calmly. "Perhaps you should supervise the opening of the door, to make sure no one is harmed and to be on hand to assess the situation and render assistance as needed. Misters Bennett and Harrison, come here, please."

The two men did, firing off salutes of their own.

"You and the rest of the men will accompany these two Guardsmen and assist them in any way you can." He turned back to the two Guardsmen. "You'll find my men cooperative, sirs. Master Bagen is my ship's physician, and he will be able to render aid to anyone who is wounded."

"Right," said the first Guardsman, nodding. "Thank you for your assistance, Captain."

"But . . ." the second Guardsman said.

"Shut *up*, Malkie. There's people in there need helping," said the first one. He turned to the men from *Predator*, his stance and bearing more authoritative and confident. "You lot, come with us. Malkie, clear those people back from the doors, eh? Last thing we need is someone to take that ax on the backswing."

Grimm watched things develop with a certain amount of satisfaction. Once given a direction, the young Guardsmen seemed willing and capable enough. It would probably eventually occur to them that they'd essentially been given orders by a civilian with no legal authority whatsoever, but they seemed to be more in their element now.

He wondered whether either of them was secretly working with the Aurorans. It hardly seemed likely—but then, good spies never seemed likely, did they?

He took a couple of steps back as the second Guardsman herded the small crowd away from the doors of the inn, and bumped into a woman who had been watching, sending her to the ground in a sprawl.

"Oaf!" the woman said, her expression a war between astonishment and anger. She wore an excellent suit of clothing in steely shades of lavender accented with grey, skirts and a bolero jacket with a matching hat. She was an attractive, sharp-edged woman perhaps a few years older than Grimm, with large grey eyes devoid of any other color, and dark hair. "How rude."

"Madame, you are entirely correct," Grimm said. "I was careless and do beg your pardon." He straightened and offered her a bow, and then his good hand. "Moreover, I ask your forgiveness. In my eagerness to comply with instructions of the good Guardsmen, I fear that I did not adequately survey the space behind me before I moved. I am entirely in the wrong."

The woman stared at him for several seconds, and Grimm had two sudden impressions: First, that she was searching his words for something that might displease her. Second . . .

Second, that this woman, whoever she was, was dangerous. The hairs on the back of his neck simply crawled.

The woman narrowed her eyes abruptly, and for a wild instant Grimm wondered whether he might have been weary enough to have accidentally spoken his thoughts aloud.

Then the moment was gone, and the woman offered him a tight, restrained smile. "Of course, Captain. You are an airship captain, are you not?"

"Indeed, madame. Captain Francis Madison Grimm of *Predator*, at your service."

Her wide, expressive mouth twitched at one corner. "Oh, indeed? My name is Sycorax Cavendish." She took his hand and rose. "Thank you."

"You are quite welcome, Madame Cavendish," Grimm said.

She smiled, though the expression was an empty bowl, somehow barren of what a smile was meant to contain. "Are you the same Francis Madison Grimm as he who took command of the *Perilous* all those years ago?"

Grimm stiffened. Was that damned ship and the choices he made upon it to haunt him for the rest of his days?

Yes, it was, he supposed. That was part of the price he had paid to do his duty.

"The same," he said.

"Oh, Captain," Madame Cavendish breathed. "I have often wished to meet you."

"Then you are an exceptional individual. Such infamy as mine does not generally draw admirers, madame."

"I am," she replied, "and as such, I am well aware that there are often two sides to any given story. Even when one side is Fleet Admiralty."

He gave her the wooden smile he'd presented to so many others over the years. "I pray you will forgive the bluntness of a simple aeronaut, madame, but I have nothing further to say about the matter."

"I can hardly fail to forgive when such a request is so politely offered," Madame Cavendish replied. There was something very hard and covered in jagged spikes behind her eyes as she said the words, as if the courtesy itself had somehow displeased her. Grimm found himself fighting a sudden desire to edge away from the woman.

There was a movement in the crowd behind her, and then several people sidled away from a large man who had approached them. He was a tall, lean warriorborn, his pale head covered in sparse, grizzled fuzz. He was no beauty, and one of his eyes was fixed slightly to one side, making his gaze vague and a bit unsettling. When he saw Grimm, he let out a low growling sound in his chest and stepped forward, his body language aggressive.

Grimm had no desire to come to blows with a warriorborn. That fight could not be won in a gentlemanly manner, and his instincts were warning him that any such action would be a mistake in the presence of Madame Cavendish. A flutter of white flickered downward in the corner of his eye as he faced the man. "Good evening, sir."

The large warriorborn scowled. He looked aside, giving Madame Cavendish a quick glance, or so it seemed to Grimm. The disparity of the man's gaze made it difficult to know for certain. Grimm was unaccountably reminded, looking at the man, of an enormous spider, something patient and lethal waiting for its prey to come within reach.

The moment the man looked away, Grimm turned on his heel, bent, and retrieved the handkerchief from where Madame Cavendish had let it fall to the ground near her feet. "Pardon, madame," he said, "but you seem to have dropped this."

"And so I did," Madame Cavendish replied. Her dark eyes glittered brightly, almost feverish in their intensity. "You have excellent manners, sir."

"My old protocol teachers at the Fleet Academy would be startled to hear you say so, I am sure," he said, adding a little bow to the words. Just then, Kettle's boarding ax crashed through the door of the Black Horse, and men began entering. "If you would excuse me, Madame Cavendish. I must attend on what happens next."

She offered her gloved hand and, he felt, only barely managed to avoid speaking through clenched teeth. "Of course, Captain. How could I do otherwise?"

Grimm bent over her hand and brushed a polite kiss over the glove, though he thought his skin might ripple entirely up the length of his spine and pile up atop his head as he did so. "It was my pleasure to meet you, Madame Cavendish." Acting again on instinct, he added, "If you so desire, I am sure I can convince a Guardsman to see you safely from this place."

Madame Cavendish's eyes flickered to the Guardsmen and back to Grimm, too wary to be the gaze of a simple woman of the upper classes. Her expression froze as she found Grimm watching her, and then the barest hint of a smile touched her lips. She inclined her head to Grimm like a fencer acknowledging a touch, and then said, "That will not be necessary. I'm sure Mister Sark can see me safely home."

The large warriorborn made another growling sound in his throat.

"Then, Madame Cavendish, Mister Sark, I bid you good evening." He bowed again, then turned and walked away. He did not allow himself to hurry. He didn't know what the two were up to, but he knew predators when he met them eye-to-eye, and it was never a good idea to show fear to such creatures.

He walked past Malkie with a firm step and a steady nod. The young Guardsman didn't seem to question his presence, and Grimm joined Kettle at the door of the inn a moment later.

The reek from inside was horrible. The first floor of the building looked and smelled like an abattoir.

"Merciful Builders," Grimm breathed. "What happened here?"

"Looks like a silkweaver attacked them," Kettle reported. "A big one, sir. Webbed the doors shut and killed a lot of people."

"A silkweaver? *Here?*" Grimm demanded. He squinted around the street. Though there were fewer lights here than one might expect in Habble Morning, it was still bright enough to clearly see objects fifty feet away. "We're near the center of the habble. How did it get here without being seen?"

"How'd it know to web all the doors shut and trap everyone inside?" Kettle asked. "Those things ain't that smart, sir."

Grimm grunted. He turned to check on the presence of Madame Cavendish and her companion, but they were no longer in sight. "And it just happens to attack this inn. Has a bad smell to it, wouldn't you say, Mister Kettle?"

"Even worse than your cooking, sir," Kettle confirmed.

Grimm glanced at the man. "That bad, was it?"

Kettle scratched at his short beard. "Naw, suppose not," he replied. "Mind you, a hundred meals like that'd be a mutiny. One is just a good story."

Grimm grinned, briefly. "Doctor Bagen?"

"Inside with the others," Kettle said.

Harrison appeared a moment later and saluted Grimm. "Captain, Doctor Bagen's compliments, sir, and he says the Lancaster girl is wounded. He needs her in his infirmary at once."

"The others of her party?"

"Alive and well, sir, but two are missing who were sent out a few hours ago."

Grimm nodded. "Have Bagen make the girl ready to move, then. Let's get them all back to *Predator* quickly. We'll leave Mister Bennett and yourself here to round up the missing members of their group."

"Sir," Harrison said, and hurried back inside.

Grimm watched the man go, and then looked around, scanning the crowd. He still found no trace of either Cavendish or Sark.

"You've got your thinking face on, Captain," Kettle noted.

"Mmm," Grimm said. "I was thinking that the Spirearch sent his team to the right place."

"Sir?" Kettle asked.

"The enemy is here, Mister Kettle," he said, "and they're clearly onto us. Let's get Master Ferus and his people out of here before the next attack."

■ ■ ■ Chapter 40 ■ ■ ■

Spire Albion, Habble Landing Shipyards,
AMS *Predator*

Grimm and the shore party headed back to *Predator*, though he had an acutely uncomfortable sensation of being watched. He walked beside a quite inebriated Master Ferus, framing the old man between himself and Sir Benedict. The old etherealist could barely stagger along in a straight line, and was humming bits and pieces from a bawdy song beneath his breath as they traveled.

"Captain," said Sir Benedict. He was walking on Ferus's other side, keeping the old man moving along with the crew of *Predator*. He dragged Master Ferus's two overloaded wagons along behind him. "The other two young ladies of our group were sent to—"

"I've left two men behind at the Black Horse to await them and bring them along when they return," Grimm said, interrupting the young man.

"But what if they do not return?" Sorellin asked, his voice tight. "They were to—"

"In that eventuality, I will dispatch a search party," Grimm said shortly, pointedly cutting him off again. "Let us not discuss anything further here where we may be overheard, shall we, sir?"

The young man scowled but then seemed to think better of it, and schooled his expression. "Of course, Captain. You are correct."

Grimm gave him a short nod, and felt a bit of his tension ease. Young Sorellin was both warriorborn and of high birth. Grimm had

met all sorts from the upper classes in his time—most of them unre-
markable in most respects. The ones who had prided themselves too
much upon their position, by contrast, could be the most obnoxious
human beings on the face of the earth, with Hamilton Rook representing the worst portion of that particular bell curve. Grimm would not
care to deal with Hamilton as a warriorborn—but this young man
seemed a more or less decent sort.

They passed the rest of the walk back to the ship in silence, and
Doctor Bagen and the men detailed to carry Miss Lancaster proceeded
directly to his infirmary.

Master Ferus tottered up the boarding ramp to the ship and promptly
wobbled about to face Benedict. "My cane, if you please, Master Sorellin."

Sorellin shrugged the strap of a carrying case off of his shoulder. A
walking cane with a leather-wrapped head was strapped to the case, and
Benedict removed it and passed it to the old etherealist.

"I'll just have a word with your ship, shall I?" Master Ferus slurred.

Grimm arched an eyebrow at him and said, "As you wish, sir."

The old man beamed and then turned and walked carefully down
the deck, his wobbling steps steadied somewhat by the cane in his hand.

"All right," Grimm said, turning to Sorellin. "What happened in
there?"

Grimm listened as the young man told him of the silkweaver attack in
terse sentences. He finished with, "And then Gwen took up a firing stance
right in front of the thing as it charged Master Ferus, and blasted half of
its little head into pulp. It had enough momentum to slam into her and
carry her into the wall, and it bit her at least once, but she killed it."

"Remarkable," Grimm murmured. "That took more than a little
courage."

Sorellin smiled, briefly. "My dear cousin has a very odd relationship
with fear—though mostly she's too busy to be bothered with it."

"I'm glad the rest of you are well. The enemy has made his first mistake."

"Sir?" Sorellin asked.

"It would have been smarter for them to do nothing," Grimm said. "To give us no clue at all as to their presence. Instead they've attacked Master Ferus."

"With . . . a silkweaver, sir?" Sorellin asked, his tone skeptical. "They've never been domesticated."

Grimm glanced up at him. "Did it seem particularly tame to you?"

Sorellin frowned.

"They've told us that Ferus is a threat to them," Grimm said. "Therefore we must be looking in the right place."

"If it isn't just a random attack of a surface creature, sir," Sorellin said. "It might be a coincidence."

"I don't believe in the stuff, myself," Grimm said, and idly flexed his wounded arm in its sling. "Though you're right. We shouldn't rule out the possibility. But how many large creatures do you think have harmed folk in the center of Habble Landing?"

"We could ask the Verminocitors' Guild, I suppose."

"An excellent thought," said Master Ferus, as he came back along the deck toward them. "If there's anything odd afoot, or an enemy force in the habble, they'll be in the ventilation tunnels and crawl spaces. The verminocitors will be the next-most-likely group to have spotted something."

"After who, sir?" Grimm asked.

"The cats, of course," Ferus said. "Your ship is quite insouciant."

Grimm found himself frowning. "Is she?"

"Terribly," Master Ferus said gravely, "but I believe she understands the importance of cooperation."

"Ah," Grimm said.

"Well, I must see what I can do to ensure that brave young Lancaster's sacrifice was not a vain one," Master Ferus said. "Master Sorellin, perhaps you and I could make inquisitions of the verminocitors."

"But, sir," Sorellin said, "Bridget and Folly are still out there."

"Folly is quite capable of taking steps to protect them both, if need be," Master Ferus said, "and time is of the essence. But I suppose if you prefer to search for them . . ."

"I'm not supposed to leave your side, sir," Sorellin noted.

Master Ferus flipped his hand in an impatient gesture. "Did the Spirearch place me in command of this mission, or did he not?"

"You may have heard about my issues with authority," Grimm said. "Master Ferus, I believe it may have become too risky for you to roam about Habble Landing without taking extraordinary precautions. And certainly I believe Master Sorellin is correct in not wishing to leave your side."

"Ah?" Ferus asked. "And why is that?"

"I met someone outside the Black Horse while we were getting the doors open," Grimm replied. "A woman who struck me as extremely odd and somewhat dangerous. She did not look like the normal sort out and about at that time of the night; nor did she behave in a manner consistent with a genuine passerby. She was accompanied by a warrior-born man. They seemed to be entirely too interested in seeing the results of the situation inside the Black Horse, with entirely too little interest in speculating upon what had happened. I suspect that they may be Auroran agents, or employed by them."

Ferus narrowed his eyes. "Odd, you say? Why so?"

"If she is indeed connected to the Aurorans, an agent here in Albion, she would have to have ice water in her veins and be somewhat addled to be standing in plain sight at the scene of an attack," Grimm replied. He added rather delicately, "The woman seemed at least as odd as yourself, sir, meaning no offense by it."

"Oh, none taken," Ferus said. He considered the crystal at the end of his cane gravely. "Inevitable that at least one Auroran operative would have talent. I had hoped it would be otherwise, but . . ." He shook his head. "You are a man of uncommonly acute instinct, Captain Grimm. What else can you tell me about this person?"

Grimm pursed his lips. "She seemed unnaturally concerned with manners, sir. I gathered the impression, in fact, that if I had slipped up, she might have become violent, or asked her companion to do so on her behalf."

"Of that I have little doubt," the etherealist replied, his expression distant.

"She said her name was Cavendish."

Ferus grimaced. "So she's calling herself Cavendish now."

"Sir?" Grimm asked. "Do you know the woman?"

"Most thoroughly, I suspect," Ferus replied.

"Then you must surely see the wisdom in keeping you here in order to protect you," Grimm said. "If she was involved in an attempt on your life once, why not do so again? More directly this time. Should a warriorborn assassin surprise you inside the habble, even Master Sorellin could be hard-pressed to defend you."

"I see your point, Captain," Ferus replied.

"That said," Grimm continued, "I find it interesting that only hours before an Auroran attack upon Spire Albion, I should be assaulted in the ventilation tunnels by creatures unknown—creatures that left poison in my blood, much as silkweavers would. You helped me then. Assuming you are capable, perhaps you could help Miss Lancaster the way you assisted me."

Ferus frowned, and his eyes began darting here and there. "Yes . . . yes, we really ought to do whatever we can for Miss Lancaster. So be it. You and Sorellin will go."

"Um, sir," Sorellin said. "Still not supposed to leave your side."

"Ah, but I will be here, and quite safe surrounded by the grim captain's ship and crew," Ferus said, smiling. He tilted his head to one side and eyed Grimm. "Correct me if I am wrong, but I seem to remember saving your life, Captain. Did I not?"

Grimm sighed. "You did, sir."

"And docs that not oblige you to me in some way?"

"It does."

"You must trust me in this. I know precisely what I am doing." The old man turned and began to walk with a determined stride toward Doctor Bagen's infirmary. Then he paused, looked back at Sorellin, and said, "I say, dear boy, could you get the doorknob for me? I never could learn the trick of the blasted things."

Sorellin gave the etherealist a perfectly bland look. Then he smiled amiably, if wearily, and strode off after him, returning a moment later.

"Shall we speak to the verminocitors?" Grimm asked him.

"What, now? In the middle of the night?"

"A silkweaver matriarch has killed some of their neighbors tonight," Grimm replied. "Word will have spread by now. I doubt any of them will sleep for some time."

Sorellin grunted and nodded, and the pair of them started down the gangplank. Halfway down, Grimm looked up to see Stern returning to *Predator*. The wiry young man was dressed in disgraceful-looking tattered rags, and covered in grease, oil, and soot. When he saw Grimm coming down the ramp, he stepped aside to let his captain pass.

"Mister Stern," Grimm said. "What is that covering you from head to toe? For a moment I took you for my shadow."

"Soot and engine grease, Skip," Stern said, grinning.

"I take it you amused yourself thoroughly this evening."

"Indeed I did, sir. All went well."

"I am relieved to hear it—but I can't have one of my aeronauts wandering about looking like a tunnel rat. Clean yourself up."

Stern grinned, and his teeth were a very white contrast to the soot. "I'll do that, sir, right away."

"Good man," Grimm said, and began striding toward the archway leading into Habble Landing.

Sorellin looked back over his shoulder as the small sailor scampered up the gangplank. "What was that about, Captain?"

"Accounts payable," Grimm replied. "Do you know where the guild has its headquarters?"

"If they haven't moved them," Sorellin said.

"Then lead on, sir."

The warriorborn took the lead, and as he did, Grimm took note of the young man's appearance. "You seem to be somewhat the worse for wear, sir. Did you take part in the fighting?"

"Some," Sorellin said. "Though it was Gwen who made the difference."

Grimm nodded. "What is her condition?"

"The bite wound was not severe, but it was poisoned. She has what might be a broken wrist," Sorellin replied, his tone wooden, but steady. "She also took a severe blow to the back of her head, and has been insensible ever since. Her head is swollen. The physician wasn't sure if her skull had been cracked or not." He showed his teeth in an unpleasant smile. "To think of all the times I ribbed her about having a hard head and a stiff neck. Now she's barely breathing."

"Hold fast, Master Sorellin," Grimm said. "I've seen men who recovered from severe concussions in a day or two. Mister Bagen knows his trade—and Master Ferus knows some things most of us don't, I daresay. There is ample reason to hope."

The warriorborn frowned. "I'm not sure how comforting that is, sir. Master Ferus is . . . I do not wish to sound disrespectful, but the man is . . ."

"One grip shy of a steering column?" Grimm suggested. "Ten degrees short of a compass? Aviating without goggles?"

Sorellin's expression flickered through surprise and amusement before he schooled it to neutrality again. "A bit eccentric, sir."

"Hardly," Grimm said. "He's mad."

Benedict frowned for a moment. "Truly?"

"Every etherealist I've ever met has been," Grimm said, as they passed into the Spire proper. "Something about the energies they work with. It affects each of them uniquely, as far as I've been able to see."

"Is that why he's so odd about doorknobs?"

"I assume so," Grimm said. He nodded toward the two piled wagons. "I've seen him demand a number of strange items from his apprentice for no sensible reason I could detect, and add them to that collection of his—the one he insists on taking everywhere with him. And you'll note that his apprentice seems unable to directly address anyone else, apart from Master Ferus."

"She's mad too?"

"She seems a pleasant enough child," Grimm said. "But yes, presumably."

Sorellin considered that for several steps. "Sir . . . is it quite *safe* to be around such folk?"

"If they were safe, I suspect the Spirearch would not have sent them into the Enemy's teeth the way he has," Grimm replied. "None of us on this mission are particularly *safe* to be around, Master Sorellin, yourself included. Of course they aren't safe. The real question is whether or not they can be trusted."

"And . . . do you trust them, sir?"

Grimm considered the question for half a block before he said, "The Spirearch has extended his trust. I am willing to do so as well."

"Even though they're mad."

"There is madness and *madness*, Master Sorellin," Grimm said.

"Ferus and Folly are quite odd, and I take considerable comfort in that fact."

"Sir?"

"In my experience, the worst madmen don't seem odd at all," Grimm said. "They appear to be quite calm and rational, in fact. Until the screaming starts." He glanced up to find Sorellin staring at him, frowning. "Let me put it this way, sir. If ever you meet an etherealist who does *not* seem odd, you will have ample reason for caution. An etherealist who speaks to things that are not there and cannot track the day of the week is par for the course. One who is perfectly well dressed, calmly spoken, and inviting you to tea? *That* is someone to be feared."

Chapter 41

Spire Albion, Habble Landing,
Ventilation Tunnels

D o permit me to pour you tea, Sergeant Ciriaco," Cavendish
purred.

Major Espira adjusted his cup on its saucer, controlled
himself from raising his voice in alarm, and said, "Madame, I pray you
will forgive the sergeant, but he has duties to which he must attend."

"Ah," Cavendish said. "Duty must be the soldier's primary concern,
of course."

Cavendish had returned to the Auroran staging area with her pet
monster wheeling a little cart behind him. The cart had produced a
small folding table, chairs, a tablecloth, and tea service, complete with
a bubbling hot pot of water ready for steeping. Sark now loomed over
one side of the table where Espira sat across from Madame Cavendish,
while Sergeant Ciriaco stood behind and slightly to one side of his
chair, watchfully facing Sark.

Espira ignored the spatters of blood on the floor and walls of the tunnel in which the little table sat. This was where Cavendish had tortured
the luckless verminocitor. Ciriaco, with his enhanced senses, would not
be able to ignore it. The smell of blood and terror was doubtless responsible for a great deal of the sergeant's tension.

"Go ahead, Sergeant, and see to the men," Espira said. Ciriaco was

380

a good man, but in his present frame of mind, the warriorborn was too bluntly spoken to survive tea with Cavendish.

"Major . . ." Ciriaco said, hesitant. Espira looked back to see the man shift his weight, eyes warily locked on Sark.

Sark, for his part, didn't seem to be looking at anyone. The grizzled warriorborn simply stood, relaxed, as if the presence of a wary, armed, and dangerous warriorborn Marine were of no greater consequence to him than the color of the cloth he'd spread over the little table a moment before.

And as long as Cavendish was there, it wasn't.

Espira suppressed a shudder.

"That's an order, Sergeant," he said calmly. "See to the men. Post a guard on the mouth of the tunnel so that we are not disturbed. Dismissed."

Espira could all but hear the sergeant's teeth grinding. But he said, "Yes, sir," snapped off a salute, and stalked out of the tunnel.

"He seemed a trifle impolite, Major," Cavendish said diffidently.

"The sergeant has had little experience with the niceties of proper society, I fear. Additionally, he was wounded in the attempt to destroy the Lancasters' crystal vattery," Espira replied. "I suspect he is experiencing more pain than he is willing to admit."

"And he is valuable to you?"

"Indispensable," he assured her.

Cavendish sipped at her tea. "I suppose allowances must be made. He is, after all, warriorborn. We cannot expect them to maintain perfect poise indefinitely." She glanced up at Sark and murmured, "Inevitably, the beast emerges."

For a second, Espira saw some kind of smoldering heat in Sark's blank eyes. The bloodstains on the walls glistened in the light of the little table's lumin crystals.

"You speak with great perception," Espira said. "This tea is excellent."

"Why, thank you, Major," Cavendish said with a smile that on anyone else would have seemed genuine. "It is my personal blend. I mixed it myself."

Espira struggled to keep his smile from becoming wooden. He had a strong instinct that he did not want to know precisely what a madwoman like Cavendish would have mixed into her tea. "Madame, you are too generous."

"That remains to be seen," Cavendish said. "The Enemy is here, Major."

Espira arched an eyebrow. He took a sip of tea and suggested diffidently, "It *is* the Albions' home Spire, madame."

She made an impatient flicking gesture with the fingers of one hand. "All the trogs of Albion cannot impede my designs," she said. "But there are other hands moving now, other minds bending their wills upon this habble. They have the power to deny us our goals if improperly handled."

"May I assume, then, madame, that this is the purpose of your visit?"

"Obviously. It is time to employ contingency measures."

Espira leaned back in his chair and cupped his tea with both hands for a moment. "Madame," he said slowly, "the timing of our strike must be precise. Otherwise we shall not have the support of the Armada nor any means of escape. Any action we take before the appointed hour jeopardizes the entirety of the plan."

Cavendish looked at him over the rim of her teacup and her expression was utterly blank. "Major. I begin to find myself disappointed in the paucity of your motivation. Must I find a way to increase it?"

"Madame, with all respect, I must remind you that my men are Marines, not spies. They fight well, but they have neither the training nor the experience to blend into the populace of an Albion habble for any length of time." He cleared his throat. "I might even suggest that your own resources might be better put to such a task."

"They have been," Cavendish replied calmly. "It was how I managed to confirm the presence of the foe. And I have been identified, I suspect, so I dare not address the matter personally from my current position. Your men will still possess the advantage of surprise."

Just then footsteps sounded in the hallway, and Lieutenant Ibarra, one of the younger officers of the force under Espira's command, appeared from the shadows. Ibarra had gone missing during the initial incursion and had been presumed lost, and the broad-chested, quick-tempered young nobleman walked toward them with tired but hurried steps.

"Major!" Ibarra called. "Lieutenant Ibarra reporting for duty, sir."

Dammit. Why hadn't the guards stopped the man? Because the young officer had ordered them to let him pass, of course. Damned young hothead. "Lieutenant, I am currently busy."

Ibarra looked strained and a bit white around the eyes, but he grinned and gave Cavendish a lecherous leer. "I can see that, sir. Rank doth have its privileges, eh? Can I afford one of those on a lieutenant's pay?"

"*Lieutenant*," Espira snapped.

"How *rude*," Cavendish said. Her smile was one of absolute pleasure. She flicked a finger. Only that.

Ibarra's eyes suddenly flew open wide in an expression of utter terror, and an instant later the man began to scream and kept screaming. His hands flew to his eyes, his palms pressing against his skull, and he staggered and collapsed to the ground one joint at a time.

Cavendish watched with flat, passionless eyes and noted, "I cannot abide boors."

Ibarra shrieked on as Espira put his tea down and lunged toward the young man. "Guard!" he bellowed.

Espira had seen this before. He desperately pried at Ibarra's wrists, but despite his strength he was unable to remove the young man's hands from his eyes.

The guards came running, but they didn't get there before Ibarra had clawed his eyes out with his own raking fingers in mindless, howling terror.

At Espira's command, and with his help, the two Marines managed to haul Ibarra's hands from his face and bind them behind his back, but the bloody ruins of the boy's eye sockets were bleeding freely by the time they were done.

"Get him to a medic, fast," Espira snapped. Then he shot a glance at Cavendish.

The mad etherealist regarded him through slitted eyes, a small smile dancing upon her lips. She was, he realized, enjoying herself—and waiting for his reaction.

"Was that necessary, madame?" he snarled.

"That depends entirely upon you, Major," Cavendish murmured. "And upon how motivated you are feeling. How many more of your men will be visited by such horrors before you elect to cooperate? You may decide."

Espira ground his teeth. He wore his gauntlet. Would he have time to prime and discharge it before Cavendish could . . .

. . . what? Twitch a finger?

And even if he did manage to kill her, what would Armada Admiralty say about the action? Cavendish was their darling.

Espira felt his shoulders sag.

"Very well," he said, and his own voice sounded ragged to him. "How many?"

"Six should be sufficient."

Six. Six men. If he sent them out on Cavendish's hunt, absolutely anything could happen. He might well be signing their death warrants.

But at this point . . . what choice did he have?

He ground his teeth and nodded. "Whom do I tell them to kill?"

She lifted her cup and took another sip of tea, briefly concealing her skeleton smile.

■ ■ ■ Chapter 42 ■ ■ ■

Spire Albion, Habble Landing,
Near the Black Horse Inn

Bridget spotted the sign for the Black Horse and felt a surge of relief—only to have it sublimate into anxiety when she realized that something was very, very wrong.

There was a crowd around the building. The front door had been broken from its hinges and lay in shattered pieces on the ground nearby. A number of uniformed Guardsmen were present—as were nearly a dozen silent, motionless human forms lying in a row on the ground, covered by bloodstained bedsheets.

Bridget promptly took Folly's arm and drew her around the nearest corner and out of sight of the Black Horse.

"Oh," Folly said, surprised. "I thought Bridget and I were returning to the master in the inn. But now we're hiding in a dark alley instead. I wonder why we're doing that?"

"Didn't you see?" Bridget asked.

The etherealist's apprentice frowned down at her jar of crystals. "One of you should tell Bridget that I was watching to make sure none of you fell out on the return trip."

"I'll watch them for a moment, Folly," Bridget said. "You should take a look."

Folly gave her a grateful smile and then crept up to the corner and peered carefully around it. After a moment, she reported dubiously, "I can see what she's talking about. But don't know what that means."

"Something has happened," Bridget said. "We don't know what. But what are the odds that so much violence would come to the same inn where our inquisition was based?"

"Oh, I can't tell her that without more points of data," Folly said seriously. "If I knew how many inns were in Habble Landing, and the general rate of violent incidents over a statistically significant duration . . ."

"Folly," Bridget said quietly. "There are dead bodies there. And we don't know who they are."

Folly stared blankly at Bridget for several seconds. Then her eyes widened, and the blood drained from her face. "She thinks one of them could be my . . . her fellow Guardsmen?" She swallowed. "Oh, I'm sure that I don't like that thought at all. We must not rush to conclusions. How can we even be sure that those are dead bodies?"

Bridget glanced up to the cat on her shoulder. "Rowl?"

"I smell death," Rowl reported.

Bridget forced herself to breathe slowly and evenly, though her heart lurched at the thought that some of the forms beneath the sheets might be her friends. She tried to address the problem with dispassionate rationality.

"One of us should go look," she murmured. "Perhaps Master Ferus and the others are simply inside. We must know what happened."

"Of course," Folly said, nodding to her jar. "Bridget is so sensible. Oh, except that . . . if there truly is an enemy nearby, he might be watching the inn. We would be revealing ourselves to him."

"I will go," Rowl said calmly.

Bridget peered around the corner again. "That is not advisable, Rowl. There are half a dozen verminocitors there now. See the scalelashes and the leather coats and boots? They might not take kindly to the presence of a cat in the middle of the habble."

Rowl made a growling sound in his throat. Cats had historically been hunted by verminocitors—and vice versa. Though there was a working alliance of cooperation between them in Habble Morning, cats and verminocitors kept communications to the absolute minimum necessary to make that alliance function. Neither group trusted the other. She had no idea what that relationship might be in Habble Landing.

"In order to harm me," Rowl said, supremely confident, "they would first need to know I was there." And with that, he leapt lightly to the ground and vanished into the shadows deeper in the alley.

"Oh, that arrogant little monster," Bridget murmured.

"Don't worry," Folly told her jar. "I'm sure Rowl will be quite careful."

Bridget sighed. "He's not one-tenth as clever as he believes himself to be."

"You mustn't judge Bridget for saying such things," Folly murmured. "She is only under strain, and I can hardly blame her. I don't want someone I care about to be dead, either. Thinking of it makes me feel as though my stomach had curled into a ball and rolled away."

Bridget grimaced. "It seems so useless to be skulking about like this. Those Guardsmen wear the same uniform I do. Or would, if we were wearing our uniforms. I should be able to walk up to them and ask questions."

"Perhaps Bridget does not remember that the Spirearch was concerned that one of the Guardsmen might be an enemy spy."

"Or they might *not*," Bridget said. "Traitors do not pose the true threat to Spire Albion. They're nowhere near as dangerous—or toxic— as fear."

Folly frowned quietly down at the ground. "And yet, what choice does Bridget have? If this situation is the result of enemy action, and the enemy *does* have a traitor within the Guard, is it not logical to assume that the traitor would be present here, watching and reporting to his Auroran masters?"

"I suppose it is logical." Bridget sighed. "But I feel no obligation whatever to *like* it."

"Oh," Folly said, more brightly. "I'm relieved that she feels that way—I thought I might be the only one."

Bridget drew back from the corner, lest someone spot her and be curious as to why a young woman might be acting in such a clandestine fashion around such dire events, and settled down to wait.

Rowl returned within ten minutes, sauntering forth from the shadows calmly and padding over to climb onto Bridget's lap.

"I know," Bridget said. "You told me so."

Rowl curled his tail around his paws and looked smug.

"What did you see?"

"I could not get close to the dead," Rowl said. "They were too closely watched. There is a very large silkweaver inside the stone box. It is most thoroughly dead. Death-scent overpowers all other smells. I could not identify the bodies. I could hear the moans of many wounded humans inside the stone box, but there is only one door leading inside, and that was too crowded and well lit to risk. Even humans would have seen me."

"Rust and rot," Bridget snarled in frustration.

"Oh!" Folly breathed, and tried to cover up the jar of crystals with her hands, as though cupping an infant's ears. "Such language."

"I do beg your pardon," Bridget said. "I'm . . . tired and overwrought, is all."

Folly nodded seriously. "Everyone begs everyone's pardon, but I've never seen a pardon. Is it near the spleen?"

Bridget blinked, then gave her head a little shake to keep the odd thought from crawling into her ear. "Folly, we need to decide on our next move."

"All right," Folly said. "What should we do?"

Rowl looked up at her, waiting.

Bridget could feel the pressure of two sets of eyes on her, and she felt her chest tighten. Somehow she had become the leader. How on earth had that happened?

"We make a sensible, conservative move," she said. "We can't know where the others are, or if they are hurt or in danger. Either way, we are ill-equipped to assist them as we are, and the chance of an enemy agent spotting us is simply too great. We will return to *Predator* and seek the help of Captain Grimm in getting back to Master Ferus and the others."

"Sensible," Rowl said, his tone one of firm approval. "I can watch for danger from the top of the ship-tree."

"Yes," Folly said. "That seems like a very fine plan to me."

"Good," Bridget said, nodding. "Yes. That wasn't so difficult, was it?" She chewed on her lip for a moment. "Rowl, could you please find us a way to circle around the Black Horse without being observed?"

"Of course I could," Rowl purred, clearly pleased as he rose. "Wait a moment while I ensure our safety and success."

The cat ghosted away and returned to lead them deeper into the alley and through an alarmingly narrow passageway to the next street over from the Black Horse. They walked in silence, with the cat padding well in advance of them, his whiskers and ears quivering as he watched for potential threats.

By the time they got back to the archway that led out onto the wooden shipyard, Bridget's alarm had begun to fade. She was simply too exhausted to sustain a case of nerves. Once they were back on *Predator*, she could report what she had learned to Captain Grimm and perhaps sit down for a few moments and rest her aching feet.

And so she was utterly unprepared when a tall, lean form detached from a shadow only a stride or two from Folly and abruptly seized her around the throat with both arms. Folly's eyes flew open wide, but she never had the chance to make a squeak. One instant she was walking, and the next her eyes were rolling up into her head while her knees buckled beneath her.

Bridget stared for a moment, trying to drag her mind into focus, to confront the threat. She abruptly remembered her gauntlet and lifted it, struggling to prime the crystal against her palm with her thoughts — only to suddenly feel her hair seized in an iron grip while something cold and terrible and sharp pressed against the base of her neck.

"Now, now, miss," growled a man with a rolling Auroran accent. "Lower your hand or I'll shove this up into your brains."

Bridget ground her teeth, hesitating, and the hand jerked her head back. She had a sudden, horrible image of her head being pulled onto the knife and let out a little sound of panic, lowering her hand.

"Alley," the man growled, and Bridget could do little as she found herself marched into a darkened alleyway out of sight of the guarded portal to the shipyard.

The first attacker seized the back of Folly's jacket in one hand and dragged her limp form along behind him. Her little jar of expended crystals went rolling free, and the odd pistoleer's belt joined it. There were other men waiting in the alley, and one of them scooped up Folly's fallen gear like a man tidying up after a mess had been made. Bridget rapidly found her hands bound behind her back, and a cloth gag forced into her mouth.

Her heart pounded with sheer panic, her weariness forgotten.

A low voice rumbled in Auroran. It was answered by the voice of Bridget's captor, its tone annoyed. A small lumin crystal appeared, being held in the fingers of a man she did not recognize. He was in his early thirties, perhaps, with fine dark hair and an olive skin tone. His eyes were dark and very, very hard. He held the light up to her face, and then up to that of the unconscious Folly, and muttered something else beneath his breath.

The first voice answered him, and Bridget recognized it even as the light from the little crystal revealed the man's features. It was Ciriaco, the warriorborn Auroran sergeant who had captured her in the tunnels of Habble Morning.

The man's eyes narrowed as he saw her, and he said, "You again."

The shorter man frowned, looking between them, and switched to speaking Albion. "You are acquainted, Sergeant."

"This girl was one of the ones we had trouble with."

"Forgive me for saying so," he said, "but she doesn't look particularly doll-like."

"This is another one," Ciriaco said.

"Ah," said the smaller man. Something about him screamed "officer" to Bridget. He was obviously the warriorborn's superior. "Then there's no real need to remain clandestine, if she already recognizes you."

Ciriaco grunted.

"Young woman," the officer said. "I hope that you believe me when I say that I truly regret the necessity of detaining you." He nodded to two of the other men in the alley, and they loped out silently, obviously intending to scout for the major just as Rowl had been scouting for them.

"Where are you taking us?" Bridget demanded, or tried to demand. The gag made it sound like a muffled echo from a distant tunnel.

The officer's expression became grim. Chillingly, he seemed to understand her question, despite the gag. Perhaps he'd had practice. "To someone who wishes to speak to you. Sergeant, take the odd little one. If this young lady tries to escape or make any sounds, cut her friend's throat."

"Aye, sir," Ciriaco said. He picked up the bound and limp form of Folly by the back of her jacket again, and drew a knife into his other hand.

Bridget felt her eyes blurring with tears of pure frustration.

"I regret the necessity of such measures, young lady," the officer said. "But I implore you not to test my resolve. It will cost your friend her life if you do. Do you understand?"

Bridget closed her eyes and felt ashamed that she had shown the man her tears. She nodded once.

"Excellent," the officer said. "Young lady, my name is Major Renaldo Espira of the Auroran Marines, and you—both of you—should consider yourselves my prisoners."

▪ ▪ ▪ Chapter 43 ▪ ▪ ▪

Spire Albion, Habble Landing,
Verminocitors' Guild

The Verminocitors' Guild was on the upper level of Habble Landing, and Grimm found it profoundly uncomfortable, somehow, to walk habble streets made of anything other than spirestone. The black stone from which the Spires had been constructed was all but indestructible, and had withstood the ravages of time for millennia — but the Builders had taken the secret of its working with them when they vanished from the world. Modern architects were skilled, but when anything collapsed in a habble, it was inevitably made of inferior masonry.

Grimm knew he was being ridiculous. God in Heaven knew that he walked far more fragile wooden decks without a qualm, both upon *Predator* and on the platforms of Landing. Nonetheless, he fancied he could feel the masonry floor beneath his feet flexing and shifting ever so slightly with each of his steps.

The guild hall was down a narrow side alley, and if Benedict hadn't been there, Grimm might not even have noticed the alleyway at all. Its battered wooden door had the faint remnants of a scalelash carved into it, worn down to a faded design by time. A single small lumin crystal hung from a string that had been fixed to the doorway above.

By its light, Grimm could see a placard on the wall beside the door. It stated, simply, "No Unauthorized Entry." A second, smaller placard immediately beneath it read, "No, You Are Not Authorized."

"Friendly," Grimm noted.

Benedict smiled tightly. "They're a breed unto themselves. And they like it that way. Which is why I'm not sure what the crystal is for."

"It's a shadelight," Grimm said quietly. "Some of my men put one up whenever I lose a member of the crew. To light his shade's way back to his bunk, so he can rest."

"A bit heathen of them, I suppose," Benedict said.

"It's a tradition," Grimm said. "Were traditions rational, they'd be procedures." He touched the light gently and then said, "We all feel a need to mark the Reaper's passing somehow." He frowned for a moment. "Were any verminocitors in the inn when the silkweaver attacked?"

"No," Benedict said.

"Ah," Grimm said. "And how many of these men do you think are killed in a given year?"

"Not many," Benedict said. "They're professionals."

"I believe it strains coincidence to consider this death unrelated to our current troubles."

"I agree," Benedict said.

"Then this," Grimm said, "is what I believe professional inquisitors refer to as a clue."

"In my considered judgment as an occasional inquisitor for the Spirearch," Benedict said, "I believe you may be correct."

Grimm nodded and said, "Excellent." Then he turned and pounded hard and steadily on the door.

The guildmaster was a man named Felix. He was grizzled and short, standing only a scant inch taller than Grimm's friend Bayard, though the resemblance ended there. Felix was blocky and solid-looking, though his nose was reddened with burst blood vessels and his eyes were sunken, heavy things lurking back beneath a heavy brow. He was dressed in breeches and a tunic of heavy leather, with matching gauntlets tucked in his belt, next to the coiled circle of his scalelash, a long braid of metal rings woven together with metal scales throughout, forming a long, flexible reptilian coil. Grimm had seen them used before. In skilled hands they could rend flesh like some kind of horrible mechanical saw.

"Gentlemen," Felix said in a low, growling tone. "I have little time to waste on foolishness." He nodded back toward a side room off the main chamber of the guild hall, where a form lay on a table, shrouded under cloth. "We've lost one of our own today, and our habble's folk have suffered. What do you want?"

Grimm considered the man for a moment and then nodded to Benedict.

"Sir, you may not remember, but we met briefly about two years ago," Benedict said. "I was in the uniform of the Guard at the time. I was taking a deposition from one of your guild members about the stolen weapons crystals."

Felix squinted at Benedict for a moment and then reluctantly grunted acknowledgment. "Sorello, right? The one that broke down the door."

"Sorellin," Benedict said, "Yes, sir."

Felix nodded. "I remember you."

"I'm in the midst of an inquisition, sir," Benedict said. "And we need to speak to you regarding any unusual activity your members may have noticed since the Auroran raid."

The verminocitor's expression turned sour. "Other than losing a man and having a rotting silkweaver matriarch tear apart half the habble, you mean?"

Benedict smiled patiently. "There were a dozen casualties, sir, some dead, some wounded, and some still hanging in the balance. One of them is my sixteen-year-old cousin, Gwendolyn, whom I love quite dearly." His smile vanished abruptly, and his feline eyes went flat and glinted with flecks of amber and gold. The barest hint of a rumbling growl came into the young man's voice. "We've all had a long evening, sir."

Felix became tense immediately, and one of his hands twitched, as if to move to the handle of his scalelash.

Benedict regarded him calmly, with absolutely no hint of hostility anywhere in his stance. Only in his eyes. Anger smoldered there, far back, and Grimm took note of it. Young Master Sorellin had presented himself as a calm and gregarious young fellow of Habble Morning's upper classes, but Grimm had, in his time, met a certain number of dangerous individuals.

Though he was young, Benedict Sorellin, Grimm judged, was one of them.

Grimm turned his gaze to Felix. What happened next would depend a great deal on whether or not Felix had the sense to see what Grimm had in the young man.

Felix was no fool. He grunted, turned away, and casually put a little more distance between himself and the looming warriorborn. He picked up a mug and swallowed whatever dregs were left in it before turning back to them and eyeing Grimm. "Who is he?"

"My associate," Benedict said calmly.

Felix grunted, looking back and forth between them. "He's Fleet. Eh?" The verminocitor snorted. "Oh, civilian clothes, sure. But them boys could be naked and you could still see their uniform." He squinted at Benedict. "You aren't in uniform either. Rot and ruin, what does that old man up in Morning think he's about?"

"Do you really want to know?" Benedict asked.

Felix shuddered. "And get drawn in further? God in Heaven, no. I have troubles enough."

"Wise man," Grimm said.

"I'd like to examine the remains of your man, if that's all right," Benedict said.

Felix shrugged and nodded. "Suit yourself."

Benedict nodded his thanks and withdrew to the side chamber. He drew the cloth back. Grimm couldn't see much of the form beneath it, and felt glad that he couldn't. What he could see was horribly torn and mangled.

Felix didn't look toward the room. He stared down at his mug, turning it in hard, scarred hands.

"What was his name?" Grimm asked quietly.

"Moberly," the guildmaster said quietly. "Harris Moberly."

Grimm nodded. "How old?"

Felix grimaced. "Twenty."

Grimm nodded. "Family?"

"Wife, brother, mother," Felix said. "Wife's expecting."

Grimm made a soft sound and shook his head.

Felix nodded. He eyed Grimm. "You know."

"Wish I didn't."

Felix let out a wry chuckle. "Drink?"

"Obliged."

The verminocitor poured from a bottle into his mug and a second one like it he took from the shelf. He held up his mug to Grimm briefly, and Grimm mirrored him. They drank. The spirits in the mug were not particularly fine, but neither were they feeble. Kettle would have loved them. Grimm swallowed it carefully.

Felix glanced into the room and then back down.

"How did it happen?" Grimm asked.

"Moberly was out on a contract on his own," Felix said. "Against the rules. Not supposed to run without a partner. But with the baby on the way, he wanted to lay in some extra money. Silkweavers got him."

"Weavers? Plural?"

Felix grunted. "Hatchlings. Matriarch like the one at the Black Horse will lay fifty eggs a day. One hatchling wouldn't have been a problem for Moberly. Six or seven wouldn't have been a problem. A few hundred, though . . ."

Grimm shuddered. "Bad way to go. You sure what killed him?"

"Those mouths of theirs make marks you can't mistake. Not hard to measure them and do the math."

"No offense meant," Grimm said.

Felix shrugged. "All right."

"What will you do next?"

"Sweep the tunnels as soon as we get enough of the lads together. Handle those hatchlings before they grow up. Coordinate with the guilds above and below Habble Landing, make sure it doesn't become an infestation."

"Difficult job?"

"Hard enough," Felix said. His eyes flattened, though his voice stayed gentle. "But we'll get it done."

Grimm nodded.

Benedict reappeared from the side room. He had covered Moberly's body again. "Hatchling marks?" he asked Felix.

"That's what we saw," Felix said. "That much venom, he never had a chance."

"I don't think so," Benedict said. "The wounds aren't right."

Felix squinted at the young warriorborn. "How's that?"

"The blood," Benedict said. "It's congealed in the wounds."

"That's what blood does," Felix said.

"What are you getting at, Benedict?" Grimm asked.

"I don't think your man Moberly was alive when those things caught up to him. He didn't bleed enough."

"Didn't bleed enough?" Felix asked. "What does that mean?"

"I think his heart wasn't beating when the hatchlings started on him," Benedict said seriously. "Did you notice his neck?"

"Neck?" Felix asked.

"We'd need to consult with a physician to be sure," Benedict said, "but I think someone broke his neck. Clean."

Grimm pursed his lips. "And then tossed him to the silkweavers?"

Benedict nodded.

"Why?" Felix asked. "Why would anyone do such a thing?"

Benedict looked at Grimm. "What do you think?"

Grimm swirled the spirits in his mug and said thoughtfully, "I think . . . they had to kill him."

"They? They who?" Felix asked.

Benedict's eyes widened in understanding. "Moberly got close to the Aurorans. He saw them."

Grimm nodded sharply and rose. "The Aurorans are here, in Habble Landing." He turned to Felix. "You say Moberly was pursuing a contract?"

"Yes," the guildmaster said.

Grimm clenched his jaw and felt his hand fall to the hilt of his sword. "Where?"

■ ■ ■ Chapter 44 ■ ■ ■

Spire Albion, Habble Landing,
Ventilation Tunnels

Rowl moved with flawless competence through the shadows behind the group of men who had seized Littlemouse and her odd friend. This meant, of course, that he was unobserved by anyone whom he did not permit to observe him.

This was all Littlemouse's fault. She had specifically asked him to seek out any possible danger lying in their way. She had said nothing whatever about danger that might steal up on them from behind, and Rowl had assumed that, between the pair of them, they might have enough wits about them to avoid being stalked and taken down like a pair of silly tunnel mice. He had therefore been *ahead* of them, looking for *reasonable* dangers, and it was quite thoroughly Littlemouse's own fault if she had not taken adequate precautions to watch over her shoulder while Rowl was busy watching absolutely everywhere else.

By the time he'd heard the half-souled human warrior and the smaller one who was the leader close in on Littlemouse and her friend, it had been too late to warn them or accomplish anything apart from exposing himself. Their enemies had been inconsiderate enough to be too many in number for Rowl to manage comfortably with only his four paws.

So instead he followed the men who held Littlemouse, and calmly plotted their deaths.

They hurried from the main human area into the ventilation tunnels on the southern side of the habble, and Rowl kept pace with them. There was a familiarity to the air of the tunnels, to the scent and the sensation, and Rowl suddenly realized that they were somewhere near the tunnel where he had battled and destroyed the silkweavers who had tried to harm Littlemouse.

So.

Was that the message Naun of the Nine-Claws had meant Rowl to receive? That surface creatures were inside his territory, along with invading humans of Spire Aurora?

It would explain much. If the silkweavers were indeed under the control of the enemies of Littlemouse's people, they would be a threat too great for the cats to face. When humans came hunting them, cats simply scattered into the endless tunnels. They moved much more swiftly and silently than any human could hope to emulate, and avoided them with relative ease.

Humans with the aid of silkweavers, though—that would be an entirely different ball of string. Silkweavers, in great numbers, could threaten the Nine-Claws, pursuing them through the tunnels the clumsier humans could not or would not use. Worse, they would use the vertical shafts as easily as the horizontal tunnels, providing them with a tremendous advantage of mobility.

Most particularly, they would be a threat to the kits of the Nine-Claws. A single silkweaver, if it struck a nursery, could kill the offspring of a generation. Working together, they could force the cats to flee through tunnels, where humans could employ their gauntlets and long guns.

Rowl suppressed a snarl. No wonder the Nine-Claws had been keeping their kits close. And of course Naun could not simply ask Rowl for help—any cat would understand that. He would probably be obliged to explain to Littlemouse the importance of a clan chief's pride of place and absolute autonomy. She would fail to comprehend it, naturally, but what else could one expect? She was human.

The warriors who had taken Littlemouse made her walk with them into a section of the tunnels that Rowl felt immediately wary of entering. There were watchers there somewhere, hidden sentries posted in the darkness, concealed even from his eyes, at least from this distance. But his instincts warned him that they were certainly there.

Rowl prowled to a particularly deep pool of shadow and had just settled down to regard the tunnel more intently when something soft flicked his whiskers and caused him to whirl about, claws and fangs bared, ready to fight.

Shadows stirred and a pair of green eyes blinked slowly and insouciantly at him from only inches away. There was a low, chuckling purr, and a small female cat curled her tail back neatly around her paws.

"Mirl," Rowl said, keeping his voice pitched below the volume a human would hear. He flicked his tail stiffly in displeasure. "I might have killed you."

"You will need to notice me first," Mirl said back, her tone insufferably pleased with herself. "O mighty Rowl."

He regarded her for a haughty moment, then sat down and composed his fur. "What are you doing here?"

"My duty," Mirl said. "Maul and Longthinker set me on a trail. It led me here. Or did you think I had come to throw myself at your paws and beg for your affection?"

Rowl gave her a gentle bump of his shoulder against hers to take the sting from his words. "I have no time for games this night."

"I saw," she said, sitting down beside him. "They took your human."

"They took *two* of them," Rowl said, disgusted, "and they will answer for it."

"Of course they will," Mirl said. "But I have been studying the Auroran defenses. I do not think there is a way to get close enough to observe them without being seen."

"Why not?" Rowl asked.

"The deepest shadows of the roof," Mirl said. "Thirty pounces back."

Rowl stared intently for a long moment at the spot she had indicated. Finally, a vague shape took form there, and a faint glitter upon a gleaming eye.

"Silkweaver," Rowl murmured quietly. "An adult."

"Others guard each passage in," Mirl said. "We can draw no closer to your humans without being seen."

Rowl lashed his tail left and right once. That was ample time to consider the situation. Then he rose.

"Mirl," Rowl said.

"Yes?"

"I will ask you to do a thing for me."

"Will you?"

"Yes," he said. "This thing I ask of you is not a command. You need not do it. I could manage it without you perfectly well."

Mirl looked at him with merry green eyes, but her voice was serious. "Of course you could, O Rowl."

"That needs to be understood."

"It is," Mirl said.

Rowl nodded once. "Excellent. This problem has some one or two facets that are beneath the dignity of cats to manage. The humans must be told of what has happened here. I will ask you to do this thing."

"Humans are too stupid to understand plain speech," Mirl said. "Am I to find one and scratch him until he runs in the proper direction? Then hope he has wits enough to notice?"

"Do not be difficult," Rowl said. "There are humans on a ship of wood with tall trees on it. As its sole purpose is to transport me, I have declared it mine, and my scent is upon it. Contact the human warrior with two red stripes upon his sleeves and a reasonably sized hat. He is less dense than most."

"That seems simple enough," Mirl said.

"But important, Mirl," Rowl said quietly. He faced her and said, "Very important to me."

Mirl tilted her head, abruptly very still. "You trust me to do it?"

Rowl sniffed. "It is a proper task for a Whisker. I am a prince. I have princely business to attend."

"What business?" Mirl asked.

"Is it not perfectly obvious?" Rowl rose and began to pad calmly toward the proper tunnels. "I am going to conquer the Nine-Claws."

■ ■ ■ Chapter 45 ■ ■ ■

Spire Albion, Habble Landing Shipyards,
AMS *Predator*

Every man to be armed and armored," Grimm said to Creedy as he strode down the deck. "Every single one, Mister Creedy, apart from Journeyman and his hired hands. They're to keep working on the ship."

"We have a little more than half the complement we had during the initial attack, sir," Creedy said, walking quickly beside Grimm. "If an entire battalion of Auroran Marines have landed . . ."

"Then it is imperative that we catch them while they're still in the tunnels to prevent them from using their superior numbers against us."

Creedy got a little paler but nodded. "Aye, sir. That will even things up. Some. But even so . . ."

"Relax, Byron. I have no intention of fighting them to the death. We're merely confirming their presence—this is a reconnaissance in force. Their security is evidently good enough to catch even someone familiar with the local tunnels, like a local verminocitor, traveling alone. I mean to find them, and I mean to make sure they don't take me the way they did that poor fellow."

"And if we do find them, sir?"

"We fight just long enough to get an idea of their numbers, break contact, leave pickets at the tunnels they can escape through, and send to the Spirearch for reinforcements. Divide the crew into five-man squads, have them pick squad leaders, and brief the leaders on the plan. Snap to."

Creedy threw a crisp salute and said, "Aye, Captain." Then he spun on a heel and went belowdecks, where most of the men were either sleeping or working on refitting *Predator*'s systems, bawling orders as he went.

Grimm stalked to his cabin, took his coat from his shoulders with an impatient shrug, and eyed his wounded arm. All things considered, he thought he might need both hands and his gauntlet for the next few hours, and he was tired of the damned nuisance of a sling in any case. So he flung it into the corner and flexed his arm experimentally.

There was pain, but not nearly so much as he had expected—and the discomfort was of a peculiar, stretchy sort, as if every muscle in his forearm had cramped unbearably and was only now beginning to loosen again. He winced and he flexed his wrist, but decided that the arm, if imperfect and uncomfortable, was serviceable. So he opened the locked cabinet, rolled up his sleeve, and strapped on his gauntlet. The wounds hurt beneath the bandages, but the cloth windings didn't suddenly turn scarlet with fresh blood. It would do.

Grimm donned his captain's coat, secured his hat firmly in place, and strode out of the cabin to find the men assembling on the deck. He checked to his right and spotted Sir Benedict pacing outside the door to Mister Bagen's sick bay. He walked over to the young Guard and nodded. "Is Ferus in there?"

Benedict nodded. His golden eyes were strained, hollow. "They're just finishing up."

"How is Miss Lancaster?"

Benedict shook his head. "They didn't say."

Grimm pursed his lips and nodded. Bagen wasn't the sort of physician to say anything he wasn't certain about. The man would always remain silent rather than risk giving false hope to those waiting on news of his patients' prospects. He didn't shirk from giving bad news, either, though.

"Then there's hope, son," Grimm said. "If she was dying, Bagen would have said so."

Benedict forced a small, brief smile to his mouth and nodded his thanks. His expression of worry did not change, but his pacing subsided.

A moment later the door rattled fitfully, and Benedict all but pounced on it in his hurry to open it.

"Thank you, my boy," Master Ferus chirped, and bustled outside. He turned, shut the door in Mister Bagen's rather startled, drawn face, and added, "Excuse me." Then he peered intently at the wood for a long moment.

"Ah," Ferus said, beaming. "I am not a braggart by nature, Captain Grimm, but I must say that in my own small way, I do excellent work."

Grimm cleared his throat. "What is the child's condition?"

Ferus rounded on him with an arched silver brow. "Child, sir? Have *you* ever slain a silkweaver matriarch?"

"Point taken, sir," Grimm said, with a small bow. "What is Miss Lancaster's condition?"

"Oh, she'll be fine," Master Ferus said offhandedly. "Assuming, of course, that she wakes up."

"What?" Benedict asked.

"She's unconscious," Ferus replied, his voice turning graver. "Both Doctor Bagen and I believe that her condition is stable, but the blow to her head was severe, and she has shown no signs of rousing. It is possible that she may sit up in the next few moments. It is also possible that she may never awaken. We simply cannot know."

"Oh," Benedict said in a very small voice. "Oh. Oh, coz." He swallowed and blinked his eyes several times. "May I see her?"

"Of course," Master Ferus said. He reached for the doorknob and fiddled with it fitfully for a moment. Then he sighed and said, "They *worked* when I was young. Standards must be slipping."

"Doubtless," Grimm said, and opened the door for Sir Benedict, who paced inside and began speaking quietly to Doctor Bagen. Grimm shut the door and turned to Master Ferus. "Sir Benedict tells me that you can locate our enemy if I can take you to the correct general vicinity."

Ferus raked a bony hand through his wispy grey hair and nodded absently. "Yes, quite probably." He blinked. "You mean to say that you've found it, Captain Grimm?"

"I believe so," Grimm said. "I mean to leave the ship and find them as soon as my men are armed and armored. I would ask you to join us."

"Yes, yes, obviously," Ferus muttered, waving a hand. His eyes were locked on what appeared to be a random point on the ship's deck. "Though . . . we won't be leaving right away, I'm afraid."

Grimm tilted his head slightly. "No? And why not?"

Ferus suddenly stiffened. His expression flickered with a rapid mix of emotions, and then a slow shudder seemed to roll down his spine. He turned slowly, pointed a stiffened finger toward the ship's boarding plank, and said, "We have no need to seek the Enemy. She has come to us."

Grimm turned in time to see Madame Cavendish stride calmly to the top of the ramp and halt, her hands folded neatly in front of her. She wore a steely lavender dress and bolero with grey accents and a matching lavender blouse. She wore her hat at a rakish angle upon her pinned-up hair, and a crystal the size of a big man's thumb glowed with gentle light at the center of a velvet choker about her slender throat.

Her gaze was focused directly upon Master Ferus even as her head rose above the level of the deck, as if she had known precisely where he would be standing long before she had actually laid eyes upon him.

Those flat grey eyes took in Ferus for a moment, and then Cavendish smiled. It was, Grimm thought, the cruelest expression he had ever seen on a human face.

Then she turned to Grimm, and her smile reminded him of nothing so much as a primed gauntlet ready to be discharged. "Captain Grimm," she said. "What a pleasure to see you again, sir. And what a lovely ship this is. Permission to come aboard for parley?"

Grimm turned his head slightly toward Master Ferus but never took his eyes off of Cavendish. "Sir?" he said quietly. "Ought we take her?"

"You can't," Ferus said, his voice roughened with emotion. "You haven't the necessary tools."

Grimm frowned. "You think we should parley with her?"

"Merciful Builders and God in Heaven, no," Ferus murmured back. "She cannot be trusted. Offer her tea."

Grimm pursed his lips. "For what reason?"

"She has us at a disadvantage, Captain, or she wouldn't be here at all. She wishes to talk, or she would simply have attacked. Let us see what she has to say."

"Is she a danger to my men?" Grimm asked.

Master Ferus's teeth showed briefly. "To all men. Invite her to take tea before the winds change." He touched Grimm's arm and lowered his voice intently. "And, Captain. Do let us be gracious about it."

Grimm frowned at the old etherealist for a moment more before nodding. Then he turned, doffed his cap, and swept a politely proper bow to the lady. "Permission granted, Madame Cavendish. Welcome aboard *Predator*. May I tempt you with a cup of tea?"

Cavendish stepped onto the deck of Grimm's ship, and her smile didn't widen so much as sharpen. "Why, what a gracious offer. Yes, Captain, tea would be lovely. Tea would please me to no end."

Grimm fought down an odd sensation of manifest dread, and offered the woman his arm. She took it, and the contact made him feel as if his flesh had begun to desperately bunch up in an effort to avoid contact with the woman's fingers.

But he allowed none of that to show in his bearing or voice.

"This way, please, madame. If I may be so bold as to ask: Do you prefer sugar or honey in your tea?"

▪ ▪ ▪ Chapter 46 ▪ ▪ ▪

Spire Albion, Habble Landing Shipyards,
AMS *Predator*

Grimm did not, as a rule, believe in extravagance. That said, he did own a rather finely made teapot.

The device was specifically made for use aboard airships, plugging into the electrical system of a ship upon two slender copper prongs. Electricity flowed into a coil upon which sat the copper teapot, and heated the water inside to the ideal temperature in well under a minute, shutting off immediately when the water was perfectly heated. As it was the deluxe model, it even had a dial on the side to adjust for altitude in order to make sure the pot was heated to precisely the correct temperature every time.

Grimm heated the water, then added the leaves and let them steep for a few moments. Then he brought the tea to the little table in his cabin around which sat Master Ferus and Madame Cavendish.

"Oh, is that the Fedori model, out of Spire Jereezi?" Cavendish asked, looking up with interest. "I'd considered acquiring one myself, for when I'm traveling, but so few airships have their passenger cabins wired for electricity."

"Something of an indulgence of mine, I'm afraid," Grimm said. "I don't mind missing meals, when it comes to that, but I simply can't do without a good cup of tea in the afternoon."

"At least you and I can agree on that, Captain," Cavendish said firmly.

"If you would care to do the honors, Master Ferus?" Grimm said.

"Why, certainly," Ferus said. He poured the tea, his expression neutral.

"I have less-than-fresh cream, I'm afraid," Grimm said. "But I believe you said that you prefer it with honey, madame?"

"Please," Cavendish said, holding out her cup to Grimm. He dipped what was very nearly the last of his rather expensive honey out of its ceramic bowl and into the matching cup upon its saucer. "Master Ferus?"

"Sugar, if you please," Ferus said calmly.

Grimm served them, added a bit of both to his own tea, and left it sitting on its saucer to cool a bit, as did his guests.

"I must say," Madame Cavendish said. "Given the innovations made in simple quality-of-life contrivances upon airships, it seems that there is vast potential in electrically powered products, such as your fine teapot, that could be expanded into the lifestyle of Spire dwellers, as well."

"In a gentler world, perhaps, madame," Grimm said.

"Oh?"

"Power crystals are valuable resources," Grimm said. "Given the amount of time required to produce them, they are nearly always slated for use aboard airships—and the expansion of each Spire's navy, in today's troubled world, is an absolute priority."

Cavendish's eyes glittered with an amusement that hardly seemed to match the topic. "Much to the loss of the poor citizens of the Spire, whom the airships are meant to serve and protect, I daresay."

"Necessity and survival, Madame Cavendish, needs must take precedence over convenience."

"Except for airship captains, it would seem," Cavendish said. "Consider the Fedori Company. Think how rapidly their shops would grow if they could supply demand for so large a market. And who knows what other products might be made available? Supplying to the citizenry of the Spires could usher in a new era of peace and prosperity."

"Well said, Cora," Master Ferus murmured. "I almost believed you meant that."

Cavendish lifted her nose and sniffed lightly. "You have always believed the worst about me, Efferus."

"And rarely have been disappointed," Ferus replied.

"Your notion seems perfectly sound," Grimm said smoothly, "in theory. But I am afraid it would suffer once exposed to the harsh realities of life."

Cavendish stared hard at Master Ferus. "A valid point, Captain. So many theories do."

Master Ferus did not quite flinch at the woman's words, but Grimm sensed the slow, long-term pain in the etherealist's face. The old man looked up at Cavendish and said gently, "It needn't be this way between us, you know. The future has many branches."

"No, Efferus," Madame Cavendish said.

Grimm was startled by the precise vitriol the woman managed to fit into the two words. They dripped with it to such a degree that he nearly checked the decking beneath the woman's chair for damage.

Master Ferus sighed and nodded. "Then you never learned to See, I take it."

"Perhaps I had a poor teacher," she replied calmly. "But in time I learned to create the future I desired."

"Oh, Cora," Ferus said. "Is that what you think this is? Creation?"

"Building a new world is never easy, my old friend," she replied. A small smile touched the corners of her mouth. "What fun would it be if it were easy?"

As a loyal son of Albion, Grimm knew more or less to the second when his tea would be cool enough to drink. He reached for his cup, and the other two moved to do the same at precisely the same time. They all sipped.

Cavendish closed her eyes in pleasure for a moment before opening them. "To business, then, shall we?"

"Of course," Master Ferus said. "Where do you propose to begin negotiations?"

Cavendish lifted an eyebrow. "Oh, Efferus. I am afraid you misunderstand me. I am not here to negotiate."

"Then if I may be so bold as to ask—why have you come, madame?" Grimm asked.

Cavendish took another sip of tea. "This is a Dubain leaf, is it not?"

"You have a discerning palate," Grimm replied. "My question stands."

"I am here for Efferus's collection."

The old man stiffened in his seat. He covered it with another sip of tea, swallowed, and asked in a mild tone, "And why, precisely, should you believe I would allow you to take it?"

Cavendish smiled pleasantly. "Because if you do not, the two lovely young women from your group have already eaten their last meal."

Ferus stared at his tea for a moment. Then he said, "If I give it to you, then you will release them?"

"Pardon me," Cavendish said to Grimm. "I fear Efferus is suffering from the first stages of senility, as I have already explained to him that this is not a negotiation." She turned to the old man and spoke in slow, measured tones. "I have them. I can destroy them with a thought. If you do not give me your collection, immediately and without protest, I will do so."

"And then?" Ferus asked, his voice roughened at the edges.

"And then, if you value their lives, I will continue to do exactly as I please with no further interference from you. I may even spare them when my business is concluded."

"I know you, Cora," Ferus said. "You offer scant hope for their survival."

Her eyes hardened until they looked like chips of glass. "No, Efferus. All I offer you is the absolute certainty of their deaths."

The old man bowed his head and did not speak.

Cavendish sat back slightly in her seat, her expression pleased. "You needn't do it, of course. Neither child is of any long-term value to your campaign. All you need do is ask yourself one simple question, Efferus."

"Oh?" the old man said. "What would that be?"

"Do you have it in you to sacrifice two apprentices in one lifetime?"

This time the old man did flinch, as if from a slap.

Grimm murmured, "Excuse me," and rose with the teapot, to take it back to its heating plate. He took the mesh leaf holder from the pot, and poured water from a ewer to cleanse it, then cleaned the pot out. He put the pot back down and rested his hand on the cabinet, out of sight of those seated at the table.

"Ah, a soldier's thinking," Cavendish said.

Grimm looked back at her. She had never taken her eyes from Master Ferus.

"Captain," Cavendish said, "you can draw that pistol if you choose, but you will wish you were dead before you can bring it to bear upon me or pull the trigger."

"You are a foe of Spire Albion, madame, and an active ally to her enemies. I am presuming, of course, it was indeed you who guided the Auroran destroyers in for their attack on the shipyards."

Cavendish tilted her head, her expression pleasant, though her eyes never left Ferus. "This is the work of that spider at the top of the Spire, isn't it? He always did have a knack for picking capable agents. I'm surprised he dared to involve himself."

"How little you know Addison, Cora," Master Ferus said quietly.

The handle of Grimm's hidden pistol was cool beneath his fingertips. He'd meant to have it ready in the event that Calliope had turned on him, if not unexpectedly then at least suddenly. Only a fool would bother to attack an etherealist with a gauntlet. The simpler, sometimes treacherous service offered by a firearm was the best weapon available for such a task. "I'm sure someone as intelligent as you can comprehend my dilemma, madame."

"Yes," Cavendish said, her tone dry. "You are insufficiently astute to understand the situation. Or do you honestly believe I would have boarded your ship without taking appropriate precautions?"

"If you would be so kind, do elaborate," Grimm said.

"Should I not appear unharmed and safely leave this vessel in the next quarter hour, observers posted nearby will alert my allies—and those two children will die horribly."

Grimm regarded Cavendish calmly, weighing his options.

The woman was clearly dangerous and capable. Master Ferus seemed extremely cautious of her. Grimm had no doubt that she would order the execution of Miss Tagwynn and Miss Folly with no more emotional investment than she might show when asking for another cup of tea. She seemed intelligent, as well. He could readily believe that she would have taken precautions to prevent some sort of assault.

And yet . . .

He had little patience for one who would callously leverage young lives against her ambitions. She was not seven feet from him. In the space of a heartbeat he could draw the pistol and discharge it, then immediately order his men to sweep the docks, and trap Cavendish's eyes and ears before he could report to the Aurorans. Information could be extracted from the watcher, and a rescue operation mounted for the young women.

Such a course seemed unlikely to succeed in the face of their foe—but judging by Ferus's reaction to Cavendish, he should think it would be at least as likely to save the young women as leaving them to Madame Cavendish's tender mercies.

She might be telling the truth about her ability to stop him. Etherealists could accomplish feats that would astound most men. But he had no proof of that. Did he not have an obligation to at least *try* to put down this foe of his home Spire?

He narrowed his eyes. Besides. No one gave him orders aboard his own ship.

His hand settled on the pistol's grip and he began the turn that would draw it from its hidden holster and into the open.

"Hold, Captain," Master Ferus said, his voice suddenly sharp. "Do not shoot."

Ferus hadn't looked at him, either. Grimm felt somewhat annoyed by that. Etherealists or not, these people should bloody well at least need to *glance* at him to know what he was doing.

"She's telling the truth," Ferus continued, his voice very quiet. "You won't be able to take the shot—and you'll be worse than dead if you try."

Cavendish's mouth split into a sudden, wide smile.

Ferus shook his head. "I wonder, Captain, if you would be so kind as to have the pair of wagons in my cabin rolled out to the deck for Madame Cavendish."

"Sir?" Grimm asked.

"I believe the Spirearch ordered you to support my mission, sir," Ferus said quietly. "Did he not?"

Grimm exhaled slowly. Then he released the grip of the pistol and lowered his hand. "He did."

"How very civilized of us," Cavendish said. She set her saucer and teacup down and rose, folding her hands in front of her. "I have porters standing by to manage the wagons, Efferus."

Master Ferus rose with her and nodded shortly. "Let it be done." He waited until she had turned toward the door before he said in a low voice, "Sycorax."

Madame Cavendish paused and looked back at him.

"If any harm befalls those girls, the world is not large enough to hide you from me."

She lifted her chin, her expression cool. "I'm not the one who has lived in hiding, old man."

Ferus ground his teeth. Then he glanced at Grimm and nodded.

Grimm escorted Cavendish from the cabin to the deck, and it was done in short order. The two little wagons, piled high with seemingly random objects, rolled down the gangplank after a couple of hired porters from one of the companies local to Habble Landing.

Cavendish watched them go, smiling, and straightened the cuffs of her sleeves. "Captain Grimm," she murmured. "Do yourself a favor. Live a little longer. Remain on your ship. Do not attempt to follow me."

"I will do whatever is necessary, madame," Grimm said. He bowed politely, and accepted her rather pensive nod in response. Then she swept down the gangplank and departed.

The moment she was out of sight, Grimm spun on a heel and marched back into his cabin. "Master Ferus, we shall leave with the shore party imme—"

He broke off his words suddenly. The old etherealist was lying on the floor curled into a fetal ball, clutching at his stomach. He rocked as if in agony, weeping silent tears.

"I can't," he said. "I can't. This isn't, grim captain, I'm not capable of it."

Grimm moved to the old man's side and knelt over him. "Master Ferus. Can you hear me?"

"I can and no matter," Ferus said, his voice twisted as if he were being crushed beneath some brutal weight. "I'll not be, not for, oh, I need thirteen needles and a ball of wax. Hat pins, a lump of green chalk and two left slippers."

Grimm blinked several more times. The old man's collection. Was that what he was babbling about? Why?

Obviously, Grimm thought, for the same reason that Cavendish insisted that he give it up: It must have been some kind of totem or fetish to the old man. He was broken and needed the collection to help him function, just as Folly needed her jar of crystals for communicating with speech—and just as Madame Cavendish seemed obsessed with the observation of courtesy. That madness seemed to follow every etherealist he had ever met. Their power, it would seem, did not come without a price.

"Folly always got them for me. Got them perfect, every time. Now she's in the dark, and it's my fault for sending her there." The old man's eyes snapped up to Grimm, clearing for a second. "You must find her. You *must* make her safe."

"I will," Grimm said. "Of course I will."

Ferus clutched at him. The man looked twenty years older. His hands shook. "*Promise* me, Captain."

Grimm took the old man's hands in his and squeezed. "Everything in my power. I swear it."

Ferus nodded once and then his face twisted in new agony and he shut his eyes tightly, muttering to himself beneath his breath at a frantic rate.

Grimm shook his head, got his good arm beneath the old man, and lugged him to his bunk. He straightened from the task slowly.

He meant what he had told Ferus—but everything in his power was worth little if he did not know where to apply it. The plan had relied upon Ferus's guidance to locate the Enemy. How was he to locate the Enemy, pinpoint where the young women were being held, and rescue them, all without being seen by his foes?

He dimmed the lumin crystals in his cabin and departed quietly, leaving Ferus to his feverish muttering. The Enemy was here, in Landing, but he did not know where. They were up to no good, though he did not know what their plans might be, or where they might strike. He had inherited a mountain of ignorance when the old man had been incapacitated, and if he acted without knowledge, the lives of those two young women might be forfeit.

Miss Tagwynn, he supposed, was a soldier in service to the Spirearch. Sacrificing her, for the good of the Spire, might be an ugly and unavoidable necessity. The apprentice etherealist was a civilian, but she too was deeply involved in this business, and in service to the Spirearch. Yet he could not throw away their lives except as a last resort.

Grimm's hands closed into impotent fists.

What was he to do?

Kettle came striding up the deck and whipped off a quick salute: "Skip," he said. "There's a cat here. Bloody little creature just came running up onto the deck."

Grimm's gaze snapped up to the pilot. "Show me."

Chapter 47

Spire Albion, Habble Landing,
Ventilation Tunnels

Bridget sat quietly, bound and taken prisoner, and fumed. It was even more annoying than it had been the first time, and nearly as uncomfortable.

She twisted her wrists, or tried to, attempting to loosen the leather cords binding them, and once again she accomplished nothing except to make the skin of her wrists even rawer and to make her shoulders ache with the effort of the motion.

She puffed out her lower lip and blew several fallen strands of hair from her face. The hair that had escaped her braid was driving her slowly insane—but her wrists had been bound at the small of her back to her own belt, and thence to her bound ankles, and there was no help for it.

She wasn't going anywhere.

She felt a terrible surge of frustration well up in her belly and rise toward her throat, and she knew that it was being lifted on a tide of sheer terror. Her heart started racing, and tears began to well up in her eyes. She struggled to fight against them, but in vain.

All she had wanted was to stay home with her father and in the places she knew. Instead she was quite probably to die here.

And Rowl wasn't with her.

At that thought, a quiet, small sound escaped her throat despite all she could do to restrain it. She shook her head fiercely. Such despair was foolish, of course. Had Rowl been captured as well, he would surely be in no position to do anything to help her. Free, he would certainly go for help, and was quite possibly her best hope of survival.

If he was free.

If he had not been killed by the Enemy.

She shook the gibbering terror away from her thoughts and forced herself to remember her survival lessons. First she had to take stock of her assets.

While Bridget may have been bound, she was at least whole. No one had shot or stabbed her, which seemed an excellent foundation from which to build, all things considered. She was trapped in the darkness of a ventilation tunnel, one that had been barricaded with a tremendous mound of broken masonry not far from where she sat. Her gauntlet had been taken, as well as her knife and her coin purse, but her captors had not mistreated her or taken her clothing away—another mercy. The tall warriorborn Gwendolyn had wounded in Habble Morning, the man who insisted that he was a murderer and not a rapist, had been one of the men to secure her bonds when she had been brought to the tunnel.

There was a paltry amount of illumination coming from the entrance to the tunnel, which had been blocked off with tarps on a light framework of some kind. Only a little illumination leaked around the tarps, barely enough to let Bridget see their outline, and not nearly enough to see her companion as more than an immobile lump on the floor beside her.

"Folly," Bridget said quietly, trying once more. "Folly. Are you awake?"

The form beside her did not stir. Bridget heard a faint, hopeless moaning sound, hardly human, as if she was in terrible pain. Bridget had seen the men remove Folly's possessions while she lay insensible. When she had woken, an hour later, Bridget had heard her move about for a moment, making frantic, animal sounds, and then let out a low keen of undiluted despair.

And then she had simply lain still.

Bridget felt abominably weary, and desired nothing so much as to lie down on her side and go to sleep. But though she was new to the business of being an agent of the Spirearch, she felt that she understood the concept well enough to know that having a nice lie-down when she and the Spire were in such dire straits would, perhaps, be unprofessional.

Bridget closed her eyes for a moment, though it hardly made a difference, and cudgeled her brain into motion. Had she anything else at her disposal?

She blinked her eyes open a moment later. She did, for what it was worth. She had a small lumin crystal in the pocket of her bolero jacket. Granted, the little thing wouldn't show her anything she hadn't already seen, even if she could get it out of her pocket, but it was something.

Perhaps a light in this darkness was what she needed most.

Bridget tried to lie down and wound up pitching over onto her side. She rolled onto her back, though it hurt her arms to do it, and began to wiggle her elbows, struggling to flap the sides of the bolero and spill the lumin crystal onto the floor.

Had anyone been able to see her, she felt certain, she would have looked utterly ridiculous.

It took her several moments of difficult, uncomfortable motion, and the skin of her wrists felt as though it had been wrapped in hot copper wire, not leather, before she was done. But then she heard it—a little click of crystal falling to spirestone floor.

The next part of the task was more difficult. She had to find the crystal, reaching awkwardly behind her with bound fingers, walking on her buttocks to scoot around the floor. That part took her at least a quarter of an hour, she was sure, and had anyone been there to see, they would have been laughing themselves sick.

And her hair kept falling into her *eyes*. Maddening.

But at last she found the crystal with the tips of her fingers, and willed the little thing to life.

Wan light rose up in the hallway, and Bridget let out a sigh of relief, and enjoyed a minor thrill of triumph, followed quickly by a wave of enervation that nearly had her falling over again for that nap.

Instead she forced herself to turn until she could get a good look at Folly.

The etherealist's apprentice was curled up in a fetal position on the floor. Though her eyes were open, they were unfocused. Her skin was pale, almost grey. For an awful second, Bridget thought that Folly might have been dead, but then she saw the girl's body rise and fall with a slow, shallow breath, and Bridget nearly wept with relief.

"Folly," Bridget said. "Folly."

The girl's eyelids flickered, and her eyes swept about for a few seconds, as though darkness still blinded her. But there was no further response.

Bridget chewed on her lip. Then she shook her head and said, "Oh, of course. They've taken your crystals. You've no one to talk to."

Tears filled Folly's eyes. She shook her head, once, slowly.

Bridget nodded, thinking. "Folly," she said, "you can hear me, can you not?"

The girl looked at her for a few seconds, and blinked.

Bridget tried to give her a warm smile. Then she said, "I've a crystal here, but I'm going to throw it away now. Do you hear me? I'm going to throw it away. It's not mine anymore."

Folly's eyes widened.

Bridget walked herself about until she could take the crystal in her fingers and flick it toward Folly.

"Oh!" Folly said, as the lumin crystal landed in front of her. "Oh, look how alone you are. And you're covered in blood, which I feel sure is not good for you, or is at least premature." She scooted her body protectively toward the little lumin crystal until she was curled into a human crescent around it.

Bridget let out a slow breath and felt her body sag with relief. Then she blinked and opened her eyes. Blood? She peered at the crystal and saw fresh scarlet smears there.

Her blood, then. The bonds must have cut her wrists while she was trying to move them.

"Folly, can you see my hands?" Bridget asked.

Folly peered at Bridget and then sighed. "Oh, poor Bridget. That must have hurt terribly."

"How bad is the bleeding?"

The odd girl shook her head. "I shouldn't think it would be deadly to her. Would you?"

Bridget nodded. "Very well then. Folly, I need to know what's happening. Why didn't you talk to me?"

"She knew already," Folly said, frowning at the little crystal. "She already said it."

"I know, because you didn't have any crystals here," Bridget said. "But I must know why you need to have them here to talk. I need to understand."

Folly frowned and was quiet for so long that Bridget thought she might have not heard the question. Then she opened her mouth and spoke very slowly, as if choosing her words with tremendous care.

"Bridget doesn't understand the toll etheric energy takes on the mind. How there's a price for power—always, always a price. How heavy it is. How it tears holes and holes and holes everywhere inside one's head." She shuddered. "And she doesn't realize how one must find other things to fill in the holes or else one simply falls into them—and falls and falls and falls."

"It's not just your speech then," Bridget said. "You couldn't have acted at all."

Folly shivered again, and whispered to the crystal, "I was falling and falling. Lying right there, but falling and falling."

Bridget inhaled slowly. "Oh," she said quietly. "I didn't know."

"We don't speak of such things often," Folly said in a sober tone. "It's bad form. Especially around someone who has practiced longer than you."

"Like Master Ferus?" Bridget asked.

"Yes, yes, my poor master. He's more holes than not, by now. And yet he holds himself together with pure will." Folly bit her lip. "Most etherealists fall, you know, eventually. They die that way. Falling while they lie in bed. One cannot feed oneself while falling." She shivered. "Someday it will happen to me and I'll not be able to come back." She closed her eyes for a moment and then whispered to the little crystal, "Be sure to thank Bridget for me. She's very kind."

"We're friends," Bridget said. "There is no need to thank me."

Folly smiled slightly. Then she moved her head, resting her cheek against the crystal, which plunged the hall into blackness again.

No more than a second later, there was a sound at the tarps at the other end of the hall, and the warriorborn man named Ciriaco stuck his head into the hall, holding up a lumin crystal of his own. He scowled at them in suspicion for a moment, but he did not come any closer. Instead he simply snapped, "Keep quiet in there." Then he departed, closing the tarp again.

Folly lifted her head after a moment and said softly, "Don't worry. I won't let the mean men take you."

Well, Bridget thought. She had made her situation that much better, at least. She had a functioning ally again, even if she was trussed up as thoroughly as Bridget herself was. If only she weren't bound, things might be less hopeless. Very well, then. What could she do to become unbound? What did the heroines in dramas and books do in such circumstances?

Frequently, it seemed, they would use their feminine wiles upon their male captors, promising them amorous attention and then turning the tables upon the foe when the moment was right (but before, of course, sacrificing anything like their virtue for the cause).

Bridget hadn't been an agent of the Spirearch for very long, but she felt that she had the concept sufficiently surrounded to see that such a ploy was unlikely to work. Even if Ciriaco had been amenable to such a thing, he had no real reason to release her from her bonds, now, did he? And, in point of fact, what captor with any professionalism at all would be taken in by such a ploy in the first place?

Besides, Bridget was not at all sure that she *had* any feminine wiles. And even if she did, she felt certain that they would not function as flawlessly in life as they did in tales and dramas.

Leather cords. She should know what to do with this problem. Part of growing the great sides of meat in the vattery was harvesting the leather casing that grew around them as they matured. Her father could strip a skin from a side of meat with several long, deft cuts and a few expertly applied tugs. Of course, they didn't tan the leather into usable form there, instead delivering the skins to a tanner with whom they had an arrangement, but all the same . . .

Bridget blinked again. Of course. The skins had to be stored in a tub of very watered-down solution to prevent them from drying out. Skins shrank considerably as they dried—and expanded once more upon being wetted down.

Bridget began twisting her wrists again, this time in earnest. It burned, and she did not care.

"Oh," Folly said. "She's making it worse. She should stop."

"No," Bridget said. She felt trickles of blood slither silently over her palms and across the pads of her fingers—and knew it had to be soaking into the leather bonds as well. "Folly, I need you to tell me when the bonds have been thoroughly soaked."

Folly stared at Bridget with her odd, mismatched eyes, and shivered. "Oh, goodness. Um. The left needs more, wouldn't you say?"

"Fine," Bridget said, and focused on twisting and wrenching her left wrist especially. It took an eternity of self-inflicted torment, but finally Folly said, "She should try it now."

Bridget nodded her thanks. Then she closed her eyes and bowed her head forward. And then, very slowly, she began to apply pressure to her wrists, straining against the bonds.

It hurt, hurt terribly, and not simply in her wrists. Her arms and shoulders ached with the strain she began to put on them. Bridget was a strong girl, strong enough to toss a hundred and fifty pounds of meat onto her shoulder and carry it from the vat to the cutting table without pausing to rest or put it down. She had never felt that it was really a terribly impressive thing to be able to do, since her father, Franklin, could toss one up onto each shoulder and walk along with them without breaking the rhythm of a working song. But for whatever her far less significant strength was worth, she pitted it against the Auroran bonds in a contest of endurance, determination, and slow power.

And though it spread fire up and down her arms, the bonds began to stretch.

It took her several tries, several painful, straining moments, but finally she rested and felt her wrists wiggle loosely. She stretched the moistened bonds one more time, and then managed to wrench her hands loose.

"Oh!" Folly said, her tone gleeful and quiet. "Oh, that should be in a play! That was amazing!"

Bridget winced as she got a look at her raw, bleeding wrists and fore-arms. "Well," she said. "It's a good start, at least." Then she leaned down and started picking at the knots on her ankles with determination. "Give me a moment and I'll get yours, Folly."

"Will it make any difference, do you think?" Folly asked.

"We shall know when we are victorious," Bridget said.

"Or not."

"When," she said firmly. After all, a few moments ago Bridget had been bound, helpless, and alone in the dark. Now she was able to move, she could see, and she was working with a friend and ally.

What had changed things? What had made the difference?

She had. All by herself. When the enemies of Spire Albion were in the walls, the great-great-granddaughter of old Admiral Tagwynn had refused to have a nice lie-down, and it was as simple and as profound as that.

Bridget looked up at the etherealist's apprentice and showed her teeth in what she felt was a very Rowl-like, predatory smile. "There's no way to know what's going to happen, Folly. But we'll bloody well be on our feet when it does."

■ ■ ■ Chapter 48 ■ ■ ■

Spire Albion, Habble Landing,
Nine-Claws Territory

Rowl hurtled down the ventilation passageways that led toward the central dominion of the Nine-Claws, taking no heed for silence. Speed was everything.

Littlemouse was in danger, doubtless a prisoner, and the humans could not be trusted to handle her rescue with appropriate violence. They might be willing to leave someone alive, and Rowl was not prepared to tolerate incompetence where his personal human was concerned. He had just gotten her properly trained.

The first of the Nine-Claws' sentinels heard him coming and emerged from the shadows to intercept him. But Rowl, kit of Maul, had been fighting for his position since the time he could walk. He was large and he was strong, he was young and he was swift—and he was in no mood to tolerate such niceties as protocol.

Rowl let out a war cry and left the first sentinel with both eyes, half his whiskers, and an entire ear undamaged once he permitted him to flee. Then he hurtled on. The scent of blood on him was enough to make the next pair of sentinels wary, and Rowl's hiss sent them leaping aside. They took up pursuit behind him—but were careful to keep their distance.

The prince of the Silent Paws scattered guardians from his path and collected a trailing tail who raced along behind him, their scents ablaze with wariness, chagrin, and, of course, curiosity.

There was nothing like playing to their curiosity when it came to catching the attention of cats.

Rowl ran an entire circuit of the Nine-Claws' central chamber, gathering up every cat within dozens and dozens of pounces of the tunnels in question, and by the time he snapped to a halt in front of Naun's central chamber, there were a hundred warriors and hunters following him.

The entire group tumbled to a sudden halt, with the Nine-Claws gathering in close to be able to observe Rowl with their own eyes—even, Rowl noted, pleased, the guardian who had been luckless enough to be the first in his path.

Two of the largest warrior cats stood before Rowl, blocking his way forward. Rowl was through with diplomacy. He padded toward them, his fur bristling, his tail lashing, and made his displeasure known with a sudden hiss.

One of the warriors flinched, and Rowl discounted that one immediately from his consideration. He stalked around the other, back arched, blood on his claws.

"I will speak to Naun now," Rowl snarled. "You will escort me to him."

"Naun has not said th—" the warrior began to say.

Rowl struck.

The warrior let out an earsplitting yowl and reeled away, spinning madly and pawing in desperate pain at the rake Rowl had fetched him across one eye.

Rowl whirled to the other guard, who skittered a half pounce away and came to guard, his own back arched.

"I will speak to Naun now," Rowl said, in precisely the same tone of voice he had used a moment before. "You will escort me to him."

The warrior looked unhappily from Rowl to his wounded companion. Then his fur abruptly settled and he looked away, lashing his tail left and right. "It is this way," the Nine-Claws said. "Follow me, stranger."

Rowl promptly pounced on the warrior's back and set his teeth in the back of the cat's neck, a death grip if he chose it to be. The cat sent up a kit's yowl and flattened to the ground.

Rowl spoke though his teeth were engaged, as it was a cat's preroga-tive to do. "I am Rowl, kit of Maul of the Silent Paws of Habble Morn-ing, and I am in no mood for insolence. Do you understand?"

"I understand, Rowl," the warrior hissed.

"Run and tell your chief that I come," Rowl snarled, and sent the warrior on his way with a sharp nip and a cuff to his ears. The other cat shot off into the chamber ahead of him, and Rowl padded after him, as if in no great hurry whatsoever.

Cats gathered around him, just as before, and Rowl could feel the eyes on him, including those of dozens of kits. Good that he had ac-complished most of the rough business before he entered the chamber. Kits were silly things at the best of times, and they would certainly have been imitating him in an instant had he engaged the other warriors before their eyes.

All kits needed to learn about blood between cats and what it meant, and what made it necessary—but while they huddled in a chamber full of frightened tribe members was an ill place indeed to begin their edu-cation. For that matter, he was pleased Littlemouse hadn't seen it hap-pen. She had such a high opinion of the cats' ability to manage conflict without violence. She had never gotten it through her gentle head that there was a time for a soft paw and a time for red claws. The burden of a chief, or a chief's kit, was to know one from the other.

Rowl entered, trailing a third of the warriors of the clan, while the other two-thirds gathered around Naun's meeting area. As he sauntered into the center of the chamber, Rowl saw Naun sitting up upon his ta-ble, staring down with unreadable eyes. The warrior Rowl had berated was crouched in front of Neen, Naun's kit, speaking quietly, his fur flattened. Neen, for his part, looked outraged.

The cats he had wounded entered, the first tattered but in essence whole. The second might lose the eye Rowl had scratched. Bad luck for both of them. They padded gingerly around Rowl to join their compatriot near Neen.

Clan Chief Naun studied the wounded warriors with steady eyes, and then drew himself up and wrapped his tail around his paws, hiding his claws. It was generally considered either a posture of peace or one of veiled fury. Naun had excellent control. Rowl wasn't sure which it signified.

"Chief Naun," Rowl said, not waiting to be addressed. "Urgent matters bring me to your territory."

"Warriors," Neen yowled to the chamber. "This creature has drawn the blood of our kin. Tear it to shreds."

A low growl rose around the room. Rowl felt a surge of something like alarm. He might not be able to fight the entire populace of the Nine-Claws warrior caste with only his own teeth and claws, though it was difficult to be certain. He did not let his . . . concern . . . show, of course. Such things were not done. He faced Naun and came to a halt, wrapping his own tail around his paws, in mirror of the Nine-Claws chief.

Something like a twitch of amusement might have shaken Naun's whiskers. Then he growled, far down in his deep chest, and the room became silent and still.

"I will hear the Silent Paws stranger," Naun growled.

"Father!" snapped Neen.

Naun's head turned toward his kit. His eyes stared, level and un-blinking.

Neen let out a low growl.

Naun regarded his kit for a moment, then turned to Rowl. "Your words will mean little to me," Naun said, "if I do not know that you see clearly what troubles my realm, young Rowl."

Rowl yawned. "Your people have been hunted like prey, O Naun," he replied.

At that, the chamber again filled with growls of outraged pride.

"Hunted!" Rowl snapped, rising and spinning toward the Nine-Claws nearest him. Offended or not, Rowl had defeated two of their warriors, one of them the chief's personal guard, without taking a scratch in return. They shied away from him. "Hunted!" Rowl said again, turning back to Naun. "Or why else have you gathered your kits into this chamber, all together, like a brood of tunnel mice? You hope to protect them."

Naun's eyes narrowed to slits. Then his tail tip twitched once, an acknowledgment. "And?"

"Your people fear the silkweavers and their brood," Rowl continued. "These are no wild creatures of the surface. These are weapons. They are under the control of a human. A human who threatened you with the death of your kits should you not cooperate with its aims."

"He knows nothing of our ways!" snapped Neen, rising and padding out toward Rowl. "Nothing of what our people may gain!"

Rowl twitched his whiskers smugly at Neen. "Ah," he said. "They have offered you both cream and claw, then. What was the bribe, should your people remain uncommitted to the human war?"

"New territory!" Neen snarled. "New tunnels and halls in which our folk can hunt, our tribe can grow! Halls free of the human plague!"

Rowl regarded Neen with pure contempt. "So said a human to you? It must therefore be true." He flicked his tail at Neen as he would at an annoying kit and said, "You are no warrior. You are no hunter. You are an idiot."

"Father!" Neen said, whirling to Naun. The fur of the prince of the Nine-Claws bristled with outrage. "Will you permit him to say such things of our clan?"

Naun made a rumbling sound in his throat. Then he turned to Rowl and said, "Our kits are our future. What would you have me do?"

"Teach them," Rowl growled, letting his voice carry to the hall. "Will you bow to the will of humans? Will you show them how to meow and purr for human charity next? To catch their mice and leave them as gifts? To besot themselves on human plants, human drink?" Rowl lashed his tail and bounded up onto the clan chief's furniture, all the way to the level just below Naun. "Naun, chief of the Nine-Claws. I would have you *show* them what it means to be *free*. To be *cat*."

Rowl turned to the room before hisses of outrage could rise. "I have climbed the ropes to the den of the silkweavers." He lifted the claws of one front paw. "I have slain their brood by the score, and my humans have slain them by the hundred. They are *dead*. Their matriarch lies *dead* and rotting in a human tavern. Their mature hunters lie crouched around the approaches to a human camp in *your own tunnels*. In territory that these *interlopers* have taken from *you all*." He whirled back to Naun. "Now is your time, Nine-Claws. They have no forces left to fall upon your kits. Now is our chance to strike them down. Give me every warrior in your clan. Let me remind them what it is to be *cat*. To deal with anything that would harm your kits with *tooth* and *claw*!"

A chorus of excited yowls and low battle cries went up with that, enough to draw Naun's gaze from Rowl to scan the chamber.

Naun's eyes came back to Rowl and his voice dropped to a low, low growl, one for Rowl's ears alone. "Is what you say true?"

"By my paws and ears, by my whiskers and tail, it is true, O Naun," Rowl said.

"He lies!" Neen screeched. "He seeks to use us! To shed our tribe's blood to protect his humans in their war! To leave our kits vulnerable and defenseless!"

Rowl spun his head toward Neen, his vision suddenly sharpened with rage, his mouth suddenly watering with a need to taste blood.

"Presently," Rowl said, "I shall grow weary of your mewling."

"I say this creature is a fool!" Neen cried. "I say that his mouth is full of lies! I say that he cannot see or hear or hunt! That this useless creature knows nothing!"

The words rang out into sudden silence, as well they might—for Neen had uttered the deadliest insult one cat could utter to another.

"Useless," Rowl purred, very quietly.

Silence quivered, tense and waiting.

"You give me your word," Naun growled finally, his eyes closing almost entirely. "You, a stranger. My kit tells me that you are filled with lies. How am I to know which of you is right?"

"With your permission, Clan Chief," Rowl said, a growl throbbing in his words, "I shall *show* you."

Neen let out a hiss, his fur rising, his claws sliding from his paws. Neen was large—larger than Rowl. His fur shone with health, and his claws were long and sharp. He stood upon his home territory, surrounded by those loyal to him, and, having not done battle multiple times in the past several hours, he was fresh.

Rowl would have no chance of surviving battle with the prince of the Nine-Claws, not with all the warriors and hunters present who would support him—but if the clan chief permitted it, he might be able to beat *Neen*, standing alone.

Naun stared hard at Rowl for a long moment, as if waiting for any quiver of movement.

Rowl faced him, completely still, showing every ounce of respect he could muster.

"Yes," Naun said then.

Rowl, prince of the Silent Paws of Habble Morning, let out the throaty music of his war cry and flung himself at Neen, claws extended, with Littlemouse's fate hanging in the balance.

■ ■ ■ Chapter 49 ■ ■ ■

Spire Albion, Habble Landing Shipyards,
AMS *Predator*

Gwendolyn opened her eyes and regretted it almost at once.

She had never drunk wine or other spirits to excess, though she had seen the effects it had produced in any number of House Lancaster's armsmen after various holiday celebrations. She had always found their winces and green faces somewhat amusing.

She suspected she would have more sympathy for them in the future.

The light did not merely hurt her eyes—it stabbed it with rotted, rusty old swords. Her heartbeat sent pulses of pain through her skull and down her neck as if on wires, and for the life of her, it was everything she could do not to simply roll to one side and commence evacuating the contents of her stomach.

Wait a moment. *Had* she become drunk? The last thing she remembered was the mad old etherealist singing sadistically unfortunate lyrics to a truly disgusting aeronaut's song, and then . . .

And then . . . an enormous surface creature? Though surely that was an artifact of the feverish barrage of nightmares she'd endured for she knew not how long. Perhaps this *was* simply a hangover. If so, she had some apology notes to write to Esterbrook and his men.

She found herself letting out a groan and *that* hurt as well, on top of everything else, as if sudden fingers of fire had dug into her ribs and her back. She put a hand to the pain, and found that it met with something a little rough and tight. She had to open her eyes to see what. Bandages. Beneath a rather thin shift, her torso had been wound with bandages until they were almost uncomfortably tight.

She had been injured, then. While drinking? God in Heaven, please no. Benedict would never let her hear the end of it.

She lifted a hand to her aching head and found *more* bandages there, for goodness' sake. Her head pounded in steady time. A head injury? Ah, then. Perhaps she hadn't humiliated herself after all. Perhaps she'd simply had her wits scrambled by a blow of some kind.

That settled, she turned her eyes to the room she was in. Wood. All wood, walls, floor, and ceiling. One wall was slightly curved. She was most likely aboard an airship, then, which would make the wall a bulkhead, and the floor a deck, and the ceiling a . . . Well. She wasn't sure what ceilings were called on airships. Ceilings, she supposed.

There was another occupant in the room, a man she didn't know, from his dress one of the sailors aboard *Predator*. He was armed with sword and gauntlet, but he was currently sitting in his chair and snoring heavily. There were bags under his eyes. The poor man looked utterly exhausted, and one of his legs was dressed with a bandage. One of the men wounded in the first Auroran attack, perhaps? Poor fellow. He was doubtless there to guard her and make sure she didn't get out of bed without speaking to some sort of physician, who wasn't there anyway, so there seemed to be no real sense in waking him. And besides, she was barely clothed.

Gwen sat up slowly. Her head spun wildly for a moment, and then settled down again. There was a pitcher and a mug on a nearby table that proved to be water. She drank three mugs down, hardly stopping to breathe, and in a few moments felt nearly human.

Gwen found her clothing lying in a heap nearby. It was stained with . . . Goodness, what *was* that horrible purplish color? And they smelled absolutely hideous. She winced with distaste, put them down

439

except for her gauntlet, and began to rummage quietly through the compartment's cabinets, until she located a modest collection of men's clothing in a trunk. She donned the shirt and the pants, found that they hung off of her like a small tent, and spent the next few moments rolling up the sleeves and legs. Then she donned her gauntlet and felt somewhat better when the cool presence of its weapons crystal rested against her palm.

She looked down at herself when finished, and felt certain that Mother would be entirely scandalized by her appearance. It would do.

Gwen left the cabin quietly to find her cousin. Benedict would mock her outfit, too, but he'd know what was going on. She opened the door and stepped into mist-shrouded, late-afternoon daylight. Afternoon? How long had she been asleep? Her last memories trailed off around eight o'clock the previous evening, and she found that gaping blank space in her mind unnerving.

Even eerier, the deck of *Predator* was utterly empty.

"Hello?" Gwen called.

There was no answer.

She frowned and began pacing the length of the ship. No one in the masts. No one in the galley or the kitchen. No one in any of the passenger cabins, and the door to the captain's cabin was locked.

Gwen rubbed wearily at her eyes, and it was just then that she heard a man's voice bawling vile curses, muffled by the planks of the deck. Gwen moved over to the hatch leading belowdecks, and the curses grew clearer and louder. She followed them, and in short order found herself in the engineering room, the beating heart of *Predator*, where the air hummed with the steady drone of an active power core crystal.

For a second she thought that the room's floor was littered with corpses, but after a moment she saw that it was covered with exhausted men who had simply stretched out on the floor and gone to sleep. Several were snoring, though that sound was being drowned out by the invective of the one man still on his feet.

He was stocky and bald, and sported an enormous, bristling mustache. His coveralls were stained with sweat and grease, and though he wasn't particularly tall, his hands looked strong enough to crush crystals in his fingers. He was crouched in front of the adjustable hemisphere of curled copper bars known as a Haslett cage, and he was working ferociously on an awkwardly placed bolt that secured one of the bars in place. The angle was bad for the wrench, but his stumplike forearms couldn't slip through the bars of the cage very easily, and he was having trouble wrangling the tool into position.

Gwen stepped over a sleeping man and said, "Excuse me, sir."

"What?" snarled the bald man, without looking up from his task.

"I'm looking for Sir Benedict Sorellin. I was wondering if you'd seen him?"

The man grunted. "He in here?"

Gwen looked around the room at the sleeping men. "Ah. Definitely not."

"Same answer," the man growled. The wrench slipped as he began to apply pressure, and he wound up gouging his hand on the frame. "Curse you for a whore!" he shouted. "Bloody strumpet! You'll be the death of me!"

Gwen blinked several times. "*Excuse* me, sir? What did you say to me?"

"I wasn't talking to you," the man bellowed, going red all the way across his bald pate. "I was talking to the bloody *ship*!" He shot a look over his shoulder and froze there, his mouth open for a moment. Then he scowled, turned back to the Haslett cage, and began trying to squeeze his arm inside to grab the wrench he'd dropped. "Fantastic. Like I don't have enough to do already. Now I have to deal with aristo-brats, too. Captain hates me. That's what it is. 'You can't go fight, Journeyman. You have to stay on the ship and fix her up enough for me to ruin, Journeyman.' God in Heaven, the man hates me."

Ah, the ship's chief etheric engineer, Journeyman. She'd heard his name mentioned when the ship was docking. Well, chief engineer or no, Gwen felt as if she should have been pinning the man's ears back—but her head hurt horribly. She really didn't feel like smashing it against any more metaphorical walls. Or literal ones. "Sir, I'll be glad to leave you to work. If you could please direct me to the captain, I'll get out of your hair."

The man's eyes whipped around to her, narrowing. "My what?"

"Lair," Gwen said quickly. "I said I'd get out of your lair."

The man scowled again and went back to reaching for the wrench. "Captain's gone. Doc's gone. Every deckhand still on his feet is gone. It's just my crew and these hired slackers left, and Tarky, but Tarky's barely able to hobble along. Guess that means your Benedict is gone, too."

"Gone where?"

"Motherless whore-spawned mistsharking tunnel rat!" Journeyman snarled, jerking his hand free.

"Oh, for God's sake." Gwen sighed. She stepped over to the cage and, before the engineer could object, slipped her slender arm easily between the bars, plucked up the wrench, and drew it back out again. She flipped it in her hand and offered it to him handle-first.

Journeyman eyed her, mustache bristling. Then he snatched the wrench and said, "You shouldn't play with a ship's systems. If you'd brushed your hand against the wrong arc, you'd have gotten the shock of your life."

"That's why I didn't touch any of the active arcs," Gwen replied calmly. "You're only running power from the topmost bars at the moment, are you not?"

Journeyman's eyebrows lowered, then rose. "Huh. You think you know something about ships, do you?"

"I know little about airships," Gwen replied. "I do possess some small knowledge of their systems."

"Sure you do," the man said.

Gwen arched an eyebrow. "I know the topmost left-side bar is out of alignment by at least two degrees. You're losing efficiency from it. Probably why the air's so warm in here."

The engineer squinted. "And why do you think you know that?"

"The tone," Gwen said. "There's a bit of a burr in it on that side."

"Huh," the man said. He pursed his lips and looked at her speculatively. Then he rose, grabbed the room's eight-foot-high scaffold, and slid it into place over the power core. He climbed up on it and thumped around with the Haslett cage for a bit. Then he climbed back down again. "All better."

Gwen tilted her head to one side and listened to the hum of the power crystal. "No," she said. "You didn't fix it. You put it out of alignment by at least another two degrees."

The engineer might have grinned for an instant, though the mustache camouflaged it. He grunted, went back up the scaffold, and thumped around a bit more. "How's that?"

"That's done it," Gwen replied.

Journeyman hopped back down from the scaffold, eyed her up and down for a second, and then flipped the wrench over in his hand and offered her the handle.

Gwen arched a brow and took it. "And what am I to do with this?"

"Saw which bolt I was working on, did you?"

"Yes."

"So loosen it," he said, "if you can."

Gwen bounced the wrench lightly in her hand. If Captain Grimm and Benedict were gone with the men, they must have been heading to a fight—but she didn't know where, and doubted her ability to run to catch up with them in her present condition. If she had to simply sit and wait for them to return, she might go mad.

She nodded, turned to the Haslett cage, and had the bolt loosened within seconds. Not because she was an expert so much as because she had smaller arms and hands and could work them into the available space much more easily than the engineer could.

"Right," Journeyman said when she was done. "Back."

She drew back and Journeyman threw the release on the lower array. The bottom half of the cage's bars began to swing out, opening away from the crystal within the apparatus, like some kind of gleaming copper flower. Pale green light flooded the chamber, glowing out of the depths of *Predator*'s power core.

Gwen stared at the rich green crystal for a second. It didn't have the proper jewel-faceted shape. It was instead formed into a much more natural-looking crystal, like a shaft of glowing emerald quartz, and then her eyes widened as she realized what she was looking at. "God in Heaven," she said.

"Uh-huh," Journeyman replied. His tone was unmistakably smug.

"That's a first-generation power core," Gwen breathed. "Before they started developing facets. How *old* is it?"

"Few thousand years, at least," Journeyman said.

"If it's that old . . ." Gwen shook her head. Unlike lumin crystals or weapons crystals or cannon crystals or lift crystals, power crystals only grew more and more capable of efficiently channeling etheric energy. A crystal was rarely considered to be working in its prime before a century of use had worn it into better condition. If the crystal was as old as Journeyman claimed, it would be able to produce more electricity from less etheric energy than almost any crystal Gwen had heard of—which would mean that the ship could sail to more places, farther and farther from the main etheric currents, and do it more swiftly. "That is a tremendously efficient core," Gwen said. "It should be in a Fleet ship."

"Well, she ain't," Journeyman said. "And she ain't going to be. She's *Preddy*'s and that's that."

"Incredible," Gwen said, shaking her head.

Journeyman's chest swelled. "Ain't she?" He squinted at her. "Where's a little thing like you learn about ships' systems?"

"From my mother."

"Who's your mother?"

"Helen Lancaster."

Journeyman frowned for a moment. Then he blinked. "Lancaster? *Lancaster*-Lancaster, you mean? The vattery?"

"I've been learning about our products since I was old enough to speak," Gwen said. "Including running system benchmarks on every crystal before we send it out, which means knowing how the systems work."

"Those Lancasters." Journeyman grunted. "Damn." He seemed to come to a decision and nodded once. "I'm going to start kicking these pansies awake in a bit. You want to be useful, meanwhile? Captain got us a little bit of a lift crystal to replace our old one. The trim crystals are all in, but I still have to rig the main one. Could use someone with a good ear for that."

"Which crystal?" Gwen asked.

"One of your new Mark IV-Ds."

Gwen blinked at him once. "You misunderstand me, sir. I mean which crystal. Which one of the Mark IV-Ds?"

Journeyman's mouth spread into a more recognizable grin this time. He nodded to the far end of the chamber, toward the ship's suspension rig. "You tell me."

Gwen went down to the rig to regard the crystal and whistled. "This is the one from the vat in section three, row two. It's one of the best of the batch. God in Heaven, if you aren't cautious, with that power core behind it this crystal could tear the ship apart."

"Tell me something I don't know," Journeyman said.

"Which configuration are you planning for its cage?"

"Standard dispersal, maximum spacing," Journeyman replied.

"What?" Gwen asked. "Why would you do that?"

"How else should I do it?" Journeyman snapped.

"Didn't you read the owner's manual?"

"*Manual?* See here, missy. I've been an etheric engineer since before you were born. I think I know how to handle a lift crystal."

"Evidently you aren't bright enough to do so, if you cannot read. We provide those manuals and specifications and procedures for a reason, you know."

Journeyman scowled. "You do everything by the book, like everybody else, you get the same results as everybody else."

"That's the idea," Gwen said in a dry tone.

Journeyman seemed to miss it. "That might be good enough for every other ship in the world, missy," he said. "But that ain't good enough for *Preddy*. I get ten to fifteen percent more out of her systems doing it my way."

"What?" Gwen said. "That isn't possible."

"Maybe not in your workshops," Journeyman said firmly. "But a ship in the open sky is different. You got to know how to treat her the way she likes."

"Well, take it from me: She's not going to like that dispersal pattern," Gwen said. "The bottom hemisphere of the Mark IV-Ds is rigged with variable sensitivity. The closer to the positive end you get, the more powerful the crystal's pathways are. You need to set your bars in an asymmetric configuration to maximize sensitivity. If you go with a standard hemisphere it will be too easy to dump too much current in. Before you know what happened, you'll be watching that crystal fly to the moon while your ship falls. Which you would know if you'd *read the manual.*"

Journeyman ground his teeth. "Always improving things that don't need improving," he muttered. "Fine. Asymmetric. Show me."

◼ ◼ ◼ ◼ Chapter 50 ◼ ◼ ◼

Spire Albion, Habble Landing,
Ventilation Tunnels

Someone shook Major Espira awake, and he blinked his eyes open to find Ciriaco standing over him, his weathered face set. "Sir. That woman's here."

Espira grunted and rose. He wasn't sure how much sleep he'd gotten, but it wasn't much, and it included dreams he planned not to remember. He climbed to his feet from his bedroll, stiff from the cold spirestone floor. "Better ready the men," he told the sergeant.

"Yes, sir," Ciriaco said, and stalked off to do so. The warriorborn man's arm, though still badly burned, was no longer held at an awkward angle, and as he moved away it swung naturally. Espira found himself wishing for a moment that his own family had carried some measure of warriorborn bloodlines. If he'd been born like Ciriaco, his back wouldn't be so uncomfortable right now.

Of course, if he'd been born like Ciriaco, he wouldn't be a major in the Auroran Marines, either.

Espira tugged on his jacket, straightened himself, and strode out of the private little side corridor he occupied in his position as the commanding officer. As he appeared, the men were already rising and gathering their weaponry and gear.

Cavendish and her pet monster were nearby, waiting. There was something tight and hard around the woman's eyes. Sark looked as he always did, but Espira had worked with the warriorborn long enough to realize that the slight dilation to the pupils of Sark's crooked eyes meant that he was tense and ready for battle.

He'd been hoping for blithe, arrogant confidence from Cavendish. Whatever business she had done with the Albions, it hadn't gone precisely to her schedule. Whatever leverage she thought the hostages had given her must not have been enough. Espira gritted his teeth for an instant, then forced his jaw to relax. The lives of the two young women were worth a little less than nothing if Cavendish decided they had no value to her—and while he had no particular cause to dislike either of the young women, and would prefer to leave them bound and in place, to be found later, he still would cut the ladies' throats himself rather than leave them in the hands of Cavendish or Sark.

"Madame Cavendish," Espira said, bowing politely.

"Major," Cavendish said. "I believe the time has come for us to act."

Espira arched an eyebrow. "You think we should begin early?"

"I will signal the Armada, Major," Cavendish said, a frosty edge to her tone.

The miracle of such rapid communication was all very well, Espira thought, but it wouldn't make an airship move any faster if it wasn't already in position. "If I may inquire as to why you believe precipitous action is required, madame?"

"I misjudged a man," Cavendish said. "The same commander who defeated your men at the Lancaster Vattery."

"He's here?" Espira demanded. "And you did not see fit to tell us this fact?"

"He's one of their Fleet washouts with a crew of privateers," Cavendish said. "They aren't professional soldiers, and their numbers have been significantly reduced—but they can make a great deal of noise before your men wipe them out, and they might sap some of your strength."

"Where are they?"

"Judging by Captain Grimm's confidence, they are coming here," Cavendish replied. "Strike the primary and secondary targets and make for the extraction point. I want your men gone by the time they arrive."

"And leave a large mobile force at large behind us?" Espira asked.

"I will attend to them," Cavendish said. "They won't be able to pursue. Where are the prisoners?"

Espira hesitated.

"Major," Cavendish said between clenched teeth.

"The hallway we blocked off," Espira said finally. He nodded down the proper tunnel. "Down there. What do you intend for them?"

"The same as I intend for the rest of the Spirearch's merry band," Cavendish said, looking away, her eyes lit with some bizarre emotion Espira could not identify. "Take your men and go, Major. If you value their lives, none of them will be standing in these tunnels five minutes from now."

Espira frowned at the woman, but she did not return her gaze to his. Then he nodded, bowed again, and withdrew.

Ciriaco fell into step beside him. The grizzled sergeant glowered back over his wounded shoulder at Sark for a moment, then turned to Espira. "We're going early."

"Yes. Dispatch the men as planned, immediately. Without the confusion of a general attack on the Spire, we'll have to move fast. Tell them to leave all camp equipment and supplies here, except for a canteen. Weapons only."

Ciriaco frowned but nodded. "Those two girls?"

Renaldo Espira had done a great many distasteful, necessary things in the course of his career. The orders of his superiors were generally given to him with the aim of benefiting those same superiors in some way. He was under no illusions about that. But even so, there was, somewhere within him, enough conscience to at least feel shame about it.

He felt ashamed of the next words he spoke to the sergeant.

"They're as good as dead, and no longer our concern, Sergeant," he said quietly.

Ciriaco glanced at the corridor where the prisoners were being kept, and clenched his large hands into fists with an audible crackle of knuckles. He exhaled once.

"Sir," he said. "World might be a brighter place without Sark and that woman in it."

"Creating a brighter world is not our concern or duty, Sergeant," Espira said without heat. "From this moment, all that we need concern ourselves with is accomplishing our objectives and getting as many Marines as possible out of this madness and back home to Spire Aurora alive and well. Clear?"

Ciriaco made a growling sound deep in his chest. But his hands relaxed and he nodded once. "Clear, sir." He looked down at Espira. "Think we can pull this off?"

"Of course," Espira replied with a confidence he was not at all sure he felt. "If each man remembers his duty and his training."

"And doesn't stand around wondering why we're doing it," Ciriaco said.

"Ours is not to reason why, Sergeant," Espira said. "Tell the captain of each force to move out. I want every single man of my command out of these tunnels in three minutes."

Chapter 51

Spire Albion, Habble Landing, Ventilation Tunnels

I t's just not natural," growled Felix to Grimm. "That's all I'm saying."

Grimm regarded askance the verminocitor walking on his left. "You can only give me a general idea of which section of tunnels your missing man had entered." He gestured to the small, utterly black cat who paced calmly a few steps ahead of Grimm. "It would seem that our companion has a more specific idea."

"Like as not the little beast is leading us into a trap," Felix predicted.

"I certainly hope so. I'd like to think that we haven't brought all these weapons for nothing," Grimm said.

Grimm's crew walked behind him in a tight, purposeful group, alongside the Verminocitors' Guild of Habble Landing. The verminocitors were a hard-bitten, wiry bunch. Very few of them were of even middling stature, or heavy of build, but they were, men and women alike, made of rope and gristle, and they all bore scars as mute testimony of dangers faced and overcome in the past.

"You say the cat belongs to a Guardsman," Felix continued.

"This one, no," Grimm said. "But I daresay our guide is acquainted with Rowl."

At the mention of the name, the little cat looked back at them without slowing her pace, focusing her lambent green eyes on Grimm. He lifted his hand and signaled a halt, and the men clattered to a stop.

"This is as good a place as any to stop and get more information," Grimm said. "I take it that is correct, ah, Miss Cat?"

The cat stopped in her tracks and turned to face Grimm. She regarded Felix for a moment, interested, then looked back up at Grimm. She moved her head up and down in a slow, deliberate nod.

"He sent you to fetch us?" Grimm asked.

Again, the cat nodded.

"Good," Grimm said. "Do you know exactly where the girls are being held?"

She nodded again. And after a moment, she shook her head left and right.

"There," Felix said. "Now, what's that supposed to mean?"

Grimm gave him a mild look. "Apparently that I need to learn to speak Cat." He frowned and called, "Benedict? Can you understand them at all?"

The tall young warriorborn shook his head. "Barely more than a greeting and a few pleasantries. It's a complex language, and takes years to learn."

At this, the little black cat looked pleased.

"Bother," Grimm said. "If we go storming in and start shooting up the place when we stumble over the Enemy, we're as likely to shoot the girls in the confusion as we are the foe. I need more specific information. She obviously knows it, or knows it better than we do, at least."

Felix huffed out a thoughtful breath. Then he reached into his coat and withdrew a thick folded sheaf of paper. He began to unfold it and laid it out on the floor. Grimm peered at it. It was a map of Habble Landing, with ventilation and service tunnels marked in several different colors, evidently to represent their respective elevations.

"Here, beastie," Felix said. "Have a look at this." He tapped a portion of the map with a thick forefinger. "I know Moberly was working in this general section of the tunnels. Which one have the Aurorans taken?"

The cat prowled over to the map and regarded it with bright eyes. She tilted her head this way and that, pawed at its surface, sniffed it, walked over it, then sat down and just stared at Felix.

"What the bloody hell is that supposed to mean?" Felix demanded of Grimm.

"It's too abstract," Benedict said. "Maps are symbols, and she doesn't have the necessary experience she needs to understand one."

"Explain, please?" Grimm asked.

Benedict moved a hand in a small, frustrated gesture. "She doesn't experience the tunnels the way you do. She doesn't just see the tunnels. She navigates them by smell and sound as much as by sight. Show her a picture that is a symbolic representation of visual dimensions alone and it's confusing to her."

Felix shook his head. "How do you know that?"

"Because it was confusing as hell to me when I was learning to read maps," Benedict replied. "It took me a while when I was young."

Felix growled. "How hard is it to read a bloody map?"

Grimm pursed his lips and regarded the cat thoughtfully. "Perhaps we don't need her to read a map for us," he mused. "Perhaps we need her to draw one."

"What?" Felix asked.

"I need a piece of chalk," Grimm said, and raised his voice. "Who has some?"

"Skip," called Stern. The little man hefted his long gun onto his shoulder, dug in his pocket, and came out with a lump of chalk, which he tossed to Grimm underhand.

Grimm caught it and turned to the cat. "Miss Cat," he said. "If you're willing, perhaps we can work out exactly where we're going so that we can take the most appropriate steps to deal with the situation."

The cat regarded him intently and then nodded once.

"Thank you," Grimm said. "I propose to have you pace out the length of the tunnels in question, relative to one another. Not at full length, of course. Perhaps one pace to every thirty you would take were you actually walking through them. I will follow you with the chalk and sketch the tunnels you show me on the floor."

Felix grunted. "Then we compare the sketch to the map."

"Precisely," Grimm said.

The cat seemed to consider the idea for a moment, then rose and turned away from Grimm with an impatient little *mrowl*.

She began walking, her head tilted at a bit of an angle, and Grimm followed her, marking the spirestone floor with chalk. The little cat walked for several moments, and Grimm followed her, hoping that he didn't look quite as preposterous as he felt, following the creature around on his hands and knees, until she turned to face him and sat down once more.

He rose, his wounded arm aching, and regarded the chalk lines. "Well, Felix?"

The verminocitor lifted his map and peered at it, and then at the drawings on the floor. "I don't think that . . . No, wait a moment. This section here. By God in Heaven, look, it lines up well enough! She must have walked all around their perimeter. They're here in the middle."

Grimm regarded the portion of the map soberly. "Four ways in. Four ways out."

"Mrowr," said the black cat, and shook her head.

Grimm arched an eyebrow and eyed her. "Less?"

She nodded.

"They've blockaded tunnels?"

She nodded again.

"Which, please," Grimm asked.

The cat paced over to an intersection of chalk lines and pawed at the floor. Then at another.

"This one and this one," Grimm said, thumping a finger on the map. "They cut down the approach to two tunnels, and left themselves two ways out."

"Your men take one?" Felix suggested. "We'll take the other?"

Grimm looked up and arched an eyebrow. "Down tunnels they've prepared to defend? We'd pay a heavy price, and never get to the prisoners before they were killed."

"What, then?" Felix demanded.

"Their only chance is for us to get in fast and hard, find the prisoners, and get out again before the Enemy can react properly. We need to go in from a direction they do not expect." He pursed his lips. "A coin toss may be the best we can hope for. Mister Stern?"

"Aye, Skip?" The lean young officer came forward.

"I trust that you brought the blasting charges we acquired from the Aurorans in Habble Morning."

Stern gave Grimm a wide, hungry grin.

Chapter 52

Spire Albion, Habble Landing,
Ventilation Tunnels

Odd clicking sounds made Bridget lift her head and open her eyes.

She and Folly had decided to resume their original positions, in the event that their captors peeked in at them. The leather cords were looped loosely around their wrists, though Bridget had been unable to devise a way to wrap their ankles in a similar fashion, one that could be shed immediately, and they'd had to simply settle for hiding their feet within their skirts.

Time passed, and not quickly. With every breath and heartbeat Bridget imagined their captors, out of sight, deciding that this was the moment in which to murder them.

The sounds came again. Rapid, irregular clicks, somehow familiar, from the Enemy camp.

"I wonder what that is," Folly whispered.

"Something's happening," Bridget murmured back. She rose and paced as silently as she could to the tarp blocking their view of the tunnel outside. She eased up to a slight gap in its edge, and peeked through it as quickly as she could.

A single glance froze her with sheer terror.

Silkweavers.

Dozens and dozens of adult silkweavers, with leathery, armored bodies and torsos the size of Bridget's own. The beasts must have weighed at least what she did—and yet they moved with that same horrible, alien grace as their broodlings had. They were flowing into the Auroran camp along the floor, the walls, and the ceiling of the ventilation tunnels, visible in the light of half a dozen small lumin crystals that had evidently been left behind by the departing troops.

Bridget blinked, and took a longer look. Everywhere she saw empty bedrolls, discarded backpacks, litter and trash—and no Aurorans anywhere. They had abandoned their camp.

And now the silkweavers were taking their place.

Bridget wanted to turn and run. But she forced herself to stay still. To look. To see. She couldn't see much of the area, not enough to get an estimate of how many Aurorans had been there. The silkweavers prowled restlessly, and she couldn't be sure how many there were. Forty or fifty, perhaps?

And there, next to a bedroll that had been neatly folded, rolled, and tied, she saw her gauntlet, her knife—and Folly's expended lumin crystals, still in their two little bags and glass jar.

Bridget took slow steps back, being as quiet as she possibly could.

She turned to find Folly staring at her, her face pale, her mismatched eyes very wide.

Bridget crouched down next to Folly and whispered into her ear, "Adult silkweavers. Dozens of them."

Folly started trembling, but nodded her head once. "Don't worry," she whispered to her little crystal. "I'll protect you."

"I found your crystals," Bridget whispered.

Folly's head snapped up, her eyes wide. She pressed her single little crystal to her lips. "Oh," she whispered. "I do hope they're all right."

"They're only about ten feet away," Bridget said. "My gauntlet is there, too. I think I can get to them. If I can get you the crystals—"

"Yes," Folly interrupted, nodding, her eyes closed. "Yes, that."

"If I can," Bridget said, "can you do anything to get us out of here?"

Folly licked her lips. Then she took a slow, deep breath and let it out. Then another. And another. When she opened her eyes they were glazed, their pupils dilated enormously. She turned her gaze slowly, left to right, then shivered and bowed her head.

"There are no currents in here," she whispered to her crystal. "But there's another blocked hall, to the left. There's a conduit there. I could use that."

"How far?"

Folly shook her head. "Fifty feet, I think, though it's a silly way to measure. Steps would be more practical. Or strides. Yes, strides."

Bridget chewed on her lip. Forty or fifty silkweavers. Ten feet to the equipment. Fifty feet to the other hallway.

They'd never make that without being seen.

She felt certain that in a drama, a heroine would have immediately devised a plan to sacrifice herself boldly for her companion. She'd rush out into the hall and fling the crystals back to Folly, and then run in the opposite direction, screaming, and drawing all the silkweavers after her. She would put up a bold fight, but ultimately die gallantly while Folly brought terrible retribution upon the surface creatures—and then finished the mission, mourning her fallen friend in the aftermath.

Heroines in dramas, Bridget felt, really ought to have more sense.

The silkweavers hadn't seen them yet, or, if they had sensed their presence, hadn't attacked. If they hadn't done so yet, they might not, at least for a while. The Aurorans, certainly, were nowhere to be seen. Perhaps the smartest thing to do would be to simply wait quietly. Their best hope, it seemed, was that Rowl would bring aid. They should stand ready to assist in their own rescue, when it came.

After all, if the silkweavers did decide to eat them, Bridget always had the option of throwing away her own life in a desperate gamble to save

Folly's. But until such time as she had no other option, she would avoid that course of action, thank you very much.

Bridget felt she would make a terrible dramatic heroine.

And then, over the clicking sounds of silkweaver legs and brushing chitin, Bridget heard voices speaking.

That sent another thrill of terror down her spine.

Humans? Near silkweavers?

There was only one real possibility that leapt to mind: These must be the people who were in control of the horrible things—and *that* was something that the Spirearch would want to know all about. Her duty as a Guardsman was perfectly clear: She must do everything she could to learn about these individuals.

Oh, dear.

Bridget swallowed and once more stalked quietly up to the gap in the partition. She peeked out, moving as slowly as possible.

A man and a woman were walking toward her through the silkweavers, as if the creatures were nothing more out of place or threatening than a crowd of schoolchildren busily playing during a recess. She was dressed impeccably, in a dress and jacket of grey-and-lavender cloth, her hair done up with pristine neatness at the nape of her neck, and sporting a matching hat and white gloves. She was a mature woman with empty grey eyes and a kind of severe, hard-edged beauty. A scarlet stone glittered at her throat, worn next to her skin on a black velvet choker.

The man walking beside her was warriorborn, like Benedict. He was taller, though, and carried more muscle on his long frame. Short hairs, dull brown sprinkled with silver, adorned his head in a sparse fuzz, matched along his arms and neck and face, giving him an especially feral appearance. One of his feline eyes was off center, and there was something about the way he moved that was just . . . wrong. Benedict did not walk so much as glide with flowing grace evident in every gesture and motion. This man . . .

It took Bridget a moment to register it.

This man moved with the grace of a silkweaver.

"Still don't see what all the fuss is about," the man said. "A fire would do. One person, in and out."

"You underestimate the Wayists," the woman said. "There are warriorborn among their number, too." Her dark eyes glittered. "Besides. A fire is not enough. A message must be sent."

The man grunted. "Seems foolish."

"We'll never destroy them while they remain in Heaven. We must therefore draw them out."

Bridget blinked at that.

"Baiting the mistshark," the man said. "Sometimes that doesn't go the way you think."

"Risks must be taken in war," the woman said calmly. "In fact . . ."

Her voice trailed off suddenly, and her eyes became unfocused, abstracted, in a manner eerily akin to Folly's a few moments before. The gem at her throat flickered with deep scarlet light.

"Ah," the woman said, her tone pleased. "My sentries. They are here. I thought as much."

The man inhaled and rolled his shoulders. He drew a short, wide sword into his hand, and the gauntlet on the other kindled to life. "Where?"

"Groups are moving toward both tunnels in," the woman said. "No more than twenty each." She moved her hand in an imperious gesture, and once more the gem at her throat flickered with sullen fire. The reaction of the silkweavers was immediate. They began to rush into two distinct groups, forming in tight ranks. The first group piled up at the mouth of a tunnel. The other rushed out of sight of where Bridget could see, but she presumed they had formed up at another tunnel mouth.

"You want any of them alive?" the man asked.

"Unnecessary," she replied. "Sark, kill the prisoners. I'd hate for the captain to think I wasn't true to my word."

The man, Sark, turned on his heel at once and strode purposefully toward the partition.

Bridget never really thought about what she did next. If she had, she would have found the idea ludicrously terrifying—she burst through the concealing partition and into a silent run in the open, in full view of a warriorborn with a primed gauntlet.

Everything seemed to slow down, and Bridget had time to note, idly, that Rowl had probably saved her life again. When other children had been playing hide-and-seek with one another, Bridget had been playing it with Rowl. She did not move with the utter silence of a cat—but she couldn't really think of any other humans who could do better than she could.

Had she made the faintest sound before she moved, the softest scrape of a boot on stone, the least careless rustle of fabric, Sark's warriorborn senses would have pinpointed her exact location. The man may well have been able to target her even concealed by the partition. But she hadn't made any mistakes. She had, Rowl would have said, behaved with acceptable competence. Sark had been taken entirely off guard.

She gained no more than a heartbeat or two of shock—time enough to reach the little pile of equipment. Then the man's reflexes took over, and he raised his gauntlet, sighting on her between the V made of his parted fingers.

It was time enough for Bridget to seize the glass jar of crystals and throw it back toward Folly.

She whirled to one side and flung herself flat on the ground—only to see Sark calmly track her motion, rather than shooting hastily. He lined up his shot, neither rushed nor slow, and the crystal against his palm brightened.

Bridget did not face her death bravely. She screamed with pure fear, lifting a hand.

The gauntlet flashed.

A tiny star tumbled into the path of the etheric bolt, intercepted it, and sent the shot curving out in a wide arc that circled around Bridget entirely.

Bridget stared in bewilderment, stunned at how slowly it all seemed to happen. The bolt wrapped around her and splashed onto the floor beyond the partition—directly into the scatter of broken glass and loose lumin crystals that marked where Bridget's throw had fallen well short of Folly.

The force of the blast did not scatter the crystals, as Bridget's common sense told her it absolutely should have. Instead it just seemed to disperse, spreading out like a wave. Where the wave spread, the little crystals burst into hot, angry light.

And abruptly and all at once, they rose into the air in a cloud of glowing motes.

Folly appeared among them, striding forward, flickers of light dancing along her candy-stripe hair, her mismatched eyes blazing.

Sark loosed several more blasts, all of which dispersed into the crystals, making them glow with even brighter light.

Folly's voice rang out, cold and hard. "We don't like it when people try to hurt our friends."

And the entire cloud of crystals flew at Sark like bullets loosed from a gun.

Sark dropped to one knee, flinging both arms up over his head. The cloud of glowing crystals tore into his flesh with a sickening, rippling sound. A fine spray of blood erupted from countless wounds. Crystals lodged in him like hundreds of tiny darts, glowing where they erupted from his skin.

A shuddering breath escaped the warriorborn.

And then he heaved himself to his feet, lowering his arms. They burned with scarlet light as droplets of blood covered the crystals. They protruded from his arms, his belly, one shin, one thigh. He bled, and glowed with the power the etherealist's apprentice had loosed upon him.

His ugly features showed not a trace of pain or fear. He flexed his hand, and the light from the gauntlet's crystal died away.

"Really?" asked the woman, something like a laugh bubbling in the word. Bridget looked up to see that she was watching with what appeared to be high amusement as she spoke to Folly. "How many years have you been his apprentice? And he's only taught you transference and kinetics?" She regarded Sark for a moment, then looked back to Folly. "Tell me that's not the entire extent of your ability."

Folly stared back at the woman. Her mouth opened, then closed again. The blood drained from her face.

The woman bent and plucked up the little bags of lumin crystals, which Bridget had not had time to throw. She tossed them to Folly. The bags landed at her feet and burst, the crystals scattering.

"It isn't polite for peers to murder one another without introduction," the woman said. "And while you are not my equal, you do have talent." She inclined her head. "My name is Sycorax Cavendish. Like you, I was once apprenticed to master etherealist Efferus Effrenus Ferus. And then he betrayed me." She smiled and flexed her fingers. "And you are?"

Folly swallowed. She looked down at the little crystals, fingers twitching, as though she had to restrain herself from stooping to pick them up. Then she bobbed a quick curtsy, her eyes on her crystals, and said, "My name is Folly, ma'am."

Cavendish burst into a merry laugh. "Folly, is it? Did he give you this name?"

"And much more than that," Folly said. Then her eyes widened and she looked up. "Oh. It's you. You're the gnat I caught."

Cavendish seemed somewhat taken aback by the comment, and arched an eyebrow. "Excuse me?"

"You were buzzing and buzzing, so I built a web to catch you. It wasn't a very pretty web, but I did." Folly tilted her head. "You . . . you were receiving orders." She chewed on her lip for a moment. "You have a new master now. Is that it?"

Cavendish's eyes narrowed. "There's nothing wrong with your mind, I suppose, Miss Folly." Her teeth showed. "Yet. Shall I show you what real power feels like?"

"I don't talk to puppets," Folly said. "They can't talk back. Not really. They just dance on their strings."

Cavendish's eyes flashed. "Sark," she said. "Kill the other one."

Sark pivoted toward Bridget and started walking forward, sword in hand.

Cavendish flicked a finger at Folly.

Folly's eyes flew open wide, and pure agony flowed from her mouth in a scream that seemed to have been ripped loose from her guts and tore up her gullet.

Bridget rolled to her feet, for all the good it would do her against an armed warriorborn.

And then there was a horrible slap against her body, and with a roar of sound and smoke, the entire world flew sideways.

■ ■ ■ Chapter 53 ■ ■ ■

Spire Albion, Habble Landing,
Ventilation Tunnels

The blasting charges blew a wide hole in the mound of broken masonry that had been used to plug the tunnel. The sound of the explosion was an invisible wall that swept through the corridor, sucking the wind from Grimm's lungs despite his protected position around the nearest corner.

Grimm forced himself to stagger out into the tunnel before he'd managed to draw a breath. He was running toward the breach in the masonry barricade before the flying bits of stone had stopped rattling to the floor, sword in hand and gauntlet primed, and he heard the clatter of boots behind him as Kettle sent the men running in his wake.

The air was thick with dust and stinking, sulfurous smoke. Bits of stone of various sizes twisted beneath his boots, threatening his balance, and his imagination treated him to an image of himself sprinting straight into a wall in the bad visibility and stabbing himself with his own sword.

God in Heaven knew, if he'd chosen the wrong tunnel, the one where the Cavendish woman had been keeping her prisoners, he'd deserve it.

The direction of his thoughts distracted him and he nearly stumbled over a block of masonry the size of a slab of fresh meat. A hand with a grip like copper-clad steel locked onto his upper arm, and Sir Benedict helped him keep his balance and continue moving forward. The young warriorborn was tense, his feline eyes bright, and Grimm knew that they were lucky to have such a resource entering the battle with them.

Grimm plunged out of the dark and smoke into an area lit with scattered lumin crystals. The dust and grit in the air gave everything an odd, flat quality, as if his depth perception had suddenly been blurred. The occupants of the chamber were still reeling, stunned by the explosion and flying debris, and Grimm had what seemed an eternity to take it all in.

Miss Tagwynn was down, lying sprawled on the floor as if she had been struck a stunning blow, her wide eyes unfocused. Not five feet away from her lay Sark, the warriorborn who had accompanied Madame Cavendish. The large man was already rolling to regain his feet, and copper-clad steel gleamed in his hand. Several yards beyond Sark, Madame Cavendish had fallen to one knee, her expensive dress and bolero covered in dust. Her teeth were clenched, and she shook her head even as Grimm dismissed the priming charge from his gauntlet and drew his pistol into his left hand instead.

His mind was still cataloging details as he strode forward, bringing the pistol to bear. Very few men could afford the expense it took to operate a pistol until they were experts in the weapon's use—and of those, a measurable percentage lost their fingers, eyes, or lives when the weapons burst from the inside, rather than propelling their loads toward the target. Any given pistol could fire only fifty or sixty rounds before the corrosive firepowder began to eat through the copper plating within the barrel, at which point iron rot would set into the steel, weakening the gun until an inevitable misfire occurred.

Grimm had dutifully gone through half a dozen barrels while learning to fire the weapon with a modicum of proficiency, but he was by no means an expert—so he strode toward Cavendish as rapidly as he could, to fire from a distance that would preclude a miss due to his dubious competence. Once she was dispatched, he could discard the pistol and bring his gauntlet to bear on the silkweavers rushing up behind her—

Silkweavers? God in Heaven, there were dozens of the deadly, fully grown adult surface creatures pouring out of one of the tunnels, rushing toward his men.

With the arrival of sudden terror, the timeless moment of detached observation ended.

"Bridget!" Benedict shouted.

Sark came to his feet, his blade darting toward the downed girl, but Benedict let out a lion's roar of pure fury, a sound that shocked Grimm's senses, and hit Sark in a flying tackle. Both warriorborn went down, struggling against each other.

The roar seemed to galvanize Madame Cavendish. She looked up, blinking her eyes, and they widened when they locked onto Grimm. She began to rise to her feet.

He wished he were closer to the etherealist, but this distance, seven or eight yards, would have to be close enough. Her hand was already rising toward him, and he had only a single instant to act. Grimm corrected his aim slightly and squeezed the trigger.

The pistol sparked and then spoke, a flash of bright light in the dim chamber.

Madame Cavendish let out a sudden, breathless cry and spun violently in place, hurled back to the ground again as though struck with a club.

The first of the silkweavers flung itself through the air toward Grimm, letting out a shrieking cry that sent another bolt of terror through him, for he had heard it before—only days ago, in the dark ventilation tunnels of Habble Morning, when he had fought back-to-back with Alex Bayard.

There was no time to prime the gauntlet. Instead he flipped the pistol, gripped it by the barrel, and brought the handle of the heavy, primitive weapon down upon the head of the silkweaver with every ounce of strength he could muster.

His arm screamed with pain, muscles and tendons protesting the abuse, but they functioned. The blow clubbed the silkweaver to the floor, and Grimm wasted no time in driving his short shipboard blade down into the silkweaver's body, where its head met its neck. He barely managed to jerk the blade clear before the beast went into wild spasms, all its legs flailing with no semblance of cohesion, its three-jawed muzzle snapping wildly, bubbling with venomous foam.

The aeronauts of *Predator* let loose a battle cry of their own, screaming, "Albion!"

And then the battle was joined. There was no time to think, to issue orders, or to do anything but survive. Gauntlets discharged. Silkweavers shrieked. Grimm dodged the pounce of another silkweaver by the barest margin, and he caught a glimpse of Madame Cavendish on the floor, her face deathly pale, pointing a finger at Grimm and wailing in primal outrage.

And half a dozen of the monsters darted toward him, following her command.

Grimm would have died where he stood if Kettle, Creedy, Stern, and half a dozen other aeronauts hadn't reached his side, their gauntlets howling. They blew two of the silkweavers into bloody, stinking meat, but a third darted beneath the blasts, seized the wiry Stern by one leg, and hauled him from his feet with abrupt violence, fangs sinking, tearing, and bubbling with poison.

Stern screamed.

Grimm struggled to get to the downed man, but it was all he could do to fend off another monster and prevent himself from joining Stern on the ground. He slashed and scored a pair of solid strokes—but the silkweaver's leathery hide was tough, and the blows drew little blood.

Stern's leg broke with an audible crack, and blood began streaming from the wound.

The scent of the blood washed over the silkweavers like a sudden wind born of primal, insane violence. Their shrieks rose up again, deafening, and Grimm felt his legs go watery. Their movements became quicker, more erratic, and the venom practically frothed from their jaws, pattering onto the spirestone floor.

With the silkweavers maddened by blood, there were now only two outcomes possible in the current situation: Either Grimm and the men of *Predator* would destroy every single silkweaver present—or else they would fall to the jaws and venom of the surface creatures.

Stern screamed again, drawing a belt knife and stabbing down at the silkweaver holding on to his leg, but the creature shook him like a cat shaking a tunnel mouse, too strong for its size, slamming the young man left and right and sending the knife tumbling.

On Grimm's other side, Creedy drove the heel of his boot into a silkweaver's mouth, only to have the thing lock its jaws onto Creedy's foot and wrench at the XO's leg. Its teeth sliced through the leather of Creedy's boot, and he shouted in rage and pain. Kettle's boarding ax came sweeping down on the silkweaver and split the thing in half in the middle of its body—but the dying front half kept wrenching and rending Creedy's foot nonetheless.

More of the damned creatures were coming, scuttling over the walls and the ceiling, using their superior mobility to surround Grimm and his men. Grimm's ground combat experience was limited—but it was not difficult to deduce that they had only moments to live.

And then Felix and the verminocitors entered the fray.

They uttered no battle cry and made no sound as they came rushing in from each of the open tunnels leading to the Auroran encampment. But as they closed the distance to the nearest silkweavers, their scalelashes began to whirl, building momentum and emitting soft, hissing whistles as they spun.

The scalelash was a deadly instrument, made of small rings of metal knitted into a tapered tube, each ring hung with a pointed, edged metal scale. The bloody things weighed as much as an ax and hit with nearly as much force—and then the scales ripped away chunks of flesh as they tore free. A strike with a scalelash could saw its way through the toughest hide, inflicting deep, horribly painful, bleeding wounds. What they did to soft human flesh was indescribable.

A dozen of the weapons whipped toward the rearmost rank of silkweavers in a unified chorus of violence.

Verminocitors prowled the darkness of the tunnels of every habble in the Spire. On a daily basis they faced the possibility that they might find themselves face-to-face with a nightmare from the surface world. It was a necessary duty. Without verminocitors, horrors from the surface could and would emerge from the ventilation and service tunnels and begin preying upon citizens of the habble—and their first victims were very nearly always children.

Men and women who took up that responsibility were by definition confident, skilled, fearless, and mildly insane. And, Grimm thought, this particular pack of madmen had a score to settle.

Scalelashes hammered and tore. Silkweavers screamed. Some of Felix's people had exchanged short, heavy spears for their lashes, and when one of their compatriots wounded or stunned a silkweaver, a spear carrier would rush in and deliver the death stroke from the relative safety of the longer weapon's reach.

Felix himself whirled a scalelash in either hand, striking left and right, smashing armor, ripping flesh, and severing the beasts' legs with a kind of dreadfully workaday practicality. With a quick motion, he struck the silkweaver attacking Grimm a savage blow that drove it flat to the ground, stunned. Then he dropped one lash, flicked the other around the neck of the silkweaver wrenching at Stern's leg, and twisted the metal weapon with professional expertise, tightening it around the creature's head.

The silkweaver began to thrash wildly, but Felix simply settled his weight onto it more firmly and held on, leaning into the strength of the pull until the creature's triple jaws snapped open and it let out a shriek of pain.

Grimm dispatched the silkweaver Felix had stunned, then stepped around behind the verminocitor. He murmured, "Excuse me," set his weapon carefully, and drove his sword into the same spot at the base of the silkweaver's skull. The thing went mad for a few seconds, thrashing wildly—and then simply sagged, like a bladder being drained of its liquid.

Felix unwound his lash from the dead silkweaver. "You boys aren't bad. For a bunch of rubbernecks, I mean."

"Thank you," Grimm said hesitantly. "Mister Creedy?"

"Sir."

"Get Stern and yourself to Doctor Bagen." Grimm turned back to Felix. "What, sir, is a rubberneck?"

Felix flashed Grimm a quick grin. "We'll get this work done and I'll tell—"

The verminocitor turned abruptly, his eyes widening, and Grimm followed the man's gaze to one of the other tunnels leading into the intersection the Aurorans had claimed. There was a chorus of shrieks and a *second* group of silkweavers, as large as the first, poured into the intersection.

Grimm watched helplessly, shouting a warning that went unheard as half a dozen of the verminocitors were buried under a wave of ripping jaws and poisoned fangs, overwhelmed by the sudden onslaught. Their screams of terror swiftly became gargling sounds of despair—and then fell silent.

Next in the path of the second group of horrors were the two warrior-born. Benedict had gained the upper hand on Sark as the two wrestled, and was more or less on top, his arms and hands moving so quickly that

Grimm could hardly see them, while Sark matched him motion for motion, countering every move the younger man attempted. As the fresh tide of silkweavers rushed toward them, the two warriorborn snapped their gazes up toward the oncoming wave.

Benedict's eyes widened and he began to hurl himself away from Sark. But the evil-looking warriorborn locked a leg around Benedict's legs and fastened his hands on Benedict's jacket. With an ugly smile, he twisted, rolling Benedict toward the silkweavers.

Benedict reversed his direction almost instantly, and instead of trying to escape Sark, he went with his opponent, twisting his own body in the same direction. He hit the ground on his back and rolled Sark over him, hurling the larger warriorborn a couple of feet clear of him and into the first rank of silkweavers. The creatures flowed over Sark like some kind of horrible, living blanket, and he vanished from sight.

Benedict barely regained his feet before the first half dozen silkweavers reached him. Had Grimm been standing in the young man's shoes, he felt sure he would not have survived—but then, he was not warrior-born.

Benedict let out a leonine roar, dodged the first silkweaver, and swept his sword from its sheath to cut another one cleanly in half as it flew toward him. One hit his arm and clamped its tripartite jaws down on his biceps. Benedict staggered, converted the momentum of the creature's leap into a spin, and slammed it into two of its fellows as if the silkweaver had been a shield strapped to his arm, knocking them aside.

The sixth silkweaver hit Benedict at the knees and sank its teeth into his thigh, knocking him down violently.

"Back-to-back!" Grimm bellowed to his men. "Group up! Kettle, on me!" He strode toward Benedict, priming his gauntlet as he went, unleashing blast after blast into the oncoming mass of silkweavers, smashing two of them to flaming pulp, and buying Benedict a few precious seconds.

The warriorborn managed to kick free of the silkweaver latched onto his leg and, with a scream of fury and pain, lifted his arm and smashed the silkweaver holding on to it into the spirestone floor repeatedly, until purplish ichor splattered and the thing fell off, body curling, legs twitching spasmodically.

Grimm and Kettle reached Benedict's side. Kettle laid about with his ax, keeping the silkweavers at bay. Grimm hauled Benedict to his feet by main force, fending off another silkweaver with his sword as he did.

"Bridget and Folly!" Benedict cried. He was bleeding freely from both his arm and his leg, but there was no time to dress the wounds — the enemy was already struggling to overwhelm them. "We have to get them out!"

"Stay together!" Grimm replied. "Follow me!"

He raised his gauntlet and began blasting the spirestone floor in the general direction of where he'd last seen Bridget lying on the ground. He hit nothing, but a handful of silkweavers that had begun approaching from that direction skittered back several feet. Grimm walked into the cleared space and blasted the floor again, sweeping more silkweavers from his path, and continued walking. He heard Kettle doing the same behind him, blasting away with his gauntlet to keep the main body of silkweavers back. He had a severe fright when a silkweaver dropped from the ceiling overhead toward his skull, but Benedict jerked Grimm aside with one hand, and with the other neatly skewered the silkweaver on his sword, holding the creature aloft for a moment as it thrashed, his arm steady, before he flung it off of his blade, twisting it as it came free of the silkweaver's body. The creature gushed foul-smelling blood as it tumbled away.

Grimm continued, and only barely stopped himself from unleashing a blast from his rapidly heating gauntlet that would have struck the prone form of Bridget Tagwynn.

"Form a circle around her!" he barked. He sheathed his sword as the men closed around them, and bent down to pick her up. She was a tall young woman, and heavier than she looked. Grimm got one of his shoulders beneath one of her arms and leveraged her to her feet. She blinked several times, her eyes not quite focused, but though her legs wobbled she was able to support most of her own weight.

"Miss Tagwynn!" Grimm shouted over the howl of discharging gauntlets. "Where is Miss Folly?"

Bridget stared at him, blinking several times. Then she said, "Tunnel. In the tunnel. Lying on the floor."

Grimm's stomach twisted in sickened horror. "Which one?"

Bridget stared around her for a moment and then nodded down the tunnel Grimm hadn't ordered blown halfway to hell.

"Captain!" Kettle screamed, his voice a warning.

Grimm's head snapped around, and his belly tightened and writhed still more as he realized the depth of their predicament.

The surprise assault of the verminocitors had been itself taken by surprise by the second wave of silkweavers. Men and women lay dying or dead, and more were being killed in front of Grimm's eyes. The stench of blood and entrails had already filled the air, mixing with the foulness of silkweaver blood. Several members of his crew were down, and others were fighting a desperate retreat back the way they had come—and he could see what had made the sudden reversal possible.

Sark was among them.

The large warriorborn moved with terrible speed, darting here and there, never predictable, moving among the silkweavers as if he were one of their number. As Grimm watched, Sark crushed a woman's throat with a casual squeeze of his hand, and hamstrung another verminocitor, dropping him to the ground, where the silkweavers could finish him. His hand moved, and a knife flickered through the air and plunged into the leg of Henderson, Kettle's apprentice pilot. The young man screamed and clutched at his leg as he fell.

Grimm tried to shout, to order Henderson not to remove the knife — but the young man jerked it clear in a small spray of blood — and every silkweaver within thirty feet flung itself upon him until he was buried under a mound of ripping, worrying bodies, and more blood scattered through the air.

Michaels, a gunner's mate on the number five gun, raised a gauntlet and discharged it twice, aiming at Sark. The first blast missed.

The second whipped out and around Sark in a tight orbit, then flew back into Michaels's head, slamming home with explosive violence, hurling a nearly faceless corpse to the spirestone floor.

Grimm's eyes darted to one side, where Madame Cavendish stood, one hand pressed against her ribs over a fresh, wet bloodstain on her dress. The other was extended toward Sark, and her eyes were gleaming.

The crew was being driven back down the breach they'd made with the blasting charges — and the silkweavers that had been finishing the last of the disabled verminocitors began to gather, darting toward Grimm and his little band in swift, agitated motions.

They were cut off.

"Fall back!" Grimm shouted. "Back down the tunnel! Keep them off with gauntlet fire until we get a defensive position!"

They retreated step by step. The copper cages of their gauntlets were smoking and smoldering with heat. Creedy's teeth were clenched over a rising, screaming sound, but the tall young XO kept blasting away with his gauntlet in steady rhythm.

They made it to the tunnel, and Bridget slid off of Grimm's shoulder and half fell down beside Miss Folly, who lay on the floor, curled up into a fetal position, quivering as though her muscles were trying to curl up even tighter. Grimm looked around. The tunnel had been blocked with more masonry, just as had the one they'd entered through. There was no way out of it, and no time to build even a meager defense out of the mound of stone.

A voice suddenly called from the tunnel beyond—Madame Cavendish. "This is the third time you've interfered with my business, Captain," she said, her words hard-edged, cold. "And as you have spilled my blood, it shall be the last."

"Madame, call off your pets!" Grimm called at once. "Guarantee the safe conduct of those with me, and I'll surrender. You can kill me however you like."

"I can do that without your cooperation, thank you," Madame Cavendish replied, her tone amused. "Good-bye, Captain."

And with that, a horde of silkweavers poured through the mouth of the tunnel—too many of the things. They were running along the walls and ceilings, spread out, moving too fast, in numbers too many to be countered.

Grimm and his people were about to be overwhelmed—and there was not a thing he could do to stop it.

■ ■ ■ Chapter 54 ■ ■ ■

Elsewhere

Folly had time to see Madame Puppet point a finger at her, and to feel a geyser of etheric energy smash into her body. Then an entire Spire full of pain crashed down upon her.

Folly thought she must surely have screamed. She knew nothing except agony, and every sensation only seemed to magnify it more. She felt herself fall, curling up into a ball, felt her eyes squeezing shut as every muscle in her body convulsed at once. She couldn't hear anything through the discordant howling sound in her head, and her throat didn't hurt—not with this new definition of pain—but it tickled a little: It seemed reasonable to assume that she must have been screaming.

That thought triggered another—how odd it was that she should have the wherewithal to process such a thought when her nervous system was so utterly overwhelmed. And that thought led to still another: How odd that she should be aware enough to notice her thought process at all.

She was still aware of the pain, pain so great that she would have welcomed the dubious relief of emptying her stomach onto the floor, if only for a change of pace. Simultaneously she could feel her thoughts drifting free of her body's limits, like a length of ethersilk snapped from a ship's web floating away upon the etheric currents.

Her body, her senses, all remained upon the floor of the blockaded tunnel, but her thoughts weren't there with them. Her mind was somewhere else entirely.

She was Elsewhere.

For a moment she floated in an empty void. And then she became conscious of solid ground beneath her feet. She looked down at it curiously and found it strange. She knelt to examine it more closely. The ground was not spirestone. It was loose earth, pale and granular. She pinched a bit up in her fingers and examined it. The earth was heavily mixed with sand.

Earth.

Sand.

Was she standing upon the surface?

The thrill of sudden terror that went through her was entirely unnecessary, unfair, and impolite, Folly felt. She knew, after all, that her body was being torn apart with pain back in Spire Albion. But nonetheless, she had spent her entire lifetime in curiosity and utter dread about the true nature of the surface world outside the Spires, the land of nightmares made flesh. In all of written history, the surface world had been a hell braved only by the mad, the desperate, and the madly, desperately greedy. Though her mind contradicted her fear, it seemed her body had an opinion of its own, and her heart raced.

She rose and turned in a slow circle. The mists were thin here, and she could see at least a hundred feet, but her cursory survey revealed nothing but more flat, dry earth and a few scattered stones.

Then the ground shook. It rumbled and quivered, and she could feel an impact through the soles of her feet. The sound came again, and then again, louder each time.

Footsteps. Enormous footsteps.

Coming closer.

The mists stirred and something vast and slow and seething with hate stopped just out of sight, so that all Folly could see was a great, dark blur. She froze in place and covered her mouth with her hands to hide the sound of her breathing.

Then a great Voice filled the air, resonant and mellifluous, like that of a particularly eloquent, poised, mature man, a professional speaker. "REPORT."

Folly hesitated. Whatever was happening to her, it seemed likely that it had not placed her in a position of leverage and power. But at the same time, her body was dying in any case. She could feel her straining heart racing so fast that she could not count individual beats. There seemed little enough point in prudence.

And besides, she was curious. She had questions. And answering questions was very nearly always more important than caution. Even the act of *asking* a question would tell her more than she now knew, if she could indeed ask it. There was no way to know but to try.

So she lowered her hands and said, "I beg your pardon. Whatever do you mean?"

She felt a sudden, awful attention from the thing in the mists, and the Voice said again, "REPORT."

"I hardly knew what you meant the first time. I've not gained an epiphany of insight in the past five seconds, I assure you."

There was a flash of red light somewhere in the fog, high above Folly's head, burning from three separate sources.

Eyes?

"YOU," the Voice said. "YOU ARE NOT CAVENDISH."

"Madame Puppet?" Folly asked. "Indeed not, and I thank you for the compliment."

"IDENTIFY YOURSELF."

Folly bobbed a quick curtsy toward the monstrous figure and said, "Folly. Who are you?"

The Voice did not answer. Instead there was an enormous boom of sound, like some utterly monstrous airship's steam-powered horn blar-

ing out into the night. A moment of silence went by, and then the call
was answered from far away, with more horn-blast sounds.

"YOU ARE A POTENTIAL ASSET."

"For you?" Folly asked. "I do not think so. I am not a puppet. You
said so yourself."

"YIELD."

The three red lights flared brighter, and Folly was suddenly sub-
sumed in a horrible, ugly *pressure* she felt inadequate to describe. It was
an enormous amount of power, one that quite took her breath away.
She could feel it scraping at her thoughts, raking them with claws, seeking something it could seize and use to hang on.

It sought to control her, just as she might control a . . .

"I *see*," Folly murmured. "You're the one holding the puppet's strings,
aren't you? You're the one holding *all* the puppets' strings."

"YIELD," the voice thundered.

The pressure increased, but Folly could feel it sliding off of her, left
and right, and it did little but make her breath come short for a few
seconds. She straightened her back and frowned thoughtfully up at the
lights.

"Are you going to be at this long?" Folly asked. "If so, I am afraid I
must decline to continue. I have an event I should attend." It did seem
fitting, after all, that one be present for one's own death, not out wandering about like a willful child shirking her chores.

There was a moment of silence and then the Voice said, "YOU ARE
OF ONE PIECE."

"I hardly think you could have said anything more obvious," Folly
replied. She squinted, trying to peer through the mist. "Yet . . . you
sought to control me, just as Madame Puppet is being directed, just as
the silkweavers are being directed."

"HOW CAN YOU KNOW THIS?" the Voice demanded.

"I look at things and think about them," Folly replied. "And use my intuition, of course, and deduction and induction, as well as any historical or theoretical models that seem to apply. Also, I was having the most horrible dreams that were evidently supposed to go to Madame Puppet, what I can only assume were instructions of some sort, so I caught one in a web and the master told me that it was an Enemy sending, and that we had an Enemy, and what he learned in the dream I caught led us to Habble Landing. . . ." Folly felt her face split into a wide smile. "Ah. Now I understand. You are the Enemy."

"IF YOU CANNOT BE MADE TO SERVE," said the Enemy, "YOU WILL BE UNMADE."

And the sandy soil suddenly began collapsing beneath Folly's feet.

Folly's belly did little flips and she began to scramble back. But it was fruitless. No matter how rapidly she retreated, the sand kept collapsing inward in a vast circle. She tried to run and felt her steps slowing, bogged down in the granules, sloughing away beneath her feet. No matter how quickly she tried to move forward, she could feel herself being drawn back—and down.

Sand, Folly thought, was a terrifying substance. She could feel it rising up, covering her ankles, and her imagination treated her to an image of it filling up her nose, her mouth, her eyes. That would be a grim sort of death, smothering on tiny, tiny pieces of glass. No wonder the Builders had surrounded humanity with spirestone. Spirestone was quite wonderful—solid, reliable, durable. One always knew where one stood with spirestone.

No sooner had Folly completed the thought than her foot came down on something hard and flat. She blinked and looked down to see a block of dark rock supporting her foot and ankle, beneath a steadily increasing torrent of sand.

"Ah, obviously," Folly said aloud. "My body is elsewhere. This is a place of the mind. In the mind, thoughts are the only reality."

She concentrated on the idea of spirestone, and took another step.

To her considerable satisfaction, her foot came down upon another immovable block of black stone.

The Enemy let out a bellowing sound, like a hundred deep, dissonant horns clamoring all at once, and Folly's heart leapt with terror. She began to run in earnest, and the spirestone blocks became a regular staircase, rising up out of the collapsing sand. She bounded up the stairs as lightly as a cat, running against a current of sand that continued trying to push her back down.

She reached the original ground level of the desert floor and continued running, her thoughts building more stairs ahead of her as she went. Behind her, there was another spine-wrenching, bellowing sound of rage, and the stairs beneath her feet shook as something utterly enormous took a great stride, and another, each coming closer and closer.

Folly did not dare look back, for fear that the sight of something terrible would shatter her concentration. She needed to escape. She fled up the staircase, trying to puzzle out how to leave this place. It seemed unfair that she should have reached it without any effort on her own part at all, only to be unable to leave.

She returned to her previous reasoning. Thoughts were reality here. If one needed to leave a place, one went out through the door.

She focused on the idea of a door, and suddenly it was there above her at the top of the stairs, set against a wall of nothing but empty air. Folly rushed up the last few stairs as glaring red light fell over her shoulders and changed the pale skin of her arms to scarlet. She hoped her theory was correct. Otherwise she was about to hurl herself through an empty doorway and down several dozen yards into a vast, collapsing pit of sand.

Folly opened the door to see what looked like a cloud of fiery red sparks hovering in the air in front of her.

The Enemy bellowed again, and a terrible shadow fell over her, a darkness and a coldness like nothing she had ever experienced.

"DEVOUR HER!" bellowed the Enemy. "DESTROY HER!"

Folly shrieked in involuntary fear and jumped through the open doorway, into the empty air, slamming the door shut behind her.

Folly sat up abruptly, clutching a batch of little lumin crystals in one hand, and blinked several times. Someone had her arms wrapped around her shoulders, and it turned out to be Bridget. There were also perhaps half a dozen of *Predator*'s crew around her, including Benedict Sorellin and the grim captain. They seemed exhausted and afraid, and they all brandished weapons in both hands. That seemed ominous.

On the other hand, Folly's general sense of herself did not seem to be anything like what she imagined death would be, as an experience, which all things considered seemed a pleasant surprise. It was important to consider the good things along with the bad.

"Oh," she said to her little crystals. "We did it! We escaped!"

Bridget jerked and stared at her. "Folly! Are you all right?"

DEVOUR HER, echoed the Enemy's words in her mind. *DE-STROY HER.*

The Enemy had been speaking to the campfire sparks, glimpsed through the doorway that had led from Elsewhere. Sparks the same ruby color as the light of the Enemy.

Folly looked up to see dozens of silkweavers pouring into the tunnel, racing along the floor and walls and ceiling, their clustered eyes glinting with little scarlet pinpoints of light.

And every single eye was focused upon Folly.

The silkweavers let out a shriek in eerie unison and then began to rush forward even faster.

■ ■ ■ Chapter 55 ■ ■ ■

Spire Albion, Habble Landing,
Ventilation Tunnels

Bridget blinked as Folly opened her eyes, sat up, and said gleefully, "Oh, we did it! We escaped!"

Bridget looked blearily from the chaos in the remains of the Auroran camp to the wall of masonry that effectively trapped them in the side tunnel where she and Folly had been held prisoner. There was a small army of surface creatures preparing to devour them, the few men Captain Grimm had rallied to his side were wounded and tired, and they had no possible means of fleeing their foe.

In what universe, she wondered dazedly, did their current predicament count as escape?

Bridget shook herself from her thoughts and saw that the etherealist's apprentice was staring blankly into space. "Folly?" Bridget asked. "Folly! Are you all right?"

"Miss Folly," Benedict said, nodding down to the two girls. He crouched down and peered at Folly, briefly putting a hand on her throat. "She's breathing and her heartbeat is strong. She doesn't seem to be injured. Perhaps she's taken a knock on the head."

"All things considered, I'm beginning to think that it would explain a great deal if we'd all taken a knock on the head," Bridget said. "What are we going to do?"

"Fight," Benedict said with a grim smile for her joke. He drew a heavy knife from his belt, flipped it so that he held it by the blade, and offered its handle to Bridget. "Here."

Bridget swallowed and took the knife. There was a reassuring heft to the blade in her hand, but she knew that if she needed to use the weapon, the silkweavers would be so close to her that it was unlikely to do her much good. More ominously, she saw that Benedict's hand and fingers were covered in his own blood, and that more of it had stained the knife's blade when he handed it to her. He was wounded, perhaps seriously. There were stains of an ugly color around the slices and gashes in his left forearm. Venom, doubtless.

Silkweaver venom could be deadly—even to a warriorborn. Bridget's heart sank a little, and she felt sick with sudden worry.

But she swallowed, rose to stand beside Benedict, and said, "Thank you, sir."

"I also saw this while we were coming here," Benedict said, and lifted his hand. He held Bridget's gauntlet. "I thought that so long as we were walking right past it, I might as well fetch it for you."

Bridget let out a huff of breath that was not quite a laugh. "Most kind, sir," she said, and began strapping the gauntlet to her arm. Her fingers did not fly with the speed and precision of a true expert, but they moved steadily and without hesitation. "Sir Sorellin?"

"Miss Tagwynn?" Benedict said.

"I suppose we are going to die here?" Bridget asked. "For goodness' sake, I would ask that you be honest with me."

Benedict regarded her steadily for a moment. He said nothing. He didn't need to. She could see the answer in his eyes.

Bridget continued strapping on her gauntlet, surprised at how calm she felt. It wasn't that the prospect of a violent death didn't frighten her—indeed, she felt terrified. But simultaneously . . .

She had chosen to be here. She stood in harm's way because she had elected to do so, to risk danger so that others could be protected. Whatever else happened this day, she knew that she had already drawn a great deal of the attention of horrible creatures and the monsters that served them away from innocents and onto herself. She had served as a shield and sword to her fellow Albions.

She didn't want to end her life that day—far from it. But all lives ended. If today was to be her last, she would have it be an ending with meaning. Surely dying in battle against such hideous foes spoke with absolute eloquence regarding her choices and her life.

Outside the tunnel, the sound of skittering and chittering grew louder.

"Here they come," said one of the aeronauts, his voice tight with fear.

"Steady," said Captain Grimm. From the excitement in his voice, he might have been talking about the weather.

Bridget glanced aside at the captain. He stood with his bloodied sword in hand, his still-hot gauntlet sending up wisps of smoke where copper cagework touched heavy leather bracer. His face was pale but calm, his eyes fixed on the entrance of the tunnel.

Her gaze continued to Benedict Sorellin, tall and straight, his breath coming a little harder than it had been a few moments before. That had to be the work of the poison. He too faced the darkness with a calm, pale face. He bounced his sword a few times in his hand, seemingly unaware that he moved the heavy steel weapon as if it had been no weightier than a cloth napkin.

If the nature of her foes would speak to the credit of Bridget's death, then surely the nature of her allies would speak even more loudly and clearly of her life.

She finished the last buckle on her gauntlet, primed it, gripped the heavy knife in her right hand, and turned to face the foe beside Benedict.

Folly suddenly drew in a sharp breath, and her eyes went wide and round. She stared for a second at the tunnel's entrance and then lifted her hands, making small whimpering sounds, scrambling away from the entrance until her back was pressed against the makeshift masonry wall.

Bridget stared at her for a second—and then remembered in a flash Folly's precognitive reaction just before the horde of infant silkweavers had come plunging out of the ceiling. She tracked the direction of Folly's gaze and whirled to shout to Grimm, "The ceiling, Captain! Fire!"

Grimm stared at her for a half second, but Bridget did not wait to see what the man would do. She raised her gauntlet and sent a howling bolt of energy flashing up toward the ceiling of the tunnel at its entrance. Even as she did, the first of a horde of silkweavers poured forward, rushing along the ceiling. Bridget's blast missed—but Grimm's shot, coming half a second later, neatly speared the lead silkweaver on a shaft of blazing light and sent it tumbling to the floor.

The silkweavers came on then, horrible and terrifyingly swift, flowing like a living carpet over the ceiling of the tunnel toward them. Their eyes gleamed, their tripartite jaws gaped, and they were emitting a chorus of hissing, whistling shrieks.

"Ceiling!" Grimm shouted, even as he loosed more blasts. "Fire, fire, fire!"

The aeronauts and Benedict followed suit, and for a moment the silkweavers were torn and blasted from the ceiling almost as quickly as they appeared. Bridget had no idea whether she hit anything, though it seemed fair to note that she could hardly have missed every blast. It was, she thought, more like pumping water at a fire than any kind of battle she had ever heard about.

Unfortunately, their pumps had a very limited amount of pressure. The aeronauts' gauntlets began overheating one by one, searing leather and the flesh beneath. Grimm was the last of his men to stop shooting, and the copper cagework around his gauntlet was glowing red-hot in places before he was through, leaving Bridget to keep firing at targets alone, her own weapon fresher and holding less waste heat than the weapons that had been engaged in lengthy battle already.

"Blades!" Grimm called, as the tide of silkweavers began surging forward now, confident and aggressive.

Sheaths rattled and steel whispered as the aeronauts drew their weapons. The first silkweaver leapt down upon them, only to be met by a group of swords and stabbed repeatedly. But Bridget could see what would inevitably happen, and her eyes blurred with tears of frustration as she watched more silkweavers pour in. There weren't anywhere near as many of them as there had been only a short while before—perhaps only a dozen. But they outnumbered the Albions two to one, and a man was a far more fragile creature than a silkweaver. They had come maddeningly close to victory—but now it was only a matter of time until death found them.

The silkweavers began to spring down upon the besieged little band.

And then Bridget heard the most beautiful music of her entire life.

When a single cat let loose a war cry, it was an unsettling sound. When two cats suddenly wailed at each other in a similar fashion, it was downright unnerving.

When *hundreds* of them caterwauled at the same time, in a single voice, the sound alone was enough to make one feel as if the skin had been peeled from one's muscle and bone, to call up horrors inherited from ancestors long since dead and forgotten, raw terror before a deadly predator. Not even the alien implacability of the silkweavers could ignore *that* call, and the surface creatures began to skitter and dart nervously back and forth.

Rowl and the Nine-Claws had come to wage war.

Cats flashed into the tunnel in a howling wave, led by Rowl, son of Maul of the Silent Paws. At his side rushed Naun, chief of the Nine-Claws, and a cadre of the tribe's largest warriors flanked them, every single one of them wearing a set of battle spurs.

The tight mass of cats seemed to explode all at once in different directions. Those who had never seen a tribe of cats at war, or at least playing war games, would look upon what came next as utter chaos. Cats dashed this way and that, seemingly at random, scratching with their claws, leaping, biting, and accomplishing nothing.

But Bridget knew better. The cats knew they were no match for the much larger and stronger silkweavers on an individual basis. Rather than sacrifice their warriors in desperate slashing piles of pure attrition, they played a different game, forcing the silkweavers to react to them, to keep them continuously spinning and turning and snapping at threats—only to have the cats they targeted sprint away before they could be pinned down. Cats darted this way and that, always passing a whisker's breadth out of reach of the silkweavers. The surface creatures, furious and agitated, could only snap uselessly at the air where a rushing cat had been, and try to keep track of every movement.

And then, once fatigue had begun to slow the silkweavers, once confusion had reduced the fantastic speed of their reflexes, Rowl and Naun struck.

Bridget watched as her friend suddenly sprinted directly at a silkweaver's open jaws. She began to shout a warning, but Rowl bounded left and right and then flung himself down flat on his back without ever slowing down. The cat slid beneath the silkweaver and promptly began raking with his battle spurs.

Rowl let out another war howl and his rear legs blurred as he raked and raked at the underbelly of the silkweaver above him. He rolled and sprinted out an instant before a rush of stinking purplish fluid and some kind of mucus burst from the silkweaver's abdomen. The silkweaver thrashed madly for a few seconds and then tottered onto its side, its many legs weaving uselessly and only slowly becoming still.

"Rowl!" Bridget called, delighted.

"Littlemouse!" Rowl caroled merrily in reply. "Do not kill any of my prey! I have a wager with Naun!" The cat bounded aside from the attack of a silkweaver Bridget would have sworn Rowl could not have seen, and rushed away, only to slide beneath another lethally harassed silkweaver on the opposite side of the tunnel. Once again he raked madly and darted clear before he could be drenched in the stinking guts of his foe.

Captain Grimm surged forward with his sword held high, bellowing, "Help the cats! Bait the silkweavers! Wear them out!"

Benedict darted forward to slash at a silkweaver who had managed to seize a cat's tail, menacing the creature and forcing it to release the cat, then kicked another silkweaver away from a wounded cat, leaping to place himself between the surface creature and the downed feline, his teeth bared in a wide grin.

Bridget held back. Given her skill with a gauntlet, it would have been foolishness to start hurling bolts of energy into *that* kind of chaos. Given how short her knife was, employing it seemed to her an excellent way to be poisoned by the silkweavers—and besides, someone had to stand watch over Folly to make sure one of the spiteful things didn't rush her helpless form.

The battle did not last long. Just as the silkweavers had outnumbered the Albions, leading to only one inevitable conclusion, the *cats* outnumbered the *silkweavers* to much the same effect. Naun, Rowl, and Naun's personal guard dispatched the creatures as each presented itself as a target—until only one silkweaver remained standing.

And at that point, Naun let out a vicious, furious howl, and two *hundred* Nine-Claws threw themselves upon the beast, ripping and tearing in a frenzy of wrath. The cats didn't *kill* the silkweaver so much as they spread it evenly over several dozen square yards of tunnel.

Bridget almost felt sorry for the beast.

Not quite, but almost.

"Bugger me," blurted a burly aeronaut. Bridget thought his name was Kettle or Keppel or something like that. "Little furry bastards don't play around, do they?"

"Mind your tongue, Kettle," Captain Grimm said. "All things considered, I think it very wise not to deliver any unintentional insults. Mmm?"

"Aye, Skip," Kettle said, eyeing the spreading stain that had been a silkweaver a few moments before. "That does seem like good sense. No offense intended, kitties."

Rowl sauntered lazily up to Littlemouse, looking enormously pleased with himself. "Five," he said smugly. "Five full-grown silkweavers in as many minutes. Maul has never done *that*."

Bridget tried to speak and found that she couldn't. Instead she dropped her knife, let out a little choking sound, and scooped Rowl up in her arms, hugging his furry warmth close to her.

"You saved us," she said.

"Of course I did," Rowl responded. "I am without flaw."

Bridget swallowed hard. And then she *did* begin to cry. "I was so scared," she said. "I thought I was going to die a long way from home."

Rowl made a deep, pleased purring sound in his chest. "How could that happen," he asked, "when you have me to protect you?"

She choked out a laugh. "You are impossible."

"I am cat," Rowl said smugly. "It is not of your doing, Littlemouse. It is natural that something so limited as a human finds me impossible. And you are squishing my fur."

Bridget kissed the top of Rowl's furry head, hugged him once more, and set him down on the floor. Oddly, he did not seem at all concerned about his fur. "I would speak to Grim Ship-Trees."

Bridget blinked. "You have given him a name?"

Rowl shook his ears as if he hadn't heard her and yawned. "Will you speak Albion to him for me?"

"I will," Bridget said. "Benedict, stay with Folly?"

"Of course," Benedict said. He nodded rather deeply to Rowl and said, "Well fought."

"He knows," Bridget said, before Rowl could actually utter an answer.

Rowl seemed to consider it for a moment, then turned with a flick of his tail that indicated the same disinterest as a human shrug. "Yes," he said. "I do. Come, Littlemouse."

Bridget accompanied Rowl over to Captain Grimm.

"Master Rowl," Grimm greeted the cat gravely. He straightened, tucked his hat beneath one arm, and swept a very low bow to Rowl. "You have preserved my life and the lives of my men. I am in your debt."

"I know that," Rowl said (through Bridget). "I have a mission to complete, as a member of the Spirearch's warriors. There are still Auroran warriors loose in the territory of the Nine-Claws. The Nine-Claws and I have saved your lives. Now you must help them defend their territory."

"Aye," Grimm said, nodding. He glanced aside and his eyes widened.

Bridget looked up to see the rest of the crew of *Predator* emerging from one of the other shadowy tunnels. The broken forms of several silkweavers dotted the floor behind them—as did motionless human forms. Evidently the larger group of men had been kept bottled up in their tunnel by a relatively small number of silkweavers. Now they emerged, gauntlets primed, swords in hand, staring warily at the cats.

"Hold your fire!" Grimm shouted. "Stand down! It's over! The cats are with us!"

The men obeyed their captain, and Grimm turned back to Bridget and Rowl. "Whatever the Aurorans put those Marines here to do, they're off to do it. They must be stopped. Will the Nine-Claws help?"

Rowl's tail flicked left and right. "The Nine-Claws do not care which humans rule the human portion of the habble. Their war was with the silkweavers. Fighting surface creatures is one thing. Fighting humans with gauntlets is another."

Grimm grunted. "What about intelligence? Can they tell us where the Aurorans are?"

Instead of answering, Rowl sat down, and a heartbeat later a little bit of shadow detached itself from a wall and padded over to sit next to him. Rowl's thirty-pound frame dwarfed that of the smaller female cat who sat down beside him, though she showed not an ounce less dignity.

"Hello, Mirl," Bridget said. "Captain Grimm, this is Mirl."

"I am pleased to know her name," Grimm said. "Thank you, Mirl, for your warning. Do you know where the Aurorans have gone?"

"Of course," Mirl said, with a sidelong glance at Rowl. "While you spoiled children have been amusing yourselves killing prey that is not even good for food, I was doing the important work."

"What work is that, please?" Grimm asked.

"Following the Aurorans, of course," Mirl said. "Incidentally, I did so entirely without getting anyone who depended upon me captured by the enemy."

Rowl's eyes narrowed slightly. "Out with it," he growled. "Where are they?"

Instead of answering, Mirl licked a paw fastidiously, for just long enough to make it clear that Rowl was not compelling her to do anything she did not wish to do.

Bridget sighed. Cats. She held up a hand for silence when Captain Grimm began to ask a question. He frowned, but complied.

After a moment, Mirl spoke. "They are in the stone house with walls and dirt and green growing things."

Benedict stiffened. "The temple. What are they doing there?"

"Killing," Mirl answered. "Burning."

Bridget's gaze shot to Captain Grimm. "Why would they do that?"

"Why indeed," Grimm replied, his eyes narrowing.

"We must help them, Captain," Benedict said fervently.

Grimm studied the young man for a moment before nodding. "We'll do all we can. Creedy, I know everyone is exhausted. But we're moving out."

Chapter 56

Spire Albion, Habble Landing,
Temple of the Way

Rowl, having defeated the army of silkweavers virtually unassisted, sat and watched as the humans floundered about in the wake of the battle.

Littlemouse, who was by far the most important human present, helped human Folly to her feet and spoke to her in a low, worried tone. That was ridiculous, of course. Human Folly could stand, and could speak, and so the odd girl was obviously well enough. Human Folly looked rather frantic for a moment, until Littlemouse placed several small lumin crystals into the other girl's hands, at which point the etherealist's apprentice cupped them as if they were more precious than kittens.

Grim Ship-Trees was visiting his fallen and wounded warriors. Rowl approved of that. Even now, Naun was making the rounds of the wounded and fallen Nine-Claws warriors. The clan chief finished the task and prowled over to Rowl, his bloodied battle spurs clicking on the ground.

"Rowl."

"Naun."

"You slew as many as I did," Naun noted.

"Did I?" Rowl asked airily. "I was not keeping track."

Naun's tail lashed in amusement. "The threat to my clan is gone. You were instrumental in making that happen."

495

"You are welcome," Rowl said.

Naun stared silently for a moment. Then he said, "You spared the life of my kit, when you had more than sufficient reason to kill him."

"I did."

"Why?"

"Out of respect," Rowl replied. He lifted his right rear leg and peered at the bloodied blade on it. "His battle spurs are excellent."

"Hardly used," Naun growled. "Keep them."

"Neen will not like that," Rowl noted.

"Neen will earn his spurs again. Perhaps this time something will sink in."

"I wish you luck with that," Rowl said. "If you will excuse me. The spurs chafe."

Naun flicked an ear in farewell. "Convey to your father my respects. His envoy is welcome in Nine-Claws territory."

"I will," Rowl replied.

Naun rose without further remark, and departed.

Rowl turned back to watching Grim Ship-Trees, and noted that the man was in the midst of detailing a few of his healthy warriors to help the human healer take the wounded to something more like safety.

If he could smell the distant smoke in the air like Rowl could, he would be moving more quickly. But that was the way of humans. Like their minds, their senses were not particularly sharp, and if that wasn't bad enough, they spent an inordinate amount of time ignoring them or dulling them even further with their drink and their alleged music and their soap. So, no matter that they were standing in the only habble in all of Spire Albion filled with flammable buildings, and that the entire place might turn into a gigantic oven and cook them all. There were human matters to fuss with before moving out to take action.

Years of living near humans had taught Rowl that there was no point in trying to hurry them, and had made him even more patient than he was puissant. They would be ready when they were ready. Meanwhile, he prowled over to Littlemouse, made himself comfortable, and started working on the laces of his new battle spurs. Knots were uncivilized creations. His thumb-paw was really not well suited to undoing the length of leather cord that kept the cuffs securely on his legs, which was why a pair of squires was generally required to secure the cuffs in the first place.

"Rowl," Littlemouse asked, in Cat. "Would you please allow me to assist you?"

"Yes," Rowl said promptly, and lay down to relax while Littlemouse saw to the knots with her indecently long and precise fingers. Each creature had something it excelled at, he supposed. Humans could manage knots easily, and cats could do everything else.

Littlemouse undid the knots and carefully slid the wide leather cuffs off of his legs. Rowl did nothing as undignified as sigh with relief once the tight, restricting things were gone, but a lesser cat than he might have done so. He felt quite filthy. The foolish silkweavers had not drenched him in their vital fluids as they had some of the slower warriors of Naun's clan, but his fur was certainly speckled with the stuff, and it smelled.

Rowl yawned and regained his feet before butting his head against Littlemouse's knee.

Littlemouse knelt down to rub the spot behind his ears, which he allowed might also be a particular expertise of human-style fingers.

"You were so brave just now, Rowl," Littlemouse said. Her voice was very soft and warm. "You saved us."

It would have been unseemly to wriggle with pleasure at her tone, so Rowl restrained himself to rising and arching his back under her hand so that it went all the way down his body, and possibly wiped off some of the filth. "I know," he said.

"How did you convince the Nine-Claws to help?" Littlemouse asked.

"I saved their clan chief's kit."

"From what?"

"From me," Rowl said. He stretched and flicked his rear legs one at a time until he felt that the fur was somewhat less disarranged. "I would knock down a Spire for you, Littlemouse."

Littlemouse made a squeaking sound and scooped him up in her clumsy human arms and gave him a smothering hug.

Rowl leaned his cheek against hers and purred. After all, *he* could hardly be called unseemly if a human, even so exceptional a human as Littlemouse, got carried away in a fit of affection.

And besides, her sleeves were cleaning his fur.

The moment lasted until the tall younger warrior beside Grim Ship-Trees called, "Everyone else form up on me! Let's go!"

And at last, only a nap or two after the last fight had ended, they finally began to move.

The smell of smoke grew stronger and stronger as the humans huffed and puffed down the cramped streets of Habble Landing. Rowl loped along beside them, amused. Of the entire group, only his Littlemouse was moving steadily, clomping along in the same boots she wore while running with the Guard. Evidently all that senseless fleeing about had done its work to prepare her for this evening. She was moving very well compared to everyone else in the little group. Not as well as a cat, of course—that was simply not possible. But better than the other humans, even the half-soul.

Rowl looked at human Benedict curiously. He had always seemed markedly less clumsy than other humans to Rowl, but that had all but vanished. His legs were moving unevenly, and he was gasping for air just like the rest of them. He must have been weary—though weary or not, he had wits enough about him to lift his nose to the air and inhale, finally noticing the smoke scent that had been obvious to Rowl since before they had begun their run.

Rowl heard something and focused on the sound.

"Littlemouse," he called. "Gauntlet fire ahead."

Littlemouse dutifully relayed the message, or tried to. The first man she told to pass it up the line to the captain was wheezing too hard to make himself understood by his fellow humans. Littlemouse shook her head, picked up her pace, and ran ahead to Grim Ship-Trees to inform him.

The humans spread out as they approached the temple and slowed their pace to a more cautious stalk—if one could even truly consider it a stalk. To Rowl, they sounded like the clump and clutter of a steam engine, except for Littlemouse, who, to her credit, sounded only as loud as a particularly clumsy, lame kitten.

Rowl had no such concerns. He would be seen only if he wished to be seen. He darted ahead.

There was a great deal of smoke billowing out of the Temple of the Way—probably due to all the fire he could see glowing within it. A number of humans had apparently tried to form a line, where they would have presumably passed buckets of water along to one another so that whichever human was most foolish could throw it at the fire. Metal buckets lay scattered everywhere, along with several corpses of the humans who had attempted to use them.

As Rowl watched, a human leaned out of the shelter of the wall around the temple, appearing in the gateway, and loosed a gauntlet blast, burning a blazing trail of tiny cinders through the pall of smoke. He quickly ducked back, just as several other blasts hammered against the stone of the wall near him, sending chips of rock flying. The humans of Landing, it would seem, were not taking the killing of their own lightly.

Rowl broke into a sprint, covering the open ground between the rest of the habble and the temple's territory at his best speed. From there, finding a convenient stone projecting slightly from the wall made it possible for Rowl to jump to the top and take stock of the situation. There were half a dozen humans inside the temple's wall, all of them armed, all of them positioned to pop up from concealment and fire gauntlets at anyone who approached.

Rowl took note of their positions and leapt lightly from the wall, rushing back to Littlemouse. He told her in rapid tones what he had seen, and Littlemouse relayed his words to Grim Ship-Trees as the group approached the temple.

Ship-Trees nodded once, his expression hard.

"Why burn a Temple of the Way?" human Creedy asked. "I don't understand."

"Why burn a library?" Littlemouse answered. "There must have been something of value in it. Something that would prompt the Aurorans to make sure that it all burned by leaving men behind to ambush the bucket brigade."

"If they aren't letting anyone in," human Benedict said, "they aren't letting anyone out, either."

"They aren't going to get away with it," Ship-Trees said in a very quiet voice. "Long guns, I believe, Mister Creedy. We've an extra with Mister Stern down. Can you use it?"

"Tolerably well, sir," human Creedy responded.

"Then you and the others will provide covering fire while I lead the charge." Ship-Trees glanced around. "Sir Benedict? I would appreciate your aid in this entry."

"Of course, Captain Grimm," human Benedict said.

"Mister Kettle, you're with me," Ship-Trees said. Then he turned to eye Littlemouse. "Miss Tagwynn, if you are willing, you will accompany Sir Benedict."

Littlemouse swallowed but nodded firmly. "I will."

The captain turned to the rest of his warriors and said, "The rest in two columns, following us. Get through the gate and blast any hostile targets you see. If the man in front of you falls, keep moving and take the shooter before his gauntlet can cycle."

"Mister Rowl," Ship-Trees said, turning to the cat. "I do not expect you to engage in undue risk in a firefight, but your senses are far better than ours. I would take it as a courtesy if you would accompany us, to see and hear anything we might not realize is happening. Will you do this?"

Rowl regarded Ship-Trees, amused. He would enter the temple—or not enter it—precisely when, and where, and as he pleased, or else what would be the point in being a cat? But Littlemouse was going, and that meant that he would go as well, to guide and protect her. Obviously. But even if she hadn't been going, Ship-Trees had consistently showed courtesy and respect above and beyond that of most humans. The very act of it was a statement of respect in itself. Rowl may well have helped him in any case, so he gave Ship-Trees a slow nod.

"Thank you," Ship-Trees said. "The rest of you, column up by twos. Keep it tight, people. Give the long guns as much room to shoot in as possible." Then, without further ado, he drew his sword and began loping toward the temple, leaving four men armed with the odd-looking human weapons behind him.

Rowl raced to catch up with Littlemouse, who was running in a strange, jerky motion, as though her body longed to break into a mad sprint toward the danger—or away from it. Her best speed would have left the weary aeronauts behind, though, so she kept the pace slow and careful. Then it was all the sound of boots striking the floor in rhythm, and the scent of sweating human, and the kindling glow of gauntlets being primed.

Then the man in the gateway popped his head around the corner again. The long guns behind them howled, sending streaks of heat and light sizzling by within an arm's length of the column. They slammed home into the stone of the gateway sheltering the enemy soldier—but these were no mere gauntlet blasts. Long rifles were an order of magnitude more powerful than a gauntlet, and instead of blowing chips of stone from the wall, they blew *stones* out of the wall, and sent them flying in every direction. Three more blasts struck only half a second later, and rock flew out in a shower as a square yard of stone wall—and the enemy crouched behind it—vanished in a torrent of radiant energy and a rumbling scream of breaking stone. The long guns began to yowl repeatedly, blowing holes in the wall near the positions Rowl had described to Ship-Trees.

Ah, that was what covering fire meant, then. It meant that *his* humans would shoot at the *other* humans and make them cower while the true threat came racing toward the front gate, along with all of his humans and his half-soul.

As they drew near the gate, Rowl took it upon himself to make things easier on the poor creatures he'd been rescuing all day, under the theory that an ounce of prevention would be worth a pound of cure. He darted ahead of Ship-Trees, exploded through the gate moving as low and fast as a cat could, and let out the defiant howl of his battle cry as he did.

Human voices shouted in surprise, and a wild gauntlet blast blew apart a brick planter several yards behind him while another splashed harmlessly onto the spirestone floor wide of him.

Grim Ship-Trees and half-soul Benedict came through the gate at almost the same instant, running, gauntlets primed. Both men unleashed blasts at their opponents without slowing down, and Ship-Trees dropped one of the enemy with a shot to the sternum that knocked the man down and cracked his rib cage with an audible snapping of bones. Littlemouse and human Kettle came in on their heels, also firing.

Littlemouse's bolt came nowhere near threatening another being with harm, but before more blasts could be loosed, the enemy warriors were lifting their hands over their heads and dropping to their knees. That would have made it significantly easier to dispatch them all, but for some reason, Ship-Trees and the other humans stopped fighting.

Rowl puzzled over that for a moment as the rest of Ship-Trees' warriors came rushing through the gates. Human Kettle took charge, took away the enemy warriors' gauntlets and blades, and bound their arms — which seemed to Rowl like an excess of preparation for cutting their throats. Over the next several breaths, it occurred to Rowl that the humans were not *going* to cut anyone's throat. What was the point in all the fighting with gauntlets if they were only going to stop fighting the moment the outnumbered fools decided the fight was over?

Rowl flicked his tail in exasperation. Humans.

This close to the fire, the heat was palpable, and the heavy smell of smoke was almost nauseating. The fire was a constant growling rumble from the interior of the temple. Now that he had time to look about, Rowl spotted several very still forms in crimson-stained saffron robes lying here and there in the gardens, like particularly morbid beds of flowers.

"Maker of Paths," human Benedict breathed, sweeping his gaze over the corpses. His eyes shone with unfallen tears. "O great Maker, show me the Path, for I am lost and cannot find my Way."

Rowl prowled over to Littlemouse and leapt up into her arms, the better to be able to see through the crowd of humans.

"Skip," human Kettle said, nodding to Ship-Trees. "Four prisoners, none seriously wounded. They say the rest of the Aurorans are already gone. They volunteered to stay behind, and won't say anything about their mission or where their officers are going."

Ship-Trees grunted and shook his head, staring at the burning temple. "Burning a library. Damned waste." He turned to one of his warriors and said, "Go inform Mister Creedy of what happened and ask him to direct the firefighting brigade here at once."

"Aye, Skip," said the man, and hurried off.

"These guys could save us a world of hurt if they start talking. You want me to persuade them, Skip?" human Kettle asked. He slammed one knob-knuckled fist into his opposite palm.

"No time," Ship-Trees said. "The Aurorans are already on the move. Why burn a *library*?"

"A diversion," human Kettle suggested. "To draw us away from their real target?"

"It's going to get plenty of attention," Ship-Trees admitted. "But . . ." He narrowed his eyes. "What if this wasn't a diversion? They only sent thirty men for the bloody Lancaster Vattery. They brought their whole force *here*. Why?"

"This entire infiltration and attack?" human Benedict asked, his voice tight and bitter with pain. "Just to burn books?"

"Books are knowledge, and knowledge is power," Ship-Trees said.

"More power than a crystal vattery?" human Kettle asked dubiously.

"Someone seems to think so," Ship-Trees said, his voice thoughtful.

Rowl heard a faint sound and snapped his head around to the proper direction in which to direct his attention. A moment later he heard the sound again—a voice, weak, choking on smoke.

Rowl turned to Littlemouse and said, "If it matters, someone is still alive in there. I can hear them."

Littlemouse blinked at him for a moment in that charmingly witless way she had, and then blurted out a translation of his words to human Benedict.

Human Benedict's eyes snapped to Rowl. "Where?"

Rowl leaned his head toward the temple and said, "Am I an oracle? No, I am not. Inside."

Human Benedict stepped up next to Rowl and tilted his head to one side with his eyes closed. They snapped open again a moment later. "He's right. We have to do something."

"The smoke could easily kill you," Ship-Trees said. "Never mind the fire."

Human Benedict clenched his jaw. And then he turned and sprinted into the burning temple.

"Benedict!" Littlemouse cried. She dropped Rowl like a sack of stale tubers and went running after him. As she did, a full quarter of the roof at the rear of the temple gave way with a rumble of falling stone and a thundercloud of rising sparks dancing madly in the whirlwind.

Rowl's heart went absolutely berserk, beating so hard that it threatened to stop up his throat. The building was on *fire*. What was Littlemouse thinking? Such things were deadly. Had she no consideration at all? Who was going to give Rowl his favorite ear rubs if Littlemouse were burned to char and ash? The very thought made him want to crouch against the ground and curl into a little ball.

It was a truly shocking discourtesy. He should let her be burned up if she was going to treat him in so cavalier a fashion—except that the very thought of Littlemouse being all burned up made Rowl's fur begin to tangle with itself.

Without any further hesitation, the cat growled and rushed forward into the burning building.

■ ■ ■ Chapter 57 ■ ■ ■

Spire Albion, Habble Landing, Lumber District

Major Espira stood wiping the blade of his sword on a white cloth as his men prepared to burn the wealth of this over-stuffed den of rats to ashes.

Gauntlet fire howled around him from nearly every direction as his men held a perimeter against the Albion citizens and odd Guardsmen who had realized that battle was upon them. There were thousands of Albions in this rat maze of a habble, and the fight at the temple, brief as it had been, had been intense. His force had been brought down to a total of fewer than three hundred and fifty men.

There would be even fewer after they fought their way out of the lumber district, but the more quickly they moved, the fewer he would lose. Though his men were outnumbered incalculably by the locals, his Marines were organized and moving together, not reacting in a con-fused herd. The most difficult and dangerous part of the mission—the wait—was over. Now it was all straightforward knifework, and no one knew fighting like his Marines.

He stood in the middle of a street of shops, trying to ignore the pres-ence of the Cavendish creature and her pet monster. Sark loomed near her, always near her, his presence a silent and constant threat. The warriorborn man was wounded and dripping blood, but moved as if he had not noticed that his forearms and belly looked like so much shred-ded and bloody meat beneath his tattered clothing. The woman clutched a book, the one book they had removed from the Great Library, open to one of its early pages, her finger tracing the lines, her eyes intent as she read, as if she stood in a reading room, and not a combat area with the cries of the wounded and dying all around her.

"Sergeant," he called. "How long?"

"Setting the fuses now, sir," Ciriaco replied.

Espira nodded and continued wiping the blade of his sword, though he knew on a rational level that he'd cleaned the blood from it long since. It gave him something to do besides wait for the proper time to give the next order.

And besides, he liked having a weapon in hand when Cavendish and Sark were so near.

The corpse of the young man who had blundered into Espira and surprised him, probably a carpenter's apprentice, lay inside one of the shops nearby. The boy had been no older than fourteen years—and probably younger. Sheer chance that he'd started up from a sleeping pallet on the floor behind a counter just as Espira had walked past in the gloom. After that, it had all been reflexes, and a gurgling scream that Espira knew he would not be able to wipe away. Now the boy's body was covered in sawdust and awaiting the fire that would take the guts out of the busiest economy in Spire Albion.

The charges were being set in small kegs, piled with sawdust from the leavings of the mills and carpenters and wood-carvers who worked this district of Habble Landing. They weren't standard demolition powder kegs, but incendiaries—a hellish mixture of fireoil, firepowder, and sticky jelly that would explode and then cling to anything it touched, burning fiercely. They were most often used to set fire to airships in close engagements, and Espira had seen their vicious efficiency at destruction with his own eyes.

"What do you think, Sergeant?" he asked. "Did the engineers get it right?"

"Sun's about to come up," Ciriaco replied, nodding. "Warm up the east side of the tower, which'll draw the air and send the fire spreading toward it, just like a chimney, but sideways. Once it starts hitting those supports, that second level of theirs will collapse right down into this one. The Albions'll be too busy to pay us any attention at all." A Marine corporal came running up and spoke briefly to Ciriaco.

"Major," the sergeant reported, "charges set, fuses ready at sixty seconds."

Espira tried not to think about the men, women, and children he was about to condemn to death by fire and asphyxiation. This area was the heart of Landing's economy, a viable target of war—and if the Albions had ignored the wisdom of the Great Builders with regard to flammable construction within a habble, that could hardly be blamed upon Spire Aurora.

Espira looked around at the wooden buildings, the wooden walkways, the wooden supports and beams, representing more wealth than any dozen habbles of his home Spire. Their greed and vanity were their weakness, and would be their undoing. He was simply lighting a match.

"Order the men to form up and begin moving out by squads," he told the sergeant. "Advance party to fire freely and clear the way, standard firing rotation."

Ciriaco had known what orders would come next. He nodded and started bawling them out even as Espira gave them, then moved out to oversee the withdrawal. Explosions began, small and scattered, as the Marines commenced throwing ceramic grenados packed with gunpowder and sulfurous ash to cover their escape with vicious shrapnel and clouds of thick, choking smoke.

"Madame Cavendish," Espira said, keeping his tone calm and civil. "Excuse me, please."

Her eyes snapped from the page up to his, coldly furious, and one of her eyes twitched in a steady rhythm. She stood stiffly, clearly in pain, and a tear and a modest stain of blood on the bodice of her dress suggested a wound sustained when she and Sark had stayed behind to deal with the group of Albions who had attacked them.

Espira swallowed and kept his expression neutral and pleasant. "Please pardon my interruption," he said, "but we are ready to withdraw to the ship, and this area will soon be on fire. For your own safety, I must ask you to accompany us at this time."

Cavendish closed her eyes for a brief moment, and when she opened them again, her own expression had been schooled into something blandly pleasant. "Of course, Colonel."

"I beg your pardon, ma'am," Espira said. "But I am a major."

She smiled, her teeth showing as she carefully closed the cover of the book and worked the latch that locked it shut. "Not after today, Renaldo Espira," she purred. "Not after today. Sark."

Cavendish turned on a heel and began marching calmly down the street, as though she were running an everyday errand. Sark moved with her, maintaining a precise distance behind her and to one side, his crooked gaze scanning steadily.

Espira let out a small breath of relief to see them go. He looked forward to the day when he did not have to deal with those creatures—even more than he looked forward to the golden insignia that would come with his new rank when he returned home to Spire Aurora.

Assuming he returned home. There was plenty of time yet to be killed.

He put his sword away, mentally cringing at the act, though he knew rationally that the blade was perfectly clean and could be sheathed without issue. Then he pocketed the handkerchief, opened his box of matches, and waited for the last of his troops to retreat toward escape. Ciriaco, as agreed, was the last of the men to fall back, and he covered Espira with an upraised gauntlet as Espira knelt to the fuses.

Then the Auroran commander struck a match.

■ ■ ■ Chapter 58 ■ ■ ■

Spire Albion, Habble Landing Shipyards,
AMS *Predator*

Gwendolyn grimaced down at her borrowed clothing. The grease on them was simply not going to come out, which hardly seemed polite to their owner, whoever he was. Perhaps she should simply dub the outfit her engine room clothing and reimburse the poor unfortunate. After all, making a mess of one's clothes was to be expected when adjusting the alignment of a Haslett cage.

It was a frustrating task at the best of times, made more so by Mister Journeyman's insistence upon using some harebrained process he had developed himself rather than the doctrine that was clearly published and illustrated in the handbook to any Haslett cage by any manufacturer worth the name. Granted, the man did seem to get results. It was vexing.

Gwen slid out from beneath the cage's assembly and said, "There. Try it."

Journeyman grunted and adjusted the controls, constricting the cage down to a smooth egg shape, rather than the usual sphere. The power core engaged the cage, a lacework of lightning suddenly branching out to it from the core crystal. A deep-throated, sweetly musical hum filled the room, a chord that made the deck beneath Gwen's feet vibrate and rattle. The bustle of the bleary-eyed contractors and engineers in the room drew to a halt as they awaited the result of the test.

Journeyman stayed rock-still and eyed the readings on several meters on the control panel.

"Well, now," he said. "Well, well. That doesn't look completely terrible."

Gwen padded over and studied the readings. "They're perfect. All well within tolerance."

"Tolerance," Journeyman said with a scowl. "Good enough for shop trogs and tramp merchant engine room slugs. Not good enough for my *Preddy*."

Gwen scoffed and began to answer him when she paused. What was that sound?

She reached over and throttled down the engine, spinning the wheel that dilated the cage out to its widest setting again. Journeyman let out a huffing sound of protest and actually slapped her hand away from the controls, but Gwen lifted a finger to her mouth and snapped, "Quiet! Shhh! Everyone!"

There was a startled moment of silence, and in that space, everyone in the compartment could clearly hear what Gwen had heard.

The howl of discharging gauntlets.

Gwen traded a look with Journeyman and then pelted up the steps from the engine room to *Predator's* deck. She hurried to the railing and stared out over the shipyard. The morning mist was thick, but glowing with the warm golden light of sunrise, and she could see out over the wooden shipyards to the entrance to Habble Landing.

Two of the habble's Guardsmen lay on the wooden deck, horribly still. Even as Gwen watched, a third, crouched beside the entrance, triggering his gauntlet wildly, was struck by a bolt of radiant energy that snapped his head back like a blow from a red-hot mallet and flung him to the deck atop the bodies of his fellow Guardsmen.

A second later, several men in grey uniforms came through the door, blades in one hand, gauntlets glowing in the other. They immediately opened fire on several stevedores who were unloading a freighter at the nearest slip, sending the men scattering for cover.

"Bloody hell," Journeyman said. "Those are Auroran Marines."

More men poured out of the opening at a quick jog, dozens of them. As heads began to peer out from ships and storehouses, gauntlets howled, wounding and killing a few, sending most scattering for cover.

"And they're coming this way," Gwendolyn noted. She heard cries and shouts, and glanced to the next ship over, a motley-looking vessel whose lettering named her the *Mistshark*. Men rushed about the deck in orderly haste. "What are they doing?"

Journeyman grunted. "Getting ready to cast off."

Gwendolyn frowned as the crew of the *Mistshark* began casting down two additional boarding planks, and sucked in a sudden breath. "They're transport for the Aurorans."

"Aye," Journeyman said. "We'd better get our heads down, lass. They'll be within range shortly."

Gwendolyn made an impatient clicking noise with her tongue and climbed up onto the rail to get a slightly better view. "Those men back by the gates. What are they doing?"

Journeyman peered. "They're setting charges," he grunted. The men suddenly sprinted away from a number of small casks. There was a loud *whumph*ing roar, and suddenly the casks were replaced with brilliant balls of light that rained drops of fire out in a wide swath. Fire began to chew brightly at the wooden decks wherever the burning rain touched.

"Merciful God in Heaven," Gwendolyn breathed. "How long will the deck hold?"

"Not long," Kettle said grimly. "And then . . ."

Gwendolyn's stomach plummeted into some unthinkable abyss as she imagined the deck, *Predator*, the engineering crew, and herself all plunging down the side of the Spire, to be crushed on the surface far below.

"We've got to get the lift crystal back online," Gwen said.

"We've got to do more than that," Journeyman said, and pointed toward *Mistshark*.

Gwen was no expert in the actual operation of airships, beyond the technical details of their engines—but even she could clearly see what was happening, and it made her fallen guts turn to ice.

The vessel preparing to transport Spire Albion's enemies was running out her guns.

"We don't get the shroud up," Journeyman said, "we're finished."

And without a further word the two flung themselves toward the engine room.

■ ■ ■ Chapter 59 ■ ■ ■

Spire Albion, Habble Landing,
Temple of the Way

I t was not the fire, or the smoke, or the prospect of immolation or
asphyxiation that most disturbed Bridget as she plunged into the
burning building behind Benedict. Instead, she found herself wishing that she had tied her hair back so that it wasn't flying behind her
like a banner, threatening to collect any random spark that might float
by, thus bursting into flame and leaving her bald.

Right in front of Benedict.

She felt that a very foolish concern, though she could not deny its
reality. The other dangers far outweighed the threat to her vanity, after
all. Or perhaps, she thought, such a tiny concern was the only one she
was allowing herself to feel. Only weeks before, she had been frightened
to leave her father's vattery. If she dared to allow her mind to grasp the
truth of what she was doing, she felt sure she would begin to weep and
then run screaming.

So she embraced her little worry about her hair. It kept her from
going mad in the face of much more horrible things.

The entrance to the temple was no more dangerous than a thick pall
of smoke could make it, but the smoke permitted them to see only ten
or fifteen feet ahead of them—and as they advanced, the pall began to
glow with a sullen, flickering light as the fire spread from the library
into the other portions of the building. The lack of visibility was disori-

enting, and she lost track of where they were within moments. What if, she thought, they simply became lost in the smoke? What if they found themselves rushing from hall to hall, struggling to find the way out, while the whole time the air grew thinner and hotter, until . . . ?

"Benedict!" she cried, her voice frail and rough with smoke. "Where are we?"

"Stay on the path!" he croaked back.

Ah, of course. Bridget looked down. She was following Benedict closely, and had only now noticed that the warriorborn moved with his feet firmly tracing the little meandering indentation in the stone flooring, letting it guide them forward. She covered her mouth and nose with her sleeve, and pressed on.

The air grew hotter, the light brighter, until they plunged from smoke into a blazing inferno. They stumbled to a sudden stop, and a blazing hot wind, like something from an enormous oven, began to lift and billow Bridget's hair.

The Great Library was being consumed by flame.

Vast sheets of it roared everywhere. The heat was so intense that miniature cyclones of flame swirled and circled around the room, being born and dying in the space of a few seconds.

At the doorway to the library, one of the heavy shelves had fallen. A man in saffron robes lay pinned beneath it and a mound of books that were slowly taking fire. His fingertips were bloodied, as if he'd tried to claw his way out from beneath the imprisoning weight, and been unable to do so. His skin was reddening, blistering under the fury of the fire.

The monk lifted his head. One of his eyes was gone, vanished into a vast, purpling bruise that swelled that side of his face to grotesque proportions—the result of a glancing hit or near-miss from a gauntlet blast. He stared at them with his bleary eye. His expression was a contortion of agony.

"Vincent!" Benedict cried, his voice anguished. He leapt into the blazing heat, lifting his arms to try to shield his face as he did. His sleeves began smoking almost at once.

"Leave me!" the monk gasped. He began to fumble weakly with his robes. "Take it!"

"No one's getting left anywhere," Benedict said. Then he knelt down, planted a foot, and reached out his hands.

Bridget stared in fascinated horror. The shelf could not weigh less than a ton in metal alone, never mind the weight of the books still contained on its upward side. And in that room, the metal would be heated to searing temperatures.

Benedict slipped his hands beneath the edge of the shelf, next to Brother Vincent's trapped body. Then he clenched his jaw and gripped it.

There was a sound like sizzling meat.

Benedict let out a leonine roar that bore only a passing resemblance to a scream of pain.

And then his lean body bowed into the effort of lifting the enormous shelf. For a second, then two, nothing happened—and then his legs quivered and the enormous mass began to move, if only by inches.

Bridget leapt forward into the oven. The heat was like a smothering blanket, painful—and getting noticeably hotter after only seconds of exposure. She grasped Brother Vincent's wrist and forearm and hauled his burned form from beneath the shelf.

"Got him!" Bridget shouted, dragging Brother Vincent toward the hallway.

Benedict dropped the shelf and it crashed to the floor, sending up showers of sparks.

They burst back into the hallway together, and the sudden lack of furious heat made Bridget start to shiver, as though she had walked into an icebox.

It wasn't until she turned to let the wounded man down gently that she saw the horribly misshapen contour of Brother Vincent's back and shoulders. The man was shuddering in pain, arms twitching and shaking.

But not his legs.

Below the shoulders he was completely, eerily still.

She looked up to find Benedict staring at Brother Vincent in horror. "Oh, Maker of Paths," he breathed. He sagged down to his knees beside the monk, as if the sight had drained the strength of his legs entirely out of him. "Oh, Vincent."

"No time, boy," Vincent said. He choked on a couple of short, hard coughs, and blood suddenly flecked his lips—which quirked into a small smile. "Literally, for me."

"Dammit," Benedict said. "Damn those Auroran sons of bitches. I'll murder every last one of them."

Brother Vincent's expression became annoyed and he slapped irritably at Benedict's leg. "Benedict. There is no time for this kind of indulgence." He fumbled at his robes again and with a grimace managed to produce a book with a very plain brown cover. "Take it."

Benedict accepted the book, his expression bewildered. "What?"

"Take it," Brother Vincent said. Blood had begun to run from his mouth. "To the Spirearch. It's the last copy. She burned the rest."

"What is it?" Benedict asked.

Brother Vincent coughed again, and grimaced in pain. The blood trickling from his mouth had turned his teeth bright red. "What they came for," he said. "The *Index*."

"I'm getting you out of here," Benedict said. "You can give it to him yourself."

A smile touched the unmarred corner of Brother Vincent's mouth. "Oh, Ben. Death is just one more Path. One you'll come to in time." He lifted a hand weakly, and Benedict gripped it tight.

"Don't let your pain choose your Way for you," Brother Vincent said quietly. "You're a better man than—"

And then the monk died. Bridget saw it. In midword, the light and life in his eyes suddenly, simply went out like a snuffed candle. What had been Brother Vincent was now . . . an inanimate object.

"Vincent?" Benedict asked quietly. "Vincent?" Then his voice broke with a ragged sob. "Vincent."

Bridget stepped up beside him and put her hand on his shoulder. "Benedict," she said, quietly urgent. "We have to go."

He nodded. He put the monk's hand down gently onto his chest, his seared fingers moving stiffly, clumsily, and then he began to rise—and suddenly pitched forward, over the corpse, to land in a limp sprawl atop it.

"Benedict!" Bridget cried. She grabbed him, rolled him over. His body was twitching in rhythmic shakes, and there was saliva and foam leaking from the corner of his mouth. His eyes were rolled back to the whites.

God in Heaven. The silkweaver venom.

Bridget shook him, slapped him, shouted at him—but he never stirred or gave any response. What was she to do?

With a roar, the doors of the Great Library burst into flame on their hinges.

Bridget ground her teeth. She wasn't sure she could find her way back, but if she didn't take action, they would both die in moments, if not sooner. She rose, seized the warriorborn, and dragged him up. His limp weight was difficult to manage, but the heat and smoke were getting thicker, and she could think of no alternatives under the circumstances. She screamed and thrashed and strained and finally managed to get him over one shoulder.

Then she started staggering toward the exit—then realized that she had forgotten the book Brother Vincent had given his life to protect. Dropping down to get it was quite difficult, but not nearly so hard as standing up again with Benedict's weight dragging at her shoulder.

She headed for the exit following the grooved path in the floor. She couldn't move very quickly. The burden was too heavy—but she dared not leave him to rush out for help. He might have choked on smoke by then. So Bridget grimly put one foot in front of the other and kept moving ahead.

She never saw the Auroran Marine before the man emerged from a cross-corridor and collided with her. Bridget fell with a cry, trying to keep Benedict from landing on his head as she crashed to the floor. The impact hurt. The Auroran landed near her, and something metallic clanged on the floor.

Bridget stared at him for a second in wonder. The man had been wounded. There was blood on his tunic and more on one leg—and a swelling lump the size of a child's fist on one side of his head. His eyes were glassy and dilated. Had he been knocked unconscious, out of sight of his companions? Surely the Aurorans had been in a hurry to leave as well. He stared at her blearily.

Bridget's eyes dropped to the source of the clinking sound. The man's copper-clad blade lay on the floor between them.

She looked up again, met the Auroran's eyes, and felt a sudden surge of terror, of confusion, of certainty that this had just become a deadly encounter—and saw the same feelings mirrored in his eyes as they stared back.

Merciful Builders, Bridget realized. *I've managed to get myself into a duel after all.*

Except that there would be no rules, no marshal, no supportive friends, no crowd of observers.

If Bridget lost this duel, no one would ever know it.

The Auroran let out a slurred cry and threw himself toward the sword.

Bridget's foot got there first, kicking the weapon from his grip. The man lunged at her, hands grasping. She twisted in the defensive maneuver Benedict had taught her, and caught one of his arms instead.

The man jerked his arm away, and seemed startled when he could not free it from Bridget's fingers.

Bridget whirled with the man, using his own strength to begin the motion, and swung him into the nearest wall. The impact made his knees wobble and he fell to the ground, with Bridget keeping the hold on his arm. He threw a punch with his other arm, and though Bridget managed to roll in the same direction to lessen the force of the impact, the blow made her see stars. There was no time for astronomy in ground fighting, she thought, and her sudden hysterical laugh turned into a scream of fear.

The Auroran got some of his weight on top of her, his hands scrambling for a hold on her throat. If that happened, she knew, she was likely as good as dead. A proper choke hold could leave her unconscious in seconds, and in the frantic terror of combat, the amount of force required to crush a human windpipe was a surprisingly minor effort. At the same time, she realized that the Marine was faster than she was, and stronger, and had more experience at this kind of business. The only reason she was still alive and fighting at all was that he was clearly injured and disoriented, barely able to move upright.

She got her forearms lined up on his chest, intersecting one of his arms and holding his weight off of her as he tried to secure a grip. One hand got to her throat, but she hunched her neck muscles against its crushing pressure and kept it to one side, where it could do less harm. The other she held off with both of her arms, straining, knowing that the longer she had to fight against not only his muscle, but against the weight of his body, the faster she would tire. She struggled to throw him clear, arching her body, but he was too strong, simply too *big* for her to move. She fought for what seemed an eternity, though she knew less than half a minute went by, and felt her arms weakening, felt the fingers of his other hand brush against her throat.

So she took a terrible gamble. Instead of trying to push him again, she abruptly relaxed her arms—and slammed her head forward, into his, as he came down. She heard a significant-sounding crunch.

The Auroran reeled back, blood fountaining from his nose, and fell, banging his head against the floor as he did. Bridget gave him no time to recover. She rolled atop him and began slamming her fists down at his skull in elemental brutality.

The Auroran tried to hold up his hands in a feeble defense, but only for a few seconds. Bridget pounded his head into the ground, and once his hands were down, she seized his hair and began using that to bash his skull onto the floor, again and again. She barely realized that she was terrified and screaming at the top of her lungs.

The smoke thickened and she began choking on it, struggling to get her breath. She stumbled away from the now-limp body of the Auroran, back to Benedict. She felt so tired. The fight had been only seconds long, but she felt as though she'd been running for twenty-four hours straight.

Once more, Bridget managed to lift Benedict to her shoulder, if only barely. At least she'd had the presence of mind to pick up the book first this time. She could not stop coughing as she staggered forward, onto the path—and realized, with a dawning sense of horror, that she was lost.

This was an intersection of corridors. Paths wandered off down all four of them—and the fall and the subsequent fight had disoriented her completely. She could not tell which hallway led out. She felt her head getting lighter, her balance beginning to waver. She did not have time to choose incorrectly. If she didn't get out of the smoke, and soon, she would fall, and could only hope that neither of them would awaken when the fire claimed them.

She turned slowly, hoping to gain a clue, but the smoke now obscured anything beyond a few feet, and it all glowed with firelight. Her already teary eyes began overflowing, and she let out a scream of rage and fear and frustration.

"Littlemouse!" called Rowl's voice.

Bridget's heart surged with sudden energy and hope. "Rowl! I'm here!"

The cat suddenly appeared from the smoke, his tail flicking in agitation. "You are *rude*. And this smoke is in my nose so that I could not track, which is also your fault. And we must *leave*."

She managed not to choke on a sudden burst of terrified laughter, and tried to answer in Cat, but her throat seized on the smoke and she began to cough instead. She nodded and gestured for Rowl to take the lead.

They had not gone twenty feet before the beams began to give way with earsplitting screeches, and the masonry of the temple began to collapse around them.

■ ■ ■ Chapter 60 ■ ■ ■

Spire Albion, Habble Landing,
Temple of the Way

I don't like it, Skip," Kettle said in a quiet tone, meant for Grimm's ears alone. "Girl running into the fire like that."

"She's not some helpless schoolgirl, Mister Kettle," Grimm replied. "She's one of the Spirearch's Guard."

Kettle snorted. The grizzled aeronaut had come through all the scuffles of the last few days with nary a scratch, Grimm noted, which was better than he could say. Kettle had a knack for standing in the right place at the right time during a fight.

"And it's not our job to babysit one of the Spirearch's Guard, Skip?" Kettle asked.

"That is correct," Grimm said.

"And you don't like it either."

"No, Mister Kettle. I do not."

"Then we go in after them."

"Don't be foolish. I'm not ordering the men to rush into a burning building."

Kettle drummed thick fingers along the hilt of his sword. "So it'll be just you and me then, Skip."

Grimm ground his teeth. He was concerned about Sir Benedict and Miss Tagwynn, and his instincts were to go to their aid—but he didn't know the building, and if he went some of his men would, in all foolish probability, follow him into the inferno. Enough of his crew had been hurt for one day. If he led his men blindly into that smoke, he might as well truss them all up himself and toss them into the building to die.

"No, Mister Kettle," Grimm said. "We wait."

Kettle grunted. "How long we going to give them?"

"Not long," Grimm said in a frank tone. "If they aren't back out in the next few minutes, they aren't coming out."

Just then, several hollow, thumping, whooshing sounds shook the air, and Grimm whirled around to stare intently out the temple gates to the habble proper.

"God in Heaven," Kettle muttered. "Skip, was that . . . ?"

"Incendiary charges," Grimm said bleakly. "Maybe a quarter mile that way."

"In the *habble*?" Kettle blurted. "God in Heaven help us. All those wooden buildings . . ."

"Yes," Grimm said. Even as he spoke, he heard an alarm bell beginning to toll frantically. "No one's going to be able to think about anything but fighting the fire for a while. A rather convincing distraction that will allow the Aurorans to escape to the shipyard quite neatly, if they're quick about it."

Kettle snarled under his breath. "Then they're already on their way."

"Don't worry, Mister Kettle," Grimm said. "We'll have our opportunity to make them answer for it."

"How?" Kettle asked.

"Trust me," Grimm replied. He took a short, sharp breath and said, "Unfortunately, this means that we need to leave immediately, before the fire spreads and traps us in this corner of the habble."

"But, Skip . . ." Kettle said.

"For all practical purposes we are now at war with Spire Aurora. We each have our own duties, Mister Kettle," Grimm said. "The Guardsmen will have to look after thems—"

He was interrupted by a roar from behind him, as the high portion of the temple, the enormous chamber of the Great Library, came crashing down upon itself, taking various sections of the building with it. Dust and smoke billowed out in a vast cloud, and the fire—that which hadn't been smothered by the collapse, at any rate—was suddenly exposed to more fresh air and blazed up wildly.

"God in Heaven!" one of the men gasped, and the cloud of smoke and dust enfolded the entire area.

"Gather on me!" Grimm shouted, his voice hoarse in the thick dust. "Gather here! Here!" He kept calling out, and his crew appeared out of the dust, squinting against it and shielding their mouths. They were covered in a thin layer of dust and dirt that gave them a phantomlike appearance in the grey flatness of the dust cloud.

Grimm took a quick head count and began to give the order to move out, when he paused to see one last phantom appear out of the haze. For a moment he wasn't sure what he was looking at. Then the phantom stepped closer, and he could see.

Bridget Tagwynn trudged out of the haze, covered so thickly in dust that she might have been an animated statue. She moved slowly, her face locked in a rictus of determination. Sir Benedict's limp form was draped over one of her shoulders, his arms swinging loosely where they hung down her back. She held one arm wrapped around the back of his thighs, keeping his weight balanced. In that hand, she clutched a dust-covered volume.

In the other hand she carried the limp form of a dust-covered cat, presumably Master Rowl. One of her booted feet left partially bloodied prints in the thin layer of dust on the ground, but she had not let the injury stop her. She simply walked, putting one foot steadily in front of the other in small, deliberate, balanced steps.

Grimm felt his eyebrows climbing higher, and for a moment he was at a loss for words. A sudden silence spread through the men of the

Predator as they took in the sight themselves. Bridget's steady footsteps were suddenly loud in the firelit dust.

"Kettle," Grimm said quietly, and the two of them stepped over to Bridget.

The girl blinked when Grimm stopped in front of her. She paused, her balance swaying. It took her a moment to focus on Grimm's face, and then she nodded to herself. "Captain Grimm," she said. "I've two for the doctor here." The hand holding the book twitched a few times. "And this is for the Spirearch."

With that, she swayed on her feet, and one of her knees buckled. Kettle caught Sir Benedict's weight across his stout shoulders, and Grimm braced Bridget and kept her from falling or dropping Rowl, who lifted his head slightly and swept a bleary, unfocused gaze around the area, before his head dropped exhaustedly again. Grimm saw a line on the cat's skull where dust and blood had caked into a scab as thick as Grimm's smallest finger.

Grimm caught up Master Rowl before Bridget could drop him, cradled the limp cat in one arm, and took the modest-sized volume from her stiff-fingered hand. To one side, Kettle and some of the men were rigging a makeshift litter upon which to carry Sir Benedict. "Very well then, Miss Tagwynn," he said, pocketing the book. "Can you walk?"

"Oh, of course," Bridget said. "I've been practicing daily for a good while."

Grimm gave her a dubious glance, but before he could call one of the men over, the little etherealist's apprentice, Folly, appeared out of the haze and calmly slipped herself beneath one of Bridget's arms, supporting the larger girl. "The grim captain is surely observant enough to realize that Bridget has a large bruise swelling on her cheek. She is obviously stunned and in pain. He will also surely note that she has friends."

Grimm regarded Miss Folly for a moment before sweeping both of the young women as low a bow as he could manage. Then he checked on Sir Benedict. He was being bundled into a shipboard coat donated by one of the men. Half a dozen hands would share the burden of carrying the unconscious young man.

"Kettle?" Grimm asked.

"Silkweaver venom, Skip, from the swelling on this arm," Kettle replied, his voice bleak. "And we got another half a dozen men down the same way, in the tunnels. Maybe if we get him back to the etherealist. Bagen said he can't do a thing with it."

"Master Ferus is unfortunately out of action," Grimm said. "But we'll do all we can."

"What did he say?" Folly asked, her voice incredulous. "The master is . . . Did something happen?"

"Madame Cavendish visited," Grimm reported shortly. "She offered to trade your lives for Master Ferus's collection. He agreed."

Folly's eyes widened. "Oh," she breathed down at a crystal strung on a bit of string about her neck. "Oh, that is not good at all. That was filling a rather large hole." Her eyes became distant, unfocused. "Where are the wagons now, I wonder?"

"Cavendish took them," Grimm replied. "Odds seem excellent that she had them thrown off the shipyard platform immediately after."

She blinked her eyes and suddenly they were alert and focused again. "He is a very good captain, but would seemingly make a very poor gambler," Folly told her crystal. "The wagons are actually moving down a street toward the shipyard. The puppet lady probably expects to riddle out some kind of pattern that would give her an advantage in future encounters."

Grimm arched an eyebrow. "Young woman. Do you mean to tell me that you . . . have the ability to simply locate Master Ferus's collection?"

"That seems rather obvious," Folly confided to the crystal. "Certain articles within it, at any rate. It might not be arrogant to say that I am its caretaker for good reason."

"Cavendish kept the collection," Grimm mused, thinking.

Folly smiled. "It seems that he understands. Clearly the master hoped to buy the grim captain enough time to rescue me so that I could recover the collection in turn."

"And perhaps he meant more, Miss Folly," Grimm said. "We shall make haste back to *Predator*."

The trek through the streets was frantic, which surprised Grimm. He had expected pure pandemonium.

A large section of the habble in the northeastern quadrant was burning. Smoke was a haze in the air that kept growing thicker, though at least the copious ventilation shafts spread throughout the habble by the Merciful Builders were circulating enough air to prevent the place from becoming an immediate death trap. Crews of citizens had turned out to fight the blaze by a variety of means—through hoses being pumped full of water from the habble's many cisterns, through lines of men passing buckets of water from hand to hand, and through crews frantically knocking down expensive wooden buildings and dragging the materials away to create a firebreak.

In fact, Grimm thought, there was a great deal too *much* organization in the chaos. As an experienced officer, he knew what it meant to hold command in a crisis situation—mostly it was, to use a particularly apt metaphor, rushing around to put out fires, one after another. It often required a great deal of shouting and potentially the measured knocking of a few heads, to one degree of literality or another. Grimm knew what chaos looked like.

And someone had taken steps to forestall it.

Firefighting crews were being directed mostly by men whom someone uncharitable would simply call thugs. Though they wore no uniforms and did not bear common gear, the men all had a certain demeanor about them, one to which their fellow citizens of Landing seemed to react. An actual evacuation was taking place—women and children being walked in calm, careful groups toward the nearest transport spiral, to retreat to a lower level of the Spire and away from the blaze. Adult men and women, freed of the need to fear for and protect their children, were able to turn their hands to fighting to save their homes and habble.

The guilds, Grimm realized. The criminal guilds of Landing had organized the response to the emergency. Which made sense, he supposed. If the habble burned down, it would take their livelihood with it along with the rest of the habble's residents'. But still, the situation had developed no more than an hour ago. By all rights, the habble should be in a state of bloody-minded panic.

Someone had warned the guilds, told them to be ready to act in the event of trouble.

Grimm's little force moved steadily through the streets. They drew attention from the guildsmen moving through the city, picking up a few shadows who followed them as they progressed, but no one tried to stop them.

They started finding bodies as the group clattered down the last few streets leading to the shipyard. They lay scattered here and there, mostly citizens of Landing, mostly armed. Here and there lay a uniformed Auroran Marine among them, but only a very few. The Aurorans knew their business well, and had been moving swiftly and working together. The scant handful of citizens and guildsmen who had opposed them had been dispatched with ruthless efficiency.

At the passage out to the shipyard, a dozen of the Spirearch's Guardsmen lay heaped together. The men had died defending the exit, and had been stacked like cordwood to one side to prevent the corpses from blocking the way out.

Grimm never slowed, leading the little column out onto the deck of the shipyard, his boots thudding on the heavy wooden beams.

Fires blazed away at two nearby storage houses, and in several of the light cannon emplacements that defended the shipyard. At least three of the docked airships were on fire, and several still forms littered the deck. Grimm's heart began to pound wildly until he spotted *Predator*, still seemingly safe and sound in her slip.

And then there was a howl of etheric cannon, and one of the unburnt gun emplacements exploded into a cloud of burning splinters and blinding light.

Grimm's eyes snapped up to where the *Mistshark* hovered in the mist perhaps a hundred yards off the shipyard. Even as he watched, her guns spoke again and again, blowing enormous holes in the wooden deck, raking the helpless, vulnerable hulls of the ships at port, and setting even more of the decking on fire. Howl after howl gave birth to thunderous cacophony.

One of the blasts ripped through the wooden hull of a vessel at the far end of the shipyard, and by luck struck its power core.

There was a burst of light and heat, so bright that it blinded Grimm, so hot that it scorched his face. He was flung from his feet as the decking of the shipyard let out a tortured moan, and tons of shattered wood went flying in every direction, shredding the ships nearest the luckless transport.

And then, with a screaming crack of protesting timbers, half of the shipyard decking fell away from the side of the Spire, broken. Airships battened down for port and unready to fly fell like so many stones, and Grimm could hear their crews screaming helplessly as they did. Dockworkers and stevedores plunged down into the misty depths along with the shipyard, lending their own screams to the din, as simple and merciless gravity claimed them all together, timber, spar, and soul.

And still, blast after blast howled down from *Mistshark*'s cannon, shattering more of the shipyard's decking like an angry man with a hammer destroying fine tableware—and claiming airship after airship with methodical precision, unleashing the full destructive power of an armed vessel upon the defenseless shipyard.

"Fall back!" Grimm screamed. "Into the Spire! Get off the deck!"

The aeronauts scrambled back into the shelter of the Spire as the cannon fire walked closer and closer. Grimm was the last one to step off of the deck, and so close was the enemy fire as he did that he could feel the force of it through the soles of his boots.

Grimm had time to turn around before, with a screaming groan, the entire shipyard began to twist and shift before what would be an inevitable fall down the obdurate height of Spire Albion to the surface. Grimm saw the level deck begin to tilt and slide, fires burning in dozens of places. *Predator* swayed helplessly in her slip.

And then the cannon fire from the *Mistshark* reached *Predator*, and Grimm's ship, his *home*, vanished in a deafening thundercloud of fire and blinding light.

▪ ▪ ▪ Chapter 61 ▪ ▪ ▪

Spire Albion, Habble Landing Shipyard,
AMS *Predator*

Gwen frantically hooked up leads to the main engineering panel, one after another, working as rapidly as she could. She lay on her back beneath the control panel, working with her arms stretched out, while around her the engineering spaces became a shouting, noisome scene of frenetic activity.

"Curse your miserable guts, get that breaker hooked up!" Journeyman bellowed. "You, there, I will personally kick you to the surface if you don't bring that resistor online!"

"Main power leads up!" someone shouted.

"Leads to lift crystal up!" called someone else.

"Blast you all to the surface," Journeyman screamed. "Get back from the core! I'm engaging the cage in ten seconds."

"The leads aren't up," Gwen growled at the engineer beneath her breath.

"They'd better be," Journeyman said. "Nine! Eight! Seven!"

Gwen frantically made her fingers fly even faster. "I can only do it so fast."

"Better be fast enough," Journeyman said. "Five! Four! Three! Two!"

Gwen slipped the last pair of lines into place and slapped the clamp down over them.

"One! Powering the core!" Journeyman adjusted the controls and the two halves of the power core's petallike Haslett cage gracefully slid up and around the core, settling into their spherical configuration. *Predator's* core crystal came to life with a deep and musical hum, and arcs of greenish energy began to flicker rapidly across the interior of the Haslett cage. Almost at once, the temperature in the room jumped by several degrees.

"Is that it?" Gwen said. "Did we do it?"

"Power core's up," Journeyman growled. "Soon as she's warmed up and ready, we get to find out if there are any flaws in any of these new crystals."

Gwen sniffed and lifted her chin. "Every crystal is thoroughly inspected and tested at the Lancaster Vattery. They're fine."

Just then there was a scream of a discharging etheric cannon, almost instantly followed by roaring thunder.

"God in Heaven, they've begun," Journeyman breathed. "General quarters! Strap up, boys! Strap up!"

Men began rushing about the cabin, frantically passing out complex bundles of leather straps from storage lockers on the walls. One of them tossed a bundle of straps to Journeyman, and a second to Gwen. "What on earth is this?" Gwen asked.

"Battle harness," Journeyman said. "Strap it on."

Gwen lifted the collection of straps dubiously. "I'm sorry?"

Journeyman's hands flew with the expertise of long, long practice, and his own ball of mysterious strapping was somehow transformed into a collection of belts that crisscrossed his torso and wrapped his waist. Each strap was liberally festooned with copper-clad steel rings. Journeyman then shook out a strap with clips on either end. He clipped one of them to a ring at his waist. He clipped a second line opposite, and a third in the center of his body at the waistline.

Howling cannon cried out again. This time there was a sound so enormous that Gwen simply could not believe that it happened. It shook the deck beneath her feet, made her stagger, slapped against her like an unseen wind, and then there was a vast grinding, crunching noise that followed it for almost half a minute.

"What on earth was that?" Gwen asked, her breath coming short.

Journeyman grimaced, and looked shaken himself. He began arranging Gwen's harness around her. "One of those shots must have hit a power core farther down the shipyard, probably that little Piker ship at the far end."

"How could you know that?"

"We're still here," the engineer answered. "If it had taken one of the bigger ships, it would have smeared us all over the side of the Spire." He thumped Gwen on the shoulder to get her to turn around, then grunted, adjusted a belt, and started clipping lines to her waist. "Three lines," he said. "Keep them hooked up to a securing ring at all times. You don't want to be standing there flat-footed when we drop a few hundred feet abruptly. Bounce that pretty head off the ceiling and break your skinny neck, likely as not."

Gwen looked around and saw that the engineers were all at their various stations, their lines hooked up to rings heavily seeded along the walls and duty stations. She watched as Journeyman began hooking up to the main panel, and followed suit.

He eyed her, grunted, and said, "Just you stay out of my way."

"I wouldn't dream otherwise," Gwen assured him.

"All right, boys!" Journeyman called.

Etheric cannon howled again.

The chief engineer clenched his jaw and said, "Prepare to engage lift and trim crystals on my mark!"

"Ready!" called engineers in quick sequence from several stations.

"Wait!" Gwen shouted. "No! Belay that!" She paused and frowned at Journeyman. "That's the proper term, correct? Belay that?"

Journeyman scowled at her. "You are exactly in my way."

Gwen shook her head impatiently. "If *Predator* suddenly rises up out of her slip, *right here* under the enemy guns, what do you think will happen? How will they react?"

Journeyman stared at her for a second and then scowled furiously. "Dammit, dammit. *Mistshark* doesn't have armor. She'll blow us to the surface for fear that we'll do the same to her if we can bring our guns to bear."

"Yes," Gwen said. "We can't take off yet. We have to sit here and not be a threat to them."

Cannon howls. Another vast sound of thunder, and a bone-deep groan that accompanied a sudden tilt of several degrees in the deck.

Everyone in the engineering compartment looked around wildly, their eyes surrounded by white. "God in Heaven," one of the men breathed. "They're shooting the shipyard out from under us."

Journeyman grimaced. "We got no pilot aboard her. We got no crew to run out her web so she can maneuver."

"Can we fight?"

"We got no gun crews! They're all off with the skipper! And we got no *time* for this!"

The shipyard shook again, enormous groaning sounds running through the air and making the deck of *Predator* vibrate as she rocked back and forth, nearly throwing Gwen from her feet. "Ungh! What can we do?"

"Go up and down," Journeyman shot back. "Down'll be real easy."

Cannon howled again, and the roaring impact was even closer. The enemy, Gwen realized, was walking his shots toward *Predator*.

"Core's hot, Chief!" called one of the engineers.

Journeyman grunted and started manipulating the Haslett cage controls. "Going to configure our shroud to cover our top half a bit thicker. Might give us an edge." He turned his head. "Trim and lift crews, stand by. We're going to start off with a little dive."

Every head in the room whipped around to stare at Journeyman.

"Dive protocol, you rot-riddled whoremongers!" Journeyman bellowed.

"I take it a dive is dangerous?" Gwen asked in a mild tone.

"With no pilot, more like suicidal," Journeyman said conversationally. "No pilot to steer, we're likely to smash up against the side of the Spire."

"What happens if we do that?"

"We go into a spin all the way down, lift crystals or not. If we're lucky, the ship breaks up and we die on impact."

"Lucky?" Gwen asked.

"Better that than to wind up on the surface on foot, with a smashed ship around us."

Gwen shuddered. "I see what you—"

Etheric cannon howled again.

Predator's core crystal flared with blinding light, and the ship lurched as if it had been struck with an enormous hammer. Thunder roared, a thing more felt than heard, and Gwen was nearly hurled from her feet despite the security straps. There was a horrible instant of complete stillness—

—and then the bottom of the world dropped out and Gwen felt her feet lift up off of the deck. There were several sharp cries and screams, until Journeyman bellowed, "Be quiet, you idiots!" He was leaning back, his feet braced on the deck, his weight secured by the taut lifelines. His expression looked precisely as maladjusted as it did when he was *not* plunging helplessly to his death, Gwen noted.

"Lift," Journeyman bellowed, "give us two percent! We have to fall slower than that shipyard debris, let it get clear of us before we stabilize!"

"Two percent, aye!" shouted another engineer.

Gwen felt her heels sink back onto the floor again, and she grasped a ring on the panel with one hand, holding on until her knuckles were white.

"Stand by!" Journeyman bellowed. Gwen heard him tapping his foot hard against the deck in steady rhythm—counting seconds, she realized.

She shook her head at this display of cool and collected thinking, of single-minded focus amidst madness—and as she did, she noticed a single loose wire sprang out from the control panel.

Gwen had no time for thought. Those wires conducted current from the Haslett cage to the ship's systems. If that wire was one of the ones running to the altitude crystal or one of the ship's trim crystals, it would not receive power when the others did, and the results could be disastrous.

Gwen unclipped one of her safety lines and lunged for the panel, all but throwing herself onto her back.

"Three!" Journeyman bellowed.

Gwen seized the loose wire.

"Two!" Journeyman shouted.

She spotted the open socket and rapidly slid the wire up into place—the starboard trim crystals. If she didn't get the system online, when the lift engineer sent power to the crystal array, the ship would begin to spin violently on its long axis and fly out of control, with disastrous, probably fatal results.

She fumbled with the wire, desperate with haste, knowing even as she did that she was too late.

"One!" Journeyman called, as his hands flew over the power switches, opening channels of current from the core. "Engage the lift array!"

■ ■ ■ Chapter 62 ■ ■ ■

Spire Albion, Habble Landing,
Former Shipyard

Blinding light from the explosion that had consumed *Predator* left a glowing blur in place of Grimm's normal vision. He shielded his eyes and blinked them rapidly, searching for his ship. The sight that greeted his eyes was almost unthinkable.

The *Mistshark*, her work done, had deployed her port-side web and was heeling over neatly. In a moment she would spread her webs wide to catch the etheric currents and begin gathering speed, heading west by southwest—directly toward Spire Aurora.

Grimm shook his head and lowered his eyes to the ground before him.

The heavy timbers of the shipyard jutted out from the spirestone for perhaps five or six feet, and then ended abruptly in edges as rough as broken teeth. Beyond that was nothing but wind and mist and emptiness where bustling industry had been only moments before.

The Landing Shipyard was gone.

And *Predator* was gone with it.

Gone.

Grimm tried to rise but made it only as far as his knees. He felt his shoulders slump, and his skull suddenly seemed an unbearably heavy burden for his neck. The world started to spiral downward. He put one hand out to the spirestone wall to prevent the world from whirling him to the ground.

Predator was gone. Home was gone.

Journeyman and his engineers and his contractors had been on the ship. So had been Master Ferus. So had been Miss Gwendolyn.

Everything had been aboard *Predator*.

Voices spoke to him, but meant little. Hands helped him to his feet. He stood, though he saw no convincing reason to do so anymore. A bright purple blur still marred his vision, the residue of the flash that had consumed his ship, his men, and his future.

". . . away from the opening, sir," Kettle was saying, his voice rough. "*Mistshark* might still fire on us."

"No, she won't," Grimm heard himself saying in a thin, wooden voice. "The shipyards, the gun emplacements, and merchant vessels bearing supplies to Albion are all legitimate targets of war. Calliope's done all she came to do at this point. Now all that's left is to get away with it. She'll run."

Kettle's hand stayed firm on his arm. "Then come away from the opening, sir. Lest your feet slip and you fall."

Grimm felt something like anger at the careful phrasing in the pilot's voice. It was a distant thing, far away, but he felt it, like a heat moving up his spine. It had power enough to lift his head and let him stare at the pilot. "Precisely what are you suggesting, mister?"

Kettle's steady grey eyes flickered with unease—and then flooded with a kind of profound relief. "Oh, Skipper. Nothing, sir. Nothing at all."

Grimm regarded the man's expression and suddenly felt everything rushing back together behind his eyes, an explosion played backward, that left his mind and will restored to some semblance of working order. There was pain, of course. There was horrible, horrible pain, a grief that he knew would, at some point in the near future, leave him a gibbering wreck.

But for the time being, his men needed him. He might not have a ship anymore, but he still had a crew. They were looking to him now, in this moment of despair and doubt. So he straightened his coat, turned his back on the horribly empty sky behind him, and faced his men.

"Well, Mister Kettle. We seem to have done all the damage we can. I'm not sure what my accounts will look like after paying death benefits to the families of the fallen, but you can be assured that I'll compensate you all as best as I am able, as well as putting a good word in one or two ears who still might be friendly to me in Fleet. Experienced hands will certainly be needed in the weeks to come. I think none of you should lack for paying work."

"Skip?" Kettle asked, his tone uncertain.

"For now, of course, we will locate Doctor Bagen, Mister Creedy, and our wounded and see to it that they have the finest care available. I believe that is their group coming along the lane now, in fact. And naturally we will lend our assistance with the firefighting effort here in Habble Landing."

"Oh," said the etherealist's apprentice. "Oh, my goodness."

"Mister Kettle," Grimm said, "please delegate a crew of four to assist the good doctor in relocating the men to a hospice of some sort. The rest of us will proceed to the fire containment effort, and join . . ."

Bridget blinked owlishly, staring past him. "Captain Grimm," she asked, her tone confused and curious, "I'm fairly new to this sort of thing, but . . . are you sure we oughtn't get on your ship?"

Grimm stared hard at Miss Tagwynn. Then at Kettle, studying the man's expression. Then the face of the etherealist's apprentice, Miss Folly, and the countenances of his crew.

Then he stiffened his spine into proper alignment, adjusted his hat, and turned, very calmly.

Rising up out of the mists, no more than a hundred feet from the opening in the wall of Habble Landing, was the absolutely beautiful, entirely flawless, pristine, and very real shape of *Predator*.

Grimm stared at the ship as she rose, steady and stately, until she hovered at the same level as the opening in the Spire's wall. Her shape blurred for a moment, but he cleared his throat, blinked his eyes once, and that illusion passed. She was whole. Her shrouds had held.

"God in Heaven," he whispered. "Thank You for Your grace."

There was a stir on the ship, and Mister Journeyman appeared from belowdecks. He peered around and let out his breath in a low whistle when he saw the broken remains of the shipyards that still clung, here and there, to the outer wall of the Spire.

"Mister Journeyman!" Grimm bellowed.

The engineer straightened his back like a schoolchild caught in the middle of some mischief, and threw a hasty salute toward the Spire. "Skipper! There you are!"

"You, you, you . . ." Grimm began. He ground his teeth and called, "What have you done to my ship!"

Journeyman repeated his salute. "Beggin' the captain's pardon, sir, but we got her all hooked up and took her for a test dive." He coughed and said, "It seemed like the thing to do, sir."

"Ah. A dive on lift and trim crystals alone, with no pilot," Grimm said. He took a breath and asked casually, "How'd she do?"

Journeyman waggled a hand. "Could use some fine-tuning," he replied.

"Very good," Grimm said, nodding, and folded his hands behind his back. "Should you *ever* do such a reckless and muzzleheaded thing with my ship again, there will be hell to pay, Mister Journeyman! Am I clear?"

Journeyman's face went a bit pale. He braced to attention and snapped off a salute. "Yes, sir!"

"*Predator* is not your personal play toy, placed there by God in Heaven for your amusement!"

"No, sir!"

"Do you hear me, Journeyman?"

"I do, sir!"

"Good. Now get my ship in close enough to throw us some lines so that we can belay you and get the planks down! Move, Journeyman!"

"Yes, sir!" Journeyman said, snapping off a last salute, and dashed back belowdecks, roaring out orders.

Grimm spun on the rest of the crew, to find them grinning at his back.

"Miss Folly," Grimm asked, ignoring them for the moment. "Can you confirm the location of Master Ferus's collection?"

The oddly dressed young woman's eyes slipped out of focus for a moment and then she frowned indignantly, muttering to her crystal, "It is moving away from the Spire rather rapidly. That horrible puppet woman has them on that ship."

"Can you follow her, miss?"

Folly frowned. "If the master's collection doesn't get too far away from us, I believe I could follow them."

Grimm nodded once, rounded on his men, and raised his voice to an authoritative roar. "What are you pack of apes gawking at?" Grimm snapped at them. "We have men suffering from silkweaver poison. Doctor Bagen cannot help them, but the etherealist can. To do so, he needs his gear, currently sailing away from us on the *Mistshark*, along with the Auroran Marines who have caused so much harm to our fellow Albions."

A round of growls, led by Kettle's deep-chested snarl, rose up among the men.

"I mean to take *Predator* after *Mistshark*, run her down, hammer her until she surrenders, and get Master Ferus his equipment so that he can save our shipmates. Given the losses we've taken, we'll be running short on hands, but make no mistake—we will speak with our cannon nonetheless. Any man who wishes to stay behind will not be censured."

Kettle glanced around at the crew, taking the measure of their stances and expressions, and nodded once. "We're all in, Captain."

"Then make ready to belay the ship and secure our loading ramp into position as soon as Journeyman warps her in."

"Aye, Skipper!" Journeyman said. "You two with me and the rest of you into two lines on either side of the hallway!"

Grimm let the pilot take charge of the situation and turned to Miss Folly and her companion. "Miss Tagwynn? How are you feeling?"

The tall young woman blinked her eyes closed and open and then managed a slight nod. She still leaned slightly against the etherealist's apprentice for support, but now cradled Master Rowl in both arms. The cat was awake, though distant, his body limp, his eyes focused on nothing. "Better, Captain."

"You've done enough," Grimm said. "I'll be sending the most grievously wounded men to the care of a hospice. You will go with them."

Miss Tagwynn pondered his words for a moment before she shook her head and said, "No, thank you, Captain. I will remain with Sir Benedict."

"I am the captain of that vessel," Grimm said gently. "We will be going into battle, and you have no training or experience that would make you useful to our cause. The decision is not yours to make."

The young woman nodded, and said, "I am certain you can have me beaten until I am not capable of boarding the ship, sir." Then she looked up and met his eyes. Her gaze was steady, penetrating, and eerily feline. "Is that what you mean to do?"

Grimm felt his mouth twitch at the corner. "No, Miss Tagwynn. It certainly is not. But if you are to insist on coming along, I will have your word that you will accept my orders as the voice of God in Heaven Himself once you are aboard."

"Very well," she said.

Grimm nodded to her. "What you did, back at the temple. That was quite remarkable." He felt a smile touch his eyes. "Sir Benedict is a fortunate man."

"He would have done the same for me, sir," Miss Tagwynn assured him.

"Of that I have no doubt."

Behind him, Journeyman had gotten *Predator* close enough to toss a pair of lines to Kettle and the crew. The men began taking them up, and working together to carefully pull the ship into position at the opening in the outer wall of the Spire. It would take only a few more moments to get the loading ramp into position.

Mister Creedy came shuffling up to Grimm and saluted wearily. The strain on his face, from carrying one of the wounded, was evident. "Captain," he panted. "What did I miss?"

"Next payday, schedule a bonus month's pay to Mister Journeyman and his engineering team," Grimm replied.

Creedy blinked. Then he glanced past Grimm, to the shadow of *Predator* hovering where the Habble Landing Shipyard had been only moments before, and his jaw dropped open. "God in Heaven," he breathed.

"It was the *Mistshark*," Grimm said simply. "The Aurorans and that Cavendish woman are aboard her. We're going to run her down and take her."

"We're short on crew," Creedy said. "We'll be light on guns."

"Yes," Grimm said.

"*Mistshark* is larger and more heavily armed than *Predator*."

"Yes."

"Very good, Captain," Creedy said. "What are my orders?"

"Get the wounded aboard and secured; then report to me on the bridge."

Creedy nodded sharply, and turned to go. He paused. "Captain . . . if *Mistshark* is already away, how are we to catch her? She's the fastest thing in the sky."

Grimm felt his mouth stretch into a wolfish smile.

Chapter 63

Folly stood on the deck of *Predator* and felt the ship rouse herself to life.

It was, she thought, really rather disturbing. The wooden deck felt quite solid, and did not at all move, and yet she could feel it shiver and flex slightly, like some enormous beast waking after a sleep, and slowly stretching its limbs. Men rushed about and began climbing her masts, plying lines and preparing to unspool the great reels of vibrating, glowing ethersilk, as bright to Folly's eyes as coiled lines of living light.

There was a deep shudder below the decks, and Folly had to catch her breath in sudden shock, as something like the beat of a great, living heart thrummed through the air. The ship quivered and creaked and then began to rise. There was a sense of focused attention, as if an enormous pair of eyes had begun to look around, and Folly felt them pass over her, as if she were a mouse that had been glanced at by a distant cat. She felt as if her heart were going to stop.

There was, she felt, a sense of gentle amusement that thrummed through the air.

And then, quite clearly, a voice said, *Peace, child. I have no quarrel with you today—and much more interesting prey to consider.*

"Oh," Folly said. "Oh, my. Pray, do not let me distract you."

A passing crewman eyed Folly with a decidedly skeptical air.

You do not, said the great voice. *Come this way, child. Pray excuse me. I have work to do.*

Just then, the grim captain called out and flicked his wrist in an authoritative gesture, and with that, *Predator* began to soar upward.

Folly stood transfixed in a sudden rush of fierce, rising joy as the ship rose up through the mists and the wind began to rush around them. Her feet drew her forward, following the current of attention and focus toward a tower that stood at the front of the ship. She climbed it, slowly and carefully, to find herself standing a few feet behind the grim captain, and the young captain, and the pilot at the controls of the ship.

"Good God in Heaven, Skipper!" the pilot called over the wind. "Can you *feel* her?"

"Aye," the grim captain called back. "Moving rather well, isn't she?"

"*Well?*" the pilot roared, laughing. He twitched the controls slightly and the ship banked left, then right, graceful and light. "God in Heaven, wait until we *fight* her!"

The sense of joy Folly had felt became suffused with an equally ferocious pride, and a sudden pulse of love so palpable that she felt tears filling her eyes.

"Steady as she goes, Mister Kettle," the grim gaptain said, his voice stern. His eyes, though, were smiling as he glanced around, and looked brighter than she had ever seen them, more alive.

"Oh," Folly breathed. "It's like seeing a caged bird suddenly fly. You never really saw it until then."

His eyes switched to her. "What was that, Miss Folly?"

Folly touched her crystal and told it, "Very revealing."

The grim captain arched an eyebrow at her. "Very good. I was just about to send for you." The grim captain turned to the young captain. "Mister Creedy, fetch the young lady a harness, if you would, and help her into it. I doubt we'll need it soon, but best we get her settled."

"Aye, sir," said the young captain. He nodded politely to Folly and went down the steep stairs to the bridge by bracing his feet and hands on the rails and sliding neatly down them.

"Miss," the grim captain said, holding out a hand, gesturing for her to join him.

Folly stepped up to the space beside the captain at the front rail of the ship and nearly lost her breath. From here she could see the great reels of ethersilk spreading like enormous wings for hundreds of feet around the ship, pulled forward by currents of etheric energy, suffused and illuminated with it, blazing through the mist like some vast cobweb of living lightning. A faint sphere of flickering light surrounded the ship at a distance of thirty or forty yards, a screen of energy that sparkled against the individual droplets of mist as the ship raced forward through them. Air and light filled her vision—the rest of the ship's crude matter vanished, here at the very prow, and only the vast, spreading space of the sky and its flow of energy, modestly veiled in mist, opened up around them.

"It's a pleasant view," said the grim captain, in a voice that told Folly that the man made a habit of taking understatement to new heights. "I never get tired of it. Do you, Kettle?"

The pilot, who stood on a small platform just behind the grim captain, let out a belly laugh as his only answer.

The grim captain smiled, an expression in his eyes that was an exact reflection of the fierce, joyous serenity of purpose flowing through the ship around Folly. He put his hands on the rail and leaned forward, into the wind, his eyes narrowed with pleasure.

"Oh," she breathed. "I see it now. *Predator* is you, and you are she."

He blinked and turned to give her a curious look. "Were you addressing me, Miss Folly?"

"Yes, Captain," Folly said. "I can, here. You are . . ." She waved a hand. ". . . appropriate."

The great voice of the ship said, *Precisely, child. Those are my feelings on the matter precisely.*

"I . . . I see," the grim captain said. "Then I hope you will not find it too inconvenient if I ask for a bit of guidance. I need to know where *Mistshark* is to catch her."

"Oh, I couldn't possibly tell you that," Folly said, shifting her feet uncertainly. "I can only tell you where the master's collection is."

The grim captain's mouth spread in a rather politely predatory smile. "That will do, Miss Folly. That will do nicely."

Folly nodded and turned her focus inward. She could see where the master's collection was, if only she gave the matter some consideration. She focused her thoughts on it, on the energy of the crystals she'd placed with the collection and marked with the proper patterns, and there it was, like a glowing star on the horizon. She could see the star blazing clearly, despite the mist, and could have seen it if a wooden wall or twenty yards of spirestone were blocking her view. By focusing on the star, she could even draw it closer, and view the space around it—an enclosed wooden space, a cabin aboard a ship with a second great beating heart, much like *Predator's* but thrumming with a labored note.

"There," she said, pointing her finger left and at an angle upward.

"She's running for the blue," said the grim captain with a certain note of satisfaction. "She'll want to stay hidden at the edge of the mist until she can get outside of Albion's defensive carousel, I expect. Two points to port and let's match her ascent, Mister Kettle."

"Two points to port and match her ascent, aye," said the pilot, his hands steady on the controls. "You called that one pretty close."

"I know her skipper," the grim captain said calmly.

"Then you know she'll have some kind of trick at hand," the pilot growled.

"This time, Mister Kettle, I struck first."

"Sir?"

The grim captain's voice grew a few shades more satisfied. "I sent Mister Stern aboard *Mistshark* a while ago. He painted the inside of their Haslett cage with what was left of that stew I almost cooked in the galley the other night."

The pilot made a choking sound. Then his belly laugh emerged again. The grim captain did not bend so far as to laugh, but the smile that suddenly suffused his features was beatific.

"I'm sorry, Captain," Folly said. "I don't understand."

"Grease and other organic material, Miss Folly," he told her. "The Haslett cage conducts power from the ship's core in the form of electricity. The closer you move the cage, the more current flows into it—and the hotter it gets."

Folly frowned. "Then . . . I beg your pardon, but wouldn't that . . . burn the soup?"

"Burn it *black*," the pilot said, an unrepentant leer in his tone. "Burn it to baked jelly and soot."

"That would . . . would not be very good for the Haslett cage, one assumes?" Folly asked.

"Precisely," the grim captain said.

"Play merry hell with their power distribution," the pilot said. "Put a huge strain on their system. Reduce the power being conducted to *Mistshark*'s web by maybe ten percent. It's the same trick that bi—"

The grim captain gave the pilot a sharp look and flicked his eyes toward Folly.

The pilot coughed. ". . . that big bunch of cheaters pulled on us in the Olympian Air Trials a couple years back," he said. "It's the only reason they beat us."

The grim captain said nothing and kept smiling—but there was a fierce glint pulsing in his eyes, and Folly could feel the ship's heart beat in time with it.

"It'll take some time," the pilot continued. "But once it sets in, we'll overhaul *Mistshark* quick enough, and have control of the engagement to boot."

"But until we do," the grim captain said, "we'll need you to stay here, Miss Folly, to help us follow them in this mist."

"I will," Folly said thoughtfully. "But I should be near the master. . . ."

She frowned and closed her eyes for a moment. She ordered her thoughts and then asked tentatively, *Can you hear me like this?*

Of course, said the voice of the ship.

Folly found the pattern of the crystals in the master's collection, found the glowing red star of retreating energy. *Do you see this?*

I do. Why are you showing it to me, child?

It is aboard the ship we hunt, Folly said. *Can you show it to the others?*

Can they not see it as you do?

I do not think so, Folly told the ship.

Poor things, the ship said, the voice suffused with fondness. *They mean well.*

Folly opened her eyes to see the point where the red star blazed suddenly echoed with a halo of red light sparkling off the sphere of defensive energy that surrounded the ship.

"God in Heaven," the pilot breathed. The ship quivered in response to the jerk of his hands on the controls, then steadied again. "Skip?"

The grim captain peered ahead at the ghostly, scarlet star of light hovering in the mist. "Miss Folly? Is this your doing?"

"Oh, yes—well, no, not precisely," Folly said. "I asked *Predator* to show you where the master's collection is."

There was a long silence on the bridge, broken when the pilot said in a flat voice, "What?"

You must forgive them, the ship's voice said to Folly. *The dear things are blind and almost deaf. Except for my captain, of course. He hears me better than all but a few, like yourself.*

"I'm sure they try very hard," Folly said aloud. Then she bobbed a curtsy to the grim captain. "*Predator* can guide you now that she knows what to look for, sir. May I go to the master?"

The stairs and guide rail rattled as the young captain began to climb them.

The grim captain turned to regard her and nodded rather deeply. "Aye, miss. As soon as Mister Creedy has shown you the harness and how to use it to stay safe. We'll be maneuvering before long, and I don't want you to be hurt."

"Yes, Captain," Folly said.

The grim captain flashed her a sudden grin and turned to face front again, hands sliding thoughtfully back and forth along the railing. "Mister Kettle."

"Aye, Skipper?"

"Follow that star."

■ ■ ■ Chapter 64 ■ ■ ■

AMS *Predator*

Bridget abruptly realized that she was sitting on a stool in a crowded room with a low ceiling. There was a plain pewter cup in her hands, half-filled with water. A thick blanket had been laid across her shoulders. She was shivering. She was thirsty. Her head hurt. Her leg hurt. Her hands ached horribly. She lifted the cup and stared for a moment at the swelling and bruises on her hands, at the torn flesh on her fingers and knuckles. Then she shivered, finished the water, and took in her surroundings carefully.

The walls and floor and furniture were all made of wood, so she must be on an airship. There were a number of wounded men in the room on pallets. Several of the men had faces she recognized from the desperate battle in the ventilation tunnels, so it stood to reason that she was back aboard *Predator*.

Bridget frowned, trying to put together her memories of the period between now and that battle. She remembered a fire, and a terrible weight on her shoulders, a sharp blow to her head from a falling stone.

And a man. A man in an Auroran uniform. A man she had killed with her battered hands.

She remembered that perfectly.

Bridget contemplated that in silence for a moment. She decided that she neither liked nor regretted the act, and that it had been absolutely awful. If she had not done it, neither she nor Benedict would have—

Bridget shot to her feet abruptly. Benedict! Where was Benedict?

The wooden room swayed, and she felt herself sink back into the chair before she fell down. She had to grip the seat of the stool beneath her to keep from falling off.

"Easy, easy," said a young woman's voice from next to her. A hand on her shoulder steadied her. "You look as though you've had quite enough adventure for the time being."

Bridget looked up at the speaker and blinked twice. "Gwen?"

Gwendolyn Lancaster looked exceptionally odd. In the first place, she was wearing men's clothing that was much, much too large for her. The clothes were covered with grease and soot, as was perhaps two-thirds of her face. Her right hand was so thickly wrapped in bandages that it could not be seen as anything but a lump, and her hair, beneath another stained bandage, resembled the spreading wings of an airship's charged ethersilk web, standing out from her head in a small cloud.

"You look awful," Bridget said.

"You're one to talk," Gwen said. She sighed, leaned back against the wall, and slowly slid down it until she was sitting beside Bridget.

"What happened?"

Gwen waved her bandaged hand. "I learned that one ought to be extremely cautious when connecting live wires during free fall."

"Are you well?"

Gwen grimaced as she looked around the room. "More so than some, it would seem." Her eyes came back to Bridget. "And you?"

"I feel ill. And my leg hurts."

Gwen nodded toward the center of the room, where a pair of aeronauts were carefully lifting a wounded man down from an examination table and over to a pallet. Doctor Bagen, looking worn, tired, and bloody, nodded to another pair of aeronauts, who lifted the wiry young man named Stern onto the table. "Doctor Bagen doesn't think your injuries are life-threatening. I'm afraid you'll have to wait the longest to be seen."

"Sitting quietly sounds quite agreeable at the moment," Bridget said. "Where is Benedict?"

Gwen's face clouded. "On a pallet on the other side of the table. He's unconscious."

Unconscious? Unconscious meant alive. He was still alive. Bridget slowly unclenched her hands. "What is his condition?"

The smaller girl pressed her lips together into a line, and her expression became a careful mask. "Less than ideal. Like several of the crew, he has been poisoned by silkweaver venom."

"Then he's"—she couldn't bring herself to say "dying"—"in serious condition."

"He's dying," Gwen said.

Bridget felt her stomach clench.

Gwen continued in a level voice. "They all are. Apparently Master Ferus can help them, if we can recover his gear from the *Mistshark*."

Bridget nodded. "And Rowl? I remember he had a cut on his head."

Gwen glanced up toward a set of cabinets on one wall and flipped her bandaged hand toward them. Bridget followed the direction of the gesture, and spotted the ginger cat asleep on top of a cabinet. One side of his head was wrapped in a clean white bandage. "He's quite the hero at the moment. The men say he saved their lives."

"Well, yes," Bridget said. "Though I almost feel that they shouldn't go about saying it aloud. He's already impossible to deal with."

Just then the world lurched sideways. Bridget all but fell off the stool. For a second she thought her head injury had caused her to lose her balance, but then she realized that several of the pallets on the floor of the infirmary had slid half a foot across the floor before being brought to a halt by tethers attached to odd rings in the walls.

"What was that?" she asked.

"Crosswind. We're under way, in pursuit of the *Mistshark*," Gwen replied. "We have been for nearly two hours."

Under way? On an airship? Then there was nothing around them. Nothing at all. No walls, no Spire, no ground. Just the vast and empty reaches of the sky. Bridget's heart labored quicker, and the aches in her head and leg increased. Rowl hurt. Benedict dying. Terrible, irrational fear knotting her guts. Blood on her hands.

That was enough for one day, she supposed.

She bowed her head and began shuddering with silent tears.

"Oh," Gwen said. Bridget could sense her make a few abortive motions before she patted Bridget on the shoulder and said awkwardly, "There, there. It's all right. All's not lost yet. Captain Grimm is quite confident we can bring the *Mistshark* to battle."

"Yes, of course," Bridget said, nodding. "But if it's all the same to you, I'm going to take a few moments to cry, in any case."

Gwen was silent for a while. Then there was the sound of ripping fabric, and she pressed a length of somewhat stained cloth torn from her too-large shirt into Bridget's hand.

The small gesture of kindness broke something. Bridget leaned toward Gwen, sobbing.

Gwen grunted a bit with the effort, but braced herself and held the larger girl steady with an arm around her. Bridget leaned against her and wept so hard that stars spun across the insides of her eyelids—but she did not make noise doing it. She simply couldn't.

She didn't give herself long. Five minutes, perhaps, passed before Bridget forced herself to steady her breathing. She sat up slowly and wiped her face with the cloth, then blew her nose. She nodded to Gwen and said, "Thank you."

"You are welcome." The heir of the most powerful family in Spire Albion regarded Bridget soberly. "I'm not a very good friend," Gwen said. "I'm willful and blunt and arrogant, and I've not had a great deal of practice. Frankly . . . I've never been good at stomaching the company of the other children of the Great Houses."

Bridget let out a short, subdued laugh. "Neither have I."

"Well, then," Gwen said. "Common ground."

Just then, outside the infirmary, a bell began to ring.

Bridget looked at Gwen in question, but the other girl shook her head. She didn't know what the sound signified, either.

"General quarters, lads!" Doctor Bagen called.

The room stirred with sudden activity. The men assisting him immediately began belting the wounded man down to the examination table with straps apparently made for the purpose. After that, they methodically, quickly did the same to the men on the pallets, while Bagen himself began clipping leather straps attached to a wide leather belt to rings set in the examination table. Another pair of aeronauts began putting jars and bottles and other supplies away in close-fitting storage cabinets, apparently determined to leave nothing sitting loose around the compartment.

"Here," Gwen said. She reached down and produced a similar wide leather belt, and began passing it around Bridget's middle. "If you don't strap up, and the ship is forced to maneuver quickly, you could be thrown into the wall or the ceiling with enough force to kill you."

Bridget let Gwen secure the thick belt on her. Then Gwen showed her how to clip the straps to rings set into the walls and floor all about the compartment, evidently for this very purpose, and how to cinch the lines in tight. Bridget felt a bit like a vegetable hung up to dry by the time the process was over, but she could see the need for it.

And then a terrible thought struck her.

"Gwen," she said. "What about Rowl?"

Gwen blinked and then turned to Doctor Bagen, who had resumed work on Mister Stern. "Sir? What about the cat? Is there a belt for him?"

"No," Bagen said, without looking up. "Nothing that small." He finished tying a knot in a length of suturing thread and looked up, frowning. "But we can't have the little blighter flying about my infirmary, can we?"

The rhythm of the ringing bell changed, and Bagen cursed. "Maneuvers! Get hold of him, quick!"

"Rowl!" Bridget called, opening her arms.

Rowl rose up, his movement slower and less fluid than it normally was, and leapt toward her.

Predator lurched, and a weight like a loaded tank from her father's vattery pressed her mercilessly to the deck.

■ ■ ■ Chapter 65 ■ ■ ■

DMS *Mistshark*

Major Espira looked around the hold of the *Mistshark* at his command. His Marines had performed with most excellent discipline. Their losses had been serious but not utterly outrageous, and if they had not accomplished absolutely every objective on their mission, their main objectives had been achieved. The presence of his force had inflicted a paralytic fear on the citizens of Spire Albion. The Landing Shipyard had been destroyed, and it would take months, if not years, to rebuild after the internal economic chaos bound to ensue in Spire Albion. Cavendish had recovered her book, though Espira had not been made privy to its significance, and every duplicate copy of the volume had been destroyed with the monastery.

He had led his men on a mission of extraordinary ambition, and extraordinary danger. More important, thank God in Heaven, Espira had also led most of them out again. His losses had been lighter than he'd dared to hope for.

Of course, he'd paid a price to do it. He'd led an attack on a Temple of the Way and its resident monks. He'd set fire to a habble full of civilians—enemies, true, but civilians nonetheless. If he hadn't, there was no way his men would have made it out with such light losses. He had traded the lives of people he did not know for those of men he did.

That was, he supposed, human nature.

He was proud of his men. He was proud of what they had accomplished, how hard they had trained, and how that training had paid off. He was proud of the blow they'd dealt to the Albion menace. He was proud that he'd taken command of them, knowing that he had a better chance to bring more Marines home alive than any other commanding officer available for the mission.

But he was not proud of the things he'd had to do to get them home again.

And, he reminded himself grimly, they weren't home yet.

The weary men were stacked fairly closely in the airship's hold. Most of his Marines, being good soldiers, were already asleep. Some were still too wound up from the action and were speaking quietly together. Some of the wounded lay quietly suffering as they waited their turn with *Mistshark*'s doctor. A quartet of seasoned veterans had simply broken out a deck of cards and begun playing, despite the dimness of the hold.

The mood wasn't as joyous as it could have been. Men had been wounded. Men had fallen. The elation that each man felt in having survived the mission was tempered by the knowledge that others like him had not been so fortunate. No, not joy. But definitely relief. Relief that it was over. Relief that the Reaper had not chosen them today. Relief that they were going home.

Though, he reminded himself again, they weren't home yet—but they had a good running start toward getting there.

Ciriaco approached through the gloom. The tall sergeant ducked under the beams that supported the airship's deck above them, nodded to Espira, saluted, and said, "She wants to see you in her cabin, sir."

"Of course she does," Espira said. He sighed and pushed himself up from his comfortable bed of lumpy cloth sacks. "Time enough for sleep when I'm dead, I suppose."

Ciriaco made a grimacing expression that passed for a pained smile. "You want me to come with you?"

"No, Sergeant. I expect that if she was going to snap, she'd have done it before now. I'll be fine."

Ciriaco frowned but nodded. "I'll ride herd on the boys for you, sir."

"Make sure everyone's strapped in and battened down. Then get some sleep. I'm sure it won't take long," Espira replied.

He started climbing the steep staircase to the deck, and hoped that he knew what he was talking about.

The *Mistshark* was not a ship of the Armada. The heavily tarred planking and decks looked smudged and dirty, though he imagined it provided excellent protection from the elements—and of course it made the ship less visible in low-lighting conditions, which was doubtless useful to a captain who was up to no good.

That said, however, the ship was run with all the professionalism of a vessel of the Armada, even if the crew looked like a pack of cutthroats and scoundrels. Certainly the *Mistshark*'s gunnery had been excellent, efficiently destroying the Landing Shipyard. Granted, any target that could not shoot back was hardly a challenge, much less one a bare hundred yards away, but not a single blast had gone to waste, and the *Mistshark* had managed to destroy some thirty times her own weight in enemy merchant craft, as well as millions of crowns of priceless Albion infrastructure.

The men around him were a crew of evil-eyed, pitiless apes—but they had done good service to Spire Aurora. He did not need to like them to respect their ability.

Espira reached the door to Madame Cavendish's cabin and raised his hand to knock.

"Come in, Major," she called, before his knuckles had touched the door.

Espira suppressed a shiver, and entered the cabin.

Cavendish sat inside at a small tea table, calmly, primly, her gown's bodice unfastened and hanging down to her waist. She was clad in only a thin shift from the waist up. *Mistshark's* doctor, a wiry Piker covered in outlandish tattoos, was tying off a bandage that had been wound 'round and 'round Madame Cavendish's ribs. Her position left an unseemly amount of skin on display, and Espira forced himself not to look at the smooth strength of the woman's shoulders or the clean, graceful line of her neck.

It would not do to permit himself to think of Cavendish as a woman. She was a monster.

She still held the slender volume in one hand, and was reading with unnervingly steady attention, even as the doctor ministered to her.

There was a bunk bed in the room. The lower berth had clearly been reserved for Cavendish, but the top was occupied by the bags of miscellaneous objects she had insisted upon bringing aboard. It took Espira a moment to notice that Sark was in the room. The bandaged, wounded warriorborn wasn't on one of the bunks—instead, he lay *under* Madame Cavendish's bunk, like some hideous spider lurking beneath an imperfect bit of decorative molding. Espira could see for a second the glitter of gold-green light reflecting from warriorborn eyes, and then it was gone.

"Major," Cavendish said, smiling faintly. "The good doctor is nearly finished ministering to me. Do sit down."

Espira doffed his hat and bowed politely before seating himself in the room's only other chair, across the small table from Cavendish. "How can I be of service, madame?"

"I need your professional assessment," she replied. "How quickly could your men seize this ship?"

For a second, the doctor's hands froze in place.

Espira frowned, staring at Cavendish, looking for some clue in her features as to how she expected him to answer.

Judging from her expression, Cavendish had noticed the doctor's reaction too. Her mouth quirked up at one corner. "Hypothetically speaking, of course."

Ah. She wanted the man to hear what he had to say. "The crew is outnumbered and outgunned," Espira replied slowly. "And my men are the best. On the other hand, we don't know what measures the crew has put in place to even the odds in such an action. But I am confident to say that my men could take this ship eight or nine times in ten."

"That is excellent news," Cavendish said. "Doctor, have you finished?"

"Ayup," the doctor muttered to Cavendish. The man never looked at her face. "Should heal up fine. Can't see as the ball tore any bone off the ribs, so no splinters. Clean it twice a day, fresh bandages each time, and don't go jumping about."

"You'll tend to it, Doctor," Cavendish replied. "I will see you after breakfast and after dinner. Plan accordingly."

The man clearly resented the command, but he only touched his fingers to the brim of a hat he was not wearing and hurried out of the cabin.

Espira waited for the man to go before turning to Cavendish and asking, "Why?"

"Our pace is too slow," Cavendish replied as she carefully slipped back into her gown. "If that does not change, we may not reach our escort before Albion's Fleet catches up to us. I notified Captain Ransom of this fact several times, and have received no reply. I do not care to be ignored. Tea?"

"Yes, thank you," Espira said.

Cavendish rose smoothly, turned her back on the major, and stopped. It dawned on him after a moment that she was waiting on him, and Espira rose immediately. "Madame?"

"Button me up, if you would, Major?"

"It would be my pleasure," Espira said, stepping forward.

"It had best not be," Cavendish said in a poisonously sweet tone.

Espira felt his spine go rigid. He forced himself to inhale and exhale deeply. Then he went about fastening up a score of buttons on the back of Cavendish's gown with quick, efficient motions.

A few moments later they both sat back down at the table for the tea Madame Cavendish prepared. As she poured, the dismal grey light of the mists outside shifted and grew brighter. The grey of the mezzo-sphere gave way to the cerulean blue of the aerosphere as the ship emerged into open sky.

A moment after that, the door opened abruptly and Calliope Ransom strode into the cabin.

Mistshark's lean captain had a vulpine air about her, and her green eyes flickered with raw anger. Her dark aeronaut's leathers were worn and of excellent quality, as were the blade at her side, the gauntlet on her hand—and a trio of pistols, slung one after another on her belt.

"Good morning, Captain," Cavendish said in a pleasant tone. "Will you join us for tea?"

"No. Thank you." Ransom stared hard at Espira for a moment, her eyes calculating. Then she nodded a few times and said, "This is my ship. And while you are valued customers, you are guests on my vessel, and by God in Heaven you will comport yourselves as such."

"Or what follows?" Cavendish asked in a gentle tone.

"You leave the ship," Captain Ransom said simply.

"Do you mean to force me over the rail, Captain?"

"No need," Ransom replied. "Santos has already opened the cargo doors in the hold below this cabin, including the one on the exterior ventral hull." She tapped a toe on the wooden deck. "Beneath this deck there is nothing but sky—and the explosive charges that will shatter this floor and send everything in the cabin tumbling down into the mist, along with you, your creepy attaché, and this sorry son of a bitch from Aurora."

Cavendish tilted her head sharply. "Excuse me?"

"If I don't come out of this cabin within the next ten minutes, Santos sets off the charges. If I emerge from this cabin acting odd or out of character, he sets off the charges. If he so much as gets a bad feeling that you're up to something, he has orders to set off the charges and kill you all."

Silence grew in the room. Espira cleared his throat. "I believe you are bluffing, Captain Ransom."

The captain's sharp smile grew sharper. "Am I?"

"I wonder," Cavendish mused aloud, "if you are truly the kind of person who would rig her guest quarters to murder her guests should they become inconvenient."

Captain Ransom cocked an eyebrow. "I wonder if you are the sort of person who would make an extremely foolish threat simply to get her extremely busy host's attention."

"Touché," Cavendish murmured. "Could you not have taken a moment to speak to me? It does seem polite."

"Polite is lovely for tea parties," Ransom replied. "It is of limited value when one is attempting to outrun the fastest and best-trained airship fleet the world has ever known." She looked at each of them. "A fact you should consider when calculating whether or not you should attempt to take my ship. You might take her, but you won't take her whole — and all of Albion will be on your heels in hours, if they are not there already."

"Meaning?" Espira asked.

"Meaning that your Marines aren't aeronauts. They can't sail like aeronauts, they can't think like aeronauts, and they can't manage the ship as well as aeronauts — and that goes double for whoever you put in charge of them. If you kill me and take my ship, you're never going to get back to Spire Aurora alive. The Albions will catch you and kill you. It's as simple as that."

Cavendish's mouth spread into a wide smile, one that looked eerily out of place on her features. "I believe I can respect you, Captain," she said. She stared at Ransom with the smile fixed in place, took a slow sip of tea, and then said, "The ship has slowed."

Ransom's brow furrowed. She kept her features composed, but Espira had the impression that she was nearly as unnerved by Cavendish as he was. "How could you possibly know that?"

"Am I right?"

"You are," Ransom said.

"Why?"

"Corrosion in the Haslett cage, my engineer says," the captain replied. She cast an aggravated glance toward the stern of the ship. "It's causing irregular power flow. We had to back off on the throttle or risk blowing out runs and relays."

"Can it be corrected?" Cavendish asked.

"Not without taking the core offline to scour the Haslett cage," Ransom said. "We would be forced to rely on wind-powered sails until the cage could be cleaned and reassembled. We can run at eighty-five percent, or we can stop using the web entirely and trust in the wind."

"And why do we not do that?"

Espira managed to keep from wincing. Cavendish might be fiendishly clever and dangerous, but the question betrayed a vast ignorance of aeronautics.

Ransom managed to answer as though the question had not sounded like one coming from a curious child. "Wind-powered sails are efficient, since they cost no energy consumption from the power core, but they lack the maneuverability offered by an etheric web," she said. "A ship running under wind-powered sails makes its best speed amongst only a limited arc of possible directions, and can be easily outmaneuvered by a powered ship. And if you don't have a good strong wind, a web-driven ship will outrun a wind-powered ship."

"You're saying that relying upon the sails creates too many variables," Cavendish said thoughtfully.

"I'm saying that it dispenses with too many options," Ransom replied. "If we disassemble the Haslett cage, all we have are the sails. No web, no shroud, no weapons. If the Fleet sighted us, we could do nothing but run, and if the wind was not favorable we would be rapidly destroyed. Once we reach the rendezvous, we can repair the cage."

"Why then?"

"Because we'll have an escort to screen for us should a Fleet ship find us," she said. "We'll be able to sail down into the mist while the escort engages the enemy." She arched an eyebrow. "This little lesson in aeronautics has cost this ship in terms of efficiency, because I was here answering your questions instead of doing everything I possibly could to keep us all alive. Enjoy your tea, madame. If I can avoid any further interruptions, this should be over soon."

Cavendish set the teacup and saucer down carefully. "I'm not sure I like your tone, Captain."

Captain Ransom put her right fist on her hip. "This is *my* ship, madame," she said. "Consequently, I'm the one who makes decisions about tone here. Do us all a favor: Drink your tea like a good trog and stop interfering with professionals."

Cavendish's eyes flashed with a spark of heat, echoed by the kindling of what looked like a tiny star in the crimson crystal at her throat.

Espira grimaced. He put down his teacup and shifted his weight slightly in his seat, so that he could throw himself rapidly to the floor should violence erupt.

"You are ill-mannered, Captain," Madame Cavendish said.

Ransom smirked. "Feel free to leave my ship whenever you wish, you arrogant bi—"

And just then a bell began to ring at frantic pace.

"General quarters!" boomed the enormous executive officer's voice, out on the ship's deck.

Ransom spat a foul curse and flung herself at the cabin's door. Just as she opened it, there was a howl of discharges from a broadside of etheric cannon, an enormous flash of light, and a sound like thousands of dry bones snapping.

"Strap in!" Espira shouted to Cavendish, even as he rose and rushed after Captain Ransom.

He dashed out onto the deck in time to see *Mistshark*'s entire starboard etheric web shot away from the ship. It was on fire, adrift and falling with lazy grace back toward the mist of the mezzosphere. The ship lurched, its drag suddenly unbalanced, its stern slewing to port as its bow rotated in the direction of the missing web.

There was a rushing sound, and scarcely five hundred yards away a lean, sleek airship flying Albion's scarlet, azure and white colors sailed up into view from beneath the *Mistshark* with seemingly effortless speed and grace. The name on the prow declared her the AMS *Predator*.

Espira clenched his teeth. Skippers in the Auroran Armada and merchant fleet alike spoke of the privateer ship in hushed, angry tones. *Predator* had been single-handedly responsible for nearly a quarter of Spire Aurora's merchant losses in the two years leading up to this war.

Before he could finish the thought, *Predator*'s guns howled again, this time firing overhead, snipping off *Mistshark*'s dorsal web as neatly as a seamstress with her shears. This time the web came slithering down onto the ship, burning, sparks flying off it with miniature lightning snaps of discharging static electricity whenever it touched nonwooden material.

Such as the *Mistshark*'s crew.

Espira looked up and saw burning web falling directly toward him. He seized Captain Ransom by the belt and pulled her back into the doorway of the cabin an instant before the web reached her. It struck the metal doorknob instead, sparking a bright flash of light that left a scorch mark on the metal. Even as the web settled, *Mistshark* became further unbalanced, her nose rising. Espira automatically snapped a pair of safety lines onto a pair of nearby hooks, in time to use their support to keep from being rocked off his feet from the ship's wallowing.

"Dammit, *how?*" Captain Ransom snarled as the web piled down atop her ship, hundreds of feet long, and a nearly equal amount across. The deck was rapidly beginning to look like the inside of a silkweaver nest.

She snapped her goggles down over her eyes. "Santos!" she bellowed. "Signal rockets *now*! Keep them going!"

"Aye!" boomed the executive officer. A second later there was a rushing sound, and a comet trailing a blazing tail of fire lifted into the sky.

"Firefighting party to the deck!" she shouted.

"Aye, Skipper!"

"Guns, fire at will!"

Seconds later, ten etheric cannon opened fire on *Predator*—but the lean ship had already altered its course and abruptly dropped lower, evading the broadside and plunging back into the mists below. Just before it did, there was a rushing sound, and rockets raced out from *Predator*, exploding a thousand yards overhead into a thick, dense cloud of yellow smoke.

Ransom stared after the vanishing ship, her eyes narrowed in thought. Then she nodded and shouted, "Pilot, course change, twenty degrees west!"

"Twenty degrees west, aye!"

"Full speed ahead! Everything you've got!"

A second pair of *Mistshark*'s blazing signal rockets raced up into the blue sky.

"Aye, Skipper!"

The ship groaned as it banked and accelerated, wobbling like a drunkard. A wooden keg that had not been properly secured bounced across the steeply angled deck and tumbled over the side of the ship into the abyss below.

"Is this wise, Captain?" Espira asked quietly.

"No," Ransom replied bluntly. "Goggles."

Espira nodded and secured his eye protection, while Ransom drew her blade and began hacking at the ethersilk webbing blocking her passage to the deck.

"We can't force him to fight with half our web shot away," she said. "We're too slow on our feet now. If we try it, he'll outmaneuver us and take out the rest of our web within minutes, or work the angles to position himself at weak points in our fields of fire and hammer through our shroud. His ship is lighter and faster, so we can't outdive him or escape into the mist, lamed as we are. Our only chance is to get to our escort before Captain Grimm turns us into a barge."

Espira drew his sword and began hacking away at the ethersilk as soon as Ransom had progressed enough to give him room to swing it. She glanced at him and nodded silent approval.

"Captain Grimm," Espira said. "There are a lot of people in Aurora who are coming to despise the man."

Ransom bared her teeth, her eyes glittering as another pair of her ship's rockets raced out above and behind them. "And to think, they weren't even married to him."

■ ■ ■ Chapter 66 ■ ■ ■

AMS *Predator*

xcellent shooting, Mister Creedy!" Grimm called out to the port-side gun crews. The shots hadn't been difficult given the total surprise they'd attained on *Mistshark,* but fully half of Calliope's web had been shot away, and at this point victory was only a matter of proper doctrine and intelligent maneuver. "Mister Kettle, stabilize us, if you please."

Kettle nodded, already trimming the ship, bringing her level again after their dive into the mist to evade *Mistshark*'s hurried reply. "'Bout there should do it, Skip," Kettle said.

Grimm nodded and turned to the gun crews. "XO," he called, "transfer the crews to the starboard battery!"

"You heard him, boys," Creedy called. "Secure your guns, unhook, and get to the other side!"

Predator's aeronauts leapt to obey, locking down the port-side guns again and crossing the ship to the bank of weapons on the opposite side. Grimm clenched his jaw. Casualties among his crew had been severe. He had only enough crews to man one bank of guns — but there was no sense in letting Calliope know that. Should she work out that he could project force from only one side of *Predator* at a time, she could complicate matters enormously.

"Captain!" called an aeronaut from the deck behind and below him.

Grimm turned to find Mister Eubanks, a stout, florid veteran with a bristling beard, waiting for him. "Report."

"We just fired the last of the signal rockets, Skip."

"Very good. You and your crew stand by for damage control."

"Damage control, aye," Eubanks said, and hurried back down the deck again.

"She's banking, Skip," Kettle noted, peering up at the red star still suspended in *Predator*'s shroud. It had begun to track more sharply to the west. Calliope was hoping to open some distance between her ship and *Predator* while Grimm was temporarily blinded by the mists.

"Adjust course, Mister Kettle," Grimm said.

Kettle grunted and did so, as *Predator* maneuvered to ascend from the mist beneath *Mistshark*, this time on her other flank, and finish the job of laming her. Calliope had no way of knowing that *Predator* could see her.

"Something wrong, Skip?"

Grimm shook his head once. "No. But it hardly seems fair, does it?"

"No, it does not, Skipper. It certainly does not." Kettle's face split into an evil grin. "Ain't it grand? Where can we get us one of those etherealists?"

"Let us survive the day first, and consider such matters later," Grimm said. "Once we're in position, we'll use the same approach as last time. But once we've fired, we'll accelerate our ascension to get above their guns' elevation instead of diving under them."

"That wasn't hardly a dive," Kettle pointed out.

"We don't dare try any more than that," Grimm said. "Journeyman says the power runs are barely holding together as it is. If we put the strain of a full dive on the ship, we could lose them entirely."

It would, Grimm thought, be a horrible surprise to find out, mid-dive, that your ship had suddenly lost the ability to *stop* diving.

"Attack run and evasive ascension on your order, aye," Kettle said. There was a sharp whistle. The pilot turned his head toward the starboard gunnery deck, and nodded. "XO reports guns are ready to fire, Skip."

"Very good," Grimm said, "stand by."

"You think *Mistshark* will surrender once we've lamed her?" Kettle asked. "She's got a good many fighting men on board."

A pulse of hot anger touched Grimm's chest. "They will surrender, Mister Kettle," he said crisply, "or so help me God in Heaven, I will scatter that ship across continents."

Kettle glanced aside at him, and Grimm saw the pilot shift his feet uneasily. Kettle lowered his voice, and his tone was cautious, concerned. "Don't get me wrong, Captain. After what *Mistshark* did to that shipyard, I'm more ready than ever to blow her clean out of the aerosphere. But would you really do that . . . ?"

. . . *to Calliope*, Kettle's tone said, though he did not finish the sentence aloud. Grimm felt something twist and writhe inside him, a halfhysterical laugh that threatened to escape his lips. He hammered it down ruthlessly. "Only if she gives me no other choice." He tried to offer Kettle a reassuring glance. "She is who she is. Do you really think she's become a loyal soldier to the cause of Spire Aurora?"

Kettle snorted. "Point. She'll yield. Unless the Aurorans don't let her."

"We are at war," Grimm said quietly. "I will do what I must."

Grimm closed his eyes for a moment and took a slow breath, trying to get a sense of the ship around him. He gauged the wind, felt the slight tilt in her deck of the weight of half her crew overloading the starboard side. He felt the quivering hum of her core crystal, a barely perceptible buzz through the soles of his boots. It was, of course, a romantic fancy that he almost felt he could hear the same subtle hum of power coming from the capacitors of the cannon on the starboard gun deck—but nonetheless his instincts confirmed what his intellect had already told him to be true.

Predator was ready.

"Sound maneuvers!" Grimm called, and the aeronaut manning the ship's bell began beating out the proper rhythm to warn the crew to secure themselves. "Stand by, gunners!"

"Gunners ready, Captain!" Creedy called.

Grimm double-checked his safety lines and snugged them tight. "Mister Kettle," he said. "Commence attack."

Predator shot up through the misty mezzosphere with the effortless grace of a cloudfin and the speed of a signal rocket. The acceleration in the ascension, driven by the enormous power of the new lift crystal, was at least as great as that the ship experienced in a dive. Grimm had to keep a firm grip on the railing of the bridge or risk being driven to his knees as the ship began to quiver and rattle—and then she began to sing.

Grimm knew that he should be presenting a stoic, solid, unmoving example to his men, become a graven image of steadfast discipline and determination—but he simply could not remain still. He could *feel* *Predator's* grace, the light and easy way she moved through the air, could feel the fierce, proud joy that filled her as she rushed into battle.

All of which was ridiculous, on a purely rational level. Grimm knew that, with his head.

His heart knew better.

As *Predator's* war song swept up in pitch and volume, a crewman erupted into a howling cry of his own. Grimm realized, with something of a start, that the scream was coming from his own throat.

The bellow from the crew, a beat later, was the loudest Grimm had ever heard, despite their depleted numbers, and he could hear Creedy shouting with the rest of them.

The grey mist abruptly lightened, turning paler grey, then pearly, then white—and a breath later, *Predator* exploded out of the mezzosphere and into the wide blue sky.

Mister Kettle had timed his approach perfectly. They emerged from the cloud cover almost directly beneath the *Mistshark,* traveling at almost exactly the same speed, only a few hundred yards out. In their first attack run, surprise had been on *Predator*'s side. Now speed was everything.

"Fire at will!" Grimm shouted.

"Fire, fire, fire!" Creedy cried, relaying the command to the gun crews.

Predator's seven cannon fired almost simultaneously. Even though his men had instructions to fire only at the enemy's web, from their angle beneath the *Mistshark* there was no way to absolutely guarantee that the blasts would miss the ship itself, but his crews performed well. The ventral web burst into flame and began drooping and falling as multiple blasts struck it. A pair of stray shots went past the web and crashed against the *Mistshark*'s active shroud, and were harmlessly absorbed as a sudden sphere of greenish light surrounded the airship.

Grimm could all but feel the shock and dismay of the enemy crew. He did not blame them. For an airship to pursue a wounded foe with such perfect precision from within the misty veil of the mezzosphere was a feat so improbable as to approach impossibility.

But more vitally, he knew that even now, the *Mistshark*'s gunners would be frantically depressing the snouts of their weapons to fire down at *Predator* the instant their pilot rocked the ship enough to give them a clean shot.

Grimm waited until he saw the enemy ship begin to roll to present her broadside to *Predator*, and then called, "Ascend!"

Mister Kettle threw the ship into her new maximum amount of climb, and Grimm staggered and nearly fell despite his grip on the handrail. *Predator* sailed as swiftly and cleanly as a worthy soul winging to its eternal reward. Eight of the enemy cannon rent the air *Predator* had just departed with their fury, and the single blast that did manage to strike home brought forth only the incandescent green gleam of *Predator*'s own protective shroud.

Grimm had timed their maneuver successfully. The *Mistshark*'s gunners tried to track *Predator* as she rose but reached the limit of their elevation short of catching up to the lighter, faster ship. In order to track back onto *Predator*, the *Mistshark*'s pilot would have to rock the ship back up to level and onto her other side, all while being dragged forward, listing and pitching, by the uneven pull of a single quarter of her web. Shifting that much awkward mass against its own momentum and inertia would require crucial seconds—seconds Grimm had no intention of giving away.

"Fire!" he called.

Again the gunners did their job. A single stray blast slipped through the web and flashed against the enemy's shroud, but the other half dozen raked through the *Mistshark*'s last remaining length of web, tearing it from the ship and setting it ablaze.

Mistshark's acceleration immediately dropped to nothing, her drunken, wallowing form now gliding forward on nothing but waning momentum. Desperate signal rockets again flashed away from her, and Grimm saw the enemy ship struggling to stabilize itself with its trim crystals alone—a tricky proposition without enough forward motion to allow the more responsive maneuvering planes to assist with the task, and until it was completed, the *Mistshark* was virtually helpless against *Predator*'s mobility. As long as Kettle could keep their ship out of the firing arcs of *Mistshark*'s cannon, *Predator* could pour fire down upon the enemy without reservation or fear of reply—and Mister Kettle knew his business as well as any man alive.

Kettle guided *Predator* into a high arc, rolling the ship onto her starboard side to present their broadside to the enemy, slowing just enough to give the gun crews the cleanest shot possible.

Grimm felt his stomach twist, and he tried to swallow through a dry throat.

He was about to find out whether or not his duty would require him to murder Calliope and her crew.

He flipped down the telescoptic on his goggles and focused his attention intently on the *Mistshark*.

"By the numbers!" Grimm shouted. "Fire!"

"Gun two!" Creedy bellowed. "Fire!"

The frontmost cannon of the starboard side of the ship howled, its blast smashing into *Mistshark*'s straining shroud.

"Gun four!" Creedy called. "Fire!"

The second starboard gun unleashed its fury, hammering down at the enemy's shroud, hungry for the vulnerable, unarmored airship beneath.

"Gun six! Fire!"

The *Mistshark*'s shroud's bright illumination grew dimmer, more translucent.

"Gun eight! Fire!"

The blast scorched the topmost mast of the enemy ship—and Grimm saw what he had been looking for: A tall, lean figure—Calliope herself, he supposed—rushed the aft dorsal mast and smacked a boarding ax down onto one of the lines running up it. The line parted, and the *Mistshark*'s Dalosian colors, a white star upon a bisected red-and-blue field, went fluttering down toward the ship's deck, in the aeronaut's universal signal of surrender.

"Cease fire!" Grimm roared. "Cease fire!"

"Cease fire!" Creedy echoed to the crews.

And the reverberating, thunderous howl of the last shot from the number eight gun faded and vanished into the open blue. The *Mistshark* lay quietly, meekly, beneath them as Kettle brought *Predator* around, keeping the enemy covered with her starboard cannon. Grimm let Creedy and Kettle handle the maneuvering, while he watched the enemy's gunners. They were, in proper form, retracting their cannon back into their secure position, where they would be unable to fire.

It would appear that their surrender was genuine—though it was

Calliope, after all. Grimm would proceed by the numbers, without dropping his guard. He felt a fierce smile stretch his lips. "Mister Creedy," he called. "Fire up the launch, if you please. Signal to Captain Ransom my compliments: 'Surrender and prepare to be boarded.'"

The cheer that rose up from his aeronauts made the planking beneath Grimm's feet vibrate, and he fancied that *Predator* was voicing her triumph along with the men who crewed her.

W/ithin a quarter of an hour, Calliope crossed to *Predator* on her launch, its steam engine chugging the little craft steadily over from the *Mistshark*. She had two crewmen with her to manage the launch, in addition to both of Master Ferus's missing wagons and a slender volume matching the one in Grimm's coat pocket, stolen from the Great Library.

If Calliope had just been soundly defeated by a smaller, less heavily armed vessel, it did not show in her swagger or her confident expression. If she was intimidated by the dozen or so primed gauntlets being aimed at her, it could not be seen from the outside.

She stepped up to the bow of the launch as it docked with *Predator* with her usual smirk on her lips. "Permission to come aboard, Francis?"

Grimm reminded himself that she was calling him by that name only because she knew it annoyed him, and that he should not surrender to manipulation. "Granted," he called calmly.

Calliope hopped down onto *Predator*'s deck and peered around the ship curiously as she paced to the bridge and ascended the steps to it. "Well, well, well," she said. "That was a bit of a surprise. What on earth have you been feeding her?"

"Enemies."

Calliope threw her head back and laughed.

"Book, please," Grimm said.

She tossed him the volume amiably, and he caught it. "You've no idea the foul looks I collected when I went to get it."

"Did the Aurorans give you any trouble about striking your colors?"

"Nothing I couldn't handle," she said breezily. "I must admit, Francis, you do gorgeous work. That was excellently done—though you'd never have beaten me in a fair fight."

"I avoid them," Grimm replied. "So do you."

Her teeth flashed very white when she smiled. "True."

Grimm nodded to Creedy, who sent several men to take charge of recovering the wagons from the *Mistshark*'s launch. They bustled the wagons away toward the etherealist's cabin without delay.

Calliope watched them go. "That takes care of the preliminaries, I suppose," she said. "What do you intend to do with my crew?"

"I mean to return them, and you, to Spire Albion for arrest and trial," Grimm said. "The Aurorans will be taken prisoners of war and treated accordingly."

Calliope shook her head. "You mean to have my crew tried as civilians for committing an act of war? They'll never submit to that. No Albion court would give them a fair trial and they know it. They'll call them pirates and hang them."

"Possibly," Grimm said. "On the other hand, if you refuse to surrender, then by the articles of war I could blast your ship down to the surface here and now. Which alternative do you think they'd find more attractive?"

Calliope's face darkened, and she clenched her jaw a few times before answering. "My crew are soldiers, fighting as soldiers. They *will* be tried and judged as soldiers in a time of war."

"Or what?" Grimm asked mildly.

Calliope stared at him, her mouth working on words that never quite formed, her eyes all but glowing with the heat of her anger. Then she closed her eyes and muttered a savage curse beneath her breath.

"Or what?" Grimm asked again, in exactly the same tone.

"You've made your point," she said in a bitter tone. "You've made your point, you bastard. I am in no position to make demands of you."

"No, Captain Ransom, you certainly are not," Grimm said.

Calliope made a face as though she had just bitten into a piece of rotten vat meat. "I . . . *request* that my crew be taken as prisoners of war and held as such, Captain Grimm. Please."

Grimm nodded slowly several times. "I want you to know something."

She frowned and peered at him.

"I know that you didn't have to use the firing pattern you did at the Landing Shipyard," he said. "You could have targeted *Predator* first, instead of last."

"Yes," she said simply.

"I also want you to know that I realize why you offered me that contract the last time you came aboard. You didn't want me to be present for what was going to happen. You wanted *Predator* out of harm's way."

Her head moved in what may have been the barest fraction of a nod.

"Why?" Grimm asked.

Calliope looked away. The question hung heavy in the silence. After a moment she said, "Once, she was my home too."

Grimm's stomach stabbed with a little ache of echoed pain he thought he'd left behind him.

"I remember," he said quietly. "Captain Ransom, I hereby declare your crew, your passengers, and yourself prisoners under the articles of war. Mister Creedy, make a note to that effect in the ship's log."

"Aye, Captain," Creedy said firmly.

Calliope closed her eyes for a moment and then nodded once to him. Her lips began to shape words several times, but evidently she could not force herself to actually say them.

Grimm had his victory. There was no point in rubbing it in any

further. "Your thanks are not necessary, Captain Ransom. I will be sending engineers back with you to board the *Mistshark* and disable your
cannon. You will sail with *Predator* back to Spire Albion. You will be
under my guns the entire way. If you deviate from any order I give, no
matter how slightly, I will open fire. Do you understand?"

"I'm not an idiot, Francis."

Grimm fought against annoyance but felt a muscle at the corner of
his mouth twitch despite his best efforts. Calliope saw it too, and her
smirk settled back into place upon her lips.

"I suppose not," Grimm said. "All the same, Calliope, the past several days have been an almighty trial. Do not test m—"

"Contact!" shouted one of the lookouts in *Predator*'s dorsal mast.
"Captain, contact!"

Grimm's head snapped around toward the lookout. "Where?"

"Inbound vessel high, west by southwest, coming fast!"

An airship coming from the west? But the Fleet was operating exclusively east of their current position. . . .

Grimm's stomach clenched and he felt his knees go a little loose and
unsteady.

He turned, flipping down his telescoptic again, and spotted the incoming airship at once, heading for them at breakneck speed. He studied her through the telescoptic carefully, and tried to ignore the way his
heart had begun beating faster and his hands had begun shaking.

"Calliope," he said quietly. "You don't need to be here. Get in your
launch and go. Now."

He heard her draw in a small, sharp breath of her own as she saw the
approaching ship. "I don't suppose I could convince you to surrender."

Grimm gave her a look over his shoulder.

Her smirk turned bitter. "Ah. No. Of course not. Duty."

She shook her head, and with a few easy strides was off the bridge
and heading back to her launch.

"Sound general quarters, if you please, Mister Creedy. Come about. Extend the web around the clock and get us moving."

The XO boomed out the orders, and once again the ship's bell began to ring. Men scrambled for their posts, quickly recinching their safety harnesses. Aeronauts swarmed into the masts, playing out the expansive lengths of the ship's web and getting *Predator* under way.

Grimm stood motionless on the bridge, watching the menacing shape of AAV *Itasca* growing larger with unnerving rapidity, and wondered whether it was already too late to escape.

■ ■ ■ Chapter 67 ■ ■ ■

AMS *Predator*

Gwen felt rather ridiculous while moving from the infirmary to the bridge. Procedure aboard a ship engaged in combat action was for every crewman to keep at least one and preferably two safety lines secured to contact points at all times. Fixing the heavy metal clips to the secure rings was not the effortless task that the crew of *Predator* made it look like. Fortunately, runner bars stretching along the length of the deck and some of the internal hallways made the task simpler, if not easy, but nonetheless it took her several minutes to travel no more than eighty feet.

She reached the bridge just as Commander Creedy began bellowing orders to the ship's crew, and the deck tilted slightly beneath her feet as *Predator* began to bank into a turn.

She was about to climb the steep staircase up to the bridge when the captain of the immobilized *Mistshark* gripped the handrails and simply slid down them, landing effortlessly on the deck and nearly bowling Gwen over in the process.

The tall woman gave her an impatient glance, took in the grease and grime on her clothes, and said, "Good God in Heaven, is Journeyman allowing women into his engine room now? What is happening to the world?"

"Excuse me," Gwen said.

"I suppose," the woman said, and moved at a gliding run down the deck, seemingly uncaring of the way the ship had begun to tilt and shudder, to where a launch had been tied up to *Predator*'s flank. She vaulted the rail to the launch, nodding to the two rough-looking men crewing it, then began untying the mooring lines.

Gwen blinked at this behavior. Was the woman not effectively a captive? Was she escaping? Why on earth was no one putting a stop to it?

"Halt!" Gwen said, in what she hoped was an authoritative tone. She began to lift her gauntlet to take aim at the escapee, then remembered as she raised her arm that she was not wearing her gauntlet, having spent most of the last day working with components of the ship's engines. Rather than abort the gesture entirely, which she felt would have looked weak and indecisive, she pointed a stern finger instead and said, "You there! Halt!"

The enemy captain looked up at her and burst out in a hearty belly laugh. Then she hauled against a lever that slowly kicked the launch out away from *Predator*. The launch began to fall behind *Predator* at once, since she wasn't being driven by any kind of etheric sail. Before the launch fell out of sight astern, the enemy captain called, "You've bigger problems than me now, girl!"

And then the launch fell out of sight behind them.

Gwen chewed on her lip for a second, then turned and laboriously ascended to the bridge.

By the time she got there, *Predator* was fully under way, sailing swiftly into the morning sun, so that she had to squint against its brilliance as she secured her safety lines near where Captain Grimm stood by the pilot's stand.

"Good morning, Miss Lancaster," Grimm said. "What can I do for you?"

"That woman, the captain of the enemy ship," Gwen said. "Did you let her go free?"

"Yes," Grimm said. A muscle twitched in his jawline.

"Why on earth would you do that?" she asked.

"I saw no point in her dy—" He paused for a moment, adjusted his peaked cap carefully, and then said, "I saw no point in giving her an opportunity to distract us during a combat action."

Gwen felt her eyes widen. "Oh, dear. Is that what we're doing?"

"Odds seem excellent," Grimm said. "Put your goggles on, Miss Lancaster."

Gwen blinked at him, then remembered and cursed herself for looking like an idiot who had never traveled by airship before. Leaving one's eyes unshielded at this altitude was an invitation to any number of etheric mental disorders, as well as to eventual blindness. She settled her tinted goggles into positon. "I'm afraid I don't understand. Why not keep her?"

"If I had, her ship, seeing help on the way, would certainly have unlimbered her guns and engaged us. We could likely have destroyed her, but doing so would have cost us precious time in delay, and we would have been unlikely to do it with our shroud intact." The captain glanced toward the rear of the ship and said, "We need every bit of power we have to keep us moving and to fuel the shroud if we are to have a chance of survival. Releasing Captain Ransom was an implicit truce, and the least evil option available to me."

"I see," Gwen said. "Am I interfering with the ship's operation by being here?"

Again he began a quick reply, and again restrained himself for a few seconds before answering. "Not at present," he said. "Currently we are under way. It remains to be seen whether we can escape *Itasca*."

"Ah," Gwen said. "I thought you should know, Captain, that Master Ferus's gear has been returned to him. He and Miss Folly are in the infirmary now."

Grimm arched a brow and turned fully to her for the first time since she'd arrived on the bridge. "Will he be able to help my men?"

"He said he would try," Gwen said. She gave her head a little shake. "The poor old man looked awful."

"He's had a difficult time of it the past few hours," Grimm answered. He flipped down the telescoptic mounted on his goggles and peered past Gwen for several seconds before he grimaced and said, "They're breaking out their chase guns."

Kettle turned his head and squinted back at the shape of an airship far astern. *Itasca*, Gwen assumed. "From there?" the pilot said, his tone annoyed. "They must have the new-model bow guns."

"So much for that advantage," Grimm said.

"Are we going to give battle, then, Captain?" Gwen asked.

"Not for very long," Kettle said darkly from his control station.

"*Itasca* is a battlecruiser, Miss Lancaster," Grimm said, by way of explanation. "She's a great deal larger and more heavily armed and armored than *Predator*. We cannot realistically survive a pitched battle with her."

"Then we are running from her?" Gwen asked.

"We're trying," Kettle said.

"I know nothing of aerial combat, Captain," Gwen said. "But . . . would it not be wise to descend into the mist and avoid action that way?"

"Under most circumstances, Miss Gwen, that is exactly what I would do," Grimm answered.

Gwen looked over the side of the ship. "And yet we seem to be ascending."

Grimm nodded. "*Itasca* was fully under way by the time we spotted her, while we were standing still. It was necessary for us to open as much distance as possible as quickly as possible, and we're lighter than *Itasca*. All that armor plate weighs her down. It takes *Predator* relatively less energy to ascend, so to keep pace with us, she has to reduce power from her other systems to maintain an ascension as she moves forward."

"By running up as well as away, *Predator* was quicker off the mark?" Gwen asked.

Grimm nodded in approval. "Just so. Doing so kept *Itasca* from catching up to us and overwhelming us immediately."

"And once you're sure we're out of her cannon range, you'll dive back down?" Gwen asked.

"Normally, yes," Grimm said with a grimace. "But Journeyman hasn't finished putting the ship back together. She's not running at her best, and she's not able to handle a combat dive yet. We could descend slowly, but if we do so, *Itasca* will be able to use her weight and momentum to make up distance on us and bring us within range of her guns."

"Then what are we going to do?" Gwen asked.

"Run like hell and pray," Kettle said.

Grimm stiffened suddenly and said, "She's firing her chasers. Evasive starboard."

Gwen turned to look behind them. There was a bright flash of scarlet-and-white light from the pursuing ship, and a brilliant little pinpoint like a tiny star appeared and grew swiftly, unsettlingly larger. Even as she saw that, the ship heaved beneath them as Kettle took her into a swift bank, then settled her down again almost immediately onto her original course. Gwen's stomach flopped and wobbled, and despite her secured safety lines, she was all but thrown from her feet.

She could not take her eyes from the incoming fire as she did. It flashed across the distance between the two ships in no more than a breath, growing and growing as it came. The sphere of energy detonated perhaps fifty yards ahead of the ship and far off to their port side, erupting into a cloud of pure fire, roiling flame dozens of yards across. The explosion was loud enough to make the planking of the deck vibrate. Gwen felt herself flinch from both the sound and the intensity of the light. "God in Heaven," she breathed. "What happens if that hits us?"

"We're at the edge of her range," Grimm replied. "When the energy of the blast is that dispersed, our shroud is best able to absorb it. *Predator* can take numerous direct hits from this distance."

"But our web isn't so lucky," Kettle said.

"I don't understand," Gwen said.

"Incoming fire," Grimm said again. "Evasive port."

Once more Gwen's stomach lurched as Kettle wove in the opposite direction for a few breathless seconds, then trimmed *Predator* neatly. Again a thundercloud of fire burst to one side of the ship—but this time there were flickers of light at the very edge of the translucent cobwebs of her starboard ethersilk web.

"As you can see," Grimm said, "our ethersilk web extends beyond the protection offered by *Predator*'s energy shroud. The web is vulnerable to incoming fire."

"Could you not shorten it to bring it within the shroud's protection?" Gwen asked. "Would that not protect the web?"

"And reduce our velocity proportionately as a result," Grimm replied. "We'd slow to a crawl. Incoming. Evasive ascension."

Gwen was all but flung down to the deck as *Predator* abruptly climbed. She felt certain that her stomach was doing its best to share her skull with her brains before Kettle leveled out again. She found herself gripping the railing desperately to maintain her footing. This time the blast exploded a shade farther ahead of the ship, if a good deal below. Which meant that *Itasca* was closer to *Predator* than she had been for the previous shot. Which meant . . .

"Then that's why *Itasca* is shooting at us," Gwen said. "She's trying to burn away enough of our web to slow us down, so she can kill us."

"We call it raking the web, Miss Gwen," Grimm said politely. "And that is exactly what she means to do. We can keep the distance open by continuing to ascend, force her to run uphill after us for a time."

"Why?" Gwen asked. "What happens then?"

"We run out of up," Kettle said with a grim chortle. "Go up too far, and the air is too thin to breathe."

Gwen felt a little short of breath already. "Then what hope have we?"

"*Itasca* is overpowered, even for her size," Grimm said. "She's running three core crystals at maximum to keep this pace with us—and she'll be running her steam turbine all-out too. That means her systems are more complex, more prone to overheating, component failure, and other technical problems."

"She can sprint as fast as we can," Kettle clarified. "But we can keep up this pace for days at a time. It's what we're made to do."

Grimm nodded. "The longer we can keep this race going, the more likely something is to give on *Itasca*. Incoming, evasive starboard."

Kettle wove the ship to one side, and this time *Itasca*'s bow gun claimed a small portion of *Predator*'s web on the port side.

"Can't you duck any further to one side?" Gwen asked.

"The more we weave side to side while *Itasca* runs in a straight line, the more distance she makes up on us," Grimm said. "Mister Kettle knows his business."

"Unfortunately," Kettle said sourly. "We don't get lucky, we're going to get to knock off work before lunch, Skip."

"I'll accept luck if we can find any," Grimm acknowledged. "But be of good hope, Mister Kettle. *Itasca*'s web is vulnerable too. She can't dodge. And she should just about be within range." He turned to a speaking tube and called out, "Stern gunnery deck, bridge."

Creedy's voice came back out of the speaking tube, tinny and distant. "Stern guns, aye."

"Rake her web, XO," Grimm said. "Fire at will."

"Fire at will, aye," Creedy said.

A second later there was a howl of discharging cannon, and a blue-white sphere of fire of their own went hurtling back toward the Auroran ship. The explosion looked tiny in the distance, and there was an odd, long delay before its cough of distant thunder caught up with *Predator*. Gwen noted a faint shimmer in the air, and realized that she was looking at a large section of ethersilk web being burned away.

"Excellent shooting, Creedy," Grimm called into the speaking tube, even as Kettle threw the ship into another sharp ascension to avoid fire. "Pour it on."

"Aye, sir!" came Creedy's voice. "Thank you, sir!"

"Why," Gwen said, "if we keep shooting like that, we'll lose her in no time."

"Except she hangs a lot more web than we do, miss," Kettle said. "She keeps a lot more web in her reels than *Predator* can. And she's got three times the chase armament we do."

Gwen felt somewhat indignant at these facts. "Well. That hardly seems fair."

Captain Grimm chuckled beneath his breath. "*Itasca*'s made for exactly this kind of work," he said.

"Then how will you defeat her?" Gwen asked.

Grimm held on as Kettle wove through another evasive maneuver. The two aeronauts took it in stride, evidently staying upright through an act of sheer, unconscious will. Gwen felt as though her stomach had decided to depart her body for warmer climes, and she desperately struggled to keep from retching in front of the captain and Mister Kettle.

"Without the ability to dive, I can't," Grimm said. "I'll keep raking her web, but eventually, probably within the next half hour, she's going to take down enough of ours to overhaul us and pound us to bits."

"I . . . see . . ." Gwen said. She swallowed. "I don't suppose her captain will give up?"

"Why would he?" Grimm asked. His teeth showed in a sudden, feral smile. "He knows it as well as I do, after all. Barring an act of fortune on our behalf, the outcome of this chase is inevitable."

"Oh," Gwen said. "You have a plan of some sort, then."

"Of sorts," Grimm said. He put a hand on the rail as the ship rocked wildly to the side again, and more web was chewed away by the heat of a blast. A distant boom marked the detonation of a shot from *Predator*'s lone stern cannon.

Gwen frowned, and considered his words for a moment. "Captain Grimm," she said. "You knew escape was nearly hopeless from the beginning."

"Yes."

"Then if your goal was simply to escape, and remaining within sight of *Itasca* was certain death, it follows that risking a dive was our most sensible option. Granted the ship may not have been able to take the strain, but it seems even the dire risk of that offers better odds for survival than this chase."

Grimm nodded again. "Precisely true."

Gwen frowned at him. "A gambit, then?"

"We've been marking our path with signal rockets since we left Spire Albion. Currently, we are following our original course back toward the Spire. If our signals have been spotted, and if any ships of the Fleet have elected to follow us, we may have support—and if so, we may be able to take *Itasca*."

"There are a great many 'if's in that statement, Captain," Gwen noted.

"Yes."

"You are risking everyone's life in an effort to take a single enemy ship."

Grimm arched an eyebrow, and his manner became intent. "Not just a ship. A *storied* enemy ship, Miss Lancaster. Whether or not official statements have been made, we are now at war with Spire Aurora— a war that they are winning, handily, given the damage they've inflicted to the Landing shipyards."

"And you believe the loss of a single ship will counter that sort of blow?"

"Objectively, no," Grimm said. "But wars are not simply about objective measurements. They are about will, Miss Lancaster, about belief. The disruption the Aurorans will cause to our economy will not be remotely equal to the loss of any single ship—but if we can counter by taking down a ship like *Itasca*, we might reduce entirely the damage done to the fighting spirit of all of Albion. It is *vital* that we not be made to seem wholly helpless in the opening moments of the war. Once a nation ceases to believe that they can win a war, that war is lost."

Gwen frowned. "And . . . you're willing to risk the lives of your crew on such a prospect."

"And yours, miss," he said quietly.

"On the chance that a friendly ship *might* have seen your signal rockets."

"It is less a gambit than a throw of the dice," Grimm said. He had turned back to watch ahead of the ship, rocking easily as Kettle took her through another evasive maneuver. "But they are *my* dice."

"What if *Itasca* breaks off? Surely she knows you are running toward Albion, toward our Fleet."

Grimm tilted his head, as if he had never considered the question before. "Hmm. Then I suppose we return home with minor damage, easily repaired. But she won't."

"Why not?"

"Her captain was sent out to bring *Predator* down last month, to make a statement. He missed us. A captain put in command of a ship like *Itasca* will be professional, brilliant, ambitious, and hungry, miss. He won't want to go home without feathering his cap with *Predator's* wreckage."

There was a sharp whistle from below, and a moment later the bridge speaking tube rattled with a tinny voice. "Bridge, ventral lookout!"

Captain Grimm turned to the speaking tube. "Bridge here, proceed."

"Contact, Skipper!" came an aeronaut's excited voice. "Five miles dead ahead of us, down at the cloudline. Skip, I think it's *Glorious*! She's descended into the mist and is ready to pop up."

"Hah!" Grimm said, smiling fiercely. "Good eyes, Mister MacCauley. Mister Kettle, when?"

Kettle squinted ahead of them and then glanced back at *Itasca*, taking *Predator* through another lateral slalom as he considered the question. "Start a gradual descent now, Skipper," Kettle said. "They'll build up speed and momentum on us. They'll close the range, but it'll keep their eyes on us and make it that much harder for them to pull out when they spot *Glorious*."

Grimm nodded sharply and folded his gloved hands behind his back. "Concur. Proceed."

Kettle nodded and, after his next evasive maneuver, put the ship on a downward angle that made Gwen's stomach rather unsettled, as the whole of the sky seemed to open up from the unfettered vista offered from the ship's bridge.

"*Glorious*," Gwen said, fighting back flutters in her stomach. "That's Commodore Rook's ship, is it not?"

"Yes," Grimm said in a severely polite, rigidly neutral tone. "I believe it is."

"Can't believe we're polishing the apple he's about to pick," Kettle muttered.

"Now, now, Mister Kettle," Grimm said. "There's a very great deal of angry *Itasca* behind us. I am well contented to have help from any ship in the Fleet, under the circumstances."

Kettle muttered something darkly beneath his breath, and Gwen frowned at the pilot. "Captain? Is there a matter for concern here?"

That Grimm paused for a thoughtful moment before he answered spoke volumes in direct contrast to his words, Gwen thought. "Not particularly," he said. "*Glorious* is a battlecruiser as well, equal to the task of engaging *Itasca*, and Commodore Rook has a solid, competent Fleet crew."

"I note, sir," Gwen said, "that you do not say that Commodore Rook is solid and competent."

"That is not my place to judge," Grimm replied steadily. "He has advanced quite capably through the ranks."

Kettle snorted heavily, soaring through another arc to avoid the rapidly expanding shape of an enemy blast sphere.

"He's a pompous, lecherous ass," Gwen noted calmly, "devoid of the wit God in Heaven gives to a simpleton, but he has a certain ratlike cunning, I suppose. He looks pretty enough in a uniform, too."

Grimm turned his head sharply toward her, and then away again. She could tell by the tightening in his cheek, seen in rear profile, that he was smiling. "I would not presume to contradict your opinion, Miss Lancaster," he said.

"That's because the skipper don't fight battles he can't win, Miss Gwen," Kettle noted.

The regular thunder of enemy munitions detonating grew fractionally louder.

"Skipper," Kettle said, a warning tone in his voice, "if *Itasca* gets any closer, there won't be time to evade. I'll have to start weaving. We might not make it to *Glorious*."

Grimm turned to the speaking tube. "Engineering, bridge."

Journeyman's voice clattered out of the speaking tube. "Aye, Skipper?"

"If there's anything else left in her, Mister Journeyman, we need it right now."

"I'm stunned she hasn't buckled on us already, Skip," the engineer called back. "Some of these runs are being held together with bloody twine. But I'll see what can be done. Engine room out."

The next few moments were, Gwen thought, uniquely terrifying. There was no kind of violent action happening near her, not an enemy to be seen as anything more than a boy's model airship, soaring in the distance behind them. There was nothing she could prepare herself to fight. Instead there was simply regular, roaring thunder and boiling fire rending the air nearby, sending gusts of hot, ozone-scented air across the deck of *Predator*, promising a sudden and violent death. The ship rocked in increasingly severe evasive maneuvers, each necessary to preserve her life, yet each also allowing the enemy to inch nearer.

She thought she might go mad with the unnerving contrasts of the brilliant sunlight, the crisp, chill breeze in the air, and the thundering violence of aerial battle. It made her feel utterly helpless.

Because, she realized, she was. There was absolutely nothing she could do to save herself from sharing whatever fate *Predator* met, apart from throwing herself over the rail at once. She had no training, no instinct, no knowledge that would help her survive in this circumstance. Her fate was, she realized, entirely in the hands of another person.

Captain Grimm stood steady in his place on the bridge, hands folded behind his back, his safety lines tight and neat, the very image of what an airship captain was supposed to be, holding all their lives in his hands, and doing it without bowing beneath the burden or complaining of the weight.

It was a form of courage that Gwen had never considered before.

There was no way in Heaven or on Earth that this man was a coward who deserved to be cast from the Fleet, whatever the records may have said.

Gwen's breath suddenly caught in her throat. In the past several moments, *Predator* had sailed down near to the misty mezzosphere, with *Itasca* gaining on her the entire while. There, ahead of them in the mist, she had spotted the shadowy form of *Glorious*, ready to burst forth into the teeth of the enemy.

"Let's not stand in Commodore Rook's way. Prepare for evasive ascension, Mister Kettle," Grimm noted, his voice entirely calm. "Steady. Steady . . ."

An endless second passed.

And *Predator*'s luck ran out.

A burning sphere from *Itasca*'s bow gun exploded exactly amidst her port-side web, sending the entire thing up in flames in a single, violently blazing sheet of burning ethersilk.

The reaction of the ship was immediate. She slowed, throwing Gwen forward against the pull of the safety lines that strained to hold her in place, the heavy leather belt around her midsection pinching hard against her flesh, cutting into her. The ship slewed heavily to starboard, pulled off balance by the preponderance of functioning web on that side, her timbers groaning and creaking at the sudden shift of forces.

Gwen actually saw one of the runs to one of the port-side trim crystals fail in a shower of sparks, finally collapsing under the strain of hard use without the stabilization of solidly established systems to support it. The port side of the ship abruptly dropped a good two feet, bang, jarring Gwen and driving her brutally to one knee on the deck. Pain flared up her leg.

Grimm was thrown to his knees on the deck as well, but he never lost concentration on the moment, his voice rising to a bellow. "Evasive ascension now, Mister Kettle! Reef the starboard web! Kettle, wheel her around to bring our starboard array into position to support *Glorious*!"

Kettle, held steady by the braces of the pilot's position, clenched his teeth and wrenched *Predator* into a sudden, lopsided climb, even as the ship lost more velocity, allowing for *Itasca* to rush in for a killing stroke—

—just as *Glorious* came surging up from the mezzosphere, her broadside to *Itasca*, firing her thirty cannon in rapid, successive, howling salvos of ten guns each.

The noise was too loud, the light simply too bright to be believed. Gwen found herself lifting her hands toward her eyes and ears and face as thunder and lightning pounded against them. *Predator* whirled with drunken grace around her vertical axis, until her own more slender but still deadly broadside came to bear on the enemy ship, and opened up in howling thunder.

Itasca vanished behind a wall of flame and deafening sound and roiling smoke. It seemed incredible to Gwen that any ship could do anything but be obliterated by such an outpouring of power.

But *Itasca* did.

The ship came sailing gracefully through the thunder and fire, her web blazing like an enormous halo all around her, her energy shroud glowing more brightly than a thousand lumin crystals. Some of the blasts had gotten through, and her prow had been smashed and warped out of shape as if some titan had taken an enormous sledgehammer to her, and two of the three cannon in her bow gunnery deck had been reduced to smoldering ruin, but the vessel was in one piece, and already slewing her stern around with more grace than any ship so large should possess, even as she ascended.

Glorious's salvo fire smashed against *Itasca*'s shroud, but as the ship rotated she brought fresh, undamaged portions of her protective sphere to bear against the fire, shrugging off the blows like a veteran brawler. Within a few breaths she had brought her own port broadside to bear, and it fired in a single titanic salvo amidships on *Glorious*.

Glorious's shroud, overloaded at the relatively smaller point of impact, gave her less protection than *Itasca*'s had. Armor rang and rent and screamed as cannon tore *Glorious*'s flank, wiping away half a dozen of her guns and smashing one of her three port-side mastworks. Secondary explosions, probably from one of the cannon, blew a hole in her guts from inside the armor, sending splinters of shattered deck and planking spinning and howling throughout the nearby compartments.

But *Itasca* wasn't finished. Rather than slowing, she kept rushing ahead, and her sharp angle of ascension carried her just over the top of *Glorious*'s glowing shroud. *Itasca* managed the roll of a much lighter ship as she went, and brought her starboard broadside to bear, aiming down at *Glorious*'s deck from point-blank range. She fired in titanic fury, and there was only so much that shroud and armor alike could do at such a range, from that relatively vulnerable angle.

Sections of *Glorious* fully thirty feet across simply vanished, charred to clouds of soot. Her main dorsal mast was cut in half and plummeted toward the deck. Human screams could not be heard amidst that destruction, but Gwen's imagination placed them for her near the small figures she could see consumed in violence that rendered even the doughtiest mortal form into a glass figurine.

Glorious listed to one side, groaning and shrieking in her pain — but even so, incredibly, the ship withstood the horrible destruction visited upon her by the enemy, wounded but not destroyed, her heavy armor enabling her to survive the punishment laid out upon her.

Itasca, meanwhile, rocked back to level, her steam turbines chugging and roaring, giving her some maneuverability even as her aeronauts labored to deploy more lengths of her ethersilk web from her masts, to harness the greater power and grace they offered. If she was not untouched, she had been marked only lightly in comparison to the ship that had appeared to have every advantage on her in the outset of the engagement, and she was ready to fight on.

"God in Heaven," Kettle swore, without a trace of mockery in his tone. "Now, *that* is how you handle a ship."

"Keep us moving, Mister Kettle," Captain Grimm snapped. "Circle us toward *Glorious* and stay in her shadow." He raised his voice to bellow, "Guns! Keep raking *Itasca*'s web! We've got to keep her lamed so that she can't get more fire into the holes she's put in *Glorious*'s armor!"

"Rake her web, aye!" Commander Creedy's voice echoed. *Predator*'s cannon shrieked, and sections of *Itasca*'s web went up in flames even as the large ship's reels spooled more out. *Itasca*'s momentum slowed, the ship hovering sluggishly for a moment — a moment in which *Glori-*

ous's massive firepower could make a proper reply to *Itasca*'s greeting of a moment before.

"Hah!" Grimm said, clenching his fist. "We can have her yet."

"Guts and rot!" snarled Kettle, sudden and furious. "Captain, look at *Glorious*!"

Grimm's head whipped around to stare at the Fleet battlecruiser. Over the distance, Gwen's stunned hearing could just barely make out a loud, frantic ringing sound. It took her only a second or two to recognize it as the same bell cadence *Predator* herself had used to signal emergency maneuvers.

And seconds later she watched as *Glorious* plunged back down into the mists, moving in a rapid, panicked-looking descent.

Gwen stared after the wounded leviathan, stunned. Only the swirling mists remained, spinning in a slow, circular vortex where *Glorious* had vanished.

"The coward!" Kettle howled. "Damn you, Rook, you rotten-crotched *coward*! Did you think you could take a fighter like *Itasca* without getting a few lumps along the way?"

Gwen shook her head dazedly, her eyes moving to Captain Grimm.

The man was staring after the vanished *Glorious*, just as she had been, and she could see the truth in the sickened horror in his eyes.

Glorious had left *Predator* behind to die.

Dimly Gwen could hear *Itasca*'s aeronauts howling in wild defiance and exultation—as well they might, having just turned an ambush back upon their attackers to send them diving out of the blue sky for the cover of the mists.

And then *Itasca* began turning, to bring her broadside to bear on lamed, fragile *Predator*.

■ ■ ■ Chapter 68 ■ ■ ■

AMS *Predator*

rimm watched as *Itasca* banked toward them, steam engines
chugging, turbines roaring, and lined up the shot that would
scatter *Predator* and her crew to the winds.

Like everything else *Itasca* had done, the maneuver was performed
flawlessly. Grimm could just see, at this distance, the outlines of the
officers standing on *Itasca*'s bridge, including the high-crowned hat of
her captain. The man's dark red uniform was marred by a blob of
white—a sling for his arm, perhaps? Some of the blast from *Glorious*'s
opening salvo must have gotten through *Itasca*'s shroud, and heat or
shrapnel from the impact upon the ship's armor must have wounded
the man. Yet he stood where a captain ought, doing what a captain
should. Grimm could respect that.

At least if he was to be gunned down, it would not be by some simper-
ing, cowardly nepotist like Rook, or by the guns of some ragged, sloppy,
desperately violent pirate. There was some comfort in the thought.

Though it was a given, of course, that he and *Predator* would not
simply lie down and die, either.

He could not outrun *Itasca*, not now. Half of *Predator*'s web had
been shot away, severely limiting her speed, whereas the larger ship
could simply deploy more ethersilk from her expansive reels. Grimm
could order the men to raise sail, but the winds were not favorable in

their current position, and turbine-driven *Itasca* would end the matter before the canvas sails could be deployed.

He could not escape in the traditional fashion—they were too far from the mist to try anything but an almost certainly suicidal dive, given that one trim crystal had already folded on them. For that matter, even a sharp ascent could be equally dangerous.

To stand and shoot it out with *Itasca* would be an utterly futile gesture. Oh, a lucky shot might strike a weakened point in *Itasca*'s shroud—she had been in a heavy exchange at close quarters with *Glorious*, after all—but a single fortunate shot from *Predator*'s guns would be unlikely to inflict heavy damage against the battlecruiser's armor with anything but luck guided by the hands of the Merciful Builders, the Archangels, and God in Heaven Himself. In contrast, it would take a similar stroke of fortune for *Predator* to survive obliteration from *Itasca*'s broadside.

Grimm turned his head to regard the flag of Albion, snapping out straight in the cold wind from the main dorsal mast. He could strike his colors. The universal sign of surrender in aerial battle would almost certainly be honored by a professional of the caliber of *Itasca*'s captain. Of course, doing so would mean the loss of *Predator*, either taken as prize or destroyed and sent to the surface as an act of war, and Grimm's soul screamed out against that course of action.

But what other option did he have?

"Captain Grimm?" Miss Lancaster asked. "What is that sound?"

Grimm frowned at her for a second and then tilted one ear to the air, listening. His hearing still rang with the fury of recent battle, but . . . yes, there was a sound coming from high above.

A sound like distant trumpets.

And it was coming from directly out of the blinding midmorning sun.

Grimm whirled to stare at *Itasca*, thundering along under the rattle of her steam engines, the roar of her turbines, and realized that the enemy ship was effectively deafened by her own propulsion. Was there time?

Yes. Yes, there might be.

Grimm felt a smile stretch his lips from his teeth and bellowed, "Hard to port at flank speed, Mister Kettle! Stay ahead of her turn! Guns! Ripple fire on *Itasca*'s bridge!"

"Sir?" Creedy called back. Grimm could hear the incredulity in the young officer's voice. Not only was he deliberately aiming for an enemy's bridge an unworthy and generally unrewarding tactic, but ripple fire — loosing blasts from one cannon after another — would accomplish nothing against *Itasca*'s heavy shroud at this distance. It would, in fact, do little more than provide a fireworks display.

"That is an order, Mister Creedy!" Grimm thundered. "Fire!"

Creedy's voice bawled out the order, and within seconds *Predator*'s cannon began hurling defiance into *Itasca*'s teeth. Blasts of fire exploded against the shroud near *Itasca*'s bow, blotting her bridge from view in intermittent washes of flame.

"Captain!" came Journeyman's near-furious scream from the speaking tube. "Port-side trim crystal array is about to fold on us! We've got to get somewhere quiet and stable and cut power!"

"Understood!" Grimm called back. "Prepare to cut power to the port trim array!"

"*What?*" Journeyman blurted.

Grimm turned to Miss Lancaster and began tightening her safety straps, checking each carefully. "Excuse me, miss."

The young woman stared at him, her eyes widening. "Captain?"

"Hold on to your straps tight with both hands, and do not adjust them, if you please," Grimm said.

Itasca continued her turn, bringing the annihilation of her broadside to bear, though Kettle kept wounded *Predator* racing ahead of it, banking into an arc that would circle around the other ship. The gesture was a futile one in the long term. Already *Itasca* was cutting her forward speed slightly to send more power screaming through the lateral thrusters of her turbines, to spin her faster and catch *Predator* in the firing arc of her own port-side guns.

The foremost trio of guns in *Itasca's* array managed to traverse enough to catch *Predator* in their sights and spat angry spheres of flame. Her heavy cannon were considerably larger than those *Predator* boasted, and the enemy fire leapt across the sky to splash against *Predator's* shroud. It illuminated in a brilliant sphere of green light, and the roar of the cannon charges felt as if they shook Grimm's very bones. Grimm could all but feel his ship's determination to persevere, feel her stubborn endurance—but he could also feel some of the heat from the enemy rounds leak through the shroud, sending the heavy scent of ozone washing over the deck.

Predator kept up her steady pounding of the area around *Itasca's* bridge, and Grimm knew that it would look like the tactic of a truly desperate man, hoping to end the threat to his ship by effectively cutting off the head of his foe. Stories and dramas often relied upon such a tactic—but in the messy practice of actual battle, targeting so precise was problematic, shrouds not so easily penetrated, and a determined enemy could usually batter through a foe's shroud amidships more accurately and rapidly than an enemy attempting to directly strike the enemy's bridge.

But, Grimm thought, it was not his goal to wreak havoc on *Itasca* with his cannon. He had something far more dangerous in mind. After all, she was already deaf.

Grimm wanted her *blind*, too.

Itasca dropped even more of her speed to sharpen her turn, her armored flanks gleaming in the sun as she struggled to catch the smaller, nimbler ship in her guns' firing arcs, like a cat whirling on a darting mouse. Grimm could feel his heart beating in pure, frantic terror as he *felt* the angles of the ships changing, felt more of the enemy's guns beginning to catch up to *Predator,* and knew he and his ship had only seconds to live. *Itasca* was determined to finish what she had begun those weeks ago, and was focused wholly upon *Predator's* destruction.

And because she was, she never knew a thing until the sound of strident trumpets suddenly rose over even the thunder of her own engines and *Predator's* cannon fire.

Commodore Alexander Bayard's AFS *Valiant* came crashing down from the sun, the heavy cruiser dropping in a descent that was very nearly as sharp as the combat dive of a far lighter vessel, her war cry a clarion call. On her flanks were her division mates, AFS *Thunderous,* roaring like a storm, and AFS *Victorious,* her spars shaking with the steady rumble of a vast war drum.

A roar of unadulterated ferocity went up from the crew of *Predator* as the three Albion heavy cruisers pivoted with the coordination of a troupe of dancers, bringing their broadsides to bear on *Itasca,* and unleashed the fury of forty-five cannon in a nearly simultaneous flash of light and sound.

The range was brutally close: Bayard had brought his ships down *between* Grimm's ship and *Itasca.*

Albion cannon blasts smashed into *Itasca's* already tested shroud, hammered through it, and gouged into her hull itself. *Itasca's* heavy armor plating had been designed to withstand guns exactly like those now being used against her, in odds exactly like those she now faced — but even *Itasca* could not ignore Bayard's opening remarks. His ships' cannon tore into *Itasca's* armor, tearing gaping holes in her outer hull and setting everything in the compartments behind them on fire. In an instant, nearly half of *Itasca's* port-side hull simply vanished, blown into clouds of ash and flame and cinder and shattered, glowing-hot armor.

And yet *Itasca's* crew was too disciplined to be rendered impotent, despite the speed of Bayard's nearly perfect execution of a classic attack. Even as the cruiser division opened fire, *Itasca* howled her defiance back at her foes, her cannon screaming—and the weight of her entire broadside came crashing down upon *Thunderous*.

The battlecruiser's heavy cannon made light work of *Thunderous's* shroud, and the greater density of *Itasca's* fire meant that *Thunderous* never had a chance. Though her outer hull was armored with copper-clad steel, at that range, and against those guns, she might as well have been protected by so much glass. Cannon charges erupted against the heavy cruiser's armored exterior, tore a hole in her large enough to sail through in a yacht, and erupted out the far side of *Thunderous's* hull in a spray of shattered armor, fire, and incinerated wood, gutting her in a single salvo.

Grimm saw *Thunderous's* starboard trim crystal array fail in a shower of small explosions, and her aft lift crystal faltered, so that she slumped abruptly to stern and starboard, her deck tilting at a precarious angle, and she began dropping swiftly. The strain on her timbers was too much, and with a cracking sound as loud as a cannon, her back broke. The rear half of the airship simply plunged—and became fouled in the long lengths of ethersilk web, jerking the forward section of the doomed, burning airship down, down, down. She vanished into the mists—but not before a quick-thinking aeronaut deployed an emergency buoy, basically nothing more than a tiny lift crystal attached to a colored pennant.

"Shift fire to her webs!" Grimm bellowed. "Let's give the commodore the chance to wear her down!"

"Fire on enemy web, aye!" Creedy responded, and *Predator's* cannon began raking *Itasca's* webs, preventing her from building any speed beyond that provided by her turbines.

Itasca kept up her original turn, trying to shelter her ravaged flank from her enemies, but *Valiant* and *Victorious* split apart like a pair of wolves circling a lumberbulk. The two Albion ships had been unable to entirely halt their descent in such a short distance, and they slid under the *Itasca*'s plane and to either side of her, each ship tilting on its axis to keep one broadside on the enemy. In response, *Itasca* rolled her undamaged starboard broadside down toward *Victorious*, exposing her belly to *Valiant*.

Itasca's fresh broadside fired first, and this time all of her cannon were focused on *Victorious*. The gun crews of Spire Aurora's prize battlecruiser knew their trade well, but had a poor shooting angle, and their hits were more dispersed. *Victorious*'s shroud flared brilliant emerald green, blunting much of the fire, but even so what got through pounded her dorsal and starboard mastworks to splinters and tore ragged holes in her starboard gun deck, taking a horrible toll among her gunners and setting much of the starboard side of the ship ablaze.

Victorious and *Valiant* fired again, but *Victorious*'s broadside was at a feeble half of its strength. Between *Itasca*'s shroud and her heavy armor, the battlecruiser shrugged off the hits, though she rang like some vast gong as *Victorious*'s fury pounded her hull.

Valiant, meanwhile, rolled almost to the horizontal as she slipped beneath *Itasca*—and then ripple-fired directly up into her belly.

Itasca's shroud held for the first half dozen impacts, but then Bayard's gunners began to gouge out great pieces of her armored hull, wrecking her forward ventral mastworks and pushing more and more deeply up into the ship, like a fine, slender knife being pressed into a man's belly beneath the ribs, questing for the heart.

Itasca shuddered and simply took the pounding, keeping her starboard guns on *Victorious* until her cannon cycled and howled again.

The second salvo was of no great accounting in terms of its accuracy, with Bayard pounding its gun crews with regular shocks of impact from below—but against wounded *Victorious*, it was enough. Though the cruiser tried to turn her mangled flanks from *Itasca*'s guns, the only thing she could do was rotate her wounded side down, exposing her only lightly armored deck to enemy fire. Her shroud failed in a catastrophic burst of sparks, and the heavy cannon of the Auroran vessel pounded her deck, tearing open huge sections, and setting dozens of fires in the unarmored compartments of her interior.

Victorious faltered and dropped like a man hit with a sledgehammer. A power surge must have hit her starboard trim crystal array, because she abruptly rolled, flipped, and began tumbling as she sank, whirling over and over her long axis, entangling herself hopelessly in her own web.

Itasca shuddered and continued her turn, descending with too much grace for a vessel so large, steam engines chugging, turning her intact starboard broadside toward *Valiant* with a ponderous sense of finality, a behemoth ready to crush the last of its smaller opponents.

The proper thing for Bayard to do would have been to increase his pace and stay ahead of *Itasca's* spin, just as Grimm had done only moments before—but instead Bayard broke in the other direction, as if seeking to disengage.

It was a seemingly foolish movement, one that might have been expected from a panicked merchant skipper or a green captain in his first action. It would only carry *Valiant* into Itasca's sights that much more quickly, and could not possibly open up enough range to make a significant difference in the accuracy of *Itasca's* gunners. Worse, the move exposed more of the ship's stern, where armor plating was thinner and the ship's superstructure more vulnerable. Grimm could all but see *Itasca's* sudden eagerness to bring her cannon to bear and destroy the last of her serious opponents.

And in doing so, to expose the gaping hole in her belly armor to *Predator*.

"Kettle!" Grimm shouted.

"Aye!" the pilot called. He had seen the opening as well, and nimble

Predator banked and dipped lower, sliding into the shadow of *Itasca*'s hull into the dead area where her guns could not reach—and where, if she rolled, *Predator* would be annihilated in a single glorious flash of luminous thunder.

"Creedy!" Grimm called. "Prepare salvo fire!"

"Salvo fire, aye!" Creedy screamed.

"Mister Journeyman!" Grimm called into the speaking tube. "*Cut the port trim array!*"

Grimm felt it when the power to the port-side trim crystals went out. *Predator*'s deck suddenly flipped entirely to the vertical, the motion a shock against his safety harness, a blow to his rib cage. Miss Lancaster let out a sharp cry of surprise, her voice tight with a terror that she quickly choked off.

And *Predator*'s starboard guns rolled up to *Itasca*'s belly from a range of fifty yards.

"Fire!" Grimm roared.

Predator's starboard cannon howled as one.

There was no shroud left to defeat the lighter charges *Predator*'s guns could throw, and *Valiant*'s heavier weapons had taken a disastrous toll on *Itasca*'s armored hull and interior armor alike. In the open space of the sky, *Predator*'s rounds may not have done much more than put red-hot dents in *Itasca*'s outer hull—but within the contained spaces of her interior compartments, the salvo of the lighter guns exploded with savage fury, a jet of fire washing back out of the relatively small opening in her armor.

Itasca staggered violently, and the salvo sent after Bayard's ship went sailing wildly in every direction. The roar of the Auroran's thrusters abruptly stopped, and for a few seconds the only sounds in the sky were the creak of timbers and the crackle of fire and the distant chugging of *Valiant*'s engines.

And then with a sound like furious thunder, *Itasca*'s boiler exploded.

The shock wave of it smashed into *Predator* like some vast, fleshy hand, and knocked the air from Grimm's lungs. He tried to give an order to Kettle, but no sound came from his lips. Kettle was already descending, though, and continuing forward, sailing out from under *Itasca*.

The enormous armored ship had been entirely deformed by the explosion, armored hull warped and dented outward by the force of the blast, torn open in dozens of places. Her mastworks were wreckage, around the clock, and multiple trim crystals had failed, so that she was listing to one side and adrift, rotating slowly. Helpless aeronauts dangled from safety lines. Her entire port-side gun deck had been consumed in fire, and aeronauts were screaming as they struggled to escape the blaze, many dying as the safety harnesses meant to protect them now trapped them within the flames.

Valiant's steam whistle wailed in triumph as she came about, taking a course that would bring her back to *Itasca* without crossing the firing arc of her remaining gun deck, and one of Bayard's chase cannon sent a single shot flashing across *Itasca's* bow.

"Hold fire!" Grimm called.

"Hold fire, aye!" Creedy echoed from the guns.

For a long moment, *Itasca* hung in the sky like a great, stunned beast, too dazed to understand its surroundings. Grimm could hear orders being shouted frantically up and down the larger ship.

And then her colors came fluttering off of their few remaining masts, and went spinning away into the breeze.

Predator drifted far enough forward on *Itasca* that Grimm could see her captain on his listing bridge, braced against the tilt of his ship, held in place by three neat, taut safety lines. He looked of an age with Grimm, a tall, lean man with weathered skin and a blaze of silver in his otherwise coal-black hair. The man stared back at Grimm, then nodded, unhooked his sheathed sword from his side, and held its handle out toward *Predator*.

Grimm straightened as much as he could in the nearly vertical position from which he depended from his own safety lines. He doffed his cap and nodded in reply to the Auroran captain.

Itasca had surrendered.

The battle was over.

■ ■ ■ Chapter 69 ■ ■ ■

AMS *Predator*

Bridget woke up almost instantly when Benedict stirred in his sickbed.

She sat up in her chair and wiped her hand at her mouth, as she always did. She had a wretched tendency to drool when she slept heavily. But she forgot, and came near to knocking out her teeth when the cast over her forearm and wrist smacked into her lips.

Bridget hissed out a curse and raised her unwounded arm to her mouth to rub at the sting. That was all she needed, for Benedict to wake up to see her lip split open and swollen.

The young warriorborn stirred and let out a soft groan. His body twitched, and then his arms moved—only to be held down by the straps of the infirmary cot he occupied. He opened his eyes and looked around blearily.

The infirmary was crowded, with men strapped into cots covering nearly every spare foot of floor space. Doctor Bagen, after laboring for nearly a day straight in the wake of the battle, was in a hammock strung up in one corner of the infirmary, snoring with the force of an approaching thunderstorm. A second hammock had been hung up in the other corner, and Master Ferus lay in it, arms folded over his belly, sleeping with a small, contented smile on his face. Folly lay curled up in the open space beneath her mentor's hammock, between the etherealist's two wagons, sleeping with her mouth open.

"Don't try to sit up yet," Bridget said to Benedict. "Here, here. Let me unbuckle it." She leaned down and unfastened the straps that held Benedict flat to his cot, and he took a deeper breath after she had, and raised his hands to mop at his face. Then he lowered them, his eyes snapped into focus, and for a moment there was something wild and dangerous in them. When they locked on her, she felt that she hardly recognized him.

Fortunately, Bagen had prepared her in advance for the kind of response a wounded warriorborn might have after a battle followed by most of two days of unconsciousness. Benedict's accelerated metabolism had burned fiercely for all that time, and he seemed more lean and dangerous than at any other time she had known him.

Without a word, she passed him a large tankard that had been sitting ready, and he all but snatched it out of her hands, clutching it clumsily due to the burns and thick bandages over his own — but he guzzled the water down with such urgent thirst that some of it spilled out around the corners of his mouth. By the time he lowered the mug, she had uncovered the large bowl of thick stew and the small loaf of bread that had been waiting with the water. He sat up, took it from her with a growl and a flash of teeth, and began eating the stew directly from the bowl, as if he couldn't get it into his mouth quickly enough. He supplemented gulps of stew with enormous bites off of the loaf of bread, hardly chewing them before he swallowed.

Bridget followed Doctor Bagen's instructions and sat very still while Benedict ate, without speaking, moving, or offering to take the bowl from him when he seemed to be done.

It was only after he had finished the bowl and the loaf alike that the wildness seemed to die out of his eyes. He blinked them several times, and then abruptly focused on Bridget again. The lower half of his face was stained with his meal. He lifted his hand to his mouth in a short, abortive gesture, and something like shame touched his eyes.

"Ah," he said, his voice low and rough. "I'm . . . I beg your pardon, Miss Tagwynn. I was not myself."

"It's all right," she assured him. "How do you feel?"

"Awful." Something deep and dark flickered in his eyes for a moment—but then it was gone. "Where are we?" he asked.

"Aboard *Predator*, in the infirmary."

He peered around him. "Ah. How did we get here? We were at the temple, the last thing I knew."

"You collapsed from the silkweaver venom," Bridget said quietly. "We knew Master Ferus could help you and the others who had been poisoned, so the captain brought everyone aboard and set out to recover Master Ferus's equipment."

"Successfully, obviously," Benedict noted. "What happened?" He blinked and suddenly sat up straight. "Bridget, what happened to your face? Your arm?" He lifted a hand and touched her bruised cheek.

His fingertips were light and hot and a tiny bit rough. Bridget thought her heart might stop. She felt her eyes grow very round.

Benedict's spine seemed to stiffen in the same moment. Then he lowered his hand abruptly and cleared his throat. "Um. That is, if you wish to tell me."

"I was struck on the face while the temple was collapsing around us," Bridget said, which was technically true. She held up her cast. "This happened as the battle began."

"What battle?"

"Oh, we chased down and fought *Mistshark*, the champion ship of the Olympian Trials, then fought something called an *Itasca* alongside several ships of the Fleet. We captured her, which is apparently quite a significant thing, and we're now bringing everyone from the battle back home." Bridget sounded to herself like a terribly nervous child reciting poetry for the first time in front of her classmates, speaking too quickly but unable to stop herself.

Benedict blinked and shook his head. "I . . . How did you say you hurt your wrist?"

"The ship was maneuvering and I was trying to hold on to Rowl. I had no idea the motion could be so violent." She shook her head and felt herself blushing. "It's nothing, honestly."

"Where's Rowl?"

"Not speaking to me at the moment," she said. "I'm afraid his pride is wounded. But he'll come around. Eventually."

Benedict smiled faintly. "And Gwen?"

"She's fine," Bridget said. "She's good."

The young warriorborn quirked an eyebrow at the thoughtful tone in Bridget's voice. "Yes, she is," he said quietly. "Arrogant, headstrong, occasionally careless, and slow to consider that she might be wrong— but she has a good heart. Beneath all the annoying bits. Occasionally a goodly distance beneath."

Bridget let out a little laugh and shook her head. "You always tease her."

"Someone must. Otherwise she'd get an enormous, swollen Lancaster head."

He grinned and looked at her for a moment. Then, moving very deliberately, Benedict Sorellin picked up Bridget's hand and rested her palm atop his fever-hot fingers. He pressed her hand between both of his. Bridget's heart raced and she felt herself blushing again and smiling and staring intently down at her own feet.

But she closed her fingers gently against his, and felt his firm, careful grip tighten in response.

It was amazing, she thought. She didn't feel a need to say anything. And apparently he didn't either. Her hand was in his, and that was saying enough and more than enough. She was exhausted and the past few days had been terrible—but now she sat quietly beside Benedict, and held his hand, and felt happier than she had in months.

*   *   *

Gwen stood very quietly on the windy deck, her goggles in place, and stared out over the railing to where a large cargo-loading platform from *Itasca* had been stacked with the cost of the opening days of the war.

There had been no room to lay the bodies of those who had died in state. Instead they had been wrapped in cloth and stacked up like cordwood, Albions and Aurorans alike. The platform now floated a hundred yards from *Predator*, tethered with a length of line.

The deck of *Predator* was crowded. The officers of surrendered *Itasca* stood, weaponless, in their dress uniforms, as did the officers of *Valiant* and *Victorious*, and the single surviving officer from *Thunderous*.

"For as much as it has pleased God in Heaven to take out of this world the souls of these men," Captain Grimm intoned, his voice calm and steady, his hat in his hands, "we therefore commit their bodies to the winds, earth to earth, ashes to ashes, and dust to dust, looking for that blessed hope when God in Heaven Himself shall descend to earth with a shout, with the voices of the Archangels, and with the trumpet of God, and when that which is no more shall be again. Then we who are alive and remain shall see a new world born of this veil of tears, and be rejoined with them in peace. Amen."

"Amen," came a general rumble from the assembled officers and the aeronauts of *Predator*.

"Funeral detail," Creedy said from his place at Grimm's right hand. "Proceed."

One of *Predator's* cannon had been adjusted for the task at hand, and what lanced out from its barrel was not the usual streaking comet of light, but a small, glowing sun. It sailed gracefully toward the float, expanding rapidly, and when it hit there was a flash of light, a cough of thunder, and a sudden thundercloud made of pure fire, so bright that Gwen had to shield her eyes against it, even in goggles.

When she blinked her eyes clear again, the float and the bodies upon it were gone, replaced with a swiftly dissipating cloud of ash and soot, already being taken by the strong breeze.

There was a long moment of silence, during which no one moved. Then, as if by an unspoken signal, scores of men suddenly redonned their hats, and the stillness of the funeral service was over. There was a brief period of mingling among the officers, in which the captured Aurorans spoke calmly with their Albion counterparts, differing only in their uniforms, and in that none of them wore gauntlets or blades.

Then men began boarding launches and returning to their ships—to *Valiant* and *Victorious*, both of them hauling the battered, gutted form of *Itasca* behind them. Then the three ships began to make their way slowly back toward Spire Albion, moving at only a fraction of the speed that had carried them away from the Spire.

Gwen waited for several minutes after the ship had gotten under way, and then watched as Captain Grimm returned to his quarters. She followed after, and knocked on his door.

"Enter," he said.

She slipped off her goggles and went in to find him sitting at the little table in his room, a fresh stack of blank pages in front of him, along with a pen and ink. He set them aside and rose politely as she entered.

"Captain. Good afternoon."

"Miss Lancaster," Grimm said. "What can I do for you?"

Gwen found herself clenching her fists on the hem of her jacket and forced herself to stop. "I . . . I need to talk to someone. But there's no one about who seems appropriate. If I were at home, I would talk to Esterbrook, but . . ."

Grimm tilted his head slightly to one side. Then he gestured for her to sit down in the other chair, and drew it out for her. Gwen sat gratefully.

"Tea?" he asked her.

"I . . . I'm not sure this is a tea conversation," Gwen said.

Grimm frowned. "I pray you, Miss Lancaster, say what is on your mind."

"That's just it," she said. "I . . . I am not sure what it is. I have a horrible feeling."

Grimm drew in a breath through his nostrils and said, "Ah. What sort of horrible?"

Gwen shook her head. "I killed a man a few days ago. An Auroran officer. I chose to do it. He never had a chance."

Grimm nodded slowly.

"And I saw that silkweaver matriarch. I saw it . . . do things."

Grimm said quietly, "Continue." He turned toward a cabinet, opened it, and withdrew a bottle and two small glasses.

"And . . . and I was here for the battle. I saw . . ." Gwen found her throat closing off. She forced herself to speak more clearly. "It was terrible. When I close my eyes . . . I'm not quite sure I need to be asleep to have nightmares anymore, Captain."

"Aye," Grimm said. He returned to the table, poured some of the liquor into each glass, and passed one to her before he sat.

Gwen stared down at the glass without really seeing it. "It's just that . . . I was among these things. I saw these things. And now . . ."

"Now you're on the way back to be among people who didn't," Grimm said quietly.

Gwen blinked and felt her eyes widen slightly as she looked up at him. "Yes. Yes, that's it exactly. I . . . I had no idea what the world could be like until I saw it. Felt it." She shook her head, unable to continue.

"How are you going to talk to someone who has no idea?" Grimm said, nodding. "How can you explain something you can't find words for? How can you get someone else to understand something for which they have no frame of reference?"

"Yes," Gwen said. Her throat tightened up again. "Yes. That's it exactly."

"You can't," Grimm said simply. "You've seen the mistmaw. They haven't."

Gwen blinked slightly at that. "I . . . Oh. Is *that* what that phrase means? Because I haven't seen a literal mistmaw."

Grimm smiled faintly. "That's what it means," he said. "You can describe it to them as much as you want. You can write books about what you felt, what you experienced. You can compose poems and songs about what it was like. But until they've seen it for themselves, they can't really know what it is you're talking about. A few people will clearly see the effect it had on you, will understand that much, at least. But they won't *know*."

Gwen shuddered. "I'm not sure I want them to."

"Of course not," Grimm said. "No one should have to go through that. Why fight, if not to protect others?"

Gwen nodded. "I thought perhaps I was going mad."

"Possibly," Grimm said. "But if so, you won't be alone."

She felt herself smile a little. "What do I do?"

In answer, he held up his glass, extending his arm to her. She picked up her own and touched her glass to his. They both drank. The liquor was golden and sweet and strong, and it burned into her as it went down.

"Talk to me about it, if you wish," Grimm said. "Or Benedict. Or Miss Tagwynn. Or Mister Kettle, if you don't mind the cursing. They've all seen the mistmaw."

"And they know how to live with it?" Gwen asked.

"I'm not sure anyone knows that," Grimm said. "But they'll understand you. It helps. I know. And in time it isn't as hard to bear."

"What we've done," Gwen said quietly. "The violence. The death." She shook her head, unable to articulate what she felt.

"I know," Grimm said very quietly. "There's a question you need to ask yourself."

"Oh?"

He nodded. "If you could go back to exactly those moments, with exactly the knowledge you had at that time—would you do it any differently?"

"Don't you mean, if I knew then what I know now?"

"No," he said firmly. "I mean exactly the opposite of that. You can't see the future, Miss Lancaster. You cannot be aware of all things at all times. In combat situations, your choices can be judged based only against what you *knew at the time*. To expect anything more of a soldier is to demand that he or she be superhuman. Which seems, to me, unreasonable."

Gwen frowned, thinking, turning the empty glass in her fingers. "I . . . If I had done anything differently, I think I would be dead right now."

"There you have it," Grimm said simply.

"But I feel horrible," Gwen said.

"Good," Grimm said. "You ought to. Anyone ought to."

"It doesn't seem very soldierly."

He shook his head. "The moment you can see the mistmaw without feeling horrible, you aren't a soldier anymore, Miss Lancaster. You're . . . something of a monster, perhaps."

"You seem all right," Gwen said.

"Seem. Yes." Grimm gave her a smile with a bitter tinge to it, and poured himself another drink. He held up the bottle, and she shook her head. He put the bottle back down and threw back the drink in a single swallow. "I'm not. But I haven't the luxury to fall apart just yet. I'll be a gibbering wreck later, I assure you, but for the moment there is work to do. I know what you are feeling."

Gwen nodded and felt a shudder go through her, and then leave her body feeling a fraction less tense, a fraction less painful.

He was right. It helped.

"It's funny," she said.

"Miss?"

"After the way I left, I suddenly find myself wanting very much to go home. But . . . it won't be the same when I get back. Will it?"

"It will be the same," Grimm said. "You're the one who has changed."

"Oh," she said quietly. They sat in silence for a moment. Then Gwen rose and put her glass back down on the table. Grimm rose with her.

"Captain Grimm," she said. "Thank you."

He bowed his head to her and said, "Of course."

Rowl crouched in his newly claimed lair and contemplated which was the greater evil—to return to his home in his current condition, or to fling himself off the side of the airship. That he could not readily discern the answer to his question spoke volumes of his situation.

Perhaps ending it all would be better. He could not face his clan as he was. Foolish humans, to make their airship in such a fashion as to maim a cat who was there only to guide and protect them. It was a wonder they hadn't exterminated themselves centuries ago.

Rowl stirred, and moved with considerable pain to rise and lie down on his other side. The inside of this crate smelled like sawdust, but its open mouth faced one of the airship's walls, so at least his crippling hideousness was not on display for every human who might walk by.

He heard when Littlemouse approached the crate for the fourth time.

"Rowl," she said. "This is foolish. You need to come out."

"Go away, Littlemouse," Rowl replied. "I am contemplating suicide."

"You can't be serious," Littlemouse said.

"Perfectly serious," he replied. "I cannot go home like this."

"Oh, for pity's sake." Bridget sighed. Her heavy boots walked away, and Rowl went back to his brooding.

He had almost perfected it when the boots approached again and someone lifted the crate and turned it ninety degrees to one side. Littlemouse leaned down and peered into the crate, frowning. "Rowl, you've been in there for two days, and we've landed back at Spire Albion. Are you ready to come out yet?"

"I will never come out," Rowl said morosely. "I am a freak."

"Merciful Builders." Littlemouse sighed. "Would you please come out and talk to me?"

Rowl shuddered. Littlemouse was his friend—but he did not owe her everything. He should not have to display his freakishness for her entertainment.

"Please," she said. "Rowl, you're beginning to frighten me."

Rowl rolled his eyes. That was a ploy. A cheap one. Trying to gain his sympathy because her odd human face was contorted with concern and affection. But . . . it was Littlemouse's ploy.

He rose, stiffly and uncomfortably, and then began his asymmetrical, halting, hideous limp to bring him out of the crate. The horrible thing on his right front leg and paw clacked against the wooden deck with each loathsome, short, unbalanced step.

"If I asked you," Rowl said, "would you kill me, please?"

"I would not."

"You are a terrible friend," Rowl said. He tried to move his leg, which itched horribly, but the deformity kept him from being able to scratch it. He had tried.

"For goodness' sake, Rowl," Littlemouse said. "It's just a *cast*. The bone will heal. Why are you so upset about it?"

"Look at it," Rowl said spitefully. "It is hideous. It is the most hideous thing there has ever been."

In answer, Littlemouse held up her broken arm, with its similar cast, and said nothing.

Rowl lowered his ears a little. "That is beside the point. Humans always look foolish and clumsy. I am a cat, and the prince of the Silent Paws. There is no comparison to be made. And my head," Rowl said. He would have shaken it for emphasis, but shaking would not make the cloth the human butcher had fastened there come loose, and it made his legs feel oddly unsteady when he tried. "Look at my head. And beneath it the fur was shaved. I look like I have mange."

"You don't have . . . Augh, Rowl," Littlemouse said. "You don't need someone to help you commit suicide. You need proper food and rest."

"I no longer need interest myself with food," Rowl said. He summoned up as much of his shattered dignity as he could, and turned to begin walking deliberately toward the stern of the airship, which protruded out into empty air.

"No," Littlemouse said firmly. She caught up to him in two strides and reached for him. Rowl tried to dodge, but the monstrous cast on his leg slowed him, and Littlemouse scooped him up, made a cradle of her arms, and hugged him gently. It gave him a brief, glowing surge of delight, which was cheating.

"Littlemouse," Rowl said, "you are squishing my fur."

She held him a little closer and said, "Yes. You are my oldest friend. I would be lost without you."

Rowl hadn't considered the issue from that angle before. "Of course you would."

"If you like, you can stay with me until Doctor Bagen says the cast can come off. Then no one from the tribe need see you."

"You are trying to bribe me out of an honorable death," Rowl said in severe tones.

"I just sent a runner to purchase your favorite dumplings."

At the very mention of the food, Rowl's stomach gurgled hungrily, which was also cheating.

He let out a heavy, heavy sigh. "Fine," he said. "But know you, Littlemouse, that I would endure this humiliation for no one else."

She rubbed her face into the fur of his back, and Rowl felt himself purring, which was cheating only if he was still trying to kill himself, which he now was not. He had decided.

So he rolled over in Littlemouse's cradled arms so that he could nuzzle her back while she nuzzled him, if only for a moment, patting her face with his uninjured front paw. Then he said, "Where?"

Littlemouse blinked. "Where what?"

"Where are my dumplings?"

Grimm sat quietly across from Addison Orson Magnus Jeremiah Albion, Spirearch of Albion, until he had finished scanning the pages of Grimm's written report. The Spirearch, Grimm noted, read very, very quickly.

"I see," Albion said, "that no mention was made of putting the captured crew of *Itasca* in chains."

"They weren't," Grimm replied.

Albion arched an eyebrow and looked up at Grimm over the rims of his spectacles.

"Captain Castillo gave us his parole, and that of his crew."

The Spirearch's other eyebrow climbed. "Just like that?"

"More or less," Grimm said. "We could have shot them down. We didn't."

Albion pursed his lips thoughtfully and then turned back to the report with a faint smile. "Tell me about our losses."

"*Thunderous* was shot down. She took heavy casualties—one hundred and fifty-three dead, including all but one of her junior officers, and forty injured—but managed to stay afloat on her trim crystals until rescue launches could find her in the mist."

"It says here," Albion said, "that special commendation should be given to Captain Castillo and his Marines, who aided in the rescue effort."

"*Itasca* had more functional launches than all of us together," Grimm said. "No Marine or aeronaut wants to see anyone fall to the surface."

"And why is that?"

"Because we all have nightmares about it," Grimm said. "The fighting was over. So they helped."

"And none tried to escape?" Albion asked.

Grimm shook his head once, firmly. "They had given their parole."

"I see," Albion murmured. "In your opinion, is *Thunderous* salvageable?"

Salvage operations were always terribly risky affairs. One never knew what horrors one might face in a simple mission to recover the precious lift and core crystals from a downed ship. After all, one had to *risk* a ship to attempt to recover a ship, and the success rate of such recoveries always wavered precariously between sustainability and throwing good crystals after bad. "I'm not a salvage expert, sire," Grimm said. "But we're in a war with Aurora now. We don't have the luxury of playing it safe."

Albion tapped a thumbnail on his desk, musing over the statement.

"Sire?"

"Yes, Captain?"

"What is going to happen to the Aurorans?"

"They are prisoners of war," Albion said. "I should imagine they will be set to work at the base of the Spire."

Grimm tightened his jaw. "No, sir."

"No?"

"No, sir," Grimm said. "I've seen that place. You might as well tie a noose around their necks and stand them on blocks of ice, if you want them to die a slow death. It will be cleaner."

"I'm not sure why this concerns you, Captain," Albion said.

"Because they surrendered to me," Grimm said. "They gave me their parole, sir. They could have fought on with no real chance of victory, and it would have been bloody. But that surrender saved blood and lives of Albions and Aurorans alike. I will not see Captain Castillo repaid with such churlish treatment."

"Mmmm," Albion said. He nodded to the report and said, "Continue."

"*Victorious* took moderate casualties among her crew, with eleven dead and forty-one injured. She took heavy damage to her hull and mastworks, but can be repaired within ten days. *Valiant* took only light damage, with no deaths and half a dozen injuries, and Commodore Bayard already has her back in fighting condition."

"And *Predator*?"

"Twenty-two men dead, in all," Grimm replied, careful to think only of numbers. "Thirty-three injured."

"We lost a single heavy cruiser," Albion mused, "and captured *Itasca*."

"What's left of her," Grimm said.

"In Bayard's report," Albion said, "he notes that the only reason *Itasca* could be taken at all was because you lured her into pursuing *Predator*."

"It was the right thing to do," Grimm said.

"Yes," Albion said, "and many men recognize the right thing to do. But when it means putting themselves at risk, relatively few will still do it."

Grimm felt a sudden flare of rage in his chest. "Rook," he said.

"Your report," Albion noted, "accuses him of cowardice in the face of the enemy."

"It does," Grimm said. "He got scared. He ran. If *Glorious* had stood fast, we wouldn't have lost *Thunderous*, and might well have taken *Itasca* whole and functioning."

"So it says in your report," Albion said. "Commodore Rook's report to the Admiralty reads somewhat differently. He claims that blast concussion shorted the leads to his lift crystal temporarily, and that he could not maintain altitude."

"He's a damned liar," Grimm said. "Ask Bayard."

"I did," Albion said. "Commodore Bayard reports that he was too far from the fighting and at too poor an angle of visibility to see what happened clearly, and cannot in good conscience swear to the truth of either report. Without his testimony, I'm afraid it is your word against Commodore Rook's."

Grimm ground his teeth. He was outcast from Fleet. Rook was the darling of one of the many factions within its command structure. "Shall I ask Captain Castillo for the courtesy of a report?"

Albion threw back his head and barked out a short laugh. "I believe you. I'm certain the good captain would back up your report. But I'm afraid his word wouldn't carry much weight with Fleet Admiralty either."

Grimm's spine felt like rigid, copper-clad iron. "So he just gets away with it, sire?"

"He gets away with it," Albion said. "For now."

Grimm heard his knuckles pop as he clenched his hand into a frustrated fist. "Yes, sire."

Albion regarded him steadily for a moment and then set aside the report and folded his hands into a pointed steeple. "Off the record," he said, "how would you review Albion's performance in this crisis?"

"We failed, sire," Grimm said.

"In what way?"

"We didn't stop the attack on Landing. Our enemies escaped, after burning down a priceless collection of knowledge. Innocents died. The Landing Shipyard was destroyed. There's only a single bright point in all of this mess."

"That being?"

Grimm withdrew two identical volumes from the pocket of his coat, and laid them on Albion's desk. "This is what Cavendish and the Aurorans were after. She took one copy and burned every other one she could find. One of the monks managed to bring one out of the fire—and I took the stolen book back from her prior to *Itasca*'s arrival."

Albion put his fingers on the books very, very slowly. He drew them both toward him and separated them so that they lay side by side. "You did not mention these in your report."

"No, sire. The Aurorans went to an awful lot of trouble to get that book. It seemed best not to mention it in any kind of record."

Albion nodded slowly. "Indeed, Captain. You did precisely the right thing." He took both books and swept them into his desk drawer. "This entire incident has been extremely unfortunate."

"It could have been more so," Grimm said.

"Ah?"

"The criminal guilds in Landing, sire. If they hadn't intervened and coordinated firefighting efforts and evacuation, a lot more people would have died. We might have lost the entire habble."

"Yes," Albion said. "We were fortunate they reacted so quickly."

"Aye," Grimm said. "It was almost like someone warned them of what was coming. Sire."

Albion blinked once, slowly, and gave Grimm a bland look. "What are you implying, Captain?"

"You couldn't trust your own Guard," Grimm said. "But you needed someone with the numbers and the muscle and the organization to do the job—and while the motivation of the guilds might be distasteful, it is utterly constant. Money."

"That is a very interesting theory, Captain Grimm," Albion said. "But it isn't terribly credible, I'm afraid. I am a figurehead of the government and little more. Everyone knows that."

"Oh," Grimm said. "My mistake."

Neither man smiled. But Albion inclined his head very slightly to Grimm, like a fencer acknowledging a touch.

"Why, sire?" Grimm asked. "Why would they want that book?"

"I'm not sure," Albion said. "I suppose we could ask."

"*Itasca's* officers and crew won't know a thing about it, beyond their movement orders and objectives," Grimm said. "That's basic military security."

"Then we must ask this Madame Cavendish, I should think." Albion looked up at him. "Can we catch *Mistshark*?"

"The moment Captain Ransom got back to her ship, she'd have taken her down into the mist and raised sail," Grimm said. "She's a smuggler. You could send half of Fleet to hunt her, sire, and never see so much as her shadow."

"And that is your professional opinion?" Albion asked, his eyes narrowing slightly.

"No, sire. It is a fact."

"Mmmm," Albion said. "Well. At least they didn't get the book."

The storm roiled all around *Mistshark*. Unpredictable winds buffeted the airship randomly and violently, sometimes shoving her back and forth, and more often sending her hurling violently up or down. Espira sat through it on the floor, his safety harness strapped tightly and securely, his back against the hull. His men were Auroran Marines, used to bad weather in airships, but even so, after three days of wind-driven propulsion, more than a few had been forced to clutch for a bucket as they lost the contents of their stomachs.

Espira closed his eyes and drifted in limbo until, some unspecified amount of time later, Ciriaco tapped his shoulder, waking him. "Again," the sergeant said.

He sighed and hauled himself to his feet. He unfastened the safety harness and began the laborious process of traversing the length of *Mistshark* to get to Madame Cavendish's cabin.

Espira was tired. He didn't feel like knocking—but simply barging in would have been impolite, and he wanted to live to see Spire Aurora again. He knocked, and a moment later Sark opened the door. The big warriorborn looked leaner, like a half-starved cat, but he was up and moving again despite the terrible injuries he had suffered. He grunted and stepped back from the door as Espira entered.

Madame Cavendish looked a fright. Her hair was mussed. Her sleeves had been rolled up, and ink smudged her fingers and made a random spatter of droplets on her lean forearms. She grimly gripped a quill, as if the muscles in her hand had long since locked into position from overuse, and she was writing furiously on a piece of paper.

A stack of several hundred more pieces of paper sat on the table beside her, their edges lined up with maniacal precision, and every one of them was covered in her bold, angular writing.

She finished the page she was on, the last, blew across it gently to help dry the ink, and then carefully placed it atop the stack. She sat back from it slowly, her eyes gleaming, and only after a moment of silence did she acknowledge Espira. "Major," she said.

"Madame."

"I need the use of some of your men. Copies must be made of these pages."

Espira frowned. Had the woman . . .

"Madame?" Espira asked. "Did you write this . . . from *memory*?"

"Why do you think I've been sitting here writing for the past three days?" Cavendish said in a waspish tone. "Why do you think I yielded the book to Captain Ransom when the Albions overhauled us?"

"I . . . I see," Espira said. "Madame, I will make inquiries about which of my men can read and write, but you should know that they aren't chosen as Auroran Marines for their penmanship."

"Acknowledged," Cavendish said. "It must be done."

"If I may be so bold," Espira said, "may I ask what was in the book that was so important?"

"Names, Major," Cavendish said, her eyes glinting with hungry, fey sparks. *"Names."*

Folly sat up screaming, and kept on screaming until she realized how uncomfortable it was. Her cries died out to little whimpers, and then she shivered and felt tears on her cheeks.

Master Ferus came clomping up the ladder to her loft, his wild white hair waving, his face concerned. "Folly?"

She tried to speak, but her voice came out very quietly. "Again, master. I dreamed it again."

"Tell me," he said.

Folly shivered. "I dreamed a Spire, surrounded in darkness, with Death pouring in through its walls. I dreamed of thousands of ships like crystal, rising from the earth—and wherever they went, people died." She shivered and took a breath before finishing in a whisper. "I saw a Spire fall. Collapse as if it had been made of sand. And I dreamed of *Predator* on fire. Burning. Breaking up. Men falling from her like tiny toys . . ."

The memory of their screams of panic brought tears to Folly's eyes again. When she blinked them free, the master was regarding her with compassion.

"Master," Folly said quietly. "These are not dreams, are they?"

"No," he said, his voice rough.

"It is the future."

"Yes."

Folly shivered.

He put a hand on her shoulder and rested his forehead against hers, his eyes closed. She leaned against him, grateful for his simple proximity.

"Why am I having these dreams?"

"Because it is beginning."

"What is beginning?"

"The end," Ferus replied.

His tone was heavy, weary.

"Master?"

"Yes, Folly?"

"I'm frightened."

"So am I, child," the etherealist said. "So am I."

About the author

Jim Butcher is the author of the Dresden Files, the Codex Alera and brand-new fantasy series the Cinder Spires. His résumé includes a laundry list of skills which were useful a couple of centuries ago, and he plays guitar quite badly. An avid gamer, he plays tabletop games in varying systems, a variety of video games on PC and console and LARPs whenever he can make time for it. Jim currently resides mostly inside his own head, but his head can generally be found in his home town of Independence, Missouri.

Find out more about Jim Butcher and other Orbit authors by registering for the free monthly newsletter at www.orbitbooks.net.